CONFESSIONS OF AN ITALIAN

IPPOLITO NIEVO was born in 1831 in Padua, then under Austrian rule. He died before he reached the age of thirty, when his ship, en route from Palermo to Naples, went down in the Tyrrhenian Sea in early 1861. He was, Italo Calvino once said, the sole Italian novelist of the nineteenth century in the 'swashbuckler, rambler' mould so dear to other European literatures. A patriot and a republican, he took part with General Giuseppe Garibaldi and his Thousand in the momentous 1860 landing in Sicily to free the south from Bourbon rule. During Nievo's short life – which spanned the better part of Italy's independence and unification drive, the Risorgimento – he produced numerous volumes of poetry, fiction and journalism, among which *Confessions of an Italian*, written in 1858 and published posthumously in 1867, is his best-known and most enduring work.

FREDERIKA RANDALL has degrees from Harvard and MIT and has worked as a cultural journalist for many years. Her translations include Luigi Meneghello's *Deliver Us* and Ottavio Cappellani's *Sicilian Tragedee*, and her English language version of Sergio Luzzatto's *Padre Pio: Miracles and Politics in a Secular Age* won the Cundill Prize for History, awarded to both author and translator. She has received a PEN Translation Fund Grant and a Bogliasco Fellowship. Randall lives in Rome.

LUCY RIALL was educated at the London School of Economics and the University of Cambridge. She is Professor of the Comparative History of Europe at the European University Institute in Florence and Professor of History at Birkbeck, University of London, and has held visiting positions at the École Normale Supérieure, Paris, the Freie Universität, Berlin, and the University of Freiburg. She is an expert in the history of nineteenth- and twentieth-century Europe, with a particular focus on the politics and culture of Italy. Her publications include *Sicily and the Unification of Italy, 1859–1866* (1998); *Garibaldi: Invention of a Hero* (2007); *Risorgimento: The History of Italy from Napoleon to Nation State* (2009); and *Under the Volcano: Revolution in a Sicilian Town* (2013).

IPPOLITO NIEVO

Confessions of an Italian

Translated by
FREDERIKA RANDALL

With an Introduction by
LUCY RIALL

PENGUIN BOOKS

PENGUIN CLASSICS

Published by the Penguin Group
Penguin Books Ltd, 80 Strand, London WC2R 0RL, England
Penguin Group (USA) Inc., 375 Hudson Street, New York, New York 10014, USA
Penguin Group (Canada), 90 Eglinton Avenue East, Suite 700, Toronto, Ontario, Canada M4P 2Y3
(a division of Pearson Penguin Canada Inc.)
Penguin Ireland, 25 St Stephen's Green, Dublin 2, Ireland (a division of Penguin Books Ltd)
Penguin Group (Australia), 707 Collins Street, Melbourne, Victoria 3008, Australia
(a division of Pearson Australia Group Pty Ltd)
Penguin Books India Pvt Ltd, 11 Community Centre, Panchsheel Park, New Delhi – 110 017, India
Penguin Group (NZ), 67 Apollo Drive, Rosedale, Auckland 0632, New Zealand
(a division of Pearson New Zealand Ltd)
Penguin Books (South Africa) (Pty) Ltd, Block D, Rosebank Office Park,
181 Jan Smuts Avenue, Parktown North, Gauteng 2193, South Africa

Penguin Books Ltd, Registered Offices: 80 Strand, London WC2R 0RL, England

www.penguin.com

Le Confessioni d'un Italiano first published in Italian in 1867
This translation first published in Great Britain by Penguin Classics 2014
001

Set in 10.25/12.25pt Postscript Adobe Sabon
Typeset by Jouve (UK), Milton Keynes
Printed in Great Britain by Clays Ltd, St Ives plc

ISBN: 978-0-141-39166-3

www.greenpenguin.co.uk

Contents

Chronology

1796 French Revolutionary armies under the command of General Napoleon Bonaparte invade northern Italy. They defeat Piedmont and sweep eastwards across the Lombardy plain in the direction of Venice.

1797–8 In Venice, the Doge abdicates and the end of the Republic of Venice is declared. France and Austria sign the Treaty of Campo Formio, which places the Italian peninsula under French control. French-dominated republics are set up: the Cisalpine Republic (northern Italy), the Roman Republic (central Italy) and the Parthenopean Republic (southern Italy).

1799 Following France's defeat at the hands of the Second Coalition, the Italian republics collapse. Italy's old rulers are restored amid horrific violence, notably in Naples.

1800 Having seized power in Paris, Napoleon invades Italy again and defeats Austria at the Battle of Marengo.

1801 Austria recognizes France's domination of Italy in the Treaty of Lunéville.

1806–1809 Napoleon consolidates his Italian possessions by directly annexing Piedmont and part of central Italy (including Rome) to France, and creating a number of new French satellite kingdoms. These years bring sweeping changes to the administrative, legal, social and economic structures of the Italian peninsula. Italians themselves, especially in the major cities, are affected by the cultural innovations of the French Revolution (1789) and by the experience of war and soldiering.

1814 The Congress of Vienna meets, following the defeat of Napoleon in Europe.

1815 The Congress of Vienna restores Italy's pre-Napoleonic rulers and partly reinstates its boundaries, but does not re-establish the Republic of Venice. Austria is now the dominant power in the peninsula, with Lombardy and Venetia part of the Habsburg Empire.

1820–1 Revolutions in the southern Italian Kingdom of the Two Sicilies and in Piedmont challenge the authority of Italy's Restoration governments. They are suppressed with the aid of the Austrian Army.

1831 Revolutionary uprisings in central Italy are suppressed, following Austrian intervention. A young nationalist, Giuseppe Mazzini, establishes a new revolutionary organization, 'Young Italy', to fight for 'the conquest of Independence, Unity, Liberty for Italy'.

November: Ippolito Nievo is born in Padua to Antonio Nievo and Adele Marin.

1834–7 Insurrections inspired by Mazzini take place across Italy. These are easily repressed, resulting in the execution, imprisonment and exile of his followers.

1837 Mazzini arrives as an exile in London, where he will live until his death in 1872.

Nievo moves with his family to Udine (Friuli).

1843 In *Del primato morale e civile degli italiani* (Of the Moral and Civic Primacy of Italians), Vincenzo Gioberti proposes the idea of an Italian federation under the Pope. The book establishes the (short-lived but popular) notion of 'neo-Guelphism' and adds momentum to the growth of moderate liberalism as an alternative to Mazzinianism.

1846 Election of Pius IX as Pope. He introduces a number of reforms in the Papal States.

1847 The periodical *Il Risorgimento* begins publication in Turin. Its editor, Camillo Benso di Cavour, is a moderate liberal.

Nievo finishes his schooling in Verona and returns with his family to Mantua, where he enters the local high school.

1848 January–March: Revolutions across the Italian peninsula lead to the granting of liberal constitutions. In Milan the

Austrian Army is driven out of the city following the celebrated *cinque giornate* or 'five days'. In Venice a Republic is declared. Piedmont declares war on Austria, and volunteers move from all over Italy to fight in the war, but the Piedmontese are defeated at the Battle of Custoza. The Pope grants a constitution in Rome, but, after the murder of his Prime Minister, Pellegrino Rossi, flees Rome for Gaeta in the Kingdom of the Two Sicilies.

In Mantua Nievo's high school is closed by the Austrians. He moves to Cremona to complete his schooling, returning to Mantua only at the end of the year.

1849 February: A republic is declared in Rome. Grand Duke Leopold flees Tuscany and joins the Pope in Gaeta, and a republican 'triumvirate' is set up in Florence.

March: Piedmont declares war on Austria again and is, once again, defeated, this time at the battle of Novara.

July: In Rome, after two months of heroic resistance by Italian volunteer armies, the French Army succeeds in restoring papal government. In Florence, the Tuscan Grand Duke is restored by the Austrian Army.

August: The Venetian Republic falls to its Austrian besiegers.

Nievo moves to Pisa and takes part in the revolutionary struggles against the Grand Duke. He begins a passionate correspondence with a young woman, Matilde Ferrari.

1851 Nievo begins studying law at the University of Pavia.

1852 Cavour becomes Prime Minister of Piedmont, where he introduces a programme of economic and political reforms. From now on, helped by the presence of Italian exiles in Turin, Piedmont becomes a beacon of liberalism in Italy.

Nievo moves to Padua. His relationship with Matilde Ferrari ends badly, provoking him to write a short novel, *Antiafrodisiaco per l'amor platonico* (An Anti-aphrodisiac for Platonic Love).

1853 A Mazzinian uprising against the Austrians in Milan is brutally suppressed.

1855 Nievo graduates in law from the University of Padua. He embarks on a literary career, concentrating on experimental verse, short stories and pamphlets clearly expressing his anti-Austrian, radical political views.

1856 Nievo moves between Udine and Milan. In the latter city he lives with his cousin Carlo Gobio and his wife Bice, with whom Nievo falls in love. In November Nievo is summoned to trial by the Austrian authorities for his short story '*L'Avvocatino*' (The Little Lawyer).

1857 The Italian patriot Carlo Pisacane's attempt to lead a revolutionary expedition to southern Italy ends in disaster at Sapri. This tragedy creates a crisis in confidence among the followers of Mazzini.

Nievo defends himself brilliantly at his trial and escapes with a fine.

December: He begins work on *Confessioni di un italiano*.

1858 A secret pact is signed between France and Piedmont, whereby Piedmont agrees to provoke Austria into declaring war and France promises to come to Piedmont's assistance.

Nievo finishes the manuscript of the *Confessioni* and spends several weeks recovering from exhaustion at Regoledo. He tries but fails to find a publisher for the *Confessioni*.

1859 In April Austria declares war on Piedmont, and France comes to Piedmont's aid. Following the victorious battles of Magenta and Solferino, France signs an armistice with Austria at Villafranca. Nationalist dreams are dashed when only Lombardy, and not Venice, is ceded to Piedmont.

Nievo volunteers to fight in the war and becomes one of the *Cacciatori delle Alpi* (Alpine Chasseurs), sent into the mountains to fight with Garibaldi. Bitterly disappointed by the Peace of Villafranca, Nievo returns to Milan and the house of Carlo and Bice Gobio, where he takes up writing again.

1860 March: Plebiscites in central Italy lead to the union of Tuscany and Emilia with Piedmont-Lombardy. In return for French agreement to the union, Nice and Savoy are ceded to France.

May: Garibaldi leads the expedition of the 'Thousand' to Sicily and lands in Marsala on the west coast of the island.

By the end of the month his forces have seized control in the capital, Palermo.

July–September: Garibaldi conquers the whole of the Two Sicilies and arrives in Naples.

September: To halt Garibaldi's progress, the Piedmontese Army invades the Papal States and the two armies meet at Teano, north of Naples.

October: Plebiscites in southern Italy vote for union with Piedmont, with Vittorio Emanuele II as king.

Nievo publishes a volume of poetry, *Gli amori garibaldini* (Garibaldian Loves) in Milan. He is among the 'Thousand' and leaves for Sicily in May, and he is given a position in government, in charge of financing the army. The post is a difficult one and Nievo is accused of financial malpractice by Cavourian agents.

1861 4 March: Nievo leaves Palermo for Naples on board the *Ercole*, carrying with him the account books from Garibaldi's expedition. The ship sinks and Nievo is drowned. Hs body is never found.

17 March: Declaration of the Kingdom of Italy, with Turin as its capital and Vittorio Emanuele II of Piedmont its first king.

1866 Venice is ceded to Italy following the Austro-Prussian War

1867 *Confessioni di un italiano* is published by Le Monnier of Florence as *Confessioni d'un Ottuagenario* (Confessions of an Octogenarian).

1870 Rome is occupied by Italian troops and is declared the capital of Italy. The Pope refuses to recognize the legitimacy of the new state and declares himself a 'prisoner of the Vatican'.

Introduction

'I have heard that there is a poet in our ranks and that he will write the epic of our battles. His name is Ippolito Nievo.'

Giuseppe Carlo Abba, 1860[1]

Italy's Risorgimento – the nineteenth-century movement for independence and unification – was the most romantic of all nationalist movements, and *Confessions of an Italian* is its literary masterpiece. The novel's young author, Ippolito Nievo, had worked, as he put it, 'day and night' ('actually more night than day') on the story and he finished the thousand-page manuscript in eight months, between late 1857 and the summer of 1858; it was, as he told a friend, 'a rather long confession'.[2] In truth, he suffered from nervous exhaustion after its completion and was obliged to take a long rest under medical supervision at a spa near Lake Como. Written in a frenzied rush, only a year before Nievo left home to fight in the final wars of Italian independence, few novels reflect the mood and tempo of the times more vividly than his *Confessions*.

'I was born a Venetian,' the eighty-year-old narrator Carlo Altoviti tells his readers at the start of the novel, 'and by God's grace I shall die an Italian.' Carlo's story begins with his childhood in a crumbling castle during the last decades of the eighteenth century and spans his youthful experiences of the Napoleonic wars in Italy and his adulthood during the long Restoration after Napoleon's defeat; it ends with his son's account of the Italian revolutions of 1848–9 and subsequent exile in South America. So Carlo's account covers virtually the entire period and shifting fortunes of the Risorgimento, starting with the collapse of the Old Regime, through the French invasions and the reversals of the Restoration period; and, most significantly, it anticipates in its opening lines the national unification that was to take place just three years after the novel was completed. 'My experiences,' he writes, 'offer a sort of model of those innumerable individual destinies that, from the collapse of the old political orders to the patching together of the present one, make up the greater Italian destiny.' The making of Carlo Altoviti becomes, in the course of his *Confessions*, the making of Italy. Figures famous in contemporary Italian history, among them Napoléon Bonaparte (1769–1821), Pope Pius IX (1792–1878) and Giuseppe Garibaldi (1807–82), take part in the action, while the fictional characters play out themes popular in Risorgimento literature; in particular, the hero's coming of age as patriot, lover and father, and his journey beyond to the wisdom of old age, symbolizes the education of a nation and the reclamation of its identity through struggle, suffering and sacrifice.

Even more than his alter ego Carlo Altoviti, Ippolito Nievo was a child of the Italian Risorgimento. Born in Padua, part of the Kingdom of Lombardy-Venetia, under Austrian control, Nievo and his family were subjects of Habsburg rule in an Italy that the Austrian Chancellor, Prince Klemens von Metternich, was later to describe as merely a 'geographical expression'. In 1815, at the end of the Napoleonic Wars, the Congress of Vienna had largely restored Italy's old internal boundaries. These divided Italy into some seven states, all of which, with the exception of Piedmont-Savoy (which served as a buffer state against renewed French expansion through the Alps), were under the direct or indirect control of Austria. The Vienna settlement, in other words, confirmed the long process of political decline that had seen Italy reduced, during the French invasions, to little more than a source of military resources and a battlefield between Austria and France.

Yet Nievo was also born at a time of tremendous and unsettling change. The year of his birth, 1831, saw revolutionary uprisings in the duchies and the papal territories of central Italy. They were swiftly crushed by Austrian armed intervention. However hopeless in themselves, these vain attempts to free Italy from Austrian influence and political oppression also helped to create a lasting tradition of heroic opposition, a tradition for which Nievo – like many of his generation – would soon come to feel an impassioned affinity. Most important of all, out of the ashes of these defeated uprisings there arose a nationalist movement that attracted fanatical loyalty and global recognition.

Giuseppe Mazzini (1805–72), the foremost nationalist of the Risorgimento, does not appear in the *Confessions of an Italian*, probably because by 1857, when Nievo started the novel, his star had waned considerably. Still, Mazzini's influence permeates every page of the book. Without Mazzini there would have been no Risorgimento, or, at least, the broader drive for political change which both Mazzini and Nievo were part of would never have attracted the unusual combination of myth, notoriety, hostility and devotion that still fascinates historians today. The failure of the 1831 uprisings appalled Mazzini. Accordingly, he resolved to set up a new movement that would not be conditioned by the defeats of the past and that would liberate Italy from its current enslavement to foreign powers. He called this movement 'Young Italy' (and he excluded the over-forties from its organization). Driven by the conviction that the Italian people were created by God and destined by geography, history and nature to be an independent nation, Mazzini blamed Italy's monarchs, its governing elites and the Catholic Church for the country's current collapse, and he called for the revolutionary overthrow of every ruler in Italy and the creation of a single democratic republic in their place. Members of Young Italy formed a 'brotherhood' and swore to dedicate their lives to this one purpose. With Mazzini, the sense of decline and the dream of change, a hope that had driven Italian reformers since the late eighteenth century, were linked to a concrete programme of revolutionary action, as well as to a mystical desire for resurrection and resurgence (the literal meaning of *risorgimento*).

In some respects, of course, Mazzini was no more successful than his predecessors. His conspiracies against Italy's governments were quickly detected; his insurrections never attracted popular support and usually met with abject failure; and members of Young Italy were obliged to flee Italy or risk imprisonment, or, worse still, were killed or executed in the most dismal of circumstances. Mazzini spent most of his own life as a political exile in London. But all of these setbacks served a purpose. Uprisings, however unimpressive in their immediate results, established a tradition of political belonging, while the repression that inevitably followed revealed the extent of government misrule; moreover, those young men who died for Italy in such tragic circumstances became martyrs, and this gave substance to a nation that had hitherto only existed in romantic imaginings. In short, during the 1830s and 1840s, as Ippolito Nievo grew up under Austrian rule in the cities of north-eastern Italy, the cause to which Mazzini and his followers dedicated themselves became famous. Before Mazzini, no one had seriously conceived of independence for Italy, still less national unification; with him, the question became a burning issue that eventually even his bitterest opponents found hard to ignore.

Young Italy created a political culture. To be sure, a sense of 'Italian-ness' (*italianità*) had long prevailed among elites in the peninsula, and, during the early decades of the nineteenth century, the pervasive influence of Romanticism had served to promote Italian themes in art and music. A new interest in, and nostalgia for, Italy's past emerged in novels and poetry and is noticeable in the growing popularity of subjects and personalities in Italian history. It was Mazzini's great achievement to have given this cultural yearning for Italy an evident political expression. Of equal importance, he realized that the great nineteenth-century 'revolution' in reading and publishing hugely expanded the opportunities for communication, so that his message could reach an ever-increasing, literate public across Europe and the Americas, whose support could, in turn, be harnessed to his political ambitions for Italy. For Mazzini and his followers writing was a form of political militancy as essential as insurgency or combat and they wrote with enormous dedication. In so doing, they helped forge a new society of radical writers and intellectuals for whom the cause of Italian freedom was a badge of common identity.

Ippolito Nievo belonged to this radical community. More

precisely, he joined it at arguably its most crucial and formative moment, that is, during the events of 1848–9, when Austria's hold over the peninsula faltered, Italy's crowned heads made major concessions and the forces of revolutionary change temporarily gained the upper hand. The revolutions of 1848–9 failed, but before they were crushed they changed Europe's political landscape for ever. That moment of liberty, however brief, brought free speech and assembly, and this, in turn, opened up new spaces and possibilities for public debate that reached places and people hitherto excluded from political life; there was a sudden increase in publishing and journalism, which, alongside the proliferation of political meetings and associations and the mobilization of men and women to fight on the barricades and as volunteers against the armies of conservative Europe, encouraged the beginnings of mass political awareness. Once started, this process of politicization proved impossible to reverse. Hence, the Italian revolution came of age in 1848–9 and, in the new era that followed, government repression seemed both harsh and ineffective, while liberalism, the main focus of its repression, assumed the form of an inescapable destiny.

For the young Nievo the years of revolution were a turning point. Admittedly, he was unfortunate to find himself with his family in Mantua, one of the great fortresses of the Austrian Quadrilateral to which Field Marshall Radetsky and his army retreated after their eviction from Milan in the spring of 1848, and an attempted uprising there against the Austrians was swiftly subdued by the authorities. Nevertheless, Nievo took part in the failed Mantua uprising; during the crackdown that followed, his school was closed and both his parents were officially classified as *compromessi* ('compromised') for their behaviour during the same events. In early 1849 Nievo left home for Tuscany, where he joined republican groups active in the coastal cities and was part of the mounting agitation that saw a democratic government installed in Florence and forced Grand Duke Leopold (1797–1870) to flee Tuscany. In May Nievo joined the resistance when the Austrian Army intervened to crush the revolution and restore the Grand Duke.

For the next five years Nievo studied law at the universities of Pavia and Padua, graduating in 1855. In this period he also embarked on a career as a writer. He read voraciously the popular novels of the day and became a prolific author of (not always published) novels, poetry, essays and pamphlets. He also joined the avant-garde movement, led by innovative writers like Carlo Tenca (1816–83), which worked to create an experimental, anti-conformist and popular literature and was a precursor of the Scapigliatura movement, based in and around Milan, which developed after Italian unification. These writers pioneered a new political journalism in Lombardy-Venetia that sought to challenge Austrian censorship, and during the 1850s they played a key role in the reshaping of public opinion in favour of liberalism. In fact, in 1856 Nievo attracted the attention of the censor and risked imprisonment when he published a satirical short story, 'L'Avvocatino' ('The Little Lawyer'), in which he disparaged the police. At his trial the following year, shortly before starting work on the *Confessions*, Nievo defended himself brilliantly and got away with a fine; as a result, he also acquired a reputation among Milanese intellectuals as a gifted militant.

The curious interplay of defeat and defiance, hope and despair, so typical a characteristic of the Risorgimento, informs Nievo's *Confessions of an Italian* with particular force. This is, at least in part, a novel about disgrace and decline. The old Count of Fratta, 'last of a dying breed'; his indulged, spendthrift wife; and their son Rinaldo, who spends his time studying the past, while his inheritance – the Castle and surrounding land – is steadily stripped away: these family members are a microcosm of culpable decay that is played out on a grander scale (and is vividly described in the novel) by the self-destruction of the 'spineless' Republic of Venice after the French invasion. 'The Republic had become a corpse unable to revive itself,' writes Carlo-Ippolito, 'a race of the living forced by long servitude to share the dead man's grave.'

A host of minor characters, among them priests, lawyers, courtesans and *cavalieri serventi* (companions or lovers of married women), contribute to the atmosphere of corruption and degeneration that pervades the dying days of Venice. Carlo's friend Leopardo, who kills himself as the French enter the city, is one of the few to escape the general censure. The central relationship of the novel, the love story between Carlo and his cousin Pisana, is at this time a source of frustration, guilt and humiliation. More than once Carlo is 'disgusted' by his lover's morals. Pisana's behaviour makes him (and another of her lovers) ill and, when they are finally united in the dying days of the Republic, he is filled with 'remorse': 'the drunken happiness she provided me came entirely at the expense of my honour', he declares, and he had risked profaning 'Venice's funeral' with his 'shameless pleasures'. When, during these same days, Carlo discovers the truth about his own mother's 'disgrace' and his role in bringing it about, he brings together all these tragedies into a single, despairing lament:

> Oh, did I weep that day! . . . And in that anguish that poured from my heart in howls and weeping were mysteriously united the *patria* betrayed, the friend who had chosen to die, the false and the unfaithful lover, and the shade of my mother, her face worn by suffering!

For Ugo Foscolo (1778–1827), the Romantic poet who has a walk-on part in Nievo's *Confessions*, Italy was a 'prostituted land' left with nothing 'except memory'.[3] 'Oh, poor Adriatic!' Nievo writes, 'Venice is but an inn; Trieste, a shop: not enough to console those shores for having been abandoned. When dawn comes to burnish your billowing mane, no issue appears but ruins and memories.' The loss and sorrow of the novel's protagonists become, in this way, the shame of Italy. Yet unlike Foscolo, who sought in the past a retreat from the misery of the present, Nievo strove to reclaim history. As a man of Mazzini's Risorgimento, made by the experience of revolution and influenced by the climate of more moderate liberalism that gained currency in the 1840s and 1850s, Nievo conveys in his novel far more than melancholy nostalgia for past glories. Instead, his message is one of opposition, education and redemption.

In this respect, we might speculate that the real hero of the novel is not its narrator, Carlo Altoviti, but rather his older companion, Lucilio Vianello. Lucilio is the 'new man' brought into being by the Risorgimento: a Byronic figure of high forehead and fierce gaze, 'doctor, patriot and republican', and a model of intelligence, fortitude, valour and dignity. He teaches Carlo and his companions the benefits of restraint and saves them from the twin perils of love and the Catholic Church; it is also Lucilio who makes Carlo a patriot, recruits him to fight in the army and sets him on the road to political maturity. 'You are dying of sorrow all your own,' Lucilio tells Giulio, Carlo's lovesick friend, 'when it is only permissible to die for the sorrow of all! Rather than surrender ignobly to the consumption devouring you, you must rise courageously to martyrdom!'

Equally, if Carlo's journey through life embodies Italy's long walk to freedom, Lucilio's strength and kindness stand for the role of family in the Risorgimento. It is Lucilio who makes the identification, common to so much Italian patriotic literature, of brotherly love with political belonging. Carlo Altoviti, we should remember, is virtually an orphan (and for part of the novel believes both his parents to be dead) and this man without a natural family builds a new one from friends, all dedicated to the cause of Italy. Lucilio is its founding member. Lucilio, in other words, represents virtue, integrity and loyalty, the most prized of Risorgimento values, and he also points to Italy's political future. At the novel's end, Carlo has this to say:

> Physically, necessity rules us; morally, justice does. The man who in temperament and convictions is just to himself, to others and to all humanity, will be the most decent, most useful, most noble. His life will be of service to himself and others, and he will leave a deep and honoured mark in his country's history. Such is the archetype of the true and integral man. What does it matter if everyone else is aggrieved and unhappy? The rest are the degenerates, the lost, the guilty. Let them be inspired by that exemplary man and they will find that peace that nature promises . . .

What of the exemplary woman? To what extent did Nievo assign her a role in this process of national resurgence? The answer is complicated. In his own life, and like many Italian male patriots, Nievo built up an extended network of female friends and relatives whom he relied on for both political advice and emotional support (Mazzini also created a surrogate family, largely made up of English women, who worked to raise money and awareness in Britain for the Italian cause). However, again like many Italian revolutionaries in this period who were unable to construct stable private lives, Nievo never married and instead pursued a series of passionate, but unrequited or unconsummated, love affairs with women who were usually beyond his reach. Yet if intimate relations were absent in practice, they were accompanied by a kind of representational obsession. Thus, in Risorgimento narratives, women assumed central roles that made them symbols of national sorrow and suffering; in patriotic literature and art the protection of a woman or vengeance for her dishonouring often served to inspire acts of national rebellion and redemption. At the same time, women played a special role in the process of national education that was so important to Nievo. Whether as daughters or mothers, they could serve either as a chilling example of the risks of bad schooling or as an edifying vehicle through which new, upstanding Italians could be made: 'Women,' Nievo writes, are 'our superiors . . . in the practical science of life', but, he continues: 'Woe to us when a woman degenerates! As the old proverb says, she is transformed into the Devil.'

Women, then, were an important presence in Risorgimento literature and activism, but their position in the patriotic hierarchy was uncertain. However much women helped Italy's Risorgimento, they were generally considered secondary figures whose main task was to support the action of men. Figuratively, they may have provided a focus for the hopes of male patriots and a form through which their anxieties could be played out, but their bodies were often no more than objects of symbolic fantasy. This ambiguity helps us to understand the complex role in the novel played by Pisana, Carlo's cousin and lover. On the one hand, she provides the pivotal point of the novel on which its narrative rests. She is spirited, beautiful and 'vivacious', with 'big brown eyes and long, long hair', and much of the modern popularity of *Confessions of an Italian* is due to a fascination with her refusal to conform to the standards of the day. On the other hand, Pisana is also a 'little devil': spoilt, selfish and capricious, 'nervous and easily riled'. She also possesses a 'feminine guile' that already, at the age of three, is 'fully developed'.

In the novel, Pisana's destructive behaviour exemplifies the degenerate consequences of a bad upbringing. In this respect, she is not a strong character at all and, although rebellious, has no power to forge her own destiny; for a great deal of the narrative she is merely manipulative and unscrupulous. In the end, moreover, she is redeemed only by humiliation – by being forced to beg in the streets of London – and by death: thus, tragedy and an act of sacrifice save her, but, unlike her lover, Carlo, she never acquires the wisdom of maturity. Carlo learns to love his homeland as a consolation for her abandonment, and Pisana comes to love Italy too, thereby effecting a reconciliation between them, but she is never a steady supporter of our hero and she never marries him or starts a family. Ultimately, she remains outside the new Italy that he helps to create.

So Pisana is an ambiguous character, reflecting both the fascination of the female and unease about women's roles in the Risorgimento. At the same time, other female protagonists in the novel are fairly routine types. Clara, Pisana's pious sister, is a heroine borrowed from the pages of Alessandro Manzoni (1785–1873), the official novelist of the Risorgimento, who presided over the literary scene in Milan as Nievo wrote his *Confessions*; Clara turns cold, distant and elderly on becoming a nun. Carlo's wife, Aquilina, is a simple woman who is devoted to him, but she is also stupid and, once their children are born, becomes a terrible nag. Another female character, Doretta Natalino, is a great beauty, but a 'trollop', too, who publicly humiliates her good husband, Leopardo, who kills himself in despair at her behaviour (and when we last hear of Doretta, she is a 'fallen woman' who is 'possessed by the Devil'). Broadly speaking, women in the novel, with the partial exception of Pisana and Carlo's Greek half-sister Aglaura (who dresses as a sailor to disguise her femininity), are either confined to the home or are a pernicious presence in public spaces. On arrival in Milan, during the days of the Cisalpine Republic, Carlo finds himself in the midst of 'a great female crowd': 'an anarchy of frivolous and flighty heads', he comments. The women are childish, silly and 'garrulous'; they scream loudly and tear at each other's hair. Carlo concludes that 'there's no creature who talks as much nonsense as a political woman'.

In my view, the novelty of Nievo's *Confessions* lies not in his treatment of women. Instead, the story's claim to originality rests on the great attention Nievo gives to rural life and to common people. It is not by chance that the novel begins in the countryside and within a domestic space: Carlo's first home, in a cavernous kitchen, which is, for him, 'the grandest monument that ever graced the earth'. We first meet the inhabitants of the Castle in or via the kitchen. Of these inhabitants, one of the most important is also the humblest: the deaf old manservant Martino, Carlo's first friend, whose 'only real task was to grate the cheese', and who acts as a surrogate father to the shunned, orphaned boy. Many of Carlo's other friends are men of modest origin who go on to accomplish great deeds: these include the country boy Bruto Provedoni and Sandro Giorgi, the son of a miller. Above all, Carlo Altoviti is himself an ordinary man. He makes mistakes and leads a life beset by misunderstandings, a life that he, in turn, regards with ironic detachment. His story, he tells the reader, is a 'simple tale . . . appended by an unknown hand' and his personal experiences reflect 'the common and national life' in the way 'a falling raindrop reflects the course of the storm'.

There is something remarkably modern about Nievo's *Confessions*. He takes an epic narrative, the Risorgimento, and plays out its grand, Romantic ambitions on a minor scale. He assigns normally trifling characters a leading role. Carlo Altoviti is, in many respects, an anti-hero whose adventures often verge on the absurd: his one meeting with Napoleon takes place while the latter is having his hair cut. 'You are a giant, but not a God', is Carlo's reaction to the news that Napoleon has declared himself emperor. Moreover, Nievo's prose reflects this attention to the commonplace. Far from adopting the grandiose tone so admired in Risorgimento discourse, he uses the first person and relies on reported conversation: he writes through the medium of the spoken word and, in particular, introduces elements of dialect and mixes dialect with the Italian language. Unusually for the time, he seeks to recover the voice of the unrefined man.

Equally, the novel itself takes a hybrid form that destabilizes the standard genres of the day. For example, with its Gothic castle, star-crossed lovers and adventurous episodes, the novel contains all the ingredients of a classic historical romance (and its basic structure owes a great deal to the Manzonian tradition), but, as the story unfolds, everyday banalities, undistinguished characters and meaningless errors subvert the heroic genre. The novel also purports to be a volume of memoirs, penned by an eighty-year-old man, and points to the prominence and influence of life-writing in Risorgimento literature. But the actual author was twenty-six years old when he wrote the book, and what he calls his confessions are really an odd mix of elements drawn from his own childhood and stories from his parents and grandparents, put together with real episodes from Italian history and linked via pure invention. It is revealing that Nievo ends the novel in the aftermath of the 1848 revolutions; that is, at precisely the moment when he might have entered the story as an adult protagonist and his *Confessions* could have derived from his own lived experiences. The genre to which this novel comes closest is the *Bildungsroman*, and it is often described as the story of an education, but, nevertheless, Carlo Altoviti's education is a strange one, made up for the most part of confusion, frustration, reversals of fortune and disappointment.

Nievo is a novelist who likes to upset readers' expectations. In this respect, the occasional ambivalence with which the narrator greets the new world that emerges from the collapse of the old is of particular interest. For instance, he observes with dismay the gradual disintegration of the Castle of Fratta, which is a symbol of the Old Regime and owned by a family that had shown him very little love. Crowd scenes and moments of revolutionary change are, in the novel, almost invariably viewed with a negative eye; the Old Countess, Lady Badoer, who had lived at the court of Louis XIV and is one of the few good aristocrats in the novel, dies a horrific death at the hands of a revolutionary mob. Especially remarkable is a long, often heart-breaking letter that Bruto Provedoni writes to Carlo from their home, in which he describes the impact of war and revolution on the old world. 'Oh, Carlino,' he writes, 'if you could see this place! You wouldn't know it any more. What has become of the fairs, the gatherings, the feast days . . . ?' he asks: these days, 'No one marries any more and rarely do the church bells ring for a baptism. When the bell tolls, you can be sure someone is dying.' The Castle of Fratta lies 'empty, silent, in ruins'. The walls still stand, but 'as for the rest: desolation! . . . The drawbridge lies rotting . . . Grass grows in the courtyards; the windows not only lack shutters, but the frames and windowsills are coming to pieces under the dripping rain.'

To this sad image of loss and decay, to this lament for the passing of feudalism and the old regime, is joined an attack on the new class of moneyed 'riff-raff' created by the revolution:

> These people, servants and peasants not long ago, are more arrogant than their former masters and, bereft of good upbringing and gentlemen's manners, don't even try to give their villainy the appearance of honour. They have lost all pretence of good and evil; they want to be respected, obeyed and served, merely because they are rich.

Nievo's *Confessions* reflect a moment of profound change in the politics and culture of modern Italy. The author's misgivings about this transformation, which he personally fought to bring about and which is expressed through the image of a vacant, rotting childhood home, mark him as a writer of enormous range and subtlety. In many ways these uncertainties anticipate doubts about the Risorgimento that were to develop after national unification, but they are also suggestive of the unstable political atmosphere prevailing in the late 1850s, when Nievo wrote his novel. On the one hand, as we have seen, Nievo was part of the growing literary and political ferment that sought to displace Austrian rule in the Italian peninsula. On the other, he was also witness to a mood of great disillusion, as the revolutionary movement founded and still led by Mazzini suffered defeat after defeat, often with the most terrible consequences.

Shortly before Nievo started work on his novel in 1857, an attempted insurrection, led by a former Mazzinian, Carlo Pisacane, in the town of Sapri in southern Italy had ended in disaster with the death of its leaders. Nievo was deeply affected by the tragedy of Sapri, and it is possible that the mood of relative pessimism and cynicism that pervades the novel is a response to these recent developments. It is also likely that Nievo was influenced by other changes in nationalist politics. Here the most notable development was the growing ascendancy of moderate liberalism, which came in this decade to surpass Mazzinian nationalism and to embody the new hopes of Italy. Under the leadership of Count Camillo Benso di Cavour (1810–61), prime minister of Piedmont, the moderate liberal movement had established a dominant role and the right to speak for Italy in Europe. Cavour's great appeal was the promise of reform without revolution, together with practical results and an end to pointless violence; moreover, in precisely the months that Nievo was writing his novel, Cavour was negotiating a secret military alliance with France that aimed to destroy Austrian power in Italy. However, to achieve these ends Cavour sought a compromise with the other forces that, for men like Nievo at least, still 'oppressed' Italy. Cavour, in short, represented political success and a victory of sorts for Italian pride, but the price of this achievement was the sacrifice of the dream of Italian regeneration.

Confessions of an Italian looks back to the Italian past. However, like all good works of history, imagined or otherwise, it engages in a constant, if silent, dialogue with the present. In the novel a sign of Carlo Altoviti's maturity is his decision to volunteer to fight for Italy; and his son Giulio atones for a 'life of dissolution' by fighting, in Rome in 1849, with Garibaldi in defence of the Republic. 'Here I am at last,' Giulio writes, after being wounded in an assault on enemy troops: 'I've taken back my name and my honour. My family and my country can be proud of me, and while I pen these lines I relish the pain of my wound and the sight of the page stained with blood.' Both Carlo and Giulio's decision to go to war points to the fact that, for a later Italian generation of which Nievo was a part, military volunteering was considered an act of genuine heroism. Indeed, for Nievo and his contemporaries, a man who chose freely to leave home in order to fight, and perhaps to die, for freedom and justice in other lands was the true incarnation of courage, virtue and manliness.

In 1859 Ippolito Nievo got the chance to imitate his own fiction. In April of that year war broke out between Austria and the allied forces of France and Piedmont. When these armies mobilized and fought each other in the Lombardy Plain and Italian Alps, there began an entirely new phase in Nievo's short life. Along with his younger brothers Carlo and Alessandro and thousands of other Italians, he left home and crossed the border into Piedmont to volunteer for the Piedmontese Army and fight against Austria; he ended up among the volunteers who were assigned to General Garibaldi and sent into the mountains to seize Austrian territory in the Alps. Nievo remained with Garibaldi throughout his victorious campaign and only returned to Milan at the end of the summer when the Peace of Villafranca brought the war to an end.

The Peace of Villafranca, by which France handed over Lombardy to Piedmont but left Venice under Austrian rule, was a bitter disappointment to the Italian nationalist movement. Far from being the longed-for moment of national liberation, it seemed confirmation of Italy's subordinate status; for volunteers like Nievo, this felt like a personal humiliation and betrayal. In response, Nievo retreated to private life and the company of his friend and cousin Carlo Gobio and his wife Bice (all the evidence suggests that Nievo was passionately in love with Bice), and he consoled himself with writing. In early 1860 Nievo published *Gli amori garibaldini* (Garibaldian Loves), a volume of poetry that recounted in verse his experiences as a combatant.

A few months later the situation changed dramatically. In May 1860 Nievo was with Garibaldi again, this time as a volunteer with the expedition of Garibaldi's 'Thousand', which sailed from Genoa to support a revolution against Bourbon rule in Sicily. Over the next five months this small army of so-called 'Red Shirts' achieved an extraordinary and entirely unexpected success. They inflicted successive defeats on their adversaries and in the course of the summer crossed to the mainland and arrived in Naples, the capital of the Kingdom of the Two Sicilies, where they met with a triumphant welcome. Although we now know that Piedmont had never supported Garibaldi's expedition to Sicily and, in fact, Cavour had sought actively with secret agents to obstruct it, it seemed at the time that the 'Thousand' and Piedmont had acted in unison towards the single objective of Italian unification. As apparent confirmation, the following year, in March 1861, the Italian peninsula was finally united as a single nation state, with Vittorio Emanuele II (1820–78) of Piedmont as its first king.

Ippolito Nievo did not live to see the unification of Italy. He had been with Garibaldi during the first clash between the 'Thousand' and Bourbon troops, at Calatafimi in western Sicily, but shortly afterwards he was given a government post and charged with the organization and financing of the army. He remained in Palermo for the rest of the summer and autumn. Here Nievo found himself surrounded by enemies; in particular, as part of the tactic to halt Garibaldi's progress towards Naples, Cavour's agents accused him and the government of embezzling funds and other forms of malpractice. Much of Nievo's time in Palermo and all of his energy was spent defending himself against these mounting accusations.

'I am done, I have had enough, I have had more than enough, I must confess that if I had known that I was leaving Genoa on the 5th of May to come to this prison I would have drowned myself', he wrote to Bice in December 1860.[4] On 4 March 1861, just two weeks before the declaration of a united Italy, Nievo left Palermo on board an old steamer, the *Ercole*, bound for Naples. He took with him the accounts relating to the administration of the expedition: his purpose was to bring the books to the government in Turin and answer the accusations against him and Garibaldi's government. But the ship never made it to Naples. Somewhere out at sea (it is thought off the coast of Capri) the *Ercole* was hit by a storm and went down, taking with it Ippolito Nievo, his account books and everyone else on board. Despite his family's attempt to search for him and recover his body, neither it nor any other trace of the *Ercole* was ever found.

The *Confessions of an Italian*, Nievo's masterwork, survived him. On the novel's completion he had failed to find a publisher, probably because of concerns about the censor, and in 1859 he had given the manuscript to Bice for safekeeping. After his death, another friend – the writer Erminia Fuà Fusinato – succeeded in finding a publisher, Le Monnier of Florence, and the novel came out in 1867 under an altered title, *Confessioni di un Ottuagenario* (Confessions of an Octogenarian); the publisher hoped to distract attention away from the novel's political content (which he described as 'hot air') by the change of title, and he also refused to publish another two of Nievo's experimental novels. It seems that Nievo's wayward approach did not fit with the more sober, conformist temper of liberal Italy and, in fact, the novel met with only moderate success on publication (the character of Pisana was considered especially shocking). A few years later the Società italiana contro le cattive letture (Italian Society against Bad Reading) condemned the novel and placed it on a list of books that were 'not advised for families or popular libraries'.

In the mid-twentieth century interest in Nievo's work revived and his reputation has grown ever since. Today very few would find *Confessions of an Italian* either scandalous or unsuitable for families. Indeed, so popular did Pisana become in the course of the twentieth century that, in 1960, to celebrate the centenary of Garibaldi's expedition and the unification of Italy, she inspired her own Italian television series, entitled *La Pisana*. Even before la Pisana's rehabilitation, however, Nievo had become something of a national treasure, a 'soldier poet' and a hero of Garibaldi's 'Thousand', whose tragic disappearance at the age of twenty-nine gave him the status of a nationalist martyr. More recently, rumours that the steamer *Ercole* was deliberately blown up or scuttled, in order to prevent the sorry truth about the financing of Garibaldi's expedition from coming to light, have revived and proved remarkably persistent. Nievo, in this version of events, was the victim of an assassination plot and his death a symptom of everything that went wrong with Italy's nineteenth-century process of national Risorgimento. We can only speculate as to what Nievo would make of his dubious present-day fame. It is unquestionable, however, that with his untimely death the nation that he had imagined in his prose and fought for in real life lost one of its most penetrating, original and subversive voices.

Lucy Riall, 2014

NOTES

1. G. C. Abba, *The Diary of One of Garibaldi's Thousand*, trans. E. R. Vincent (Oxford: Oxford University Press, 1962), p. 15.
2. To Bice Gobio Melzi, 29 July and 17 August 1858, in M. Gorra (ed.), *Tutte le opere di Ippolito Nievo. VI. Le lettere* (Milan: Mondadori, 1981), pp. 511, 515.
3. *Ultime lettere di Jacopo Ortis* (1798) and *Dei sepolcri* (1807), quoted in C. Duggan, *The Force of Destiny: A History of Italy since 1796* (London: Penguin, 2007), pp. 3, 35.
4. 2 December 1860, in I. Nievo, *Lettere garibaldine* (Turin: Einaudi, 1961), p. 114.

Further Reading

Banti, A. M., *La nazione del Risorgimento: Parentela, santità e onore alle origini dell'Italia unita* (Turin: Einaudi, 2000)

Davis, J. A. (ed.), *Italy in the Nineteenth Century, 1796–1900* (Oxford: Oxford University Press, 2000)

De Francesco, A., *L'Italia di Bonaparte: Politica, statualità e nazione nella penisola tra due rivoluzioni, 1796–1812* (Turin: UTET, 2011)

Duggan, C., *The Force of Destiny: A History of Italy since 1796* (London: Penguin, 2007)

Ginsborg, P., *Daniele Manin and the Venetian Revolution of 1848–49* (Cambridge: Cambridge University Press, 1979)

Isabella, M., *Risorgimento in Exile: Italian Émigrés and the Liberal International in the post-Napoleonic Era* (Oxford: Oxford University Press, 2009)

Laven, D., *Venice and Venetia under the Habsburgs, 1815–1835* (Oxford: Oxford University Press, 2002)

Mack Smith, D., *Cavour and Garibaldi, 1860. A Study in Political Conflict* (1968; Cambridge: Cambridge University Press, 1985)

Patriarca, S. and Riall, L. (eds), *The Risorgimento Revisited. Nationalism and Culture in Nineteenth-Century Italy* (Basingstoke: Palgrave Macmillan, 2012)

Riall, L., *Risorgimento: The History of Italy from Napoleon to Nation-State* (Basingstoke: Palgrave Macmillan, 2009)

—, *Garibaldi: Invention of a Hero* (London: Yale University Press, 2007)

Sarti, R., *Mazzini: A Life for the Religion of Politics* (London: Praeger, 1997)

G. M. Trevelyan, *Garibaldi and the Making of Italy* (London: Longmans & Co., 1911)
—, *Garibaldi and the Thousand* (London: Longmans & Co., 1909)
—, *Garibaldi's Defence of the Roman Republic* (London: Longmans & Co., 1907)

Note on the Translation

'In this year 1858 of the Christian era I am now over eighty years old,' begins Carlo Altoviti, the narrator of the *Confessions*, an old man just about ready to 'dive into that time which is no longer time', writing his memoirs from his home in the country, where he has 'watched the last, farcical act of the great drama of feudalism'. Despite the pondered tone, there is something about Carlo that immediately belies his senescence. For Ippolito Nievo was just twenty-six when he wrote his novel, and his octogenarian protagonist can barely contain his young creator's verve and energy. When the venerable Carlo is not being grave and solemn, he is a sly, witty, cheeky twenty-something. Here, for example, is how he speaks of the Count of Fratta, the precarious patriarch of a tottering mainland Venetian noble family:

> The Count of Fratta was a man past sixty who always looked as if he had just stepped out of his armour, so stiffly and pompously did he sit in his chair. But his elaborate bagwig, his long cinder-coloured, scarlet-trimmed *zimarra*, and the boxwood snuff container forever in his hands detracted somewhat from the warrior pose. True, there was a sliver of a sword stuck between his legs, but the sheath was so rusty you could mistake it for a roasting spit, and in any case, I couldn't swear there was really a steel blade inside, nor had he himself perhaps ever taken the trouble to find out.

That witty, first-person voice, the youthful high spirits and pointed comic gift are some of the keys to Nievo's style, which could not be more different from that of the other great novelist of Italy's Risorgimento against whom he's often measured, Alessandro Manzoni. Manzoni, who worked and reworked his masterpiece, *The Betrothed*, publishing separate versions in 1827 and 1842, is considered the first real stylist of modern literary Italian. *The Betrothed*'s reputation, however, was not built on its literary merits alone. Manzoni's pessimism, his conservatism and his Catholicism struck just the right note with the monarchical and conservative side of the Risorgimento that would emerge victorious in 1861.

Nievo was in the other camp: a radical, a free-thinker and a democrat. He wrote the way he talked, like a virtuoso conversationalist, and like his vivid, intimate letters. His sentences sparkle with fireworks, but also with dry wit; sometimes he is flamboyant and theatrical, sometimes impish and ironic. The translator's first task is not to betray that conversational voice (*voice* being, perhaps, the most important device in persuading us to suspend disbelief). But 'conversational' does not mean the writing is either simple or straightforward.

To begin with, that voice is by no means always polished on the page. Nievo uses odd turns of phrase and sometimes mixes his metaphors. The language of the *Confessions* is also studded with archaic verb forms, Venetianisms and colloquial expressions from as far away as Dalmatia. Only some of that idiomatic variety can be conveyed in translation without resorting to hackneyed English vernacular, which is rarely a good equivalent to Italian local speech. And while it seemed right to stay close to the same historical register as Nievo's in English, too much fussy 'period speech' would be jarringly wrong. For Nievo's spontaneity, his relaxed, immediate, first-person mode, his anti-heroic protagonist and his stormy, half-emancipated first lady, la Pisana, still sound fresh and modern today. (By comparison, the omniscient narrator of *The Betrothed* has aged greatly along with Manzoni's good and earnest principals Renzo and Lucia.)

If translation is the business ('sleight of hand', someone called it) of transferring words, meanings and atmosphere from the ever-changing river of one language to another, then even simple terms can depart from their dictionary definitions as time passes and the two rivers flow at different rates, as they approach or recede. The Italian word *patria*, which appears frequently in the novel and is not quite the same as what we mean in English when we say 'nation' or 'country', is often translated as 'fatherland' in English. The word 'homeland' might also come to mind. Yet both those English terms come with heavy twentieth- and twenty-first-century ideological baggage that prejudice the novel's great enthusiasm for Italian nationhood. Therefore, this translation sticks with *patria*, in the hope that the non-English word will sound more neutral in English.

The use of the article 'la' before a woman's name was standard practice in Nievo's time. Although it is disappearing as the Italian language ceases to reflect an exclusively male perspective, I've retained it here in English for one character: it marks la Pisana out as special, as a woman who can't be dismissed, who's high-handed and demands attention.

This is a book of ideas, for Carlo-Ippolito was one of the new men of his times and his views about society, about justice, about men and women, about sex, about science and politics, often rather radical, are expressed with verve in the novel. Ideas and enthusiasms spill out in a hundred convoluted digressions punctuated with all the intellectual references and scientific terminology a new man of his day would pride himself on knowing. Whether the subject was star formation, Roman history, vine blight, Venetian law or dried fruit and nut imports from the Balkans, he was up to date and well-informed.

The *Confessions* is also a tale of emotion and psychology, a treatise on love. And some of its currents are anything but easy to engage with today, great flights of fancy and gusts of feeling. Nievo's vocabulary of sentiments is especially tricky to translate. While ideas that have become obsolete merely seem quaint, antiquated emotion and sentiment can make us uncomfortable. By the standards of postmodern restraint, the intense and melodramatic pronouncements of a character in a nineteenth-century novel can make us squirm – yet those sentiments and emotions are needed to bind readers to the story. The translator has to negotiate the sensibility gap between those earnest, archaic hearts and souls and the fallible, contradictory human beings we moderns hold ourselves to be.

And then there were a few instances where fidelity to Nievo's style proved a real challenge. One was his passion for triples: he liked his adjectives and participles to come in threes. By the more austere standards of twenty-first-century taste, that is two, perhaps even three modifiers too many. Yet in the end I grew to appreciate all those triplets; for one thing, they provide an unexpected rhythm to Nievo's prose.

The *Confessions* has never before appeared in English in its entirety, although an abridged English edition was published in 1957, translated by the prolific Lovett F. Edwards, best known for his translations from Serbo-Croatian, especially *The Bridge on the Drina* by Ivo Andrić. Edwards had come upon the *Confessions* in a camp library while a prisoner of war at the Castle of Montechiarugolo near Parma in the early 1940s. His translation is lively and a labour of love. But it has aged and the three hundred or so pages cut from the text leave a somewhat distorted idea of what the novel is about. Imagine *War and Peace* without many of Tolstoy's asides: such was the 1957 edition. It was given the title *The Castle of Fratta*, which did justice to Nievo's marvellous portrait of *ancien régime* Venice in the shape of one tiny castle, but swept aside the novel's broader political and historical reach.

If there was one aspect of the novel that the earlier translation was often deaf to it was Nievo's frequent use of free indirect discourse. While the narrative is framed in the first person, Carlo's reminiscences are so lengthy and extensive that in telling an anecdote he will slip out of his own voice and into the point of view of another character he is telling us about. It is an expedient Nievo uses to good effect, broadening his optic to illustrate the thoughts and prejudices of the many characters that populate his tale, like a dazzling drawing-room raconteur sketching out all the parts in his story. Take away that profusion of voices and not only sense, but much humour and psychological insight, are lost.

Finally, a personal note: I am pleased to have brought this

book into English not only for its literary qualities, but because I think its spirit and its message (for this is also a book with a message) remain extraordinarily vital. So long as the ideals of liberty and justice have not been fully realized, the *Confessions* has something to say. And, unfortunately, across Europe and beyond, that is still the case today.

This translation is based on the first scholarly edition of Nievo's novel published in 1952 by Sergio Romagnoli. The Italian editions that post-date Romagnoli differ only very slightly from that standard text, largely in their interpretation of the author's omissions and errors.

I would like to thank Eva Cecchinato of the Università Ca' Foscari, Venice, who helped with various historical matters, and David Laven of the University of Nottingham, who was generous with his extensive historical knowledge of nineteenth-century Venice. I'm grateful to Alberto Mario Banti, Sara Bershtel, Anne Edelstein, Marion Faber, Adam Freudenheim, Edith Grossman, Eva Hoffman and Lucy Riall for help and encouragement. My editors Jessica Harrison, Anna Hervé and Ian Pindar were all marvellous, both eagle-eyed and sensitive to the novel's eccentric use of language. My thanks also to Lovett F. Edwards, Nievo's first English-language translator, whose (posthumous) enthusiasm for the *Confessions* was contagious. And, finally, to Vittorio, *grazie infinite*. All errors are mine alone.

Cast of Characters

AT THE CASTLE OF FRATTA:

Carlo Altoviti, author of these *Confessions*, patriot, soulmate to his cousin, la Pisana

The Count of Fratta, lord of the Castle, last of a dying breed

The Countess of Fratta, a lady of Venice domiciled with the Count in the provinces

Their children:

Contessina Clara, the saintly

Contessina Pisana, the rebel

Young Count Rinaldo of Fratta, the bookworm

The Old Countess, Lady Badoer, wife of Venice's ambassador to France in Louis XIV's day

Monsignor the Canon, a man of moderate religious vocation and a healthy appetite

The Clerk of Fratta, the clerk and scrivener of the chancery

The Steward of Fratta, administrator of Fratta properties, rent collector

Marchetto the Bailiff, the server of chancery sentences, torturer

Martino, who grates the cheese

The Captain, the officer of the Cernide militia, and his wife Signora Veronica

Marocco, the Captain's dog

Germano the Porter of Fratta, the gatekeeper

The Chaplain of Fratta, guardian of Castle souls
Fulgenzio the Sacristan; his sons Domenico and Girolamo
Faustina, the maid

BEYOND THE CASTLE, IN VENICE, THE FRIULI AND OTHER PARTS OF THE NOT-YET-ITALIAN NATION:

Lucilio Vianello, a doctor, patriot and republican, Clara's suitor
Partistagno, lord of the castle
Venchieredo, lord of the castle
His son Raimondo Venchieredo, one of Clara's suitors
Gaetano, bailiff and *bulo* of Venchieredo
Signor Antonio Provedoni, elder of the commune of Cordovado
His children:

- Leopardo Provedoni, a true man of the people
- Bruto Provedoni, a humble patriot enlisted in the French Army, where he is badly wounded
- Aquilina Provedoni, a country girl with a good heart, limited horizons

Doretta Natalino, daughter of the clerk of Venchieredo; wife to Leopardo Provedoni
Spaccafumo the smuggler
Sandro Giorgi, son of the miller, later General Giorgi
Monsignor di Sant'Andrea of Portogruaro, confessor to the Countess
His Excellency Mauro Navagero of Venice
Senator Almorò Frumier of Venice; his son Agostino
Avvocato Ormenta of Padua, a shady reactionary
Padre Pendola, a tireless defender of Church privilege
Madre Redenta, abbess of the convent of Santa Teresa

Todero Altoviti, Carlino's long-lost father

Apostulos, Greek banker in Venice

Spiro, his son, and Aglaura, his daughter

Countess Migliana, a well-connected Milanese courtesan

The Princess of Santacroce, influential Neapolitan aristocrat who helps Carlo and la Pisana

Francesco Martelli, Neapolitan patriot, Carlo's fellow officer in Carafa's legion

His sons:

Arrigo, who goes to Greece to fight for the independence of Italy's Greek brothers

Claudio, an engineer working in Brazil

Carlo's children with Aquilina:

Luciano, Donato, Giulio and Pisana

HISTORICAL PERSONAGES:

Napoléon Bonaparte

Joséphine de Beauharnais, his consort

Lodovico Manin, last Doge of Venice

Ferdinand I of the Kingdom of the Two Sicilies

Cardinal Fabrizio Ruffo, a royalist, leader of the anti-republican peasant army, the Sanfedisti

Ettore Carafa, Duke of Andria, Count of Ruvo; a patriot, republican general

Ugo Foscolo, poet

Mahmud II, Ottoman Sultan

George Gordon Byron, poet

Pope Pius IX, 'the reformer'

General Giuseppe Garibaldi, the Hero of Two Worlds

Emperor Dom Pedro I of Brazil

And many more . . .

F. R.

Italy after the Congress of Vienna
SWITZERLAND
AUSTRIA
AUSTRIAN EMPIRE
HUNGARY
Lake Geneva
Lake Maggiore
Lake Como
Trento
Udine
Lake Garda
Verona
Vicenza
Trieste
CROATIA
PIEDMONT-SARDINIA
Milan
LOMBARDY–VENETIA
Padua
Venice
Turin
Mantua
BOSNIA
Piacenza
Alessandria
Parma
Modena
Ferrara
PARMA
FRANCE
Genoa
Bologna
OTTOMAN EMPIRE
Ravenna
MODENA
MASSA
LUCCA
Lucca
Pisa
Florence
Pesaro
DALMATIA
Nice
Livorno
Ancona
Ligurian Sea
Siena
TUSCANY
Perugia
PAPAL STATES
Adriatic Sea
Bastia
Elba
CORSICA
(to France)
Ajaccio
Viterbo
L'Aquila
Pescara
Rome

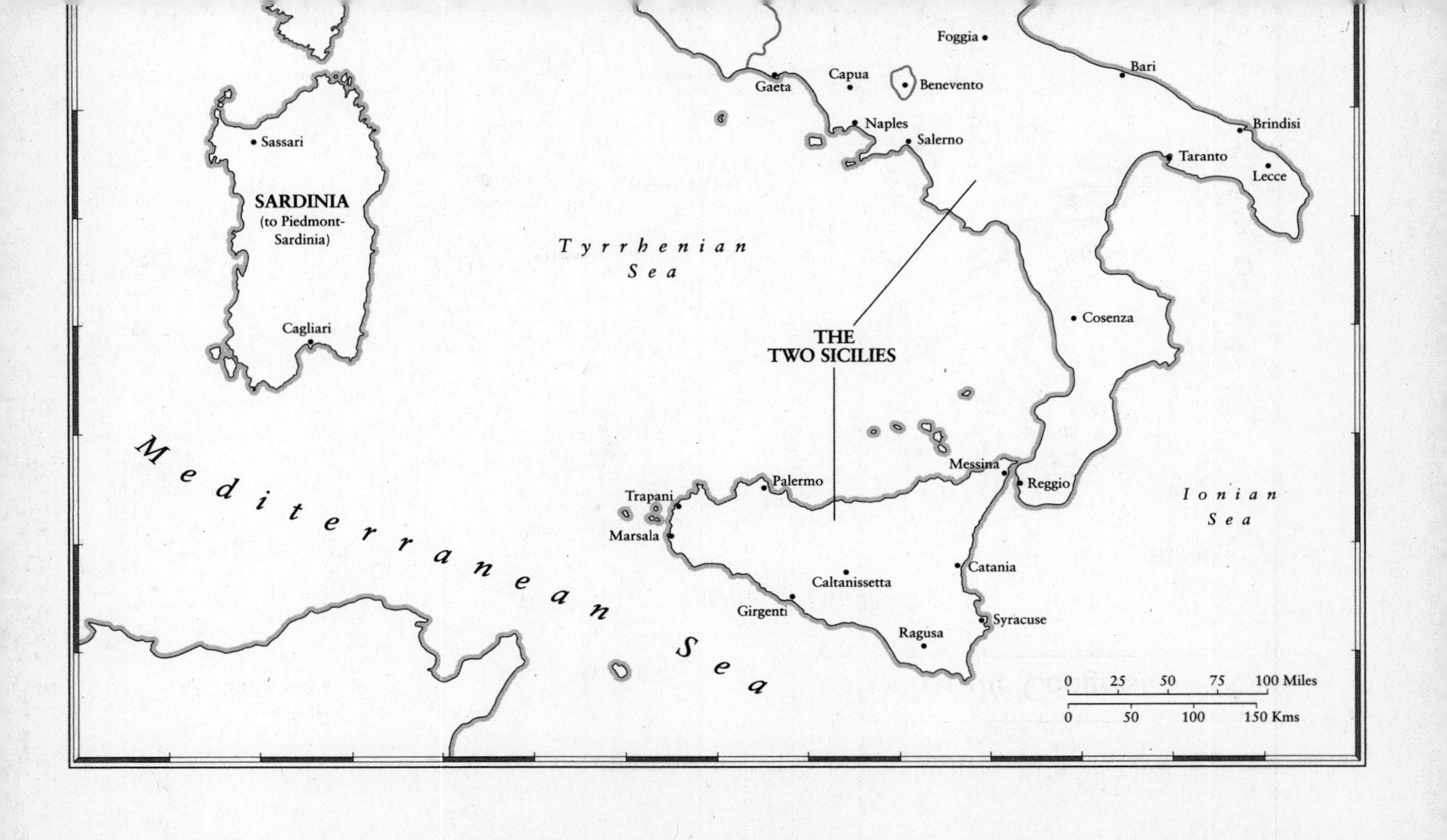
Foggia
Bari
Gaeta
Capua
Benevento
Naples
Salerno
Brindisi
Taranto
Lecce
Sassari
SARDINIA
(to Piedmont-
Sardinia)
Tyrrhenian
Sea
Cagliari
THE
TWO SICILIES
Cosenza
Mediterranean Sea
Messina
Reggio
Palermo
Trapani
Marsala
Ionian
Sea
Catania
Caltanissetta
Girgenti
Syracuse
Ragusa
0 25 50 75 100 Miles
0 50 100 150 Kms

CONFESSIONS OF AN ITALIAN

ONE

A brief introduction to the motives inspiring these Confessions of mine, to the famed Castle of Fratta[1] *where I spent my childhood, the kitchen of that aforementioned castle, as well as the masters, the servants, the guests and the cats who lived there around the year 1780. The first invasion of dramatis personae, interrupted here and there by many sage observations on the Venetian Republic, the military and civilian orders of the day, and the significance given to the word patria – native land – as the century came to an end.*

I was born a Venetian on 18 October 1775, the day of Saint Luke of the Gospel, and by God's grace I shall die an Italian,[2] whenever that Providence that so mysteriously governs the world deems it right.

That is the moral of my story. And since it wasn't I but my times that wrote the moral, it occurs to me that a simple account of how my times acted upon my life might be of some use to those destined one day to know the full consequences of what was just beginning here.

In this year 1858 of the Christian era I am now over eighty years old, and yet younger of heart than perhaps I ever was in my pugnacious youth and industrious manhood. I have lived and suffered much, but never without those consolations (often forgotten among the trials that overwhelm us in our weakness and intemperance) that later grant peace and serenity when we recall them, infallible talismans against adversity. I refer to those sentiments and those opinions that are not shaped by external events but rule victoriously over them. My nature, my talents, my early training and what came after were, like all things human, a mixture of good and bad. To be quite honest, I might add that the bad was rather more abundant than the good.

But none of this would be unusual or worthy of note had my life not spanned these past two centuries: a time destined to remain memorable, above all for Italians. It was then that we saw the first real fruits of that political speculation that between the Trecento and Settecento emerges in the works of Dante, Machiavelli, Filicaia, Vico,[3] and those many others whom my mediocre culture and near-ignorance of literature prevents me from recalling. The fortune (some would say misfortune) of having lived through these years has made me wish to set down what I have seen, heard, done and felt from earliest childhood to the verge of senility – when an old man's aches and pains, a wish to step aside before the young, the taming of opinions with age, and, may I say, the many, many troubles of my later years have confined me to that country dwelling from which I've watched the last, farcical act of the great drama of feudalism.

My simple tale adds no more to history than a note in the margins of an ancient codex appended by an unknown hand of today. The private life of a man who was neither so mean and so petty as to pretend not to see the hardships of others, nor so stoic as to fight them with great determination, nor so knowing or so arrogant as to ignore them in contempt, reflects, it seems to me, the common and national life he is a part of, the way a falling raindrop reflects the course of the storm. My experiences may thus offer a sort of model of those innumerable individual destinies that from the collapse of the old political orders to the patching together of the present one, make up the greater Italian destiny. Perhaps I am mistaken, but might not some young men, reflecting on my tale, shy away from false temptations, others get fired up about this endeavour slowly being realized, and yet others forge certain beliefs from those vague aspirations that make them try a hundred directions before they find true civic office? Thus at any rate it has seemed to me during these nine years when I have been putting down these notes as whim and memory suggested.

I began them, full of confidence, on the eve of a great defeat, and carried them to term during the penance of these long years of further struggle, and they have helped to convince me that there is more stamina and greater hope today than in the past's feeble, degenerate example.

And so, as I sit down to make a fair copy, I wish in these few words of preamble to set out those ideals that have forced me (an old man and not a writer) to try, perhaps in vain, the difficult art of writing. The clarity of the ideals, the simplicity of the sentiments and the veracity of the tale are my excuse and compensation for my poor command of rhetoric. Instead of fame, I'll have the sympathy of my good readers.

As I near the grave, alone in the world, left behind by friends and enemies alike, with no fears and no hopes that are not eternal, freed by age from those passions that so often deflected my judgement from the true path, and freed, too, from the fleeting siren call of my not very bold ambition, I see that I've harvested a single fruit in my life: peace of mind. I live content in this, I trust in this; I commend it to my younger comrades as the most enviable treasure and only shield against the seductions of false friends, the deceit of the vile and the abuse of the powerful.

One other truth I must declare (and here the voice of an octogenarian perhaps adds some authority): I have found life to be good. That is, so far as humility permits us to count ourselves as infinitesimal actors in a great universe of life, and habits of friendship accustom us to consider the well-being of the many above that of ourselves alone. Now that my earthly existence approaches its end, I am happy for the good I have done, certain to have made amends as best I could for the bad, and have no other faith nor hope beyond that which flows into the great sea of being. The peace I now enjoy is like that mysterious gulf from which the able sailor finds his way to the infinitely calm ocean of all existence. But my thoughts – before I dive into that time which is no longer time – rush ahead once more to mankind's future.

To those men of the future I faithfully confide my mistakes to be corrected, my hopes to be met, my vows to be carried out.

My early years were spent in the Castle of Fratta: today no more than a pile of rubble from which the peasants gather stones to brace their mulberry trees, but once a great edifice with towers and turrets, a huge drawbridge now rotting with age, and the loveliest Gothic windows to be found between the River Lemene and the River Tagliamento. In all my travels I have never seen a construction that cut a more bizarre figure in the landscape, nor that had edges, corners, protuberances and indentations to please all the cardinal and mid-points on the weathervane. Not only this, but the angles were built with such bold imagination that not one matched another, as if the T-square had never been near them, or an entire engineer's office had fallen asleep part-way through the job.

The castle was wonderfully protected by a deep moat where sheep grazed when the frogs weren't croaking, but some stubborn ivy had crawled in on hidden paths to cover it, and shooting over here and climbing up there, had ended by creating such an explosion of festoons and arabesques that you could no longer see the reddish colour of the terracotta bricks. No one dreamed any longer of cutting that aged mantle from those lordly walls; only the shutters, blown here and there by the northern winds, risked chopping off a shoot or two.

Another peculiarity of that house was its multitude of chimneys, which from a distance made it look like a half-finished chess game (and let me say that if the lords of long ago kept one armed man per chimney, this must have been the best-armed castle in Christendom). Otherwise, the courtyards with their high arcades were full of mud and chicken mess, their internal disorder nicely in keeping with the promise of the façade. Even the bell tower of the chapel was cracked at the top from repeated thunderbolts. But persistence must be rewarded, and since a storm never brewed but the castle bell tower gave it a welcome, so the storm was obliged to deliver a few bolts of lightning. Some said the merit for this comedy belonged to the stand of age-old poplars that gave shade around the castle; according to the peasants, the Devil lived among those trees and from time to time received a visit from his old friends. The masters, used to the fact that the bell tower alone got struck, began to look on it as a lightning rod and thus happily abandoned it to heavenly wrath, so long as the barn roof and the big chimney over the kitchen went unharmed.

And now we come to a matter that demands a rather detailed

description. Let me put it this way: I, who have never seen the Colossus of Rhodes or pyramids of Egypt, believe the kitchen at Fratta and its hearth to be the grandest monument that ever graced the earth. The Duomo of Milan and the great temple of St Peter's are something, yes; but they have nothing like the same size and solidity. The only thing remotely similar I can recall is perhaps Hadrian's Mausoleum, although its transformation in Castel Sant'Angelo has made it seem much shrunken. The kitchen at Fratta was a huge space with an undefined number of walls each a very different dimension from the others; it rose towards the sky like a dome and plunged into the earth like an abyss; it was dark, nay, black with ancient soot from which glittered like so many diabolical eyes the bottoms of casseroles, roasting tins and carafes hung on their nails; it was cluttered everywhere with huge credenzas and giant cupboards and endlessly long tables; it was ploughed every hour of the day and night by an infinite number of grey and black cats, which lent it the semblance of a workshop for witches.

Such was the kitchen proper. But in its deepest, darkest corner there opened the jaws of an Acherontean den, an even grimmer and more frightening cave where the darkness was split by a crackling flicker of coals and by two greenish openings secured with double bars. Here was a dense swirling of smoke, an eternal bubbling up of beans in hideous cauldrons; here, on creaky, smoke-darkened planks sat a congress of grave, surly, somnolent figures. This was the hearth and the domestic Curia of the lords of Fratta. But just let the evening *Ave Maria* sound, let the murmur of the *Angelus Domini* cease, and the scene would suddenly change as the hour of light came to this gloomy little world. The old cook would light four lamps with one taper; she hung two under the hood of the hearth and two at either side of a Virgin of Loreto. With a huge poker she beat the coals hidden under the ashes and tossed a handful of brambles and juniper on top. The lamps beamed their calm yellow light back and forth, the fire sputtered and smoked and sent whirling plumes up to scald the bars of two giant andirons bossed in bronze, and the evening inhabitants of the kitchen showed their various faces under the light.

The Count of Fratta was a man past sixty who always looked as if he had just stepped out of his armour, so stiffly and pompously did he sit in his chair. But his elaborate bagwig, his long cinder-coloured, scarlet-trimmed *zimarra*,[4] and the box-wood snuff container forever in his hands detracted somewhat from the warrior pose. True, there was a sliver of a sword stuck between his legs, but the sheath was so rusty you could mistake it for a roasting spit, and in any case, I couldn't swear there was really a steel blade inside, nor had he himself perhaps ever taken the trouble to find out.

The Count was always shaved with great care, as if he had just left the barber's hands. Morning and evening he wore a blue kerchief under his arm, and although he rarely went out on foot and never on horseback, he wore boots and spurs to put Frederick the Great's couriers to shame. It was his tacit declaration of sympathy for the Prussian side, and although the German wars[5] were long over he never ceased to threaten the Austrians with his fierce boots. When the Count spoke the flies fell silent, and when he had finished, each man agreed in his own fashion, with his voice or with a nod of the head, and when the Count laughed, all hastened to laugh, and when he sneezed, even when tobacco caused the sneeze, eight or nine voices shouted out: 'Long live!' 'His health!' 'His happiness!' 'God save the Count!' When he got up, all got up, and when he left the kitchen, everyone, even the cats, breathed deeply, as if a millstone had been lifted from their breasts. And the one who breathed most deeply and noisily of all was the Clerk, on those days when the Count didn't signal him to follow, but left him to the warm ease of the hearth.

However, this miracle seldom happened, I must say. Almost always the Clerk was the shadow incarnate of the Count. He rose with him and sat down with him and their legs strode back and forth together so rhythmically that they seemed to obey a drum beat.

There had once been a time when the frequent absences of his shadow led the Count to turn around every three paces to be sure he was being followed according to his desires. But soon the Clerk grew resigned to his fate and spent his afternoons and evenings collecting the master's kerchief, wishing him good health at every sneeze, agreeing with his observations, and telling him what he imagined would please him with regard to various juridical matters. For example, if a peasant, accused of having stolen vegetables from the master's garden, replied to the Clerk with blandishments, or by stuffing a half-ducat into his hand to avoid *la corda*,[6] the Clerk would tell the Count that the miscreant feared the severe judgement of His Excellency and had asked for mercy, that he had showed remorse and was willing to make amends if that was deemed appropriate. The Count then inhaled enough air to fill Goliath's lungs for a week, and replied that the clemency of Titus must certainly be conjoined with the fair justice administered by the courts, and that yes, he would be willing to pardon anyone who was truly sorry.

The Clerk, out of modesty perhaps, wore clothes as poor and ragged as his master's were sumptuous and magnificent. Nature itself counselled such modest dress, for it would be hard to find a body more wretched and ruined than his. He was cross-eyed out of habit, they said, but few cross-eyes had more reason to be considered genuine. His aquiline nose managed to be hooked and snub at the same time: a Gordian knot of many aborted noses all together. His mouth gaped beneath it so menacingly that at times the poor nose sniffed as if in fear of falling in. His legs in their boots of Russian leather splayed out on either side, lending as much support as possible to a man who otherwise seemed about to collapse with every gust of wind. If you subtracted the boots, the wig, the clothes, the sword and the frame of bones – I do not jest – the Clerk of Fratta weighed no more than twenty *libbre*,[7] and at least four of those belonged to the goitre he tried to hide under a huge, white, starched collar. Despite all this, he enjoyed the happy delusion that he was anything but unattractive, and there was nothing he loved to talk about more than comely women and the gallant arts.

How Milady Justice felt about being in his hands, I couldn't honestly say. I do remember seeing more contrary faces than cheerful ones coming down the covered stairway from the chancery. Outside the anteroom on days when audiences were held, it was also trumpeted about that anyone with a good pair of fists, a loud voice, and gold in his pockets was likely to find himself in the right before the court. What I can say is that twice I saw *la corda* applied in the Castle courtyard, and both times this punishment fell to poor fellows who certainly didn't deserve it. Luckily for them the bailiff who applied the penalties of high and low justice was a man of discernment and he knew how to raise the rope in such a way that the dislocated joints would heal inside a week. And so Marchetto (also known as Bone-Bender) was as much loved by the poor as the Clerk was hated.

As for the Count himself, hidden away in the clouds of Olympus like destiny among the ancients, he eluded both the hatred and the love of his underlings. They doffed their hats to him as towards an alien saint from whom they kept their distance, and they would drive their carts right into the ditch when the coachman, still half a mile off on his high perch, shouted at them to make way.

The Count had a brother who was nothing like him, and he was the honorary canon of the Portogruaro Cathedral. He was the roundest, smoothest, most mellifluous canon in the whole diocese: a true man of peace who divided his time judiciously between the breviary and the table, without letting it be known whether he preferred the one or the other. Monsignor Orlando, as his Christian name testified, hadn't been begotten by his father to be dedicated to the Mother Church. The family tree of the Counts of Fratta could boast of military glory in every generation, and Orlando was destined to carry on the family tradition. But man proposes and God disposes: for once the hoary old proverb wasn't wrong.

The future general's first act was an unusual show of affection for his wet nurse. He could not be weaned until he was two, and then it wasn't clear whether 'pap' or 'pappy' was the one word he could pronounce. When he succeeded in getting up on his two legs they began to give him wooden swords and paper helmets, but he immediately ran off to the chapel to ply a broom with the sacristan. As for getting him accustomed to real weapons, he had an instinctive revulsion for table knives and preferred to cut his meat with a spoon. His father tried to overcome this disgraceful reluctance by getting one of his guardsmen to take the boy on his lap, but little Orlando was so terrorized he had to be handed over to the cook. After the wet nurse, the cook was his second love.

The boy's vocation remained hazy. The Clerk of those times maintained that captains ate heartily and that the little master could well become a famous captain. But the old Count was not cheered by this augury, and he sighed as he turned from the puffy, lost face of his second-born to the rugged, protruding chins in the old family portraits.

The last gasp of the old Count's procreative faculties had been an ambitious try at inscribing a Grand Master of the Order of Malta or an Admiral of the Serenissima[8] in the family annals. He couldn't abide the thought he'd gone to all that trouble just to have a frightfully hungry captain of the Cernide[9] militia at his table. And so he redoubled his efforts to stimulate Orlando's bellicose spirits, but to no avail. Orlando went around building little altars in every corner of the castle, he recited the Mass, high, low, and ceremonial, with the sacristan's daughters, and if he saw a shotgun he would run to hide under the kitchen credenza. And so they tried more persuasive methods: he was forbidden to hang around the sacristy or sing vespers through his nose, as he had heard the parish choristers do.

His mother, however, was alarmed by this severity, and quietly began to take her son's side. Now, Orlando enjoyed playing the little martyr, and because his mother's sugar-coating neutralized his father's needling, the vocation of priest became ever more desirable. The cook and serving maids sniffed out a certain odour of sainthood on him; he, in turn, swelled up with pride and would go to great lengths to keep the women worshipping him. In the end, the entire family was against the old Count and his martial zeal. Even the rude guardsmen, who backed the cook when their lord wasn't in earshot, felt it was a sacrilege to try to dislodge San Luigi[10] from the true path.

But the Count was stubborn, and it was only after twelve years of fruitless siege that he finally abandoned the field and stowed away Orlando's future laurels in the chest of vanished hopes. One fine morning the boy was called with great ceremony before his father. Despite the Count's determination to maintain an absolute ruler's autocratic scowl, he was as vacillating and contrite as a general in the act of surrendering.

'My dear son,' he began his speech, 'the calling of the warrior is a noble calling.'

'Yes, sire,' said the boy, putting on a saintly face only slightly sullied by the sly glance covertly aimed at his mother.

'You bear a proud name,' the old Count continued with a sigh, 'as you must know from Ariosto's poem,[11] which I have so often urged you to study . . .'

'I read the Office of Our Lady,' said the boy humbly.

'Very good,' added the old man, tugging his wig forward on his brow, 'but Ariosto is also valuable reading. Orlando was a great knight who freed France from the rule of the Moors. And if you had also glanced at your Tasso,[12] you would know that it was not with the Office of Our Lady but with great strokes of the sword and thrusts of the lance that Good Godfrey took the Holy Sepulchre from the Saracens.'

'The Lord be praised!' exclaimed the boy. 'Now there is nothing more to accomplish.'

'What do you mean, nothing more?' said the old man. 'Know, you wretched boy, that the infidels recaptured the Holy Land and that even as we speak the Sultan's pasha rules Jerusalem, to the shame of all Christendom.'

'I will pray to the Lord that this shame may cease,' added Orlando.

'Pray? You must act. Act!' shouted the old Count.

'Pardon me,' intervened the Countess, 'but you don't mean you want our little one to carry out a crusade all on his own?'

'Nonsense – he is no longer our little one!' replied the Count. 'He turns twelve today.'

'Even were he to turn one hundred,' said the lady, 'he wouldn't get it in his head to conquer Palestine.'

'We shall never conquer it as long as we let our sons play girls' games with rosaries,' shouted the old man, purple with rage.

'Oh, all we need is to hear some of your blasphemy,' the Countess went on patiently. 'Here the Lord has granted us a son who wishes to do good, and we show our gratitude by not recognizing his gifts?'

'Gifts, gifts,' muttered the Count. 'A gluttonous little saintlet he is . . . half-fox and half-rabbit!'

'Mind that the boy never said anything so very dire,' added the lady. 'He said he prays to God that the places of His passion and His death be returned to Christian hands. It's the best you could hope for today, when Christians are busy cutting each other's throats and the soldierly vocation has been reduced to a school for assassins and butchers.'

'O Sainted Body of His Worship the Doge!' swore the Count. 'Had the mothers of Sparta been like you, Xerxes would have oiled his way through Thermopylae with three hundred jugs of wine!'

'Well, had he done so, it would have been no great loss,' replied the Countess.

'What?' shouted the old man. 'You would go so far as to deny that Leonidas was a hero and the Spartan mothers were exemplary?'

'Oh, we've been over this ground before,' said the Countess quietly. 'I know little of Leonidas and the Spartan mothers, although they are often cited to me; but I'm willing to take it on trust that they were excellent people. But remember that we have called our son Orlando before us to be enlightened about his true vocation, and not to argue in his presence about these ancient trifles.'

'Women, women, born to raise hens!' grumbled the Count.

'Husband mine,' said the lady sitting up straight, 'remember that I am a Badoer. You will agree with me, I hope, that the hens in our family are not more numerous than the capons in yours.'

Orlando, who had been holding his sides for a while, burst out laughing at his mother's fine jest – but he shrank back like a wet hen at the severe look she gave him.

'You see?' she added in the direction of her husband. 'We're going to end by tossing out both wheat and chaff. Rein in your temper, for the Good Lord wants you to know that he doesn't approve of it, and think instead about the soul of this boy, as is fitting for a proper husband and father.'

The old man, still impenitent, bit his lip and turned towards the lad with such an ugly face that the boy ran to hide his head under his mother's apron skirts.

'So,' the Count began, not looking at the child, because when he looked at him he felt his bad temper rising. 'So, my son, you do not wish to take your place on a fine horse harnessed in gold and red velvet, with a great, glittering sword in hand, before six regiments of Schiavoni[13] each four arm-spans tall who await no more than a signal from you to rush forward and be killed by Turkish scimitars?'

'I want to say the Mass,' whimpered the lad, still under the Countess's apron.

The Count, hearing that whining voice muffled under the folds of her skirts, looked around to see what it was, and, catching sight of his son with his head buried like a pheasant, could not contain his rage, or perhaps it was shame as much as anger.

'Then *go* to the seminary, you bastard!' he shouted, fleeing the room.

The poor little devil then began to sob and, knowing he was safe from doing himself any harm, to pull at his hair and beat his head against his mother's lap. She took him in her arms to console him, saying, 'Oh my pretty one, do not fear, we'll make you a priest, and you will say the Mass. No, you are not made, like Cain, to shed the blood of your brothers.'

'Ooooh, I want to sing in the choir! I want to be a saint!' whimpered Orlando.

'Yes, yes, you will sing in the choir, we'll make you a canon, and you'll have your rochet and those nice red stockings! Don't cry my dearest. These are trials you must endure to show the Lord you are worthy,' she said.

The lad calmed down at this – and thus we have the story of how Count Orlando, despite his Christian name and his father's opposition, became Monsignor Orlando. But as much as the Curia was eager to satisfy the Countess's devout ambition, Orlando (who wasn't the sharpest of blades) needed no less than twelve years of seminary and another thirty of humble waiting before even half of her wishes were met. And the Count triumphed by dying many years before the red ribbons were tied to Orlando's hat. However, it cannot be said that the young man wasted all those years of waiting. First, he developed a respectable familiarity with the missal; and then his collar expanded to the point where he was surely the equal of his softest and most expansive colleagues.

Now, a castle that had within its walls two juridical and clerical dignitaries such as the Clerk and Monsignor Orlando, could not but also have its military luminary. Captain Sandracca would have given anything to be a Dalmatian, but it seems he was born at nearby Ponte di Piave. He was certainly the tallest man in the jurisdiction,[14] but the goddesses of grace and beauty had not presided at his birth. All the same, he spent a good hour each day before the mirror making himself much uglier than nature had, practising some new expression, some new arrangement of his moustaches, that made his scowl even more formidable. To hear him tell it – after he'd downed his fourth glass – there hadn't been a war from the siege of Troy to that of Belgrade in which he hadn't fought like a lion.

However, when the fumes of the wine had cooled, his pretensions shrank to more modest proportions, and he was content to talk about the twelve wounds he'd received in the Battle of Candia, always offering to drop his trousers so we could count them. And God only knows what those wounds looked like, for as I think about it today, it seems to me quite unlikely that a man who barely admitted to being fifty had taken part in that battle some sixty years previously. Maybe his memory was playing tricks on him, making him think himself the hero of some blusterer's tale heard in Piazza San Marco. The good Captain often got his dates wrong, but on the first of the month he never forgot to ask the Steward to pay him his wages of twenty ducats as commander of the Cernide. It was his day of celebration.

At dawn he sent out two drummers the length and breadth of the jurisdiction to raise a din that didn't cease until midday. And then, after the noon meal when the militia was gathered in the castle yard, he'd come out of his quarters with such an ugly face that his looks alone were almost enough to send his troops running. In his hand he held a sword big enough to pace an entire column. At the least infraction he liked to whack it fiercely across the bellies in the front line, and so whenever it seemed he was about to lower it, the first rank would fall back into the second and the second into the third, and the confusion was such that not even the arrival of the Turks could have occasioned worse.

But now the Captain smiled happily and raised his sword to reassure the troops. And so those twenty or thirty ragged peasants, their guns hoisted like shovels on their shoulders, began to march towards the parish square to the beat of the drums. But because the Captain marched ahead of them on legs that were longer than theirs, no matter how fast they tried to go he always got there before them. And then, sword outstretched, he would turn with fury on that useless herd of riff-raff, but none of them was such a fool as to stand and wait. Some simply picked up their legs and ran away, some scaled the ditches, others slipped through doorways and sneaked into haylofts. The drummers had their instruments to defend them. It was thus, in the domain of Fratta, that the monthly parade of the Cernide almost always concluded. The Captain wrote a long report, the Clerk entered it in the records and no more was said about it until the following month.

Today such clownish political and military methods may seem a wondrous thing. But that is how things worked in those days. The Portogruaro district, to which the commune of Teglio and the parish of Fratta belonged, now makes up the eastern reach of the Province of Venice, which includes all the territory on the plain next to the laguna,[15] from the lower Adige where it meets the Po Valley, to the lower Tagliamento. In the times of which I write, things stood as nature had made them and as Attila had left them.[16] The Friuli, however, answered to sixty or seventy families originating beyond the Alps and naturalized here after a century's residence; to them were entrusted the various jurisdictions, with powers both limited and full, and their votes, those of the free communes and of the peasantry made up the Friuli's Parliament of the Patria, which met once a year to take a consulting vote alongside the Representative sent out to Udine from Venice.

Although I have few sins of omission on my conscience, one of the gravest of them is never to have attended one of those

Parliaments. It must have been a wonderful spectacle. Few of the lords-and-magistrates knew anything of the law, and the country folk certainly did not know a great deal more. I doubt that all of them understood Tuscan[17] and the fact that none could speak it is rather evident from their decrees and deliberations, where, following a brief salvo in Latin, a mixture of Italian, Friulian and Venetian comes forth that is not without charm for those who enjoy a laugh. All seems to point to the fact that when the Magnificent Universal Parliament of the Patria petitioned His Serene Highness the Doge for the licence to pass a law about some matter, the tenor of that law had already been meticulously worked out between His Excellency the Representative and the Most Excellent Council of Ten.[18] That the jurists at the Bar of Udine also had a voice in those preparatory agreements I wouldn't seek to deny, especially where those jurists had the good sense to back the Signoria[19] in its designs. Of course all matters relating to private and feudal rights were naturally excluded from such negotiations; the lords would never have allowed their privileges to be put into question, nor would the Signoria have dared to deprive them of any, out of those inscrutable motives that often amounted, simply, to fear.

The fact is that having been granted permission to express itself on a particular matter, the Magnificent Universal Parliament then proposed, discussed and approved all in a single day, 11 August, to wit. The motive for haste and the reason that particular date had been chosen was this: the feast of San Lorenzo fell on that day, thus offering all the parties in the Parliament the opportunity to meet at Udine. While the San Lorenzo fair was on, however, few were inclined to neglect their private business in favour of public matters, and so it was felt that twenty-four hours was more than sufficient to dispose of public affairs. The Magnificent Universal Parliament then begged the ruling Serenissima to endorse what had been proposed, discussed and approved, and when that confirmation came the trumpeters loudly hailed as universal and sacrosanct the decision of the Magnificent Universal Parliament.

This is not to say that every law so approved was unjust or silly; as the publisher of the Statutes of the Friuli put it, *Laws are a digest of justice, maturity and experience, and are always directed toward salutary and commendable aims*. But grave doubts do remain about what merits the Magnificent Deputies of the *patria* could claim.

In 1672 it seems that the Most Excellent Carlo Contarini informed the Most Serene Doge that the old laws must be reformed. Thus in *Dominicus Contareno Dei gratia Dux Venetiarum*, etc., the Doge wishes *the wise and noble gentleman Carlo Contarini health and serenity* and then goes on to illustrate the limits of the licence granted. *Having duly considered not so much the instances of the* patria *or the Parliament as what you have pronounced in your own sworn statements with regard to these*, etc., we resolve *to comfort the souls of your beloved and faithful subjects*, and to grant them *general consensus for the reform of those articles* we believe *necessary to serve them*.

One year later, the Most Serene Doge having read and reflected upon those reforms he had approved, was pleased to permit their publication, along with his letters to the *very wise and noble gentleman Girolamo Ascanio Giustiniani* (this gentleman was then governor for the Friuli): *As here below there are some alterations in certain of the following articles which we wish to see reduced to their true essence without appendages and amendments*, etc., etc., *must be omitted*, etc., *public decrees being sufficient in this regard. In article one hundred and forty seven in which it is proposed to eliminate the damage inflicted on the lord-magistrate by the ville and the communes a penalty of fifty lire was applied to the lord-magistrate, and because this penalty was not printed in the Latin it must be removed and struck from the printed record. Such will permit the law to be applied, with the proviso that the old statutes and other laws be preserved for all those instances and recourses that may be made to Our Signoria. Ducal Palace, 20 May 1673*.

Following all these formalities, the Friulian statutes[20] were finally put on record and began to serve as the law at the beginning of the present century. The motives of the reform were thus expressed by its compilers in a solemn preface: *It has been decided to renew the laws of the* patria *of the Friuli, many of them having become impracticable over a long course of time, others debatable, and many the circumstances upon which no rules had been expressed*, etc., etc. *And because we deal here with judicial matters that must be known not merely to the judges themselves but to all*, etc., etc., *it has been resolved to take down the present volume of Laws in the vulgate and in the simplest and most easily understood form possible*, etc., etc. *To offer a fitting foundation for this profitable and praiseworthy undertaking, we shall begin with the First Constitution.*

No mention is made of why the First Constitution and not the Second should offer a fitting foundation for this profitable and praiseworthy undertaking. But perhaps the reason is that the First specified that observing the Christian religion was obligatory, and stipulated how Jews and blasphemy were to be treated. That even these matters ought to be among the 'salutary and commendable aims' that according to the publisher are always the goal of the law, I'm loathe to believe, no matter how blindly I place my trust in the selfsame publisher's interpretive faculties. The Statutes go on to establish the *feast days in honour of God and those for the needs and necessities of men, so they may easily and with no distraction harvest that which the earth, irrigated by a divine hand, produces.* There follow the regulations regarding notaries, solicitors, lawmen and advocates, about whom the legislator, having observed that *arms decorate and letters arm the State*, concludes that *their office being so noble, they must also be subject to appropriate remedies.*

Here the attribute 'noble' oddly seems to mean 'infirm' or 'dangerous'.

Numerous articles concerning procedures follow, among them, under the heading 'False Testimony', the sage proviso that *any convicted of such in a civil suit will be liable for a fine of two hundred lire, or if insolvent, have his tongue excised*. In the event of a criminal case, *the same punishment awaiting the accused will be applied to the witness*. Contracts, dowries, last wills and testaments, evictions, rents, are discussed in subsequent paragraphs. Article one hundred and forty-one deals specifically with assassins, *any of which, should he fall into the hands of justice* – an exceedingly rare event, which helps to explain why the law is so tentative – *is condemned to be hanged by the throat, in such a way that he dies*. From the paragraph dealing with assassins, we move to impoundments, to hunting and grazing laws, to that economically sensible statute proclaiming that *communes are forbidden to condemn the accused to fines more than eight* soldi *for each infraction*. There is a chapter entitled 'Castles' in which the reader is advised to see under the rules on 'Fiefs'. And finally there is a last heading, 'The Leasing of Houses', under which the dwellings of our subjects are regulated with rare paternal solicitude: *Any whose lease is less than fifty years long*, states the provision, *must be notified of eviction at least one month before the execution*. In that span of time he can settle himself for the next fifty years, and may the Lord grant him the longevity of Methuselah so that he can enjoy many such leases.

It would seem quite a wondrous thing, this statute book of a hundred pages that puts order in so many very different matters, and the jurists of the Magnificent Parliament found it so handy that they took the opportunity to insert here and there laws and recommendations on guardians, nurses and sorcerers, on the assailants and the annoyers of public officials, who were to pay a fine of forty-eight *soldi* if men and twenty-four *soldi* if women. They include a list of fees for sworn expert opinion and a smart reprimand for peasants using their carts to haul on feast days. The statutes also follow the wise custom of endorsing platitudes, as when, having established that summonses in different places falling on the same day should be served one after the other in order of precedence, the lawmaker adds, as the motive for this provision: *because a person may not in several places simultaneously be*. Our modern codes of law are not very logical; they simply impose because they impose. But that doesn't mean we can't appreciate the charming naivety of the old ones.

You might think that the business of the judge or the advocate would be quite simple when the statutes were so concise. But there was a small stumbling block. In those cases not covered by provincial law, Venetian law was meant to take effect, and anyone who has any idea of the volume and confusion of the latter code can just imagine how easily court transactions grew entangled. And then there was customary law, and, finally (to confuse matters further) came feudal law, which, when mixed with other rules and decrees in a land cluttered with castles and jurisdictions, always ended up in that place where oil settles when it is mixed with wine.

The way the arbitrary conjunction of so many laws and so many codes produced never-ending inconvenience for the administration of justice moved the souls of the Most Serene Signoria to mercy, and it was decided to remedy the situation by sending three examiner-inquisitors to the mainland, where, able to touch with their hands the distress *of the dearly beloved subjects and the poor peasantry*, they could bring swift and sound redress. And, in fact, the three ever-so conscientious inquisitors traversed the *patria* of the Friuli far and wide, and the very first fruit of their peregrinations was a fiery proclamation on taxes owed to the public purse, which concluded: *the zeal of the Gentlemen Representatives stands aroused and ready to ignite collection efforts and to periodically appraise properties, rents and incomes belonging to revenue-shirkers, confiscating and selling off the same goods and effects to the benefit of public coffers; and this they are unfailingly bound to do, or risk losing their offices at the discretion of justice*. What 'justice' I'd be eager to ask of them.

Having brought suitable order to such arguments with half a dozen similar proclamations, the Illustrious and Most Excellent gentlemen examiners turned their minds to a matter of real and immediate benefit to the dearly beloved subjects, with a further decree that stated: *We* (new paragraph) *With regard to the wines of Istria and Isola* (new paragraph). *The obstacles to the sale of the wines of this most loyal* Patria *have drawn the attention of Magistrates*, etc., etc., *and prompt us to make known here* (new paragraph). *Under the law*, etc., etc., *it is absolutely forbidden to introduce in this* Patria *and Province of the Friuli, any type of wine from Leeward*[21] *or Isola d'Istria, if the Duty has not been put in the hand of the Collector at Muscoli*. And here followed a couple of pages listing the punishments.

With this decree the gentlemen inquisitors considered they had done their duty for the immediate benefit of the loyal *patria*, and so began to turn out proclamations: *concerning the Grist Tax*[22] *and Ducats per Barrel, concerning Baker's Ovens, concerning Oil, Salt and Tobacco, concerning Contraband*, and they didn't stop giving voice to these concerns until they had voiced a quite paternal and far-sighted one *concerning Mourning Customs*, which stated that *in the event of a death in the family, to prevent extravagant mourning displays that would impose pointless and superfluous obligation, leading a family to ruin and preventing familial duties from being carried out* (such duties as paying taxes) it was forbidden, among other things, *to wear those long cloaks otherwise known as mourning dress, a penalty of six hundred ducats to the transgressor, to be paid one-third to the Gentleman Chamberlain, one-third to the coffers of the magnificent city, and one-third to the informer.* I feel sure that after this measure was introduced all those who had lost a relative during the past decade must have shortened their normal cloaks by half an arm's-length so as not to risk paying so dear a price.

That first set of examiners was vigorous and sharp-sighted, but those who followed were even more adept at exacting profit. Special mention must go to the ones who in 1770 handled the reorganization of the Cernide, the local militias raised by the communes or the fief-holders and charged with maintaining order in the jurisdictions. *The Gentlemen Examiner-Inquisitors permit the Cernide, their Corporals and Heads of Hundreds*, which is to say, their captains (Captain Sandracca was Head of Hundred, or perhaps of fifty or of twenty, depending on the good will of his subordinates, and claimed the title of Captain because of his glorious past) permitted them, as I was saying, *to freely carry an unloaded musket in town and in transit through fenced territories, never in church, at fairs, markets or when accompanying townsmen. They may also*, the Very Illustrious Examiners went on, *when serving in small, medium and large military parades and on patrols, be armed not only with a musket but also with a bayonet, but never a dagger, permanently outlawed if now wantonly replaced by the knife, a weapon that is an abomination to any sort of militia and which is condemned under all legal codes.*

That clause struck less at the Cernide than at the high-handed lords of the castles, who, recruiting their famous *buli*,[23] would arm the most ruthless of them to the teeth and keep them on hand for regular acts of violence. Here, however, one must praise the Counts of Fratta, whose *buli* were famous all around for being especially meek and mild, and who, if the Count retained them, were more the beneficiaries of sheer habit than belligerence. Captain Sandracca, the one-time hero of Candia, looked with horror on this vulgar rabble of marauders and irregulars, as he put it, and had pressured the Count until he banished them to a little room next to the stables, and even Marchetto the bailiff, who served when necessary as their chief, was not allowed to enter the kitchen unless he first laid down his pistols and his cutlass. The Captain explained his horror of these weapons according to the arguments of the gentlemen examiners: such weapons were an abomination to any sort of militia. He said he was more afraid of a knife than of a cannon – and this was plausibly true at Fratta, where no cannon had ever been seen.

Having taken care of the difficult matter of weapons in this somewhat wholesale fashion, the gentlemen examiners moved to regulate the no less important matter of coinage. But the first problem meant so much to them and was causing so much disorder that they quickly returned to it. In that very same year they repeated their *prohibition on the carrying of weapons by anyone without the necessary permission*, extending this ban *also to feast days and public ceremonies*, with the proviso that *breaches of this rule may be denounced in secret and a prize of twenty ducats will be awarded to the informer*.

This matter was evidently of the utmost importance to the Maggior Consiglio, on whose authority the examiners were turning out proclamation after proclamation. Their energy, however, only betrayed the fact that their results were modest. In truth, it was not easy to control weapons in a province divided and subdivided into a hundred jurisdictions overlaid and interwoven with each other, bordering on other countries such as Gorizia and the Tyrol, furrowed at every step by streams and rivers that lacked not just bridges but ferries, and rendered ten times larger than it is today by crooked, rutted, utterly disgraceful roads more suited to overturning passengers than to speeding them along. Between Colloredo and Collalto, a stretch of four miles,[24]

I can recall that up until twenty years ago a pair of strong, swift horses would sweat for three hours to haul a coach, which had better be strong enough to resist the pounding it received from ruts and rocks. And then there was a good mile in which the road became a ditch or a creek, and to pass that stretch a team of oxen was indispensable. And these carriageways were no better or worse than in the rest of the province, and so we can just imagine how much executive power the authorities could bring to bear on persons protected at every turn by so many natural obstacles.

Here, I will leave aside for the moment the venal complicity of the guards, the bailiffs and even the clerks of the chancery, forced to stoop to such compromises to compensate the crushing meanness of their fees and the proverbial miserliness of their masters. Among the lords, for example, was one who rather than pay his clerk or scrivener, demanded a portion of the fines received – and I recall the clerk who was forced to fine people double in order to satisfy the greed of his master and at the same time earn enough to live. Another lord, during his penniless moments, himself denounced supposed infractions so as to skim off part of the fees the condemned man paid to the clerk.

Not that the master and the Clerk of Fratta were so inclined, although I do not recall ever hearing their justice much praised. The Clerk, when freed from his shadow ministry and when not gossiping about low women or intrigues of the flesh, complained unceasingly about how mean his fees were; and, according to him, any officer of the courts unable to prove categorically to St Peter that he had died of hunger could not even think about getting into paradise. I don't wish to judge how right or wrong his complaints were, but I do know that the fee for questioning one or more criminals was one lira, or one-half franc, and I think it's unlikely that anyone could enjoy justice at more cut-rate prices. But in justice, as in other things, he who spends more, spends less (proverbs rarely being mistaken). The same thing held with the posting of letters: to send one right across the Friuli cost just three *soldi*, and considering the devilish condition of the roads that was a real bargain. But what difference did it make when you had to send ten to get one delivered, and then even that arrived only by chance, and so late it no longer mattered? Looked at in a certain way, those who hold San Marco[25] sacred are not entirely wrong, but in a thousand other ways apart from that one, I would bless all the other saints in Heaven and not bother with the second evangelist and his lion. I am old but not enamoured of age, and as for antiquity, I worship the beard itself, not whether it is black or grey.

Certainly, those who had inherited many rights and few duties and who wished those conditions to endure, found San Marco a convenient patron. No conservative – not even Metternich or Chateaubriand – was more conservative than he. The Friuli remained just as it had been when it was handed to him by the patriarchs of Aquileia; never mind his jurisdictions, his statutes and his parliaments. All these represented a mere ghost of public life that once, perhaps, had harboured sparks of vitality, but under the Lion's wings was reduced to profound indifference and weary resignation to the Republic's senile command. The short-lived raids of the Turks at the end of the Quattrocento had saturated this far corner of Italy with a great, near-superstitious fear, so that the tie to Venice – the old victor, as it had been, over Ottoman power – was thought very fortunate indeed. But Venice, shrewd old trader that she was, knew that to hold her new domain without weapons she must rely on the lords in their castles, who had grown to be ever bigger bullies protecting the countryside during the last Turkish incursions.

And so the old feudal order was indulged, the way much was indulged in that boggy, infirm realm of the Republic. Nobles were still holding court in their castles three centuries after their compatriots had already become citizens. Their one-time virtues had become their vices, as the changes all around them extinguished the very air they breathed. Courage became brute force, pride became hauteur; hospitality, bit by bit, became the arrogant and illegal custom of harbouring the worst gallows-material. San Marco slumbered, or when he was awake and punishing, meted out justice darkly: cruel and inexplicable; pointless, and therefore providing no example.

Meanwhile the patrician class of the Friuli began to split into two factions: countrymen, who were cruder, rougher and less inclined to be ruled by the laws of the Republic; and the city folk of Venice, who tended to flabbiness due to their daily exposure to the city aristocracy. Family habit and nearness to the lands of the Empire drew the former to the imperial side, while the latter, with their city ways, grew more and more sheep-like in obeying their governors. The first were rebellious out of instinct; the second, cowards because they were so insignificant. Worse than just useless, both were harmful to the good of their country. And thus it was that numerous mainland grandees served the Court of Vienna for generations, while others who had married into Grand Canal society enjoyed high office in the Republic.

But the two sides were not so much at odds that they didn't sometimes conspire. The most wilful of mainland lords could occasionally be seen in Venice to make amends for his crimes, or to supply the senators with large purses full of *zecchini*[26] so they would turn a blind eye. And then there were those charming noble-fellows, so *venezievoli* – so sleek and mild after three months of winter in Venice, that is – who when they went back to their towers and turrets turned more ferocious than ever, although their bluster mostly involved fraud, not violence, and often they had arranged things ahead of time so that no punishment would be applied.

As for justice, it was much the same as between cats and dogs: no one took it seriously except for those few who lived in fear of God and risked making giant blunders out of ignorance. But on the whole, justice was the reign of the cunning and the sly, and it was only with cunning and trickery that the poor could find a way to compensate themselves for the bullying they endured. In the law courts of the Friuli, the administrators' sleight of hand replaced the principle of *equitas* in Roman law, and the greed and superiority of the officials and their respective masters marked the confines of *strictum jus*.

In any case, on this side of the Tagliamento the signori adhered to the Venetian party, to which the Counts of Fratta boasted they had belonged since time immemorial. On the other, the imperial faction boldly held sway, and if they were less popular and wealthy they were far more energetic and daring. Nevertheless, there were the hot and the cold among them, too, and then there were the lukewarm, and these, as usual, were the worst. The stern sentences handed out by the Council of Ten to careless individuals accused of plotting for the Emperor and to the detriment of the Republic, tended to discourage sedition. Such rebellions, however, were too rare for the fear to last long. And as the times grew less propitious, the plots became more frivolous and innocuous, and the people cared little about these artificial and undesired novelties.

In the days of Maria Theresa's rule, three signori from the foothills – a Franzi, a Tarcentini and a Partistagno – were accused of stirring up unrest in the land and of trying to turn popular opinion against Venice. The Council of Ten spied on them diligently, and learned that the accusations were not untrue. Above all it was Partistagno, whose property stood near the border with Illyria, who openly backed the imperial side, who scoffed at San Marco, and who had raised his glass in the dining hall to the day his honour the Representative and (I repeat the words of his toast) those other *gentlemen who shit in the water* got a kick up the backside that sent them past the Tagliamento. All present had laughed at this and the man's audacity was admired and imitated, as best they could, by his vassals and other signori all around. In Venice, the Council was convened and it was decided that the three agitators should be summoned to justify their behaviour. And as everyone knew, 'justification' was the certain stairway to the *piombi*, the dungeons.

The much-feared Messer Grande[27] then appeared in the Friuli with three sealed letters, to be opened and read in the presence of the respective accused, containing orders to proceed forthwith to Venice to submit to the Most Excellent Council of Ten. Such injunctions were usually obeyed without question, because the power of the Lion still seemed formidable to the far-away and the ignorant and it was considered pointless to try to flee. And so the Messer Grande made his solemn visit to Franzi and Tarcentini; and each bowed his head in turn and went of his own accord to the dungeons of the Inquisitors. He then took the third letter to Partistagno, who had already been informed about his companions' humble behaviour, and who awaited the

Messer Grande in the great hall on the ground floor. The Messer Grande entered, his great red robes sweeping up the dust, and solemnly took the letter from his breast and, having opened it, read out the contents. *Therefore*, his nasal voice intoned, *the Noble and Distinguished Signor Gherardo di Partistagno is invited within seven days to appear before the Most Excellent Council of Ten*, etc., etc.

The Noble and Distinguished Signor Gherardo di Partistagno stood before him with his forehead bowed to his chest, trembling, as if hearing a death sentence. Faced with such dismay, the Messer Grande's voice grew more and more threatening, and when he finally read out the names of the signatories it was as if his nostrils were puffing out all the terror inspired by the Inquisitorial Council. In a shaky voice Partistagno replied that he would obey immediately, and held out the hand he'd been resting on the table to a servant, as if to call for his horse or a litter. The Messer Grande, proud to have annihilated in his usual fashion that presumptuous feudatory, turned to leave the room, head high. But he had not yet taken a step when seven or eight *buli*, summoned by Partistagno from a castle of his in Illyria the day before, jumped him, and with a bashing here and a pounding there, left him in such a state that the poor Messer Grande couldn't even get a squeak out of his throat. From time to time, Partistagno urged the ruffians on:

'Oh yes, ready to obey! Get him, Natale! Hard, hard on that parchment mug of his! Coming here to my castle with his proclamations! Thinks he's clever, by Diana! . . . Oh, what a mess you look! Good work, my boys! That will do it, now; leave him enough breath to get back to Venice and deliver my news to those good gentlemen.'

'Oh woe is me! I'm betrayed! Oh mercy! I am killed!' whimpered the Messer Grande as he floundered about on the floor trying to get himself upright.

'Oh no, you're not, my little kitten,' replied Partistagno. 'See? You can stand up tolerably well, and with a bit of mending, that nice red dressing gown of yours won't show any sign at all of this nasty incident. Now go,' and here he conducted him out the door, 'go and let your masters know that Partistagno takes orders from no one, and if they wish to invite me, then I will invite them to come and meet me in my castle at Caporetto[28] above Gorizia, where they will receive a triple dose of that potion you've been given.'

With these words he conducted the Messer Grande by great leaps and bounds to the castle gate, and gave him a push that made the man tumble head over heels for a good ten paces, and all the onlookers laughed. And then while the Messer, gingerly prodding his bones and his nose, proceeded down towards Udine in a litter he had requisitioned along the way, Partistagno and his *buli* hurried off to Caporetto, never to be seen again in the lands of the Serenissima. And not only that, our old men tell us, but not a word was ever heard again of those two companions sent to the dungeons.

Such bagatelles took place in the Friuli just a century ago; tales from Sacchetti,[29] they might be. It was in the nature of those mountain towns, where the granite peaks maintained the templates of old times at length, but because the Friuli is a small compendium of the universe – mountain, plain and swamp in sixty miles from top to bottom – there was also another side to the coin. During my childhood at the castle of Fratta, the signori of the Highlands were always spoken of with horror, so Venetianized had those good counts become. I'm quite sure they were as scandalized as the Inquisitors themselves at the refreshments Partistagno served up to the Messer Grande.

However, matters of justice – high, low, public, private, legislative and executive – in the *patria* of the Friuli have drawn me away from that majestic hearth around which, by lamp light and the flames of the crackling juniper branches, I was convening the characters who used to sit there during the long winter afternoons of my childhood. The Count and his shadow, Monsignor Orlando, Captain Sandracca, Marchetto the bailiff and Ser Andreini, *primo uomo* of the Commune of Teglio. The last is a new personage I've not yet spoken about, and it would require a long speech to explain what *primo uomo* meant back then, that order of rural intermediaries between the signori and the peasants. To say what they really were is to seek to make sense of a mishmash; to say how they wished to be seen needs no more than two strokes of the pen. They wished to be the humble servants of the Castle and men in the confidence of the signori; in short, to be the number two masters in town. Those blessed with a good nature achieved this singular ambition well; those who were stingy, or swindlers, or just nasty, tended to be the lowest, most infamous hypocrites. And Ser Andreini was a leader among the first: he was shrewd and amiable, a good man at heart, who wouldn't have pulled the wing off a wasp that stung him. The servants, the footmen, the bugler, the scullery maid and the cook were as friendly as could be with him, and when the Count was not around, he would joke with them and help the Steward's little son pluck birds for the skewer. But when the Count appeared, he drew himself up and paid attention only to him, as if it were a sacrilege to do anything else but bask in the charmed presence of the great man. And depending on the latter's probable wishes, Andreini was the first to laugh, to say yes, to say no, and even to reverse himself if he had erred in his first try.

There was also a certain Martino, who had been His Excellency's father's valet and who was always hanging around the kitchen like an old hunting dog among the infirm, sticking his nose in the credenzas and the casseroles to the cook's great dismay, and grumbling about the cats underfoot. Because he was deaf and not very interested in gossip, he never much joined the conversation. His only real task was to grate the cheese. True, his natural lethargy, exacerbated by his great age, and the unusual consumption of soup coming from that kitchen, meant that this task consumed many hours of the day. I can still hear today the monotonous sound of cheese rinds pushed up and down the blade with very little respect for fingernails; and old Martino's fingertips, in reward for his parsimony, were always cut up and plastered with cobwebs.

I'd really rather not make fun of Martino, however. He was, you might say, my first friend, and if I wasted a lot of wind getting my words to strike his eardrums, I also had, for all the years he lived with me, a tender reward in terms of his affection. It was he who came looking for me when I had been banished from the family for some impertinence; he who made peace for me with Monsignor, when rather than assisting him at the Mass,

I ran out in the garden and climbed the plane trees looking for birds' nests; he who would vouch that I was ill when the curate came hunting for me to do my doctrine lessons; and when they sent me to bed, it was he who would take my Jalappa, my purgative, for me. In short, Martino and I were like hand and glove, and if, on entering the kitchen I couldn't see him for the deep shadows that reigned there all day long, some inkling always told me when he was there, and I would go right for him to tug his wig or grab his knees and ride them. And if he wasn't there, they would all laugh at me because I stood there so bashfully, like a chick bereft of its mother hen, and then, vexed, I'd take to my heels – unless the Count cleared his throat and left me rooted to the floor. In that case I would stand so still that not even the Epiphany witch could have dislodged me, and only after he had gone would I regain my freedom of thought and movement. I never understood why that tall and pompous old man had such a strange effect on me, but I suspect it was the scarlet braid on his coat that mesmerized me, just as the sight of something scarlet is spellbinding to a turkey.

Another of my great friends was the bailiff who would sometimes put me on his shoulders and carry me around while he posted the banns and did other duties. Now I did not detest knives and pistols by any means as much as Captain Sandracca did, and along the way I would always dig into Marchetto's pockets and steal his dagger, which I used to swipe at and duel with the rude fellows we would meet. Once, when he had grabbed his pistols on the run and had ridden out to Ramuscello to deliver a summons to the lord of the castle there, Marchetto caught me rummaging through his pockets despite the smacking he had just delivered, and I set off the trigger and ruined a finger – and it is still somewhat twisted and lacking the final joint, in memory of my judicial adventures. But the punishment by no means cured me of my passion for weapons. Marchetto always insisted that I would have made a good soldier and that it was too bad I didn't live in one of those towns up in the hills where boys grew up learning to use their fists – not running after country girls and playing *tresette*[30] with priests and old ladies.

Those country rides of mine didn't go down well with Martino, though. People who lived in town, if not as fractious and brawling as those in the hills, were quite hard-headed and often paid no heed at all to the sentences from the chancery, and would jeer at the bailiff when he came to deliver them. Hot-blooded as Marchetto was, you never knew what might happen. He insisted that my presence stopped him flying off the handle, while I, in turn, boasted that should the occasion arise, I could give him a hand by reloading the pistols or by waving my billhook madly around, and, little thing that I was, I didn't see how people laughed at such hyperbole. Martino would bow his head, and unable to hear much of what we were saying, would grumble that it was unwise to expose a boy to the reprisals that a bailiff might face when he went out to collect bail or post notice of new taxes and duties. Those very peasants who cut such a sorry figure in the ranks of the Cernide, who trembled when the Clerk eyed them in the chancery, knew very well how to use a gun and a cleaver in the fields or in their own homes, and if once upon a time that discrepancy astonished me, now I think I've discovered the real reason.

We Italians have always had a natural antipathy for clowns and puppets and we laugh at them quite readily, yes – but we laugh even more readily at those who would like to pass themselves off as prodigious, something to doff our hats at. Those bands of men – herded together like sheep, kept in line by drumbeat and driven forward by a fife, their worth measured by the commander's curt orders – they've always seemed like a troupe of clowns to us, haven't they? That is because such parts as they played were forever to their detriment, and rarely to their advantage. And given that this was how things unfortunately stood, the idea of going on that stage and playing the puppet naturally turned sour, and any wish to perform well, any sense of dignity, escaped us. I speak, of course, of times past; today the knowledge of a greater purpose may have improved our natures in this regard. Yet even today one might not be wrong, philosophically speaking, to reason as we once did, for the wrong is this: one cannot insist upon being sage and follow the rules of sagacity when all the others are mad and act according to their madness. And in fact it has been said and repeated a hundred times, proven and re-proven, that one of our men, breast to breast against any strong man of any other nation, can hold his own and make the other turn tail. And yet, sad to say, in no other nation does it cost more effort to raise an army and keep it as firm and disciplined as modern military arts require. Napoleon, though, taught us – and once and for all – that what is involved here is not the courage of a nation, but the will and tenacity of its leaders. Such reluctance of ours to abandon free will can perhaps be explained not only by an independent, reason-loving national character, but also by an utter lack of military tradition.

But this is quite enough with regard to the people of Fratta, and as for their quaking before the authorities, there is probably no need to add that it was not so much the consequence of cowardice, as that age-old reverence and unease that unlettered folk show before those who have some learning. The Clerk who with three strokes of a pen could at his fancy toss two, three or twenty families out of their homes and into misery and starvation, must have seemed no less than a sorcerer to those poor people. Today, when things work according to laws that are more reasonable, even the most ignorant regard the courts more favourably, and don't fear the law as the gateway to the hangman's noose or the bailiff's seizure of their property.

Along with those members of the household I've mentioned up to now, the Rector of Teglio, my teacher of doctrine and calligraphy, used to pass assorted hours at the great hearth, sitting across from the Count and showing him much deference each time he was addressed by him. He was a great big priest from up in the mountains, no friend of the monks and abbots, scarred by smallpox so that his cheeks always made me think of *stracchino* cheese when it is nice and fat and full of eyes, as the cheese-lovers say. He walked very slowly, spoke even more slowly, never failing to divide each of his utterances into three points, and this habit of his was so deeply lodged in his bones that whether eating, coughing or sighing it always seemed that he ate, coughed or sighed in three points. All of his actions seemed so carefully weighed and considered that should he ever have committed some sin (betraying his generally placid and reverent habits) I doubt that the Good Lord would have been inclined to pardon him. Not even his gaze moved without cause and only with great difficulty penetrated those two hedgerows of protective eyebrows. He was the very idea of premeditation, incarnate in the body of a mountain man from Clausedo, his head tonsured by the Bishop of Portogruaro, wearing the longest cloak that ever battled with the shins of a priest. His hands trembled slightly, a defect that rather limited his abilities as a calligrapher, but which didn't keep him from leaning heavily on his India walking stick with ox-bone knob. As for his moral faculties, he was a model of ecclesiastical independence for a man born in the Settecento, and the deep respect he showed the Count did not prevent him from looking after mortal souls in his own fashion. Perhaps it was his way of saying: 'Most Excellent Count, I certainly revere and respect you, but for the rest, in my own home I am the master.'

The Chaplain of Fratta was instead a cowed and cowardly little mite who would have been willing to deliver the benediction with a kitchen ladle had the Count got such a bee in his bonnet. Not because he lacked reverence, no; it was because the poor thing was utterly overwhelmed by any man holding a title and lost all sense of what he was doing. Thus he was always terribly nervous while at the Castle, and I believe that if one wanted to put him in true purgatory now he is dead, you would merely have to bring him back to life as a resident there. There was no one who could rival him when he sat hour upon hour without raising his eyes or opening his mouth, the others observing him, and at the same time he had a miraculous ability to disappear unseen, even from a group of no more than ten persons. It was only when he trailed behind the Rector of Teglio that some glint of ecclesiastical dignity lit up his face, but you could see what an effort it was to keep up with his superior. He was so busy trying to train his mind on his part that he neither saw nor heard anything, and was capable of putting hot coals in his mouth instead of hazelnuts, as the Steward proved after taking a wager.

Signor Ambrogio Traversini, steward and actuary of Fratta, was the Chaplain's scourge. The two kept up a steady flow of those jokes and pranks that were once so much the fashion and took the place of reading the newspapers in country circles. The Chaplain, always the butt of those jokes, needless to say, was compensated with various invitations to luncheon – a reward even crueller than the original punishment. But very often the distress about those invitations brought on a case of double quartan fever and then he no longer needed to resort to lying to confect his excuses.

Whenever he had occasion to set foot beyond the castle drawbridge, no man, I believe, was happier than he, and this was his compensation for all the suffering. He leapt, he ran, he rubbed his hands, his nose, his knees; he took tobacco, mumbled prayers, flipped his walking stick from one hand to the other, talked, laughed and waved at every creature that passed him by, be it a boy, an old lady, a dog or a heifer. It was my glorious and naughty fate to be the first to observe the Chaplain's peculiar jubilation when he left the Castle, and after I'd made the discovery, everyone clustered around the windows of the dining hall when he left, to enjoy the spectacle. The Steward swore that one day the Chaplain's overwhelming relief would land him in the fish pond, but it must be said in the poor man's favour that this never happened. The greatest measure of happiness I ever saw him show was the day he joined some rascally boys to ring in the feast day down at the church.

He had got off very lightly that day, it was true. A high prelate from Portogruaro, the Canon of Sant'Andrea, was at the Castle: a leading theologian, quite intolerant of other people's ignorance, he had honoured and continued to honour the Countess with his spiritual patronage. Along with Monsignor Orlando and the Rector, the Canon had sat down before the fire to indulge in some dogmatizing on morals. The Chaplain, passing by to learn how the Count's digestion was faring, as was the after-luncheon custom, came very close to falling into the trap, but halfway into the kitchen he had heard the theologian's voice, and under cover of the shadows, was able to take to his heels, blessing every saint in the calendar. Did he or did he not have reason to ring the bells with happiness?

Along with the two priests and other canons and seminarists from the city who came to visit the Monsignor of Fratta, the

Castle was also frequented by the local gentry and minor signori from all around. They were a motley crew of drinkers, slackers, odd wits and artful dodgers, who passed their time hunting, duelling, flirting and taking suppers without end; a merry procession that showed off the Count's aristocratic reserve. When he appeared, it was pandemonium. The best casks were uncorked, bottles of Picolit and Refosco lost their tops, and the young ladies who helped the cook ran to take refuge in the scullery. The cook herself acknowledged neither friend nor foe, she raced back and forth, elbowing Martino in the stomach, tramping on Monsignor's toes, plucking ducks, gutting capons, and she wasn't more busy than the spit itself, which squeaked and sweated oil on all its pulleys for having to spin around four or five skewers of hares and game. Tables were laid in the dining hall and in two or three nearby rooms and the great fireplace in the hall was lit, so big that to fill it up you needed half a cord of wood. And after the first flames rose up the company had to retire to the far corners or the next room, in order not to get singed.

It was these gentlemen who made the greatest uproar, but the wittiest member of the party was usually some young graduate, some budding seminarian, some poet from Portogruaro who never failed to come running when the scent of festivities beckoned. Down at the bottom of the table a sonnet or two was improvised (of which the poet probably had drafts complete with corrections back home), and if his memory failed, he could always round off with thanks and apologies for the *liberties* the company had taken (to swarm in and drink the wine and praise the infinite merits of the Count and the Countess). He who most often performed this office was a sleek and powdered attorney who had, in his youth, courted many a Venetian lady, and now lived on with his memories and his quibbles in the company of his housekeeper. A churlish young fellow named Giulio Del Ponte often came with him and he liked to compete for who declaimed the cleverest verses, amusing himself by filling the attorney's glass once too often until he became incoherent.

The comedy ended up in the kitchen with much laughter behind the graduate's back, but this young man, who had studied at Padua, was so clever that he nonetheless had the best of it. He and a pale, taciturn young fellow from Fossalta named Lucilio Vianello are the only ones I still recall from the ranks of the semi-plebeians. Among the gentry a Partistagno, perhaps a relative of the one who dealt with the Messer Grande, stands out: tall, bold, robust and blessed with a certain proud reserve sharply distinguished from the drunken excess of the many. Even back then I recall noting some sidelong glances between him and Vianello that suggested they were not on the best of terms. And this despite the fact that by all rights these two should have got along with each other, the rest of the company being a uniformly worthless bunch of fools and rogues.

By the time I was old enough to make sense of myself and annoy the chickens in the courtyard of Fratta, the Count's only male offspring Rinaldo had already been away a year in Venice studying with the Somascan Fathers, who had educated his own father. And so I had no memories of him apart from a slap or two that he had given me before leaving to make it clear he was the master, and I myself in any case was then only a babe scarcely big enough to teethe on a crust of bread. But old Martino took my side from the start, and I recall the time he surreptitiously tugged at the ears of the young master, who shrieked loud enough to bring down the rafters, so that the Count scolded Martino at length. Fortunately for Martino, he was deaf.

As for the Countess, she never appeared in the kitchen but twice a day in her capacity as supreme director of household affairs: in the morning to deliver flour, butter, meat and other ingredients for the meals of the day; after the last course at luncheon, when she put aside a portion of what was left for the servants, and the rest in smaller dishes for the evening meal. She was tall, sharp and short of words, a noblewoman (a Navagero of Venice) who took her snuff one nostril at a time and never went anywhere without her keys rattling from her apron. She wore a white lace cap with pink ribbons at the temples, like a new bride, not, I think, out of vanity but merely out of habit. Over the black silk scarf around her neck lay a thick braid of Spanish gold attached to a cross of diamonds – worth enough, according to the cook, to provide a dowry for all the young ladies in the jurisdiction.

She also wore, attached to her bosom with a gold pin, a portrait of a handsome young man wearing pigeon-wing side curls, who was certainly not her dear husband, for he had an outsized nose while the fellow in the portrait had a pert little one, a bauble suited to smelling rose water and Neapolitan *parfum*. In short, the way I later heard it, the lady had only very reluctantly accepted to marry that nobleman from the mainland, a marriage she considered pretty much the equivalent of falling into the hands of barbarians, accustomed as she was to the amusements and the delicacies enjoyed by the city girls of Venice. Forced to make a virtue of necessity, she would drag the Count to Venice from time to time, where she compensated for their provincial estate by enjoying the gallantries and courtship of all the upcoming young dandies. The portrait she wore on her breast seems to have been that of the boldest of these young fellows, but it was said he had caught a chill while they were out one evening in a gondola, and died on her. Afterwards, she was inconsolable and had retired forever to Fratta, much to the Count's satisfaction.

When this terrible event took place, the Countess was near forty. She passed long hours at her prie-dieu, and whenever she met me at the kitchen door or on the stairs, she would tug, but not very hard, at the hair on my scalp, the only kindness I ever recall from her. A quarter hour daily was devoted to giving orders to the maids, and the rest of her time was spent in the sitting room with her mother-in-law and daughters, knitting and reading the life of the saint of the day.

The Count's mother, old Lady Badoer, was still alive in those days, but I never saw her but four or five times, for she was confined to a chair and I was not allowed to enter any room but the one where I slept with the second maid, the 'baby-maid', as she was called. The old lady, who was almost ninety, was rather fat and her appearance suggested kindness and good sense. Her voice, sweet and calm despite her years, was so enchanting to me that I often risked getting a slap when I would go and put my ear to her door. Once, the maid opened the door while I was at the keyhole, and the old lady saw me and beckoned me to come in. My heart nearly jumped out of my breast with gratitude when she put a hand on my head and asked me very gravely, but not meanly, what I was doing behind the door. I told her, in all innocence and trembling with emotion, that I was there because I enjoyed listening to her speak, that I liked her voice very much and would have wished my mother to have a voice like hers.

'Very good, Carlino,' she said, 'I shall always speak kindly to you as long as you deserve it for behaving well, but no one, least of all young boys, should be listening behind closed doors. When you wish to speak to me, you must come into the room and sit beside me, so that I can teach you to pray to God and become a good boy.'

The effect of these words on my poor self was to send a flood of tears down my cheeks. It was the first time anyone had spoken to me from the heart, the first time I had received an affectionate look, and this gift came to me from an old lady who had seen Louis XIV! I say 'had seen' and I mean it literally, for Lady Badoer's husband, the old Count who was so keen on grand masters and admirals, had, a few months after his wedding, gone to France as the ambassador of the Serenissima, and he had taken along his wife, who had been for two years the toast of the French court. And when she returned to Fratta, she kept the same charming manners and speech, the same rectitude, the same high, pure sentiments, the same moderation and charity, so that even when her youthful beauty had faded, the young swordsmen and townsmen continued to give their hearts to her, just as the courtiers at Versailles had done. For genuine grandeur is admirable and admired everywhere, and neither becomes nor feels small even when it changes seat. And so I wept hot tears as I held and kissed the hand of that remarkable woman, and promised myself I would often accept the invitation to come up and sit with her, when suddenly the real Countess, the one with the keys, came in, twitching with indignation to see me there against her orders. This time the tug on my scalp went on for a long time, accompanied by a harsh scolding and an eternal interdiction against entering those rooms unless I was called to do so. As I went down the stairs at the back wall, rubbing the nape of my neck, crying this time more out of anger than pain, I could hear the old lady's voice, softer and sweeter than ever, as she tried to intercede in my favour. But a shout from the Countess and the sound of the door slamming violently behind me barred me from witnessing the rest of the scene. And so, one leg following the other, I climbed down the stairs to the kitchen to be consoled by Martino.

Even this familiarity of mine with Martino annoyed the Countess, and also the Steward, who did her bidding. According to them, my protector should instead have been a certain Fulgenzio, part-sacristan, part-scrivener, and reputed to be a spy and informer inside the castle. But I couldn't stand this Fulgenzio and used to play such tricks on him that I'm sure he didn't find me tolerable either. For example, once – but this was some time later – when I was standing behind him at the morning Mass on Maundy Thursday, I took advantage of his absorption in the ceremony to detach a lit taper from the stick he used to light the candles, and twist it around his pigtail. When the taper burned down his pigtail caught fire and soon the tow of his wig was in flames, too. Fulgenzio began to hop around the choir and the boys who played the rebecs ran after him shouting 'Water! Water!' And in the confusion, the rebecs went tumbling to the floor, and there was such pandemonium that the ceremony had to be delayed for half an hour. No one ever got to the bottom of that scandalous affair, and I, who was suspected of being the mastermind, had the good sense to play dumb; nevertheless, I had to pay the price of a day confined to my room on bread and water, which certainly didn't endear Fulgenzio to me, just as the fire in his wig hadn't made me very popular with him.

Now I said that the Countess spent most of her time in the sitting room with her daughters, knitting. The youngest of them, in my earliest memories a mere infant and younger than myself by several years, slept in the same room as I did with the 'baby-maid,' Faustina. The Contessina Pisana was vivacious, nervous and easily riled, had beautiful, big brown eyes and long, long hair, and at the age of three her feminine guile was already fully developed. She seemed to be living proof of the notion that women are never children but come forth as full-blown females, with all the possible feminine wiles and vices. Not an evening went by that I didn't bend over her crib to watch her at length, as she lay there with her big eyes closed and one arm that had worked itself free of the bed clothes, the other draped over her forehead: a sweet, sleeping angel. But just as I was thinking how pretty she looked, she would open her eyes and leap up beside me on the bed, pounding me with pleasure at having fooled me into thinking she was asleep.

Such things happened when Faustina wasn't looking or had forgotten her orders, for the Countess had told her to make sure I kept my distance from her little darling and that I didn't become too friendly with her. My companions were to be Fulgenzio's sons, whom I considered even more abominable than their father, and on whom I never missed a chance to play a trick, not least because they had taken it upon themselves to tell their father they had seen me give a kiss to la Pisana, and carry her in my arms all the way from the sheep manger to the dam. And because the young lady cared as little as I did for what other people thought, she began to be fond of me and tried to make sure it was I who looked after her instead of Faustina or Rosa the 'key-maid' (today we would call her the chambermaid). I was happy and proud to have found another creature who considered me of some use, and I even put on certain airs and would say to Martino: 'Give me a nice piece of twine, because la Pisana needs it!' La Pisana: that's how I spoke of her with him, but with the others, I always called her la Contessina.

However, my pleasure was not without pain, for in childhood (just as in every other stage of life) there is truth to the proverb about every rose bearing a thorn. When the local *signori* came to visit the castle, their children all dressed up in modish finery, with their little ruff collars and their little plumed hats, la Pisana would desert me to play the charmer with them, and I would work up a terrible temper watching her mince around and twist her neck like a crane, enchanting them with her bright, careless chatter. And so I would run to Faustina's mirror to make myself handsome, too, but sadly I would soon find it was impossible. My skin was dark and smoked like that of a herring, my shoulders drooped, my nose was scratched and mottled, my hair stuck out at the temples in hedgehog spines, my pigtail was all twisted and messy: a blackbird that has just pulled free of the trap. As much as I tortured my scalp with the comb, my tongue emerging with the effort and great thought I was putting into the matter, those difficult hairs always seemed to return to their original position. One time it occurred to me to oil my hair as I had seen Faustina do, but as chance would have it I took up the wrong bottle, and instead of oil I doused myself with the ammonia that she kept on hand in case of fainting fits. For at least a week I went around bathed in a chamber pot smell to turn your stomach.

In short, I was quite unlucky in my first attacks of vanity, and rather than endear myself to the little one and distract her from her flirtations with her guests, I made myself a laughing-stock, and found new reasons to feel angry and even somewhat humiliated. It was true that once the guests departed, la Pisana would be happy enough to lord it over me once again, but the bad feelings aroused by her disloyalty lingered, and not knowing how to rid myself of them, I found her whims oppressive and her tyranny somewhat hard to bear. The little devil paid no attention at all. Perhaps she had already sensed what stuff I was made of, and so by doubling her bullying, doubled my affection and submission; for in some of us, devotion to our tormentors is even greater than our gratitude to those who make us happy. I have no idea whether such persons are good or bad, wise or foolish; but I know I am one of them, and that I've had to carry this fate of mine with me through the many long years of my life. And at heart I'm not unhappy about it, and if I'm not unhappy, who is – at least in my own house?

I must also say, however, that if from an early age it was evident how wilful, fickle, and cruel la Pisana could be, she could also be quite generous, in the manner of a queen who, having slapped and humiliated a too-bold suitor, will intercede on his behalf with her consort, the king. At times she would smother me with kisses like her little dog and tell me all her secrets; then turn and ride me like a horse, mercilessly whipping my neck and cheeks with her willow switch. But just let Rosa or the Steward interrupt our games – as I have said the Countess had forbidden them – and la Pisana would howl and stamp her feet and shout that she loved me more than all the others put together, that she only wanted to be with me, and so on, until, thrashing and shrieking in the arms of whoever was dragging her off, she would finally fall silent in front of her mother. These tantrums of hers, I confess, were the only reward I had for my abnegation; not that it didn't often occur to me that there was more pride and obstinacy in them than love for me. But we mustn't let the rash judgements of maturity sully the pure illusions of childhood. The fact is, I didn't mind getting beaten for presuming to join the Contessina in her games, and afterwards went happily down to my kitchen to watch Martino grate the cheese.

The Countess's other daughter Clara was already a young lady of marriageable age when I first opened my eyes on the things of this world. The firstborn, she was pale, fair and melancholy like a lady in an old ballad or Shakespeare's Ophelia, although she had certainly never read any ballads or even heard of *Hamlet*. The many months she had spent at the side of her invalid grandmother had left the shining reflection of a serene and respectable old age on this young woman's face. No daughter ever looked after her mother with more diligence than Clara devoted to guessing her grandmother's most secret cravings, and she could guess them with no more than a glance, because they had spent so many hours together. The Contessina Clara was beautiful in the way of a seraph who moves among men without ever touching the earthly mire and without knowing anything of filth and impurity. To many, however, she could seem cold and this coldness could even be mistaken for lordly hauteur. And yet there was no soul more simple, more modest than hers, and the maids considered her a model of sweetness and goodness – and as we all know, when it comes to praise for their masters, the vote of just two maids is as good as a great many sworn witnesses. When the old Countess wanted a coffee or a cup of chocolate and there was no maid in the room, Clara wouldn't ring the bell, she would go down herself to the kitchen to speak to the cook, and while the cook prepared, she would stand patiently with her knees resting lightly on the rim of the hearth, so that she could reach out and take the pot off the fire. When she stood there like that, the kitchen seemed to be lit up with an angelic glow and was no longer that dark, sad place we were accustomed to.

Now here, some of you may ask why, in this tale, I continue to return to the kitchen, why my characters appear there and not in the dining hall or the sitting room? A natural question and an easy one to answer: the kitchen – my friend Martino's habitual abode and the only place where I could stay without being shouted at (perhaps because the dim light hid me from everyone's attention) – was where I largely spent my youth. Other citizens recall with delight those public places where they used to play as children; in my case, my first memories are pitched in the smoke and gloom of the Fratta kitchen. There I met my first human beings; there I experienced and pondered my first loves, first sorrows, first opinions.

And thus, although my life, like that of other men, was led in various countries, various places and various houses, my dreams almost always take place in kitchens. Perhaps not a very poetic location, but then I write to put down the truth, not to entertain my readers with poetic inventions. La Pisana looked with horror on that deep, dark, badly paved domain and the cats that lived there, and she rarely set foot in the kitchen unless she was running after me with a stick. But young Contessina Clara showed no disgust at all, and she would come in whenever necessary without pursing her lips or lifting the hem of her skirt the way even those prissy maids did. I used to be delighted to see her there and if she asked for a glass of water I felt blessed to give it to her and hear her say in her charming way, 'Thank you, Carlino.' And then I would crawl back into my den, thinking, 'Oh, how lovely are those three words, "Thank you, Carlino"!' If only la Pisana had thanked me even once in a voice so kind and loving.

TWO

In which at last we learn who I am and my nature is first described, along with the temperament of the Contessina Pisana and the habits of the lords of Fratta. And more: how the passions of mature men can first be detected in childhood; how I learned to sound out my letters with the Rector of Teglio and the Contessina Clara, and to smile from Signor Lucilio.

The principal effect of chapter one on my readers will most likely be a great curiosity to finally learn just who this Carlino is. In fact, it has been quite an accomplishment on my part – or maybe just simple fraud – to send you rambling through an entire chapter of my life, always nattering on about me, without first introducing myself. But sooner or later I must tell you, so let it now be known that I was born to a sister of the Countess of Fratta and am therefore first cousin to the Contessina Clara and la Pisana. My mother had made a marriage – had eloped, I should say – with the ever so illustrious Signor Todero Altoviti, 'Gentleman' of Torcello:[1] that is, she had run away with him aboard a galley to the Levant and had married him in Corfu. It seems that her taste for travel was quickly sated, because just four months later she was back without a husband, brown with the sun of Smyrna,[2] and with child. After she had given birth to me I was quite unceremoniously sent off to Fratta in a basket, and so became a ward of my aunt on the eighth day of my life. How welcome, anyone can imagine.

Meanwhile my mother, poor thing, having been expelled from Venice by her family, had set up with a Swiss captain in Parma, and returning from there to Venice to beg her aunt for mercy, had died in the hospital without so much as a dog paying her a visit. I heard these facts from Martino, and hearing him tell them made me cry, but I never knew how he himself had learned them. As for my father, it was said he had died in Smyrna after my mother fled; some said from heartbreak at being abandoned, others out of desperation for his many debts, others from dropsy due to drinking too much Cyprus wine. I was never able to learn the true story, but there was even a vague rumour among the Levantine merchants that before dying he had become a Turk. Whether or not he was a Turk, I was baptized a Christian at Fratta, for they weren't sure whether it had been done in Venice, and since the choice of my name was left up to the priest, he gave me the name of the saint of the day, who happened to be San Carlo. He was a priest without any preferences among all the saints in paradise, nor did he wish to trouble himself coming up with any special name for me. And I am grateful to him, for experience has shown me that San Carlo is worth not one whit less than the others.

The Countess had only abandoned her glittering life in Venice a few months before the basket arrived, so you can just imagine how overjoyed she was to see its contents. With all the troubles and vexations bothering her, now there was this baby that had to be nursed – and not only that but the baby of a sister who had disgraced her and the family – and then there was that bungled marriage with a delinquent from Torcello that nobody had yet been able to get to the bottom of! And so from the first the Countess eyed me with a most sincere dislike, and it wasn't long before I felt the consequences. She decided at once that it was pointless to take a wet nurse into the house and pay her to feed a little grass snake who had emerged from who knows where. And so Providence was assigned to look after me, and they sent me around from house to house wherever there were breasts to suck, like St Anthony's pig or a foundling of the Commune. And thus I am milk-brother to all the men, the calves and the kids born in the domain of Fratta in those days, and was nursed by all the mothers, goats and cows, all the old women, and the old men of the township. Martino, in fact, told me that once or twice, seeing me shivering with hunger, he had mixed up a certain concoction of water, butter, sugar and flour, with which he stuffed me until my throat was full and I could no longer cry. And the same happened in other houses where the breasts that were charged to feed me that day had already been milked dry by some other hungry big baby of eighteen months old.

Miraculously, I thus survived my early days. The porter of the castle, who was also the winder of the tower clock and district armourer, had the honour with Martino of standing by me while I took my first steps. Mastro Germano was a ruffian of the old school who most likely had many homicides on his conscience, but who had found a way to make his peace with the Almighty, and would laugh and sing all day as he collected leavings along the road in his cart to manure a field he rented from the master. At the tavern he drank great draughts of fine Ribola wine with true patriarchal serenity. You would have thought he had the cleanest conscience in the parish. The memory of Germano leads me to think that we each adjust our conscience to a personal scale; what is a sip of a fresh egg for one, is for another a grave crime. If Mastro Germano had committed quite a few during his youth in service to the lord of Venchieredo, he believed it was the master who would have to answer to God for such trifles, and so, having made his yearly confession, he considered himself as pure as spring water.

These were no mere quibbles to quiet his remorse, but a general philosophy that armed his soul three times around against any sort of melancholy. When he moved to the payroll of the Castle of Fratta as chief cut-throat, he took the habit of saying his rosary, as was the practice there, and so had succeeded in purging himself of the old, bad seed. And so when, having reached seventy years old, he celebrated his jubilee by becoming porter and superintendent of the hours, he was firmly convinced that the road he had taken was that leading straight to sainthood. As you can imagine, he and Martino did not always agree. Martino, born expressly to be Cappa Nera[3] to a Rialto patrician; Germano, expert in all the mischief and coercion of the bully boys of his day. The first, diplomatic servant of a powdered milord; the second, hired sword of the most despotic chieftain of the Bassa, the lowlands. And whenever they disagreed, they turned on me, and then each tried to wrestle me away from his adversary, claiming he had more rights over me. But most of the time they were in accord, and tolerated each other, and so they jointly enjoyed the progress I was making on my little legs and, one on each side of the Castle drawbridge, they watched me toddle from the arms of one to the other.

And when the Countess, going out with the Rector and some visitor from Portogruaro on her post-prandial walk, came upon them in this pedagogical exercise, she beamed them both one of her excommunicating stares, and if I should stumble between her legs she never failed, even then, to encourage me with one of those raps on my head. And I, howling and shaking with fear, would run to Martino's arms and the Countess would press on, grumbling about the foolishness of those *crazy old men*, as my two guardians were known in the kitchen. Whatever the case, thanks to those two crazy old men, I learned to stand on my own two feet and even to run all the way to the linden tree at the parish church whenever I saw my aunt's white cap appear in the entrance hall. I can call her aunt now, poor thing, that she is dead a good half-century, but back then, as soon as I was capable of speaking, they taught me, at her command, to call her Madam Countess – and so it always was, our family relationship forgotten by tacit agreement.

Those were the days when I began to grow up, and because the Countess didn't wish to see me there on the bridge every day, she decided to hand me over to Fulgenzio the sacristan, about whom I have already told you. The lady thus hoped to detach me from la Pisana by tossing me in with the sacristy children. But that contrary instinct that even children have against those who order them around without good reason, made me stick even closer to my capricious young friend. It's also true that as we grew up and found that two were not enough to play the games we wanted, we enlarged our circle with stray children from all around, much to the horror of the maids, who, afraid of what the Countess would say, came to drag la Pisana away whenever they found us. But we were not much bothered, and because both Faustina and Rosa had little on their minds beyond their sweethearts, it wasn't so difficult for la Pisana to steal away and join us again.

As the band grew, so did her ambition to hold court, and as she was quite a precocious girl, as I've said, and liked to play the little lady, there were soon flirtations, jealousies, marriages, separations, reconciliations: all in childish fun, of course, but still, a fair indication of la Pisana's nature. And may I suggest that there was not so much innocence in all of this as people would like to believe: it astonishes me to think how the Contessina used to roll around in the hay and ride piggyback on one boy or another, how she would pretend to marry and go off to sleep with her husband, driving away all unwelcome witnesses from that tender scene.

Who had taught her such things? I can't be sure, but it seems to me she was born with innate knowledge of such matters. What was worse was that she never kept the same lover or the same husband for two days running, but changed them constantly. And the local lads, whether because they were embarrassed or out of respect and deference, allowed themselves to take part in this comedy; they didn't object. But I, who had my own fixed ideas about these matters, would suffer terrible bile and unspeakable heartbreak when I was discarded and replaced by the Steward's little boy or the son of the druggist from Fossalta. And she wasn't even very particular about who she chose. The main thing was to change partners, although it must be said that she tired quickly of the filthiest and most unattractive.

If I think back with equanimity (these being matters of some eighty years ago) I can only feel proud that at times I enjoyed her favours for three days running, and that if the other boys had their turn just once a month, mine came up nearly every week. Her invitations were as gratifying and imperious as her rejections were wilful and arrogant. One had to obey at all costs, and adore her as she demanded, and smile and laugh into the bargain, because if she sensed her consort was moody, she was mean enough to hit him. I don't think any medieval Court of Love was ever ruled by one woman with such tyranny.

Now I have my reasons for dwelling at length on these childish affairs; for one thing, they don't seem to me as childish as the moralists would argue. Left on their own, even children, as I have said, can have vices. And that childhood freedom that stimulates the senses before the sentiments are developed seems to me in no way desirable, and it can even be a grave risk to a person's moral equilibrium for a whole lifetime. How many men and women of great sagacity inherit lascivious ways from their childhood habits? Let us be frank. That metaphor that likens a man to a tender plant that bends or grows straight according to the talent of the cultivator has frequently been used. My views, however, are better represented by the example of the vein that once opened, may not be closed. All the humours flow to that side, and it is best to let them drain out, or risk worsening the condition of the whole organism. When the senses are aroused, as they can be in the early years, reason will certainly come along to express shame or sorrow about their sordid influence, but whence comes the strength to master them and put them back in their rightful place?

We grow according to the path sketched out by our beginnings, however much we may value reason, and however much we may blush; and thus are formed those half-creatures, no, those double-creatures in which depraved habits are joined with high intellect and even with high sentiments. Sappho and Aspasia[4] belong to history, not to Greek mythology, and they are two examples of those souls capable of great passions but not great sentiments, the kind that flourish in our times of sensual licence, when children lose their innocence before they are capable of experiencing guilt. Now, a Christian upbringing is supposed to extirpate the pernicious effects of these early vices. But apart from the fact that extirpation is time wasted when one could be building something, I believe that a Christian education does more to conceal than remove vice. We all know what torment it was for St Augustine and St Anthony to overcome the temptations of the flesh; today, few can be said to be as holy as they, but many practise the same abstinence. In effect, we're content to take things at face value; we are content with the mere appearance of decency, like the crafty cat who covers her droppings with earth, as Ariosto writes in his verses.

Yes, I say it and I repeat it: young and old, great and small, believers and unbelievers, there are few among us today who wish to do battle with our own passions or confine our senses deep within the soul, where nature would have them be. Vice is with us, but these are not times in which the mortification of the flesh can be a remedy. Upbringing and education can do much, by cultivating reason, will and vigour before the senses prevail. Not being a religious man myself, my objective is not the pure good of the soul. I preach for the good of all and for the good of society, for healthy manners are as necessary to society as healthy humours are for the well-being of the body. Physical strength, loyal sentiments, clear ideas, a strong spirit of sacrifice: these are the corollaries. These fine capacities, reinforced by long practice in individuals and so brought to operate in the social sphere, will inseminate, protect and hasten an entire nation's positive destiny.

Wild, lax and sensual habits, on the other hand, ensure that the soul can always be distracted from some high purpose by low and unworthy necessities, its false enthusiasm suddenly collapsing or oscillating wildly between struggle and failure, effort and humiliation. It is the festering of such bad habits under the sparkling tinsel of civilization that makes will become mere wishing; facts become words; words, chit-chat; science, purely utilitarian; harmony, impossible; conscience, venal; life, vegetative, dull and intolerable.

How can we expect millions of men to conduct a great national drive lasting one, two, ten or twenty years, when not one of them is capable of keeping up that drive for three straight months? It is not harmony, not concord, we lack, but the basis for concord, derived from strength and perseverance. The concord of the flimsy is no more than a mouthful, like the mouthful that 'little corporal' Bonaparte[5] made of Venice. Now, when we need four times that much strength, we find that for the most part our forces are weakened, defeated, and instead of taking one step forward, have taken two steps back. (Here you may think our discourse has moved far from the petty libidinousness of childhood, but if you look carefully you will see that subject approach and grow large, like sunspots viewed through the lens of a telescope.)

I myself, by nature anything but tepid, can count myself exempt from those moral disorders owing to the precocious senses. As far back as I can recall, it seems that the spirit had awakened in me before the flesh, and I was lucky enough to love before I began to desire. Not that any of this was to my credit, just as it was not la Pisana's fault that wilfulness, arrogance and childish malice stirred her nervous, impetuous, changeable nature and her fickle and provocative instincts. From the sort of life she was allowed to lead as a child and young woman, great heroines come forth, but never prudent, level-headed women, never good mothers or chaste wives, never trusted friends, but creatures who would sacrifice their lives for a cause today, that they wouldn't give a penny for tomorrow. Hers was the sort of school in which the supreme and fleeting talents and the great and enduring vices of dancers, singers, actresses and adventurers are tempered.

From early childhood la Pisana demonstrated an unusual intelligence, but this was spoiled by the frivolity and vanity she was allowed to enjoy. Her teacher was Signora Veronica, wife of Captain Sandracca, and she needed great patience to focus that girlish brain for a quarter-hour on the sentence she was meant to compose. Certain she could understand everything with ease, la Pisana would read the first part of the lesson and leave the rest, but this practice, far from helping her to learn, taught her to forget. At times, praise goaded her to do her best, but then some whim quickly set her meagre ambition to one side. Accustomed to pursue whatever course her talents followed, she liked to change her tasks and amusements at will, and didn't know this is the way one becomes bored with everything, until one can no longer find peace and contentment in life, and ends by never feeling happy because one has tried too hard and in too many different ways.

The science of happiness lies in the art of moderation, but the little one was unable to see this and merely pursued her whims, not least because she was allowed to do so. When a girl is happy to command and be the first in everything, when the world is ordered according to her likes, is it surprising she will tell tales if it means she can make others have the high opinion of herself she holds? And when the others all flatter her and pretend to believe her, she will take that good opinion seriously, and no longer even bother to make her fibs credible. It often happened that to make good one lie, la Pisana would have to invent two, and then four to make good the two, and so on to infinity. But she was prodigiously quick and inventive; she never lost her composure or showed any concern that others might not believe her, or bothered to think through all the implications of the stories she wove. She was, I believe, so accustomed to playing her roles that after a while she no longer knew the real from the imagined.

It was I, of course, who was left holding the sack, and I held it so gracelessly that the fibs were quickly apparent: not that she ever seemed annoyed or resentful; rather she seemed to be inclined not to expect much better from me, or perhaps she thought herself so superior that she needn't put her own assertions in doubt, merely because a third party had questioned them. True, the punishments all fell to me, and here there was no particular merit to her aplomb. And alas, they fell to me often and harshly, because my daily adventures with la Pisana constituted one long infraction of the Countess's rules; and while no effort was made to determine who was to blame, I was first to be punished because my crimes were open and repeated. Anyway, no one apart from her mother would have dared punish the Contessina, and the Countess paid not much more attention to her than to any other woman's daughter. La Pisana was the responsibility of the 'children's maid', and until she reached the age of ten maternal vigilance was pretty much confined to paying Faustina her two ducats a month. Between ten and twenty there was the convent, and from twenty on, Providence. Such was the tutelage that, according to the Countess, was sufficient to acquit her of all obligation to her female offspring. Clara had left the convent when still quite young in order to nurse her grandmother, it was true, but her grandmother's room was her cell, and differed from the convent only in name.

The good Countess, abandoned by youth and by such passions as had given her a hint of something beyond herself, was now so deeply concentrated on nursing her temporal and eternal health that beyond her rosary and a good digestion, she found no other suitable occupations. If she knitted stockings it was merely out of habit, or because no one else had a light enough hand to make them clothe her delicate skin without binding. When it came to household affairs, she was firm, perhaps because she knew that any laxity would have made the family too carefree and cheerful, and she didn't like cheerfulness in others when she enjoyed so little herself. Envy is the sin and the punishment of stingy souls, and I fear that the back of my head owed its daily torments to the Countess's pique at finding she was old, while I was but a child. For similar reasons, she detested Monsignor Orlando as much as she did me. That face of a man content at heart, those hands clasped on his belly as if to contain an excess of joy, annoyed her no end; she simply couldn't understand how someone could grow old so cheerfully. Heavens, there was a reason, of course! Monsignor Orlando had confined all happiness to satisfying the pleasures of the stomach, a passion that can burn – and rather brightly too – in old age. While she on the other hand . . . oh please! I don't wish to go on, now that her skeleton has been polished by fifty years underground.

Meanwhile we were growing up, our temperaments becoming more defined; what had been mere fancies became real passions, and the mind stirred and began to reason. Already the horizons of my desires had widened, so that the kitchen, the courtyard, the hayloft, the bridge and the piazza no longer served as my universe. I wanted to see what was beyond them, and left to my own devices, every step I took beyond my usual circle brought me that joy Colombus knew on discovering America. I would get up very early, and while Faustina was busy with the housekeeping or down in the mistress's rooms, I'd steal away with la Pisana to the garden or the banks of the fishpond. They were blessed hours, when the little imp pestered me less than usual and repaid my servitude more graciously. The morning hours, I have often observed, encourage peace of mind: in the morning even the most complex natures find some measure of simplicity and rectitude. As the day goes on, habit and deference begin to lord it over us, and towards evening, we see the most grotesque affectations, the worst lies, the most helpless outbursts of passion. Perhaps one reason is that the daytime hours are often spent in the open air, where men feel less slaves of themselves and more obedient to the universal laws of nature, which are never entirely wrong. I cannot say, however, that la Pisana, even when alone with just me, spoke or moved differently. It was all too clear that she enjoyed my admiration quite a bit more than my friendship or my intimacy, and I never ceased to be a sort of audience, however narrow and habitual, for her pantomimes.

But I should say that this became clear to me later, not that it was clear then. Then, I revelled in those blissful hours, I was sure that the young lady so desirous of pleasing me was the true one, that it was the fault of the others if her manner changed during the day.

When it came time for Mass (celebrated by Monsignor Orlando in the Castle chapel) the entire family – masters, servants, clerk, bailiff, steward, captain and guests – would collect in the appropriate pews. The Count had his own prie-dieu in the choir facing Monsignor, and from there he gravely acknowledged Monsignor's nods when he entered and exited, as well as the three waftings of incense during the Mass. When he recited the benedictions and the *Oremus* Monsignor never forgot to make a deep bow in the direction of His Most Excellent and Most Mighty Lord and Magistrate, who in turn gazed out into the middle distance towards the rest of the church, as if to measure the lofty heights that separated him from his flock of vassals. The Clerk, the Steward, the Captain, the Porter and even the maids and the cook drank up what fell on them of that gaze, and then trained a similar gaze on those in the chapel whose place was lower down than theirs. The Captain twirled his moustaches and placed his hand noisily on the hilt of his sword. When the Mass was over, all sat with their heads bowed in prayer (towards the Altar of the Rosary if Mass had been celebrated at the high altar, or vice versa), until the Count rose, cleared an ample space before himself with a great sign of the cross, and, replacing his missal, his handkerchief and his snuffbox in his pocket, moved gravely and stiffly towards the holy water font. Here there was another sign of the cross, and then he left the church with a slight nod towards the altar. Behind him came the Countess with her daughters, family and guests, all of whom bowed somewhat lower, then the servants and the officials, who bent one knee, and then the peasants and the townspeople, who bent two. Today, when we think of the Lord as very, very far away, he might seem to be equally distant from all the grades of society, just as the sun does not warm the top of a bell-tower more than it does the base. But in those days, when He was required to live rather closer to us, the greater and the lesser distances were easily observed by all, and the lord of the castle was considered much closer to God than the others, enough to permit a greater familiarity.

Half an hour before the Mass they usually came out to look for me to assist Monsignor, who, in choosing me meant to show I was more in his special favour than Fulgenzio's sons. But I felt no particular gratitude for this distinction and took steps to be sure that whoever came out to find me nearly always came back empty-handed. Most often I hid with Mastro Germano and never emerged from his den until the last bell had sounded. In the meantime they had put the surplice on Noni or on Menichetto, who in their wooden clogs always risked breaking their noses on the altar stairs. Then I would come into the church, certain the way was now clear. When these tricks of mine were discovered, Monsignor hauled me over the coals quite a few times at the kitchen hearth. I tried to excuse my repugnance, saying I didn't know the *Confiteor*.[6] And in order to fortify this excuse, the few times I did have to serve at Mass, I always stopped and began the prayer over again when I got to *mea culpa*, repeating this move three or four times until an impatient Monsignor finished the prayer himself. On those unhappy days I had the pleasure to be closed up in a little room below the dovecote until an hour before vespers, with a missal, a glass of water and some dark bread. I doused the book in water and made crumbs of the bread to feed the doves and when Gregorio, Monsignor's valet, came to release me I would run to Martino, who was certain to have put aside some lunch for me. During those long hours I had to listen to la Pisana romping with the other children and showing no regret at all about my imprisonment. It made me so furious at the *Confiteor* that I balled it up into pellets and threw it down on those little snakes in the courtyard, along with as many chips and flakes of plaster as I could scrape off the walls with my fingernails. Sometimes I would throw myself against the door with all my might and beat on it with my elbows, feet and head, and after half an hour of such a racket the Steward never failed to come up and repay me with four strokes of his whip. And he would repeat this dose in the evening when he discovered I had wet and torn up my missal.

On ordinary days after the Mass everyone went off to do his own business until mealtime. My business was to try to defend myself against the Rector's minion, who came to get me for my lessons. Run here, run there, me ahead and him behind; I ended up being captured, half-dead with vexation and fatigue, and then I had to trot the mile between Fratta and Teglio to make up for lost time. When we got there I busied myself studying the landscapes of Udine that hung on the walls of the rectory, and with some effort they closed me into a study, in which, after several days' experience, they locked me up rigorously to pay for my cheek. Among other things, I amused myself drawing sketches of the Rector on the walls: two great bushes of eyebrows and a big hat on his head that left no doubt about the artist's satirical intentions. Often, while I was exercising my artistic skills, I would hear the quiet footsteps of Maria, the Rector's housekeeper, who came to spy on me through the keyhole. Then I would leap over to the desk and with my elbows smartly lifted and my head bowed to the paper, would trace out some A's and some O's that filled up half the page and with four or five other big ugly letters that looked even more Arabic, exuberantly complete my assignment for the day. Or I would begin to shout *bi, ba, be, bo* in such a wild, mad voice that the poor woman fled to her kitchen, deafened.

At half past ten the Rector would appear and scold me for the messes on the wall, adding a second round of rebukes for the terrible penmanship and a third for the scant attention I paid to his finger tracing the lines of the lesson. As I recall, I used to get distracted by some big red books behind the glass of a bookcase, and instead of following the order of the alphabet, jumped inevitably to the V line: *vi*, *va*, *ve*, *vo*. At this point my recitation was interrupted by the third rebuke mentioned above, and I never learned why my memory preferred the letter V, unless it was that it was one of the last. The mistakes, the tugging at my ears and my nose, the foolishness I came out with during those lessons stick in my mind as proof of my bad behaviour and of the Rector's exemplary patience. If I had to teach such a little pig as I was then to read, I'm sure I would pull off his ears in the first two lessons. I instead suffered no inconvenience beyond going home with ears slightly lengthened. But that inconvenience, which persisted from when I was six until I was ten, permitted me to read all the printed letters and even to write them fluently, so long as there were no capitals. The parsimony with which I've used full stops and commas throughout my life I also owe to the easy-going and liberal instruction of the excellent Rector. Even now, as I put down my story, I've had to rely on a friend of mine in the prefect's office for the punctuation; otherwise the tale would be told from beginning to end in a single sentence, and no orator would have the wind to pronounce it.

On my way back to Fratta, when I didn't get lost chasing *sposi* (as we call dragonflies) or salamanders in the ditches, I would arrive just as the family was sitting down to eat. The dining hall was connected to the kitchen by a long, dark hallway that rose several arm-lengths along the way, so that the dining hall was high enough to see it was daytime through the windows. It was a huge, square room half-occupied by a table covered in green cloth, as large as two billiard tables. Between two embrasures facing the moat stood a huge fireplace, and at the other end, between windows looking out on the courtyard was a drop-leaf walnut credenza. In the four corners of the room stood four tables with candles ready for the evening card games. The dining chairs weighed at least fifty pounds apiece and they were all the same: wide in the seat, feet and back bolt upright, covered in black Morocco leather and stuffed with nails (or so it seemed from their pliant cushioning).

The table was usually laid for twelve: four on each of the long sides; three on the end closest to the hallway for the Steward, the Chaplain and the registrar; with the free side left to the Count. To his right sat her ladyship the Countess with the Countess

Clara; to his left, Monsignor and the Clerk. Between them and the other side of the table sat the Captain with his wife, and the guests. If there were no guests their places remained empty, and when there were more than two the Captain and his wife sought refuge among Steward, Chaplain and registrar. The Chaplain, as I've said, nearly always avoided the master's table, and more often than not his cutlery came back clean to the kitchen. Agostino, the pantry-keeper, delivered the serving dishes to the Count, and he, from his high chair – for he alone sat on a kind of throne that brought his knees almost up to the height of the table – gave the signal to carve. When Agostino had finished, the Count grabbed the choicest morsel and then signalled again to pass the plate to his wife, but even as he was signalling with his right hand he was already eating with his left.

The footman and Gregorio also served at table, but they offered slight assistance, for their time was taken up pouring wine for Monsignor or loosening his napkin or delivering great slaps on the back when he began to choke on a mouthful. La Pisana, I should say, did not dine with the others; that was an honour conferred on girls only after they left the convent. She ate, along with the maids, in a pantry between dining hall and kitchen. As for myself, I gnawed bones in the kitchen along with the dogs, the cats and Martino. No one ever came to tell me where my place was and which was my cutlery, for my place was where I found it, and instead of cutlery I had only my fingers. No, that's not entirely true. When it came time to eat my soup, the cook did give me a ladle, so broad it widened my mouth a good two fingers. But they say my smile was more expressive as a result, and since I've always had strong, white teeth, I can't complain. Because Martino and I were not counted among those who sat in the dining hall, nor among the servants with whom the Countess divided the remains after the meal, it was our privilege to scrape the pots and pans and casseroles, and make our luncheon from the scrapings. But there was always a basket of cooked polenta hanging on a hook on the kitchen wall, and when the scrapings left me hungry, I had only to point at the polenta. Martino understood: a slice was toasted and it was farewell, hunger!

The Bailiff and the Sacristan, who had wives and children, did not usually eat with the masters, nor did Mastro Germano, who cooked for himself, mixing up certain concoctions all his own that I never knew how the human palate could endure. From time to time he would grab one of the many cats that populated the Castle kitchen and make merry with stews and roasts for a week. And so, although he often invited me to dine with him, I was careful to decline. He insisted that cat is a delicious and flavorful meat and an excellent remedy against many ailments. But he never said such things in the presence of Martino and so I was sure he meant to fool me.

After the meal and before the Countess appeared in the kitchen, I would bolt outside to find the local rowdies who assembled in the piazza at that hour, and many of them would follow me into the courtyard where la Pisana would arrive, ready to engage in that coquetry I've already mentioned. You may well ask: why did I go to call those very rivals who then annoyed me so much? But the Contessina was brazen enough that she was capable of calling them herself, and this persuaded me to do myself what I would anyway – double mortification – be forced to endure. The Countess's serene digestive processes and the duties that kept the maids busy after luncheon freed us to enjoy our games for long hours. And if there had been a time when the old Countess had wanted to see her granddaughter in the afternoon, la Pisana behaved so badly that her mother soon dismissed her to preserve digestive peace.

And so we were free to shriek, pull each other's hair and race around the garden, the courtyards and the colonnade. Just one terrace – on to which looked the windows of the Count and Monsignor – was forbidden us under Gregorio's sharp-eyed watch. Once, when a few of the most defiant tried to break that rule, Gregorio came flying out of the door of a secondary staircase with a broomstick and laid into those boisterous boys until all saw that it was pointless to disobey. The Count was supposed to be taking care of chancery business in those hours, but if he was, he was gifted with quite exceptional eyesight, because his windows were always firmly shuttered until six o'clock. As for Monsignor, he slept and admitted to sleeping, but even had he wished to deny it, he snored so loudly that the infinite far corners of the castle would not have believed him.

Between six and half past six, weather permitting, the Countess went out for her stroll, and the Count and Monsignor went out to meet her half an hour later. They had no reason to fear they wouldn't find her, because every evening she invariably trod at the same pace to the first house of Fossalta and then, at the same pace, retraced her steps, a stroll that took sixty-five minutes unless she unexpectedly met someone. I need not add that along with the Count went the Clerk, walking a pace behind the master, and kicking pebbles from the road into the ditch when he wasn't honoured with any questions. But usually the Count would ask him about the morning's business, and he would tell him of the examinations he had made and about those cases for which he had 'provided information' for His Excellency. 'Information' referred to the sentences to which His Excellency would then pride himself on affixing his signature, armed with two pairs of spectacles and all the sweat of his brow his calligraphic expertise could muster. While the two secular judges thus took care of worldly affairs, Monsignor Orlando strolled on, polishing his teeth with his tongue and patting his belly. When the two parties met at a little path of stepping stones that connected the two villages along the road, the Clerk came to a halt with his hat sweeping the ground; Monsignor stood by, a hand raised in greeting, and the Count advanced halfway across the stepping stones to give his hand to the Countess. The young Countess Clara then came forward (when she was there, for often she remained at home with her grandmother), followed by the Rector or the Chaplain or Signor Andreini or Rosa or whoever else was part of the contingent. They then returned to the Castle in that order, two by two or sometimes in single file, because of the dreadful state of the road. When they arrived Agostino ran to light a great silver lamp in the dining hall which bore, instead of a handle, the family coat of arms: a boar flanked by two trees, with the Count's coronet behind. The boar was larger than the trees and the coronet was larger than all three. If the Count held this piece of craftsmanship dear, it was nevertheless quite apparent that Benvenuto Cellini had never been near it. Meanwhile the cook was putting a huge coffee pot on the fire, and the company continued their conversation in the dining hall.

But the afternoon followed this programme only during the fine months and when the weather was dry. Otherwise, neither the Count nor Monsignor left their rooms except to settle down by the kitchen hearth, and there the family gathered to pay them court until it was time to play cards. On such days they took coffee in the kitchen and proceeded to the dining hall, where the card tables were set up, and the whole party followed on tiptoe. The Countess was there alone to receive them, for young Countess Clara did not come down until an hour later when she had put her grandmother to bed. Some days the Captain's wife was granted the honour of taking coffee with the Countess, and this was a sign that things had gone ever so well that day. Signora Veronica was rather vain about this privilege and stared sternly at her husband when he stood before her, as he often did, twirling his moustaches before sitting down.

When the occasion was confined to family, they would play *tresette* at two small tables, but when there were guests – and there were guests every autumn evening and on Sundays the rest of the year – they would crowd around the big table to play *mercante in fiera*, *sette e mezzo* or *tombola*. The puritans like Monsignor and the Clerk, who disliked games of chance, withdrew to a corner to play *tresette*, and the Captain, who thought luck was always against him, retired to the kitchen to play the Game of the Goose[7] with the Bailiff or Fulgenzio. In truth, I suspect that the two *soldi* stake they put down in the dining hall was too risky for him, and he was happier with the *bezzo* (or *bezzo-e-mezzo*, one and a half of those sturdy little coins) stake that was customary in the kitchen.

In the meantime, having played with la Pisana until nightfall, when Faustina came to take her to bed, I squeezed in at the hearth to listen to Martino or Marchetto tell stories. And so I remained until my head bobbed on my breast, and then Martino would take me by the arm and, crossing the courtyard so as not to pass through the hall, conduct me up the stairs to Faustina's door. I would lurch in, rubbing my eyes, and having unbuttoned my trousers was naked and ready for bed, for no shoes, no vest, no stockings, no drawers, no scarf ever complicated my life before I was ten – and a jacket and a pair of those linsey-woolsey breeches the servants wore composed my entire wardrobe, along with a piece of twine to tie my pigtail. I also had a few shirts, so large they repaid all their other defects, because Monsignor passed his on to me when they wore out, and no one ever took the trouble to make them fit, except by shortening the tails and the sleeves a little.

As for my head, one winter when the temperature was often freezing – I was about seven, I believe – Mastro Germano adorned it with a fur cap he'd worn back when he was a *bulo* at Ramuscello. That cap would have slipped down to my chin had the Rector not previously readied my ears to resist the force of gravity. Behind, where I had no ears, it fell to my neck and Martino said that with that thing on my head I looked like a cat whose fur has been rubbed the wrong way. But perhaps he said so to spite Germano, and I am grateful to the latter and to his cap, which saved me from many a chill. How many years I wore it, I cannot say for sure. Certainly I still had it when I was already a young man, and I would save it for feast days, because once my head had grown I thought it suited my looks admirably and gave me a fearsome flair.

One day, at the fair in Ravignano on the other side of the Tagliamento, where there was dancing on the planks, I went so far as to make fun of some of the Cernide at the service of the Savorgnani, who had come to keep order at the fair with their shotguns in one hand and a napkin full of eggs, butter and salami in the other, the makings of a mangy omelette, as they say. Those fellows of the Cernide with their wooden clogs and their threadbare linsey-woolsey jackets, those faces that you could see were stupid a mile away, had me laughing fit to die. I and some other bold fellows from Teglio and nearby began to make vulgar gestures at them, and ask them were they good at flipping omelettes, and would they cook them with their shoes? One of them replied that we had better go and dance, and so I stepped forward and said I would begin the dance with him. And so I did, taking him by the arms just as he stood there with his shotgun on his shoulder, and spinning him around in the strangest *furlana* that has ever been seen. But he had put his provisions on the ground, and so as we spun around we tramped on the eggs and made the omelette all too soon.

At this point his brave companions, who hadn't lifted a finger when their colleague was derided, were suddenly moved by the destruction of the eggs and threatened to attack me with their bayonets. But pulling my pistols from my pockets and pushing my dancing friend to the ground before them, I began to shout that the first man to move was dead. Instantly my companions all clustered round to defend me, one with his knife unsheathed, another with pistols just like mine. There was a pause and then the heavens opened, and how we found ourselves one on top of the other, without firing our guns or using any arms but the butt ends, I don't know, because in truth the dispute wasn't worth it. A beating here and a pounding there; those poor Cernide ended up the worse for wear and so did their eggs. But just then their captain arrived with the rest of his band, and he drove us away with dire threats, saying that if we didn't stop squabbling he would open fire on all of us without regard for friend or foe. And so witnesses were called to say who was at fault, and they declared (as they always did) that we were in the right and the Cernide in the wrong, and so we were allowed to leave without further ado.

But while I was going, and boasting about this triumph to my companions, that fellow who had danced the *furlana* with me shouted out that I had better watch my step dancing and not lose my fur headpiece, for he would take it for a trophy to put on his ass's head on the second day of the fair. And I replied with a vulgar gesture to say, take it if you can, and that he and the ass would always make two, but he would never get my headpiece. And there the captain cut us short and we went to dance with the prettiest girls at the fair, while the Cernide lit some fires to make omelettes with the remaining eggs.

That evening I stayed at the fair longer than perhaps I had intended, to see what that bounder who had challenged me was good for, and so did some of my companions. And finally, at an hour when the night was as dark as Hell itself, we headed towards the Mendrisio ferry, where, on the other shore, a steward's cart was waiting. The road twisted among fields thick with trees, and was in places so narrow that four of us could barely walk abreast, and since each of us, having downed abundant quantities of Ribolla, needed room enough for four, we were always about to lose one of us in the ditch. We were laughing and singing as best we could with the wine nearly bubbling up in our throats, when at a turn in the road I saw a black figure leap over the ditch and throw itself on me like a bomb. I took a step back and the figure said to me, 'Aha, it's you!' and gave me a good pounding on the back that sent me tumbling into the mud like a sackful of sausage meat. I raised myself up on my elbows and watched that figure leap back over the ditch and disappear into the country darkness. Only then did I realize I had lost my cap, and bent down on the road searching for it – and here I have to say either that the road could be seen from the fields rather well, or that the darkness was in my own eyes, because the fellow who had jumped the ditch saw me bend down to look and he shouted at me from afar to resign myself, because it was he who had grabbed my cap, to prettify his donkey at the fair next day. When I heard these words I recalled the incident with the Cernide, and my companions were much relieved, for the whole apparition had seemed to them the Devil's doing. Now that we knew the truth, they were clamouring for revenge, but the ditch was wide and none trusted his legs enough to make the leap (and perhaps we still had a glimmer of good sense about us). And so we went on our way, promising to take reprisals on the morrow, and we all stayed the night at Mendrisio, and the next day went to the fair to inspect all the Cernide and all the asses we came across. And when we found the one who had, between his ears, my fur cap stuck to his forehead with pitch, we gave his captain such a whipping that they had to send him home on the donkey's back. And my cap, now no longer fit to wear, we stuck firmly to his face, telling him he should keep it as a souvenir. Thus I lost Mastro Germano's gift, which had done me such good service for so many years, and out of these events came a criminal lawsuit that kept me very busy, as I will report in due course.[8]

Meanwhile, I pray you not to think badly of me if at this point in my life you find me revelling with peasants and drunkards. I promise you will see I'm a man of some importance, but just now I'll return to my boyhood, so as to tell my story in order.

I've mentioned that I used to go to bed while they were still playing cards in the hall, but the games did not go on very long, because at half past eight precisely they got up to recite the rosary, at nine they sat down to supper and at ten the Count gave the signal to rise from the table when he ordered Agostino to light the lamp. The company then filed out of the door leading to the great stair, opposite the door to the kitchen. I say 'great stair', but in fact it was a stairway like any other. At the first landing the Count would always stop and tap the wall to extract his prognostication for the following day. If the wall was damp he would say, 'Bad weather tomorrow,' and the Clerk behind him would repeat 'Bad weather,' and all chimed in contritely, 'Bad weather!' If instead he found the wall dry the Count would call out, 'We shall have a fine day tomorrow!' and the Clerk would echo 'A very fine day!' and all, right down to the bottom stair, would concur: 'A fine day!' During this ceremony the procession would halt on the stairs to the Countess's great distress, for she feared that all those draughts would bring on sciatica. Monsignor instead would begin to drift off to sleep, and Gregorio had to hold him up and shake him or he would have tumbled over onto Signora Veronica, who stood behind him. When all had made their way up the stairs, the business of saying good night began, after which they disbanded and went to their respective rooms, and some of them were distant enough so that three paternosters, two Ave Marias and three Glorias could easily be recited before reaching the door. At least that is what Martino said; after he retired, he had been assigned a tiny space on the second floor, next to the bare room where the friars slept when they came begging.

The Count and his wife occupied rooms that from time immemorial had housed all the lords of the noble family of Fratta. Theirs was a great, high-ceilinged chamber with a terrazzo floor that in winter gave you the chills just to look at it, and bare beams up above decorated with blue and yellow arabesques. Floor, walls and ceiling were all covered with boars, trees and coronets, so that one couldn't cast an eye around without meeting a pig's ear, a leaf or the point of a crown. In their vast bridal chamber the Count and the Countess were literally assailed by spectres of crests and family trophies, and that glorious display, imposing itself on the mind before the lights were dimmed, could not but have imposed an aristocratic bearing on even their darkest and most secret matrimonial functions. If Jacob's ewes could bring forth piebald lambs[9] just by looking at some dappled rods at the spring, the Countess could not but conceive offspring blessed in the lustre and excellence of their line. If subsequent events did not always confirm this hypothesis, perhaps the fault lay more with the Count than with the Countess.

The Contessina Clara slept near her grandmother in the apartment that opened on to the hall across from her parents. Her room resembled a nun's cell, and she had hidden behind a pile of books (most likely without thinking about it) the only boar impressed in the stucco on the mantelpiece. The books were the remains of a library that was rotting away in a ground-floor room, neglected by the Count and Countess and exposed to the unfriendly attentions of worms, mice and damp. The Contessina, who during her three years in the convent had taken refuge in reading to escape boredom and the nuns' gossiping, on her return remembered that room piled high with disintegrating old treatises and parchments and decided to fish around for whatever little of value remained. A few memoirs translated from the French; some of those old Italian tales recounted in a homespun way without too much rhetoric; Tasso, Ariosto, Guarini's *Faithful Shepherd*, and nearly all the comedies of Goldoni, only recently published: this was all her prize amounted to. Add to these one Little Office of the Blessed Virgin Mary and several devotional works and you have the catalogue of that bookshelf behind which the boar crest hid in Clara's room. After she had silently stolen over to her grandmother's bed to be sure that nothing disturbed her placid dreams, holding her hand before the lantern to prevent the light reflecting too violently off the walls, she would withdraw to her little cell to study some of those books. Often all the inhabitants of the Castle would be deep asleep while the lamp-light still shone from her balcony window, and when she took up *Jerusalem Delivered* or *Orlando Furioso* (those same volumes that had not been able to impress a military career on her uncle) the oil in the lamp would fail before the young lady's ardour for the book. She trailed Erminia through shady groves and followed her to shepherds' huts; with Angelica and Medoro she wrote songs of love on mossy walls, and raved with mad Orlando and wept tears of compassion for him. But above all her gentle heart was won by Brandimarte's death, when at that fatal hour the name of his beloved was arrested on his lips, and then he seemed to go on uttering it and repeating it forever in the happy eternity of love. When she fell asleep after reading those pages, she sometimes dreamed she was herself the very widow Fiordelisa,[10] and a black veil fell from her forehead over her eyes and down to the ground, as if to conceal from the common gaze the sanctity of her inconsolable tears, that sweet, sad, eternal grief that swelled in her heart like a distant echo of faint harmonies. And from the purest substance of that grief came something like a ghost of hope that, too light and ethereal to amuse itself on earth, ascended far into the heights of the heavens. Were these fancies or premonitions? She did not know, but she did know that the feelings of the Fiordelisa of her dreams were exactly those of Clara.

A soul untouched by this world's imprint, she was as God had made her amid the frivolity, the vanity and the vulgarity around her. The devout beliefs and gentle ways of her grandmother, purified by the serene reflections of old age, were reborn in her with all the spontaneity of virginal youth. She had spent her childhood at Fratta, a faithful companion to the elderly woman. Even as a child she seemed to be the thriving young chestnut shoot that grows from the old stump. A solitary existence had protected her from the dissolute company of the servants and from what she might have learned from her mother's example. Pure, serene and simple, she lived in the Castle like the sparrow that hides its nest in the barn's rafters. Her beauty grew with her, as if the sun and the air she imbibed from morning till night with all the nonchalance of a country girl had mingled inside to enlarge and illuminate her. But it made a benign, pleasant light not unlike that of the moon – not the harsh and flickering glare of the lantern. She shone, she reigned, like a Virgin among the candles on the altar. And, in fact, her countenance emanated an almost heavenly peace, and it was apparent just from looking at her that beneath that gentle and harmonious frame ardent devotion was mingled with pure imagination, lit by the most innocent delicacy of feeling. The fire of the south, reflected off the adamantine white glaciers of the north.

The peasant women all around called her The Saint, and they remembered with veneration the day of her first Communion, when, just after taking the mystical bread, she fainted from solace, fear and humility, and they said that God had brought her to ecstasy, for she was worthy of a true marriage with Him. And Clara, too, recalled that heavenly day with joy and trembling, tasting again and again in memory the sublime rapture of her soul, invited for the first time to participate in the sweetest, most noble mystery of her religion. You must remember that I am writing about a time when faith was still in fashion, and produced in the elect those miracles of charity, sacrifice and worldly detachment that remain miracles even in the misbelieving eye of the philosopher. I don't preach doctrine or condemn or defend systems, and I know very well that faith – or zealotry, as faith is expressed by false and depraved souls – can twist consciences worse than any other kind of perversity. And I repeat that I am not a believer, and perhaps I regret that because it costs me great pains to find another path toward life's true and decent worth.

So often I must traverse, disillusion by my side and desperation before my eyes, the deeps of the metaphysical abyss; I must force myself to enlarge my diffident, myopic soul before the infinite expanse and duration of human affairs; I must close my eyes to the frequent, harrowing instances in which happiness, science and virtue contradict one another; I must, as a sociable creature answerable to the laws of society, retreat to the fortress of conscience to know sanctity, eternal vitality, and those moral laws that today are derided, trampled and violated in every way; and finally I must – a man who would boast of his reason and his dominion over the universe – sink and annihilate myself, one invisible atom, in the immense and immensely harmonic life of the very universe in order to find excuses for that struggle we call existence, and motives for that spectre we call hope. And even this excuse quivers before mature reason as a candle flame buffeted by the wind, and late in life I've understood that faith produces more happiness than does science. I cannot, however, repent of my moral persuasion, for necessity admits no remorse; I cannot and must not be ashamed of it, for a doctrine that, in practice in society, combines stoical determination with evangelical charity must never be ashamed of itself no matter what its philosophical underpinnings.

But how much effort, how much grief, how many years, how much constancy are needed to get there! Only the patience of the ant – knocked flat by the wind, losing his burden one hundred times, and hoisting it up on his back one hundred times over again to make his long trek by tiny footsteps – only that patience made it possible. Few would have imitated me, and few did imitate me, in fact. Halfway there, most toss aside that capricious compass that so often leads astray, abandoning themselves to the whims of the wind. And when the time comes to bring the sails into port, most run aground. There are charming young ladies and polite young gentlemen whose every effort goes into material pleasures: things of enjoyment, parties and celebrations are their sole desires; their only care the money that provides rich loam for those desires. Their spirits seek no nutriment but to appear beautiful in others' eyes and to avoid embarrassment. Their minds know no pleasures that are really their own.

Ask one of them if he would have liked to have been Scipio or Dante or Galileo and he will tell you that Scipio, Dante and Galileo are dead. Life is all for them. And when they must abandon it? They don't want to think about that! They don't want to, they say; I would add that they are unable, that they don't dare. And if they did dare, their choice would be between the pistol – bodily suicide – and despair – the soul's suicide. Thus is the destiny of the strongest, and of the most wretched.

In its time, religious faith was an ideal, a force, a comfort, and those who had not the courage to question could bear what came their way by believing in heaven. Now faith is disappearing, and science – alive and in full – is not yet with us. Why then should we so glorify these times, that even the most optimistic call times of transition? Honour the past and speed the future, but live in the present with the humility and determination of one who knows he is impotent, but still feels the need to make sense of life. Raised without the beliefs of the past and without faith in the future, I sought everywhere, in vain, a place of repose for my thoughts. And finally I understood that justice is the goal of human life, and man the minister; and that history expiates by counting up the sacrifices on behalf of humanity. Old in years, I rest my head on the pillow of the grave and offer these words of faith to those who no longer believe, but still wish to use their minds in this age of transition. Faith cannot be imposed, not even on oneself. To those who object that my virtuous but pointless effort will have no recompense in time eternal, I say: I am master before other men of my temporal and eternal being. It is not your business to intervene in any accounts between God and me. I envy your faith, but cannot impose it on myself. Believe, therefore, and be happy, and leave me in peace.

Contessina Clara was not only a believer, she was devout and ardent, for faith was not enough for her soul: it also wanted love. What's more, her reputation for goodness was not merely based on fervour, but on continual good works of the most saintly kind. Her manner was not that of the humble scullery maid or housekeeper, but that of the countess who derives her social superiority from God and who before God considers herself equal to the most abject member of the human family. She had what is called second sight when it came to her intuition of others' afflictions, and the gift of simplicity, which permitted her both to advise and console. The value she attributed to wealth was that assigned by the needs of the poor: the right value, as any healthy economy would suggest, to earn her credit with humanity. People said she was a spendthrift, and it was true, but she was unaware of it; hers was a duty done automatically, the way we are not aware of blood that circulates or lungs that breathe. She was utterly incapable of hatred, even of the wicked, because she never doubted they would repent.

She was a friend to every creature in the universe and nature never knew a daughter more loving and grateful. She couldn't bear to see a mousetrap in the house and would step aside to avoid trampling on a flower or a clump of green grass in the fields. And yet – no poetic exaggeration – her footprint was so light that the flower merely bent its head a moment under her heel and the grass did not register being trod on. If she kept birds in a cage it was to free them in the springtime, and sometimes she grew so close to those delightful warblers that it broke her heart to free them. But what did her own regrets matter to Clara when the good of another was involved? She would open the birdcage, her smile glistening with a tear or two, and sometimes the little birds came to peck at her fingers before flying off, and then they would hover near the Castle, returning confidently to the window where they'd spent the cold season as happy prisoners. Clara recognized them and was grateful for how affectionately they remembered her.

And so she believed that the things of this world were good and that human beings could not be evil if goldfinches and tits were so grateful and loving. Her grandmother smiled from where she sat in her armchair at Clara's tender, touching, childish fancies. She took pains not to scoff at her, because the old lady knew from experience that, indulging such delicate girlish feelings, Clara would store up for later life an inexhaustible font of pleasures – modest, but pure, neither ephemeral nor envied by others. During the three years she stayed in the convent at San Vito with the Salesians, she was readily mocked for her foolish habits, but she was good enough not to be ashamed and true enough not to change her ways. And so when she emerged to take up, at her grandmother's side, her vocation as a nurse, she was still the same simple, modest, obliging young woman, quick to laugh and quick to weep for any joy or any sorrow that was not her own.

The Countess, after she had made the move from Venice to Fratta and found the village somewhat primitive and savage, had first intended to civilize Clara with the usual ten years in the convent, but after three she began to say that the girl was clever and perhaps three were enough. The truth was that she found it burdensome looking after her mother-in-law, and to avoid having to sacrifice one of her maids to do the job, decided to double her savings by bringing her daughter home. It was also true that her erstwhile fashionable life in Venice had cut rather deeply into the family's finances, and, concerned about how she would provide for her son's education, she thought it best to cut back on spending for daughters. There were already two of them, because the Countess was with child when she decided to take Clara away from the convent, and she never doubted for a moment that she would give birth to a girl, for whom she'd already chosen a name in honour of her mother, whose surname was Pisani.

And this is how things stood while I was sucking at the breast and gulping down my pap in all the houses of Fratta. By the time I was nine years old and la Pisana seven, and young Count Rinaldo was finishing up his studies with the reverend Somascan Fathers, the Contessina Clara had already grown up to be a charming young woman. She was, I believe, about nineteen years old, but she looked younger, for her delicate colours always kept her looking young and fresh. Her reading had enriched her mind with useful knowledge and with the right thoughts to enhance her compassionate and reflective nature. Her sensibility – without having lost any of its girlish charm – had found useful expression in the aid she distributed to women of the poor. She still loved her flowers and little birds, but spent less time thinking about them now that her hours were taken up with human charity. Her serene nature was as solid as ever and even more enchanting now that her soul was lit up by heavenly certainty.

When she came down to the dining hall after putting her grandmother to bed, and sat by the table where her mother was playing cards, white work in one hand and needle in the other, all eyes were drawn to her and her presence was enough to quiet the voices and soften the comments for a quarter hour. The Countess, who was anything but dull, noticed the effect her daughter produced and was even somewhat jealous, for her own lace cap and all the presumption of the Navagero line etched in her physiognomy had never been able to accomplish so much. Although she had often sought to damp down the gossipy, vulgar tone of the conversation, when that pause came she was annoyed and began to prod the Captain or Signor Andreini not to be shy. The Count would gloat to see his wife enjoy the local tittle-tattle, while Monsignor stole sideways glances at her, unable to understand what accounted for these unusual and somewhat indiscreet outbursts of amiability. I was just a little thing then, but from the keyhole through which I sometimes spied I could sense when the Countess was peevish and when good-humoured; and so could Clara, for I also remember that a blush would spread across her face when the Captain or Andreini said something rude in front of the illustrious mistress's guests. I can still see her, that angel of a girl, dig into her embroidery and twist her thread around her fingers in her haste. And I'm sure her blush derived mostly from concern that the thought crossing her mind at that moment was really quite vain. Did Monsignor suspect or understand any of this? I was nine and he was past sixty; he was a canon wearing his surplice and red stockings, and I was practically a foundling, shirtless and shoeless. He was named Orlando and I, Carlino: with all of this, it was I who knew more of the world and of morals than he. He was the most simple-minded theologian in all the clergy of Christendom, I swear!

Around these times, visitors to the Castle of Fratta, mostly young men from Portogruaro and nearby, began to show up more often. Not just on a Sunday or during the vine harvest, but all year round, even on the coldest, most icy winter day, some courageous visitor would arrive on foot or on horseback, gun on his shoulder and lantern held high. I don't know whether the Countess thought it was she who was attracting these visits, but certainly she took pains to seem vivacious and charming. Yet even supposing her respectable and really quite mature age held any attractions, the eyes of those young men wandered rather a lot until they came to rest on Clara's charming little face. Lucilio Vianello, who lived closest by at Fossalta, was the most assiduous, but Partistagno wasn't far behind, although his castle at Lugugnana was near the coast beyond the pine forest, a good seven miles from Fratta. The distance perhaps conceded him the right to come early and often he arrived just as Clara was setting out to meet her mother on her afternoon promenade. Custom then granted him the role of her companion and Clara accepted politely, although the rude and determined manners of the young man were not much to her taste.

When the card games were finished the Countess never failed to invite Partistagno to spend the night at Fratta, because the distance was great and the darkness perfidious, but he always declined with a bow, and aiming Clara a look that was rarely returned except by chance, went out to the stables to saddle his rugged Friulian steed. Wrapping himself tightly in his stout jacket and shouldering the strap of his gun with its indispensable lantern on top, he would leap into the saddle and pound over the drawbridge, searching in his saddlebags to be sure his pistols were still there. And so he rode out, a ghostly figure between dark roads and deep ditches, but most of the time he would stop for the night in San Mauro, two miles on, where he had furnished for his use four rooms in a farmer's house on one of his properties. The people nearby had the greatest respect for Partistagno and for his shotgun, his pistols and even for his fists when he had no weapons on him. A blow from those fists was powerful enough that if you took a couple in the stomach, you didn't need a cannon ball or even a bullet to send you to your Creator.

Vianello instead came and went each evening on foot, the lantern on the top of his walking stick thrust forward like the sacristan's collection bag during the intervals at the sermon. He seemed to have no weapons on him, although had you searched his pockets you might have found an excellent double-barrelled pistol, rather unusual for those times. But no one dared bother him, for he was the son of the doctor at Fossalta and thus profited from some of his father's inviolability. In those days popular opinion held doctors to be magicians and few were bold enough to risk medical retaliation. Today there's quite a lot of that (retaliation), even unintended, but in the last century there was six times as much – and just imagine if there had also been premeditation! When plague decimated the province, doctors were pretty much held responsible; I know one high-born family who even today when they call the doctor will recite long prayers to the Virgin, begging protection.

Nothing about Dr Sperandio ('Trust-in-God', a name that all by itself supplied good advice to the ailing) suggested he didn't deserve the reputation for witchcraft he and his colleagues enjoyed. He wore a large inky black wig of wool or horsehair that protected his brow, ears and neck from the wind, and on top of that a three-cornered hat as big and black as a thundercloud. Arriving from afar on his gaunt, tired mount – ash-grey, more donkey than horse – he seemed an undertaker, not a doctor. And when he dismounted and stood before the patient's bed, glasses perched on his nose to inspect the tongue, he was the picture of a notary come to take down a last will and testament. Ordinarily he spoke a mixture of half-Latin and half-Friuli, but after lunch it was three-quarters Latin and towards evening, when he had downed the chalice of the Ave Maria, it was pure Cicero. If in the morning he ordered a palliative, in the afternoon he inclined to the drastic; a few leeches after lunch, but by night-time, abundant blood-letting. His courage expanded with the hour: after supper he was ready to excise the brain of a madman in hopes the operation might cure him. No doctor, surgeon or phlebotomist had lances longer or rustier than his; I suspect they were the very lances of the Huns or the Visigoths, dug up in the ruins of Concordia. Yet he employed them with singular skill and in his long career spoiled but the arm of a paralytic, and the only (frequent) nuisance was the copious flow of blood from the deep wounds. When Dragon Powder did not stem the tide, he would fall back on just letting the blood flow, quoting a Latin phrase all his own, to wit: *No peasant ever died with his veins open*. And, in fact, Seneca was no peasant, but a philosopher!

Dr Sperandio held the arts of Galen and Hippocrates in the highest esteem. And well he should have, for he had not only earned a living from them, he'd had enough left over to buy a house and farmland in Fossalta. He had studied at Padua, but considered the School of Salerno and the University of Montpellier superior. His prescriptions relied greatly on medicinal herbs, mainly indigenous plants from the bogs and hedgerows, and this most un-Christian method put him at odds with the town druggist. But the doctor was a man of conscience and, knowing that the druggist made his imported medicines from local herbs and flowers, he thus exposed the fraud by the awful simplicity of his own remedies. As for his ideas about society, he was somewhat Egyptian. Let me explain. He believed that the professions should belong to families and wished at all costs to see his son inherit his clients and his lances. But Lucilio did not share this opinion and thought that the Great Flood had come for nothing if not to sweep away that fetid, old doctrine of hereditary tyranny.

The young man had done his duty, though, and spent five years studying at the very ancient, very learned University of Padua. As a scholar he was distinguished in his negligence, yet he didn't cut a bad figure when he did show up. He quarrelled with the noblemen and the guardsmen, and every time it snowed he was the first to arrive at the waiting room of the Convent of Santa Croce to announce the news. It was more or less established that the nuns would reward whoever got there first with a nice basket of millefeuilles. And Lucilio Vianello had emptied many such baskets before attaining his laureate.

But now we come to the eternal question between Lucilio and his father. There seemed to be no way that the elder could induce the young man to finish that blessed degree. He would put the travel money, to Padua and back, in his pockets, along with the cost of a month's lodgings and the fee for the first exam, and see him to the postal boat for Venice. But Lucilio would depart, lodge and return without the money and without having taken the exams. Seven times in two years he was absent this way, sometimes one month, sometimes two, and the professors of the Faculty of Medicine had still not had a taste of their first fees.

Whatever was he doing during those absences? That was what Dr Sperandio was doggedly determined to find out, but his efforts seemed to be in vain. On the seventh trip he finally learned that his son didn't take the trouble to go all the way to Padua, but having arrived in Venice was quite content to stay there and saw no reason to go further in order to spend his father's money. He learned this from his patron, a certain nobleman and senator by the name of Frumier, related by marriage to the Count of Fratta, who spent the summer months at Portogruaro; this Frumier wrote warning the Doctor about Lucilio's rather suspect behaviour in Venice, on account of which the good gentlemen Inquisitors were keeping a paternal eye on him.

Oh mercy me! What next? Dr Sperandio burned the letter and stirred up the ashes with a poker, casting a sour look on Lucilio who sat nearby, drying off his cow-hide gaiters, but for a long time did not speak to him again about the degree. However, he did drag him along on his visits to test out his erudition in the science of Asclepius, and when he found himself satisfied with the result, began to send him around to examine the tongues and the urine of the various country folk whom the doctor had already visited that morning. Lucilio took out his notebook and marked off separate pages for Giacomo, Toni and Matteo, with triple columns for pulse, tongue and urine, and as he completed the visits he would fill up his charts with the information requested and take it all back in good order to his father, who was at times astonished by the erratic reactions and sudden reversals not typical, in his view, of the illnesses of common labourers.

'What? Tongue clean and moist, Matteo – who's been in bed since yesterday with fever and putrid gut? *Putridum . . . fluxum ventris . . . purgationes resolvitur*, he would mumble. Tongue clean and moist? This morning it was dry as tinder with two fingers of patina on top . . . Zounds! Gaetana, a racing pulse? When today I counted fifty-two beats a minute and ordered her up a potion of *vinum pepatum et infusione canellae*? Whatever can this mean? We shall see tomorrow! *Nemo humanae natura pars qua nervis praestet in faenomenali mutatione ac subitaneitate*. At times the doctor's Latin grew somewhat nonsensical.

On the morrow, Sperandio would go out on his rounds and find Matteo's tongue was coated and Gaetana's pulse was sluggish, despite the wine, the pepper and the cinnamon. The reason for these miraculous improvements and reversals was that Lucilio, who hadn't felt inclined to make his visits that day, had invented and copied out his charts at leisure under the shade of a mulberry tree. He then handed them back to his father to make him despair of his theories about the signs and symptoms of diseases.

There were certain occasions, however, when the young man didn't mind having a putative licence in medicine from the Paduan University: when, for example, as soon as he arrived home, Rosa came to ask him to go and see the old Countess, who was subject to irritation of the nerves and wanted some laudanum and distilled water to calm her pains. It seemed Lucilio held this near-centenarian in a sort of holy veneration and no remedies or attentions were ever enough to preserve a life so worthy and precious. When he listened to her it was with something like stunned amazement; the sound of her words seemed to evoke blissful pleasure, a sort of melodious pins and needles of the soul. Although he was by nature reticent and closed, when he talked to her he warmed with involuntary candour and did not hesitate to speak of himself and his affairs, as if to a mother. No one, in his view, had suffered being an orphan as much as he (for Dr Sperandio's wife had died in childbirth with this only child). He seemed to seek comfort for his painful loss in this near-maternal figure. Little by little the old woman grew accustomed to the young man's presence, and she would call for him even when she didn't need a doctor and listen with pleasure while he recited the news of the day, finding him, to her satisfaction, quite different from the other young fellows who frequented the Castle. And, in fact, Lucilio did merit that distinction, for he had read widely and had a great love for history. Knowing as he did that every day is a page in the annals of the people, he was keeping an attentive eye on those first upheavals appearing on the European horizon.

At that time the English were not well regarded by the Venetian patriciate, perhaps for the same reason that the bankrupt man cannot look kindly on the new owners of his goods. It was the adventurous Americans and the eminent citizen Washington (who had freed an entire New World from submission to the Lords) who captured the Venetian imagination. The old lady would listen happily as Lucilio told of battles that invariably went badly for the English, and she shared his enthusiasm for that pact of federation that had deprived them forever of their American colonies. And when he spoke, tight-lipped, of events in France, of ministers who were rapidly ousting one another and the King who no longer knew which side to turn to, and the intrigues of that Germanized Queen, then Old Lady Badoer spoke up to tell how things had been in her time: the splendours of the court, the intrigues, the servile courtiers, the Great King's[11] proud if somewhat lugubrious solitude as he outlived the glory his contemporaries had attributed to him and saw the frivolity and debauchery of his heirs. She spoke with dismay of the openly lewd customs that the younger generation was then already welcoming and thanked heaven for having protected the Republic of San Marco from that pestilential invasion.

She also recalled Venice as it had been at the dawn of the Settecento, when she had left the Court of France for the Castle of Fratta, when the Republic was not yet unworthy of a place in the Maggior Consiglio of European states. Little did she know that in the meantime the monstrosities of Versailles and Trianon had been amply copied in false and tinselled elegance on the Rialto and the Grand Canal. When her granddaughter read to her from some of Goldoni's comedies she was scandalized and made her skip certain pages; she even took away several volumes and locked them up. She simply couldn't see that what to her were the loose language and decadent thinking of the comedies that played at the San Benedetto or Sant'Angelo were, in fact, a blow struck against customs even more brazen and corrupt.

Sometimes they would touch on the reforms undertaken by Joseph II,[12] especially in ecclesiastical matters, and the devout old lady could not decide whether she abhorred that infamous deed against her religion – or was consoled it had been done by such an enemy of the Republic (who would later surely be punished by the hand of God). The Venetians, especially in the Friuli, had long felt the pressure of the Empire, and if they had resisted by force during their one-time military supremacy, and by using careful diplomacy while they enjoyed mature civic judgement, now that both force and diplomacy had perished in universal decadence, the best simply relied on Providence. A strategy understandable in an old woman, but not in a senate expected to govern. We all know that Providence matures its own designs using our thoughts, our sentiments, our works, and that only the desperate and the petty expect ready-made results from Providence. And so when the elder Countess resorted to this kind of foolish faith, Lucilio could only nod his head, but he did so biting his lip and suppressing a little smile that escaped the corners of his mouth, pushing it back behind thin, black moustaches. I wager that the Emperor's reforms and the decline of San Marco didn't displease him as much as he pretended.

But the conversation didn't always deal with these exalted questions; in fact, it dealt with them quite rarely and only when no more immediate topics presented themselves. In those days steamships, telegraphs and railways had not yet realized that great moral creed, the unity of mankind, and every little society – left to its own devices because communications were difficult and jurisdictions almost completely independent – occupied itself above all with *itself*, taking no interest in the rest of the world, except as a place for curiosity to graze. Molecules spun away from one another into chaos; centripetal force had not yet condensed them into systems fitting one inside the other, held together by reciprocal active and passive influences. And so the inhabitants of Fratta lived, much like Epicurus' gods, with a very high opinion of their own importance, and whenever they enjoyed a respite from their business and their pleasures, would shoot a glance – indifferent or curious – to the left or right, as fancy dictated. This helps to explain why there was such a shortage of statistical notions in the past century, and why geographers wasted their time recording strange customs and travellers' tales, rather than the real conditions of the provinces. The fault lay less with the means and the ignorance of the writers than with the aptitude of their readers. For them the world was not a marketplace, but a theatre.

Most often it was local gossip that concerned our two conversationalists: this or that Commune which had usurped the rights of this or that fief-holder, and the squabbling that had burst out in front of the Most Excellent Representative, and the sentence he issued, and the soldiers sent on foot and by horseback to punish the Communes with a special tax, and how they wolfed down the expected revenues. Future marriages were bruited; those already effected were murmured about; and the disputes, the tyrannies, and the bickering of the lords of the castles usually occupied much of the discussion. The old lady expressed herself with tact and composure, as if looking down upon the earth from the great heights of her age and station, but her manner was not particularly intimidating and it was frequently softened by a goodly dose of simplicity and Christian modesty. Lucilio was the perfect young man seeking to learn from the wise, and his discretion (in such a green young fellow with a smattering of letters) earned him the old lady's esteem and affection. To watch him hover around her and meet her every need, you would have said he was her own son, or at any rate someone obliged to her because of special grace or favours. In fact, it was nothing like that: it was merely his good heart, his good breeding . . . and, yes, his cunning. You hadn't guessed? Well, now I will tell you all.

When Lucilio left the old lady to go down to the dining hall or to return to Fossalta, it was Clara who remained by her side. And when they were alone, Old Lady Badoer never tired of praising the young man: his excellent manners, his kind soul, his wise intellect; she even found reason to praise his good looks, the mirror, she thought, of his inner excellence. Now when an old woman is sincere and good and begins to love someone she will tend to invest in that one love all the tenderness, concern and even the illusions of all the loves that have left a trace in her heart. And so it is hard to say whether a lover, a sister, a wife, a mother or a grandmother would have embraced a man with greater affection than the old Countess embraced Lucilio. Little by little he had rekindled a flame in that ageing, weary but not yet moribund heart, until finally he was loved so much that a day didn't pass that he was not desired or called upon for company. And Clara, for whom her grandmother's wishes were decree, had come to desire him just as much, and so his arrival was greeted with joy by both of them.

The old Countess, meanwhile, never suspected that the young man might have anything on his mind but good deeds or perhaps a wish to escape the noisy, foolish conversation downstairs. Lucilio was the son of Dr Sperandio. Clara was the firstborn of her own firstborn, and that was that. Had any suspicions crossed her mind, she would have been ashamed – what a rash notion, what a disloyal, unreasonable thought! – before that pearl of a young man. And let us be frank: she was simply too fine, too aristocratic, to be touched by such concerns. Her affection for Lucilio had become a real weakness; she behaved towards him as she had done with little Orlando when it came to defending his freedom to follow his vocation. And no surprise, she didn't deduce from their frequent encounters and conversations that the two young people's hearts had grown entwined. Clara herself was not aware and Lucilio used his every artifice to conceal it from her. Have I explained myself? He sought the blind faith of the older woman to conquer the young one.

Now it is not an easy task for me to try to lead you through the labyrinth that was and is this young man's soul, to try to make sense of his temperament and sort out its assets from its defects. He had one of those vigorous, ardent natures that contain the germ of all qualities both good and bad; he had the tinder of an unbridled imagination to keep those qualities alight, and a steadfast and calculating will to maintain and correct them. Servant and at the same time master of his own passions – more than other men, certainly – both demanding and patient, a man who valued his own strength highly but did not like to waste an ounce of it, an egoist both generous and cruel when necessary, a man who despised in others any obedience to those passions he considered he ruled in himself, and who believed that the lesser must by natural law concede to the great, the weak to the strong, the petty bully to the noble and generous, the simple man to the clever. His largeness, his strength, his generosity and his cleverness were all invested in his very tenacious will, in his ability to use all and risk all to satisfy his own will. His was the temperament of men who do great things, whether good or bad.

How did the narrow and humble world of his origins bring forth a nature so strong and determined – if not noble and perfect in every regard? I really cannot say. Perhaps his reading of old historians and new philosophers, his observations of society in the various communities in which he'd lived, had forged of his will a high and mighty resolve. He believed that everyone, great or small, must possess that resolve in order to have the right to call himself a man. Such a temperament leads the great man to command, and the little man to contempt: and of those two types of presumption, I don't know which is more similar to Lucifer and his ambition.

If Lucilio's soul lacked that sensitive, almost feminine part in which true kindness and mercy abide, it was backed by a powerful intellect that sustained him all the same, an intellect far superior in its breadth of vision and strength of intent to the modest station that his birth and humble conditions had prepared for him. His brow, a vast repository of great ideas, seemed to go on rising beyond the fine hair that shaded its summit; his deep and penetrating eyes looked past the faces of others to their hearts and souls; his nose was straight and fine; his mouth was sober yet mobile, denoting strong intent and perpetual cogitation. He was relatively small in stature, as most great men are, with a neat, elastic musculature that suited his turbulent and energetic spirit. He was a handsome young man in every way, but if you had put the question to the crowd, they would have found a thousand others more handsome – or anyway would not have chosen him among the first. His dress displayed a certain elegance, it is true – a portent almost of that English simplicity that would take the place of powder and trimmings – an elegance that compensated for its ordinary manufacture and made it look outstanding. He wore no wig or powder, no laces or fine shoes, even on great occasions. Rather, a round Quaker hat, trousers tucked into his Prussian boots, a jacket without ornament or enamelled buttons, and a waistcoat of plain green or grey that hung not more than four fingers below the waist. His style had come with him from Padua; he said he liked to be comfortable in the country, and he was right. The rest of us, used to parading around in our finery like Pantaloon,[13] used to laugh at his sober attire, without any gold trim, fringes or bright colours. La Pisana called him Signor Merlo – Mr Blackbird, Mr Booby – and when he appeared the little boys at the Castle would flutter around squealing that nickname to annoy him. He neither smiled as if he enjoyed this childish harassment, nor took offence like a fool annoyed in earnest; he merely walked on as if absorbed by other things. And that bothered us. That air of indifference made us dislike him, just as his dress seemed to us ridiculous. And when he met la Pisana or myself inside the Castle and gave us a smile or a pat on the head, we let him know his niceness was unwelcome and would run off, throwing ourselves into the arms of anyone else we found nearby or stopping to play a game of catch with the Captain's dog. Childish reprisals! And yet, while we were avenging ourselves he would gaze at us and I can still remember the intensity, even the colour, of those gazes. He seemed to say: 'My children, if I thought it was worth my while to make you adore me, I could do it in an instant.'

And, in fact, when it was worth his while, he succeeded every time.

When I think of his constancy, of the long, long path he took to reach Clara's heart by means of her grandmother's praise and affection, it seems astounding to me. But he was always like that and I can think of no matter, great or small, that he embarked upon without that same constancy, whether the wind was for or against him. His rugged character, which at first had little appeal for me, later aroused the admiration that strong things merit in these listless times. And his love for Clara, ignited and tended in long years of silence, protected by a thousand small acts of prudence, a fire inside him of invincible passion, was so evidently sincere as to compensate for any other of his less attractive sentiments. Astute in the use of his means, determined in his ends: if this was self-interest, it was the self-interest of a Titan.

The old Countess, meanwhile, who saw no more in him than he would let her see, was more in love each day. The few other visits she received were not enough to diminish the glow of his. There was the Count, who around eleven in the morning came to enquire how she had passed the night, on his way to the chancery to sign whatever papers the Clerk put before him. Monsignor Orlando, who from eleven to twelve sat yawning energetically in anticipation of the noon meal along with the

Countess and Clara; the Countess herself who sat for long hours, silent and upright, knitting, and never opening her mouth except to mourn the good old days; Martino, her dear departed husband's servant, who kept her company in his way, his words few and his replies nonsensical, while Clara went out for her afternoon walk. There was la Pisana, brought to her, shrieking and scratching, by Faustina: this was the sum of those who passed before her every day, monotonous as the figures in a magic lantern. It wasn't strange, therefore, that she was impatient for the afternoon to begin, when Lucilio would come and make her laugh and lighten with a glimmer of cheer Clara's mild but grave countenance. For youth is life's heaven and the old adore cheerfulness, the eternal youth of the heart.

When Lucilio saw that the good cheer he instilled in the old woman had also touched the younger one, that she was ready to reply to his smile with one of her own, he began to hope his reward might be near. When two people meeting make each other smile they are much inclined to fall in love, and even two melancholics will show their sympathy with smiles before the fervour of love sets in. Their joy in melancholy stems from the pleasurable likeness we detect between our own sentiments and those of others. Most of what we call passion is, in fact, compassion, fellow feeling. Lucilio knew this, and much more. Month by month, day by day, hour by hour, smile by smile, he watched – solicitous, in love, but also patient, calm and sure of himself – the affection he was implanting in Clara's heart grow. He loved, but he also observed: something of a miracle where love is concerned. He observed her pleasure in her grandmother's enjoyment of his company turn into gratitude towards him; and then into sympathy, stoked by the praise of his rare and brilliant gifts that rang constantly in her ears. Fellow feeling begat familiarity, and familiarity the wish to see him, to speak to him, to please him.

And finally Clara began to smile of her own accord when he came in and asked the old Countess how her nerves were, and removed his glove to take her pulse. This, as we've said, was when Lucilio's hopes first rose, when he saw that what he had sowed had budded and a new shoot was coming forth. Even during his first visits, Clara had smiled, but this was different. Lucilio was even better at diagnosing souls than he was bodies. For him, the lexicon of glances, gestures, of emphasis, of smiles had as many entries in it as any dictionary, and rarely did he get his meanings wrong. Clara was not aware that she took more pleasure in his presence than she once had; he already knew, with no fear of misreading her, that he could send her one of those glances that said, 'You love me!' He didn't, however, venture sending that glance to innocent Clara. If resolve was his master, it was tempered with reason. Passion, so potent and tyrannical when awakened, was shrewd enough to know it was blind, and to let those other sharp-sighted operators command. Clara was deeply religious; it would be foolish to alarm her. She was descended from counts and countesses; it would be foolish to delve into her heart without first ridding it of all patrician pride. And so Lucilio paused before his victory, like the Roman general Fabius Maximus Cunctator ('the Delayer') before Hannibal. Perhaps, wise and perceptive as he was in human affairs, Lucilio enjoyed tarrying in that first and enchanting stage, when love is requited.

Still, sometimes on the road from Fossalta, when he joined the Fratta party returning to the Castle on its usual promenade and met Clara, his face would pale slightly. Often Partistagno was walking beside her, peacocking because of his post of honour, and when the two parties met he never failed to look down on the young doctor from Fossalta as if from a great height. Lucilio held his gaze, just as he endured the children's ragging, with an indifference that was three times prouder and more contemptuous. The indifference was all on his face, though; his heart sang a victory hymn. Clara's own face – solemn and rather glum before Partistagno's crude if honest courtship – would light up with pleasure when she glimpsed from afar that fine, grave figure who had become her grandmother's adopted son. While Partistagno eyed her with a long, sideways look of admiration, Lucilio scarcely glanced at her. Both were intoxicated: one with vain hopes, the other with the logical certainty she was in love with him.

As for the Count, the Countess and Monsignor Orlando,

their thoughts were too exalted (that is, they were too preoccupied with their own magnificence) to pay attention to such minutia. The others in the party dared not raise interfering eyes, and so these matters unfolded among the three young people without any other intrusive glances.

Martino would sometimes ask me:

'Did you notice whether Doctor Lucilio came by today?' He called him Doctor, although he had no degree, because he had looked at many a tongue and felt many a pulse in the nearby villages.

'No, I didn't see him!' I would shout at the top of my voice. This exchange invariably took place just as Clara was going out in the afternoon, alone or with Partistagno, but looking less cheerful than usual. Perhaps Martino saw more than any of the others, but this was the only hint he ever gave. As for la Pisana, she would often say: 'If I were my sister I'd marry the gentleman with the nice ribbons on his jacket and the fine horse with the gold saddlecloth, and I'd put that Mr Blackbird in a birdcage and give him to Grandmother for her name day!'

THREE

The kitchen of the Castle of Fratta compared with the rest of the world. Part two of the Confiteor, and the roasting spit. My first adventures with la Pisana and my bold excursion all the way to the Bastion of Attila. First verses, first sorrows, first amorous follies, in which I surpass even Dante Alighieri's rare precocity.

The first time I left the kitchen at Fratta and ventured out into the world it seemed to me beautiful beyond all measure. Yes, making comparisons is despicable, but I could not help comparing things back then, at least with my eyes, if not my brain. And let me say that between the kitchen of Fratta and the world, I wouldn't hesitate an instant to give the victory palm to the second.

To begin with, nature prefers light to darkness, the sun in the heavens to any sort of flame in the hearth. Second, in that world of grass and flowers, of leaps and bounds, of heads over heels, wherever I put my foot there was neither the Count's fierce scarlet braid nor Monsignor's scoldings about the *Confiteor*, nor Fulgenzio's persecutions, nor the Countess's unwelcome caresses, nor any smacks from the maids. And finally, while I was a lowly subject in the kitchen, two steps beyond the door and I felt myself master to breathe at will and even to sneeze and say to myself, 'Your health, Excellency!' and then to reply, 'Thank you!' without anyone finding anything to object to.

As long as I can remember I had envied the good wishes the Count received on those auspicious occasions when he sneezed, and it seemed to me that a person wished so many good things must be of great importance and the highest merit. As I grew older I corrected that peculiar belief, yet even today I cannot sneeze but feel the itch of a certain desire to hear many voices wishing me long life and happiness. Reason matures and grows old, but the heart stays a child forever: hearts are probably best educated with loud scolding, in the Rector of Teglio's patriarchal way. As for the Mutual Instruction Method[1] so popular today, hearts have little to gain and much to lose when sentimentalist banknotes are exchanged in place of real currency with its genuine metallic ring. It would be a mutual instruction of tricks and falsehoods to no one's advantage, for the many always carry along the few, as the saying goes. But to return to that world that looked so beautiful to me at first sight, let me also say it was by no means paradise on earth.

From the stable courtyard a small wooden bridge led across the moat at the back of the castle to the kitchen garden. There stood two pergolas twined with ancient vines, laden with bunches of golden grapes that were courted by wasps from all around. Then came green expanses of turnips and maize, and finally, beyond a low, tumbledown wall, great rolling meadows alive with silvery brooks, flowers and crickets! Such was the world behind the Castle. As for those to the front and the sides, I would only meet them later. I was kept so tight on the leash between Fulgenzio, the Rector and the roasting spit, that I never entered the world of plants and free air, the great temple of nature, except when no one was looking and by the back door.

And now a word about the spit, which has been on my mind for a while. Everyone in the Castle did their duties daily, except for the iron roasting spit, which was employed only on ceremonial occasions. It wasn't considered worth troubling His Excellency the Roasting Spit for the usual two chickens. Now, whenever His Excellency was enjoying his mute and dusty ease, the turnspit was me. The cook would thread a couple of chickens on the skewer, affix the point of this to a notch in the andiron, and pass me the handle so that I could turn it smartly and with isochronal constancy until the victims turned a nice golden brown. The sons of Adam – and maybe Adam himself – had done the same, and I, a son of Adam, had no right to complain about this task imposed on me. How many things aren't done, aren't said, aren't thought, unless there be due consideration of one's rights!

I sometimes even thought – remember, there was the huge iron spit roast sitting in the hearth – that it was dead wrong to make a spit of me. Was it not cruel enough that I must punish my teeth gnawing the bones of that blessed roast? Must I also scorch my face turning it back and forth, back and forth, in eternal tedium? Sometimes, turning a skewer of birds, I watched them with their legs pointed up, sagging over the coals and almost touching the flames, their tiny heads raw and bloodied. My head would sag along with theirs and I wished I were one of those chaffinches in order to take my revenge by sticking in the throat of some unwary diner. When these nasty fancies stirred in me, I would grin with malign pleasure and turn the spit as fast as I could. Then the cook would shuffle over and smack my hands, saying: 'Slowly, Carlino, birds must be treated nicely!'

If the fear and vexation hadn't stopped me from speaking, I would have asked that grease-stained old hag why she didn't treat Carlino at least as nicely as a chaffinch.

La Pisana, when she knew I was at the spit, would overcome her loathing for the kitchen and come down to watch my furious humiliation. Oh, to have given that shameless girl a slap for each of those silly grins of hers! Instead, I had to swallow my bitterness and turn my spit, while an evil rage swelled my heart and made me grind my teeth. Martino was ready to relieve me, I think, but first, the cook would have none of it, and second, the good man was busy with his cheese rinds and his grater. Instead, when the soup was put on to boil, I was treated to Monsignor's ultimate consolation: when he caught sight of me there all tear-stained or half-asleep, he would urge me in mellifluous tones not to be foolish or wicked, but to repeat again and again the last part of the *Confiteor* until I had it by heart.

Enough! No more! Even just thinking about it, I can feel all the sweat of all those roasts run down my back, and as for Monsignor, I would happily send him to that place where he's been for quite some time now, if I didn't have a certain respect for his bygone red stockings.

The world therefore had this one very important advantage over the kitchen of Fratta: that I was not nailed in martyrdom to the spit. Out there, alone, I leaped, I sang and I talked to myself;

I laughed out loud at the pleasure of being free, and contemplated what nice courtesy I could do along the lines la Pisana favoured, to make myself more appealing to her. And when I was able to drag that enchantress of mine along with me through the corn rows and the thickets, they seemed to me all that I could wish for and all that she could desire. There was nothing that I didn't consider mine or that I didn't think I could obtain to make her happy; and if she was mistress inside the Castle, out in the fields I was the master, and I treated her to all the honours, as if it were my fiefdom. From time to time, to remind me of my ragged condition, she would put on a serious little frown and say, 'These fields are mine; this meadow belongs to me!'

But she didn't make the slightest impression on me with her assertions of feudal rights, because I felt – I knew – that when it came to nature I was the master; I had the upper hand of love. Just as Lucilio felt indifferent to Partistagno's superior glances or the little boys' mocking, so I felt when la Pisana played at being a princess. And thus, far away from lordly turrets and crenellations and the smell of the chancery, my heart swelled with that sentiment of equality that allows brave and honest souls to look down with equanimity even on the heads of kings. I was a fish returned to water, a bird released from the cage, an exile come home. I had so much wealth, so much happiness, that I needed someone to share it with, and, lacking friends, I was ready to hand it out to strangers or even those who wished me ill. Fulgenzio, the cook and the Countess herself would have had their share of fresh air and sunlight, had they come to ask politely, without smacking my hands or pulling my pigtail.

La Pisana would follow me happily on my forays into the fields, whenever that puerile populace who paid her homage didn't show up at the Castle. In that case she had to be content with me, and having studied all the pictures in Clara's volume of Ariosto, she wanted to play Angelica pursued by Rinaldo, or the warrior maiden Marfisa, or even Alcina, who falls in love with all the knights who come to her island and turns them into stones. I played, with a certain forbearance, the part of Rinaldo, staging great battles against dragons (the poplar row) or desperately fleeing some treacherous sorcerer, my lady-love behind as if on the back of my horse. Sometimes I would undertake a long, imaginary voyage to the Kingdom of Cathay or the republic of Samarkand, but there were always terrible obstacles to overcome: a hedgerow that passed as a forest, a levee that grew to a mountain, a brook that expanded into a mighty river. We would then comfort each other with brave deeds or confer in whispers, looking around cautiously and holding our breath. Having decided to risk it, we were off at breakneck speed through bramble bushes and puddles, leaping and shouting as if possessed. We would usually make it over the obstacles, but la Pisana's dresses often got ripped or her feet wet when she sloshed through the water in her woollen shoes. My own jacket was well acquainted with thorns and I could have spent a hundred years in the water, like an oak tree, before the damp seeped through the tough soles of my feet. And so I'd get to work consoling, mending and drying her off, for these little misfortunes would make her sulky, and to keep her from crying or scratching me I'd take her on my shoulders and make her laugh, leaping over ditches and brooks with her weight on my back. I was strong as a young bull and the pleasure I felt when she laid her head on my neck and her hands around it and laughed out loud gave me wind enough to reach if not Cathay or Samarkand, at least Fossalta, still carrying that load.

Thus we would spend the early hours of the afternoon, but we soon began to venture farther from the Castle, getting to know more distant roads, paths and places. The meadow where we made our first excursions descended west towards a wide watercourse that snaked across the plain beneath broad shadows of poplars, alders and willows, a country maid with time to spare and little wish to work. You could hear the perpetual trill of small birds, and the grass grew tall and thick like the carpeting of a lady's most secret chamber. All around, leafy paths wandered to and fro among thickets of bramble and sweet-smelling scrub, offering the most secret hideaways, the softest seats for innocent merriment or for lovers' earnest conversations. The water's murmur rendered the silence harmonious and made our light, silvery voices doubly magical. We would sit down on the greenest, softest hillock and a green lizard would scuttle away to a nearby thicket, and from there stop to look at us, as if he wished to pose a question or spy on us. We usually chose, for that pleasant moment of repose, a point along the banks of the stream where, after a labyrinth of whispery, whimsical twists and turns, the water ran straight and silent for a good long way, like a madwoman who has suddenly taken religious vows. The gentle slope calmed its course, but, according to la Pisana, the water was simply tired of running and we ought to imitate it and sit down. But you mustn't think she was still for long, the little minx.

After she'd embraced me once or twice, or had yielded to my hankering to dally, she would get to her feet as heedless of me as if she had never met me and lean out over the stream bank to study her reflection or thrash her arms in the water or slip into the thicket in search of snail shells to make herself bracelets and necklaces, with never a thought that her frock might rip or that her sleeves or shoes might get soaked. I would speak up then and urge her to be careful – more because I wished to preserve the playful mood between us than out of any concern for her clothing – but she never took the trouble to reply. Now, let a single thread on her collar get snagged in some game of another's devising and she was more than capable of raising a fuss. But when she was playing the mistress of ceremonies she was just as ready to rip and destroy anything, including her long, black hair, her round, pink cheeks and her small, plump hands. Sometimes I'd be unable to divert her from these solemn and solitary pursuits of hers for the remainder of our ramble. She would struggle half an hour to make a hole in a snail shell with her teeth or her nails, so that she could string it on a willow shoot and hang it on her ear. And if I ventured to try to help her she would growl at me and stamp on my feet, elbowing me in the stomach, close to tears. As if I had done her some great wrong! But it was all the play of her moods.

Fickle as a butterfly that will not rest two seconds on a flower before beating its wings and moving off to suck another, she would shift from great familiarity to great hauteur in an instant; from loud chatter to obstinate silence; from cheerfulness to irritation, and even to cruelty. Why? Because her temperament did not change in any of love's stages: she was forever the little tyrant of Fratta, able to make a fellow happy in order to try out her powers in one direction, and then to make him rage and cry, to try them out in another. In sensual and impulsive natures (unless they be cooled by a wise education that arms reason against excess and secures sensibility against instinct's plunder), in such natures, whim becomes law, and self-regard, order. Otherwise, no matter how many good qualities such a soul may have, it cannot be trusted, being a slave to sensuality. La Pisana was, then, just a girl, but what is a girl if not a slip, a sketch of a woman? Painted in oil or in miniature, the lines of a portrait remain the same.

In any case, the new horizons opening up to me offered a haven from these first, stubbornly painful childish trials. I could rest in nature's great bosom, with her beauties to distract me from anger's dour company. The vast countryside I now roamed was nothing like that little dungeon stretching from the garden to the fish pond that had given me such pleasure between the ages of six and eight. When la Pisana abandoned me to flatter or torment other boys, when she disappeared midway through one of our rambles in the hope that some visitor had meanwhile appeared at the Castle, I no longer made a fool of myself by showing a long face and my rebellious back; I would go and let my troubles subside in the coolness of a meadow on the banks of a stream. Every step brought forth new prospects, new marvels. That spot where the stream broadened to become a tiny lake as bright and silvery as the face of a mirror. Those lovely fronds of water weed moving back and forth as if a magical breeze caressed them, and the little pebbles glimpsed between them, white and smooth as pearls escaped from their shells. The ducks and geese honking on the banks, then throwing themselves boisterously in the water and bobbing up again after a momentary dive, and coming together, their wings beating, in the graceful, orderly ranks of a naval fleet on manoeuvres. It was a delight to watch them advance, draw back and pivot round without disturbing the transparent surface of the water, but for the slightest ripple that would hit the banks and expire in an even tinier swell. All around me stood a thick wood of ancient trees on whose branches the wild grape vines wove the greenest, most whimsical constructions. Here, they crowned the top of an elm; there, they moved to enjoy the solid support of an oak, and, clasping it on every side, fell down around it in graceful festoons. From branch to branch, from tree to tree they twisted and turned as if they were dancing, the tiny black clusters of grapes inviting the starlings to feast and the pigeons to squabble with them to get their share.

Just beyond that point where the lake went back to being a brook stood two or three watermills and their wheels seemed to race around behind them, spraying water at one another in antic frenzy. I would sit there for long hours, watching and tossing pebbles into the vortex to see them bounce up, then fall again and disappear under the giddy turn of the wheel. You could hear the millstones pounding away inside, and the millers singing and the boys making a racket, and even the rattle of the chain in the hearth when they were stirring up the polenta. The smoke that began to plume out of the chimney told me so, just before that rattling began to sound in the great concert. Out in the yard in front of the mills, sacks and figures dusted with flour took part in a constant exchange. Farm wives from the villages nearby stood and talked with the mill women, while their corn was being ground. Meanwhile the donkeys, freed of the heavy sacks they had been carrying, ate ravenous portions of the bran served up to reward them for their trips to the mill, braying with joy and spreading out their ears and their legs when they had finished, while the mill dog barked and raced around them, feigning a thousand attacks and retreats. It was a very lively scene, let me tell you; I, who knew nothing of life but what Martino, Mastro Germano and Marchetto had told me, could not have wished for more. It was here that I first began to look at things with my own eyes and to reason and to learn using my own mind; to understand what work was and what wages were; and to distinguish among the various duties of the housewives, the farm wives, the millers and the donkeys. Such thoughts amused me and kept me busy, and I would return to Fratta with my head in the clouds, studying the marvellous colours that lit them up as the shifting light directed.

My rambles grew longer and longer; and longer and bolder were my spells of freedom from Fulgenzio's grip and the Rector's studies. I had been too small when I rode around on horseback with Marchetto for what I saw to be impressed on my memory, and later he didn't want to risk setting me astride an old nag that was wise, yes, but weak of leg. And thus everything I looked at now was new and unexpected: not merely the mills and the millers, but the fishermen with their nets, the peasants with their ploughs, the shepherds with their goats and sheep – everywhere, everything around me was cause for amazement and delight. And finally, the day came when I thought I'd lost my head or landed on the moon – so marvellous, so unimaginable were the things I beheld. I want to tell you about this, for it was an experience that made me forever a worshipper of that simple and poetic religion called nature, a solace for every kind of human sorrow, I found: sweet and constant in its quiet pleasures.

One afternoon la Pisana had a visit from three of her cousins, the children of one of the Count's sisters who had married a nobleman from the Highlands. (He also had another sister who lived in grand style in Venice, but I only met her later.) That afternoon la Pisana was so annoying, she offered me up so barbarously to the mockery of her cousins, that I stomped out in fury, wanting only to put the greatest possible distance between us. And so I escaped across the bridge behind the stables and set off over the ploughed fields, shame and vexation chasing me from behind. I walked and walked, eyes fixed on my feet and heedless of my surroundings, until suddenly I looked up and found myself in a place I'd never been before. I stood for a moment unable to think, or rather unable to free myself from the thoughts that were hammering in my mind.

'Can it be?' I thought when I did get free. 'Can I have walked so far?'

I had, it seemed; the place where I now found myself was not within the bounds of my usual forays, for I knew the length and breadth of the territory two miles behind the Castle very well. This instead was a sandy, empty place that ran downhill towards a muddy, stagnant canal; on one side stood a meadow infested with canes that spread out as far as the eye could see; on the other there were neglected fields in which the unkempt bare earth was punctuated by outbursts of luxuriance, some few large trees growing in addled rows. Looking around, nothing I saw seemed familiar.

'Confound it! This is all new to me,' I said to myself, happy as a skinflint who has found a great treasure. 'Let me go on and have a look.'

But going on was not so simple: before me was a wide, marshy canal covered by a thick mat of yellow-flowered weeds. The great pasture of the unknown and the infinite spread out in one direction; in the other was that arid, abandoned countryside I had no desire to explore. What to do here? I was much too curious to turn back and too foolish to fear that the canal was deeper than I really wanted it to be. I rolled up my breeches past my knees and waded into the swamp, my hands and feet entangled in the water lilies and weeds. Pushed to one side and pulled to the other, I made my way forward through that floating brush, but the way forward was ever downhill and the water weeds spread a slippery, icy slime over me. When God willed it the bottom began to rise again and the worst I had to endure was fear – but I think I was so determined that I wouldn't have turned back even had I drowned. When I put my foot on grass again I flew up like a bird, for the meadow ahead rose gently and it was growing late for me to reach the high point and look out on my great conquest. I did get there in the end, but so out of breath I was like a dog come back after chasing a hare. I looked out and I will never forget the dazzling pleasure, the stupefaction, the awe I felt.

A vast green and flowered plain spread out before me, crossed by great canals like that I'd just forded, but wider and deeper. These reached out towards an even larger expanse of water and beyond this rose a cluster of hillocks, some of them crowned with bell towers.[2] Even further out was an infinite blue space that my eye could not fathom, but which looked to me like a piece of sky that had fallen to earth and been flattened, made of translucent azure blue streaked with silver, that far, far away melted into the slightly less potent blue of the air.

It was the hour before sunset and the hour told me I had walked a long way.

It was that moment when the sun 'looks back', as the peasant saying goes: when, having descended through a thick curtain of clouds, just before setting, it finds an opening to send a final gaze towards earth, a moribund gaze from beneath lowered lashes. All of a sudden the canals and the great lagoon into which they merged turned fiery red and that distant, mysterious azure blue became an immense rainbow flickering with a multitude of brilliant colours. Now the flaming sky was reflected in it and minute by minute this spectacular view expanded and grew more beautiful to my eyes, taking on all the perfect and improbable aspects of a dream.

Would you believe that I fell to my knees, like Voltaire at Mount Grütli[3] when he declared before God the one article of his faith? God came to my mind, too: that great and good God that is in nature, father of us all and for us all. I worshipped, I wept, I prayed, and I must confess that when in later years my spirit was battered by greater tempests I often took refuge in the memory of that boyhood moment to recover a glimmer of hope. No, this was not the act of faith the Rector taught me with great tugging of my ears. It was a new, spontaneous, vigorous impulse of a new kind of faith that slept ever so soundly in my heart, only to spring to life at nature's maternal invitation. In universal beauty I sensed that there was something like universal goodness, and I became convinced that just as winter storms cannot spoil the stupendous harmony of creation, so human passions can never darken the fair skies of eternal justice. Justice is among us, above us, inside us. It punishes us and it rewards us. Justice alone is the grand unifier of things; it offers souls happiness in the great soul of humanity. Yes, these are ill-defined sentiments and we know not when they may become ideas, but they come from the heart and send poetry to the minds of certain men, and I am one; poetry, however, that lives and becomes flesh, verse by verse, in the annals of history. They are the feelings of a soul tested by life's trials, yet budding already in that sense of joy and the sacred that made me, a mere boy, bend my knee before the majesty of the universe!

Poor little me, however, had I tried to think such exalted, such ineffable, thoughts back then. I would have lost my way in the back lanes of philosophy, and I certainly wouldn't have made it back to Fratta that night. However, when dusk began to obscure that wonderful spectacle before me, I suddenly became a child again and nearly began to cry in fear that I didn't know my way home. I had run to get there and ran even faster on my return, and when I arrived at the canal it was still twilight. But once across, when I ventured into the fields, the look of things began to change; night came down black and murky, and I, who had arrived lost in thought, was now just lost. A feverish trembling and a desire to run somewhere, anywhere, overtook me. However long the way was, I thought, running would propel me there faster than walking. But my calculus was wrong, because haste made me overlook those signs that might have helped me keep on my northward course. And also, the effort wore me out and I needed all the fright stirred in me by the thought I might not make it home to make my legs go forward. Luck kept me going straight enough so that I didn't fall into the swamps, where I would certainly have drowned, and at last I found a road. A road? My God! Today no one would use that word; it would be called a death trap or worse. I thanked Providence, nevertheless, and began to walk along with a certain tranquility, thinking, reasonably enough, that I would ask directions at the first house I came to.

But what fool would have put up a house in those hollows? I remained hopeful and pressed forward. The first houses would appear sooner or later. I had gone no further than half a mile on that road when I heard a horse galloping behind me. I made the sign of the cross and threw myself as deep in the ditch as I could, but the way was very narrow and the horse, spooked at my presence, shied back suddenly, causing its rider to unleash a string of curses.

'Who goes there? Out of my way, rogue!' he shouted in a voice so rough it froze my blood.

'Have pity on me. I'm a lost boy and I know not where this road is taking me,' I said, just barely loud enough to be heard.

My childish, pleading tone evidently moved the man on the

horse, because he drew on the reins to halt the beast, although he had already planted his knees in its belly to ride over me.

'So you are a boy?' he said, leaning down slightly in my direction so that I could see a huge black figure wrapped in the folds of a great cloak, that of a smuggler or a sorcerer. 'Yes, I see you are a boy. Where are you going?'

'To Fratta, if the gentleman will help me,' said I, drawing back in fear.

'But what brings you to these parts, where no living soul ventures at night?' asked the mystery man, somewhat suspicious.

'Well,' I said, 'I ran away from home because I was unhappy, and I walked and walked until finally I came to a beautiful place where I saw a lot of water, a lot of sun and many beautiful things I'd never seen before. But on my way back I found myself rather confused, for it was getting dark and I didn't remember the way, and running this way and that I came to this place, although I don't know where it is.'

'You are behind San Mauro towards the pine wood, my lad,' the man said, 'and you have at least four miles before you get home.'

'Sir, you are very good,' I said, the greater fear driving out the lesser – the fear that I must ask him which way to go to get home fastest.

'So you think I am good?' said the horseman in a peculiar tone. 'Oh yes, by Diana, you are right, and I am going to prove it to you. Jump up behind me and I'll let you down by the Castle, for I am going that way.'

'I live in the Castle, you see,' I continued, not sure whether I should accept help from this perfect stranger.

'In the Castle?' he exclaimed, surprised, but not amiably. 'And who in the Castle do you belong to?'

'Oh, heavens! I belong to no one! I am Carlino, who turns the spit and studies with the Rector.'

'Oh well, all right. If that's the case, jump up, I say. My horse is strong and won't notice a thing.'

Half-relieved, half-trembling, I climbed up on the animal's back and he gave me a hand, saying I shouldn't be afraid of falling. In those parts children are practically born on a horse and every boy is told, 'Get up on that colt' the way you might say, 'Go ride that broomstick.' When I was seated as best I could, he took off at a furious gallop, as if skirting the edge of a continual precipice on that road. I held on with both my hands around the horseman's chest and I could feel the hairs of his very long beard scratching my fingers.

'What if he is the Devil?' I thought. 'He might well be!'

After a rapid examination of my conscience it was clear that my sins were grave and he had every reason to carry me off. But then I saw that his horse was afraid of my shadow and it seemed to me that the Devil's horses would not have the same fears as ours do, and so I was somewhat reassured on that front. However, if not the Devil, he might be his deputy – some robber or assassin, something of the sort. This didn't frighten me, for I had no money and thus felt sure I was well armed against robbery of any kind. But now, having decided who he wasn't, I began to try to ascertain who my nocturnal guardian was. Worse and worse! I would defy a Neapolitan to reach conclusions more certain than I did, but meanwhile I determined that I wanted to know nothing. Suddenly the dark object of these fancies turned his big beard towards me and asked in the same, not very charming, tone: 'Is Mastro Germano still at Fratta?'

'Yes sir,' I replied, starting with surprise at his unexpected growl. 'Every day he adjusts the clock on the tower, opens and closes the gates and sweeps the courtyard in front of the chancery. We are great friends and he often takes me up to look at the clock works, along with la Pisana, who is the Countess's daughter.'

'And does Monsignor di Sant'Andrea often come calling?' he asked with a great laugh.

'He's the Countess's confessor,' said I, 'but I haven't seen him for a while. Now that I've begun to go out and see the world I spend as little time as I can in the kitchen.'

'Very good! Good boy! The kitchen is for clerics,' he said. 'You can get down now, boy. We've arrived at Fratta. You're the best horseman in all the territory, allow me to congratulate you!'

'Certainly,' I said, jumping to the ground, 'I always used to ride behind Marchetto.'

'Oh, so you're the little parrot who was his shadow some years back,' he said with a snort. 'Now take this,' here he gave me a good whack on the neck, 'and give Marchetto a taste of it, this sweet-bun, on my behalf, but since you are his friend, don't tell him you saw me anywhere around here. Don't tell him or anyone else!'

At these words the man with the big beard turned and began to gallop along the trail towards Ramuscello and I stood there with my mouth open, listening to the pounding of his hoof-beats. When the sound began to fade I walked around the moat and saw Germano on the Castle bridge, peering out as if he were waiting for someone.

'Oh you rascal! You wicked boy! Roaming around at this hour! Coming home so late! Who taught you such pranks? You're going to get it from me now!'

Such was the scolding with which Germano greeted me, and the most heated parts cannot even be put into words. The good Germano propelled me forward with slaps and whacks from the Castle gate to the kitchen door. And there it was Martino who pounced on me: 'You little rogue! Good for nothing you are! You'll never try that again, I swear! Outside, at night, in such darkness!

Here, too, words were the least of it; it was the raps on the head I recall. And if this was the reception I got from my friends, just imagine the others. The Captain, who was playing Goose with Marchetto, merely gave me a good whack on the backside and proclaimed that my problem was simple idleness and they had better hand me over to him. Marchetto tugged jovially at my ears; Signora Veronica, who was warming herself at the fire, picked up the spanking where Germano had left off; and the cook, that greasy old crone, gave me such a nice kick in the behind that I landed with my nose on the spit.

'There you go! Just in time!' the harpy said. 'I had to put the roasting spit on, but now that you're here, we don't need it any longer.'

She had already loosed the rope from the pulleys and handed

me the spit handle, having released it from its iron grip. And so I began to turn it round and round, from time to time assailed by each of the serving boys and maids as they came into the kitchen. And while I turned I thought about the Rector, Fulgenzio, Gregorio, Monsignor, the *Confiteor*, the Count, the Countess and my scalp! Had they strung me up from end to end on the spit that night, the agony of my fear would not have been less. I would surely have rather had my scalp roasted than let the Countess at it for just three minutes, and as for being plucked and dressed, I've always thought St Lawrence, who was grilled, was luckier than St Bartholomew, who was skinned. So long as all were waiting for their turn to beat me, no one asked what I had been doing during my long absence, but once I was nailed to my spit they began to lob demands and questions from all sides, until I, who had been brave during the smacking, began to weep under this new assault.

'What's the problem now? What are these tears?' asked Martino. 'Wouldn't it be better to answer the questions?'

'I was down at the meadow by the watermills. I went down to the river there to catch crickets. I did! And then . . . it got dark . . . and . . . I was late!'

'And where might these crickets be?' asked the Captain, who sometimes took part in criminal interrogations at the chancery, and liked to imitate the style.

'Well, you see,' I said in an even more teary voice, 'I don't know! They must have escaped from my pocket, you see! I have no idea! I . . . I was down by the river catching crickets, and . . .'

'Move that spit, you liar,' shouted the cook, 'or I'll tan your hide myself!

'Don't frighten him too much, Orsola,' said Martino, who could see the menacing intentions on the old witch's face.

'Oh, bones of St Pancras!' shouted the Captain, slamming his fist down on the table so that all the plates and cutlery set out for the servants' supper went flying. 'Three times in a row those damned dice had to come up nine! Never saw anything like it! What a miserable game! Enough! Now remember, Marchetto, that's three *bezzi* I owe you from Sunday and two and a half tonight . . .'

'And then there were the seven from last week,' said the Bailiff cautiously.

'Ah yes, seven and five, that makes twelve and a half,' said the Captain, ruffling his hair. 'Just one half *bezzo* more to make six *soldi*. I'll pay you tomorrow.'

'Why, certainly. As you wish,' said Marchetto with a sigh.

'As for you,' said the Captain, turning towards me so as to change the subject, 'as for you, you little sneak of a chicken roaster, I'd like to get my hands on you and set you straight! Isn't it true, Veronica, that I am famous for setting people straight?'

'Fool! You say that because you'd like to see him bent!' said his wife, walking away from the hearth towards the dining room. 'I'm going to tell the Countess not to worry any more, for Carlino has come back.'

I had no mirror before me, but I can swear her words made my hair stand up like so many lightning rods. But just then fresh exhortations from the cook got me turning the spit again, and so I just stood there more stunned than resigned, awaiting developments. I did not have to wait long. Even as the Countess broke her daily rule – appearing for the third time in the kitchen, Signora Veronica on her right hand – from the opposite direction came Fulgenzio, his anchorite's bulk buried deep in the collar of his jacket. Never did the image of Christ between the two thieves seem more appropriate, but there was no time to enjoy the thought, for I knew that neither of these thieves intended to repent. The Countess came towards me, the tail of her gown dragging dramatically behind her, and halted a hair's breadth from my face. The glow of the hearth lit up her eyes like two coals and made the droplet that hung from her beaky nose glisten like a carbuncle.

'And so,' as she stretched out a hand I doubled over, chills running down my spine, 'and so, you ugly little tadpole, this is how you repay our goodness, we who took you in, raised you, fed you and even taught you how to read and write and serve at Mass? Oh I am sorry! I predict your wrongdoing will lead you to perdition, and that you will be a criminal like your father and end up hanged, for you already display all the right talents!'

At this point I could feel the noose tightening around my

neck. But no, it was not: merely the Countess's fingers, seeking their usual hold on me. I shrieked so loud that the Rector, the Clerk, Clara, Lucilio, Partistagno and, a few moments later, even the Count and Monsignor, came running from the dining hall. All of them, along with the kitchen staff and the maids and manservants who had also come running, made up a fine audience for my Passion. The spit lay still and the cook intervened to detach my hands from my head and put me back to work, but I was still too dismayed by the Countess's rabid performance to pay any heed.

'Now tell me what you've been up to, roaming around all night long!' The Countess now put her two hands on her hips, to my great relief. 'I want to know the truth, and none of your nonsense about crickets, and no whining!'

Signora Veronica gave me a nasty grin, as only hateful old women and the Devil do. For my part I sent her a look that spoke a hundred curses.

'Speak up, jailbird!' howled the Countess, going at me with hands bent like cat's claws.

'I walked out to a place where there was a lot of red water and a lot of sun. And then . . .'

'And then?' demanded the Countess.

'And then I came back.'

'You certainly did come back to trouble!' the Countess went on. 'I can see that and there's no need for you to tell me, but if you do not tell me what you've been doing all this time, I promise you, on my word as a noblewoman, that you'll never taste salt again!'

I was silent, and then I shrieked for a while when she gave me another rap on the head with those monkey fingers, and then I fell silent, and even, like a fool, began to turn the spit once again, because the cook had put the handle in my hand.

'I'll tell you, Madam Countess, what this little knave has been up to,' Fulgenzio spoke up. 'A little while back I was in the sacristy cleaning the vases and the ampullae for Easter and I went out to get some water from the moat when I saw a fellow on horseback coming from San Mauro. He let down the young man and said something to him I couldn't follow, and then he rode off on his horse towards Ramuscello and the young man walked around the moat to come in by the gate. That's what he's been up to!'

'And the man on the horse: was that you, Marchetto?' asked the Countess.

'Marchetto spent the whole afternoon with me,' said the Captain.

'So, therefore, who was that man?' the Countess turned to me.

'He was, it was . . . nobody,' I mumbled, recalling the mystery man's kindness and his warning.

'Nobody, nobody,' scowled the Countess. 'We shall soon find out who this nobody was! Faustina,' she said to the nursemaid, 'take Carlino's bedding up to the closet between Martino's quarters and the friars' room and put him in there when the roast is done. And, my little cherub,' she said turning to me, 'you won't get out of that room until you've told us who was that man on horseback who set you down at the turning for Ramuscello.'

Faustina had lit the lamp, but she had not yet gone to move my bedding.

'So, will you tell us who he was?' demanded the Countess.

I looked towards Faustina and I felt my heart break, knowing that before I lay down to sleep I would no longer be able to gaze at la Pisana's face or risk kissing her sleeping eyelids and her plump, dewy mouth. And I even had the power to keep Faustina from going!

'No, I saw no one! I came with nobody!' I suddenly said, more boldly than before.

'Very well,' said the Countess turning towards the dining hall and nodding at Faustina to leave and carry out her orders. 'Be it as you wish!'

She put her hands in her pockets and left the kitchen, taking behind her the whole party, each of whom, on leaving, beamed me a couple of nasty looks to signal agreement with the lady's sentence. The Count further exorcised me with a wave of the hand, as if to say, 'This fellow is possessed by the Devil.' Monsignor went off, shaking his head, as if he'd never hear the *Confiteor* again; the Rector pursed his lips in an 'I don't understand anything' sort of way, and Partistagno turned and walked off cheerfully, having grown tired of all the fuss. There now remained just the Contessina Clara, who defied nasty looks from Signora Veronica, Fulgenzio and the Captain and came sweetly to me to ask if I had really told the truth. I took a look around and said yes, bending my chin down to touch my breast. Then she patted me on the head in a kindly way and went out with the others, but before she left, Lucilio came to murmur in my ear, telling me that the following day I should stay in my bed and ask for him to be called, and that he would adjust everything and I was not to worry. I raised my head to look at him to see if he was in his right mind to speak to me so lovingly, but he had already gone, pretending not to notice the grateful glance Clara had sent him from the doorway.

'What did you say to the poor child?' she asked.

'Oh, nothing much,' said Lucilio.

She smiled and together they returned to the dining hall, to which, the dinner hour approaching, they were followed by the Captain and his wife. Now there was no one but Fulgenzio and the cook, but Marchetto and Martino got me released, insisting that the roast was cooked and I should be off to bed. Then Martino lit a lamp and led me up to my new chamber via a long, long course of stairs and corridors that never seemed to end. He arranged my bedding in a corner of that tiny room – it was no more than the space under a stairway – and he helped me undress and pull the blankets up to my neck so I wouldn't be cold. I let him do it, as if I were dead, but after he had gone, when by the light of the lamp shining in the corner I saw the crumbling walls and crooked ceiling of that dog hole, I was seized by such desperation at not being with la Pisana in her pleasant, white room that I beat and scratched my face until I saw my hands were red with blood. In the midst of my outburst, I heard a quiet rasping sound at the door and as if I were a mere child, desperation rapidly gave way to fear.

'Who's that?' I warbled in a faint voice, sobs still wracking my breast.

The door opened and la Pisana, half-naked in her nightdress and barefoot and trembling with cold, leapt into my bed.

'You? What's wrong? What's this?' I said, not yet myself with surprise.

'I came to find you and to kiss you, because I love you,' she said. 'I woke up while Faustina was taking up your bedding, and when I learned they didn't want to let you sleep in our room but had put you in with Martino, I came up here to see how you were and find out why you ran away today and didn't come back.'

'Oh my dearest, dearest Pisana,' I cried, squeezing her hard to my heart.

'Don't make so much noise or they'll hear you in the kitchen,' she said, stroking my face with her hand. 'What's this?' she went on, feeling her hand was wet and studying it under the moonlight. 'Blood, it's blood. You're all bloody! There's a wound on your forehead here that's spilling out blood. What's happened to you? Did you fall or stumble into some thorns?'

'No, no, it was nothing . . . just the latch on the door.'

'Very well, whatever it was you must let me make it well,' she said, and with that she put her mouth on my wound, kissing and sucking like the good nuns of long ago did upon the breasts of their Crusader brothers.

'Enough, Pisana, enough! I'm better now: I hardly even know I'm wounded!'

'But no, there's still a spot of blood,' she said, applying her mouth to my forehead with such force she didn't seem a child of eight.

Finally the blood was staunched and the conceited little thing now grew cocky to see how much I enjoyed her ministrations.

'I came up in the dark, one hand on the wall all the way,' she told me. 'I wasn't afraid they would find out; they're downstairs, having their supper. But now that I have cured you, I must go down again so they do not find me on the stairs.'

'And if they do find you?'

'Oh, I'll pretend I'm sleepwalking.'

'Yes, but I'm not very happy that you should risk being punished by your mother.'

'That you're not very happy means nothing to me, or rather,

it pleases me,' she replied, tossing her head back to free the curls that had fallen on her face in a great show of imperiousness. 'You know, I like you better than anyone, and when you're not wearing those ugly clothes of yours – as you're not right now, my darling Carlino, so that I can see you just as you are – I like you three times over! Oh why don't they dress you up nicely like my cousin Augusto today?'

'Oh, I'll get those nice things!' I shouted, 'I shall have them at any cost.'

'And where will you get them?' she asked.

'Where, where? I shall work and earn money – and with money, Germano tells me, I can have anything.'

'Yes, work, you must work,' said la Pisana. 'And I shall love you all the more. But why do you not smile? You were so happy a moment ago.'

'Let's see if I am smiling,' I said, putting my mouth on hers.

'No, I can't see you! Let me go! I want to see if you are smiling. Don't you understand I want to look at you?'

I did as she asked and even made an attempt to form my lips into a smile, but in my heart I could only think how much she would love me when I could dress as a gentleman.

'That's nice. Now you please me,' she murmured in that little voice of hers that still delights my ears in memory. 'Goodbye Carlino, farewell. I must go downstairs before Faustina returns.'

'I'll carry a lamp for you.'

'No, no,' she said, jumping from the bed and holding out a hand to keep me from doing the same. 'I came up in the dark and I can go down in the dark.'

'But I don't want you to hurt yourself; let me light your way down the stairs.'

'Don't you dare move!' Now she changed her tone and left me free to move, sure that her confidence alone would stop me. 'You're making me angry. I tell you I want to go down without a lamp. I'm brave. I'm afraid of nothing and I want to go down as I please!'

'And what if you should trip or get lost among the corridors?'

'Trip? Get lost? – I? Are you mad? I wasn't born yesterday!

Farewell now, Carlino. You must thank me, because I was good enough to come and find you.'

'I thank you, I thank you!' I said, my heart swelling with contentment.

'And I must thank you,' she added, kneeling and covering my hand with kisses, 'for you go on loving me even when I am beastly. It's true! You are the best and handsomest boy around and I don't know why you never punish me for all the meanness I sometimes show you.'

'Punish you? But why, Pisana? Rather, I beg you to get up now and let me light your way. With this cold, you're going to fall ill!'

'Never! You know I never fall ill! But before I go I want you to thrash me and pull my hair hard for all my wickedness towards you.' And here she took my hands and put them on her head.

'Goodness, no!' I said, withdrawing my hands, 'I'd rather kiss you!'

'I want you to pull my hair!' she said, taking my hands again.

'And I don't want to!' I replied.

'What do you mean, you don't want to? I want you to!' she began to scream. 'Now pull my hair, pull my hair – or I shall shriek so loud that they'll come up here and take me to my mother for a whipping.'

To shut her up I took a lock from one of her braids between two fingers and wound it around my hand playfully.

'Pull it, now! Pull my hair!' she said somewhat crossly, yanking her head back so that I had to follow with my hand or cause her pain. 'I tell you I want to be punished!' she shrieked, beating her feet and knees against the rough floor made of broken stone.

'Don't do that, Pisana, you'll hurt yourself!'

'Very well then, pull my hair!'

I pulled gently on the lock in my hand.

'Harder! Harder!' She was growing wild.

'Like this, then,' I said, pulling a little harder.

'No, not like that! Harder!' She was in a fury now. And while I stood there, uncertainly, she jerked her head back so forcefully and so suddenly that the lock was left in my fingers. 'You see?' she said happily, 'that's how I want to be punished when I ask to be punished! Goodbye now and do not move from here or I shall never come to play with you again.'

And there I stood, stunned and immobile with that lock of hair between my fingers, while she bounded out of the door and closed it behind her. I tried to run after her with the lamp, but she had already disappeared down the hall. Now, had her mother ever punished her by pulling out even one of those hairs, I'm sure she would have made a racket to turn the house upside down. I marvel even today to think she could bear such pain without blinking, but such was the power of her will and her wildness, even in childhood. Was this a moment of pleasure or regret for me? I still wonder. The heroic way she had defied the labyrinthine passages of that dark house to come and find me, defying, too, the punishment awaiting her, had put me in seventh heaven. But then her stubbornness had intervened to clip my wings considerably, because I sensed (I say 'sensed', because at nine or ten one is too young to know certain things), at any rate I sensed that her heroism was made up less of affection for me than of vanity in being able to boast of such a feat. And so the first gush of my enthusiasm had been somewhat stifled, and I wondered if that lock that remained in my hand did not speak more of my own subservience than of her good intentions toward me.

Yet right from the beginning the material proofs of my joys, my sorrows and my vicissitudes were always very dear to me, and I wouldn't have given away that lock of hair for all the beautiful gold and mosaic buttons and all the other bounty the Count wore on his person on great ceremonial occasions. Memory for me is like a book and the objects that recall certain of its annals are like those ribbons we use to mark the most interesting pages. Your eye picks them out immediately, and without having to shuffle through the pages to find that point in a story or that sentence that struck you; you can simply rely on them. For many long years I've carried a museum of minutiae behind me: locks of hair, little stones, dried flowers, ribbons and tassels, broken rings, slips of paper, little jars, even bits of clothing and kerchiefs that correspond to events in my life both foolish and grave, sweet and painful, but in any case memorable. That museum grew steadily, and I preserved it with all the devotion of an antiquarian for his medal collection. If you, my readers, could inhabit my soul, I would merely need to inscribe in it that long list of trinkets and reliquiae, the way the Egyptians inscribed their hieroglyphics, and the whole story of my life would spring to your minds. As for myself, I can read it in them very clearly, the way Champollion read the story of the Pharaohs at the Pyramids.[4]

Unfortunately, my soul has never offered any lexicon to the public, and so, to separate that soul from its secrets, I have no choice but to waste my breath in words and reasoning. Do you forgive me? I hope so, at least for my good intentions – to allow you to profit from my long experience – and if the effort on my part gives me some pleasure or relief, would you prefer I forgo it and sternly mortify my spirit? I confess, I'm not much of an ascetic. Those emblems of the past are to the memory of an individual what a nation's monuments of stone and of art are to posterity. They recall, they celebrate, they compensate, they fire us up: they are Foscolo's Sepulchres[5] that take us back in thought to speak with the dear departed, and every day for us is a dear departed, an urn of ashes and flowers. Such peoples as have great monuments to inspire them never disappear completely; and when moribund, come back to life larger and more vigorous than ever. So the Greeks, emboldened by their statues of Hercules and Theseus, were able to fight off Xerxes and the Persians, and so today they rise up courageously against Mahmud,[6] bearing in mind the Parthenon and Thermopylae.

In his devotion to his own history, man never lets go of passing time; he shapes manhood from his youth, and preserves both youth and manhood in the weary, thoughtful repose of old age. They are a treasure that accumulates, not small coins to be spent day by day. Memory is a habit that seems to mark the good and the honest; the unhappy man has little to gain and much to lose in looking back, and he will try to destroy, not preserve, the physical traces of his actions – for remorse seethes from every one, like warriors from the teeth that Cadmus sowed.

Perhaps it is a habit that marks an excessive attachment to life, so that the cult of the past inexorably becomes gluttony for the future? Perhaps it does work that way for some, but by no means for all – and I am proof of it. He who collects and worships only flowers and jewels during his earthly pilgrimage will probably go trembling to that gate where the tax collector relieves him forever of his lovely burden. But when the memorial chapel holds both smiles and tears, roses and thorns, and there are emblems to remind us of all the ups and downs of our lives, the spirit resigns itself more easily to the final necessity, and the tax collector appears both exacting and merciful.

All depends on the temperament of the person who has assembled the museum; for our fates, I believe, are inscribed in our temperaments. Temperament is that internal rule that gives a value to outer events and things, and temperament decides whether life is idleness or pleasure, sacrifice or struggle or mere formality. He who errs in that decision must either accept he's been wrong or endure despair. Very often those who consider life an opportunity for pleasure do not think so when the time comes to depart.

That lock of twisted black hair, so evidently ripped from her head, was the first cross hung up in my domestic shrine of memory. I often came to pray, to meditate, to smile, to weep before that cross, its suggestion of both joy and trouble already hinting at those sharp, reckless, feverish pleasures that would later consume my spirit, but also replenish it. That lock of hair would be the A of my alphabet, the first mystery of my Via Crucis, the first relic of my beatitude, the first word of my life, as close to inscrutable as the lives of any of us. I sensed its importance immediately; indeed, my first thought was that I did not have any safe place to keep it. And so I folded it inside a blank page torn from my missal and hid it between the bedcovers and my pallet. What a strange thing! When I thought about the inestimable worth of those few hairs, they seemed to scorch my fingers. Whether it was the fear of losing them or an instinctive horror at the terrible promise they held, I do not know.

I had already hidden that lock of hair and lay silent, pretending to sleep, when Martino came up and, imagining I was asleep, took away the lamp and retired to his own room. Little by little my feigned sleep then became real sleep, and sleep in turn became a knot of dreams and ghosts and metamorphoses that made that night seem to last an entire lifetime. Perhaps time is not measured by the motions of the pendulum, as it seems, but by the sum of sensations? It may be, but equally it may be that such a question is really just a game of words. Certainly there were nights when in but an hour's dream I lived many long years, and it seems to me this phenomenon can be explained by likening time to a distance and the dream to a steam engine. The views remain the same, but they pass by more quickly; the distance doesn't shrink, it is devoured.

The following morning I awoke so grave and serious I felt like a grown man, such were the years that seemed to have been condensed in my last twenty-four hours. The memories of the previous day unfolded before me as clear and alive as the pages of a fine story. La Pisana's baiting of me, her smirking cousins, my dejection, escaping from the Castle, coming to my senses on the banks of the canal, the perilous fording of the waters, the great meadow, my climb to the heights, the wonders of that stunning view of grandeur and mystery, the fall of night, my fears, my pell-mell race across the countryside, the hoof-beats approaching, the fellow with the great beard who pulled me up on his horse, the wild galloping through fog and night, Germano's whipping when I arrived at Fratta, my other torments in the kitchen, the spit and the Countess, my determination (despite the terrible punishment threatened) not to betray the man who had come to my aid, Clara's kindness and the words of Signor Lucilio, my agitation, my desperation on going to bed, the sudden appearance of la Pisana, both humble and imperious, kind and cruel, thoughtless, outlandish and beautiful as ever: was all this not too much for the brain of a small child? And there, wrapped in a slip of paper under my pallet was a talisman that forever after could bring that rich and varied day to life again whenever I wished.

That morning, recalling Signor Lucilio's words and seeing I could profit from them, I began to shout for Martino at the top of my lungs. Aware, however, that before the old man's eardrums reacted to my howling I could have been drawn and quartered, I jumped out of bed and went to his room, where, in fact, he was nearly dressed. I told him I had a terrible headache and that I hadn't slept a wink all night, and would he call me the doctor, because I was afraid I was about to die. Martino told me I was delirious and that I should get right back into bed and he would go for the doctor, but first he went down to the kitchen to steal me some broth (at which, owing to the darkness down there, he succeeded wonderfully), and I drank the broth patiently, although I had a great hunger for sweet buns, and lay down under the blankets, promising I would try to sweat. Between the gash on my head and the fatigue, the hunger and the sweat produced by the hot broth, I think I must have worked up a nice fever, so that when Signor Lucilio arrived after about an hour, the hunger had been replaced by a terrible thirst. He took my pulse, studied my tongue and questioned me about the gouge on my forehead, then smiled at me in a kindlier way than before, hearing the sound of a skirt rustling in the hall. So Clara, too, came into my closet and after hearing from the doctor what ailed me, reassured me that in view of my illness the Countess would not insist on punishing me all that harshly, and if I were to tell her the truth about what had happened the night before, she was even inclined to pardon me. I replied that I had already told the truth and would continue to repeat it, and if it seemed strange to them that I had spent almost an entire day roaming around without knowing where I was, so it also seemed strange to me, but I did not know what to do about it.

Clara then questioned me about that wonderful place I said I had been, so full of sunlight and colours, and after I had once again described it all in vivid detail, she said that perhaps Marchetto was right, that I might have been at the Bastion of Attila, a bluff along the Lugugnana sea coast, where, according to local tradition, the King of the Huns, coming from Aquileia, had pitched his camp before meeting Pope Leo.[7] But from there to Fratta it was seven good miles even by the speediest roads and she could not understand how I had not got lost on the way back. She then told me that the immense, beautiful, azure, many-coloured thing I had seen mirroring the sky was, in fact, the sea.

'The sea!' I cried. 'What a joy to spend one's life upon the sea!'

'You think so?' said Signor Lucilio. 'I have a cousin who has savoured that joy for many years and he is not so very pleased about it. According to him, water is designed for fish and it was quite nonsensical for the old Venetians to have settled down in it.'

'It may be nonsensical today, but once upon a time it wasn't,' Clara went on, 'when on the other side of the sea stood Candia, the Morea, Cyprus and all the Levant.'[8]

'I myself intend to stay on the sea forever without any concern for what's on the other side,' I said.

'In the meantime, cover yourself and get well, you little devil,' Signor Lucilio said. 'Martino will bring you a little flagon of water from the druggist, as tasty as jam, and you will take a spoonful every half hour, do you understand?'

'And meanwhile we'll try to arrange things with Mother,' said Clara. 'Since you continue to say this is the truth, just as you said last night, my hope is she'll pardon you.'

Lucilio and Clara went out; Martino followed, on his way to the druggist, and I was left with my sweating, my thirst, and such an uncontrollable desire to see la Pisana that I really didn't care whether I was pardoned or not. But the young lady did not appear, although down in the courtyard I could hear her and her little companions squealing as they played their games. I was afraid to be seen, however, or taken away by Martino or denounced by some other little boy, so I didn't get up and dress myself and go down to the courtyard as I would have liked. I stayed where I was, ears tuned to their screams and my heart in such tumult I could scarcely hear. About an hour later, however, I heard la Pisana shouting at the top of her lungs:

'Martino! Martino! So how is Carletto?'[9]

Martino must have heard her and even replied, but I heard nothing. Not long after, he appeared with the medicine and told me he had met the Countess on the stairs and the good lady had asked him whether it was true I had bashed my head against the wall in desperation.

'Is that true?' asked Martino.

'I don't know,' I told him. 'Last night I was so upset that

I could have behaved very foolishly without being able to remember today.'

'You don't remember?' said Martino, who hadn't understood much.

'No, I don't remember,' I replied. But he wasn't at all happy with my reply, for it seemed to him that having done so much damage to my face I should have had an excellent memory of it for quite a while.

The medicine worked, better and faster than anyone expected, for that very day I got up – and as for the Countess's threatened punishment, it was never spoken of again. Neither, however, was my return to Faustina's chamber mentioned, and so I continued to sleep in my dog hole next to Martino. As you might guess, my desire to see la Pisana after her unexpected night-time visit played a great part in my sudden recovery, and when I descended to the kitchen my first thought was to look for her. The family had just finished the noon meal and Monsignor, quite unusually, gave me a pat on the chin when we met on the stairs and peered at the gash on my forehead, which was not very serious. He told me that I must not be such a plague as I was thought to be, if I had done myself such damage out of remorse at being considered a liar. But I should be more judicious in the future and ask God to relieve my troubles, and learn the second part of the *Confiteor*. I recognized Clara's gentle spirit in Monsignor's kind words and knew she had provided that edifying reason for my odd behaviour; and so I was granted, if not a full pardon, at least a clement, blind eye. I later learned from Marchetto that Signor Lucilio had depicted me as a shy and sensitive lad, my health and strength easily weakened by any kind of displeasure, and that he and Clara had so strongly guaranteed my sincerity that the Countess could no longer insist I was a liar. She did take the trouble to question Germano, but he had surely been coached by Martino, and replied that yes, indeed, he had heard a horse's hoof-beats the night before, but long before my return, and so I couldn't have arrived on that horse. Fulgenzio's testimony was thus ignored and I was left alone and didn't have to lie further to salve my conscience.

Let me say, though, that what some might think was just a

boy's frivolous obstinacy seemed to me then and seems to me now fine proof of loyalty and gratitude. It was the first time pleasure and duty battled in my soul and I didn't hesitate a moment before choosing duty. If in this case the duty doesn't seem so very binding – for neither did the stranger seem to be wholly serious, nor did I promise anything, nor was it clear what my silence about something so ordinary as a man on horseback was worth to him – I nevertheless proved my rectitude three times over. Perhaps this first sacrifice, which I undertook so willingly and so lightly, set my character on that path that I've kept to ever since, usually in much more solemn circumstances.

Whether fate makes the man or man governs his fate is a matter that has long been debated. But perhaps not enough attention has been paid to discriminating between what is and what ought to be. Philosophy certainly elevates man above the influence of the stars and the comets, and yet the stars and the comets were circling above us long before philosophy taught us to defend ourselves. And often it is chance that comes to nurture reason, even before reason is developed. Although the circumstances of childhood do not determine the tenor of an entire life, they often frame beliefs that, once formed, become the incentives that guide us. Therefore, pay attention to the child, my friends; if you care about the man, always pay attention to the child. Do not let childish passions turn wicked; do not let careless tolerance or unbending tyranny or murderous neglect allow the child to think that what pleases him is right and what he dislikes is abhorrent. Aid the child, support him, guide him. Offer him those occasions to find virtue to be beautiful and saintly, and vice ugly and unpleasant. A grain of right experience at nine is worth a course of studies in morality at twenty. Courage, honesty, love of family and of country – those two great loves that give all others meaning – are learned as languages are. Infancy is very much the right age to learn, but woe to those who don't. Woe to them and woe to those who must deal with them, and to the family and the country that hopes for aid and decency from them. The bud is in the seed and the plant is in the bud: I shall never tire of saying so, for experience has proven to me the truth of this old axiom. Sparta, master of men, and Rome, queen of the world, trained their warriors and their citizens from the cradle, and thus their peoples were warriors and citizens. Today we look on children as spoiled and pleasure-loving – and our mob is made up of the spoiled and the pleasure-loving.

Now perhaps I am altogether blinded by self-regard, but when I search my memory I find no more worthy deed than when – a mere boy – I bravely defied a thrashing to keep a secret asked of me and to show gratitude for a favour received. It was a rule I later clung to, for I would have been ashamed to show myself less of a man than I had been as a boy. This is what I mean when I say that circumstances frame beliefs. I had risen to the occasion and did not wish ever to descend again. And when I did fall, I felt remorse; but I don't mean to write about remorse here, but would rather use my pen to start afresh and put down my actions according to their merits. Those times I did err I was all the more guilty, for it wasn't in my nature or my practice. Yet who is blameless among us mortals? I'm always comforted by the story of Christ's noble words for the woman taken in adultery: he that is without sin among you, let him cast the first stone.

And so that afternoon (as I was saying) I went looking for la Pisana, but to my great disappointment I could not find her anywhere. I asked all the maids, but since they were guilty of not having kept an eye on her, they were doubly annoyed at me. Nor did Germano, Gregorio or Martino have any idea. I was by now very upset and went out behind the stables to ask the gardener whether he had seen her leave the Castle. And, indeed, he had seen her head out into the fields with the druggist's son, but that was two hours ago and most likely the young mistress had already returned, because the sun was hot and she didn't like getting burned. But I was less certain, knowing her fickle nature, and so I headed out into the fields myself. A scorching sun glanced off my head; the soil was dry and parched under my feet, but my heart was so full of misery I was aware of nothing. By the side of a ditch, I found a shoelace. It was hers, and I continued, certain that my great desire would lead me wherever she was. I searched the woods and thickets, the trees along the ditches, the hidden places where we used to rest when we were out larking; my eyes roamed up and down, haunted by jealousy, and if that druggist's son had happened to turn up, I think I would have given him a good thrashing without stopping to ask myself why.

As for la Pisana, I knew her very well indeed and had foolishly become accustomed to her faults, in fact was close to loving her for them, the way a great horseman will prefer among all the animals in his stable the one that rears, the one that resists the reins and the spurs. No circumstance makes a thing more cherished and dear than when it seems about to elude us, but if a weak spirit is discouraged by such a fear, it merely arms and strengthens the steadfast. You might think la Pisana had cast a spell on me, were it not for the fact that my pride continually pricked me to prevail over the other pretenders. I was her favourite often, but I wanted to be her favourite always. The sentiment that drove me was love of the purest kind: a love that later grew and changed its colour and its nature, but which even then overwhelmed my heart with all its madness. And love at the age of ten is as excessive as every other desire in that ingenuous time of life, all unaware of where the impossible resides.

Here, a dearth of words makes me say 'love' instead of that noun, whatever it is, that we ought to be using, for such a varied passion encompassing the purest heights of the soul as well as the lowest bodily functions (where the first bow to the second and the second aspire to be the first; and sometimes the two mix in an almost divine ecstasy and at other times in a truly bestial convulsion); such a passion would need twenty names instead of a single generic name that is suspect both for good and for ill, depending on the case, and seems deliberately chosen to disturb the modest and condone the shameless. I said 'love' and I could not say otherwise, but each time I shall use that word in the course of my story I shall feel obliged to add a line of comment to supplement the dictionary. At that time the Pisana I loved was the companion of my games, and since games at that age are everything, I wanted her all for myself: and if that doesn't constitute the purest form of love, take it up with the dictionary writers.

Despite my furious hunt for her, she didn't let herself be

found that afternoon, and in the course of searching here and peering in there, of running and jumping and walking around, I began, without noticing it, to follow the same path that had taken me so far afield the day before. By the time I did become aware, I stood at a rough crossroads where some country lanes met, and a sad-looking San Rocco sat atop a crumbling stone wall, showing off the sore on his leg to pious travellers. His trusted dog was by his side, tail down and nose up, as if to observe what the saint was doing. All this I saw in a glance, but as I was looking away I caught sight of a ragged and bent old woman praying very earnestly before that San Rocco. She looked to me like Martinella, a local beggar woman who would stop and take a pinch from Germano's snuffbox every time she passed by the castle bridge at Fratta. I approached her with some uneasiness, because hearing Martino's tales I'd come to suspect all old women were witches, but the fact that I knew her, and, of course, my need, pushed me forward. She turned round, looking annoyed, although she was usually the most patient and affable of beggars, and snarled at me, asking what I was doing in that place at that hour. I said that I was looking for la Pisana, the Countess's daughter, and was getting ready to ask whether she had seen the girl come past with the druggist's son.

'No, no, Carlino, I didn't see her,' she told me hastily and rather sharply, although she seemed to want to show she was friendly. 'While you were looking she probably went back home another way. Go back to the Castle. I'm sure you'll find her there.'

'I don't think so,' I said. 'She has just now finished her luncheon . . .'

'I tell you, go there and you won't fail to find her,' the old lady interrupted. 'As a matter of fact, now that I think of it, I believe I saw her going down past Montagnesi's fields just five minutes ago.'

'But I came up that way just five minutes ago myself!'

'And I tell you that I saw her!'

'No, that's not possible!'

While I insisted on standing there and arguing, and the old woman was doing her best to send me away, what did we hear but a horse galloping along one of the four roads that approached us? Martinella turned from me suddenly with a shrug of her shoulders and moved towards the hoof-beats, as if preparing to put out her hand for alms. A moment later a horse burst out of a hollow in that rutted road: a strong and fiery colt with flaring nostrils and a slight foam at the mouth. Atop the horse was a giant wearing rags, with a wild grey beard blown to the four winds and a big, weathered hat that covered his face to the nose. He had no stirrups, no saddle or bridle, only the end of a lead, which he used to beat the animal's shoulders and put some fire in it. Right away I thought of that bearded fellow who had carried me back to the Castle the night before, and I knew I wasn't wrong when I heard a deep, harsh voice reply to the beggar woman. She turned to him with a glance towards me, and he brought his horse near her and bent over to whisper some words in her ear.

'God and San Rocco will reward you for your good deed,' she said. 'And as for the alms, I trust you: don't forget now, at the end of the week!'

'Yes, yes, Martinella! Don't fail me,' the man said, digging his knees into the horse's flanks and racing off down the road towards the laguna. Some way off, he turned and pointed to show the old woman the road he had come by, and then horse and horseman disappeared behind the dust raised by the animal's hooves.

I watched the scene intently until, at last moving my eyes from the spot where the horseman had vanished, I glanced out over the fields to the other side, where I saw la Pisana and the druggist's lad running towards me in great haste. I, in turn, began to run towards them, and Martinella shouted, 'Oh, and where are you going now, Carlino?'

'She's there! La Pisana is there! Don't you see her?'

When I reached the young lady she looked so pale and stricken it was pitiful.

'My heavens, Pisana, what's the matter, are you ill?' I said, holding her up.

'Oh mercy me, what a fright, what a chase . . . They are over there with their shotguns . . . and they want to cross the stream,' wheezed la Pisana all out of breath.

'Who is over there with shotguns, who wants to cross?'

'You see,' came the reply from the druggist's boy, Donato, who was now somewhat less breathless and terrified, 'here is what happened. We were playing on the bank of the mill stream when on the far side out jumped four or five men with some very ugly faces, carrying guns in their hands that would frighten you to death, and they seemed to be looking for something and even getting ready to cross. And so la Pisana ran off and I ran after her with as many legs as I could muster, but two or three of them began to shout, "Wait! Did you see a man on horseback come by here?" but la Pisana didn't answer them and neither did I, and we kept on running away and now we're here. But those men will certainly come this way, too, for high as the water is, the mill bridge isn't far off.'

'Let's run away! Let's run away!' la Pisana shouted in utter terror.

'Courage, my young lady,' the beggar woman intervened, having heard all these remarks. 'The Cernide are not looking for you but for a man on horseback, and when Carlino and I stand here and tell them that the only man on horseback we've seen is the caretaker of Lugugnana going to take care of the hay at Portovecchio . . .'

'No, no! I want to get out of here. I'm afraid!' screamed la Pisana wildly.

But there was no time to get out of there, because just then four *buli* suddenly materialized before us and, peering up and down the four roads, turned to the old woman with the same question they had previously asked the two children.

'I saw nothing but the caretaker of Lugugnana, who was going towards Portovecchio,' Martinella told them.

'The caretaker of Lugugnana? It was probably him!' said one of the four.

'Listen, Martinella,' said another, 'you know Spaccafumo, don't you?'

'Spaccafumo!' spat out the old woman, making a nasty face. 'That scoundrel, that bandit who lives beyond the law and the fear of God, like a Turk? No, thanks be to God I don't know him, although I saw him one Sunday in the stocks at Venchieredo, it must have been two years ago.'

'And you didn't see him in these parts today?' It was the first *bulo* once again.

'Did I see him today? But they say he was drowned at the end of last year!' the old lady went on. 'And then, I must confess to your Excellencies, that my eyesight is not what it should be.'

'Listen to this! It *was* him!' the fellow went on. 'Why didn't you say right off that you are blind as a bat, you wrinkled old hag? All right, let's go! To Portovecchio, boys!'

And the four set off toward Portovecchio, in the opposite direction from that taken by the bearded horseman a quarter of an hour before.

'But they're going the wrong way,' I blurted out.

'Quiet!' Martinella whispered. 'Let those bad fellows go away and we'll say a paternoster to San Rocco, who has rid us of them.'

During our conversation with the Cernide la Pisana had recovered her courage, until finally she seemed the most confident of us all.

'Oh no,' she said, 'before we do any praying we must run to Fratta and warn the Clerk and Marchetto about those terrible fellows we saw. It's the job of the Clerk to keep the criminals out of Papa's lands, isn't it?'

'Yes, indeed,' I said, 'and he even puts them in prison when he pleases.'

'Well then, now we must go and put those four bad men in prison,' she said, pulling me towards Fratta, 'because I don't – I really don't – want them to frighten me again!'

Donato followed behind, deliberately ignored by the capricious young lady, while Martinella had resumed her place on her knees in front of San Rocco, as if nothing had happened.

FOUR

Don Quixote the smuggler and the Provedoni family of Cordovado. A pastoral idyll at the spring of Venchieredo with some observations about love and perpetual creation in the moral universe. The chaplain's maid at Fratta; a diplomatic exchange between two lords and magistrates.

Spaccafumo was a baker at Cordovado, which is a picturesque little plot of land between Teglio and Venchieredo. A man at war with the local authorities, he had earned the title Spaccafumo because he was capable of great speed when chased.* In his first exploit he took on some customs and excise officers who wanted to impound a certain bag of salt found in the possession of an elderly widow who lived next door to him. I believe, in fact, that old lady was Martinella herself, who in those days was still able to work and hadn't yet become a beggar. Spaccafumo's punishment was two years' banishment, but Signor Antonio Provedoni, elder of the Commune,[1] had commuted the sentence to twenty ducats. However, after the scuffle with the customs officers, Spaccafumo picked another fight with the Vice-captain of the jail, who wanted to incarcerate a cousin of his, because he'd been found with weapons on his person at the Venchieredo Fair. And so our baker spent three days in the stocks on the village square, and then two months in jail, and was sentenced to exile from the territory for twenty-eight months.

At this point he stopped making bread, and that was as far as his compliance with the sentence of the Venchieredo crim-

* In the somewhat Venetianized Friuli dialect of the place, Spaccafumo means *sbattipolvere*, 'dust-raiser', but I would be loathe to un-name him by translating it thus, and I don't recall ever knowing his real name.

inal court went. For the rest, he went on living in sundry places around the district and exercising his own private ministry of justice for the public good. The constables of Portogruaro had been sent out after him twice, but he raised the dust with such speed and knew the tricks and secret hiding places of the countryside so well that they had never been able to catch him. As for surprising him in his lair, that was even more difficult, for all the peasants were on his side and none knew where he went to sleep or how he stayed out of the weather. And while the city constables of Portogruaro proceeded with too much pomp and circumstance to be able to steal up on him unannounced, the guards and the Cernide militia, who served the landed lords, were in too tight with the villagers to seriously chase after him.

Sometimes, after months and months when he hadn't been heard of, he would turn up ever so coolly at Mass in Cordovado. The whole town was delighted to see him, but he listened to the Mass with one ear only, the other tuned to the main doors, ready to run out the side if he heard the slow, heavy tread of the patrol approaching. That the police would be clever enough to guard both doors was out of the question (by which I don't mean they were not in good faith). After Mass he would join the circle chatting in front of the church, and at lunchtime he would head straight off to Casa Provedoni, the last house on the way out of town towards Teglio. Signor Antonio would close an eye and the rest of the family would join Spaccafumo in the kitchen with great pleasure to hear about his adventures and laugh at the wit that coloured his tales. From childhood he had been treated as a neighbour and friend in that household, and so it continued as if nothing had happened, and no one was surprised to see him sitting there in front of the chimney, eating that sour turnip soup called *brovada*.*

The Provedoni family was respected in town for its long lineage and reputation. I myself remember seeing the name Ser Giacomo della Provedona in the minutes of an assembly

* A soup of turnips grated and soaked in brine, then put to the boil with pounded ham. Martino grated many of these turnips and I recall that I ate them very happily, raw as they were, before supper.

meeting held in 1400 and from that time on, the family had always been one of the mainstays of the commune. But the fortunes of the poor communes were not all that luminous, hedged in as they were by the aristocracy, and even more wretched were the fortunes of their leaders compared with those of the fiefholders. San Marco was popular, but distantly and mostly ceremonially, and in the end, he prized the deference of the nobility, especially in the Friuli, over that of any of those scarecrow communes. So Venice tolerated any commune that was already established and did not pretend that the law be strictly applied, but kept them all in a humble condition with many constraints and restrictions – and as for establishing any new ones, that was out of the question. When a feudal domain expired because the holder was charged with felony[2] – treason – or other grave crimes, and the territory returned to the Republic's jurisdiction, San Marco, rather than declare a commune, would name some local official to administer the fief. And thus, a double goal was quietly achieved: the numbers of nobles (unfortunately, one had to keep them on one's side) was formally reduced, while the population was maintained in strict servitude and kept as far away from public affairs as possible.

In any case, while the communes, in their disputes with the lords, were usually in the wrong as far as the law books went, they were *always* in the wrong when they went to court – in part because of the connivance of the patrician local representatives sent year after year from Venice by the Doge to preside over the mainland tribunals. There was, of course, a means that made all ranks equal before the holy impartiality of court, and that was money. But if one thinks of how a love of litigation battled in those communes with their very parsimonious habits, it is easy to understand why the communes rarely sought justice by those means. While the lord had already paid out his gold ducat, the commune was still bickering about whether it should be a *bezzo* or a *petizza*. He had the sentence in his favour already in his pocket – and they were still squabbling about some phrase in their riposte.

And so avarice, which often tends to become rooted in the government of the many and the humble, shrank those already weak powers granted to the communes even further. The lords kept their militias well armed and hired the roughest fellows in the territory as their guards, while the communes had to choose from the others' rejects and often a whole platoon of their militia might have just four old, worm-eaten, broken blunderbusses among them – every shot from which was a mortal danger to the shooter. And, in fact, they prudently shied away from danger, and when fits of bravery overtook them, resorted to their gun stocks.

Just as each jurisdiction reasoned and acted for itself before the State, not seeing any value in common cause, so individuals behaved before the commune, distrusting (not without reason) its authority and seeking their own justice or authority. Which meant that there were endless private retaliations; and the communes deferred to the aristocrats nearby, which was even more damaging and cowardly, because unnecessary (although necessary in one sense: that natural law dictates that the weak should serve the strong). Not without reason, we Italians have been accused of fawning, of pretence, of excessive regard for the individual. And the public habits I've mentioned tend to encourage those faults in the national temperament. Hypocrites, parasites and highwaymen will flourish like weeds in a savage, uncultivated place. Ingenuity, shrewdness and defiance, aimed at evading laws applied unfairly, can also evolve into wickedness and transgression. The lowly, by cheating or by stealing, move to get what has been denied them by a biased court, whether because the judge is ignorant or in somebody's pocket.

For example, there was a law that said that the accounts kept by merchants and gentlemen were legally valid. How, then, were their opponents to take their cases to trial if they could boast no coat of arms and didn't belong to the merchants' guild? Bribes and protection: these were the additional articles that supplemented an imperfect legal code. Sometimes even the judge who imposed the fine on the miscreant took his cut – and against those judges who made it clear they would be quite happy to pocket such earnings, what remedy was there besides threats, either from the wrongdoer if he was powerful or from a powerful friend if he was not? Oftentimes the judge would be willing to take his contribution under the table and sign a decree of innocence, happy to avoid trouble and risk. But this fine custom – private veniality sparing the worst of public justice – was not tolerated by those judges cut from Venetian cloth, who weren't greedy enough to take the guilty man's wool and give half to their ministers.

Signor Antonio Provedoni deferred to the nobility out of genuine feeling; he wasn't servile and boot-licking. His family had always acted that way and he had no intention of behaving otherwise. The respect he showed, polite but not profuse, made people respect him; that's how it was in those days: a man who didn't make a great show of deference was considered a worthy person. I don't mean by this that he was able to resist the bullying demands of the nearby lords; he just didn't go out looking to make them offers, and that was already something. Privately, he considered their presumption a sign that the real nobility, the one that matched grandeur with courtesy, had fallen low. In their greed and bullying, there wasn't much difference between them and the guardsmen. But you would never hear such a thought escape his prudent lips; he was silent and bowed his head, the way the peasants do when Providence sends them a hailstorm.

He and his forebears had always watched the sun, the moon and the stars move in one direction – whether the year was rainy, dry or it snowed. When there was a bad year it was followed by many good ones; after a good year came many bad ones: this was the reasoning he applied to the things of this world. Things went well or they went badly all by themselves; it was his turn to hit a bad patch, and that was all. But he had great faith that things would improve for his children and his grandchildren, and he merely had to make sure they came forth abundantly to guarantee that the family wasn't cheated of its share of happiness in the future.

Only the second-born of his large family, whom he had named Leopardo, gave him any reason for concern. But then, how could a boy named 'Leopard' be meek and docile? In this regard, the elder statesman of Cordovado had been rather careless. The names he had given to his sons and daughters were all pretty ferocious and bestial; they didn't denote those habits of tolerance, silence and complicity that he knew were appropriate to persons of their rank. The firstborn was named Leone, the second, as we said, Leopardo, and then there was Bruto, Bradamante, Grifone, Mastino and Aquilina.[3] In short, it was a real menagerie, and Signor Antonio didn't seem to understand that with such names, proper peasant deference was either impossible or came across as mockery.

If in his times they had still used the name Bestia ('Beast', 'Wild Animal'), as they did among the ancient Romans, Signor Antonio would have certainly given that to his firstborn, keen as he was on zoology. But since that generic name wasn't available, he chose one perhaps even grander and more threatening, the king of the beasts, according to Aesop. Leone never proved himself to be any less a sheep than the times – or his parental example – demanded. Growing up, he learned to put up with much, he sighed a lot, and then, like his father, took a wife and had children – and there were already a half dozen babies by the time his brother Leopardo began to frequent young ladies himself.

And so we arrive at that point where family discord first arose between Signor Antonio and his second-born.

Leopardo was a young man of few words and many deeds – that is, of few deeds, I should say, but in those few he was so stubborn there was no dissuading him. Scold him about anything at all and instead of replying he would turn on his castigator with a growl in his throat and his two eyes pinched together – and the scolding rarely went beyond the preamble. For the rest, he was as good as gold and as serviceable as the five fingers on his own hand.

For two hours a day he did what he pleased and not even the Devil could make him do otherwise. The other twenty-two they could set him to split wood, plant cabbages or even to turn the spit as I did and he would never grow restless. He was the most docile leopard that ever lived. Most attentive to his duties, observed the Mass and said his rosary: a good Christian, that is, as was customary in those days. He was also literate and learned far beyond the standards of his peers.

Nevertheless, it wouldn't be an overstatement to say he was rather stubborn. He was born that way, perhaps, but while others might be stubborn in conscience alone (and otherwise all too servile) he was, as they say, a mule inside and out, and would have given even the Most Serene Doge himself a kick in the face if the fellow had dreamed of contradicting him. Hard-working and passionate as he was, he became leaden and inert if diverted from his course, like a factory wheel when the belt is cut. His belt was his conviction and without it he advanced no further than an ant. As for allowing himself to be persuaded, Leopardo was as persuadable as a fanatical Turk.

Perhaps the reasons for his stubbornness lay in an upbringing of solitude and silence; his thoughts were not delicately grafted together, they were the thousand tendrils of a sturdy oak root that had grown slowly before budding and bearing fruit. Now, a branch may be grafted over another graft, but roots cannot be pulled up, or when they are, they shrivel. Leopardo's head was made in such a way that it could only sit on the shoulders of a great and generous man – or on those of a madman. All or nothing: that was his essence, the motto on his nature's coat of arms. The precepts of his parents and masters coincided so little with his own views that he asked nothing of them, nor they of him.

The root of all his troubles, however, was the spring at Venchieredo. Once he began to drink from that spring, his father began to hammer at him with questions, advice, reproofs. And because none of his remarks in any way corresponded to Leopardo's own opinions, he began to growl and look surly. And thus, as Sterne would say, the animal spirits in his name prevailed – in short, Signor Antonio's passion for animals cost him rather dearly.

This riddle needs a bit of explanation.

Between Cordovado and Venchieredo, about a mile away from each, lies a large, crystalline spring whose waters are reputed to be salubrious and very refreshing. The nymph of this spring, however, did not wish to rely on the quality of the waters alone to attract her worshippers, so she framed it with such a lovely horizon of woods and sky, such a hospitable, shaded grove of alders and willows, that in truth her retreat was a spot worthy of Virgil's pen. Meandering secret paths; tiny murmuring brooks; sweet, mossy banks: nothing was missing from the picture. It was all that a sorceress's pool should be, that clear blue water bubbling up silently from a floor of tiny white pebbles, reflecting in its own bosom the picturesque pastoral setting. The sort of place that brings to mind the inhabitants of Eden before there was sin. And one that makes us think of sin (without second thoughts) now that we are no longer inhabitants of Eden.

Pretty girls from Cordovado and from Venchieredo, girls from Teglio, Fratta, Morsano, Cintello and Bagnarolo, not to mention other villages nearby, had from time immemorial gathered at that spring on holiday evenings. They would laugh and sing, talk and eat their picnics, until their mothers, their *innamorati* and the moon came to take them home. Is it worth mentioning that along with these maidens there were young gentlemen? You could probably make that deduction yourself. When you count things up at the end of the year, I'm certain there were more visits to the spring of Venchieredo for the purpose of love-making than for water-drinking, and in any case, more wine than water is drunk there. It's a question of complying with the picnic hams and sausages rather than with any superstitions about spring water.

I myself visited that enchanting fountain many a time, but only once did I dare to profane the virgin splendour of those waters. Exhausted from the hunt, I was weary and burning with thirst, and not only that but my flask of white wine was dry. Were I to go back again, I would no doubt drink great rejuvenating draughts, but old age's need to take the waters would not make me forget those rowdy, cheerful bouts with the good wine of those times.

Now then, a few years before me, Leopardo Provedoni had made the acquaintance of the spring at Venchieredo. That quiet, solitary, peaceful place fitted his imagination as neatly as a suit can fit a person. His every thought found a natural correspondence there, or at least none of those willows ever disagreed with what he was thinking. He embellished, coloured and peopled the empty landscape to suit himself, and although still not yet at war with anyone on earth he nevertheless instinctively felt himself different from the rest, so it seemed to him that he was happier there than anywhere else because he was alone and free.

Leopardo's love for the spring at Venchieredo was his first act that did not admit contradiction. The second was his love, not so much for the spring, as for a pretty girl who often came there and whom he met all alone one lovely spring morning. To hear him tell the story was like listening to Tasso's *Aminta*[4] read aloud, except that Tasso shaped his verses first and then he read them, while Leopardo merely remembered, and as he remembered, improvised – and yet as you watched and listened, your brow was actually touched by poetry's cold sweat.

He had left the house on a sunny May day with a gun on his shoulder, more to satisfy the curiosity of any passers-by than with hostile intent towards snipe and partridges. He was walking along, head in the clouds, when he reached the edge of the woods that surround the spring on two sides, and there he stopped to listen for the familiar call of a nightingale. The nightingale had in fact been observing his approach and cooed out its usual trill, but not from the usual tree; that day, the call came out softly and timidly from a more hidden perch, as if the little bird was indeed greeting him, but with a certain diffidence due to that weapon slung over his shoulder. Leopardo peered though the branches looking for his mellifluous friend's new perch, but as he glanced here and there his eye fell on something that, in fact, he wasn't looking for.

Oh, why was it not I who fell in love with Doretta? Old as I am, I would write a page to astound my readers, I would lay siege to the high seats of poetry. Oh, let youth sketch the lines, let the heart colour them, let youth and the heart shine out of every corner of the fresco with such magic that the good, out of mercy, and the bad, from envy, will put down the book. Poor Leopardo! You alone could bear it; you who for your whole life bore that scene of love inside you, painted on your eyes and hewn out of your heart. Such loving innocence shines through even the distant memory of your words that I cannot but shed a tear as I write these lines.

To repeat: he was looking for a nightingale and saw instead, sitting on the verge of a little brook that runs down from the spring, a young lady with one foot in the water and the other, bare and white as ivory, tracing curves and circles around the minnows darting to the surface. She was laughing and clapping her hands as from time to time she managed to catch one of these little fishes with her toes and lift it out of the water. And then the shawl fluttering over her breast would open to reveal the whiteness of her half-bare shoulders, and her cheeks would redden with pleasure, enhancing her innocence. The minnows, if briefly frightened, soon returned to her side, for she had in her pocket the secret of their trust. She would slip that other merry little foot very, very quietly into the stream, and take from under her apron a piece of bread and crumble it into tiny pieces for her playmates. And then there would be a to-ing and a fro-ing, a darting and a tugging, a stealing one from the other among that whole quicksilver family, while the young lady bent over them as if to receive their thanks. And when the repast was all laid out, she would splash about under the water with her feet to watch the darting, greedy fish, frightened for a moment but quickly growing bold so as not to miss the best morsels. That stirring of the water allowed a glimpse of the delicate outlines of a supple, round leg, and as her shawl fell back from her shoulders, her woollen bodice barely seemed to contain her breast as it rose and fell with mirth.

All ears when it came to listening to the nightingale, Leopardo was now all eyes, and not even aware of the metamorphosis. Her simple, innocent, happy girlishness; her unwitting and unselfconscious allure; that immodesty so childish it made one think of naked angels at play in Pordenone's paintings; those thousand charms of a delicate, slender form; the golden brown hair in curls on her forehead like those of a baby; the fresh, sincere smile that seemed designed to show off two rows of small bright teeth as neat as crystal rosary beads: all this, I must add, coloured her with wonder in the eyes of the young man. He would have given anything at all to be one of those fishes so intimate with her; he would have been happy to stand there all his life, looking at her.

Because, however, he was a young man of conscience, these

stolen pleasures, this ecstatic rapture, awoke in him a certain guilty remorse. And so he began to whistle heaven knows what song, how tunefully you can only imagine, those of you who know exactly what effect the first blandishments of love have on the lips and the voice. Whistling without tune and without tempo, Leopardo pushed through the branches awkwardly and tumbled onto the verge of the spring, staggering worse than any drunkard.

The young lady settled her shawl around her shoulders, but had not had time to take her feet out of the water, and so she sat there half-embarrassed and half-amazed at this inopportune entrance. Leopardo was a good-looking young man, good-looking in the sense that includes beauty, strength and calm: as handsome as you could wish, in a way that hinted at divine perfection. His gaze was that of a babe, his brow that of a philosopher, his form that of an athlete, but the simple peasant fashion of his clothing made him look something less than distinguished. And, therefore, the young lady was not at first as upset as if the intruder had been a *signore*, and felt even more reassured when she raised her eyes to his face and recognized it, and murmured, with something like pleasure,

'Oh, it is Signor Leopardo.'

Hearing that muffled comment, for the first time the young man felt that his name was not sweet enough, not gracious enough, to rest upon lips so lovely. But his heart leapt up to learn that the young woman knew him and that he could thus make her acquaintance.

'And who are you, my lovely young lady?' he said, stammering, addressing her reflection in the spring, because he did not yet have the courage to look at the original.

'I am Doretta, daughter of the clerk of Venchieredo,' she replied.

'Then you are Signora Doretta!' exclaimed Leopardo, ever more desiring to look at her, but all the more unable, because he feared he had treated her at first with little respect.

The young lady raised her eyes as if to say, 'Yes, and I really don't see why you should be so astonished.'

Leopardo, ready to plunge in again, clutched all his reserves of courage to his heart, but he was such a novice in this business of asking questions that it was no wonder he cut a very mediocre figure this first time.

'It's very hot today, is it not?' he resumed.

'Deadly,' replied Doretta.

'And do you think it will remain so?' he said again.

'Well, it depends on the almanacs, doesn't it,' said the girl, somewhat nastily. 'Schieson says yes; Strolic says no.'

'And what do you predict?' continued Leopardo, going from bad to worse.

'Oh, it's all the same to me,' said the girl, who was beginning to be amused by this exchange. 'The rector at Venchieredo says prayers both for drought and for frost, but as far as I'm concerned, praying for one is no more trouble than praying for the other.'

'She's so lively and full of fun,' thought Leopardo, and the thought diverted his brain from the difficult inquiry he had been carrying out so manfully up to then.

'Have you taken a lot of game?' Doretta decided to ask, for he had fallen silent and she didn't want to miss this rare opportunity to amuse herself.

'Oh!' exclaimed the young man, as if he had just at that moment noticed the gun slung over his shoulder.

'I must warn you that you've left the flint at home,' the clever young lady continued, 'unless that is a new sort of gun?'

Leopardo's harquebus harked back to the first generation of firearms, and you only had to look at it to see the hint of malice in her coy pretence.

'It's an old family weapon,' the young man replied gravely, for he knew the gun well, every moment of its life story. 'It fought in the Morea[5] with my grandfather's great-great-grandfather. My own grandfather shot twenty-two snipe in a day with this gun, although that might sound hard to believe when you think that you need a good ten minutes to load it, and that after the powder lights in the flash pan, the shot takes a good half-minute to emerge. And, in fact, my father never hit more than ten and I've never got more than six up to now.

'The snipe, though, are getting cleverer and cleverer, and in that half-minute when the shot delays in the barrel, they've already flown half a mile away. The day will come when I'll need mounted artillery to catch them. Meanwhile, I point my gun and fire, but the flintlock has grown loose, and so at times I aim and pull the trigger, but after half a minute, when the shot should have fired, I discover that in fact the flint is missing. I must take it to Fratta to have Master Germano repair it. I could also, it's true, ask Papa to get another, but I'm sure he'd tell me the family doesn't want me introducing novelties. And, in truth, I agree with him. If the gun is slightly the worse for wear after the Morea campaign and those twenty-two snipe in one day, one can see why. Still, I believe I *will* take it to Master Germano to be mended. Am I not right, Signora Doretta?'

'Certainly,' said the young lady, withdrawing her feet from the brook and drying them on the grass. 'And the snipe will thank you a thousand times over.'

Leopardo was, meanwhile, gazing lovingly at his gun and wiping the barrel with the sleeve of his jacket.

'For now, this is how we contend with it,' he continued, reaching into his pocket for a handful of flints and selecting the most suitable one to place in the flintlock. 'You see, Signora Doretta, how I must be prepared for all contingencies? I must always carry a pouch full of flint, but then it isn't the gun's fault if old age has filed down its teeth. A man carries a powder horn, tinder and shot – so he can also easily carry flints.'

'Undoubtedly. You're strong and wouldn't be put off by that,' said Doretta.

'Certainly not. Four little flints! I'm not even aware I'm carrying them,' said the young man, replacing them in his pocket. 'I could even carry you very quickly all the way to Venchieredo without breathing any more heavily than the barrel of my gun does. My legs are good, my lungs excellent; I can walk all the way to the Lugugnana marshes and back in the space of one morning.'

'Goodness, how rash!' the young lady exclaimed. 'The Count, when he goes there to hunt, goes on horseback and stays away three days.'

'I am more fleet-footed; I come and go like lightning.'

'Without bagging anything, however.'

'What do you mean, without bagging anything? The ducks, fortunately, haven't become as clever as the snipe; they would sit while my gun warms up not a half-minute, but half an hour. I never come back from there without my sack full. It's true that I go to look for the game where it lives – and I am not afraid to go into the marsh up to my belt.'

'Oh mercy!' cried Doretta, 'Aren't you afraid you'll sink in and be buried?'

'I'm afraid of nothing but the real ills that I have met,' replied Leopardo, 'and even those do not worry me very much. The rest I don't even think about, and because up until now I have never died, I don't have the least fear of dying, not even were I to see a row of muskets pointed at me. What a silly thing, to be afraid of something you've never met. That's all I need!'

Doretta, who had up until now been having fun at the expense of the young man's simplicity, began to look on him with some respect. And Leopardo, having cleared the first obstacle, now wanted to reveal more of what was in his heart, perhaps for the first time. He was no less curious to hear the sincere and spontaneous confessions that came to his lips than was the young lady. He had never before been bothered to peer deeply into his own soul, and so he heard his own words as if they were news of the greatest interest to him.

'Tell me the truth now,' he said, sitting down beside the young lady, whose eyes stopped wandering in search of her clogs. 'Tell me the truth. Who was it who taught you to love the Venchieredo spring so well?'

The question disturbed Doretta somewhat, and now it was her turn to fall silent. She knew how to chatter and tease well enough, perhaps too well, but a serious reply was something she could not deliver without a great deal of concentration and solemnity. However – and here was the strange thing – faced with this good fellow Leopardo she was unable to make a joke of it and had, instead, to reply, stammering, that the spring was close to the hamlet where she lived with her father and so she had played there from childhood and continued to do so because it pleased her.

'Excellent!' said Leopardo, who was too modest to notice Doretta's sudden shyness, just as he was too earnest to have been aware of her previous jests. 'But you wouldn't be afraid, I suppose, to play with the water of that brook?'

'Afraid?' said the young lady, reddening. 'And why should I be afraid?'

'Well, because you might slip in and drown,' said Leopardo.

'Oh heavens, I never even think about such dangers,' replied Doretta.

'Just as I do not think of them – or any,' said the young man, fixing his large, calm blue eyes on her small, sparkling ones. 'The world goes on with me and it could go on without me. This is my consolation, and anyway the Good Lord takes care of all. But do you come often here to the spring?'

'Oh, yes indeed,' said Doretta, 'especially when I feel warm.'

Leopardo was thinking to himself that if they had met this time they might also meet again, but the thought seemed to him over-bold and so he confined himself to gazing at her with hope and desire. Meanwhile his lips had begun to chatter about the heat and the season, and he said that as far as he was concerned, spring and summer were all the same. There was really no difference, except for the leaves which budded and later fell.

'Oh, I love spring above all,' said Doretta.

'As do I!' exclaimed Leopardo.

'What? Did you not say it was all the same?' said the girl.

'Well, that's true . . . so it seemed. But today is such a beautiful day that I'm inclined to give the prize to this very season. I believe that what I meant when I said it was "all the same" was that I was referring to the heat and the cold. But as for the pleasures of the eye, spring is certainly the best.'

'There's that varlet Gaetano at Venchieredo who always defends winter,' the young lady continued.

'That Gaetano truly is a varlet,' replied Leopardo.

'What's that? You know him too?' asked Doretta.

'Yes. That is, he's the porter, is he not?' said Leopardo stammering. 'That is, I have a muddled memory that I have heard him mentioned.'

'No, he's not the porter, he's the bailiff,' said Doretta, 'and he's one of those who gets carried away with his jesting. I never want to hear winter mentioned, and to spite me he's always praising it to the skies!'

'Oh, I could make him be still,' exclaimed Leopardo.

'Yes? Well then, I pray you come by sometime,' said Doretta, standing up and putting on her clogs. 'But be sure you come with a good supply of patience, for that Gaetano is as stubborn as a mule.'

'I shall, I shall,' said Leopardo. 'But you will also come to the spring again, will you not?'

'Oh yes, when the fancy takes me,' said the young lady. 'And on holidays I am always here with the other young girls from nearby.'

'Feast days, holidays . . . ,' murmured the young man.

'Oh you must come,' said the young lady, 'you must come and see what a Paradise we have here.'

Doretta turned towards Venchieredo, Leopardo trailing after her, a dog following its master after it has been chased away. From time to time Doretta turned to look at him, smiling, and he smiled, too, but his heart was pounding so hard his legs were trembling, until finally they reached the gates of the hamlet.

'Goodbye, Signor Leopardo,' said the young lady from a distance.

'Goodbye, Signora Doretta,' replied the young man, gazing at her so long and hard that he seemed to beam his very soul towards her. He bent down, blushing, to retrieve some flowers she had dropped, I believe, with a certain coy intention. Then, when the vines on the trellis finally interfered with his view of Doretta's dear, slim and gracious body as she hastened toward the castle, his gaze fell to earth: so grave, so profound, that he might have wanted to bury it there forever. After a long while he raised his eyes with some effort and a sigh, and took the road home, his head full, if not of new thoughts at least of very new and strange fancies. He pinned the little flowers to his heart and never took them off again.

In short, Leopardo had fallen in love with the young lady. But how and why did it happen? How? It was certainly by looking at and listening to her. Why? We shall never know, just as we will never know why one person likes the colour sky-blue, while another prefers scarlet or orange.

He had seen girls as pretty as Doretta and even three times prettier at Cordovado, at Fossalta, at Portogruaro, and while the daughter of the clerk of Venchieredo was far more lively than she was perfect, he hadn't fallen for any of those others, despite the opportunity to stay and talk with them. Instead, he had fallen like a ripe pear at first sight, at the first word from this one. Perhaps familiarity and conversation subtract rather than add magic to feminine charms? I don't say that now; that would be a grave injustice to women.

There are some who don't strike one at all at first, but whom, when one has known them for a long while, begin ever so slowly to warm the heart, and finally light such a fire that it can never be extinguished, while the mere sight of others scorches, and often such a flame leaves nothing but cinders. But just as there are men of straw who, even heated very slowly, end up in ashes, so there are iron hearts that once fired up, never cool down again. Love is a universal law with as many different corollaries as all the hearts that answer to it. To draft a full treatise one would have to build a library in which every man and every woman left a volume of personal observations. One could read the most generous things and the most vile, the most heavenly and the most bestial to be found in the imagination of any storyteller. But the problem would be to ensure that these accounts were sincere and truthful, for many fall in love with preconceived notions in their heads and prefer to use those notions, and not the force of sentiment, to explain their actions. Thus the abuse of that terrible word *forever*, employed with such carelessness in amorous talks and promises.

There are many who believe (and with some justice) that eternal, faithful love is superior, and so they reach for it. But it is not enough to believe in a great and powerful feeling; one must be able to achieve it. And most people, set to the task, will be blind to the many ways they don't measure up to their own ideals of truth and constancy. It's as if I, a writer of cheap non-sense, said to myself: 'The highest peak of human knowledge is metaphysical philosophy. I therefore am a philosopher like Plato and a metaphysicist on a par with Kant.' Fine reasoning, truly worthy of a dunce.

That very arrogance that we would not condone in any of the intellectual orders, we quite happily grant to ourselves in measuring our sentiments – and never mind how foolish this is, because sentiments, far more than intellect, do not bend to the will. No one would dare to measure himself against Dante's mind, but all think themselves his equal in love. Yet Dante's love was even rarer than his genius, and men are mad to think it available to all. Truly great souls are no more common than truly great minds; to feel and nourish love in one's loftiest essence one must free oneself from human frailty even more than the poet frees his mind in the highest spheres of his imagination. If only you pygmies trying to measure up to giants would cease for once and remember instead the fable of the frog and the ox! Must we flatter ourselves and human nature, only to worsen matters with disgraceful lies and remorseful betrayal? We would do better to beat our breasts and blush, rather than raise a hand to swear falsehoods. Taking oaths is better left to those who've looked deep within themselves, but such oaths are anyway superfluous. As for those who swear with every intention of swindling, they are too foolish or too wicked to waste words on. If a madman playing the saint is ridiculous, the villain doing so is a sacrilege.

I've known yet others who mistook the strength and momentary ardour they gained from nearness to some fervent soul for their very own sentiments. They think, like that young man, that the moon has fallen in the well because its picture is floating on the water. But then the moon sets and the picture vanishes. And so they wave their arms about to keep as warm as at first; they snort and sigh in the best of good faith. The fervent soul observes it all with pity, and that love mixed with mercy, doubt, memories and contempt becomes a martyrdom. Superlatives do not take one to Heaven, and volition alone will not keep a lamp alight when the oil is dry. It is pointless to try.

Meagre hearts should be wary of themselves and especially of their own most intense passions, for while a tepid love can long endure and be happy, a violent love is a meteor, a flash of lightning that leaves all the more unhappiness the more hopes it kindles. That unhappiness, however, is all for the others, because the frivolous aren't made to feel it. And so they take no trouble to avoid occasions for it, and only with extreme difficulty manage to obey that old precept: 'Know thyself.'

But then, who would dare to confess or even think himself meagre-hearted? One must, finally, leap beyond the reach of these arguments, an infinite labyrinth of vicious circles that clarify nothing beyond the fact that strong and superior natures are most likely to fall prey to misfortune, on account of the tricks and false certainties of the inferior. Yes, we bow our heads reverently before these mysteries, to which justice is alien. And yet we believe that in our own hearts the altar of justice holds no mysteries. Conscience tells us that it is better to be generous and treated meanly, than to be tepid and yet desired. And thus we suffer, but we love.

Now Doretta of Venchieredo did not seem at all suited to supply the needs of the grave, warm, intense heart of Leopardo. Nevertheless, she was the first to command his heart and to order him to live completely and forever for her. It was a mystery no less obscure or painful than any other. Why did other girls who might have satisfied his heart's demands not move in him any of those desires that constitute love? Is that how the moral order is made, that likes flee from each other and opposites attract? Even this rule is negated by the many exceptions.

One can only suspect that if material things roving confusedly through space have been, over many centuries, subject to some ordering force, the inner, spiritual universe still awaits, in a state of chaos, to know what rules govern it. Meanwhile it is a battlefield of sentiments, of forces, of judgements; a tumultuous, formless stew of passions, of dampenings, of deceits; a bubbling up of cowardice and ardour, of magnanimous acts and filth; a genuine chaos of spirits not yet well formed by matter, and of matter pressing dangers on the spirit. Everything grows excited, moves and changes; and yet I must repeat that the core of the future order is already shaped, and every day attracts to itself new elements, like those nebulae that, as they swirl around, grow larger and thicker and draw density and confusion from the atmosphere of atoms around them. How many centuries does that nebula need to grow from an atom into a star? Only the astronomers can tell us. How many centuries before human feelings become conscience? Only the anthropologists can tell us. But just as that star near the far, disordered edge of the universe is perhaps creating another solar system, so conscience promises the sentiments' internal disorder a stable and truly moral order. In a man's thought there are stretches of time that can be confused with eternity. But while thought may be faulty, hope nevertheless springs forth. Humanity can long hope, and wait patiently.

Poor Leopardo, too, although he did not have centuries of life before him, had to wait patiently until Doretta showed she had noticed his attentions and was grateful. Vanity, I believe, is what persuaded her. First of all Leopardo was handsome; then, he was one of the most desirable matches around; and finally, he offered her so many proofs of his near-religious devotion that it would have been true foolishness not to take advantage of them. And then, his simplicity, his naivety, was amusing; and that calm, gallant heart of his, enchanting. She noticed that while he was meek and tolerant with women even when they made fun of him, he was by no means meek towards the young men around. He merely had to look at them and they would fold their wings, and for her it was no small feat to have at her command one who could so easily dampen the high spirits of others.

And so Doretta let herself be found at the spring more and more often; she celebrated the holidays with him in a very friendly fashion; and although it took her some time to return his courtesies, between one thing and another, she finally did. At that point Leopardo was no longer content to see her only on those mornings when they happened to meet or in the middle of the crowd at the festival; he went every evening to Venchieredo and they walked up and down the stairs of the chancery or around and around the village until suppertime. Then he said farewell, more with his heart than with his lips, and returned to Cordovado, whistling his favourite song with great confidence. And so the two young people joined their lives together.

For the older generation, it was another story. The distinguished Dottor Natalino, clerk of Venchieredo, let matters take their course, because he had seen so many flies buzzing around his Doretta that one more, one less, made little impression on him. But when Signor Antonio became aware of the matter, it put his nose out of joint and he began to show a hundred other signs of his dismay. A man of country stock and country manners, he did not like the fact that his son was frequenting people of the other sphere. He began, therefore, with disapproval, a sentiment that had no effect on Leopardo, and seeing that this was not enough, he grew cooler, more ill-tempered, and addressed him rather stiffly, as if to say, 'I'm not at all happy with you.' Leopardo, who was extremely pleased with himself, thought he was showing Christian patience by enduring his father's meddling. And when the older man got to the point, as they say, of breaking eggs and laid out clearly and plainly the reasons his nose was out of joint, Leopardo felt obliged to lay out clearly and plainly in return his iron determination to continue on the path he had chosen.

'What? Are you shameless? Do you mean to go on wallowing in those pretty little dresses? Have you thought what they'll be saying in the village? Don't you see that even the Venchieredo *buli* think you're a fool? Just how do you think this game is going to end? Aren't you worried that one of these days the lord is going to have his retainers run you out of town? And you want to get that signore all riled against *me* when you already know how troublesome he is?'

With this and other such lines of questioning the prudent elder of the Commune went after his handsome, defiant Absalom, but Leopardo didn't give a damn about such rubbish, as he called it, and replied that he was a man like any other, and that if he loved Doretta it was no laughing matter and he did not mean to drop her when mocked by the first man who came along. Signor Antonio's voice went up, so did Leopardo's back, and each stuck to his own opinion. As a matter of fact, I think these disputes considerably warmed the young man's already heated heart.

It soon became clear, though, that the elder man's misgivings were not misplaced. While Doretta always received Leopardo amiably, the other inhabitants of Venchieredo were not so friendly. Among them was Gaetano, chief of the castle *buli*, who perhaps felt he still had some claims on the young lady and who certainly could not digest those daily visits by the handsome young fellow from Cordovado. It began with jesting, proceeded to loud altercations and once ended up in a fist fight. But Leopardo was so calm, so sure of himself, so deliberate, that it was the *bulo* who had to slink off, tail between his legs, and that defeat, played out in the public square, certainly did not quell his animosity. Meanwhile Doretta, in whom vanity was stronger than any love for Leopardo, was delighted to see war breaking out all around her, and did nothing to stop it. Gaetano dropped so many hints in the ear of his master – the young Provedoni was much too insistent; the young Provedoni was not very respectful of high-ranking persons and in particular of the lord himself – that finally the lord gave in and began to look on Leopardo with an even more beady eye than he turned on everyone else. The look meant 'Keep out of my way!' and it was well-known for ten miles around that a beady eye from the lord of Venchieredo was worth a sentence of banishment for at least two months.

Leopardo, however, was looked at, looked back, and calmly went about his business. Gaetano couldn't have asked for more; he knew that unspoken challenge would count for a hundred crimes in the view of his all-powerful lord. And, in fact, the latter was extremely annoyed to see that Leopardo took so little account of his beady eye, and, after having met him two or three times in the castle courtyard, one day he told him to halt and warned him fiercely that he was much too idle and that all that walking between Cordovado and Venchieredo would give him a pain in the backside. Leopardo bowed, not understanding, or pretending not to understand, but continued walking back and forth without fear of any injury. Now the lord began to feel Leopardo was getting up his nose, as they say, and, seeing that half-measures were useless, he had him summoned one fine afternoon and told him very clearly that he didn't keep his castle for the convenience of young men from

Cordovado, and that when Leopardo was in heat he should look to relieve himself with other maidens besides those of Venchieredo, and that if he wanted to bring a good beating upon himself, he merely had to turn up that evening for his usual tryst and he would get as much as he wished.

Leopardo bowed once again and said not a word, but that evening he didn't fail to come to visit Doretta, who, it must be said, was so proud to see him dare stir up a tempest on her behalf that she was doubly tender with him. Gaetano quivered with rage, his master cast a beady eye on everyone, even his dogs, and everything seemed to indicate they were plotting some nasty trick. And indeed one fine night (the very one when la Pisana came to me, after I had returned to Fratta on horseback with that mystery man) Leopardo, having taken leave of his sweetheart, was climbing over the hedgerow to go back to Cordovado when three evil fellows leapt on him and began to beat him with their knife handles, and he was thrown to the ground, overwhelmed by the sudden attack and unable to defend himself. But just at that moment, a wild black shape leapt out of the hedgerow and began to hammer at the assassins with the butt of his gun, so vigorously that it was their turn to defend themselves, and Leopardo, recovering from his initial shock, soon began to deliver some blows himself.

'You filthy dogs! You'll get it now!' the new arrival shouted, chasing those three rowdies towards the castle bridge.

But they ran so fast that he and Leopardo didn't reach them until they were just at the castle gate. Fortunately this was barred, and so however much the three shouted for the gate to be opened right away, they had plenty of time to receive a few blows. As soon as the porter got it partly open, they hurled themselves inside the hatchway like fugitives from the Devil.

'To hell with you! I know you!' said one of the them – Gaetano, in fact. 'You are Spaccafumo and you will pay dearly for your presumption and for interfering in matters that don't concern you!'

'Yes indeed, I am Spaccafumo,' the other shouted from outside, 'and I am not afraid of you, nor of your ill-born master, nor of all the thousands of others like you!'

'You heard that! You heard that!' said Gaetano, securing the gate with heavy chains. 'God is my witness: the master will have him hanged!'

'Perhaps, but first I'll string you up!' replied Spaccafumo, turning to go with Leopardo, who was still reluctant to move from that gate barred in his face.

The smuggler now went behind the hedgerow and untied his horse, offering to accompany the young man to Cordovado.

'How is it that you happened to appear just at the right moment?' asked Leopardo, who was feeling more ashamed than pleased to owe his skin to another's assistance.

'Hah! I'd already got wind of what was going to happen and so made it my business to be there,' said Spaccafumo.

'Scoundrels, brutes, traitors,' the young man snorted.

'Silence! It is their job,' said Spaccafumo. 'Let's talk of other things, if you will. How do I strike you in my guise as a horseman? A while ago I decided to give my legs a rest (for they are no longer so young) and so I've replaced them with that special breed of colts that pasture around the laguna. Today it was this one's turn and we made it from below Lugugnana to here in less than an hour – and we even carried a boy who was lost in the marshes back to Fratta.'

'You'll tell me how you came to know of their plot,' said Leopardo, who was still stewing over the nasty turn events had taken that night.

'No, I'll tell you nothing,' replied Spaccafumo, 'and now that you have arrived at your doorstep, I bid you farewell. We'll meet again soon.'

'What? You won't come in and sleep at our house?'

'No, the air here doesn't agree with me.'

And with that Spaccafumo and his horse were off and I couldn't say where he spent that night. The next day at noon, however, he was seen visiting the Chaplain of Fratta, his spiritual father, who was said to receive him with great respect, because he was terrified of him. Later that day four ruffians from Venchieredo turned up at Fratta looking for him and, hearing he was with the Chaplain, went straight to the rectory. They knocked and they knocked, they shouted and shouted and finally a very sleepy Chaplain came to open up and asked what they wanted, all innocence.

'Oh, what do we want?' said Gaetano furiously, dashing out into the fields behind the rectory, where a man could be seen galloping off on horseback. 'That's what we're looking for! Come along, hurry, boys! The Chaplain will make it up to us later.'

The poor priest, faint with terror, collapsed into a chair, while the four *buli* raced off across the furrows in hopes the orchard rows and the ditches would slow down the fugitive's progress. But the way the peasants saw it, Spaccafumo was not a man to let himself be captured on foot, and even less to let such a misfortune happen now that he was fleeing on horseback. So the esteemed *buli* were wasting their breath.

Back at the Castle of Fratta, these matters were already known and being treated as grave and inexplicable happenings when we three – la Pisana, the druggist's lad and I – came back. The Count and the Clerk were running up and down in search of the Captain and Marchetto; Fulgenzio had raced up the bell tower and was tolling the alarm as if the hayloft were on fire; Monsignor Orlando was rubbing his eyes and asking what was the matter; the Countess bustled around, ordering that the doors and windows be barred and the fortress readied to defend itself. In God's good time the Captain appeared with three men, two muskets and a blunderbuss, and they lined up in the courtyard to await his Excellency's orders. His Excellency commanded them to proceed to the square to see whether order had been disturbed and to offer assistance to other authorities against all criminals, and especially against the afore-mentioned Spaccafumo. A grumbling Germano let down the drawbridge and the brave troops went out into the countryside.

But the good Spaccafumo had no intention of showing himself that day in the piazza at Fratta, and with all that the Captain flaunted his ugly face and twirled his moustaches in the tavern doorway, no one came forward who dared to defy such a very menacing frown. It was a source of great pride to the Captain, and when the *buli* of Venchieredo came back that evening from their futile chase as worn out and deflated as hunting hounds, he didn't fail to make much of it. A scornful laugh was Gaetano's not very polite response, whereupon the three Cernide of Fratta took fright and disappeared into the tavern, abandoning their boss. But the Captain was a man of sword and law book, and was able to mount a fair defence against Gaetano's insults, pretending to have learned just at that moment that Spaccafumo had escaped on horseback over the fields. The way the Captain told it, he expected that scoundrel to leap out of his hiding place at any moment, and then he would make him pay dearly for his affront to the noble lord and magistrate of Venchieredo. To such foolish bluster Gaetano could only reply that his master was more than able to extract payment all by himself, and would they tell the Chaplain they would take care of settling the bill for Spaccafumo's overnight stay?

No one dared to leave the Castle that afternoon, and so la Pisana and I spent some fairly dull and nasty hours bickering in the courtyard with Fulgenzio's children and the Steward's brats. That evening, each time someone came to the gate, Germano questioned them sharply from inside, and only when he heard the reply did he lower the drawbridge. The rusty chains squeaked on their pulleys, as if annoyed to have been put to work after so many years of pleasant ease, and all who walked over the wobbling planks looked down uncertainly through the cracks. Lucilio and Partistagno both stayed later than usual that evening, their laughter barely sufficient to calm the nerves of the Countess, who saw the entire domain of Fratta already up in flames as a result of the hostilities between Spaccafumo and the Count of Venchieredo.

The next day, Sunday, there were other, striking new developments in town. At half past seven, just as the population was returning from Mass at Teglio, a great clatter of hoof-beats was heard and the lord of Venchieredo showed up in the piazza with three of his *buli*. Red-haired, sturdy and middle-aged, the Count of Venchieredo (from his eyes you couldn't divine whether he was more devious or more cruel) was certainly very arrogant, as his voice and manner attested. He halted his horse abruptly, and rudely inquired where the Reverend Chaplain of

Fratta lived; the rectory was pointed out and he stomped through the door in lordly style, handing the reins to Gaetano, who was stuck to his side like a shadow.

The Chaplain had just been shaved and the maid was now trimming his tonsure. They were at work in the kitchen, and the poor fellow, having recovered somewhat from his fright the day before, was teasing Giustina, telling her to shear his noddle well, not like the last time when the whole church burst out laughing after he took off his biretta. Giustina, however, was so intent on her task that she didn't even reply to his jests, but a shear here and a shave there, the tonsure was getting larger, a drop of oil expanding on the priest's poor head, and although he had made clear it was not to be larger than a half ducat, there was by now no coin in the realm big enough to cover it.

'Ah Giustina, Giustina,' sighed the Chaplain, one hand exploring the extent of his new tonsure, 'I think we're quite close to this ear.'

'No doubt about that!' replied Giustina, who was about thirty years old but looked forty-five, a good peasant woman if a maladroit barber. 'If we're close to this ear, we'll not be far from the other.'

'O Lord be with me! Do you mean to pluck me like a friar?'

'No, no, I've never plucked you!' she replied. 'And I won't pluck you today, either!'

'I tell you, stop! Let it be! That's enough!'

'It's not enough, let me finish! Be silent and don't move for a moment.'

'Oh, you women are the Devil!' murmured the Chaplain. 'Little by little, you'd be capable of persuading us to shave our . . .'

We can only guess what he might have said after 'shave our' if he hadn't stopped, hearing a clicking noise at the door, like spurs. He leapt up, pushed Giustina away, pulled the towel from his neck, and, wheeling around, found himself face to face with the lord of Venchieredo. Oh what a face! What eyes! What a figure did the poor priest cut then. Well, you can imagine! He stood there stock still in that awkward state of curiosity, terror and astonishment in which the ominous appearance of Venchieredo had surprised him; his towel fell to the floor and his hands, between the folds of his jacket and his thighs, were fumbling around in a way that clearly said 'We're done for!'

'Well, my dearest Chaplain! And how is your health?' Venchieredo began.

'Hmm, I don't know . . . That is, please come in, it's my pleasure,' the priest stammered.

'It doesn't look like a very great pleasure,' the other said. 'Your face is whiter than your collar, Reverend. Or maybe,' he went on with a mocking glance towards Giustina, 'I'm distracting you from some canonical business?'

'Oh not at all!' the Chaplain said in a whisper. 'I was just . . . Giustina, put the water on for coffee – or perhaps chocolate? Would the Count . . . His Excellency . . . prefer chocolate?'

'You go look after the chickens. I want to speak to the Reverend alone,' Venchieredo went on.

Giustina didn't wait to be told twice, but slipped out to the courtyard, the razor still in her hand.

Now Venchieredo moved closer to the Chaplain and, taking his arm, dragged him towards the hearth, where the priest, without even thinking about it, found himself sitting on a bench.

'And now for our business,' the Chaplain's guest went on, sitting down to face him. 'A fire just lit doesn't harm the skin, even in summer, they say. Tell me in all good conscience, Reverend: are you a priest or a smuggler?'

The poor man felt a quiver run down his entire body and he twisted his face around so badly that however much he smoothed his collar or scratched his lips, he was unable to put it right.

'They are two quite different professions and I don't wish to make comparisons,' the other continued. 'I merely ask for my own information which of the two you intend to exercise. For priests we have alms, tithes and capons, while for smugglers we have firing squads, prison and hanging. But everyone is free to make his own choice and I don't say I would necessarily have chosen the priesthood. I would have thought, however, that the laws must forbid the double exercise of these professions. What's your view, Reverend?'

'Oh yes, sir . . . Excellency . . . I quite agree,' the priest stammered.

'Well, now then, let's get to the point,' Venchieredo continued. 'Are you a priest or a smuggler?'

'Excellency, you are joking!'

'Joking? I? Certainly not, Reverend. I rose at dawn and when that happens I am never in a mood to joke! I come to tell you loud and clear that if the Count of Fratta is unable to protect the interests of the Serenissima, I am here, not far away, and consider myself thoroughly capable of it. You welcome contraband and smugglers into your house . . . No, no, Reverend, there's no point in shaking your head, we even have witnesses, and, if needed, we can bring you to trial in court – or make an agreement with the Curia.'

'Oh Mercy!' exclaimed the Chaplain.

'Therefore,' said Venchieredo, 'as it doesn't please me one bit to have such bands of thieves nearby, I would ask you to make a change of venue as you desire, before it becomes necessary to make you change by force.'

'A change of venue? What do you mean? I should change venue? How is that? Please explain, Excellency!'

'Well, I mean that if you could obtain parish wages in the mountains, it would be a great delight to me.'

'In the mountains?' The Chaplain was ever more astonished. 'I, in the mountains? But that's impossible, Your Excellency! I don't even know where the mountains are!'

'Right over there,' said the other, pointing out of the window.

However, Venchieredo hadn't counted on the priest's extreme timidity. There are certain individuals – rough, simple, modest, but whole and uncomplicated – for whom timidity sometimes takes the place of courage, and so for the Chaplain, having to begin life anew in a new place with new people seemed a grimmer and more daunting fate than simply dying. He had been born in Fratta, his roots were there, and he felt that to tear him up and move him from that place was equivalent to a death sentence.

'No Excellency,' he said in a much firmer tone than he had spoken before. 'I will die in Fratta as I have lived, and as for the mountains, I doubt I will ever get there alive if I am sent there.'

'Very well,' the other said, getting up from his bench. 'You may get there dead, but I can assure you that one way or another an accomplice of Spaccafumo will not remain the Chaplain of Fratta.'

That said, the noble gentleman rattled his spurs loudly against the hearthstone and strode out of the rectory, followed by the priest with lowered head. The latter made a final bow as he watched the other mount his horse, and then went back inside to complain to Giustina, who had been eavesdropping on the entire conversation from behind the courtyard door.

'Oh no, they won't stow you away in the mountains!' the maid whimpered. 'Some terrible evil will strike you if you have to go so far away! And your souls: they are all here, aren't they? How will you answer the Good Lord on your day of reckoning?'

'Away from me with that razor in your hand, child!' the priest replied. 'And be silent, for I am surely not going to the mountains. They can put me in the stocks, but not in another parish, certainly not! Just imagine if at the tender age of forty years old I were to find myself among all new faces and had to begin again that struggle my life has been from infancy up until now! No, no, Giustina! I've said it and I'll say it again: I intend to die in Fratta and although it is a heavy cross that now falls on my neck, I will bear it with sainted grace. Oh, that fellow! What an ugly snout! But rather than move away I will bear even this and if he plays some terrible game on me, it won't be the worst thing. I'd rather deal with his *buli* than somebody else's! At least I know them, so I'll be less intimidated by their beatings.'

'Oh what are you saying?' the maid said. 'Those *buli* will be intimidated by *you*. What do you think, that a priest is just the head on a nail to be knocked about?'

'Little more than that, my child, little more than that, in these times of ours. But there's not much we can do!'

Just then the sacristan came in to say that everyone was waiting for the Mass to begin, and the poor man, remembering that he was already very late, rushed out to do his duty with his tonsure only half-finished. In vain, Giustina chased after him, razor in hand, all the way down to the piazza, and there the priest's crooked tonsure and Venchieredo's visit, on top of all the events of the day before, gave rise to many a choice comment.

The following day the Count of Fratta received a momentous letter from the lord of Venchieredo, in which the latter, not beating about the bush much, asked his illustrious colleague to evict the Chaplain in the briefest possible time, accusing the priest of a thousand crimes, among them defrauding the Serenissima of customs duties by storing the contraband of the most ruthless lowland smugglers. *The Inquisitors' statutes speak clearly*, the letter said: *heads are at stake. For money is like the blood of the State, and he who by his own negligence conspires to drain away that truly vital fluid, conspires against the State.*

It was obvious that Venchieredo had hit the right chord, and the Count of Fratta, hearing the Clerk read these opening verses, twisted and turned so much on his great armchair that his usual majesty was somewhat marred. As much as the Count would have liked to keep the matter secret, the Chaplain's summonsing, the visit he had received the previous morning, his great dismay, and the conversation with Giustina had spread the word across town and a genuine uproar had ensued. The Chaplain was loved by all as a good friend, and, furthermore, the people of Fratta, accustomed to their lord's paternalistic and Venetianesque rule, had this odd notion that they shouldn't let themselves be trodden upon. There was much muttering against the despotism of the lord of Venchieredo, and, to the Count's great dismay, even the inhabitants of the Castle itself, his stubborn, immodest servants and retainers, seemed to want to bring bad weather upon him. I had never seen the Count and the Clerk more stuck to one another than in those days; they looked like two flimsy beams leaning one against the other, hoping to ride out a storm, so that if one moved, the other felt he was falling and moved too, so as not to lose his balance. They tried various remedies to tame that perilous agitation of souls, but the medicine was always worse than the disease. The fruit seemed particularly tasty because it was forbidden, and tongues that were kept in check in the kitchen went wild in the piazza and the tavern.

It was Mastro Germano who groused the most about his former master's tyranny. The virulence of his invective and the boldness with which he defended the Chaplain had all but made him the ringleader of the revolt. Every evening, from his bench at the tavern, he loudly preached that this last representative of the common people, the priest, must not be removed. Those despots could rage as much as they liked, he said. There were all kinds of justice – and some past sins might very well come to light that would send the judges to jail and set the accused free.

Fulgenzio the sacristan, manoeuvring in that shameless way of his in these turbulent waters (inside the Castle his official manner was more prudent), never failed to prod Germano cautiously to learn just how much truth there was in those threatening insinuations of his. One evening, when the porter had drunk far more than he should, he prodded him so much that he lost all control and bellowed and shouted to the four winds that the lord of Venchieredo had better desist or, if not, he, a poor broom-pusher, would make known certain old stories that would be very bad news for the gentleman.

Fulgenzio could not have asked for more. He artfully changed the subject, so that the inebriate's words either went unnoticed or merely seemed the mad ranting of a drunkard. And then he went home to say the rosary with his wife and children. But the next day, which was market day at Portogruaro, he went out early and came back later than usual. He was even seen at the offices of the Vice-captain of justice, but because he was a sort of unofficial scrivener in the chancery that did not seem so very unusual. But the fact is that eight days later, when the Curia had already begun to move its wheels so that the Chaplain could be sent to take the mountain air, the Clerk of Fratta received precise and formal orders from Venice to halt any further action and to mount instead a secret inquisition of the person of one Mastro Germano, with regard to certain revelations of great importance to the Signoria that the man could and must provide about the past life of the Most Illustrious Lord and Magistrate of Venchieredo. A meteorite falling from the moon to interrupt the gay carousing of a band of merrymakers could not have produced more amazement and awe than this decree. The Count and the Clerk felt the ground give way under their feet, and because they had not thought to assume their usual reserve during their first, bewildered moments, the fears of the Countess and Monsignor – and the joy of the rest of the family celebrated in a thousand ways at the news – worsened their deplorable spirits three times over.

They were, unfortunately, in a hard place. On one side, the proximate, proven effrontery of a nobleman accustomed to scorn all laws, divine and human; on the other, the imperious, inexorable, arcane justice of the Venetian Inquisition. Over here, the hazard of sudden and fierce revenge; over there, the nightmare of secret, terrible, unimpeachable punishment; to the right, a fearful picture of *buli* armed to the teeth, of blunderbusses hidden behind the hedgerow; to the left, the sinister apparition of Messer Grande, deep dungeons, blazing hot prison cells, nooses, pincers and axes. The Count and the Clerk suffered a bad case of vertigo for forty-eight hours, but in the end, as perhaps was predictable, they decided to throw the sop to the biggest dog, for pleasing both of them or getting them to agree was not even a consideration. Here, I can't hide the fact that Partistagno's urging and Lucilio's wise counsel helped to tip the balance in that direction, and the Count felt just that little bit more secure knowing himself to be backed by such brave and sensible persons.

That didn't mean that Germano's trial wasn't veiled in the most impervious gloom of mystery – nor that the gloom was so impervious as to prevent curious eyes from peering through by force. In fact, it was immediately trumpeted around that Venchieredo's former *bulo*, terrified by the Inquisitor's decree, had come forward with certain old documents that did not corroborate his former master's perfect loyalty to the government of the Serenissima. And if upon these hypotheses (and let us be clear, they were no more than hypotheses, because after the trial began the Count, the Clerk and Germano, the only three involved, were all but deaf and dumb), if upon these hypotheses, castles were built in air, well, I leave that to you to imagine.

As you might suppose, one of the first to learn of these developments was Venchieredo himself, and it seems that his conscience was not entirely clear, for his first reaction was a much greater fright and unease than he would subsequently reveal. He thought about it, considered it, weighed it and thought about it again, and at last, one fine day when they had all just risen from the table at Fratta, his visit was announced to the Count. At the mention of his name I believe the Chaplain, who was in the kitchen, came near to having a fainting fit, while the Count sought counsel in the eyes of his fellow diners, no less astonished and no more certain than his own, and then, stammering, told the serving man to show the visitor into the sitting room upstairs, and that he and the Clerk would be up immediately. There were too many risks, threats and displeasures pending on the visit to even hope to withdraw into a prior advisory council, and, what is more, the two gentlemen were not really bright enough to make such a deliberation in two minutes. And so, resignedly, they put their heads in the sack and went upstairs to face the fearful arrogance and the no-less fearful cunning of their all-powerful neighbour. The family remained in the dining hall, hearts pounding like that of the family of Regulus[6] as the Senate deliberated whether to keep him in Rome or send him back to Carthage.

'Your humble servant!' Venchieredo shot out, as soon as the Count and his shadow set foot in the hall. He then threw a glance at the shadow that turned the latter very much darker and more livid.

'Your Excellency's most humble servant!' replied the Count without lifting his eyes from the floor, where he seemed to be searching for inspiration to get him out of this mess. When inspiration did not rescue him, he turned around to seek enlightenment from the Clerk, and felt very uneasy, seeing that the man had retreated right back to the wall. 'My good man,' he tried to continue, addressing the Clerk.

But Venchieredo cut him short.

'It is pointless,' he said, 'pointless that the Clerk be distracted from his usual business to waste time listening to our chatter. As we know, he has in hand some very important trials that demand diligent examination and rapid prosecution. The good of the

Signoria comes before all, even before life itself, is that not so, my good man of the chancery? In the meantime you can leave us here in private, for our conversation has nothing to do with legal matters and we can dispose of everything ourselves.'

The Clerk had barely the strength to drag his legs out of the room and his crossed eye was so far off true that he hit his nose on the door latch going out. The Count made him a last, silent and impotent gesture of entreaty, fear and desperation, a gesture like the arms of a drowning man who seems to gasp for air before he abandons himself to the current. But when the door closed the Count straightened his *zimarra* and its scarlet braid and raised his eyes cautiously, as if to say, 'Well then, let me wear it with dignity!'

'It is a pleasure to me that you welcome me so confidentially,' said Venchieredo. 'I can see we shall end up in agreement. You have done well, because in fact I come to discuss a private matter. I believe we understand each other, do we not?' the old fox said, coming closer to take his hand slyly.

The Count, somewhat relieved by this sign of affection, waited slightly impatiently until the handshake was done, and as soon as his hand was free he thrust it into his pocket. I think he couldn't wait to go and wash it, to be sure the Vice-captain would not smell that handshake all the way from Portogruaro.

'Yes, sir,' he said, producing a bungled little smile that made two tears fall from his eyes with the effort. 'Yes, sir, I believe . . . That is . . . we have always understood each other!'

'Well said, by God,' said the other, sitting down in an armchair beside him. 'We have always understood each other and we'll understand each other this time, too, in spite of various meddlers! We of the nobility, whatever our differences of manners, ties or temperament, nonetheless have common interests, and a wrong done to one of our members is a wrong to all. And so we must remain united and give each other a hand, and do what we can to keep our privileges intact. Justice is all very well, indeed *very* well – for those who have need of it. I find that I want justice in my own house, but that anyone who wants it at my expense annoys me dreadfully. Is it not true, my dear sir, that you also dislike the presumption of those who seek to interfere in our affairs?'

'Oh, no . . . Yes . . . It is all quite clear!' stammered the Count, who had also sat down, quite mechanically, and out of all his visitor's words had only grasped confused sounds and a droning noise, like a millstone grinding in his ears.

'What is more,' Venchieredo went on, 'the justice of these others is often neither expeditious nor well served, and that fellow who would obey it like a sheep may find himself facing someone of different views, someone who commands another sort of justice that is much more rapid and effective!'

These remarks, pronounced one after the other and (I ought to add) emphasized by the hard and uncompromising tone of the speaker, shook the Count's ears deeply and forced on his face a look that was either scandalized or terrified, for having understood them. But since to take offence might expose him to unpleasant clarifications, he chose the path of diplomacy, producing for a second time that smile, which obeyed him less unwillingly than before.

'I see that you have understood me,' the other continued, 'and that you are capable of weighing the force of my arguments, and that the favour I've come to ask will therefore seem neither strange nor excessive.'

The Count's eyes widened and he withdrew his hand from his pocket to place it on his heart.

'Some evil tongue, some miserable, lying tattletale to whom I intend to give a whipping, have no doubt,' Venchieredo went on, 'has done me the favour of blackening my name with the Signoria for some old foolishness that doesn't even deserve to be remembered. Trifles and trickery, everyone agrees; but they must proceed with the case so as not to contravene their regulations. You understand, were they to overlook frivolous denunciations, they might then neglect the greater ones; having adopted a rule, they must accept all the consequences. In short, I know for certain that it was ordered down there to take up this trial only very unwillingly. You understand me . . . that secret document . . . that Mastro Germano is responsible for . . .'

'If only the Clerk were here . . . ,' murmured the Count of Fratta, a ray of hope lighting up his face.

'No, no, I do not wish the trial to be blabbed about,' replied Venchieredo. 'I merely want to remind you that it was not because of any suspicions about me, nor because the matter was important, that the decree was issued, but merely out of habits of good government. It's quite pointless that I should dwell on it further. And even Venice, it seems, would not be unhappy to put an end to this business. It always happens, when applying the law, that one must soften and correct whatever is too rough and too broad in the rules of state. Now, my dear sir, it is up to us, between good friends as it were, to interpret the tacit intentions of the Inquisitors. The spirit – you know this better than I do – goes before the letter; and I can assure you that if here, the letter commands you go forward, the spirit advises you to cancel it all with a stroke of the pen. In confidence, I've even had communications along these lines from Venice, and you can probably guess by what means. With an honest compromise . . . with some happy medium, one could . . .'

The Count's eyes widened even further and his fingers tortured the lace on his shirt, and at this point all the breath he had forced into his breast in his great agitation came out in a noisy snort.

'Oh, don't be intimidated by all this!' the other went on. 'It is all much simpler than you think. And even if it were difficult, we would have to try, so as to obey the spirit, the intentions, of the Most Serene Council of Ten. The spirit, remember, not the letter! For the Serenissima cannot wish that an excellent gentleman, such as you are, should suddenly find himself in grave embarrassment for having followed too faithfully the literal meaning of a decree. Can you imagine? Setting one lord in conflict with all his peers! It would be most ungrateful of them. It would be an unpardonable wrong against you!'

The poor Count, who understood these comments wondrously well, with all that acumen fear provides, had cold sweat running down his temples, like wax dripping from a taper on a procession day. The need to reply, the wish to say neither yes nor no, was such a torment to him that he would have gladly given up all the privileges of his noble rank to be free of it. But finally, it occurred to him there might be a way out. How brilliant he was! He had actually discovered something never before tried!

'Well . . . with time . . . we shall see . . . We shall work something out . . .'

'Bah! Time waits for no man!' Now Venchieredo leapt up in a real rage. 'For no man, my good Count! I, for example, if I were you, I would say immediately and for my own good reasons, "Tomorrow, this trial will no longer be spoken of."'

'I don't understand! How is that possible?' the Count exclaimed.

'Aha, I see we are once again beginning to understand one another,' Venchieredo continued, 'for he who is looking for the means is already persuaded of the rule. And the means are at hand. Insofar as you, my dear Count, agree (as duty compels) to satisfy the secret wishes of the Council of Ten. And mine!'

That *mine* came out like the explosion of a blunderbuss.

'Just imagine! I couldn't agree more!' the poor fellow stammered. 'When you assure me that even those above us wish the same . . .'

'Certainly, it's the lesser evil,' Venchieredo went on. 'Of course it's understood that all must happen by chance: that's the key. A word to Germano, you understand . . . a pinch of tinder and the flint-steel, and that will be the end of those papers.'

'And the Clerk?'

'He will say nothing, have no fear! I'll have a word with him, too. It is thus that those in high places desire, and thus I desire – not that the matter could have any harmful consequences for me, but it would grieve me to have to make reprisals against a man of your merits. Venchieredo brought to trial by one of his peers? Can you imagine? The code of honour does not permit it. I shall press to have the trial transferred elsewhere – to Udine, or some such place – and there I shall clear myself, there I shall defend my name. Here, as you can see, that would be impossible, and I will not tolerate it, I must not tolerate it when the cost is not one, but one thousand, dead!'

The Count of Fratta was trembling from head to foot, but by now he was accustomed to that troublesome quaking and found the breath to reply: 'Very well, Excellency, but might one not actually send those meaningless papers to Venice?'

'Piddle,' Venchieredo hastened to interrupt. 'Didn't I say I want them burned? What I mean is, as they are meaningless, there's no reason to trouble the postal courier with them.'

'If that is so,' the Count said in a faint voice, 'if that is so, we shall burn them . . . tomorrow.'

'We shall burn them immediately,' Venchieredo said, raising himself from his chair.

'Immediately? Immediately, you wish?' The Count raised his eyes, for he felt not the slightest desire just then to raise himself from his chair. We may suppose, however, that the face of his interlocutor was quite expressive indeed, for he added straight away, 'Yes, yes, you are right! Immediately! They must be burned immediately!'

And now he stood up with great effort and moved towards the door, hardly knowing in which world he found himself. But just as he touched the latch, a meek, whining voice spoke up, asking permission to enter, and then the humble Fulgenzio came into the room with an envelope in his hand.

'What is the matter with you? What is it? Who told you to come in?'

'The Bailiff has come back from Portogruaro with this very urgent message from the Signoria,' said Fulgenzio.

'Oh, be off! That is business for tomorrow!' said Venchieredo, looking somewhat pale and taking a step beyond the door.

'Begging pardon of their Excellencies,' Fulgenzio said, 'but the order is binding. To be read immediately!'

'Oh, poor me . . . Yes, I'll read it right away,' the Count said, putting his glasses on his nose and opening the envelope. But no sooner had he cast an eye on its contents than such trembling ran through his person that he had to lean against the door frame to keep his legs upright. Meanwhile, Venchieredo had also got a glimpse of those papers and guessed their content.

'I see we shall not reach an understanding today, my dear Count,' he said in his usual high-handed way. 'You had best put yourself under the protection of the Council of Ten and of Sant'Antonio! My pleasure to have paid you my respects.'

Having said this, he went down the stairs, leaving the Count of Fratta completely befuddled.

'Is it true? Has he gone?' he said when he had recovered from his state of confusion.

'Yes, Excellency! He has gone!' said Fulgenzio.

'Well, well, what do they write to me?' said the Count, handing the papers to the sacristan.

Not much surprised, he saw there a formal mandate to arrest Venchieredo as soon as the occasion arose to do so without causing any disorders.

'Now he's left, he's good and left, and it is not my fault if I cannot stop him,' said the Count. 'You are my witness that he left before I had fully understood the meaning of these papers.'

'Your Excellency, I shall be the witness of anything you command!'

'Still, it would have been better if the Bailiff had come a half hour later . . .'

Fulgenzio smiled to himself, and the Count went off to find the Clerk to let him know about this new and terrible predicament.

Fulgenzio's identity, and his functions, I shall leave you to guess as I did myself. There were many similar cases in which the Signoria of Venice employed the humblest of servants to keep an eye on the loyalty and zeal of their masters. As for Venchieredo, despite his great hauteur, the message left him in a frank state of terror, for he understood instantly that they meant to finish him off without mercy, and so, at first, the arguments of fear won out. But soon enough he was back, trusting in his own guile and cunning, and in his powerful connections, and in the government's weakness, and then suddenly he was once again looking for ways out. His first idea was to run away to Illyria,[7] and we shall see whether he was right or wrong not to pursue it. But then he began to think that it would not be so easy to capture him without a great fuss being raised, and if the worst came to the worst, he could always flee across the Isonzo any time it seemed necessary. The thought that he could avenge himself in one blow on Fulgenzio, the Chaplain, Spaccafumo and the Count, and perhaps even make the Signoria show some respect, won over that stormy, ferocious soul. And so it was that fear drove him to become even more rash.

FIVE

The last siege of the Castle of Fratta in 1786 and my first accomplishments. The happiness of two lovers, the anxiety of two monsignori, the peculiar behaviour of two Capuchin friars. Germano, porter of Fratta, is killed; the lord of Venchieredo goes to jail, Leopardo Provedoni takes a wife, and I study Latin. Of them all, it seems I am not the most unfortunate.

Here is the truth of the story of my life, as it is of all lives, I believe. It begins all alone in a cradle; it joins, strays from, commingles with the great throng of human affairs; and it ends up once again alone, rich only with sorrows and memories, approaching the peace of the grave. So the waters that irrigate fertile Lombardy spring from some Alpine lake or some torrent on the plains to divide and subdivide and break up into a hundred streams, a thousand tiny rills and freshets; and then further on those waters meet once again in a single, slow, silent, pale current that becomes the Po. Is this heartening or discouraging? Modesty demands I call it heartening, for my own case would be of little moment, my thoughts, my reversals, my twists and turns unworthy of study, if they were not woven into the stories of other men who found themselves on the same path as me, who briefly travelled with me on our pilgrimage of this world.

But are these the *Confessions* I set out to write? Or are they not more like those of the foolish woman who tells the priest, instead of her own sins, those of her husband or her mother-in-law, or all the tittle-tattle of the village? Well, so be it! A man is so much part of the century in which he lives that he cannot reveal his own innermost soul without also passing judgement on the generation to which he belongs. Just as our notions of time and space lose themselves in infinity, so on every side, man loses himself in humanity. Egoism, self-interest, religion: these provide a brake, but are not enough; our philosophy may work in practice, but the inescapable wisdom of primitive India overwhelms our boastful little systems with the great truths of eternal metaphysics.[1]

Now, in the meantime, you will have noticed that in this account of my childhood the characters have begun to multiply around me in a terrifying way. I myself am frightened, like that witch who was frightened by the devils she so foolishly summoned. An entire phalanx has appeared to march alongside me, and the noise and the chatter it makes is badly inhibiting me in my haste to go forward. Have no doubt, though: if life is not a pitched battle, it is, however, a tangle of daily skirmishes and tussles. Those phalanxes do not fall in ranks as if brought down by cannon fire, but are broken, decimated and destroyed by desertion, ambush and disease. Our companions of youth abandon us one by one to the other (rarer, more cautious and more self-interested) friendships of manhood. From here to the desert of old age is but a short step full of grief and tears. Let us not hurry matters, my friends! After I've walked you round and round in the cheerful, various, densely populated labyrinth of my younger years, you will end up sitting in an armchair where an old man who can barely move his legs nonetheless – with some courage and much thought – invests his hopes in a future that goes far beyond the tomb.

But for now let me show you the old world, the one still playing its childish games at the end of the last century, before the magical life force of the French Revolution renewed both flesh and spirit. The people of those times were different from us today: look at them and imitate them in that little that was good; correct them in all that was not. A survivor of that brood, I have the right to speak plainly and you will have the right to judge us after I have spoken.

Just a few days (I no longer remember exactly how many) after the strained encounter between Venchieredo and the Count, the village of Fratta was disturbed one evening by a sudden invasion. First came rough country folk and bandits on the run, followed by Cernide, *buli* and bailiffs, who were chasing them every which way, shouting in the piazza, thrashing peasants in their path and making the greatest uproar imaginable. At the first murmurs from that rabble the Countess, who had gone out for her afternoon walk with Monsignor di Sant'Andrea and Rosa, hurried back to close herself up in the Castle, and had her husband awakened so he could see what was going on. The Count (who for a week had been sleeping with only a single eye shut) went rushing down to the kitchen, and soon thereafter the Clerk, Monsignor Orlando, Marchetto, Fulgenzio, the Steward and the Captain had gathered round him, showing the world's most terrified faces. By now everyone had understood that it would not be very easy to return to the peace and tranquility of before, and each new wave of the storm doubled their fear, just as a hint of a relapse terrifies the convalescent. Once again that evening it was Captain Sandracca's turn to play the lion-hearted and leave the Castle, three of his men by his side. But not five minutes had gone by than they were back with their tails between their legs and little desire to try again.

That band rioting in the square were Venchieredo's guardsmen and they didn't seem at all disposed to retreat. From their headquarters at the tavern Gaetano swore and swore again that he would cut the smugglers to pieces and that any who hid in the Castle would be treated even more harshly. According to him, there was a league in town set up to defraud the tax officers, and the Chaplain and the Count were the ringleaders. But now the time had come to exterminate that band of thieves, and because those who should be enforcing the law had shown themselves to be the law's worst enemies, it was up to him and his friends to make the Signoria's decrees stick and show their own great merits in the process.

'Germano! Germano! Raise the drawbridge and bar the gate well!' the Count began to shriek when he learned of this long-winded list of insults and invention.

'I've already raised the bridge, Excellency!' shouted the Captain. 'And for greater safety I had it thrown into the moat by three of my men, because the pulleys weren't hauling well.'

'Excellent, excellent! Close the windows and chain all the doors,' the Count added. 'Let no one dare leave the Castle.'

'I defy anyone to leave now that the bridge is down,' the Bailiff observed.

'I believe the bridge behind the stables will provide us an attack route in case of need,' observed the Captain sagely.

'No, no, I don't want any attacks!' the Count began to shout again. 'Knock down the bridge behind the stables as well! I now declare this Castle in a state of siege.'

'May I point out to his Excellency that once that bridge is down there will be no exit from which to go out and acquire the day's provisions?' said the Steward with a bow.

'It doesn't matter! My husband is right!' said the Countess, who was the most frightened of all. 'You just obey and destroy the stable bridge right away; there is no time to lose. We may be assassinated from one moment to the next here!'

The Steward bowed even lower and went out to take care of the task assigned. A quarter of an hour later communications between the Castle of Fratta and the rest of the world were completely cut off and the Count and the Countess breathed easier. Only Monsignor Orlando, who was by no means a hero, dared to show any uneasiness about the problems of procuring the usual quantities of beef and veal for the morrow. The Count, hearing his brother's laments, thus had an opportunity to show off the sharpness and speed of his administrative skills.

'Fulgenzio,' said he in a solemn voice, 'how many piglets has your sow?'

'Ten, Excellency,' replied the sacristan.

'Well then, we have provisions for the entire week,' replied the Count, 'for the pond will supply us for the two fish days.'

Monsignor Orlando sighed miserably, thinking about those lovely sea bream from Marano and those succulent Caorle eels. Alas, there was no comparison between them and the muddy little fish and frogs from the pond.

'Fulgenzio,' the Count went on, 'have two of your suckling pigs killed; one to be stewed and one to be roasted. Do you understand, Margherita?'[2]

Fulgenzio and the cook now bowed one after the other, but then it was the turn of Monsignor di Sant'Andrea to sigh, for on account of an intestinal ailment he could not digest pork and the prospect of a week-long siege on such a regimen did not appeal to him at all. But the Countess, who had read the distress on his face, hurried to assure him they would put aside a pullet hen to stew for him. The prelate's face then brightened to saintly serenity, for with a decent hen coop even a week's siege would only be a mild purgatory. Finally, when the orders had been imparted to take care of this vital kitchen business, the garrison broke ranks to ready the fortress to defend itself. Some ancient muskets were stuck through the embrasures; two dusty old catapults were dragged into the courtyard, and the doors and balconies were barred. Finally, the bell was rung to say the rosary and none said it with more conviction than on that evening.

The Countess was much too taken with her own worries at that moment to concern herself with anyone else, but when the daylight began to fail, her mother-in-law asked what had become of Clara, who was very late in bringing her usual bread and milk. Faustina, la Pisana and I called and searched for her up and down, but we could find her nowhere. The only one who had seen her was the gardener, who said she'd gone over the bridge by the stables some two hours before, but that was all he knew and he thought she had probably returned to the Castle by the front gate with the Countess, as she usually did. However, it was clear she couldn't have come in that way, for the Steward had carried out his orders so thoroughly that no sign of the bridge remained. By now it was getting very dark and it was obvious she could not be still roaming around outside. And so we began to search for her again, and only after another hour of meticulous and fruitless searching of the Castle did Faustina decide to go down to the kitchen to relay the unhappy news that the Contessina had disappeared.

'By Bacchus!' the Count exclaimed, 'those murderers have certainly carried her off!'

The Countess would have very much liked to weep and wail, but her own worries were too pressing.

'Just imagine,' her husband went on, 'what they're capable of, those wretched rogues who dare call me a smuggler just so they can turn the whole district upside down! They'll pay for this, oh yes they will!' he muttered softly, for fear someone outside might hear him.

'Oh, idle talk, nothing but idle talk!' the lady continued. 'Talk will do nothing but pile more wood on your pyre! Here we are, we've been caught in this trap for three hours and you have no idea how to get us out! They make off with your daughter and you waste your breath muttering that they will pay for it! For what she costs you, you won't get much from them!'

'What, my dear wife? For what she costs me? What do you mean to say?'

'Sharpen your wits if you don't understand. I mean to say that you give as much thought to your own children and myself and our health as you do to straightening the top of the bell tower' – here the Countess furiously inhaled a pinch of tobacco. 'Let's see what ideas you have for getting us out of this mess. How do you intend to search for Clara?'

'What the deuce? Behave yourself! Clara, little Clara . . . There's no reason to get so excited. You know how good and well behaved she is. My view is that even were she to spend a night outside the Castle, no harm would come to her. As for us, I hope you don't wish to bring the shotguns on us. (Here the Countess looked horrified and impatient.) So, therefore, we must try to parley.'

'Parley with thieves? Oh, by Diana, that's good!'

'Thieves? Who says they are thieves? They are officials of the court, perhaps slightly over-hasty, maybe somewhat drunk, if you will, but nonetheless vested with legal authority, and when this folly is finished, they'll listen to reason. They were merely over-zealous about chasing some smugglers, and the wine went to their heads and they became convinced that the criminals were hiding out in Fratta. What's so strange about that? Once we persuade them that there has never been a trace of smugglers here, they will go home as meek as lambs.'

'Excellency, you forget one thing,' interrupted Monsignor di Sant'Andrea. 'It seems that the fugitives here are really assassins disguised as smugglers, sent out ahead to create a pretext for a great scuffle. Germano says he recognized some Venchieredo criminals among them.'

'And what does this have to do with me? What am I to do about it?' the poor Count exclaimed in desperation.

'Well, in the meantime we could send someone out to study the situation in secret and find out about the Contessina,' the bailiff said.

'Oh heavens above!' said the Countess. 'That would be most unwise, for now that we are short of help here in the Castle, it is not the moment to send away those with experience!'

La Pisana, who was hunkered down with me between Martino's knees, came boldly forward towards the hearth and volunteered to go out and search for her sister, but they were all so distracted that no one beyond Marchetto even seemed to register that touching, childish act of bravery. But her example was by no means wasted, for then I, too, spoke up and offered to go out looking for Clara. And this time, the offer was heard by someone.

'Would you really take the chance of going out to have a look?' the Steward asked me.

'Certainly,' I said, raising my head and gazing proudly at la Pisana.

'We'll go together,' she said, wishing to show herself my equal.

'Oh no, this is no matter for a young lady,' said the Steward, 'but Carlino might just be able to slip out of any difficulties nicely. Isn't that right, Madam Countess, that it's a good idea?'

'For lack of anything better, I won't say no,' she replied. 'Here inside a boy isn't much use to us, and outside he wouldn't raise suspicions and could stick his nose in everywhere. The fact he's as insolent and disobedient as the Devil may for once be useful to him.'

'But I want to go out too! I want to look for Clara too!' la Pisana began to scream.

'You, young lady, will go to bed right away,' said the Countess, making a sign to Faustina to carry out the command immediately.

There followed a small battle with howling, scratching and biting, but Faustina triumphed and the little savage was carried off to bed.

'What shall I say to the elder Countess about the Contessina Clara?' the maid asked as she was departing to the sound of la Pisana's shrieks.

'Tell her she is lost, that we cannot find her; that she will be back tomorrow!' snapped the Countess.

'It might be better to let her think that her aunt from Cisterna came to get her, if I may so advise,' the Steward suggested.

'Yes, yes, make something up,' continued the Countess, 'so that she doesn't drive us to distraction, because we have enough problems already.'

Faustina went off and la Pisana could be heard howling down the corridor.

'As for you, little snake,' said the Steward, grabbing me ever so politely by the ear. 'Let us hear what use you will be to us when you are outside the Castle.'

'Well, I'll go out for a walk in the countryside, and then, as if by chance, I'll stop in at the tavern where those bad fellows are, and begin to cry and lament about not being able to go back inside the Castle, and I'll say I went out in the afternoon, along with the Contessina Clara, and got lost chasing butterflies and could no longer find her. And then anyone who knows anything will surely tell me, and I'll come back to the stables and let out a whistle, and the gardener will hand me a plank and I'll put it in the moat and cross it as I did when I went out.'

'That's excellent, you're a real warrior,' the Steward said.

'What's all this?' asked Martino, who was anxious about all these speeches he saw me making and had not really understood anything.

'I'm going out to search for the Contessina, who hasn't yet returned,' I said as loudly as I could.

'Very good, you do well,' he said, 'but please be very careful . . .'

'Not to compromise us,' said the Countess.

'And while you are at it, stay a while and listen to the comments of those bandits at the tavern to hear what their intentions are,' said the Count. 'That way we can prepare for further operations.'

'Yes, yes, and come back quickly little one,' said the Countess, kindly patting those unfortunate hairs on my head that had so often been treated otherwise. 'Go, observe and come back to report what you see faithfully! That the Lord made you so cunning and bold is all to our benefit. Go now and may the Lord bless you, and remember we are here waiting for you in great agitation.'

'I shall be back as soon as I have guessed anything,' said I, self-confidently, for already I felt myself to be a man in that company of rabbits.

Marchetto, Martino and the Steward came out with me, offering encouragement and counselling me to be cautious and prudent. A plank was tossed into the moat, and I, who was pretty good at this sort of navigation, arrived happily on the other side, and, giving it a push with one hand, sent the raft back to them. And then, while they were saying a second rosary in the Castle kitchen at Monsignor Orlando's suggestion, I slipped into the night's thick shadows and set off on my brave expedition.

Clara, meanwhile, had indeed left by the back door of the Castle, as the gardener had reported, and still had not returned. Expecting to meet her mother along the road to Fossalta, she had walked all the way there, one foot after the other, without encountering a soul. At this point she wondered whether it was not later than she'd thought and whether the company from the Castle had perhaps returned while she was rounding the orchard on her way to the road. So she began walking quickly home herself, but she had not gone a stone's throw when the sound of footsteps behind her forced her to turn around. It was Lucilio, calm and thoughtful as always, but lit up in that moment by ill-concealed happiness (perhaps he did not even try to conceal it). He scarcely seemed to move, but he was at her side in a flash, and yet that flash was not as instantaneous as the desire of both would have it. Nothing exceeds the speed of thought: the steam engine already looks too slow, and one day electricity will seem lazier and duller than a coach horse. Believe me, it will happen, and in the last analysis the proportions will be the same, as they are in the picture enlarged by a lens. The fact is that the mind senses a dazzlingly high, distant and inaccessible world beyond itself, and our every circle, step and spiral that doesn't bring us closer to that paradise seems not movement, but sloth and tedium. What does it matter that we can go from Milan to Paris in thirty-six hours instead of two hundred? What difference does it make that we can see the four corners of the earth ten times in forty years, instead of just once? The earth does not grow larger or life longer as a result, and thinking too much will only take us beyond those limits into the infinite, the mystery without illumination.

That instant in which they approached each other seemed to Clara and Lucilio to last forever, while the time they walked together before reaching the first house of Fratta passed in a flash. And yet their feet moved forward quite reluctantly, without noticing how often they stopped along the way to talk of Clara's grandmother, of the lord of Venchieredo, of what they thought about them, but also of themselves, their feelings, the lovely sky above, which they found enchanting, and the beautiful sunset that made them stand in rapturous contemplation for a very long time.

'Ah, this is how I'd like to live!' said Clara innocently.

'How? Oh tell me immediately!' said Lucilio in his nicest voice. 'Let me see if I'm able to understand your desires and share them with you.'

'Well, I did say I would like to live like this,' said Clara, 'but I wouldn't know how to explain that wish. I'd like to see with the eyes of this splendid light from Heaven; hear with the ears of that happy and harmonious peace that engulfs nature when she is sleeping; feel with the heart and mind of those sweet thoughts of solidarity, those attachments without prejudice and without measure that seem to spring from this pageant of the simple and the sublime!'

'You would like to live that life that nature has prepared for men who are equal, judicious, innocent,' said Lucilio sadly. 'A life that in our dictionaries is defined as dream and poetry. Oh yes! I understand you perfectly, for I, too, breathe the sweet air of dreams and confide in the poetry of hope, not wanting to respond with hatred to injustice, with despair to grief. Look how badly we are equipped: he that has brawn has no brains;

he that has brains has no heart; and he that does have brains and heart has no authority. God is above us, and He's said to be just and prophetical. We, God's blind, unjust, enslaved children, deny Him constantly in our words, our writings and our deeds. We deny His providence, His justice, His omnipotence! It's a sorrow vast as the world, protracted as the centuries, that pushes us, chases us, brings us down, and that one fine day will make us recognize that we are all equal – all of us – but only in death!'

'Death, death! You must say in life, in that true life that endures forever!' said Clara, inspired. 'That is where God rises again and makes sense of earthly contradictions.'

'God must be everywhere,' said Lucilio in a tone that a devout man would have found lacking in the heat of faith. But Clara sensed no doubt in his words, as he very well knew she wouldn't or he would not have said them.

'Yes, God is everywhere,' said she with an angelic smile, gazing at all four corners of the heavens. 'Does he not see, hear and breathe everywhere? Right thoughts, kind feelings, sweet passions: if they don't come from him, where do they come from? Oh, I love my good Lord, the source of all beauty and all goodness!'

Now if ever there was an argument to persuade a doubter there was any truth in religion it was the heavenly look that shone on Clara's face just then. Immortality was written in divine light on her serene brow and no one would have dared say that nature had only provided such intelligence and sentiments, such beauty, as a breeding ground for worms. Yes, there are hard, stony faces; lewd, crooked glances; coarse and grovelling persons, whose filthy example can stir the materialists' fantasies and make them deny the eternity of the soul, as we deny eternity to animals and plants. But out of that crew of half-dead galley slaves come a few faces that seem to glow with divine light, and seeing them the sceptic can only stutter in confusion, unable to arrest that quivering in his heart that is either the hope or the terror of a future life. What life? the philosophers ask. Don't ask me, if you are one of those unfortunates who is not satisfied by that centuries-old wisdom we call faith.

Ask yourselves. But certainly, if organic matter, once divorced from human existence, continues to ferment and live its material life in the earth's womb, then why should not the thinking soul also continue to live its spiritual life in the great sea of thoughts? Why should movement, which never ceases in that whirring mechanism of veins and nerves, come to a halt in the limitless sphere of ideas?

In something close to ecstasy Lucilio stopped to admire his lovely companion. A blaze of light washed over his face and for the first time a feeling that was not his own, but was imposed on him by the feelings of another, penetrated the dark folds of his heart. He recovered, however, from that brief setback to become master of himself again. Sadly.

'Divine poetry!' he said, shifting his glance from the fine sunset now fading into dull twilight. 'The first who soared up to immortal dreams in poetry was mankind's true consoler. To teach men happiness we must train up poets, not scientists and anatomists.'

Clara smiled in sympathy and asked, 'Do I understand, Signor Lucilio, that you are not so very happy?'

'Oh yes, just now I am happier than I may ever be again!'

The young man suddenly took her hand. At that, the immortal splendour of faith disappeared from the girl's face and the sweet, tremulous light of sentiment glowed like a bright full moon emerging after sundown.

'Yes, happier than I may ever be again,' Lucilio went on, 'happy in my desires, for my desires are full of hope, and hope beckons at me from afar like a lovely garden in flower. But oh, do not pick those flowers, do not sever them from their slender stems! No matter how much care you take, they will begin to wither after three days, and after five will lose their lovely colour and their sweet perfume. And finally they will sink irrevocably into memory's tomb.'

'Oh no, do not call memory a tomb!' said Clara boldly. 'Memory is a temple, an altar! The bones of saints we worship are in the ground, but their virtues shine in Heaven. The flower loses its freshness and its perfume, but the memory of that flower stays in our souls as sweet and undecayed as ever!'

'Oh God, forever! Forever!' cried Lucilio, the vehemence of his feelings rushing in to fill up the solemnity of the moment. 'Yes, forever! Be it an instant, a year, an eternity, it must be filled up, satisfied, beatified by love! Oh yes, Clara, love seeks out the infinite by every means, and if there is a supreme and immortal part of us it is surely that. We must trust in love so as not to become clay before our time, so as not to lose the soul's natural poetry that alone makes life beautiful. Yes, I swear, I swear to remember always this rapture that makes me greater than myself! Desire so strong transmutes into faith; our love will live forever because really great things never die!'

His words, spoken in a deep, resounding voice, deliciously awakened Clara's confused desires. She was not terribly surprised, because the things she now heard had already been long imprinted on her heart. Lucilio's glances, his conversation, his patient, subtle priming, had prepared a secure place in her soul for that ardent declaration. To hear his lips repeat what her heart was expecting all unaware, suddenly woke in her a latent, timid joy. What happened in her soul was like what happens when the photographic plate touches the acid: the hidden image comes forth in all its particulars. And so if Clara was surprised at that moment it was because she was not really surprised at all. A mysterious, utterly new kind of agitation kept her from replying to the young man's passionate words, however; and as she sought to withdraw her hand from his, she looked about for something to lean on, for she felt herself swooning with delicious pleasure.

'Clara, Clara, please answer me!' said Lucilio, holding her up anxiously and looking around to see if there were anyone nearby. 'Just one word, answer me! Do not kill me with your silence; don't punish me with this show of your unhappiness! At least pardon me, at least that!'

He looked as if he might fall to his knees, he was so overcome, although perhaps it was just a studied gesture to force matters along. The young lady came to quickly and gave him a smile, her sole reply. One of those smiles a man could not but remember his whole life. A smile that begs compassion, promises happiness, that says all, pardons all: the smile of a soul giving herself to another soul; a smile that in no way reflects its worldly surroundings but glows with and for love only; a smile that encompasses or perhaps dismisses the entire world, that lives and makes another live all by itself; a smile that in a single flash opens and conjoins the mysterious depths of two souls in a single desire for love and eternity, a single sentiment of bliss and faith. The heavens revealing divine sights and indescribable splendour to the eyes of a saint could not be more enchanting than that meteor of happiness that races by, radiant (and sadly often fleeting) in the shape of a woman. It is a meteor, a flash: but in that flash the confused horizons of the future are more evident than in ten years of meditation and study.

And yet, how often after that flash disappears, does the clear sky of hope within us cloud and our thoughts plunge, cursing, into the great void, like unhappy Icarus when his waxen wings melted! So many rapid, painful flights from the empty ether where myriad spirits float in oceans of light, to the dead and frozen abyss that never sees a ray of sun, that will never in many centuries give birth to the spectre of a thought! Meanwhile, science, heir to a hundred generations, and pride, the fruit of four thousand years of history, flee like slaves caught stealing when feeling threatens to erupt. We poor, lost pilgrims: who are we? Where are we going? What guides us towards the right, the fortunate path? A thousand voices sound around us; a hundred mysterious hands point to even more mysterious paths; a fatal, hidden force pushes us left and right. Love, the winged Cupid, invites us to Paradise; love, the mocking devil, demolishes us. Our only comfort: the faith that sacrifice may lighten the burdens of the others.

But Lucilio? Ah, Lucilio was not thinking about all this. Thoughts follow happiness as night follows nightfall, as the frozen winter follows the golden, harmonious autumn. He had loved for years; for years he had directed his every thought, his every art, his every word, to stoking the pleasure of that moment in the distant future. For years the shrewd and patient

Lucilio had walked down a difficult, solitary road lit only here and there by a ray of hope. Slowly, tirelessly, he had approached that flowered height, from which he now looked down and possessed all the joy, the delight and the riches of this world. He was monarch of the universe. He had produced the philosopher's stone; laboriously mixing glances, actions and words to bring forth the pure gold of love and happiness. The victorious alchemist now tasted his delightful triumph with all his senses; the passionate, spirited artist could not get enough of his own work: that divine smile that glowed on Clara's face like a beautiful day dawning. Another's heart would have pounded with gratitude, devotion, fear. In him, pride swelled to unchecked, tyrannical joy. I (and thousands like me) would have given thanks tearfully; he rewarded Clara's acquiescence with a fiery kiss.

'You are mine! You are mine!' he said to her, raising her right hand to the heavens. He meant: 'I deserve you, because I have conquered you!'

Clara did not reply. Without knowing it and without speaking, she had loved him even before then, but the moment when love becomes aware of itself is not the moment when love speaks. All she knew was that for the first time she was utterly in another's power, which merely changed her smile from one of joy to one of hope. First she had been delighted for herself, now she was delighted for Lucilio; this second was easier, for it demanded only her sympathy, her modesty.

'Clara,' said Lucilio again. 'It is getting late and they will be expecting us at the Castle.'

The young lady roused herself as from a dream and, rubbing her eyes with her hand, felt they were wet with tears.

'Do you wish to go?' she asked in a faint, sweet voice that did not seem her own. Without a word, Lucilio set out on the road again with Clara by his side as meek and mild as a lamb with its mother ewe. The young man desired no more that day. Now that his treasure had been unveiled he wanted to enjoy it at length, as a miser does, not squander it producing more miracles and then find himself poorer than before, weighed down with faint memories.

'Will you always love me?' he asked after a few silent paces.

'Always!' she said. No angel's harp ever played a sweeter chord than that word pronounced by those lips. Love has Paganini's genius: harmony steeped in the soul's goodness.

'And when your family finds you a husband?' Lucilio's voice was pained and sharp.

'A husband!' the girl exclaimed, lowering her head.

'Oh yes,' said the other, 'they will sacrifice you to ambition; in the name of religion they will force you to accept a love that religion forbids in the name of nature.'

'Oh, no, I love no one but you,' replied Clara, who seemed to be speaking to herself more than anything.

'Swear it by all you hold sacred! Swear it by your God and by your grandmother's life!'

'Oh yes, I swear,' said Clara calmly. To swear what she felt an irresistible force compelled her to do, seemed quite simple and natural to her. Now they were able to see the first houses of Fratta through the darkness and Lucilio dropped her hand and walked respectfully by her side. But the die was cast; their two souls were joined forever. Self-restraint and tenacity on one side, meekness and mercy on the other: the two fused in love's blaze. Lucilio's will and Clara's abnegation were two sides of the same coin, like those twin stars that eternally approach one another in the heavens.

Two armed men came forward as they drew near the village, but Lucilio moved on, thinking they were two country guards waiting for someone. Then one of them ordered him to halt and told him it was forbidden to come into town that night. The young man was astonished and annoyed by such presumption and tried a technique he knew from experience never failed in these situations: raising his voice and berating the men. In vain! The two *buli* took him politely by the arms and told him that the police of the Signoria had ordered that no one be allowed to enter Fratta until they had finished investigating some smugglers they were seeking.

'I suppose, however, that you do not wish to prevent the Contessina Clara from returning to the Castle?' said Lucilio, glowering and pointing to the young lady (he was holding her tightly by the arm in protection). Clara made a move as if to calm his rage, but he paid no attention and repeated his threats to walk on. Now the two *buli* grabbed his arms again and warned him they had precise orders and were authorized to use force against all who disobeyed them.

'And I am permanently authorized to use force, and I use it quite a lot against bullies!' said Lucilio, ever more heated, breaking free of the guards' hold. But another movement on Clara's part persuaded him that such violence was dangerous and inopportune. He calmed himself and inquired of those two who they were and on what authority they prevented the lord's daughter from returning to the Castle. The men said they were Cernide militiamen from Venchieredo and that because they were chasing smugglers they were authorized to act beyond their jurisdiction, and that the proclamations of the authorities were very clear in this regard, and that in addition this was the order of their captain, and they were there to make sure it was respected. Lucilio wanted to protest further, but Clara humbly begged him to refrain, and so he turned back with her, unable to do much more than threaten the two *buli* and their master that he would bring down the full ire of the Representative and the Signoria on them (although he knew how little that was worth).

'Be silent! It is useless,' Clara whispered in his ear, drawing him away from the two guardsmen. 'Of course it is very late and they will be concerned about me at home, but if we take the long road around we should be able to enter by the stables.'

And so they headed out into the countryside to find the path to the back Castle gate, but they hadn't gone a hundred paces when they met another two guardsmen.

'We're under attack!' said Lucilio angrily. 'It's outrageous that a noblewoman should have to pass the night outdoors to satisfy the whims of some young scoundrels!'

'Watch your words, Illustrious One!' said one of the *buli* with a furious thump of his musket butt on the ground.

Young Lucilio, quivering with rage, had a hand on the trusty pistol in his pocket, but with his other hand he could feel Clara's arm trembling in terror, and thus, showing true courage, was able to restrain himself.

'Let us understand each other here,' he said, still infuriated. 'What will it take to get you to allow the Countess through? I don't suppose you think she is carrying some contraband?'

''Lustrious One, we don't think anything,' said the man, 'but even if we could close an eye and let her pass, the inhabitants of the Castle think differently. They've already knocked down both bridges, and so the Countess could not go in except by walking on water like St Peter.'

'Oh dear, but then the danger is very great!' said Clara weakly.

'It is nothing! Just panic! That's my opinion,' said Lucilio, and, turning to the *bulo* once again, asked, 'Where is your captain?'

'The 'Lustrious Captain is down at the tavern drinking up the best wine, while we're out here watching the bats,' said the fellow.

'Very well. I hope you won't decline to take us to the tavern so we can discuss matters with him.'

'Oh, well, we don't have any orders about that,' said the man, 'but it seems to me we might be able to help you, especially if Your Lordship would like to pay for a glass or two.'

'Look sharp then, and come with us!' said Lucilio.

And so the guardsman advised his companion to stay where he was and not fall asleep – advice of little cheer to one who had nothing to down but the fog, while his friend looked forward to a nice pitcher of Cividale wine. Grumbling, he resigned himself, however, and Clara and Lucilio once again set out for the village, preceded by the Cernide militiaman. This time the two guardsmen let them pass and soon they were at the tavern, where there was such a racket going on it sounded more like Carnival than a hunt for smugglers. Gaetano, having supplied his men with plenty to drink, was now offering wine to perfect strangers. And these, although they were slightly uncouth, did communicate perfectly with him in that silent and expressive language of theirs. Those who'd already been watered called their friends, and the company expanded and went on drinking. And so – stir it around once or twice – in half an hour the *buli* of Venchieredo had become one big happy family with the peasants of Fratta, and the tavern-keeper couldn't stop praising the magnificence and rare largesse of the ever so worthy captain of the Cernide of Venchieredo.

As you might expect, that magnificence was not without ulterior motive. The Count of Venchieredo himself had suggested it, to keep the local population quiet and prevent them from taking the side of the Count of Fratta against them. Gaetano was clever and his master's aims were well-served. Had he wanted to, he could have had three hundred drunkards shouting 'Long Live the Lord of Venchieredo!' And God only knows how the Castle of Fratta might have reacted to that menacing cry.

When Lucilio and Clara got to the tavern the revelry was at its height. The young lady would certainly have been aggrieved to see the family's most faithful tenants celebrating with Fratta's foremost enemies, but she didn't notice, and her surprise and shock at all the commotion prevented her from understanding. She feared that her family was in grave danger and wished she could be with them, not thinking that if they were in danger for being holed up inside a twenty-foot moat, her own situation was rather more serious, with just a single man to defend her against an entire rowdy mob.

Lucilio, however, was not inclined to let anyone tell him what to do. He went straight to Gaetano and ordered him in quite a high-handed way to allow the Contessina to return to the Castle. The *bulo*'s arrogance and the wine he had drunk made him flaunt his Head of Hundred title even more shamelessly than usual. He replied that the Castle was inhabited by a perverse breed of smugglers and that he had ordered they should be kept locked up until they had consigned the criminals and the stolen goods to him; and as for the Contessina, he would take care of her, because she was quite within his reach. Lucilio raised an arm to slap him for his impertinence, but halfway up he changed his mind and began to tug his moustaches furiously in the manner of Captain Sandracca.

The best he could do now was to leave that wild place and find somewhere secure where his companion could spend the night. But Clara disagreed and wanted at all costs to get to the

Castle bridge to see if it really was down. Lucilio went with her (although it seemed dangerous to venture out with a young maiden among all those drunken rogues roistering in the piazza), for he didn't want to be thought lacking in courage or to have missed any chance to take Clara home. But once they had seen the broken bridge and called for Germano a couple of times without reply, it seemed wise to leave in a hurry, because the commotion was growing steadily, and the *buli* were beginning to gather and provoke them with jeers and insults. It was costing Lucilio great pains to restrain himself, but the greater problem was how to keep the young lady safe and sound, and so he headed down a village side street and, taking the road for Venchieredo, strode quickly along to the meadow by the windmills, pulling her along behind. There they stopped so she could catch her breath.

Weary and morose, she sat down by a hedgerow and the young man bent over her to contemplate her pale face, upon which the newly risen moon seemed to reflect itself, enchanted. The dark turrets of the Castle rose before them and here and there a light escaped from the barred balconies, then hid itself like a star flickering in a stormy sky. The dark foliage of the poplars stirred lightly and the noise from the village, softened by the distance, interrupted not at all the nightingales' loud, amorous trilling. Glow-worms sparkled in the grass, the stars quivered in the sky and the moon's pale, slanting rays slid over vague, shadowy shapes. Nature's summer bridal bed was concealed behind shadows and silence, but her great palpitating heart from time to time released a breeze that promised fruit to come.

It was one of those hours when a man does not think but feels; that is, when he absorbs fine thoughts and deeds from the universe he belongs to. Lucilio, a thinking, sceptical soul par excellence, felt small despite himself in that deep and solemn stillness. Even the joy of love cast a long, sweet, melancholic futility over his soul. It seemed to him that his feelings expanded like a cloud of dust sped along by the wind: their shapes grew vague; their colours faded; he felt himself grow larger, but less strong; master of all, but not of himself. It seemed to him that Clara, sitting before him, was illuminated by a fiery flash of light in her eyes and that he had to close his own eyes, as if struck by a thunderbolt. Where did this strange thing come from? He did not know himself. Perhaps it was night's solemnity, squeezing superstitious fears into weak souls, bending the spirits of the strong to show them, in the darkness, the shade of that destiny that tames all. Perhaps it was the girl's grief reigning over him, as not long before he had ruled over her with the force of his will.

Poor thing! Now her eyes did not flash fire, although her face still shone with tremulous tears. Overflowing with happiness and love just half an hour before, her heart had now fled to her grandmother's side, to that quiet, well-ordered chamber where Lucilio had spent so many hours, and where after he had gone he still hovered in the air as a cherished memory, an invisible, enchanting fiction. Oh how hard it would be for the poor old woman to go to sleep without her granddaughter's usual kiss. Who would be there to sympathize, to console her for that absence? Who would even give her a thought among the perils facing the Castle that night? Pity, divine pity, swelled the young woman's breast again, and the hand that Lucilio held out to help her to stand was bathed in tears.

But when they were on their way again, his usual readiness and composure returned. The dreams dissipated, the thoughts that sprang to his head were manly and resolute; his will, no longer bowed, righted itself energetically to take command. The story of his love, of Clara's love, the extraordinary events of that evening, his sentiments and the young woman's sentiments resolved themselves in a single, sharp, consistent picture. He studied its overall outlines with the eye of an eagle, and decided that – alone or with the young lady – he must at all costs find his way into the Castle before the night was finished. Love imposed this duty on him, and let us add that love's interests also warmly advised it. Clara prayed to the Lord and the Virgin; Lucilio summoned all his enterprise and courage; and arm in arm they walked silently towards the mill. What self-control! some would say of Lucilio. But any who say so . . . well, either I've explained myself badly or they didn't properly understand when I described his temperament.

Lucilio was neither devious nor reckless, he merely wanted to plumb the depths of human affairs, identify the best and be capable of getting it. He knew that he could achieve these three purposes if he tempered them with good sense, so he never allowed himself to be led by his passions, but kept the reins firmly in hand. He knew how to check passion on the very brink of a precipice, as well as on the seductive verge of a broad green meadow. And so they entered the mill, but found no one there, although a fire was burning in the hearth among the embers. The remains of polenta on the board made it clear not everyone had eaten; perhaps some of the men had stayed late in the village to watch the excitement. This was probably the household the Contessina knew best, where she wouldn't mind being taken in for the night.

'Listen, my dear one,' said Lucilio, stirring up the embers with a poker to dry off the damp that clung to her from the fields. 'I'm going to call out now and entrust you to one of the women here, and then I shall break into the Castle one way or another to tell them of your whereabouts and find out how they are doing in there.'

Clara blushed deeply under the young man's gaze. It was the first time that their silent language of love – in a room and before a blazing fire – had entered her heart. She blushed without any shame, for she didn't think she had violated any of the Lord's commandments; there seemed to be little difference between that silent love and the act of confessing love one to another.

'You lie down now and rest,' said Lucilio, 'and I will meanwhile warn the Vice-captain of Portogruaro of what is going on in Fratta, so that he can break up these scoundrels' plans. They certainly haven't come here for no reason at all, and behind all this zeal of theirs to capture smugglers I sense some vendetta or a reprisal, perhaps even a brawl stirred up on purpose to put an end to the mess of that trial. But I will reveal matters in their true light and the Vice-captain will determine where the Signoria's true interests lie. Meanwhile, my dear Clara, don't worry, sleep peacefully; tomorrow, if they do not come from the Castle to fetch you, I shall come myself, perhaps even during the night if things turn serious.'

'Oh . . . you, no! . . . You must take no risks! For heaven's sake!' the girl murmured.

'But you know how I am,' said Lucilio. 'I couldn't but go out and try to accomplish something, even if only strangers were involved. Just imagine when it's your own family in question, and our dearest old friend.'

'Poor Grandmother!' Clara exclaimed. 'Yes, be off to comfort her and then come back at once to call me, for I'll be waiting anxiously.'

'I tell you that you must lie down to sleep and I will call one of the women.'

'No, no, let them sleep, for I cannot,' said the girl. 'Oh, I'm astonished, almost ashamed to think I could stay here and not run out there myself.'

'To do what?' said Lucilio. 'No, by God, do not move from this place. No, you must lock yourself in well, for they have been foolish enough to leave the doors wide open at midnight . . . Marianna! Marianna!' the young man began to shout from the doorway at the bottom of the stairs.

Soon another voice responded from above, and then two clogs were heard and after a minute Marianna, her neck and shoulders bare, descended to the kitchen.

'May God forgive me!' she said, clutching her nightdress over her bosom. 'I thought it was my man! But you, Signor Dottore? And the Contessina? The Devil take me; what has happened? How did you get in?'

'Heavens, what do you think? Through those four armspans of open doorway!' said Lucilio. 'But there is no time for chatter now, Marianna. The Contessina cannot return to the Castle because there are riots all around.'

'Riots? What do you mean? And what about our men, then? Oh, those good-for-nothings! They haven't even eaten! They went out to have a look and left all the doors wide open!'

'Listen to me now, Marianna,' said Lucilio, 'your men will be back and they are in no danger.'

'What do you mean no danger? If you only knew what a rash fellow, what a brawler mine is. He's capable of picking a fight with an army, that one!'

'Very well, but rest assured that tonight he won't pick one! I'll go out and look for them and send them home. You, meanwhile, make sure the Contessina has everything she needs.'

'Oh, my dear lady! That such things should happen to you, too! Oh, please do excuse me if I'm dressed like this, but I really thought you were my man. That scoundrel! Running away without his supper and leaving the doors open! Oh, he'll pay for this! But now, my lady, what are your orders? I'm afraid nothing here measures up to what you're accustomed to!'

'I leave her in your hands, then, Marianna!' said Lucilio again.

'Have no fear; my hands are capable. I am sorry to be so undressed, though. But you, Signor Dottore, are used to seeing such things, and the Contessina is a good lady!'

As she bustled about the fire, Marianna showed off her lovely shoulders, which were very white in contrast to the brown of her face and arms. Perhaps she wasn't really so very unhappy about showing them off, and thus her many apologies.

'Farewell! Love me, love me!' Lucilio spoke softly in Clara's ear, and when he had intercepted a glance full of love and expectation from her, slipped out the door into the misty countryside. Clara followed him to the doorway and when she lost sight of him, sat down again in the kitchen, but not beside the hearth, because the fire was hot and had already dried her clothes thoroughly. Her head and her wrists burned like red-hot coals and her lips and throat were dry, as though she had a fever. Marianna was determined to get her to eat something, but Clara was utterly opposed and would only take a glass of water. She then stretched out an arm along the back of her chair and rested her head on it as if to sleep, while Marianna tried to persuade her to go upstairs to sleep in the mill-wife's own bed; she would make it up with fresh sheets. But then, seeing that her words were wasted, the miller's lovely wife fell silent, and having turned the key in the door lock, sat down herself on a stool.

'I want you to go and sleep,' said Clara to her, for the Contessina, no matter how many concerns and fears she might have for herself, never ignored another's welfare.

'No, Madam! I must stay here to open the door to our men,' replied Marianna. 'Otherwise, rather than hauling someone over the coals I'll be hauled myself!'

Clara once again rested her forehead on her arm and sat there, dreaming with her eyes open, while Marianna, after her head had nodded for a while, rested it on the table and began to breathe with the calm, regular rhythm of a strong country woman who is fast asleep.

Meanwhile, as Signor Lucilio approached the moat behind the castle, taking every care not to be seen, I, who had been sent out to scout the area, was moving with equal caution, hoping to walk around and enter the village by the other side so as not to raise suspicions about my real purposes. When I'd walked a stone's throw towards the meadow, I thought I saw the shape of a man in the dark, advancing warily through the vine leaves. I squatted down in the wheat rows and watched, protected by my small size and by the wheat around me with its handsome fronds already blond and bending down. Between one frond and another, one vine and another, I scanned the situation, and what did I see there in a clearing lit up by the moon? Signor Lucilio! I scanned again; he came back into view. Now I stood up and cautiously approached through the wheat, ready to dive back in like a hare at the slightest excuse. I looked again: it was really him! What a lucky turn of fate, I thought. Signor Lucilio was the confidant of the old Countess and of Clara; he had shown he cared about me somewhat on the occasion of my outing to the Bastion of Attila, and no one could be better help in my investigation. And because he had a reputation as a man of science, our meeting seemed to augur well. And so, when I was some ten paces away from him, I hissed: 'Signor Lucilio! Signor Lucilio?' My voice was so low it seemed to be very, very long and very thin.

He stopped and cocked an ear.

'It's Carlino from Fratta! Carlino the turnspit!' said I in the same low voice.

From his pocket he extracted something that I later learned

was a pistol and, coming towards me, looked me hard in the face. I was in the shadow of the wheat and he seemed to have trouble recognizing me.

'Yes, yes, by the Devil, it is I,' I said, somewhat impatiently.

'Be quiet! Silence!' said he in a very low voice. 'There's a guardsman nearby and I wouldn't like him to hear us.'

He was speaking of that guardsman who had been left behind when his companion escorted Lucilio and the Contessina to the tavern. But solitude is sometimes a bad counsellor and the guard, after a valiant battle lasting more than half an hour, had finally allowed himself to be conquered by sleep. Thus Lucilio and I were able to speak in full confidence that no one would disturb us.

'Come close to my ear and tell me if you come from the Castle, and what news comes from there,' he whispered in my ear.

'The news is: they're frightened to death in there,' I said. 'They have knocked down all the bridges so as not to be murdered by Venchieredo's *buli*, and the Contessina Clara has disappeared, and since the hour of the Ave Maria they have said the rosary twice. But now they've sent me out to have a look around and try to find out something about the Contessina, and then to come back and give them the news.'

'And how will you do that, little one?'

'The deuce! How will I do it? Well, I'll go to the tavern, pretending to be lost, as I was that other time – do you remember? The time I had the fever – and then I'll listen to what the *buli* are saying, and then I'll ask a peasant or two about the Contessina, and then I shall go right back the way I came, crossing the moat atop a plank laid over it.'

'You know, you're a clever little fellow! I didn't know you had so much wit in you. You'll be happy to know that luck has spared you some real bother. I've been to the tavern and I have delivered the Contessina Clara to safety at the mill, and if you can show me how to get into the Castle, we can take them the news together.'

'Can I show you how? I just need to whistle and Marchetto will toss the plank over. Then you must let me show you how, and you will be able to cross without getting wet, so long as you take the trouble to copy me and keep your balance on the plank.'

'Let's go then.'

Lucilio took me by the hand and, squeezing up against some thick hedgerows behind which a person cannot be seen even in daylight, I led him rapidly to the moat. There I whistled as per our agreement and Marchetto ran out to toss me the plank.

'So soon?' he said from the other side of the moat, for his amazement won out over all caution just then.

'Quiet!' I said, showing Lucilio how to balance on the plank.

'Who's that?' Marchetto said with even more surprise, for he was now able to pick out two figures instead of one.

'Friends. Be quiet!' said Lucilio, and then he, too, as if he were practised at it, pushed off and landed, planting a clean kiss on the other shore.[3]

'It is I,' he said, 'and I bring good news of the Contessina Clara!'

'Really? Heaven be praised!' said Marchetto, moving aside to let me pull the plank from the water.

As we entered the kitchen they were just finishing saying the rosary, and the fire had gone cold (in any case, they would never have been able to survive the summer heat in there) and nobody was thinking about supper, although Monsignor Orlando glanced uneasily at the cook from time to time. Only Martino, taciturn and unruffled, stood there, grating his cheese; the rest wore faces worthy of a funeral. Lucilio's appearance was no less than a ray of sunshine in the midst of the storm. An 'Oooh!' of wonder, anxiety and pleasure sounded all around, and then everyone stopped to look at him in silence, as if they doubted he was a body at all and not a ghost. And so it was he who began to speak first – and the words of Moses when he came down from the Mount were not heard with greater attention. Even Martino stopped grating, but as he could not understand a word of what was being said, he finally took hold of me and made me tell him a part of the story in signs.

'To begin with, I have good news of the Contessina Clara,' said Signor Lucilio. 'She had gone out into the countryside towards Fossalta to meet the Countess as always, and when she was prevented from returning to the Castle by the ruffians who stand guard on all sides, I myself had the honour of conducting her to safety at the mill on the meadow.'

Those ruffians standing guard on all sides of the Castle rather badly spoiled the good impression made by the news of Clara. All smiled with their lips at this dove of good tidings, but fear sank even deeper into their eyes, which smiled not at all.

'So, therefore, we are really under siege as if there were Turks out there!' the Countess exclaimed, wringing her hands.

'You may be relieved to know that the siege is not all that intense if I have been able to enter the Castle,' said Lucilio, 'although it is true that all credit must go to Carlino, for had I not met him it's unlikely I'd have found my way here so quickly and got Marchetto to toss me the plank.'

The eyes of the company then turned to me with a certain amount of respect. They had finally understood that I was good for something besides turning the roast and I enjoyed my little triumph with dignity.

'Did you also go to the tavern?' the Steward asked.

'Signor Lucilio will tell you everything,' said I, modestly. 'He knows more than I because he dealt, I believe, with those gentlemen.'

'Ah! And what do they say? Are they planning to go away?' the Count enquired nervously.

'They plan to stay,' said Lucilio. 'For now, at least, there's no hope they'll leave. It will need a word from the Vice-captain of Portogruaro to put their tails between their legs.'

Now Monsignor Orlando sent another, more expressive glance towards the cook, and Monsignor di Sant'Andrea loosened his collar with a slight yawn: in both men of the cloth the needs of the body were starting to speak louder than the afflictions of the spirit. If that was a sign of courage, the two were the most courageous men in the Castle just then.

'But what do you say? What's your opinion on this emergency?' asked the Count, as nervous as before.

'There is but one opinion,' said Lucilio. 'Are the walls strong? Are the gates and windows well barred? Are there muskets and catapults at the embrasures? Are there enough men here to defend the Castle for the night?'

'You, Captain!' screamed the Countess, looking poisonously at the would-be Dalmatian warrior, who did not emanate self-confidence. 'Answer Signor Lucilio, then! Have you taken care of things so that we may feel secure?'

'Well,' the Captain stammered, 'I have only four men, including Marchetto and Germano, but the muskets and catapults are in place and I've handed round the gunpowder. As we lack bullets, I've distributed my hunting shot.'

'Oh, excellent! You think those assassins are sparrows!' the Count shouted. 'Fine shape we'll be in, defending ourselves with bird shot!'

'Never mind, for five or six hours, bird shot will be enough,' said Lucilio, 'and if your lordship can keep those criminals at bay until daylight, I think the Vice-captain's militia will be able to intervene.'

'Until daylight! How will we ever hold on until daylight if those bandits get it into their heads to attack?' shouted the Count, tearing at his wig. 'We kill one, the blood will go to the heads of the others and we'll all be finished before the Vice-captain so much as gets his slippers on!'

'No, don't look at it that way,' said Lucilio. 'You punish one and, believe me, the others will see the light. There's never any harm in showing one's teeth, and as Captain Sandracca doesn't seem to be in his usual fine spirits, I offer myself and declare and guarantee that I alone will defend the Castle and will trounce those blowhards out there at the slightest move from any of them.'

'Bravo Signor Lucilio! You will save us! We're in your hands!' the Countess squealed.

And, in fact, the young man spoke with such confidence that he put some courage back into all of them, and life began to course once again through those figures limp with terror, and the cook moved toward the credenza, to Monsignor's great satisfaction. Lucilio now asked that the whole affair be recounted from the beginning and decided that it was all most likely some trick on the part of the lord of Venchieredo to interrupt his trial by attacking the Fratta chancery; and in his first act of authority, he had all the papers and protocols relating to the matter delivered to an inside room. He examined the moat, the gates and the windows carefully and posted Marchetto and Germano behind the bolted gate. The Steward was ordered to take up guard duty by the stables, while the two other Cernide, the remaining part of the garrison, were stationed at the embrasures overlooking the bridge. He then handed out munitions, ordering that the first man who dared cross the moat be shot dead without hesitation. Captain Sandracca was right behind him while he was handing out these orders, but the Captain didn't have the courage to put on a sour face, and all his wife's glances, her elbowing and admonishments were needed to keep him from declaring he had a stomach ache and retiring to the barn.

'What do you think, Captain?' asked Lucilio with a somewhat derisory grin. 'Would you have done things as I say?'

'Oh yes sir! It's what I would have done already,' the Captain stammered, 'but my stomach . . .'

'Poor fellow!' Signora Veronica interrupted. 'He's been busy up to now and if the assassins haven't already broken into the Castle, the credit is certainly due to him. But he's no longer so young and work is work, and a man's strength is not at the command of his good will.'

'I need to rest,' the Captain murmured.

'Yes, yes, rest as much as you like,' said Lucilio. 'You've proven your zeal quite enough; you can now get between the sheets with a clear conscience.'

The hero of Candia did not wait for a second invitation; he flew up the stairs like an ascending angel and, although his wife was right beside him, shouting to watch his step and to be careful not to fall, he was up in his room in an instant, door barred and well locked in. That business of looking out of the embrasures had made him dizzy, and he felt much better between the bedclothes and the mattress. God would take care of future perils; he was more afraid of present ones. Signora Veronica began to complain quietly about how worthless he was, but he replied that dealing with thieves was not his calling and that if it had been a matter of genuine pitched battle they would have seen him at his post.

'These young fellows!' exclaimed the brave Captain, stretching out his legs. 'They act like they are heroes because they have the gall to risk a bullet by sticking their heads above the ramparts! My God, more than that is required! Oh, Veronica, you mustn't leave the room, you know! I intend to defend you as my greatest treasure!'

'Thank you,' the woman said, 'but why have you not undressed?'

'Undress! You'd like me to undress with this wee tempest raging all around us? Veronica, stay close by my side! Anyone who tries to offend you will do so over my dead body!'

She too, then, threw herself on the bed fully dressed and, courageous as she was, might even have gone to sleep, had her husband not leapt up at every passing fly, begging her to say whether she had heard anything, exhorting her to rely on him and not to abandon her legitimate defender.

Meanwhile, down below a decent meal improvised of eggs and chops had calmed the hunger pangs of the two Monsignori, and now, their hearts filling up once again with fear, they wondered aloud to each other about how strapping their assailants were and how many there might be: one hundred, three hundred, one thousand? In any event they were certainly all jailbirds, the best of whom had most likely escaped the noose because the hangman was feeling indulgent that day. If they were shouting about smugglers, it was just an excuse for pillage and plunder; and the way they were howling and singing in the piazza, they must be dead drunk, so neither reason nor mercy could be expected from them. The rest of the company looked alarmed at these arguments, and even more so when one of the sentinels came in to report sounds heard and movements detected near the Castle.

Lucilio, having gone up to visit the old Countess and having supplied (he, too) some fiction about Clara's absence, returned to comfort the poor devils downstairs. He wrote out and had the Count sign a long and urgent appeal to the Vice-captain of Portogruaro, and asked to be allowed to go and deliver it personally. Mercy! How could ever he think such a thing? The Countess practically fell to her knees before him; the Count took hold of his coat so tightly he nearly ripped it to pieces; the canons, the cook, the maids and the servants all crowded around, barring any escape. With eloquent eyes and signs, with sharp monosyllables, they struggled to make him understand that if he were to leave he would deprive them of their last hope of salvation. Lucilio thought of Clara, but he decided to stay.

However, someone was needed to deliver the letter and once again I came to mind. Taking advantage of the general confusion, I'd been upstairs in la Pisana's room, where she scolded me for having defrauded her of a great adventure *extra muros*. When they began to call me, I was shrewd enough and lucky enough to be found on the stairway, however. They stuffed my head with instructions and advice and sewed the letter into my jacket, and off I went for the second time on an important diplomatic mission. It was then ten o'clock at night and the moon was quite immodestly bright, and I was troubled by both things: the hour, owing to the witches and the witchcraft Marchetto had told me about, and the moon, because I was likely to be easily spotted. Nevertheless, I was fortunate enough to arrive safe and sound at the meadow. At first I trembled a bit, but along the way I began to feel calmer, and when I entered the mill, as instructed, I assumed an air of importance that did me justice.

I reassured the Contessina Clara and answered all her questions politely, and then I told Marianna to wake the eldest of her sons, and while she was gone I tore the letter from my jacket and casually placed it in my knapsack. Sandro was a young lad just two years older than I, of unusual cleverness and courage; thus the Steward had suggested I go to him to have the letter carried to Portogruaro. He accepted the task without a second thought and, tossing his jacket on his shoulders and putting the letter in his shirt, went out whistling, as if he were just going off to water his oxen. The road to Portogruaro headed away from Fratta and there was little chance he'd be caught and intercepted. No longer concerned, I was now quite gratified to see that the tasks entrusted to me had come off so well, and could already hear my praises being sung in the Castle kitchen. Although Signor Lucilio had warned me I must stay with the Contessina Clara until the messenger returned, I was burning to be on my way again; all the comings and goings, the mystery, the secrecy, the dangers, had set my childish imagination reeling and I could not sit still without some great enterprise to embark on.

And so I decided to return to the Castle to report on the first part of my mission and its success, and then to go out once again to get the reply from Portogruaro. Clara, when she heard my scheme, asked me if I was bold enough to get her across the moat, too. My small heart was pounding with more pride than unease and I told her – my face aflame, my arm tensed – that I would rather drown than let so much as the hem of her dress get wet. Marianna tried to discourage the young lady's plan with many wise warnings, but Clara was quite determined and I was so excited I could hardly wait to be outside with her.

Leaving behind the miller's wife and her worries, we thus crossed the fields and were soon at the Castle moat without incident. The usual whistle, the usual plank; the crossing, just as successful as before. The Contessina couldn't have been happier about the makeshift raft and almost seemed to enjoy her passage over the moat, laughing like a child as she knelt on that contraption. The surprise, relief and celebrations on the part of the family were a story in themselves, but Clara's first thought was to ask about her grandmother – or if not her first thought, that was her first word. Lucilio told her that the good woman, having happily swallowed the tales they'd fed her, was peacefully asleep and it would be unwise to wake her. And so the young lady sat down with the others in the dining hall, but while they strained their ears to hear the noise from the village through the cracks in the windows, she beamed her silent messages to Lucilio's eyes, thanking him for all he had done for them. And, in fact, they all agreed that it was to Signor Lucilio that they owed that tiny bit of security and hope that had lifted the spirits of the Castle's inhabitants after their earlier discouragement. It was he who had comforted them with good suggestions, he who had rapidly armed the Castle against an attack, he who had devised the superb idea of turning to the Vice-captain.

Here, I came back on stage. I was asked about the letter and to whom it had been entrusted and all were overjoyed to learn that in a few hours I would return to the mill to receive the reply from Portogruaro. Everyone wanted to embrace me; I was the man of the hour; Monsignor forgave my ignorance of the *Confiteor* and the Steward showed remorse for having treated me like a spit-roast. The Count sent me sweet looks and the Countess couldn't stop patting my head. It was justice – a little late, but deserved!

But even as the company were falling all over themselves flattering me, the noise outside suddenly increased and Marchetto the bailiff, gun in hand and eyes wide, burst into the dining hall. What was it? What was the trouble? All jumped up and began to shout and clamour; chairs were overturned and so were candlesticks. The trouble was that four men had leapt out of a dry water channel behind the Castle and had jumped on him and Germano, and the latter, who had been knifed two times in his side, was in a bad way, and Marchetto himself had just had time to escape and lock himself in. At this news the screaming and the distress increased threefold and everyone lost all sense of what they were doing: like bagged quail in a basket they poked their heads foolishly and aimlessly this way and that. Lucilio talked himself breathless urging calm and courage, but it was a dialogue with the deaf. Clara alone heard him and tried to help by urging the Countess to trust in God.

'God, God, yes, it is certainly time to turn to God!' said the lady. 'Call my confessor! Monsignor, commend our souls!'

Monsignor di Sant'Andrea, to whom these words were addressed, had scarcely any soul of his own left – imagine how much he wanted to or was able to commend those of others! Just then many gunshots were heard exploding and a shouting, threatening mob seemed to descend on the Castle. The chaos could not have been more complete. The scullery maids went one way, the house maids, la Pisana and the serving men the other, the Captain, more dead than alive, appeared, held up by his wife and shouting that all was lost. From outside, the shrieks and prayers of Fulgenzio's family and that of the Steward could be heard, begging to be let into the master's house, the safest place around. From the dining hall, awed and terrified faces appeared and disappeared at the window and there was a general bowing in prayer and making of signs of the cross, of women crying, men cursing and Monsignori exorcizing. The Count had lost his shadow, the Clerk having decided it was wise to retreat even further, under the rug on the table. The Countess, who was close to swooning, squirmed around like an eel, while Clara tried to quiet her as best she could. As for myself, I had taken la Pisana in my arms, determined I would let myself be cut to pieces before I gave her up to anyone.

In all this pandemonium only Lucilio kept a clear head. He asked Marchetto and the servants whether the gates were locked, and then queried the Bailiff about whether he'd seen the two Cernide before abandoning the tower. He hadn't seen them, but in any case two men were not enough to chase away that huge noise that could be heard outside, and Lucilio came to the rapid conclusion that some new development was taking place. Had their appeal to the Vice-captain already brought results? It seemed too soon, especially since militias of the time didn't err in their overwhelming zeal. However, some aid apparently had arrived, unless the assailants were so drunken as to be aiming their guns at each other! At that moment, the howling of Fulgenzio's and the Steward's women gave way to men pounding on the doors and shouting to open up and rest assured, for all was finished. The Count and the Countess, resting anything but assured, thought all this was merely a ploy to steal into the Castle. Everyone crowded nervously around Lucilio, awaiting counsel and salvation. The Contessina Clara was poised at the door to the stairway, ready to run up to her grandmother the moment danger became imminent. Her eyes replied bravely to those of Lucilio: he should look after the others, because she felt strong and steady enough to face whatever might happen. I was holding la Pisana ever tighter in my arms, but the young lady, wanting to imitate my courage, shouted for me to let her go; she could take care of herself! Pride worked so hard on her imagination that she reckoned she could face an army. Meanwhile, Signor Lucilio went to the window and asked who was knocking.

'Friends! Friends! From San Marco! From Lugugnana!' a chorus of voices sounded.

'Open up! It is Partistagno! The criminals have been driven away!' said another, well-known voice, and the party, caught between fear and hope, exhaled collectively.

A shout of relief went up, shaking the windows and walls of the dining hall, and if they had all gone mad together they wouldn't have produced a stranger and more grotesque expression of joy. I remember (I will always remember) the Count, who at the sound of that friendly voice put his hands to his temples, raised his wig and held it aloft towards the heavens, like an *ex voto* for grace received. I laughed so much that, luckily for me, the great happiness of the group distracted the general attention from my person. The doors were finally unbarred and the windows flung open; lights, lamps and candelabra were lit, and under the festive glow of full illumination, to the sound of triumphal marches, the *Te Deum* and the most devout of prayers, Partistagno and his liberating army invaded the ground floor of the Castle. There was no end of embraces, tears, thanks and amazement, and the Countess, ignoring all propriety, threw her arms round the neck of the young conqueror, and the Count, Monsignor Orlando and Monsignor di Sant'Andrea were ready to follow suit. Clara thanked him very warmly for sparing her family countless hours of fear and distress and perhaps even some less imaginary misfortunes. Only Lucilio did not join in the common approval and euphoria. Perhaps he wasn't convinced the scoundrels had been routed, or would have preferred that the router be anyone but who he was. He was too clever and fair-minded, however, not to disguise his unseemly feelings of envy, and thus was the first to question Partistagno about how he had accomplished his good deed.

Partistagno explained he had come to pay his usual visit to the Castle that evening, but slightly later than usual, due to some canal embankments that he'd had to repair at San Mauro. Venchieredo's *buli* had stopped him from entering the village, and he'd raised a great hue and cry against their despotism, but to no avail; and finally, seeing that his words were wasted and that their campaign against smugglers was merely a ruse concealing God knows what devilry, he decided to retreat and come back with better arguments than the verbal ones.

'Because I'm not the intimidating sort as a rule,' said Partistagno, 'but if need be, I, too, can accomplish things and make myself respected.' As he said so, he tightened the muscles of his wrists and showed some long, sharp teeth that resembled a lion's.

And, in fact, he had galloped back to San Mauro and gathered together some of his trusties, along with quite a few of the Lugugnana Cernide, who were still working on the embankments, and they headed back towards Fratta. They arrived just as the tower was being invaded by four scoundrels and, having rather easily dispersed the drunken crowd in the piazza and the tavern, he began to ford the moat with some of his men. With some trouble they reached the other side without being rebuffed by the men in the tower, who were busy smashing locks and hinges, trying to break into the archive where the incriminating documents about Venchieredo were stored. And then, after some gunfire (exchanged in the dark, more for show than for protection), he overpowered the four criminals and they were now locked up in the very tower they had broken into with such brazen infamy. Among them was the ringleader, Gaetano. As for the Castle porter, Germano, he was already dead by the time the Cernide of Lugugnana got to him.

'Oh, poor Germano,' Marchetto said.

'Is there really no more danger? Have they really all left? They won't be back to take their revenge?' asked the Count, who could hardly believe that such a terrible storm had simply dissolved into thin air without some great cracking of thunder.

'The leaders are well tied up and will be as good as gold until the hangman takes even better care of them,' said Partistagno, 'and as for the others, I wager they will soon wish to forget the smell of the air of Fratta, and that they will have no wish at all to breathe it again.'

'God be praised!' shouted the Countess. 'Dear Partistagno, all that is ours is yours in recognition of the immense service you have done us!'

'You are the greatest warrior of modern times!' chimed in

the Captain, wiping from his brow the sweat that fear had deposited.

'It seems that you, too, provided an excellent defence,' said Partistagno, 'for the windows and doors were so well sealed that not an ant could have got through.'

The Captain fell silent and advanced towards the table to conceal the fact he was not wearing his sword. With one hand he gestured towards Lucilio, as if to confer on him all the credit for those precautions.

'Ah, so it was Signor Lucilio,' said Partistagno with a hint of irony. 'Certainly, greater caution could not have been used.'

Now a paean to caution voiced by one who had just shown great audacity was a bit too much like a slur to escape Lucilio's notice. His soul had to soar quite high to reply to those ambiguous words with no more than a modest bow. Partistagno, who believed he had demolished him, or just about, turned to see how this new triumph over his small, unlucky rival looked on Clara's face. He was quite surprised not to see her at all, because the young lady had run upstairs to listen at her grandmother's doorway. The old lady was fast asleep, protected from all the musketry by slight deafness, and so Clara was soon back in the dining hall, very happy about what she'd learned.

Partistagno looked her over with pleasure, receiving a glance of pure benevolence in return that confirmed all the more his pity for the sad little doctor. Meanwhile, he was assailed with questions about this and that from all sides: about the number of criminals, about the method he had used to cross the moat, and, as always happens after some great danger, all enjoyed themselves imagining the danger to have been enormous and reliving their emotions. The mood of a man who thinks he has escaped a mortal threat is much like that of a man who has received a favourable response after declaring his love. The same gaiety, the same loquacity, the same magnanimity, the same nimbleness of body and spirit, or, to put it another way: all great joys are alike in their effects, while great sorrow varies greatly in its manifestations. Hearts know a hundred ways to feel pain and woe, just one for happiness. Nature knows little of the temperament of a Guerrazzi; she's better able to conjure up the sorrows than the joys of life.[4]

The first who observed that the new arrivals might need some refreshment was Monsignor Orlando, and I suspect it was his stomach, rather than his gratitude, that alerted him. They say that good humour is the most powerful of the gastric juices, and Monsignor had digested his dinner in fear, so good humour only stimulated his appetite more. Two eggs and half a chop! That was scarcely enough to satisfy the appetite of a Monsignor! They got to work right away and Fulgenzio's suckling pigs were soon dispatched. Fears of a long siege had vanished; the cook was working triple time; the scullery maids and serving men had four arms apiece; the fire seemed ready to cook anything in a minute. Martino, weeping, having learned of Germano's death from the Bailiff just at that moment, grated half a pound of cheese in three strokes.

La Pisana and I – forgotten in the general celebrations and happy as we could be – had our own festivities; if only the Castle were under siege every month, so that we could enjoy such Carnival! But the memory of poor Germano often clouded my happiness. It was the first time death had come near me since I'd reached the age of reason. La Pisana entertained me with her chatter and chided me for my fitful spirits; but my reply was, 'What about Germano?' Then she would sulk a while, but soon she was back to chattering, demanding all the details of my nocturnal expeditions, arguing that she could have done even better, and celebrating with me because the cook had deigned to put the roasting spit in motion, rather than making me do service. Thus I was distracted from my grief, and my bossy little friend, needing my admiration, kept me too busy with myself and my self-importance to think very much about the dead man.

It was at least half past midnight before supper was ready. Nobody bothered with quarters of nobility and all that. In the kitchen, the dining hall and the pantry everyone ate and drank where and what he wished. Fulgenzio's family and the Steward's were called to the great table, and between a toast and a mouthful, Germano's death and the disappearance of the Chaplain and Fulgenzio raised only a rare sigh. But the dead lie in the ground, while the living move around. And, in fact, Fulgenzio and the priest appeared soon thereafter, so pale and limp they looked as if they had been closed up in a flour bin. They were greeted with a round of applause and invited to tell their story. In fact, it was very simple. Each of them, without consulting the other, they said, had hastened to Portogruaro to seek help when the enemy arrived. And now here they were, the valiant crusaders of Pisa.[5]

'You mean to say there are brave soldiers out there?' said the Count, who hadn't yet noticed he had lost his wig. 'Bring them in! Come now, bring them in!'

The brave soldiers numbered six, including a corporal, but they had the appetite of a regiment. They arrived just in time to finish up the remains of the roast pig and to revive the general good cheer, already sinking into lethargy. When they were sated and Monsignor di Sant'Andrea had recited an *Oremus* to thank God for sparing us, we were ready for bed in earnest. At that point it was every man for himself – one here, one there – everyone found himself a den: the high-born in the guest rooms, the others in the friars' room, the cupboards or the hayloft. The next day the Count ordered that the soldiers, Cernide and guardsmen be granted a nice gratuity, and everyone went home after hearing three Masses – at none of which did anyone force me to recite the *Confiteor*.

Thus we returned to life as usual after that terrible onslaught. The Count, however, warned us to enjoy our great victory quietly, because he very much wanted to avoid any reprisals.

Given his frame of mind, you can well imagine that the investigation based on Germano's evidence did not proceed very rapidly, nor did it seem there was really any intention to punish those four scoundrels Partistagno had taken prisoner. When Venchieredo was cautiously questioned about them, he said that, to tell the truth, he had sent them out on the trail of some smugglers thought to be hiding out near Fratta, and that if his orders had been surpassed in some way punishable by the law, the matter did not concern him, but the chancery of Fratta.

The Clerk of Fratta, meanwhile, seemed little inclined to get to the bottom of the affair, and made sure not to lead the prisoners into any hazardous confessions. Germano's example spoke clearly, and the Clerk was a quick study. And so he let the main investigation lie dormant, and in his inquiry about the assault on the tower he was pleased to find the four accused men to have been inebriated. Thus he hoped to wash his hands of the matter. The dust of forgetfulness would providentially drift over those unwelcome protocols.

Matters had been proceeding in this halting way for a month or so, when one evening two Capuchin friars came to the Castle, looking for a bed for the night. Fulgenzio, who knew every Capuchin and his beard in the province had never seen these two, but when they said they came from Illyria (and their accents bore this out) they were courteously taken in. In any case, had they come from the moon itself, no one would have risked turning away two Capuchins with the sorry excuse they were perfect strangers. In a fine show of saintly humility, they begged off from the lively discussion in the dining hall and went instead to the kitchen to edify the servants with some of their holy tales and such stories from Dalmatia and Turkey as pass for parables in those parts. They then asked to be shown to their beds and Martino took them up to the friars' room, which was divided from my sleeping hole by a mere board that afforded me a view of them through a crack. Not long after, the entire castle was asleep – except for me, who was spying through my crack, because those Capuchins had a way about them that rather piqued my curiosity. As soon as they were in the room, they secured the door with two stout bolts, and then I watched them take things that looked like labourers' tools from under their habits, and also two big knives and two pairs of pistols, such as friars don't often carry. I held my breath I was so terrified, but I wanted very much to know what those implements were intended for, and I kept on spying. One of them then took a chisel and began to pick at the wall facing me (which backed onto the tower) and, one stealthy blow after another, began to open a large hole.

'The wall is thick,' said the other man softly.

'Three arm-spans and a half,' said the one who was chiselling. 'We'll need two and a half hours before we can get through.'

'And if someone discovers us in the meantime?'

'So much the worse for him! Six thousand ducats is well worth a knife in the ribs, or two!'

'And what if we can't get out because the porter wakes up?'

'Don't be foolish! He's just a lad, Fulgenzio's son! We'll frighten him and he'll give us the keys so we can get out easily, or else . . .'

'Oh, poor Noni!' I thought, watching that killer interrupt his chiselling with a threatening swipe of his hand. I had never been able to tolerate that hypocrite Noni, especially because of the nasty way he spied on la Pisana and me, but just then I wasn't thinking about how spiteful he was, just as I wasn't thinking about his brother Menichetto's mean and envious religious fanaticism. Sympathy silenced all other feelings, and, of course, the threat applied also to me, should they suspect I was watching them through a crack in the board. Now that I was accustomed to adventures, I hoped to show off my mettle that night too.

So I opened the door to my cupboard very slowly and crept on tiptoe into Martino's room. Not daring to speak, I unlatched the shutters to let in some light (because there was a very bright moon) and then I approached the bed and tried to wake him. He leapt up, shouting, 'Who is it? What is it?' but I put my hand over his mouth and signalled him to be silent. Luckily he recognized me right away, and with signs I persuaded him to follow me, and, leading him down the stairs to the landing, I explained all. Poor Martino's eyes were as big as lanterns.

'We must wake Marchetto, the Count and the Clerk,' said he, anxiously.

'No, only Marchetto,' I said, quite sensibly. 'The others will simply add to the confusion.'

And so he woke the Bailiff, who agreed that the thing must be done very quietly, with no clamour and few participants. The hole at which the Capuchins laboured gave on to the chancery archives, an ugly, dark room on the third floor of the tower, full of documents, dust and mice. The best plan would be to have two big, trusted fellows wait there and seize the two friars as they broke through, and then properly bind and gag them. And so it was. The two men were Marchetto himself and his brother-in-law, who served as the Castle gardener. They stole into the archive using the Count's keys (as always in the pocket of the master's breeches, hanging in his dressing room) and they hid there, one to the right and one to the left of the spot where the faint sounds of two chisels could be heard. Half an hour later a ray of light penetrated the archive and the two defenders stood stock still. They had armed themselves with pistols and hatchets for all eventualities, but they hoped to do without them, because the friars were busy at work without much concern.

'I can put my arm through,' one of them said.

'Just two more blows and the worst is done,' said the other.

They rapidly enlarged the hole in this fashion so that one person could just pass through, and then one of them, who seemed to be the ringleader, put his head through, and then one arm and then the other, and, crawling forward, hands on the archive floor, sought to pull his legs after him. But just when he was least expecting it, he felt a friendly force assisting him, even as a sturdy fist grabbed his chin and forcing open his jaw, stuffed it with something that nearly stopped him breathing, let alone shouting. A stout cord around his wrists, a pistol at his throat and the job was done: he had no wish to move away from the wall against which he had been pushed. His fellow friar was surely rather uneasy about the silence after his boss's passage, but then he took heart, imagining that the other wasn't breathing because he was afraid he'd be heard, and he, too, got up his courage to poke his head through the hole. He was treated with even less consideration than the first: as soon as he had that head in his hands, Marchetto began to tug on it so hard he'd have torn it off had the patient not dislodged some stones from the wall with his shoulders. When he, too, had been gagged and bound, they searched him up and down, along with his companion; their arms were taken away and they were led to a nasty, damp, remote and airless corridor, where each was secured in a small cell, like two real friars. There they were left to their meditations, while the family was awakened and the great news conveyed.

Oh, just imagine the excitement, the wonder, the relief! This new offensive had come from Venchieredo's side, certainly, and therefore it was decided to keep the matter as secret as possible until the Vice-captain of Portogruaro could be informed. Fulgenzio was charged with this mission and it was carried out so nicely that Venchieredo was still waiting for the two friars to return when a company of Schiavoni surrounded his castle, took charge of his person, bound him well and transported him to Portogruaro. It was clear that Fulgenzio had used some strong arguments to persuade the cautious Vice-captain to take such drastic measures. Pale with fear and rage, the prisoner bit his lip for having fallen like a fool into the trap, and he rued those lovely fiefs of his beyond the Isonzo, wise too late. The prisons of Portogruaro were very solid and the fact he'd been captured so swiftly convinced him he'd be a fool to think he could escape.

A great weight had now been lifted from the inhabitants of Fratta, and all roundly condemned the effrontery of that bully, and great and small flattered themselves that they deserved thanks for his capture. When several days later an order came to deliver the four men charged with armed invasion, the two false friars and the papers relating to the inquiry on Germano to the messenger from the Council of Ten, the Count and the Clerk were seized with joy. They were much relieved to have cleaned that pitch off their hands and they arranged for a *Te Deum* to be sung, 'for reasons regarding their souls', when, months later, reports came downwind that the six rogues had been condemned to life in the galleys, while the Count of Venchieredo was to be shut up for ten years in the Fortress of Rocca d'Anfo near Brescia for high treason and conspiracy with foreign potentates against the Republic.

The letters that Germano had supplied to the authorities were part of a long-ago secret correspondence between Venchieredo and some noblemen of Gorizia, in which they vowed to press Maria Theresa to take over Venetian Friuli,[6] assuring her of the loyalty and cooperation of the landed nobles. The letters had remained in Germano's hands because of the many difficulties he'd had transporting and delivering them, and he had been able to avoid returning them, saying they had been destroyed to guard them from those chasing him, or for some other urgent reason. Thus he hoped to defend himself against his master in case that gentleman (as was his custom) should try to get rid of him. As fate would have it, what he had prepared for defensive purposes was used to mount an offensive against an unjust and tyrannical man.

When Venchieredo's criminal trial was done, a charge of felony – cause for him to lose his fief – was filed in the civil courts. But whether the government was loath to deprive the Friulian nobility of too many privileges or whether the advocates were especially clever or the judges very lenient, it was decided that the guilty man's young son, who was studying with the Scolopi Fathers in Venice, would continue to hold the domain of Venchieredo. In short, the sentence for treason against the father would not be allowed to prejudice his heir's rights.

And so it was that Leopardo Provedoni – Gaetano and every other obstacle removed – was finally able to marry Doretta. Signor Antonio had to condone it, just as he condoned having Spaccafumo, defying all bans and sentences, grace the wedding banquet with his distinguished presence. The young couple were judged to be the handsomest seen in the territory in the previous fifty years, and no one bothered to count the fireworks shot off in their honour. Doretta made her triumphal entry into the Provedoni household and the gallants of Cordovado had an extra beauty to ogle during Sunday Mass. If Leopardo's sternness and Herculean strength discouraged their attentions, his wife's flirtatiousness was a constant encouragement. And, as we all know, temptation is stronger than fear in such cases. The Clerk of Venchieredo, who was all but the absolute master of the castle while the young lord was still a minor, shone part of his splendour on his daughter Doretta, and on feast days she preferred the arm of her father to that of her husband, above all when she went to show herself off at the festive gatherings around the spring.

In those days my fate, too, had changed greatly. I wasn't ready to take a wife yet, but I was now all of twelve years old, and exposing those false Capuchins had raised my standing in popular opinion. The Countess no longer despised me and sometimes seemed close to remembering we were related, only to firmly abjure any tender impulses. However, she did not object when her husband took it into his head to have me trained for the courtroom and apprenticed me as a scrivener to the Clerk.

I finally had my place at the table, right next to la Pisana, because the economic straits of the family, made worse by bad administration, had led them to rule out the convent for the younger daughter, too. I continued to grouse, play and suffer beside her, but now my greater importance counterbalanced the humiliations I was still forced to bear. Whenever I could walk by her, reciting the Latin lesson I was to repeat before the Rector the following day, I felt myself superior in something. Oh, poor Latinist! How little did I know!

SIX

In which a comparison is drawn between the French Revolution and the patriarchal tranquillity of the domain of Fratta. Their Excellencies the Frumiers take shelter at Portogruaro. My importance, feelings of jealousy and knowledge of Latin grow, until I am appointed a scrivener in the Clerk's office. But the arrival at Portogruaro of the learned Padre Pendola and the dashing Raimondo di Venchieredo give me pause.

The years that came and went at the Castle of Fratta, as unvarying, modest and unremarked as humble country folk, bore famous and terrible names in Venice and the rest of the world. They were called 1786, 1787 and 1788: three numbers that are numbers like any other, but which in mankind's chronology will always stand for one of its greatest upheavals. No one today believes that the French Revolution was the madness of one people alone. The impartial muse of history has shown us that a hidden fever for liberty had long incubated in men's souls, before it burst out – heedless, inexorable, supreme – in the social order. Where deeds thunder, you can be sure that an idea has struck. The impetuous and reckless French nation was the first to plunge from doctrine to experience; France was considered the brain of humanity when it was but the hand: a bold and dexterous hand that often destroyed its own work, even as the design grew clearer in the universal mind of the people.

In Venice as in every other European state, opinions began to emerge from their familial haunts to circulate in the wider sphere of civil affairs; men felt themselves to be citizens[1] and, as such, wanted to see their homelands well governed. The governed and their governors: the first judged themselves capable of having rights; the second became aware they were bound by duties. Between two forces previously in accord, hostile looks were exchanged and battle lines drawn, and there was a new daring on one side, fear and suspicion on the other. The inhabitants of Venice were less inclined than others to break the laws, however; the Signoria rightly trusted in the happy somnolence of its peoples. And that prince from the North[2] who visited in those days was not wrong when he said that in Venice he had met a family, not a state.

But what is provident and necessary in a family may become tyranny in a republic; the differences of age and experience that induce children to obey and parents to protect are not always found in governors and authorities. When good sense matures in the people, the rules of justice of an earlier time are an obstacle barring their way. Pressing on with the metaphor, children who have grown in strength, reason and age have the right to be freed of parental authority. That family in which the right to think is granted to an octogenarian but denied to an adult person is certainly not designed according to nature's wishes, and, in fact, it will stifle the holiest of human rights, which is liberty.

Now, Venice was such a family. The ruling aristocracy was decrepit; the people weakened by indolence, although the divine spark of philosophy was rejuvenating their self-awareness. The Republic had become a corpse unable to revive itself, a race of the living forced by long servitude to share the dead man's grave. But then, who is not familiar with those charmed islands, graced by the heavens and caressed by the sea, where even death casts off its black mourning dress and ghosts would dance on the water singing Tasso's amorous verses? Venice was the tomb where Juliet lay down to sleep dreaming of Romeo's embraces, where to die with hope's consolation and rosy illusions of bliss would always seem life's delicious pinnacle. No one understood that those long, boisterous Carnivals were nothing less than the Republic's funeral march. Doge Paolo Renier died on 18 February 1788,[3] but his death was not announced until 2 March, so that the Carnival euphoria should not be interrupted by any public mourning rites. A shameless act of frivolity, marking how little love or faith connected subjects with their ruler, sons with their father. Live and die as you will, but please don't disturb the masked balls and the Ridotto gambling hall:[4] so the people reasoned, and with them the nobility who disguised themselves among the people, to spend less and enjoy greater safety.

The same indifference greeted the election of Doge Lodovico Manin on 9 March; his election, however, may have been pushed forward to break the grim monotony of Lent. And thus it was during the fast that the last Doge took the seat once held by Enrico Dandolo and Francesco Foscari;[5] but Venice failed to see the penance that was to be paid. In all the heedlessness, decay and incompetence, there were those who vaguely foresaw that times were changing, and called on the Signoria to take appropriate measures. Perhaps the remedies proposed were neither appropriate nor adequate, but it should have been enough to examine the patient and let others find the right medicines. Yet the men of the Signoria averted their eyes and denied that any medicines were needed, believing quiet and calm meant Venice was healthy, not infirm (they did not understand that the most dangerous infirmities are the painless ones).

Not many years before, Angelo Querini, Avogadore[6] of the Commune, had twice been sent to prison by the Council of Ten for having dared to expose the tricks and abuses by which the Maggior Consiglio constructed false majorities. The second time, after it was decided to debate the matter, he was locked up even before any such debate took place. Such was the independence enjoyed by that body, such the powers accorded it; no one noticed (or all pretended not to notice) that Querini had been imprisoned, because no one wished to follow him.

But now the time had come when reform could not be arrested. By 1779 the administration of justice and the public good were so neglected that even the most patient and cheerful of people reacted. Carlo Contarini urged the Maggior Consiglio to correct the abuses and proposed changes in the constitution, and his arguments were so persuasive and at the same time so moderate that, with astonishing unanimity, it was decided to call for the Signoria to carry out rapid reforms. What we might call the liberal party in that debate wanted to restore authority to the entire patriciate, and to dissolve that oligarchic power which time and habit had assigned to the Signoria and the Council of Ten. The reforms they sought were superficially of little importance; they were trying to enlarge the sphere of sovereignty, to return to the original balance, insisting on the long-forgotten maxim that the role of the Maggior Consiglio was to command, of the Signoria, to carry out those commands, and that the authority of the second was conditional.

Faced with such arguments, the party of the oligarchy fumed, and the many and muddled statutes offered them a thousand subterfuges to avoid taking any action. The Signoria, pretending obedience, proposed silly, inadequate remedies. After a year of continuous disputes, during which the Maggior Consiglio continued, in vain, to support the reform programme, the Most Serene Doge was drawn into the controversy. His proposal was to appoint five 'correctors' to examine the defects complained of in the Republic's institutions; he urged this expedient (which would change nothing) for the same reasons that would have persuaded a cleverer politician to reform everything, and right away. Renier spoke at length of Europe's monarchies, grown powerful at the expense of the few republics, and concluded that harmony and stability were paramount. 'I myself,' he pronounced in his patriarchal Venetian, 'I myself was present in Vienna during the disturbances in Poland, and I heard it said many times: *These Polish gentlemen are behaving unwisely, but we will take care of them*. If any state is in need of harmony, it is our own. We have no power, neither terrestrial, nor maritime, nor any alliances. We exist by chance, *by accident*, and our only motto is governmental prudence.'

Speaking thus, the Doge showed himself to be more cynical than courageous, I think; the best he could oppose to so much ruin was mere inertia. It was: 'If we move one stone the house will fall! Don't breathe, don't cough or it will fall on us!' But it was so ignominious of him to say this before the Maggior Consiglio that he should have been made to throw off his horned bonnet[7] in shame. Procuratore[8] Giorgio Pisani shouted out that the republican reforms were vital, and if they were not approved, it should be written in the public record, so that our descendants might pity their ancestors for their futile wisdom, not curse their negligence and toss their ashes to the wind. But the Maggior Consiglio backed the Doge and the five correctors were elected, among them Giorgio Pisani.

And when that momentary revolt was tamed and the Inquisitors of State took their revenge (and without the least concern for sovereign decree confined Pisani to the Castle of Verona for ten years, and sent Contarini to die in exile at the Gulf of Kotor,[9] and banished and condemned many others) no voice of censure or mercy was heard. For the first time in history what the Supreme Council of the Republic had judged useful, opportune and correct was determined to be a crime. Bowing their heads to this outrageous insult, permitting those officials charged with carrying out their decrees to languish in exile and prison: such was the political order, and such was the patience of the Venetian people. In truth, rather than live this way, *by accident*, as the Most Serene Doge had it, it would have been more civilized, more prudent and more generous to risk death in any other way.

But finally came the day when the menace of the new thundered far louder than a few weak-voiced orators. The very day the Estates General were convened in Paris, 14 July 1788, Ambassador Antonio Cappello informed the Doge. He pointed out some of the difficulties the Republic might face as a result and suggested a plan of action. But the Most Excellent Savi, the Elders, tossed the dispatch in the stack of unread letters and the Senate was not informed. The Inquisitors, however, doubled their vigilance. There began a spate of imprisonments, spying, threats and vexations, of bans and proclamations (that without reducing the danger made clear it was imminent), until a mood of diffidence mixed with fear and hatred pervaded Venice. From Turin, Count Rocco Sanfermo, Venice's ambassador to Piedmont and Switzerland, told of the disorders in France and the secret plots among the Courts of Europe; Antonio Cappello, back from Paris, loudly called for a speedy debate. The danger grew to such proportions that it no longer made sense to try to wait it out without making an alliance with one side or another. But the Signoria was not accustomed to look beyond the banks of the Adda and the Isonzo; it did not see why agitation among the others should disturb its own peace and tranquillity, and it considered neutrality both useful and salutary, not understanding, instead, that it would be untenable. Outside, the disorders in France grew; inside, the whispers, the fears, the vexations increased. The government sought to show a calm self-confidence, but every member despaired in his heart. Under such conditions, the cleverest avoided trouble by leaving Venice. Left at the helm were those very few concerned about the public good, the many vainglorious, and the multitudes of the heedless, the foolish and the poor.

The Most Excellent Almorò Frumier, brother-in-law of the Count of Fratta, owned vast lands and a magnificent house at Portogruaro. He was among those Venetians who, without understanding much of the upheavals taking place, caught the whiff of a bad smell from afar and had very little wish to dirty his hands. In agreement with his wife, therefore (she wasn't unhappy to return to those provinces where her family enjoyed almost sovereign privileges), he moved to Portogruaro in the autumn of 1788. His wife's health served as pretext for their departure (she 'had need of her native air') and once they had left they decided they would not set foot again in Venice until the last little cloud from those storms had dissipated. The gentleman's two sons looked after the interests and the welfare of their household, and as for Frumier himself, the fawning of the illustrious provincials and indeed of an entire city, more than compensated the perilous honour of being able to hold forth in the Senate. With a great train of trunks and chests, of armchairs, of bibelots, the mature bride and groom set forth in a carriage and, having suffered a long and anguished martyrdom of tedium and mosquitoes, arrived after fifty hours of travel through swamps and down canals to disembark at their country villa on the River Lemene. So the Venetians called any house of theirs on dry land,[10] be it in Milan or Paris or even Portogruaro.

The Lemene just touched the foot of their garden, and as soon as they arrived they were consoled to find assembled there the best the city could offer of every social order. The Bishop, Monsignor di Sant'Andrea and other prelates, priests and seminary professors, the Vice-captain and other government dignitaries, the Chief Magistrate and other officials of the Commune, the superintendent of taxes and duties and the guardian of the Customs House with their respective wives, sisters and sisters-in-law, and, finally, the nobility, in swarms, so many of them that among the five thousand inhabitants of the place there were enough to furnish all the cities of Switzerland, which by misfortune had none. From Fratta, the Count had come with the Countess and their daughters, his brother the Monsignore and the inseparable Clerk. And I, who meanwhile had prompted great expectations with my rapid progress in Latin, had been granted special dispensation to climb on the back of the carriage; and so, tucked away in my corner, I was allowed to enjoy the spectacle of that solemn reception.

The great patrician conducted himself with proverbial Venetian amiability. From the Bishop to the greengrocer, no one was deprived of the favour of his smile, and, kissing the ring of the first, he gave the second a slap with equal modesty. Turning to the boatmen, he warned them to take special care with his armchair when unloading the furniture, and went inside offering his arm to his sister-in-law, his wife behind him with her brother. In the great hall where refreshments were served he complained that the terraces were chilly, and the usual greetings, usual exchanges, were had. The girls were handsome and much grown, the lady was looking much younger, the gentleman was fresh as a rose, the voyage had been long, hot and fatiguing, Portogruaro was flourishing as never before, the guests were charming and commendable, the welcome most agreeable: the niceties took up a good hour and more. After which, the visitors took their leave and the family was left to speak very highly of itself and make a few nasty remarks about those who had left. In this, too, they adopted that Venetian sweetness and discretion that contents itself with slashing the clothing without scraping the flesh to the bone.

Towards the hour of the Ave Maria, the Fratta party said their farewells, making it clear they would return to visit often. Certainly, the noble Frumier had very great need of company, and let us also say that the Illustrious Count of Fratta was rather proud of his familial ties and intimacy with a Senator.

The sisters-in-law gave each other a careful peck on the cheek, the brothers-in-law shook hands, the girls made their bows, and Monsignor and the Clerk raised their hats all the way to the carriage footboard. They were then stuffed in as best they could be, and I took up my usual place, and four strong horses had quite a job to pull that heavy carriage over the cobblestones. The Most Excellent Senator returned to the hall, quite satisfied with his first appearance at his country villa.

Portogruaro was one of those small cities on the mainland that copied and recopied the Serenissima with the greatest faithfulness. Large, spacious houses adorned with a triple window in front were lined up on both sides of the streets and only the water was missing to complete the likeness with Venice. Every third door boasted a caffè with the usual awning in front, and, beneath it, many tables and a fair number of idlers. There were packs of winged lions on top of the public buildings; easy women and boatmen perpetually chattering in alleyways and fruit stalls; pretty girls standing at balconies behind canaries in cages and pots of carnations and basil; black-gowned advocates, tail-coated notaries, and patricians sporting greatly venerated scarlet-trimmed *zimarre* up and down in the piazza and by the city hall; four Schiavoni standing guard before the prison; a smell of salt water in the Lemene canal; a cursing of boat-keepers and a whirl of barges, anchors and cables; a constant tolling of church bells and recitation of sermons and psalms; little stucco Virgins decked with flowers and festoons at every corner; pious mothers on their knees with rosaries; blonde daughters entertaining young men behind the doors; abbés eyeing their shoe buckles, cloaks drawn modestly over their bellies: nothing was missing, the miniature was identical to the painting. Even the three flags of San Marco had their imitation in the piazza of Portogruaro: a red-painted mast from which the colours of the Republic flew on solemn occasions.

What more? The Venetians of Portogruaro, after many centuries of study, had managed to discard the barbarous, bastard Friuli tongue used all around them and now spoke a Venetian more Venetian than the originals themselves. Nothing annoyed them more than the fact that their city was governed by Udine, reminding them of their long ties with the Friuli. They were like the low-born man ennobled who despises the cord and awl that bring to mind his father, the cobbler. Alas, however, history is written but once and cannot be erased. The people of Portogruaro took their revenge by preparing a very different version for the future, and in their new-coined lexicon the term 'Friulian' meant vulgar, boorish, penny-pinching and flea-bitten. Once beyond the city gates (they had built them ever so narrow, as if they were expecting gondolas, not carriages and hay carts) they were like fish out of water, like Venetians out of Venice. They pretended not to know the difference between wheat and maize, although every market day the grain sacks were there to be seen; they would stop and stare at trees like young dogs, and marvel at the dust on the roads although their shoes betrayed a daily familiarity with it. Talking to the country folk, they all but addressed them as 'you dry-land people'. Portogruaro, in their imaginations, was a sort of hypothetical island built in the image of the Serenissima, not in the lap of the sea but between four nasty canals of muddy, greenish water. That this was not dry land, the many walls, the sagging bell towers and house fronts testified in their way. I believe they even built them on weak foundations for this reason.

But it was the ladies who were the real, dyed-in-the-wool Venetians. The fashions of the capital were imitated and exaggerated with keen attention. If at San Marco wigs were two fingers tall, at Portogruaro they grew to a couple of handswidth. The hoop-skirts spread out until a small knot of women became a veritable flood of lace, silk and trimmings. Necklaces, bracelets, brooches and chains cascaded over their persons, and while I wouldn't want to swear that all the gems came from the mines of Golkonda[11] or Peru, they were dazzling to the eye and that was enough. In all events, these ladies arose at midday, spent four hours at their toilettes and paid visits all afternoon. In Venice the great topics of *conversazione*,[12] that is the salon, were theatre, opera buffa and tenors, and here, too, they felt obliged to keep to the same arguments; so that while the theatre of Portogruaro was open but one month every two years, it nevertheless enjoyed the rare privilege of being on a hundred pretty lips for all the twenty-three intervening months. When this subject was exhausted, they slandered each other with truly heroic resolve.

Each of them, you understand, had her own *cavalier servente*, and each tried to steal him from another. A few took this fashion so far as to have two or even three of them, with rights variously apportioned. One to pass the lady her fan; one her lorgnette or her handkerchief or her snuffbox; to one, the pleasure of escorting the lady to Mass; to another, of joining her on her promenade. This last amusement was enjoyed rather soberly, though; the divine silkiness of the gondola being unavailable, and the mere sight of a carriage going though its barbarous motions so appalling, that they had no choice but to go out on foot, an intolerable exertion for their dainty Venetian feet. Oh certainly, some country wag or boorish local lord liked to say this was just the fox eyeing the grapes: that so far as carriages went, those ladies could desire one with all their hearts as long as they wished, but they'd never see one. Who was right, I cannot say, but based on their sex alone I would side with the ladies. As a matter of fact there are many carriages in Portogruaro today, even though our treasure chests aren't worth much compared to those of our great-grandparents. True, in those times a carriage was an affair for a king; when the Count of Fratta drove by in his, all the rabble in town came out to watch.

In the evenings (when they weren't 'going out to the theatre'), night came late, after long card games: in this, too, they followed Venice fashion, and if that passion didn't ruin entire households as it did in the capital, the credit went to Portogruaro husbands and their guarded liberality. On the green baize, instead of gold *zecchini*, they played with *soldi*; but this was a town secret that no one betrayed even for gold itself, so that when outsiders heard talk of the triumphs and the excitements of the night before, they could well believe that the fortunes of an entire family – and not a mere twenty *soldi* – had been at stake in every game. Only the wife of the Correggitore exceeded that limit, and she sometimes bet up to half a ducat, although the envious muttered of greed and cheating. This lady's primacy was contested by certain Venetian wives married into

Portogruaro families or residing there for reasons of office, who had joined forces with the local women. But not only was she beautiful, she knew how to use her tongue like a real Venetian and a glance from her was as flattering as anyone could ever desire. The young men clustered around her at church, at the caffè, in the salon, and I couldn't say whether the admiration of the men or the envy of her rivals was more appreciated.

The wife of the Podestà, who gesticulated much with her fine, white hands, liked to say that the other lady's hands were those of a scullery maid. The Superintendent's sister maintained that one of her eyes wandered, and, in so saying, flashed her own large, blue eyes (which she thought were the city's most beautiful, although they were merely the largest). Each of them singled out as common, ugly and defective in her that part considered perfect in herself, but when the maid came back to report these jealous whispers, the lovely object of their denigration merely smiled at her mirror. She had two lips so rosy, thirty-two teeth so small, white and neat, a pair of cheeks so round and dimpled with love, that all she had to do was smile and she proved them wrong.

As you might imagine, Lady Frumier was soon surrounded by a swarm of these simpering females when she arrived. She herself had reached a certain age and more, it was true; yet being a Venetian, she no longer remembered her birth date, and her manner, her glances, her coiffure all vaunted that perpetual youth that is the singular privilege of the ladies of Venice. Now as I've said, there were a fair number of Venetians living at Portogruaro, but all of them belonged to the middle classes or the lesser nobility. A grande dame, a gentlewoman of high standing versed in all the arts and refinements of *conversation*, had until then been missing. They were, therefore, overjoyed to finally possess an example, to contemplate her, idolize her, imitate her according to their rank, and to be able to say, at the end: 'See! I speak, I laugh, I dress, I walk like Madam Senator Frumier.'

She herself, clever as the Devil, was enjoying the game immensely. One evening she would chatter like a magpie, and the following, amuse herself watching the ladies compete for who could say the most words in a minute. Every table was transformed by a great twittering. Another evening she played at languor and suffering, speaking only in a low voice, in sobs; and immediately all the chatterers fell dumb and put on faces like so many women in childbirth. One day she wagered with a gentleman from Venice that she could get the first lady of Portogruaro to dress her head with capon feathers. And then she appeared in public with this bizarre adornment atop her hair, and that very same day the wife of the Podestà plucked an entire henhouse to deck out her own head that way. But Lady Frumier was kind enough to the capons not to insist on this fashion, for, had she continued, within three days there wouldn't have been one still wearing the dress Mother Nature had provided.

Lady Frumier's conversation eclipsed and absorbed all others instantly. They were but preambles, corollaries to hers. Fine sayings, eloquent glances and gestures were prepared for the great appearance – or what had been said and done chez Frumier the night before was repeated. Let me add that the coffee was nicer in that household, and that from time to time a bottle of maraschino and some cakes made by the nuns of San Vito added to the group's enjoyment.

Frumier, too, found something there to sink his teeth into. If, in practice, he behaved little differently from his grandparents, he had a passing knowledge of modern philosophy and, when necessary, could quote some phrase from Voltaire or Diderot in his broad Venetian accent. Among the advocates and clergy of the city there were some inquiring spirits like himself, who rigorously separated principles and practice, and therefore did not fear to question or even negate that which (if necessary for professional reasons) they would readily declare certain and indubitable. We know how relaxed customs were in the last century in this regard; in Venice they were more relaxed than elsewhere, and in Portogruaro relaxed beyond all measure, for the men, too, like the women here, were not content merely to follow the example of the capital, but wanted to go courageously beyond it. To cite just one: Monsignor di Sant'Andrea, supreme syllogist among theologians, who once detached from the Curia and sitting down to reason with his peers in confidence was not ashamed to turn some of his own syllogisms upside down. And as for the young seminarists, there were one or two who, in terms of dangerous views, far exceeded most of the medical men in town. And doctors, if I may say so, were even then not considered great spiritualists.

However, among the labourers in the Lord's vineyard, there was a side (crude, traditional and incorruptible) that opposed this elegant, long-winded, somewhat reckless scepticism with all the force of inertia. And if there were any old priests of broad-minded opinions who also observed that simplicity and integrity which priests are called to, they were rare specimens indeed. More often, whether young or old, those who fell into philosophical anarchy did not excel at piety, chastity and the other virtues special to the clergy. Their lax discipline and dogmatic indifference could not but injure the genuine priesthood, those who had studied St Thomas's *Summa Theologica* and believed that faith was immutable truth, and their ministry holy. Such men, their unbending consciences and their austere manners ill-suited to gentlefolk and the moral gambits of the city, adapted nicely, however, to the patriarchal rule of country parishes.

Now the mountains are often the seedbed of the country clergy and this side I call traditional was kept alive by the many vows taken in Clausedo, a large mountain village in the diocese. The 'secularians' (so their adversaries designated those whose opinions and habits approached unbridled secularism) came from comfortable families in the cities and on the plain. On the traditional side, the gravity, reserve and faith (not to mention enthusiasm and priestly self-abnegation) perpetuated itself from uncle to nephew, from rector to chaplain. On the other side, classical culture, philosophical freedom, elegant manners and religious tolerance were instilled by the family, and boys became priests either thoughtlessly, obediently or because they were keen to have an easy, untroubled life. Both the first and the second had their defenders in the seminaries and the Curia, and sometimes one, sometimes the other was dominant, and every bishop that commanded the diocese was accused of favouring either the secularians or the Clausedans. Clausedans and secularians fought like cats and dogs; the one side was accused of ignorance, tyranny, nepotism and penny-pinching; the other of licentiousness, irreligion, worldliness and setting a bad example. In general, the city supported the second side; the countryside, the first; but the Clausedans, by temperament and because of what they believed, tended to agree more among themselves, while petty obstinacy and personal lack of seriousness prevented the others from finding any rule of conduct or order.

Such dissension among the clergy naturally fed gossip and intrigue in society. Armed with sharp wit, those bright young seminarists who enjoyed the good life were, if unable to demolish that ascendency their adversaries had acquired in centuries and centuries of sobriety, at least able to hit back. Young ladies tended to favour the young seminarists; only the odd, elderly paralytic backed the rigorists, more out of envy than conviction. In short, the Senator found a select group of conversationalists even among the clergy, men who were cut from the same cloth as he, accustomed to his way of looking at things and his equals in learning and culture, who could offer him some very pleasant company. He enjoyed talking, reasoning and arguing freely; telling and hearing clever tales and gossip; and conversation sprinkled with jokes and popular sayings without any prudes around to turn up their noses. He found his sort of people there. Even drops of mercury do not chase each other and meld together so stubbornly as the like-minded form a society. And so, when the Senator entertained, a group began to form, dividing itself from the others and shaping itself around their host. In truth, all would have liked to join it, but not everyone had the courage to participate in a discussion without understanding it, to laugh when others laughed without knowing why, to take a kick in the foot with a smile on the face, to remain in a group of fine fellows without ever being asked a question or daring to say a word.

And so the ignorant, the fools, the hypocrites, the genteel and well-bred were quickly refined out, leaving pure gold: the sophisticated, the cultivated, the wits. There was Monsignor di Sant'Andrea, Avvocato Santelli and a few other men of the law; the young Giulio Del Ponte, Professor Dessalli and several other professors of belles-lettres; a certain don Marco Chierini who had a reputation as a most elegant abbé; and three or four counts and marquises who loved both books and women, both the study of antiquity and modern manners. And now that I mention it, let me say that in those days there was no such thing as an educated man who did not have the constitutions of Athens and Sparta at his fingertips. The words of Lycurgus, of Socrates, Solon and Leonidas were the subject of regular gymnasium lessons: a curious contradiction in the midst of so much obsequious, blind obedience, so little regard for honesty and liberty. In any event, while the ladies and the rest of the company cut the cards and played *tresette* and *quintiglio*,[13] the Senator's little academy met in a corner of the drawing room to discuss politics and banter about all the most scandalous news in town. Theirs was a motley music, a veritable serio-comic opera of melodies both absurd and sublime, silly and serious, cheerful and gloomy; a verbal mosaic of bons mots, debates, lengthy stories and coy restraint, an example of that masterpiece of Venetian invention that can be admired in the finest detail in the work of Benvenuto Cellini. The events in France and Germany were spoken of in the most liberal terms, along with Pius VI's travels, Joseph II's aims, Russia's intentions, Turkish manoeuvres. Machiavelli, Sallust, Cicero and Aretino: a wide assortment of views were brought to bear. Events of the day were compared with chapters from Livy, and such serious reflections never failed to be interspersed with jests and jokes. Any excuse to laugh was welcome.

Those who believe the origins of humour are to be found in England have evidently never lived in Venice or passed through Portogruaro. There they would have found a southern sense of humour – the fruit of centuries of ease and leisure, of excellent meals and quick, bright, clever minds – that is as different from its northern cousin as the heavy nocturnal fog of the moor is different from the bright, vaporous horizon of a summer's gloaming. Life and all that is in it, equally derided: here lies the parallel between the two. But all viewed through a carefree, joyful lens: here lies the difference. In England, instead, they incline to melancholy; they brood, grow passionate and kill themselves. These are two forms of immorality, two different types of folly, and I do not wish to choose between them. The mind would go one way, the heart the other, depending on whether dignity or happiness is most admired. But let me assure you that for these Venetian pranksters to leap from Catherine II's Russian scandals to the adventures of a certain local lady or cavalier was no leap at all. One name conjured up two more; two names, four; and so on without end. Neither the absent nor the present was exempt, and these wits had the good manners to endure a joke without retaliating immediately, waiting for the opportune moment that would arrive sooner or later. There was much cultivation, superficial if you will, but broad and not at all pedantic; a great deal of wit; finely pared repartee; and, above all, infinite tolerance in the conversation of that fun-loving little court of Athens (as I think of it).

Notice that I refer to fun-lovers here, not knowing how better to translate the French *viveurs*, which first came to mind. Having lived at length among the French I often have this problem and I am not always familiar enough with my own language to resolve it. Here I write 'fun-lovers' to mean those who fashion their purpose in life out of what fate provides, taking from life as from philosophy the happy and enjoyable part. If by 'fun-lover', you understand an idler, a material pleasure-seeker, well, none of these gentlemen was one of those. All had their business to take care of and all took their share of pleasures, only they took them as pleasures, not as obligations and moral necessities. 'Spirited' and 'spiritual' are more often opposites than synonyms, they knew.

The lords of Fratta, finally rid of their bête noire at Venchieredo, had resumed their usual routines. The Chaplain remained at his post and had not stopped receiving his old friend and penitent, Spaccafumo, at least once a month. The Count and the Clerk closed an eye; the Rector of Teglio scolded him from time to time. But the paltry little priest of Fratta, although quite unable to stammer out a reply to those lectures from his superior, was perfectly able to carry on as he liked once the Rector had turned his back. Meanwhile, for reasons of office and of proximity, Dottor Natalino, clerk of Venchieredo, had drawn closer to the Count and the Clerk of Fratta. Signor Lucilio, who was good friends with Leopardo Provedoni, had also got to know his wife, and from time to time the vivacious Doretta also joined the evening gatherings at the Castle. But now, two evenings a week, there were far more interesting gatherings! They were expected to spend the evening at Portogruaro and join in the Frumier salon. It was quite a perilous enterprise, given the roads of the day, but the Countess was so determined not to be outshone by her sister-in-law that she got up her courage to try. One of her daughters was already old enough to be married, the other was growing up a bad weed; the first had just a dusting of manners, while the second was utterly virgin. They must be introduced in society so as to learn how to behave. And they must be pushed forward, because marriers think with their eyes above all, and those two silly girls would lose nothing by being looked at. Such were the arguments put forward by the Countess to convince her husband to venture out in the carriage twice a week on the road to Portogruaro. First, however, the cautious Count sent out a dozen workmen to adjust the roughest stretches and the deepest holes along the way, and then he had the coachman conduct the horses at a walk, and sent two footmen out ahead with lamps. The two footmen were Menichetto, Fulgenzio's son, and Sandro from the mill, made to wear scarlet livery for the occasion cut from two old parade saddlecloths. I stood on the rear footboard and all the way (which was three good miles) I amused myself looking at la Pisana through the carriage window. Why it was that I, too, went along on those visits only to nap in the Frumier kitchen, I will tell you presently.

Just as the Count dragged the Clerk behind him, so the Clerk dragged me. I was, in short, the shadow of a shadow, but in this case I didn't much mind being a shadow, because it offered me a pretext to accompany la Pisana. Our love continued quite whole-heartedly, interrupted and varied by the usual jealousies, then bolstered again by necessity and habit. Now, between a lad of thirteen and a girl of eleven, such an affair is no longer mere foolishness. But I was enjoying it, and she, too, for lack of anything better, and her parents were not troubled at all, and the maids and serving boys, after my memorable venture and my promotion to the chancery, had begun to treat me like a little gentleman and left me to do as I pleased. Our games thus continued and grew ever more serious; and I was already beginning to design certain romances that if I were to recount them now would make these confessions go on forever.

In any case there was also a change in my feelings, for if once la Pisana's embraces had seemed to me entirely due to her goodness, now, feeling myself more important, I ascribed some of the credit to myself. What the deuce! Little Carletto the turnspit, dressed in the servants' cast-offs and Monsignor's rags, was now a Latin scholar, neatly combed with a black pigtail on my shoulders, shod with two brass buckles, nicely dressed in a blue velvet tunic and garnet-hued breeches. What a difference! Even my skin, no longer exposed to the sun and the elements, had grown much more civilized. I found that it was actually white and that my large brown eyes were as good as those of any other; I saw my frame grow taller and slimmer every day, and found my mouth was not disagreeable, with a fine row of teeth inside that (even if they weren't so close together as to annoy one another) nevertheless shone like ivory. Only those damned ears, and here the Rector was to blame for pulling them, occupied too much space on my head, but I was trying to correct this defect by sleeping one night on one side, and the next night on the other, to give them a more attractive angle.

Oh, enough! I'm pressing at those ears now and recognize I was not all that successful. But Martino never ceased to admire me, saying, 'The truth is that beauty does not bud unless it is mistreated. The fact is, you are the handsomest Carlino around, and you came forth from the ashes of the hearth, and most of the mother's milk you had I gave to you myself.' As I grew up, the poor man grew ever more bent over; now his legs were getting weak, and he grated his cheese sitting down and couldn't hear a thing, even if you shot off a cannon by his ears. It didn't matter, though: he and I were still able to communicate with signs. To have been alone in the world without me would have been an equal curse, I think. As for his former mistress, the old Countess, he would go up to keep her company when Clara was absent, but their different habits and the distance between their lives meant they did not have those common signals with which the deaf are able to communicate.

In the meantime, after the Count and Countess of Fratta, and above all after the Contessina Clara appeared at the Frumier salon, a new element of castle dwellers and petty rural gentry also began to arrive. Partistagno, who had become a sort of guardian angel to the family after aiding the Count during Venchieredo's attack, was one of the first to show up. It must be said that he wore his glorious halo rather ostentatiously, but the facts were all in his favour, and you could laugh perhaps, but not deny them. The young cavalier's superior bearing pained Lucilio greatly, but his pain owed more to envy than to jealousy of Clara. He was pained that the services rendered to the Count of Fratta had not been rendered by him. But he felt sure of Clara's feelings and every glance from her offered him new hope; and even the calm way she accepted Partistagno's gallantries seemed a guarantee that no danger would ever come from that side. How could he not trust a heart so pure, a conscience so upright and earnest?

After that first declaration of love, he had spoken to her often when the two were alone in the dining hall or during one of their promenades; almost every afternoon he sat with her an hour in her grandmother's chamber and he was ever more devoted to her innocent, angelic beauty, her ardent, yet virginal heart, so silent and calm. His fiery, tyrannical nature demanded a matching soul that would grant him the quiet security that he was loved. He had found it, loved it (the way the Capuchin at the end of life loves his piece of Heaven), and now his heart, his intelligence and the thousand arts of an imaginative spirit and an all-powerful will were at work binding to himself that other, necessary part of him that lived in Clara. For her part, she yielded deliciously to this powerful love, loving in turn with all her soul and not thinking of what might follow, for God protected her innocence and happiness, and she was happy enough to fear nothing and blush at nothing. That dreary, false precept holding that it is shameful and unnatural for young maidens to fall in love had never been one of the articles of her religion.

Instead, love was her rule and she had always obeyed and still obeyed devoutly. And so she made no effort to conceal that sweet sentiment that Lucilio had inspired, and if the Count and the Countess were not aware of it, it was possibly because such a thing was so very unthinkable that it raised no suspicion. In any case, maidens of the times were by no means forbidden to fall in love, as long as the matter went no further. Inside the Castle it was already whispered that when Clara married, Signor Lucilio would be her *cavalier servente*.

But when one day Rosa made a joke on the subject, I watched him blanch and bite his moustaches in fury. Even the old Countess, I suspect, had discovered Clara's secret, but she was too taken with the young man herself to think of her granddaughter's happiness. Her imagination, come to the unconscious aid of her interests, probably offered her a thousand arguments against believing him in love. Lucilio was so guarded that Clara would calm down in the end, she thought. The old lady knew – or thought she knew – something of those lovely gilded clouds that race across young girls' imaginations.

'They are only clouds!' she reasoned. 'Clouds that will pass at the first breeze.' The breeze would be the offer of a good match and an order from her parents.

How well she understood Clara's temperament and how much, or how little, it resembled her own, we shall soon learn. But certainly Lucilio's cool bearing lulled her into placid security, for if she had examined the matter more carefully she might not have thought those clouds would disperse so easily; but then, if she destroyed those impossible castles in the air the two young people were building, she'd be deprived of the only delights remaining to her. As things were, she felt sure she could trust Clara's discretion and calm nature, and could even say to herself when Clara left the room to light Lucilio's way, 'Ah, what a good and wise young man! You wouldn't think he's afraid to raise his eyes and show he's attached to my granddaughter, would you? He raises them only to look at me – at his age! It is quite miraculous!'

But Lucilio found other moments to let his soul to take flight, and in those moments his good and wise eyes were often unfaithful to the older woman. While they played at cards in the dining hall and he seemed quite wrapped up in Monsignor's game of *tresette*, or sat petting the Captain's dog Marocco attentively, a dialogue of glances was always flickering between him and Clara – an angel singing in the heart, while the din of cracked bells attacked the ears. Oh precious, how precious those divine harmonies that beatify the soul without troubling those rude drums of our ears! The religion of the imperceptible and that of the eternal join together in the mind like light and colour in a ray of sunshine. A sentiment imagined triumphs over bodily sensation, proving that the soul exists even without material support. Love born in the spirit does not perish in the body; it surmounts human fragility to flow, pure and eternal, into that immense love that is the one God. Lucilio felt the divine magic of this without it troubling his medical judgement. Such things were phenomena beyond nature and, indulging in them, he merely took on greater warmth and more obstinate passion.

When her parents introduced her to her aunt's salon, the young doctor of Fossalta found he could quite easily join the group as well. Venetian etiquette was never so unjust as to bar the well-educated, the witty and the meritorious from its patrician halls, even when there was no coat of arms to enhance those fine qualities. Lucilio was greatly admired at Portogruaro and was a favourite and an intimate of several young seminary professors. They presented him to the illustrious Senator and he soon thanked them for the favour. In any case, the Senator had long known Dr Sperandio, who relied on him for all his needs in Venice. And so Frumier nicely took the young man to task for relying on third-party sponsors to present him. That first evening, as they said their farewells, the Senator remarked that all the fine things said about the young man were nothing compared to what he himself intended to say in future. Lucilio bowed, modestly pretending to have no words to match such kindness.

In fact, Lucilio's conversation was so lively, so varied and amusing, that few others were as pleasurable to listen to; only Professor Dessalli was more erudite, and the prize for wit and cleverness was evenly divided between Lucilio and Giulio Del

Ponte. If Del Ponte was sometimes quicker and more profuse in his arguments, Lucilio took the palm for irony and profundity. He appealed to those who enjoyed mature wisdom, while Del Ponte had youthful spirit and charm on his side. But making men think leaves deeper traces on their souls than making them laugh, and charm fades quickly before admiration. For admiration is no mere gift from one man to his equal, but a genuine tribute imposed by the great on the small, by the strong on the weak. And Lucilio knew how to impose it gallantly, to demand it discreetly, so that the others were made to pay well and even to be grateful.

When Lucilio appeared, the Senator's intimate circle was suddenly lit by fresh enthusiasm. All those nicely appointed dabbling minds, a bit tepid, a bit worn, were invigorated by his company. He brought all that was youthful and alive in them to the boil. They forgot what they had been and what they were and borrowed youthful dreams from him. They laughed and chattered and bantered and argued not like men looking to kill time, but as if they were in a hurry to understand it, make use of it. Their lives seemed to have acquired purpose. They breathed a single breath of hope, noble and mysterious; they were one brow shining with undying intelligence. The Senator, once alone and returned to his usual apathy, was amazed by that hot enthusiasm, that combative spirit, those disputes and rows that carried him away like a schoolboy. He attributed it all to the presence of the young, when instead it was the very flame of life stirred up in him by a powerful spellbinder, a flame that, although unable to warm the frozen fibres of his heart, filled his head with fire and roused his tongue.

'You might almost think I'm serious about all this sophistry we whip up to kill time!' he mused while he awaited his supper in his favourite armchair. 'And just think that it's forty years since I smelled the venerable dust of a schoolroom! Perhaps it's true that men are no more than eternal boys! Eternal, eternal,' said the old man, patting his sunken, wrinkled cheeks. 'Yes, God willing!'

Once Lucilio had unleashed the enthusiasm of the Senator's little circle, those at the gaming tables, especially the ladies, were often distracted. That perpetual hum of questions and answers, accusations and replies, of banter, laughter, exclamations and applause stimulated the card-players' curiosity, and, may I add, even their envy. The charms of *quintiglio* and the thrill of *tresette* were considerably less exciting, and when a *capot* hand[14] set off the usual ironic congratulations and the usual promises to take revenge, that was the end of it, and they all went back to the monotonous to and fro of the game like old carriage nags. In that one corner of the drawing room, however, the conversation was forever various, cheerful and animated. All ears began to turn that way, while eyes turned glassy over cards.

'Signora, it's your hand. Or didn't you see I called you?'

'Oh, I'm sorry, I've a touch of headache' or 'Oh, I didn't notice, my mind was elsewhere!' Such were the reproofs and rejoinders flying across the tables; the offenders sighed and returned to their card-play. Lucilio had much to do with those sighs, and he knew it. He knew the effect he had on the Senator's salon and he knew it would earn him much gratitude from Clara. Love has its own sort of vanity. On the one hand, it wants to aggrandize and please the many, on the other, it is terribly proud to find that what aims to please just one, pleases the many. Giulio Del Ponte, who like Lucilio had reason to try to make himself appealing to the ladies, had to use all his wits to keep up with his friend, and the rest of the company duly competed with them in cleverness and verve, in all the weightiest arguments that could be concocted out of the odd sentence in the *Gazzetta di Venezia*, the mother – no, the Eve – of all newspapers. In truth, the Venetians of the time had need to invent the *Gazzetta*, for it became, in turn, a real and legitimate element in their imaginations, the source from which they spun their library of gossip and wit. Every week the Senator received his *Gazzetta* and it brought forth great comments, but in that labour of polish and intarsia, Lucilio was far ahead of the others. No one knew better than he how to find the reasons in one corner of the globe for what had happened in the other corner.

'What an eye you have, dear Dottore,' they would say to him in wonder. 'For you, England and China are at the end of a spyglass and you are able to find as many links between them as between Venice and Fusina!' And Lucilio would reply that the Earth is but a ball that turns and moves as one, and that since Columbus and Vasco da Gama had put it back together as it was created, we should not be surprised that blood had once again begun to circulate through that great body from the poles to the equator. Whenever they were sailing through such waters, the Senator would close one eye, and, half-closing the other, ruminate about certain past times when young Lucilio had left a few black marks on the books of the Inquisitors of State. Yes, those distant concerns did sometimes disturb his scrupulous Venetian mind, but on the other hand, Lucilio had not left Fossalta for several years, and was happily living his comfortable country life, and by now the Inquisitors must have forgotten about him, and he them, and his youthful superstitions. On a diplomatic visit to his distinguished patron, Dr Sperandio reassured him, confessing that in the old days he had never dreamed that his son could be as quiet and well-behaved as he was in his present simple, hardworking life.

'Oh, if only he would decide to take his degree!' the old doctor said. 'Without stopping in Venice, of course!' he added remorsefully. 'But I say, if he would only take his degree I have a fine clientele ready for him!'

'There is still time, there is still time,' said the Senator. 'You, meanwhile, see to it that your son straightens up, that he gets rid of his bizarre ideas and keeps his liveliness and good humour, without taking seriously any of those writers and their literary fantasies. The degree will come one day or another, and there will always be plenty of sick people for a doctor who knows how to make them well.'

'*Morbus omnis, arte ippocratica sanatur aut laevatur*,' added the doctor. The Hippocratic arts can treat or cure any disease. And considering that this exchange took place in the afternoon, he most likely went on citing another half-dozen texts, but I don't know that for certain and would rather spare my readers having to make sense of them.

So Lucilio had become, as they say, the darling of the ladies. Those flighty things, who in spite of all the capricious laws of love will let themselves be ensnared by anyone showing off in any way. There can be no greater pleasure than to be envied by all. But Lucilio permitted none of them that pleasure. Jovial, sparkling and clever on those rare occasions when he ventured among the card tables, he would return to the Senator's circle without showing so much as the tip of his handkerchief to any of those odalisques. On his way back and forth, however, he would light up Clara's whole person with one of those glances that envelops everything in fire, as the salamander does. At that sudden, sweet flame, every fibre of her being trembled, yet her innocent soul went on speaking its peaceful smile through her eyes. It was as if a magnetic current touched her veins with a thousand invisible barbs, without in any way disturbing the deep recesses of her soul. Her conscience was more insuperable than an abyss, more solid than a rock. Her modesty, even more than the inconspicuous seat she chose, protected her from other ladies' inquisitive eyes. She could make herself be forgotten with ease, and no one suspected that Lucilio's heart beat for the one lady who did the least to win him over.

The wife of the Correggitore[15] was not so discreet. From the very first evening her attentions, her flirtations, her affectations towards the desirable young man from Fossalta had caught the eye of the Podestà's wife and the Superintendent's sister. Those two, in turn, had made themselves conspicuous for being miffed. In short, Paris among the goddesses could not have been more contested than Lucilio among those ladies. He floated through by noticing nothing at all.

There was, however, another young lady who more than any other, more than Madam Correggitrice herself, was fascinated by Lucilio's triumphs, who never took her eyes off him, who blushed when he drew near, who was not shy about approaching him to touch his arm or brush his sleeve or study him by gazing into his eyes. Who was this shameless young lady? La Pisana. Imagine! A coquette of twelve, still immature; a lover not yet four feet tall? And yet it was the case; the all-seeing eye of jealousy told me so. The third or fourth time we went to the Frumiers, I watched the young lady take special care to curl and crease and decorate herself. None of her dresses was good enough for her; no primping too great, no concentration enough to dress her hair and polish her nails. Now I hadn't seen this agitation on our first or second visit, and immediately I guessed it couldn't be put down to the usual feminine vanity or any wish to be admired by the ladies. There had to be some other purpose behind it, and I, a fool in such matters then as always, decided I would clear it up once and for all. Even back then, the martyrdom of certainty seemed less terrible to me than the torment of doubt (and yet when I acquired that cruel certainty, the forsaken joy of being able to go on doubting plagued me every time!).

And so when the servants came up to bring the coffee, I slipped into the drawing room with them and, half-hidden behind the door, stood on the lookout. I saw la Pisana with her eyes fixed on Lucilio as if she wanted to eat him. Her head turned towards him like a sunflower to the sun, and when he became animated or turned away from his circle I saw her little bosom swell with vanity like that of a grown woman. She didn't speak or breathe or see anything at all but him; she didn't move or smile except for him. Her behaviour showed all the signs of a most intense and violent love; only her tender age saved her from the comments and suspicions of the ladies, just as modesty had saved her sister. I trembled from head to foot, sweated as if I had a fever; I ground my teeth and clutched the door, feeling close to death. Suddenly I understood why la Pisana had been so sulky in those past few days, why she didn't laugh and talk as usual, why she was so pensive, so cross, so enamoured of her solitude and the moon.

'Oh, traitor!' my poor heart wailed, and I was in anguish. My unfortunate love gave way to a consoling swell of hatred. I would have liked to clutch a bunch of thunderbolts in my hand and hurl them at Lucilio's high, detested brow; I wished my soul were a poison that could enter into his every pore, dissolve his every fibre and torture his nerves to death. I cared nothing for myself then, for I was tasting life's bitterness for the first time and I hated it (almost as much as I hated Lucilio) for being the occasion if not the reason for all my ills. And then I had to watch that vain little fool, all innocence, take the cup of coffee from the servant and give it to the young man herself. She was as red as hot coals, her eyes were sparkling like rubies (more than I had ever seen) and suddenly she was no longer a child but a fetching and charming young lady, and, what was worse, in love. When Lucilio took the cup from her, she was trembling slightly and spilled a few drops of coffee on her dress. Lucilio smiled fondly and bent to blot them with his handkerchief. Oh, if you had seen that little lady! Her face wore an expression more voluptuous than any Greek ever gave to a statue of Venus or Leda. Her eyes were lost in a mist of beatitude and her little person began to sag so weakly that Lucilio had to put an arm around her to hold her up. I bit my hands and my lips, tore at my breast and my face; I felt an impulse pushing me to throw myself in rage at that odious spectacle, but also a mysterious force that held my feet stuck to the floor. God being merciful, Lucilio finally went back to his conversation and la Pisana sat down next to her mother. But that sweet turmoil attached to her person went on tormenting me until the servants began to carry out the trays.

'Oh, Carlino! What are you doing here?' one of them said to me. 'Move out of my way and get back in the kitchen; this is not your place!'

His words, which should have added insult to my injury, had the opposite effect, of a chilly and providential poison that calmed and relieved it.

'Yes, indeed,' I said to myself in gloomy despair. 'This is not my place.'

And so, staggering like a drunken man, I returned to the kitchen and there I stayed, my eyes fixed on the coals in the hearth, until they came to tell me that the horses had been harnessed and it was time to go. Then I had another chance to see la Pisana as she followed Lucilio stubbornly down the stairs, a little dog close behind her master. Indifferent to anything else, she climbed into the carriage looking only at him, and I saw her lean out the window to stare at the spot where he'd been, even after he was gone. Meanwhile, I took up my usual place; poor, disinherited soul that I was, and God only knows what my thoughts were for that hour it took us to return home.

Thoughts, perhaps, is not the word: ravings, curses, grief, imprecations. I knew very well what that narrow partition of leather that divided my place from hers meant for my future. A thousand times I'd imagined that day when the accursed force of human affairs robbed her from me forever and gave her to another. But in my mind that other was never desired, never loved, only barely tolerated. It comforted me to imagine her pale, tearful and suffering under her white wedding veil, to see her go to the altar a victim, and in the gloom of the nuptial chamber, offer herself cold, trembling and broken, neither loving nor desiring, to the master she had been sold to. Her heart would remain mine, our souls would go on loving; I would have been happy indeed to see her in passing with her children sometimes; it would have been a joy to take one of them aside when she wasn't looking and squeeze that child to my heart, to kiss and love and look in that little face for the traces of her own, and to delude myself that the mysteries of her spirit transmitted to that child had also been mine, when she loved me alone, and with all the force of her heart.

Although I was still a flimsy lad of not yet fourteen, I knew a great deal about the things of this world, for the careless chatter of the maids and manservants had taught me perhaps more than I needed to know. Nevertheless, I was quite willing to subdue my confused and agitated senses, to ground my soaring, enamoured fantasy; I wanted no more than sweet sorrows and melancholy pleasures. Yet all my efforts and devotion were met with negligence and ingratitude. She didn't even neglect me for another love; then, at least, I might have had the comfort of a struggle, of hatred and revenge. No, I was discarded like some useless instrument so that she could run after her vain ambitions of superiority, grow intoxicated with her monstrous, impossible dreams. My initial antipathy to Lucilio slowly devolved into a furious contempt for la Pisana. For her, Lucilio was an old man who had seemed neither handsome nor desirable; the admiration of others had been necessary to make her appreciate his merits, too fine and manly to impress her childish mind. I felt I was being mercilessly sacrificed to her vanity.

'No, there's not a trace of kindness in her, not a glimmer of memory, nor a speck of shame. Oh, I despise her for what she is, I will always despise her!' I wailed to myself.

Poor boy! For the first time I loved and despised simultaneously, one of the worst torments nature prepares for her sons and daughters: a war on and perversion of every moral principle; a desperate humiliation in which the soul, although able to recognize and love the good, is compelled to kneel and pray before the idol of evil. My heart was too large, my memory too long, and thoughts of our early, childish affections pursued me ruthlessly. In vain I tried to flee; in vain I sought to fight those memories with reason, but they predated reason and knew all my soul's folds and hiding places. Their fatal breath stirred up a tempest in me, a storm of desire, fury, rage, tears. So think hard on these two words that embody the entire tale of my disgrace and my shame; think hard on them and then tell me whether, even with all of passion's eloquence, all pain's lessons suffered, all the candour repentance brings, it is possible to say what they mean. I *loved* and I *despised*.

You will probably laugh at this tale of two children pretending to be adults, but I swear to you that I'm spinning no romance here: this is simply the story of my life. As I recall it aloud, I write what I recall. And I would wager that if all of you could return in memory to your infancies, many would find there the germ, if not the whole, of those passions that later swelled in you. Believe me, when they speak of girls being born little women, it's often forgotten that boys, too, can be men prematurely. The tutor's lash and the iron circle of obligation will generally keep them tamed until a certain age. But allow them to move and think and do as they please, and you will soon see them – as if under the narrow shaft of a microscope – animated by the spark of mature passions. La Pisana and I were allowed to grow up as God willed and as was the habit of those times, at least when the easy way out, the convent, was not chosen. It was such an upbringing, in the midst of the worst models, that created that sheep-like flock of men without faith, strength or illusions who reached the threshold of life already half-dead, then wallowed in pleasures and oblivion until death. The worms that awaited them in the tomb could well have been their companions in life, too.

For my part (by luck of temperament or because adversity hardened my soul from my earliest years) I was able to remain honest and not soil myself so much as to remain forever stuck in that mire. But la Pisana, although endowed (more than I) with great gifts and good inclinations, was deprived of them despite all the chances she had to save herself. Even her mind, so lively, so flexible, so clever, grew cloudy and sterile in that frenzy for pleasure that overtook her, in that fire of the senses in which she was allowed to burn up the noblest part of her soul. Courage, mercy, generosity, imagination: all the best qualities of her nature degenerated into so many instruments to satisfy unbridled cravings. If, from time to time, they shone anew, they were merely passing flashes, bizarre impulses, not conscious acts of real virtue.

This lamentable decay began in early childhood, and in the period I now refer to was already so advanced that although it might have been possible to arrest it, the consequences could not be erased. And when later I could touch it with my hand and see in it the reason why la Pisana's infantile vices grew steadily worse over the years, there was nothing on earth that could make it better. Oh, what tears of love and desperation I shed! How I mourned the miracles and conversions of past centuries! With what ardent hopes did I devour books telling how to save souls with affection, patience, sacrifice! With what humility and courage did I offer up piece after piece of myself so that this fallen angel, whose charmed beauty I had looked upon at the dawn of her life, could regain her light! But either the books lie or la Pisana was already beyond man's power to change her. One day the heavens opened above her and I saw what my reason doubted but my heart held most dear. That day of recompense and infinite sorrow seems so near! But when she lived at the Castle of Fratta it was very far away indeed and I would have been horrified to think that my love's greatest reward would be bestowed by death.

In the days following that evening when I suffered so much,

I began to look so wan and haggard that everyone feared some illness. They very much wanted Signor Lucilio to take my pulse, but I was firm in my refusal and as long as I grew no worse they left me alone, convinced I was just a stubborn boy. The maids were well aware that feelings between la Pisana and me had cooled greatly, but they didn't know this was the reason I was so emaciated. They were accustomed to these intervals of cooling and paid little attention to such childish foolishness. After a few days la Pisana, too, noticed my pallor and my lack of appetite and, almost as if she had guessed my secret, made an effort to stay with me. I had already moved on from furious desperation to weary sorrow and my aspect was somewhat melancholy and pitiful. She wasn't at all pleased with these spirits of mine and pretended I'd said I didn't need her and left me there like a dog. Oh, if only she had thrown her arms around my neck! I would have been simple (or cowardly) enough to press her to my heart and forget those cruel moments when she'd made me suffer. But perhaps it was better this way, because the next day the suffering would have returned and found me weaker than before.

Despite my poor health, each time the family went to Portogruaro I did not fail to go along, and each time I savoured my misfortune with bitter pleasure. My soul grew stronger, but my body suffered mightily and I certainly couldn't have carried on that way much longer. Martino was always asking me what caused me to sigh so much; the Rector was amazed to find my Latin exercises were not as correct as before, but he didn't have the courage to reprimand me, for my debilitation moved him to compassion; the Contessina Clara was always at my side with embraces and attentions. I grew thinner before their eyes and la Pisana pretended not to see, and if she did allow a merciful glance to fall on me, she would retract it quickly. It was thus that she hoped to punish me for my pride. But was it pride? I was dying of heartbreak and still I felt sorry for her, the reason I was dying. I pitied her and I loved her, when I should have despised her, disdained her, punished her. Tell me then, was this pride?

In those very days the Countess fortunately fell ill; I say

fortunately, because our visits to Portogruaro were interrupted and so I did not die. Lucilio continued to come to the Castle, now even more often because his medical ministrations were needed, but la Pisana was by no means as enchanted with him at Fratta as she was at Portogruaro. Once or twice she paid him some court, but then without much effort she stopped and slowly returned to her usual indifference. And as Lucilio began to exit her heart I began to re-enter, and my joy at her change of mind was so intense I resumed all confidence in our love. I was a boy and I trusted her blindly. Just as I had trusted her once, despite her passing flirtations, sure that there was no one in her heart but me, now I convinced myself that her transformation must be eternal. It was almost as if her apparent infidelity and her readiness to return to me were but one more proof that she could not live without me.

And so I said not a word about my suffering and avoided replying to her questions, guessing perhaps that a confession of jealousy was by far the best way to incite fresh infidelity. Touchy spirits, an unexplained malady: these were my excuses to cease investigating the matter and simply give full rein to my joy and open that heart of mine that so long had been closed. La Pisana romped with me quite impulsively, and her momentary fancy seemed to have left no trace in her memory or conscience; I found this comforting, but if I had been more thoughtful I should have found it dismaying. I thus abandoned myself completely to that current of happiness bearing me along and was delighted to find the young lady easy-going, loving and even humble and patient, which she had never been. Was this an unspoken compensation, unconsciously offered, for the wrongs she had done me? I cannot say. Perhaps her shy admiration for Lucilio had weaned her soul of its violent and tyrannical bent, and so I reaped what another had sowed. But such a doubt, which today seems so demeaning, did not even cross my mind then. One must live and philosophize at length to master the exquisite art of self-torture.

Although the Countess was only slightly indisposed, her recovery was slow. Her qualms, anxieties and complaints were such that all of Dr Sperandio's Italian and Latin eloquence,

Lucilio's patience, Monsignor di Sant'Andrea's comfort, her husband's and Clara's attentions and four good potions a day were not enough to calm her. One morning, however, a visit from her sister-in-law Frumier was announced and she immediately came round, forgot her infinite woes, washed, brushed her hair, put on the prettiest cap in her wardrobe and had her bed decorated with cushions and coverlets trimmed with lace. From that moment on it was certain she would recover and a *Te Deum* could be sung in the chapel to celebrate the most excellent mistress's new-found health. Monsignor Orlando sang that *Te Deum* with great earnestness, for never had he eaten so badly at Fratta as during that lady's illness. Everyone had been busy brewing up special teas, concocting soups and carrying up bowls of broth, and meanwhile the pots and pans remained empty and luncheons were the fruit of improvisation. No less than four or five visits from Lady Frumier were needed to restore order to family affairs and convert the Countess's long convalescence into excellent good health, and by then we were in the midst of winter. But the robust glow of those precious cheeks was now assured for another thirty years.

Monsignor Orlando watched happily as fat casseroles and ebullient stew-pots little by little repopulated the hearth. If he'd had to go on with that diet of semi-abstinence he would have paid for the Countess's recovery with his life! La Pisana and I had meanwhile gained a few months of peace and harmony. Harmony in a manner of speaking, for in effect we were back to the old way of life: first affection, then insults, jealousy and reconciliation. At times Donato, the druggist's son, and Sandro from the mill had me seething with rage. But now things were quite different. I had been used to these little dramas for some time and la Pisana, however brusque and hardnosed she might be in showing tenderness to me, was three times that with those other boys. Nor did I see in her, vis-à-vis them, that transformation that made her so humble, quivering and anxious when near Lucilio in her aunt's drawing room. The anguish I'd suffered then had in truth left no trace in my heart, but I did recall the reasons and often it was on the tip of my tongue to mention the matter to la Pisana and see what she remembered of it and how. Still, I hesitated, and would probably never have fulfilled that desire of mine had she not given me an occasion one day.

Lucilio, after a visit to the Countess, who was by now practically restored to health, and to the old Countess Badoer, was coming down the stairs heading towards the stable bridge, now rebuilt under Captain Sandracca's direction with all those clever devices necessary to defend the Castle. Clara was by his side on her way to the garden to pick a few lemon verbena leaves and any geraniums still battling frostbite. Many days had gone by since they had seen each other and their souls were agitated: full of those sentiments that from time to time need to be expressed boldly and freely, or become twisted up inside as if turned to poison. They longed to be free, to be alone, and once they had crossed the bridge and were sure they were indeed alone, they dipped into that pleasurable repetition of love's sweet questions and eternal answers which is quite enough to constitute a conversation between lovers. Words said and heard a thousand times, always with fresh meaning and pleasure: enough to prove that the soul alone is capable of the magic of thought, and that lips, moving, produce no more than a vain, monotonous stammer lacking internal harmony. Lucilio was just about to open the floodgates to all that love that had been choking him for days, when behind him he heard the skipping footsteps and high-pitched voice of la Pisana.

'Clara! Clara, wait! I want to come and pick a bunch too!' Lucilio bit his lip and was unable, or thought it unnecessary, to hide his dismay, while Clara, who had turned round towards her sister with her usual goodness, would not have been unhappy herself had she not seen the young man's pained face. As for herself, the happiness that bunch of flowers promised her sister might well have repaid that much-desired, forfeited conversation with her lover. Clara was good, good above all; and in such souls even violent passions can be domesticated by concerns for the pleasures of others. But Lucilio didn't like her easy resignation and his dismay increased. He turned towards La Pisana with a scowling face and asked if she had left her grandmother alone.

'Yes, but she herself gave me permission to come and pick

flowers with Clara,' the girl replied testily, for Lucilio didn't have the right to question her in that way.

'Were you generous and kind, you would know not to take advantage of certain permissions,' said Lucilio. 'An old woman who is ill and in need of company must not be left alone, however much she seems to permit us to do so.'

Tears of rage rose to la Pisana's eyes and she rudely turned her back and didn't even reply to Clara when she was told to stay, not to be so sensitive. She went running into the Chancery antechamber where my desk stood and, red with shame and indignation, threw her arms round my neck.

'What's happened?' I said, throwing down my pen and getting up from my chair.

'Oh, I'll make him pay for this, Mr Blackbird! Oh yes, he'll pay for it!' said la Pisana, stuttering and shaking.

I had quite forgotten hearing her use that name and had no idea who she was talking about.

'And who's this Mr Blackbird, what's he done to you?'

'Oh, it's Mr Blackbird of Fossalta, who wants to meddle in my business and question me and correct me as if I were one of his little serving girls. While I am a countess and he's nothing but a bloodletter, fit for the beggars and the peasants!'

The thoughts that raced through my head at those words made me smile, and only later did I understand the particular reason for her terrible ire. In the meantime I took advantage of my opportunity to get more out of the young lady.

'At first I didn't understand who you meant with your Mr Blackbird,' I said. 'The truth is, it's a long time since you called Signor Lucilio by that name.'

'You're right,' said la Pisana. 'It's been a century. And I've been so foolish! There was a time when I liked him; most of all, at my aunt's house in Portogruaro; I was enthralled listening to him talk. Heavens above! All those people, so impressed, so hanging on his every word. I would have given anything to be him and make such a fine impression.'

'You loved him very much,' I said, quivering inside.

'I . . . loved him?' she whispered, thinking it over quite sincerely. 'I can't say . . .'

At this point I watched the lie work its way up her face and I saw that at last, if not before, she understood the nature of her affection for Lucilio. She was ashamed and furious to have made such a confession to herself and, in revenge, redoubled her abuse of him.

'He's ugly. He's arrogant. He's nasty. He dresses like Fulgenzio!' Every curse, every sin in the book was thrown at him; I don't recall when I'd heard la Pisana go on at such length and with such vehemence as in that tirade of hers against Lucilio. And so, for my part, I felt secure. But that very virulence, had I thought about it, should have given me pause, not confidence, in a temperament as wild and extreme as hers. And indeed, when the twice-weekly jaunts to Portogruaro were resumed, la Pisana cooled on me and stood once again stupefied watching and listening to Lucilio. Those speeches and protestations of hatred for him were forgotten and, once again, without the least shame or surprise, she adored the man that just days before she had vilified. This time my suffering was less impetuous but deeper, for I understood what a seesaw of hope and disenchantment I had hitched my fortunes to. I tried to get la Pisana to see how displeased I was and make her think about the wrong she had done, but to no avail. I did notice, however, that her devotion for Lucilio was now mixed with a dose of jealousy. She had realized that she came second to Clara and suffered bitterly as a result; but this didn't harden her heart either towards her sister or Lucilio. Rather, she seemed content to love, or certain to love so deeply that one day she would come first.

All these sentiments that I read in her eyes were of little consolation to me. Not knowing whom to blame – not Lucilio, because he'd never notice, not la Pisana, because she paid me no more attention than she did the wall – I ended up once again blaming myself. But my suffering, as I said, was, if deeper, also more reasoned: I came to terms with pain, and rather than let it foment idleness and boredom, sought distraction in my work and studies. I sat myself down to read Cicero, Virgil, Horace, translating long passages and commenting on them in my own style, and making up my own compositions on such topics. In short, I believe I can say that la Pisana's second lapse was rather beneficial to my classical studies. The Rector declared himself very pleased with me and praised me to the Count and the Clerk for my love of study, and so everyone was happy (everyone but me) about my rapid progress.

Don't think this was but a matter of hours and days, it was actually weeks and months. There were the usual intervals, the usual lulls. Bad weather or bad roads or the terrible heat or evenings that were too short or the Frumiers' jaunts to Udine: at times the Count and Countess of Fratta suspended their visits to Portogruaro. Then la Pisana's love for me would revive, along with the usual store of blandishments for Sandro and Donato, and, finally, she even seemed aware of my unhappiness while in the heat of her infatuation with Lucilio and pitied me and offered me a glance or even a kiss in charity. I took whatever I was given like a real beggar; my suffering made me *cleave unto the dust*, as the psalm says,[16] and I would have let myself be stepped on, flattened and spat upon without complaint.

None of this meant that I didn't become a more worthy Latinist every day, and I sweated so much and grew so pallid over my books that Martino sometimes said he'd rather have seen me turning the spit, as I'd done in the past. No matter. For I had discovered all by myself what a great aid work is in dealing with life, and whatever Martino thought, I'm sure I'd have been much more miserable had I spent my pain in dissipation or allowed it to flourish in idleness. In any case, just after I turned fifteen I was in a position to sit exams in grammar, Latin, composition, prosody, rhetoric and ancient history at the Seminary of Portogruaro, and to emerge in greatest glory. Imagine, in scarcely three years I had learned what the others took six to accomplish!

After such a triumph it was decided in the family to send me to Padua to take a degree, but in the meantime I was given the post of junior official in the Chancery with an annual pay of sixty ducats, equal to fourteen *soldi* a day. Little, very little, certainly; but I was quite happy to pocket those coins and think, 'These belong to me, because I earned them myself!' The new level of dignity I'd risen to also meant I had a place at the masters' table and could enter the Frumier drawing room and sit beside the Clerk and watch him play *tresette*. That occupation didn't suit me much, but I was happy to have la Pisana always in my sights, where I could brood constantly over the foolish things she did to show her love for Lucilio. Really, when I think about it now, I can only laugh aloud, but then, matters were different. My heart wept tears of blood.

In the meantime, la Pisana had also grown up to be a real young lady. Not yet fourteen, she was already mature and perfect. She wasn't very tall, no, but she was very finely shaped, especially around her shoulders and her neck: a real bust of Giulia, Emperor Augustus' granddaughter, her head rather large but corrected by the beautiful oval of her face, her hair a great downpour, eyes languid and glistening as if with hidden fire, the finest eyebrows and a mouth, oh, a mouth made to be painted and to be kissed. A full and sonorous voice, the kind that doesn't trill from the head but draws its sound from the breast, where the heart lies. A bearing, now quiet like someone not very discerning; now bouncing and sure of herself like a schoolgirl on holiday; now mute, closed and pensive; then suddenly open, laughing, even chattering if you will; but already the foolish chatter had abandoned her and at fourteen years old you could see that other thoughts preoccupied her enough to keep her tongue silent. Thus she was the perfect lady while in the salon, but once she had left and was free of social constraints, the rights of youth took hold of that well-turned young body and made it do great somersaults and the most bizarre contortions ever seen. She was too much the tomboy then, just as in the salon she played the languid, simpering female. This is how I remember those years of transition: now a genuine little girl, now a mature woman, but the defects of the girl were so precisely repeated in the woman's soul and temperament that I never really noticed at what point the one superseded the other. The second was merely the continuation of the other, its natural evolution.

Now, here I've come to the point where a new torment was about to hit me, or rather, one already there was about to grow worse. Just about that time Signor Raimondo di Venchieredo left school and came to live in his castle near Cordovado. As he hadn't yet reached his majority, his guardian, a maternal uncle from Venice, had placed him under the watch of a tutor, a certain Padre Pendola, who (having arrived in Venice from . . . no one was exactly sure where) had acquired a great reputation for erudition. This mysterious fellow certainly had his very good reasons for taking up the post, and, between us, I think that on the sly he was one of those blue-eyed boys of the State Inquisitors. He was said to hail from Romagna, but he travelled on a Russian passport; we know that when the Society of Jesus was suppressed[17] the Jesuits fled to St Petersburg and the Republic of Venice never offered to be their protector. In any event, the Signoria had abandoned the political precepts of Paolo Sarpi[18] by the time Padre Pendola settled down with his pupil at Venchieredo, and both he and the young Venchieredo made a great impression on Portogruaro society, which hastened to invite and to celebrate them. When this young gentleman appeared at the Frumiers', la Pisana often paid attention to him and neglected Lucilio. While I, seated next to the Clerk, was gnawed to the core by jealousy – and flung my meaningful glances to the winds.

SEVEN

A panegyric for Padre Pendola and his pupil. Two marriages go up in smoke for no good reason. The Countess Clara and her mother move to Venice, where they are followed by Doctor Lucilio, who comes to be quite at home at the French Legation. Why I tire of la Pisana and begin to delight in various exponents of the fair sex all around; why I end by embracing the study of law at the University of Padua, where I remain until August 1792, sniffing from afar the scent of the Revolution in France.

It seemed at first that the Countess's ambitions to find a match for Clara would soon be satisfied. The young men of Portogruaro all had, you might say, eyes only for her, and she would merely have had to choose to be awarded that fellow among them she liked best. First, there was Partistagno, who was convinced she belonged to him, and when he saw another looking at her too earnestly, made sure his intentions were very, very clear. When he first visited the Frumier salon he had incautiously tried to join the master of the house's inner circle, then had to retreat, for he was not such a fool that he could not see the sorry figure he made. And so he sat down with two old ladies and a monsignor playing *tresette*, and from there kept Clara under constant fire from his conquering eye. His behaviour didn't much please his fellow card-players, and there was a continual murmur of calls and complaints. But the young cavalier was unmoved; he paid for the games he lost, or made his partner pay, never losing his composure. As luck would have it he was both young and handsome, and so the old ladies pardoned his distraction, and the monsignor, who was the spiritual father of one of the ladies, was forced to pardon him too.

Young Marquis Fessi, the Count Dall'Elsa and a few other

titled young popinjays about town were also courting Clara. But rather than just besiege her with glances, discreetly, they bowed and scraped and proffered compliments and praise. They joked and jested about, arms akimbo, thrusting a leg forward, and dressed up in their Sunday suits with trimmings, their enthusiasm was uncontainable. Circulating among the ladies' chairs, they would bend over this one or that, advise this player, now that one, always being supremely careful not to get involved in any of the games. The young seminarians and Prof. Dessalli, in particular, were also quite willing to hover for a quarter-hour around Clara, for their solemn garb protected them from any malign comments and the young lady's composure nicely matched their priestly gravity. In short, the fair young lady of Fratta had set all the heads in the room spinning and had the very peculiar modesty not to know it. Giulio Del Ponte, who was not by far the least keen, was amazed and annoyed by her reserve, and had gone even further and formed some suspicions about Lucilio, although without any proof. For only a heart already occupied by great affections could so coolly resist that carousel of love whirling around her. And who but the young doctor of Fossalta could have opened that breach?

So Signor Giulio thought; and from thought to a whisper of something the path was no greater than an ant's pace. Those whispers were just beginning to circulate when Padre Pendola appeared to present young Venchieredo to the Frumiers. The Count of Fratta was somewhat embarrassed, for he hadn't forgotten that with his assent, if not by his own doing, Venchieredo senior was eating black bread in the prisons of Rocca della Chiusa.[1] But the Countess, a woman of rare talents, let her imagination run ahead and conjure up a plan that could remove any bad blood between the two houses. Partistagno, in whom she'd initially placed great hopes, gave no hint that he intended to make a move; what harm could there be, then, in drawing Venchieredo into a good match with Clara? Once the two families' interests were united, one could to take steps to free the condemned man, and then gratitude and happiness would draw a line through the bad memories of the past, and, of course, the worthy protection of Senator Frumier was a guarantee that this happy conclusion might be reached. Padre Pendola was a priest of conscience and tact, and once he had understood the advantages of these nuptials he would surely have persuaded his pupil; therefore, one must begin there. The clever lady immediately got to work. The Reverend Father was not one of those who can barely see past their noses but want it to be thought they can see a mile, oh no. Rather, he could see quite far off, but wore spectacles with a great, rascally appearance of resignation. I think, though, that he didn't have to raise his eyes twice to read the Countess's mind and, pleased to be courted, responded to her attentions with a truly edifying modesty.

'Poor thing,' the lady said to herself, 'he thinks I'm so nice to him because of his rare qualities! Well, let him think so, for he will serve us more willingly.'

Young Venchieredo, meanwhile, met the Countess's frank designs with great enthusiasm. He'd fallen in love with Clara at first sight, you might say, and was as enamoured as an ass – or a young man just out of school. He sought to please her in every way; he plotted to sit as near her as possible so as to touch, at least with his knee, the folds of her gown; he stared at her constantly; and the few, timorous words he uttered were all addressed to her alone. Her far-sighted mother was overwhelmed with joy, for both the tutor and his charge were falling innocently into the net she'd so cleverly devised. But Padre Pendola was not particularly alarmed by the young man's amorous outbursts; he knew his pupil better than the Countess did and would let things take their course so long as it suited him.

To put it plainly, Signor Raimondo (so the young Venchieredo was called) loved, rather more than Clara herself, the fair sex in its entirety. He'd given notice of this essential aspect of his temperament as soon as he'd set foot in his jurisdiction, running a wild chase after all the beauties in the territory. Fathers, brothers and husbands quaked at those bellicose sorties, and the hearts of decrepit old ladies beside the hearth beat faster, recalling the days of his father. This wild colt soared over ditches in a single bound, bored through hedgerows without mercy, paid no attention to a jerk on the reins or a warning voice, delivered kicks left and right to penetrate to his desired pastures. His authority, however, was not yet so great that from time to time his high-handedness didn't exasperate someone. Some father, some brother, some husband would raise a fuss, threaten reprisals, recourse, revenge. But then the Reverend Father would appear with his bowed head and pained face.

'What do you expect? These are the penalties of Providence; unpleasant, yes, but they must be borne like any other trial for the greater glory of God. My heart, too, bleeds to see this blackguardery! But I put my faith in the Lord, I shed my tears before Him; He comforts me. If He so wills, this will go no further than boyish pranks, but the good that only the Lord may concede must be earned with patience. Join me, my children! Let us weep and suffer together, that we may have our reward together in a better world than this.'

And the good people wept with that fine fellow and suffered with him; was he not the guardian angel of their families, the saviour of their souls? Oh, what calamity had he not been with them! How many scandals and crimes would have turned the town upside down? Blood might even have been shed, for the indignities had exceeded all decency. But the good father comforted them and he calmed them, and soon they were once again sheep to be shorn (and worse, with resignation). Then, having properly led them back to their place, he took the heedless young man aside and delivered a bellyful of good advice. No, that was not the way to gain the people's affection and preserve the eminence and the decorum of the house! Yes, there had been some sinners even among the Venchieredo elders, but at least they behaved with some care; they didn't go around trumpeting their mischief or foolishly exposing themselves to public ire; they avoided setting a bad example and, above all, they didn't arouse their neighbours to that filthy Turkish sin of excommunication: the vendetta. Oh, blessed the prudence of his ancestors!

The young fellow, as you might expect, took from this advice the part that suited him best, and so he began to plan his deeds in advance and to conceal them well when he was finished. People didn't complain so much, and the women and the girls in town got a nice brooch or a silk apron, and Padre Pendola was blessed by all, and the young lord owed him if not his soul's well-being, certainly that of his body. Early reports of Raimondo as the consummate scourge of chastity were silenced, and he gained a reputation as a polite, respectable young man, who liked to jest, but not beyond measure, and who never failed to be courteous to all. For example, he adored husbands who had young, graceful wives, and whether they were prosperous fellows or cowherds, he was never the least bit impolite to them. He listened patiently to their long-winded tales, spoke up for them with the clerk and the steward; he would carry the notice of a petition granted or a bill paid all the way to their houses. And if the good man then happened to be absent on some business, he would wait patiently for him, and the wives were generous in their praise for the young master's urbanity and his modesty. The truth was that Padre Pendola alone was capable of effecting such a conversion, and the entire population and clergy all around proclaimed him a sort of miracle worker.

Doretta Provedoni was among the first to attract Raimondo's ready compliments, but Leopardo could not stomach the young cavalier's simpering ways, and, despite great squeals of complaint from his wife, he found ways of fending him off. To hear her tell it, the young lord was certainly well within his rights, for they had been siblings at the breast and had played together as children, and so it wasn't at all strange that he had affectionate memories of her. The elder Provedoni, Leopardo's brothers and his sisters-in-law, all fearful of getting on the wrong side of young Venchieredo, backed her and treated Leopardo like a jealous, churlish misanthrope. So long as Raimondo kept up his reckless ways, Leopardo had reason on his side and Doretta wore her pout, unable to counter them. Then the conversion came and people began to talk about Padre Pendola's miracle and the young man's wondrous mending of his ways. And suddenly everyone turned on Leopardo with great disapproval, and Doretta said nothing, didn't shout, she merely acted offended by her husband's insulting suspicions. And he, who was honest, guileless and ready to give in to her on any matter at all, because he loved her so blindly, admitted he had been unjust and, not wishing to see her suffer, allowed her to go to see her father at Venchieredo, as she had used to do before Raimondo finished school.

The young lord received his milk-sister quite humanely and spoke of his surprise on never finding her at Cordovado when he went to pay his respects, and even expressed anger that she had never introduced him to her husband. In the end Leopardo was convinced that appearances had deceived him about Raimondo's intentions. As much in love with his wife as he was, he heard her out and ended up apologizing, and then he hastened to pay a visit with her to young Venchieredo and came home edified by so much affability and discretion – he, too, praising Padre Pendola and agreeing to let his wife go as often as she liked to Venchieredo. So Raimondo had begun the business of perfecting his lordly arts, and when he met Clara his idolatry of her taught him cleverer and more discreet methods. Meanwhile, the Countess, fearing he might cool off, decided it was time to sound out Padre Pendola. Numerous times she invited him to luncheon, she sat him by her side at the evening card games, she abandoned Monsignor di Sant'Andrea and went to him for confession, and when it seemed to her that the ground was ready, she determined it was time to sow.

'Oh, Father,' she said to him one evening at Casa Frumier, having abandoned her card game on some pretext or other and retired to a corner of the drawing room with him. 'You are fortunate indeed to have a pupil who does you such justice.'

The Countess cast a quasi-maternal eye on Raimondo, who was standing ramrod straight in front of Clara, waiting for her to finish her coffee so that he could take the cup. The Reverend Father beamed much the same kind of glance towards the young man, glowing with equal parts of affection and humility.

'You are right, Madam Countess,' he said, 'I am quite fortunate, because in any case a tutor plays but a small part in his pupil's merits. To grow good wheat on good soil all that is needed is to harvest it, while poor soil will grow nothing, no matter how many buckets of sweat go into it.'

'Oh no, Father, don't say such a thing!' the Countess replied. 'I envy you precisely because you are worthy of such good fortune and have been able to procure it. As I see it, the proper upbringing of a young man so well positioned to do good is the greatest merit one can boast of!'

'That of a gentlewoman who forms and educates excellent mothers is certainly no less,' replied the Reverend.

'Oh, Father, we put little into it. If the Lord gives us good and pretty daughters, we must thank Him. Wise economy, an orderly home, a goodly fear of God and the gift of modesty make up our daughters' virtues.'

'And you say that is nothing, Madam? Economy, order, fear of God, modesty! It is all there, all of it! I should say there's even some left over, because order teaches thrift, and fear of God leads to humility. Believe me, Madam Countess, were there women of this kind on the greatest thrones of this earth, they would do us justice indeed!'

The Countess's heart swelled like a rose under the rain. Her eyes moved from the good Padre Pendola to Clara, from Clara to Raimondo, and from there once again to the good father. Her gaze went round like the theme of a symphony she was preparing to play.

'Listen, Reverend Father,' she went on, drawing near to his ear, while from his piquet table Monsignor di Sant'Andrea was exterminating her with two basilisk eyes. 'When Signor Raimondo first appeared here, were there not rumours about him . . . about . . . certain things . . .?'

The Countess stammered, as if she hoped the excellent Padre Pendola would offer her the missing words, but the Reverend was on guard, as they say, and replied to her stammering with an air of astonishment.

'You understand,' the Countess went on, 'I accuse no one. I merely repeat what people said. It seemed that Signor Raimondo's predilections were not, well, exemplary . . . As you know, judgements tend to be hasty in this world, and often mere appearances . . .'

'Regrettably, regrettably, my dear lady,' the Reverend interrupted her with a great sigh. 'Do you think either of us is safe from that cursed monster, calumny?'

The Countess bit at her lips with her teeth and raised a hand to check that the ribbons on her bonnet were in place. She would also have liked to blush, but these days she grew pink only when coughing.

'Whatever are you saying, Father?' she went on in a demure voice. 'Believe me, a hundred thousand souls would join in a single voice to praise your saintliness. And as for me, I'm much too small and wretched a thing to merit . . .'

'Oh, Madam Countess, surely you jest. A great lady in these times of ours is worth an entire seminary of priests, and she alone has the privilege to make an entire city speak well or ill. As for us, it is already more than enough if they raise their hats to us.'

The Countess, who was much too vain to let a compliment drop, and not clever enough to lop off the useless branches of this conversation immediately, let her tongue be carried where the reverend was leading, getting further and further away from the destination she'd had in mind at the start. For Padre Pendola was no fool, and before getting embroiled in certain inconveniences he wanted to be sure what good would come of it and with whom he might have to associate. The moment, he decided, was not the right one to pursue the matter, and he steered the conversation so cleverly that when they rose from the table to leave the Countess was recalling – if I'm not mistaken – the delights of her youth, the fine times she'd had in Venice and God only knows what other ancient rubbish. When she saw it was time to leave, she felt a bit rueful for a moment; but the hour had raced by so solicitously and the good father had entertained her with such interesting subjects that the principal argument, alas, had remained stuck in her throat. As for suspecting that the good father had led her, as they say, around in circles, the Countess was very far from it. Rather, she was annoyed at herself for talking too much and vowed she'd be more restrained the next time, and forget about the past and concentrate on the present.

But the second time was as the first, and the third as the second, and it wasn't as if the Reverend was avoiding her or seemed unhappy to see her. Not at all: he sought her out and visited her often, and he was never the first to take his leave, unless the table laid for luncheon or the late hour forced him to do so. It was just that the occasion never presented itself to bring up the matter or that it slipped the Countess's mind just when the moment was perfect.

Now, of course, Padre Pendola did not remain idle in the meantime. He studied the town, the people, the governors, the clergy; he made his way into the graces of this gentleman or that lady; he accommodated himself to the tastes of others so as to be welcome everywhere and by everyone; and above all he pursued every path that could bring him into the favour of Senator Frumier. But this could only happen by small degrees, and he knew it, and he chose the long, cautious way over taking a tumble at the first step. After a few weeks he had become a necessary participant in the Senator's inner circle. Up until then there had been a genuine anarchy of opinion. Pendola intervened to bring agreement, to set rules, to draw conclusions. True, his conclusions were weak and sometimes all it took was one of Lucilio's epigrams to bring them tumbling down to the company's loud laughter. But the ever-so-patient Reverend Father would stand them up again and then strengthen them with new props, until finally his friends and adversaries alike grew so weary they would end up saying he was right.

The Senator grew to like these dialectical exercises. By nature methodical and accustomed by long practice to academic debates, he enjoyed those discussions in which half an hour of amusement was followed by an attempt to arrive at something like the truth. And Padre Pendola succeeded where he had failed with that bunch of whimsical and spirited minds that clustered around him. He therefore granted high esteem to Pendola's perfect logic, in his opinion the greatest honour that could be bestowed on anyone. He didn't enquire whether Padre Pendola was consistent with his own logic or whether that logic changed legs every three steps to keep advancing. He was content to see it advance, whether on Lucilio's crutches or those of Prof. Dessalli.

Now it must be said that the excellent Padre Pendola had a special gift for seeing into men's souls, and, therefore, he had not only understood in just a couple of evenings that Senator Frumier's affections could be won by talk, he had even grasped what sort of talk was necessary to do the job. Lucilio, whose eye was by no means inferior to the Reverend's, quickly understood what sort of a beast this was, but it was not so easy to see into his soul. That black soutane was woven so very, very finely that to look on it was to blunt one's gaze, and so Lucilio was forced to work with his imagination.

At last the day arrived when Padre Pendola unveiled to the Countess that plan he had so long cherished. He had learned all that he needed to know, prepared what needed to be prepared; he no longer feared – nay, he was eager – that the Countess should turn to him with a request, so that he could ever so courteously reply, 'My dear Madam, certainly I promise you that, if you will promise me this other thing!'

Now perhaps you are wondering: what did the excellent Reverend Father want? A trifle, my children, the merest trifle. You see, when Signor Raimondo was married to the Contessina Clara, his tutor would be no more than an extra mouth to feed in the Castle of Venchieredo, and so he hoped to be appointed chaplain in Casa Frumier. Lady Frumier was reputed to be quite devout; he had put a finger on that key, and the key had responded nicely; and therefore it was up to the Countess to complete the job, if indeed she wanted to see her daughter so excellently matched. Poor Padre Pendola was tired, he was old, he was devoted to his studies; this was a position he could retire to that seemed the very antechamber of Paradise. The priest who held the post now wished instead to be taking care of souls; he could be satisfied and at the same time so could Pendola, who no longer had the necessary energy or the wisdom to work productively in the Lord's vineyard. Of course, the excellent father hinted at this request in such a way that the Countess seemed to be dragging it out of him, when really he was entreating her.

'O saints in Paradise!' the Countess exclaimed. 'What a comfort for my brother-in-law! How his excellent wife's spirit will be soothed if you, Reverend Father, if you really do intend to devote yourself to the paltry role of chaplain.'

'Yes. That is, when my charge marries,' replied Padre Pendola.

'Oh, he will marry! He will marry! Don't you see them? They seem to be made for each other.'

'In fact, if I were to say the word, Raimondo . . . But enough! Allow me to study their temperaments, let me observe them awhile myself.'

'Pray, what is the point of studying the hearts of twenty-year-olds? Don't you see them? You merely have to peer into their eyes, and their thoughts, their affections, are clear. Oh, you must trust me! It's three months now, you know, that I've been studying them every evening. Imagine, Padre Pendola, that for six weeks I've been thinking of discussing this matter with you and I could never get up my courage?'

'Truly, Madam Countess? Oh, you astonish me. That you should lack the courage to call me aside for an act of such great charity, an act so useful, that brings such great lustre to two entire families!'

'It is a good idea, isn't it, Father? And wouldn't it be a nice wedding present if the Inquisitor could be persuaded to suspend the rest of that other poor fellow's sentence? And put an end to all those disputes, misfortunes and disasters that have tormented the good souls of the district!'

'Oh, yes, certainly! I would retire quite happily if I could confide my spiritual son's happiness to such a well-bred young bride, but these are matters, my dear Lady, that must be considered at length. And precisely because I have much influence where Raimondo's soul is concerned . . .'

'Yes, and just for that reason I pray you make clear to him all the advantages that would accrue to both houses from this marriage.'

'What I mean to say, Madam Countess, is that precisely because of the responsibility I'm charged with, one must proceed with shoes of lead.'

'Oh mercy, Father, you need but a glance to see it all! Oh, how I long to see this excellent alliance forged! And the Senator – how delighted he will be to have a man of your calibre in his household. Tomorrow they'll look to provide a stipend for the present chaplain right away. In as much as he already wishes it, what could be better?'

'However, Madam Countess . . .'

'No, Father, no objections, please! You must promise me to do this favour for my brother-in-law! Since you let slip a word, do not retract it.'

'I'm not saying I'm retracting . . . but . . .'

'But, but! Let there be no buts! Just look at Signor Raimondo and my Clara! See how they look at each other: don't they look just like two turtle doves?

'If the Lord so wills it, there will never have been a more perfect couple.'

'But we must assist the Lord in His designs, Father. You, above all, His most worthy minister.'

'Unworthy, most unworthy, Madam Countess!'

'In any case I'll expect you for luncheon tomorrow, and then you'll tell me something about your Raimondo.'

'I'm pleased to accept, Madam Countess, but I don't know . . . so much haste . . . No good will come . . . Enough! It will cost me dearly to separate myself from that fine lad.'

'Oh, I can assure you that the Frumiers will pay you back a hundredfold for what you are about to lose.'

'Yes, I imagine so, I hope so. But . . .'

'Now, Father, until tomorrow. We will speak. We'll organize matters. I'll drop a hint to the Senator this very evening; as it happens we'll be staying for supper with him.'

'Heavens, Madam Countess, let us not be too rash about this! Don't compromise me so. It would be a great sacrifice for me . . .'

'Oh, I see! For selfish reasons you would prefer to deprive that fine lad of a bride? What a miserable guardian! Until tomorrow, then, Father, and come in time so that we can discuss matters while the rice boils.'

'Your most humble servant, Madam Countess, I will certainly be there. And may God guide our intentions to fruition.'

The good father, once he had left Casa Frumier with Raimondo and sunk into the comfortable seats of his carriage, began to praise the young man for the exemplary life he was leading and the profitable use he had made of his advice. However, he should not forget that man's intentions were illusory, his passions domineering – and efforts to contain them with sacred and legitimate bonds could never be commended enough! Raimondo was now approaching twenty-one years; the moment could not be better, and the excellent father was offering his long and discerning experience to assist him in his choice.

'Oh Father, do you speak seriously?' said Raimondo. 'You urge me to marry? But just a year ago did you not insist on the rule that one must be mature in years and good sense before deciding to plant a family? And that the aid of a guardian of sound heart and mind was worth far more than some slight and inadequate female sustenance.'

'Yes, my son,' said the Reverend, all innocence. 'Yes, I did give you that advice during the last year I taught you in school, and I was convinced it was excellent counsel. But I had not yet observed you in full liberty then, and now that I know you better in the practice of life, I am not ashamed to confess I was mistaken and to change my mind. Note that I speak to my own detriment, for when a bride enters the castle by one door, I must necessarily go out by another.'

'Oh no, Father! Don't say that! Don't deprive me of your aid and counsel! Believe me, I'll never forget what I owe you! Just two months ago those ferrymen at Morsano would have finished me off if you hadn't brought them to reason with a small monetary reward. And I hadn't touched so much as a finger of that sister of theirs, I swear, Father!'

'Yes my son, I believe you. But you must not try my modesty by recalling such trivial merits. I pray you to forget them or at least to speak of them no more. What has been, has been. As I say, I've changed my mind about what I thought useful to you a year ago. Now I would like to see you settled, permanently and honourably. Knowing you have a good, patient, devout wife at your side, I can retire quite contentedly to my old man's retreat.'

'But Father! Have you not always insisted that even when I married, you would remain as my peacemaker, my comforter, the spiritual bond between myself and my wife? That you would never agree to part from me for all the gold on earth?'

Padre Pendola had indeed often spoken in just such terms. But then, fishing the troubled ecclesiastical waters of Portogruaro he had spotted something more advantageous, and now he cast his words in a different light.

'I did say that and I don't deny I said it many times,' he went on. 'My spirit will always be with you, because its best part has been transfused into your soul through the holy channel of education. And as for your bride, since I've taken great care to select her according to the precepts of good morality, she will be one with my aims in trusting her to you. This, Raimondo, is that spiritual bond forged in the secret depths of my heart that will always tie you and your wife together!'

Listening to these explanations from his tutor, Raimondo did not seem quite as unhappy as he might have been three months earlier. But just then they reached the castle and their exchange was interrupted until after supper, at which time they resumed it of common accord, because the young man was eager to know the name of the bride destined for him in Padre Pendola's mind.

'But Raimondo, you know the name!' said the priest, all charm, in a voice of sweet reproof. 'I can read it in your eyes. You've shown a lack of confidence in your only friend not to have told him of your heart's vows.'

'What? Can it be true? Her, Father? You have guessed so soon?'

'Yes, my son, all can be divined when a man is in love. And I confess that even though your reticence grieved me, I was much consoled by the fine choice you've been afforded; it will not fail to furnish your life with abiding joys.'

'Oh Father, isn't she as beautiful as an angel? Have you seen what eyes, what shoulders? Oh my God, I've never seen such lovely rounded shoulders!'

'These are fleeting qualities, my son, mere outward ornaments that count for little if the vessel does not contain a fragrant, unspoiled perfume. But I can assure you that the Contessina's soul is all that her appearances promise. She may really be an angel, as you were just saying . . .'

'But will they give her to me, my most beloved Reverend Father? Will they consent to give her to me in marriage? You can't imagine my haste; I'd like to have her with me tomorrow, today, if that were possible, but she is still so tender, still almost a child.'

'You are wrong, my son; her modesty and innocence make her seem younger than she is. Her age suits you very well; she is only slightly younger than you.'

'What? What is this you tell me? The Contessina Pisana is nearly my age?'

'Raimondo, you mistake their names. The Contessina is Clara, not Pisana. The other is her younger sister, that little girl sitting between you and Monsignor di Sant'Andrea this evening.'

'But that is just what I wished to speak of, Father! Did you not see how she looked at me? I've been smitten to death since yesterday! Oh, there's no point in living if I can't make her love me!'

'Raimondo, my son, have you gone mad? Have you no eyes to see, no mind to comprehend what you are saying? That one is but a child of ten at the most! You cannot be infatuated with her; your heart certainly deceives you and makes her seem so delightful because she is the Contessina Clara's sister.'

'Not at all, Father, I assure you . . .'

'But it is certainly so, my son; allow yourself to be guided by one who knows better, let me put some order in that heart of yours: I know it better than you and surely I have the right, after all these years in which I've studied it and tried to direct it. You love the Contessina Clara. I know it because you've been so attentive and courteous to her.

'Yes, Father, until last week, but now . . .'

'Now, because the Contessina is too modest and well brought up to return your affections openly and without her parents' consent, you believed she wasn't moved at all by the interest you showed her, and so you have tried to approach her by becoming familiar with her sister. And the little one responded with glee, with that innocence that is characteristic of her young age, and you mistook for love the gratitude you feel for her kindness! Think about it, my son: it would be terribly foolish, positively shameful!'

'It doesn't matter, Father. It's evident that you have never observed her as carefully as I have done these past two evenings.'

'Rather, I have observed her very carefully and if you have any intentions in her regard, my dear Raimondo, you must resign yourself to seven or eight years of waiting, and then she may change her mind in the meantime. And just think how everyone will laugh when they see you are in love with a little girl! It is perfectly silly, you know, to fall in love with a green fruit when you can already pick one that is ripe and flavourful.'

'I wouldn't know what to do with it, Father. I wouldn't know!'

'Think, my son, think carefully. Let me now employ your same arguments. Do you really think that la Pisana will one day be more lovely and graceful, her skin whiter, her form more perfect, than that of the Contessina Clara? Keep that in mind, Raimondo! Do you really think you can resist her?'

'I don't know, Father. I don't know. But she certainly has no interest in me.'

'Nonsense, believe me; appearances and nothing more. The mere effect of modesty and shyness.'

'Well, that may be, but such chilly temperaments do not appeal to me.'

'Chilly, my son? It's evident you lack experience. It is just those hearts that are most composed, most reserved, that conceal the most intense passions, the most exquisite pleasures. Trust me, for I have studied the human heart.'

'Perhaps, Father. Rather, I'm sure that is the case, nevertheless . . .'

'Nevertheless, nevertheless! What do you wish to say? Nevertheless, I'll tell you! Nevertheless, it is neither charitable nor wise to torment the heart of a lovely young lady who beneath her outward guise of serenity and modesty loves you heedlessly, lives only for you and is ready to make you a gift of the most saintly pleasures that our merciful Lord permits us to taste!'

'Oh Father, is it true? The Contessina Clara, in love with me?'

'Certainly, I assure you. I swear it. If you must know, I was told by someone in her household. She's in love, poor thing, and perishing with the desire to please you!'

'If that is so, Father, I was mistaken. Seven years are long! And I myself was in love with the Contessina Clara, and now that I think about it again . . .'

'Aha! You have confessed it, my son! You have confessed it! May the Lord bless you! My ministry is now complete and I can retire in peace, knowing the happiness my two hands have prepared for your beloved creatures. Raimondo, I have uncovered your heart's secret; now let me act so that all will conform to your desires.'

'Go slowly, Father. I wouldn't like great haste to . . .'

'A solution is urgent, my son. Just think of your beatitude when, in this very castle, in this very chamber, you press to your heart a bride so lovely, so docile, so inflamed with thoughts of you! Oh God! You've never felt anything like it!'

'Very well, Father, you are right; please go ahead. Although, in truth, it was my intention . . . but now, after mature reflection, and so long as you assure me that the girl is in love with me . . .'

'Oh yes, Raimondo, I couldn't be more certain.'

'Very well, Father. Could we not have the wedding on Sunday?'

'Heavenly might! Sunday, you say, and then you tell me not to act in haste! We will need a few weeks, perhaps even a few months, my dear child. The things of this world proceed at a certain pace, which cannot be disturbed. However, in the meantime you can see your fiancée and talk with her, and stay with her at length at the Castle of Fratta when her parents are present.'

'Oh what a consolation, Father, for that way I can also continue to see la Pisana!'

'Of course, and love her and treat her with the honest intimacy of a future brother-in-law. Rest easy, my son; confide in me and pass your nights in tranquil sleep, so that your venerable uncle's hopes will not be disappointed, and when I tell him of your marriage I can assure him that I've made you both good and happy!'

The young nobleman wept with tenderness to hear these words and kissed the hand of his diligent guardian, and went up to his bedchamber with la Pisana and Clara dancing together confusedly in his imagination. He knew not which, but felt quite certain that either of them would have been welcome that night. Padre Pendola had counted on this happy outcome to distract him from that thoughtless fancy for la Pisana and reignite the flames for Clara, and his plan didn't fail. Only when he, too, went up to bed did he stop to be astonished and congratulate himself for having so boldly headed off this new crisis.

'Oh, that little rascal' he thought. 'Of course I'd noticed there were thirty years of malice hidden away in those fourteen years of hers. But such daredevilry – I'd never have thought it. Perhaps those who say the world's in constant progress are right after all!'

These thoughts in mind, the Reverend Father lay down to sleep, unclutching those pamphlets by the esteemed Jesuit Bartoli[2] that were his accustomed bedtime reading. What came as such a surprise to him, however, would not have surprised me at all. For I had been following young Venchieredo through the various phases of his love for Clara, and after he had lost hope of moving her heart, I'd watched him during the past two evenings become aware of la Pisana and draw close to her, and in an instant begin to burn with greater heat than two months of courting her older sister had awakened in his heart. How very much this dismayed me anyone can imagine, even those who've little understood my feelings for that ingrate! But soon I was to be surprised, for la Pisana, when Venchieredo had paid his humble respects, suddenly reassumed that kind and affectionate manner towards me that she hadn't employed except with guile and almost forcing herself.

To what did I owe this strange new thing? I was utterly unable to make sense of it back then. Today I would guess that when she was so haughty with me it was because she was vexed at being treated like a child, despite her wanton desire to please. For as soon as she began to please someone, she went back to treating me normally. Or rather, better. For nothing makes us as good and obliging towards others as ambition satisfied. I confess that I took my share of that affection shamelessly and without scruples, and that, little by little, my grief at Venchieredo's triumph began to be transformed into a bitter kind of happiness. It now seemed to me that la Pisana did not seek the pleasure of being loved by others, she sought novelty; it was pride and vanity at play. Thus she had abandoned Lucilio and attached herself to Venchieredo as soon as the novelty of the second had drawn more attention than the spirited arguments of the first. At the time it consoled me to think that no one had loved her or would ever love her as much as I, and that every time her heart sought true love I was sure she would fly to my arms. Foolish and cynical I was to be satisfied with such an illusion, but step by step I had thus descended, growing so accustomed to degradation, servile aspirations and jealousy that I'd already become a feeble, disenchanted fellow when all imagined me a carefree, hearty young lad. Nobody was keeping track of our youthful passions, our adolescent romances! They considered us novices in life, when we'd already set out the warp complete (the weft being merely a manual task to which we're driven by fatal, ineluctable forces).

Padre Pendola, once he was sure the young man was still firm in his intentions of the night before, told the Countess of Fratta of the excellent results he'd achieved, omitting (it wasn't necessary to mention!) all that concerned la Pisana. The lady all but threw her arms around his neck, and by way of thanks assured him that the mere hint he might wish to join the Frumier household had been greeted with such joy by the Senator and his wife that it seemed likely the matter would soon be settled.

'And now,' the Countess whispered in the Reverend's ear, for he had sat down beside her in spite of Frumier etiquette, 'now you may leave things to me. Even before Clara suspects anything (girls must be led gently to these things) I want my esteemed kinsmen to be blessed by your company.'

'Poor Raimondo,' sighed Padre Pendolo between one mouthful and another.

'Oh, don't be too sorry for him,' said the Countess in a low voice, eyeing her daughter, 'such a bride will certainly suit a young man of twenty-one years better than a priest does.'

Needless to say, the following week all Portogruaro had heard the news. The celebrated, illustrious, learned – the sainted – Padre Pendola, weary after his long missions, was to retire in Casa Frumier. There he intended to take his rest, for although he was not terribly elderly he did suffer from some of those discomforts that inconvenience the old. The former Chaplain had been transferred (at his request) to a post just outside Pordenone, and the Senator and his wife were overcome with happiness to have such an ecclesiastical luminary in his place. Raimondo had pretended to be cross that the Reverend was to leave him before his bride had settled at the castle, but the good father did not need to say much to persuade him that a young man soon to be married hardly wanted the services of a guardian, and for many reasons it was best that he leave Venchieredo somewhat before the wedding celebration.

Raimondo shed few tears to see him go and he continued to visit the Castle of Fratta, finding that la Pisana's forthright friendliness somewhat compensated for Clara's icy reserve. As Clara had not yet been informed of the fate awaiting her, he attributed her coldness to the effort she was making to hide her fiery passion for him. In any case he didn't go to any great trouble, for if he failed to get Clara he would be quite happy to fall back on her sister. Such were the philosophical reflections of the young lord of Venchieredo, but the Countess did not see matters the same way.

After she had allowed the two young people to become politely familiar, she began to prepare Clara for the young man's request, but although she alluded to the matter many times, she was somewhat dismayed to see the Contessina remain forever cold and unmoved, as if it all had nothing to do with her. One fine day the Countess spelled out Raimondo's probable intentions in the clearest of terms, but even this last move did not disperse the cloud resting on the young lady's brow. She lowered her lashes; she sighed; she said neither yes nor no. Her mother began to think she was a fool, something she had always suspected, seeing her so grave, so modest, so different in every way from what she herself had been in her youth. But even fools react when husbands are mentioned and so Clara's stupidity must be of a rare type indeed if that did not move her.

At last she approached her ageing mother-in-law, who had always been Clara's confidante, and begged her to find a way to make the girl understand the family's intentions for her. The old woman spoke, she listened, and then she told the Countess that Clara had no intention of marrying and wished to remain by her grandmother's side, nursing her in illness and keeping her company.

'Nonsense! That is old wives' twaddle!' the Countess snapped. 'I suppose she thinks she'll just keep showing that poor fellow her back until he finds some pretext to disappear. When parents want something, it is a girl's duty to obey, at least in this house, and there won't be any changes in that regard, no there won't! As for yourself, Madam, I do hope you don't intend to encourage this madness, and that you'll help the Count and me show the girl what's best for her.'

The old lady nodded her assent and was quite happy to see her daughter-in-law leave her chamber after this outburst. Still, she was no less willing to try to persuade Clara to accept the match, noble and worthy in every respect, that was being offered. But the young woman either remained utterly silent, or replied as before that God did not call her to matrimony, and that she would be very happy to live out her life in the Castle beside her grandmother. There was a great hustle and bustle on everyone's part: her grandmother, her mother, her father, her uncle Monsignor, but Clara always produced the same refrain. And so the Countess, although secretly furiously angry, decided not to say anything immediately to young Venchieredo and instead ask Padre Pendola, so wonderfully wise, to suggest some means to bring Clara to obedience without having to resort to any violence or harsh methods.

Now, none of the girl's obstinate resistance was at all apparent outside the family; Lucilio seemed quite unaware of it and continued to behave exactly as before, and Partistagno appeared at the evenings in the Castle and at the Frumier salon ever more smiling and triumphant. When Padre Pendola was told about this grave problem, he offered to mediate between the Countess and the young lady, and great hopes were entertained by all; and when he met with Clara in private, some of the curious hid behind the door to eavesdrop.

'My dear lady,' the Reverend began, 'and what do you think of this fine weather?'

Clara bowed, slightly confused and uncertain what to say, but Padre Pendola resolved the matter for her by continuing:

'A season like this we haven't enjoyed for quite some time, and just think that we have scarcely emerged from winter! The

Most Excellent Senator has allowed me – I should say he has begged me – to go and visit my dear old pupil, that fine young man, that ever so well-bred cavalier that you must surely know. But as I was passing by I thought I'd like to see you all and hear news of your family.'

'Thank you, Father,' the young woman stammered, for he did not seem inclined to go on.

Her timidity, the Reverend thought, was a good omen. If he'd managed to extract that 'thank you' from her, he'd be able to make her say and promise anything he liked, he reasoned.

'My dear young lady,' he went on in his most mellifluous voice, 'your mother has confided in me, and today I hope to hear from you what my heart has long desired. In this regard you have but given me halves of words and it appears that you have not understood your parents' right and godly purposes. But I hope that when I've explained them to you better, you will not hesitate to accept them as the Lord's commandments.'

'Please speak, then,' said Clara modestly, but now calm and sure of herself.

'My dear, you have the means in hand to restore joy and harmony not merely to two illustrious families, but you might say to an entire district, and yet from what I have been led to believe, because of some pitiful scruples, you do not wish to use those means. Allow me to think that your reply has not been interpreted correctly: that what appears to be unreasonable refusal and scandalous rebellion is really nothing more than modest hesitation or excessive charity?'

'Father, perhaps I explain myself badly; I only hope that by repeating the same thing many times, in the end all will understand me. No, I do not feel myself called to matrimony. God leads me along another path; I would be a terrible wife, but I can go on being a worthy daughter and my conscience commands me to adhere to this second way.'

'Excellent, my lady. Certainly I do not wish to condemn you for respecting the rules of your conscience. Quite the contrary, that redoubles my esteem and makes me hope we will be able to bring our views closer together. Will you permit my very humble but devout good sense to help you illuminate a conscience that has grown somewhat upset, somewhat obscured, with all its recent vacillations and conflicts? No one, my child, is so saintly as to trust his own conscience blindly and reject all the suggestions and counsel of others.'

'Please do speak, Father, please. I am here to listen and to confess I am wrong, as soon as I am persuaded of it.'

'Oh, they say she's a dimwit!' the excellent Father thought to himself. 'Dimwit, my foot! I can see I've got a mean cat to skin here, and if I succeed, I'm pretty good!

'Well then,' he went on, now speaking aloud, 'you know better than I that obedience is the first rule for conscientious, God-fearing young women. Honour thy father and mother that thy days may be long upon the land . . . God himself decreed it, and up until now you have always followed that divine precept. But obedience, my dear child, permits no exceptions, it seeks no way out; obedience obeys, and that is all. That is conscience as we poor ministers of the Gospel understand it.'

'And that is how I understand it, too,' said Clara very humbly.

'I've convinced her already?' the Reverend said to himself. 'I wouldn't bet a damned penny on it!' However, he pretended he believed it and, raising his hands to the heavens, exclaimed,

'Thank you, my dear daughter in Christ! Thank you for these good words. This path of abnegation and sacrifice you have chosen leads to the highest grade of perfection, and thus (and it is to your great profit) you can now profess to be an even more excellent wife and mother than you have been a good and decent young woman. Oh, it will not be such a great trial, I assure you! A husband such as the one Heaven has destined for you is not easy to find these days! I've brought him up myself, my lady; I've shaped him with my own spirit's purest marrow and the holiest precepts of Christendom. God will reward you for your great piety, your sense of filial duty! May He continue to bless you, and may He be praised for having allowed me to light up your soul with persuasion.'

The good father, his hands and eyes still pointing towards the heavens, made to leave the room, so he could report the good news to the Countess. But Clara was too honest a girl to let him entertain such a grievous misconception. And here her candour came to her aid as much as any guile, because the good father, convinced she was faint-hearted, innocent and simple, believed she would allow herself to appear persuaded, simply because she was loath to contradict him. He was, therefore, quite astonished to feel the young lady touch his sleeve, although he understood what that gesture must mean. Nevertheless, he struggled to control himself and turned towards her with true paternal unctuousness.

'What is the trouble, my child?' he said, sweetening each word with a seraphic smile. 'Oh, I see: you would like to be the one to deliver such a great consolation to your parents! After having tormented them so (perhaps in a good cause) you would like to throw yourself at their feet, implore their forgiveness, assure them of your filial subjection! Let us go, then. Come along.'

'Father,' said Clara, who was not at all dismayed by the priest's feigned assurance, 'perhaps I understand obedience differently from you. In my view, to obey means to surrender not merely to the letter, but also to the spirit of our superiors' commandments. But when we do not feel we can fully observe one of these commandments, would it not be hypocrisy to pretend to submit merely on the level of appearances?'

'Oh, my dear child! Whatever do you mean? These are scholastic quibbles. St Thomas . . .'

'St Thomas was a great saint; I respect and venerate him. As for myself, may I repeat what you must tell my good mother, my grandmother, father and uncle? I cannot promise to love a husband I will never love. To obey, to give myself to this man, would mean to obey with my body, with my lips, but not in my heart. In my heart I could never obey. Therefore, Father, you will permit me to remain unmarried.'

'Oh, my dear lady! Think and think again! Your reasoning is faulty in both form and substance. Obedience is not so long-winded!'

'Obedience replies when it is questioned and, had I not been questioned, I assure you I would never have replied, Reverend Father.'

'Halt right there, my child! Let me speak! Must I explain

everything? Must I spell out every Christian virtue that is to be expected from an exemplary daughter? You say you are ready to obey every one of your parents' commands that you feel able to carry out. Excellent, my child! But what do your parents command? They command you to marry a young man who is noble, honest, polite, wealthy, with whom your alliance will bring great benefits to both families and to the entire city! As for your heart, they do not command it at all. You will deal with your heart later, but meanwhile faith requires that you bend it as best you can, and you may be sure that as a reward for your submission God will grant you the ability to carry out perfectly all the duties of your new condition.'

This fine moral sophistry left Clara puzzled for a time and Padre Pendola began to regain some hope he had brought her to heel, but his victory was brief, for the young lady's puzzlement was soon resolved.

'Father,' she said resolutely, with the air of one who's come to the end of a discussion and no longer wishes to hear more, 'what would you say about a man riddled with debts and stripped of all assets, who posts surety for eighty thousand ducats to be paid on the morrow? I would call him either a madman or a scoundrel. I believe you understand me, Father. Aware as I am of my poverty, I do not wish to post surety for one penny.'

After she had spoken, Clara bowed and moved to leave the room. It was now the Reverend who would have liked to detain her with some further speech or with fresh objections, but seeing that this would be entirely useless, he contented himself with following her out, as desolate as a hound returning to his master without bringing him any game. Those who'd been listening behind the door were just in time to rush into the dining hall, but not so clever as to hide all they'd learned. And so Padre Pendola had not yet whispered a word to the Countess but she had already attacked Clara with all sorts of threats and curses, her shrieks alerting many as far away as the kitchen. The Count and Monsignor then stepped in to restrain her, while Padre Pendola beat a timely retreat, washing his hands of the matter like Pontius Pilate. Once he was gone it was his turn to take the abuse and the good lady began wailing that he was a great big hypocrite, a worthless fellow, a bare-faced liar who he had got what he set out to and then shamelessly left her in a shambles. Monsignor begged his sister-in-law for God's sake not to insult an abbé who, after just a few days' residence at Portogruaro, was already taking charge of the clergy and even had a hand in the Curia's business. But when a woman's tongue is itching, she has quite something else on her mind!

Before she could listen to Monsignor's advice the Countess had to let out that great surge of gall in her. And when that subject had been exhausted, she began to scold Clara again, and as the curious kitchen-dwellers gathered round, the Count and Monsignor also began tormenting the Contessina. The young lady bore it all, and not with that cold resignation that stems from contempt, but with the true suffering of one who would like to – but cannot – do what others ask. Her torture went on for days, for the Countess was bitterly determined that she would marry Venchieredo or be sent to a convent straight away.

Meanwhile, Lucilio was already being whispered about and had to behave even more cautiously than before. Yet when word of Clara's obstinate refusal to marry Venchieredo began to spread, there were many who blamed it on a secret love she harboured for Partistagno. This party was led by Partistagno himself, who, after he learned of the matter, began showing up at the Castle more smiling and sure of himself than ever and looking down on the whole family, and you would have been hard put to say whether, in those tender glances that he reserved for Clara alone, love exceeded pity or vice versa. Whatever the reason, this hypothesis lodged itself in the Countess's mind, too, and since she did not deign to suspect Lucilio, it seemed to her quite likely. But that blessed Partistagno never made up his mind to act! For years he'd been working those eyes of his, those smiles, without ever once speaking his mind. Raimondo, instead, came, you might say, ring in hand and all that was needed was a nod and he would be grateful and delighted to put it on Clara's finger. These considerations didn't temper the Countess's bad blood towards her daughter one bit, especially since recent developments hadn't put any fire at all under the glorious young lord from Lugugnana.

When, therefore, one day the Frumiers invited their Fratta relations to luncheon to distract them from these family troubles, the illustrious Count grew quite uneasy when his brother-in-law called him aside in a separate room. Each time he found himself separated from his trusty Clerk, he was like a candle without a wick. But he made a virtue of necessity and, with many a sigh, followed the Senator down the hall. Frumier closed the door, turned the key twice in the lock, drew down the green shades on the windows and with great care opened the most secret drawer in his desk, taking out a document and handing it to him.

'Read this, but in silence, for mercy's sake! I trust in you because I know you well.'

The poor Count's eyes had misted over and he rubbed and scrubbed at the lenses of his glasses with the lining of his coat (to gain time more than anything else), until finally and with some effort he was able to decipher what was written there. The letter, unsigned, seemed to be written by someone well versed in the views of the Signoria, and it was a confidential reply to the noble Senator with respect to clemency for old Venchieredo. First, the writer was astonished by such a request, for this was not a moment when the Republic could afford to free its fiercest enemies, while instead it was busy investigating them and rendering them harmless as far as possible. None of the nobles up in the hills were at all well-disposed towards the Signoria, and the example of Venchieredo was needed to correct them, and perhaps it was not even enough; only supreme indulgence had exempted his family from having the property confiscated. For nothing is more malign than powers granted to an enemy's affiliates; evil must always be cut out at the roots so that it does not re-grow. Not having done so was the Signoria's only regret.

Now, of course, this wasn't addressed to the Senator, who was above suspicion and had only been drawn into this affair by the suggestions and pleas of others, but the friends of Venchieredo had better not try to hide their faltering loyalty (or their views perhaps tinged by the great sedition from abroad that threatened to destroy the ancient and venerable orders of San Marco!); no, they had better not try to hide behind the sovereign benevolence Frumier enjoyed! Troubled times demand the greatest caution: this must be their creed, for no one was exempt from the State Inquisition's vigilance.

The Senator, patrician of Venice that he was, observed with a certain satisfaction the various shades of astonishment, pain and distress that passed over the Count's face as he worked his way through the letter. When he had finished, the page fell from his hand and he stammered out various excuses and protests.

'Do not fear,' said the Senator, picking up the letter and putting a hand on his shoulder. 'It is merely a warning. But, you see, it was all but by the grace of God that your daughter refused that marriage. If she had consented, the wedding would already have been celebrated by now.'

'No, by all the saints in Heaven!' exclaimed the Count, horrified. 'If she should now consent, or if my wife in all her frenzy should try to force the match, it won't take but two words from me . . .'

'Shh!' the Senator warned him. 'Remember, this is a delicate affair.'

The Count just stood there with his mouth open, like a guilty boy caught in the act, but finally he downed the lump in his throat and went on: 'Praise God, for He has been good to us and we are saved from a great danger. My wife shall know that for powerful, secret and incontrovertible reasons this marriage must never again be spoken of; it must be as if it had never even been imagined. She is wise and will act accordingly! Holy Lord in Heaven! I fear she has been duped by Padre Pendola!'

Here he fell silent with his mouth open once again, for a grimace from the Senator told him he was about to say, or had already said, something very foolish.

'Just between us,' said Frumier in that patronizing voice the master adopts with his student, 'from a few words the worthy Father let drop, I believe it was not by chance that he was assigned to young Venchieredo. It might be that when he saw your wife was so eager to give your daughter to the young man, Pendola pretended to agree. But then, you know, he wishes you well and he wishes me well and . . . without wanting to trouble anyone . . . well, in that talk he had with Clara . . .'

'Oh, not at all! I was right behind the door and I can assure you . . . ,' the Count began.

'And what do you know about it?' the Senator snapped. 'There are a thousand ways to say something with one's lips and make another be understood by one's expression or by keeping silent about certain things. The Reverend perhaps suspected that you and your wife might be listening; in any case I promise you that if the marriage did not go through, the credit must go to him.'

'Oh, bless our dear Father! I must thank him . . .'

'Mercy, no! What an idea! After all the care he's taken to conceal his role and make you think he approved your plans! Really, sometimes you are a true mastermind!'

Who was the true mastermind in this case I couldn't say. Padre Pendola, when at luncheon the day before he had heard the Senator smartly disapprove of that marriage between his niece and Venchieredo (until that moment favoured by the good Father), had sniffed out if not the letter from Venice, then something like it. And so with headshakes and half-words and other means at his disposal he allowed the Senator to believe quite the opposite of what had happened. And the latter, when he got up from the table, shook his hand in a most enigmatic way, saying: 'I see, Father. My thanks to you on behalf of my family!'

Now if the Senator was shrewd – and he had given much evidence of that in his long public and private career – this was certainly that case which proves the proverb, to wit: in a day, each of us has our quarter-hour of asininity. For there is no thief so clever that he cannot be robbed by another cleverer than he.

When the Count and the Senator had finished speaking and the fatal letter had been duly burned, they went back to the dining hall, talking of Clara and how lucky it was she could be settled with Partistagno. The Count did have a few misgivings, for not every relative of the young man was in the Serenissima's good books, but the Senator suggested he should not be overly concerned, for the relatives in question were distant ones, and recently young Partistagno had shown himself to be so deferential to the Republic that it made another point in his favour.

'There is another problem,' the Count went on. 'As much as we think Clara to be in love with him and he with her, he doesn't seem inclined to declare himself.'

'Let me take care of that,' said the Senator. 'I like that young man. We need people like him: devout and respectful, yes, but also strong and bold. Let me handle this, and he will soon declare himself.'

And so these matters were set aside for the rest of the day and only that evening, deep in the silence of the nuptial bed, did the Count dare to hint to his wife about that grave and mysterious danger spared them by Clara's refusal of Venchieredo. The Countess was keen to know more and began to screech that she didn't believe a word of it, but as soon as the Count whispered the name of the Most Excellent Senator Frumier, she quieted, and didn't even insist on trying to guess her most illustrious brother-in-law's arcane secrets. The Count also told her that Frumier was convinced Clara should marry Partistagno, and was even willing to help bring the young man to a formal declaration. The two then had a joint attack of matrimonial glee and I wouldn't like to think how far beyond that it went. But it was Clara who was most joyful, for without even knowing why, she had several days of respite from her torment, when she could respond without the least aloofness to those passionate, grateful glances Lucilio was sending her on the sly.

Meanwhile, the Senator had been true to his promise to use every means to get Partistagno for Clara's hand. The Correggitrice, who was the young man's counsellor, was delighted to help Frumier in this design, and she was so good at prompting the youth's courtesy and his vanity – his main qualities – that she succeeded even more rapidly than she had hoped. Partistagno, loath to let a young lady perish with love for him and flattered to be considered worthy of becoming the nephew of a senator, confessed that he, too, had long been in love with the young lady and that only his natural indolence had kept that love from leaving the platonic sphere. After saying that last part, he snorted as if from the great effort it had cost him to invent it.

'Courage, then, and let's be quick about it!' the lady said. And he took his leave with the most sincere assurances that the girl's condition moved him to pity and that he would act as quickly as possible.

But the Partistagno line came forth with a head full of etiquette, and before the young man had prepared all the ingredients necessary for the ceremonious request of Clara's hand, quite a few days had passed. During that time he came to Fratta as always and looked at Clara the way the steward's wife looks at the turkey she is fattening up for Easter dinner. At last one day, two cavaliers astride white saddle horses harnessed in purple and gold presented themselves at the Castle drawbridge. Menichetto went running to the kitchen to announce the arrival of the great mission, while the two horsemen, grave and swell-chested, advanced towards the stables. One of them was Partistagno in a three-cornered hat with plumes and the lace billowing a good foot out of his shirt front, and enough rings, pins and brooches to make him resemble a pin cushion. Along with him came a maternal uncle, one of the thousand barons of Cormons, all dressed in black with silver embroidery, as befitted the solemnity of his office. Partistagno sat bolt upright on his horse like the statue of Gattamelata,[3] while the other dismounted and, handing the reins to the coachman, went in by the main door, which was held wide open for him. He was led into the great hall, but there he had to sit and wait a while, because the Count and Countess of Fratta also knew their etiquette and did not wish to appear any less illustrious than their ever so illustrious guests.

Finally the Count, wearing a waistcoat entirely woven of braid, and the Countess with twenty yards of pink ribbon on her bonnet, came down, offering a thousand excuses for the involuntary delay. Clara, dressed in white and as pale as wax, came out, holding her mother's hand, while the Clerk and Monsignor (who was clutching a napkin which he stuffed into a pocket) stood at either side. A deep silence followed, then great bows on both sides, and they looked as if they were about to dance a minuet. The maids, la Pisana and I, who were watching through the keyhole, were all stunned by this majestic spectacle. The Baron put one hand on his breast and, extending the other, began to speak his lines magnificently.

'In the name of my nephew, the Most Illustrious and Most Excellent Signor Alberto of Partistagno, Baron of Dorsa, Magistrate of Fratta, Dean of San Mauro, etc., etc., I, Baron Duringo of Caporetto, have the honour of requesting the hand in marriage of the Most Illustrious and Most Excellent lady Countess Clara of Fratta, daughter of the Most Illustrious and Most Excellent Signor Count Giovanni of Fratta and of noblewoman Cleonice Navagero.'

A murmur of approval greeted these words, and the maids were about to begin clapping their hands. It was just like at the puppet shows. The Countess turned towards Clara, who was clutching her hand and looked like she was closer to death than to marriage.

'My daughter,' the Countess began, 'accepts with gratitude this distinguished offer and . . .'

'No, Mother dear,' Clara interrupted, her voice choked with sobs, but nonetheless marked by a force of will that conquered any quavering of emotion or deference. 'No, Mother, I will never marry. I thank the Baron, but . . .'

Here her voice died on her and all living colour drained from her face and her knees seemed about to give way. The maids, not thinking they were thus confessing they'd been eavesdropping, rushed into the hall, shouting, 'The young mistress is dying! The young mistress is dying!' and took her in their arms. Behind them la Pisana and I, curious, came in, and with us all those who'd gathered to enjoy the spectacle. The Countess was shaking and clenching her fists, the Count bending this way and that like a weathervane that had come unstuck; the Clerk stood behind him, ready to prop him up should he collapse. Monsignor drew the napkin from his pocket and mopped his brow; the Baron alone stood impassive with his arm out, as if it were he with that magical gesture who had created the general pandemonium. The Countess tried for a moment to revive her daughter and command her respect and obedience, but when she saw Clara open her eyes, shake her head no, and all but faint again, she turned towards the Baron in fury.

'Sir,' she said, 'As you can plainly see, an unforeseen incident has spoiled today's celebration, but on my daughter's behalf I can assure you that no young woman was ever so honoured as by the proposal made in the name of the Most Excellent Partistagno. He can be certain his wife will be obedient and faithful from this moment on. I merely beg you to delay his first visit as fiancé until another, more opportune moment.'

The maids then dragged Clara out of the hall, while she, although nearly unconscious, continued to shake her head and wave her hands about. But the Baron paid her no more attention than any other piece of furniture in the house and merely began to recite the second and last part of his speech.

'My thanks,' he began, 'on behalf of my nephew to the noble bride and to all her most excellent family for the honour bestowed in accepting him as a husband. When the banns have been duly posted, the marriage will be celebrated in the chapel of this Castle of Fratta. I, Baron of Caporetto, volunteer as of this moment to be his ring-man, and may Heaven's blessings fall gently on this most happy grafting of the ancient and illustrious lines of Fratta and Partistagno.'

Here he bowed thrice, turned on his heels and descended the stairs with all the dignity he had used to come up.

'What now?' asked his nephew, preparing to dismount.

'Stay, my dear Nephew,' replied the Baron, putting a hand out to prevent him from getting down from his horse, and mounting his own. 'For today, you are excused from your visit. The bride was taken ill with joy and I myself am still very much affected.'

'Really?' said Partistagno, blushing with pleasure.

'Look!' replied the Baron, revealing two teary, bloodshot eyes that looked as if they had seen the bottom of many a wine glass. 'I believe I wept!'

'Do you think the diamond necklace will be enough of a wedding present?' asked Partistagno, pulling abreast of him as they left the Castle.

'Well, in light of this new incident, let us add the emerald clasp,' replied the Baron. 'A Partistagno must show what he's worth and that he's obliged for the love he inspires.'

And thus they rode back to Lugugnana dreaming of the splendid feasts that would be held to celebrate the wedding.

Imagine the amazement of both when the following day they received a letter from the Count of Fratta expressing his dismay at his daughter's wish to consecrate her virginity to the Lord by entering a convent! The young man did not really believe that a young lady could prefer a convent to him, but now he had no choice and he found it somewhat humbling. Far worse, he then learned from the tittle-tattle going around that it was not the girl who wanted to retire to a convent, but her parents, who were sending her there in punishment for having refused such an excellent match as himself, and that further, it was Lucilio Vianello who was his rival for Clara's heart.

The Baron went all the way back to Caporetto to hide his shame, while Partistagno remained, howling to the four corners of the province that he would revenge himself on Lucilio, Clara and her family, and woe betide them if – nunneried or un-nunneried – they didn't send him his bride! He swore he was certain she was in love with him, just as he was sure it was her family's ill-will or the doctor's evil arts that prevented her from showing it.

Meanwhile in Portogruaro a great family council was held in Casa Frumier about what to do, for the problem was a new one: young ladies of the time who set themselves so stubbornly against their parents' wishes were few and far between. They thought of appealing to the Bishop, but Padre Pendola immediately rejected this plan. All concurred that unfortunately the popular gossip was probably true and Lucilio Vianello was the root of the scandal. There was no way to send him away and so it was Clara who must be sent. The Senator's palazzo in Venice was empty and the Countess did not seem unhappy about going to stay there. After much discussion, therefore, it was decided they would move to Venice. To avoid all ceremony and occasion for large expenses, only she and her daughter would take up residence there and the family would continue to live at Fratta. Whatever nonsense Clara had in her head, she persuaded herself it would soon pass and should that not happen, there were plenty of convents in Venice where she could be brought to reason. The Count complained a little about having to remain at Fratta, for he was quite terrified of Partistagno, but Frumier assured him he would be all right and that he himself would guarantee it.

And so just one month after this discussion the Countess had already moved to Palazzo Frumier in Venice with Clara, but so far, she had to confess, she had made little progress changing her daughter's mind. Meanwhile at Fratta we were all happier than ever. The cat was away, the mice at play.

But something very unexpected happened to disabuse the Countess of her illusions. Lucilio, who had wasted many years not getting his degree, now got it in his head that he wanted to do so, and, despite Dottor Sperandio's opposition, he left for Padua, became a doctor and then rather than return to Fossalta, settled in Venice, where he had decided to practise medicine. By the time they heard this astonishing news in Portogruaro he had already procured himself a clientele that relieved him of any need to depend on his family. A true calamity! There were those who wanted him arrested, those who thought the Countess and Clara should depart immediately, those who proposed that the entire family go to Venice to do battle with his insolence. In the end nothing was done. The Countess wrote that she wasn't concerned, that Clara seemed serious about her vocation and that in any case even if they were to change city, Lucilio, now that he was a doctor, could follow them halfway around the earth.

And so Frumier was asked merely to write to some colleague of his in the Council of Ten with a request that an eye be kept on the young man, to which came the reply that an eye was trained on Lucilio day and night, but this must be kept quiet, because he was said to be protected by a secretary at the French Legation, a certain Jacob, who was the de facto ambassador in those days, for he was the only one trusted by the ringleaders of the Revolution in Paris. When the Count heard this dreadful news he was like a man possessed, but Frumier urged him not to lose heart and to pay more attention to his wife, who was constantly lamenting his parsimony in sending money. The poor man sighed to think he had been relegated to Fratta for the sake of economy, while she spent more than enough to support the entire family in great style. He sighed, as I say, but still he raked together those meagre ducats in his half-empty casket and made them into stacks that sank with all the others into the Venetian deep. At that pace, the Steward warned him, his incomes would soon be mortgaged for fifty years to come. But the master said there was no help for it, and with that philosophy ploughed onward. Monsignor, at least, was happier, because oblivious, and just went on transforming the ducks and capons bestowed on him into flesh.

As for myself, I had finished my humanistic and philosophical studies, somewhat haphazardly it is true, but I did finish. And when I took the exam they determined that I was no more of an ass than those who had followed the courses regularly. The time had now come when I should have been sent to Padua, but the Count's finances did not permit such munificence – and justice demands I give credit for a good deed where it is due. Padre Pendola was not the sort of man to waste away as a mere house chaplain at the age of fifty, just at that age when ambition shrinks back to aim higher and become more stubborn. As chaplain and special counsellor of Casa Frumier he'd been able to garner the esteem of the many priests and monsignori who were guests there, for he never lacked either those saintly maxims or those agile mutations of conscience that allowed him to attract both the one and the other; and the better he was at it, the more cleverly he showed off his triumph, so that when even the Bishop heard of him, he was said to exclaim at every predicament afflicting the diocese, 'Oh, if only I were Padre Pendola! Oh, if only I had Padre Pendola in Curia!'

That humility of his, that diffidence, called even more attention to the Bishop's opinions, and when his secretary died there were priests among both the Clausedans and the plain-dwellers who begged Frumier to press Padre Pendola to take the job, each side thus hoping to strengthen its own party within the episcopate. Frumier spoke to the good father, who showed great reluctance, refusing the crown as Caesar, but then accepting it as Augustus,[4] and suddenly he was in: secretary to the Bishop, and being so clever and adept at manoeuvring, soon in charge of the whole diocese. Great things were sure to come, and if for the moment all were somewhat confused, they were also glad, because they expected much from him. He had just assumed his new office when the Rector of Teglio, during a visit by the Bishop, presented me to the good Father. I pleased him, it must be said, and he promised to try to interest Senator Frumier in my case. The Senator had the right to name someone to attend the free college for poor students at the University of Padua and, as the position was vacant, I was assigned it to begin in November. He even chided the Count for not mentioning me before, saying he would have provided for me very happily. But the prize had come in time, and so I fervently thanked my benefactor as well as the useful intermediary. I saw no further than that, and hadn't yet learned to ring the coin on the table to see if it was good.

In any case, I wasn't unhappy to change my surroundings. La Pisana – after Lucilio had left town and Venchieredo no longer came – was making eyes at Giulio Del Ponte, and this time it was serious, for she was now fifteen and looked, and certainly considered herself, eighteen. It was then that I – to distract myself from so much heartbreak – began to go out to carouse and chase girls with the town *buli*, and I quickly became the beau of all the young ladies, both the peasant girls and the town girls. Coming home from some fair on the little grey horse I'd borrowed from Marchetto, playing my fife like a mountaineer, I always had a dozen or so of them following me and dancing the *furlana* along the way. When I think about it now, I must have looked like the rising sun as painted by Guido Reni[5] with its cortège of dancing hours before it. However, I must admit that this life tired me, and it was interrupted by a grievous incident: the death of Martino, who expired in my arms after a brief attack of apoplexy. I believe I was the only person to shed tears at his grave, because it was decided to say nothing of his death to the old Countess, who was nearly one hundred years old and befuddled by Clara's absence.

La Pisana, consigned to that fox-without-a-tail Signora Veronica for her education, became wilder every day, and idleness worsened the bad side of her nature. The day before I was about to leave for Padua I saw her come in from her afternoon walk, all red-faced and angry.

'What's the matter, Pisana?' I asked, my heart swollen with sympathy, but also, let me confess, with that love for her that was stronger and bigger than I.

'That coward Giulio didn't come!' she replied, enraged.

And bursting into tears she threw her arms around my neck, howling,

'But you love me! Yes, you do love me!' and then she kissed me and I kissed her back furiously.

Four days later I was attending my first lesson in the law, but not a word of it made sense to me, because the memory of those kisses made my head spin diabolically. There was great excitement and much discussion among the students about the news from France, ever more on a war footing and ever more contrary to the old regime. As for me, I gnawed at the college's scanty bread rations and the abundant glosses on Roman jurisprudence disconsolately, my mind always on la Pisana and the joys – bitter or sweet but always precious in my memory – of our childish years. And thus the great year 1792 came to an end. Although do I recall that at the end of January of the following year, when news that King Louis XVI had been beheaded reached us, I said a *Requiem* for his soul. Proof of my moderate views at the time.

EIGHT

In which are reviewed the first Italian revolutions, the customs of students in Padua, my return to Fratta and my growing jealousy of Giulio Del Ponte. How the dead may console the living, and the devious convert the innocent. Padre Pendola entrusts me in my innocence to the Avvocato Ormenta in Padua. Not all that glitters is gold, however.

France had beheaded a king and abolished the monarchy. The volcano rumbled, announcing the coming eruption, and all the old regimes studied each other in fright and pushed their armies forward to crush revolt. They no longer fought to defend royal blood, but their own skins. Under siege by implacable republican legions, Nice and Savoy, Italy's western gates, had raised the *tricolore*. The might of the invaders was already evident in the great promises they brought with them; the urgent danger visible in the uprisings on the boil. Treaties and alliances were being forged everywhere. Naples and the Pope shook off their shameful fear, while old Europe, raised from its sleep by a bloody spectre, struggled up and down its length to exorcize it. What, meanwhile, did the Most Serene Republic of Venice do? The Maggior Consiglio of Savi ingeniously decided that the French Revolution was to be nothing to them but a footnote to history, and spurned all alliances: with Austria, with Turin, with Petersburg, with Naples, convincing the Senate to cling unanimously to the foolish and ruinous policy of unarmed neutrality.

On 26 January 1793 Jean Jacob was recognized as the new French ambassador, when Savio Gerolamo Zuliani noisily overrode Francesco Pesaro's stately argumentation. That decision to accept the King's envoy was not in itself vile or despicable, for neither family ties nor common interests nor sworn pacts obliged the Republic to take a stand in favour of Louis.[1] But Zuliani was so venal and the Senate so quick to ratify his proposal, that it would take on the colours of genuine, vile treason.

The news of the King's death, soon to arrive, made Venice's foolish compliance with the French monarch look like outright complicity. On the one side, contempt for the Serenissima grew; on the other, outright hatred. All the scheming and the hopes of the new men of Venice concentrated on the French Legation, and this, in turn, led other emissaries to drive the Ottoman Porte against the Empire and the Serenissima, which led the Russians and the Germans to arrive on the scene. The College of Savi, ever renewed (the retiring elders transmitting their stolid certainties and apathy to the new) and ever imbecile, hid these perils from the Senate. They had endured fourteen centuries[2] while other orders and empires fell into ruin, and collapse seemed unthinkable. They were like that tottering old man who has lived ninety years and thus concludes he will never die.

Finally, in the spring of 1794, after France had violated Genoa's neutrality (at Piedmont and Lombardy's expense), Francesco Pesaro warned his fellow Venetians there was imminent danger of a conflict between the imperial forces descending from the Tyrol to the Duchy of Mantua, and the French, who opposed them. Even the sleepy Senate reacted to this, and against the advice of Zuliani, Battaja and other scared rabbits more rabbity than the rest, issued a decree to arm the mainland with fresh troops from Istria and Dalmatia, and to reinforce all the fortresses and supply them with artillery. Venice would save face, not the rule book. But the Savi, Zuliani in the lead, made certain that face would also be lost. To avenge themselves for the defeat suffered in the Senate, they decided to obstruct that decree using the method of Boerhaave,[3] who sweetened the pills he gave to his patients to disguise the bitter medicine. They argued that because the treasury was empty, they could do little, and very slowly. And they did nothing, ever.

And so the decree was implemented with just seven thousand men, mustered with great difficulty and little by little posted around Lombardy. Pesaro, his brother Pietro and Filippo Calbo (one of the Savi, whose name, at least in this, was cleared of the common ignominy) told the Senate these were delaying tactics, but the Senate had by then fallen back into its old blind stupor and swallowed the sweetened pill of the Savi without noticing the bitterness – although it was soon to know its poisonous effects.

Thus my life began to unfold among the ruins and my judgement grew stronger every day in long and furious study, and alongside the strength to master unhappiness and grief grew the strength and the will to act. Love tortured me; I had no family; my country was dying. Yet how could I ever love – or rather, how could that sluggish, waterlogged, enervated country ever have inspired in me a useful, active, worthy love? Corpses are mourned, not loved. The dignity of rights, the sanctity of laws, the pride and the glory that give one's *patria* a near-divine majesty: for a long time none of these had lived under the Lion's wings. Nothing was left of Venice but the old, broken limbs; the spirit had fled. If Venice was the most insignificant and foolish of Italian governments, all of them, from the best to the worst, were dying from a lack of ideas and moral vitality. And thus there were many more souls here who worshipped liberty and the other rights of man proclaimed in France, than anywhere else. It was this – more than the servitude we lived under or any likeness of brother races – that helped the captains of France undermine the rotten regimes of Venice, Genoa, Naples and Rome, in short, of all our governments. For just as happens in individuals, when the seed, the core, the spiritual fire is lacking in groups and human institutions, not even the physical organism can long survive. And if no violent force comes to destroy it, the life within will nevertheless grow weaker until it ceases by itself.

My life in Padua was very much that of the poor student. I looked like the serving boy of some priest, and I wore the colours of the Italian nation, as was then the custom among students, almost as if we were in the times of Galileo, when Greeks, Spaniards, Englishmen, Germans, Poles and Norwegians attended that university.[4] Gustavus Adolphus is supposed to have been a disciple of the great astronomer – a fact which adds little to the biography of either one. My fellow students in the free college were for the most part mountain oafs – rough, ignorant and filthy – this being the seedbed for future clerks of high-handed lords or venal notaries for the criminal courts. Carousing and brawling among themselves, they were always picking fights with guardsmen, butchers and tavern-keepers, and especially with this last group, who clung to the peculiar idea that the young men should not be allowed to leave the tavern until they had paid their bills. The quarrel would end up before a court, where the judges always had the good sense to side with the students, thus avoiding their implacable, however unjust and immoderate, wrath.

The students from the patrician ranks put as much distance as possible between themselves and this rabble, more out of fear than from arrogance, I suspect. There was also a middle rank of the many, the hesitant and the cautious, who, during the fat days of the month joined in the expensive pleasures enjoyed by the wealthy, and in the lean days at the end, fell back on the thieving revelry of the others. They would disparage one side to the other and then the other to the first, while making fun of both among themselves: genuine forerunners of that brainless, soulless middle class that believes itself to be democratic because it is as incapable of obeying as it is of commanding.

In the meantime, the upheavals in France arrived to rouse the frivolous, empty hearts of us students. When veins are young, the blood boils and wants to boil at any cost; the young are like flies that even when headless continue to fly around, buzzing. Among the patricians there were armchair reformers who cheered and timid doctrinaires who quivered. Among the plebeians a few roared like Marat, but the Inquisitors soon taught them what to think, while most remained docile admirers of San Marco, rebelling against the faraway French with the typical bravado of those who bow and serve the signore nearby. Those in the middle waited, hoped and babbled on: it seemed to them that the natural force of things would move the reins of government from the nobility to themselves, and that having got their hands on them, they had better hold on. But this they didn't shout out loud: they murmured, they whispered like those who are saving their voices (and their skins) for better times.

The Inquisitors, as you can imagine, had a thousand eyes trained on this varied swarm of ideas, hopes and passions, and, once in a while, a hornet that buzzed too loud fell into the trap set for him by some spider. The hornet was carried off on a barge to Venice and once he had passed the Bridge of Sighs his name was never heard again. With such wiles and tricks (good to frighten an infant people) they thought to save the Republic from impending slaughter.

As for myself, I had too many memories to hold on to, too much grief to contend with, to think what these upheavals could mean for me. The news from France came from such a faraway region that I could not understand how the madness going on there could possibly affect us. What was happening seemed to me madness and nothing more. The autumn after my first year of jurisprudence nearly put the seal on my neglect of politics. Travelling on foot all the way to Fratta; seeing la Pisana once more; love reawakened and then snuffed out again because of new whims, new jealousies; the duties granted me, experimentally, by the Clerk; praise from the Count and the Frumiers; Venchieredo's bullying and his escapades; troubles in the Provedoni family; quarrels between Doretta and Leopardo; Spaccafumo's eternal exploits; advice from the old Rector and strange counsel from Padre Pendola all gave me so much to think about, to do, reflect on, enjoy and suffer, that I did not regret having left the matters in France and the reading of newspapers to my university companions. In any event those affairs all had the effect on me of an evening's comedy, compared to what la Pisana alone put me through in those two months!

If I said her disposition had improved in the meantime, no one would believe it and I would be a barefaced liar. Her form and her face, however, had grown much more beautiful. She had become a real woman: not one of those delicate flowers that the first breath of November robs of its perfume and its colour, but a proud, strong, self-confident figure softened by a rosy freshness and a lively expression, at times outlandish, but always charming and beguiling. When that proud, marbled brow of hers bowed for an instant before the provocative glances of a young man, and her eyes, as if puzzled, looked down, her entire being emitted such a flame of desire, pleasure and love that the air around her seemed to have caught fire. I was jealous of all who looked at her. And how could I not be, I who loved her so much and knew her from my very innards?

Poor Pisana! Was she at fault if her nature (left entirely to its own devices) had spoiled that miracle of intelligence, beauty and virtue that art's sweet cunning was preparing? And was I wrong to love her nonetheless, to love her always, however ungrateful, wicked and unworthy, when I knew I was the only person on earth who could forgive her? Was her sin and error not to be redeemed by any solace here below?

Memory, memory! Our torment, comfort and tyrant, you devour our days hour by hour, minute by minute and restore them to us in the shape of an instant, a symbol that stands for eternity. You take all and return all, destroy all and preserve all; you speak of death to the living and of life to the departed. You are the sun of wisdom, the creed of justice, the ghost of immortality, the earthly and finite image of God who is infinite and ubiquitous. Yet you, memory, served me rather poorly, binding me, a youth and a man, to the whims of a childhood passion. Still, I forgive you, for I believe it is better to remember too much and suffer, than to forget and take one's pleasure. The tale of how I suffered during those few weeks at Fratta would be a long one. But I confess (and it is to my credit) that it was pity more than jealousy that afflicted me, for there is no cross worse than to be forced to pity as well as blame the object of one's love. Her whims were often quite unjust, and seemed wanton when I forgot how heedless she was.

And her sympathies towards others no longer had any reason, pretext, duration or method. One week you would hear of her great, reverent affection for the old Rector of Teglio, and she would go out with a black veil on her head and her lashes lowered, and stop and talk with him at the door of the rectory with her back to the passers-by, and listen patiently to his advice and even to his sermons. She had got it into her head to become Santa Maddelena and she would arrange her hair just like the Magdalen's in the little painting above her bed. Then, the next day, as if by magic she had changed and her favourite was no longer the Rector but Marchetto the Bailiff, and he had to teach her to ride at all costs, and she would race up and down the pastures bareback on an old nag, like an Amazon scratching her knees and her brow against the branches. And she wanted no one by her side but peasants and poor folk, and aimed, I think, to impersonate a lady of the Middle Ages, walking along the stream on the arm of Sandro the miller's lad; and even Donato, the druggist's boy, was too well-dressed and well-mannered for her. A few days later and once again a change of heart: she wanted to be driven morning and afternoon to Portogruaro, and she wore out her father's horses in the muddy ruts of those terrible roads, always insisting they proceed at a gallop. She delighted in outdoing the Podestà's wife and the Correggitrice and all the other ladies and maidens in town. Giulio Del Ponte, the liveliest and most desirable beau, served as her mirror, and she would talk and pose with him, not because she had anything to say, but to be thought witty and sharp-tongued. And Giulio was madly in love with her and swore she was wittier than all the sharpest tongues of Venice. She, instead, was always discontented, always tormented by vague desires and by a reckless need to please everyone, and that was all she thought about, all she worked at, and she rarely listened when others spoke.

One of the singular qualities of her character was this: so long as she felt sure it would please someone, there was nothing, no matter how difficult or unpleasant, that she would refuse to do. Had a cripple, a halfwit or a monster made it clear he wanted a charming smile from her, she would immediately have beamed him a long and fiery one worthy of the brightest young dandy around. Was this generosity, thoughtlessness or arrogance? Perhaps all three together made her what she was. No one around her was so base and hateful that he could not, with a bit of pleading, get pity and familiarity from her, if not actually affection and esteem. At times she would even cozy up to Fulgenzio to the point of sitting down at the hearth with him while the polenta was cooking. But once she'd left the room, the very thought of that grease-spotted, unctuous sacristan made her shudder.

And yet she couldn't resist a fawning gaze. Signora Veronica had understood this and though she had seemed highly disagreeable to la Pisana at first, she had been able to transform herself by force of adulation into bearable, even almost likeable. And you can just imagine how la Pisana's upbringing benefited from the self-interested flattery she got from her tutoress! Veronica even played procuress to gain la Pisana's favour, and would run and warn the girl and help Giulio Del Ponte escape by the stables whenever the Count or Monsignor woke up earlier than usual. Nor was Faustina the best companion. So often these little slips of girls, bred in town and reduced to country life, became experts in vice, and Faustina was worse than many others, for she was not by nature very shy. Gaining her mistress's complicity was the guarantee of her own impunity, and, believe me, she was her zealous helpmate and fired her up with suggestions and her own example.

It still amazes me that no terrible scandal ever broke out under the Count and Canon's eyes. Perhaps things looked worse than they were, in truth, and the physical exertion and the wild, vagabond life Pisana led attenuated her hot-blooded and sensual instincts. I was in any case more inclined to see black than white here, for having been witness and companion to her childhood exuberance I found it hard to believe that adulthood would damp down in her that which it excites in others. From time to time, inebriated by love and memory, I was overcome with feeling for her and found myself in her arms, but when I did not see her tremble and sigh as I liked, I was riven by jealousy. These were the ashes of a fire that had burned for others, I thought; the lips from which I hoped to taste the joys of paradise instead served up inferno's torments. She would pull away from me, disturbed by my coldness and my perpetual anger, and I would run off with my hands in my hair, desperation making me think of revenge and murder.

Then Giulio Del Ponte would come to mind, his fiery expression, so bold and full of life, his eyes forever sparkling with pleasure and emotion, the mocking, impudent smile of a Greek faun, his ready banter, so clever and suave. Those great gifts of nature that allowed him to charm women made me detest him, and I liked to think he was neither handsome nor strong nor graceful, and that the most cross-eyed maiden in the district would have preferred my broad shoulders and my healthy form to his gaunt, haggard and twisted little figure. With all that, I felt insignificant compared to him before la Pisana, and I knew that if I were a woman I myself would have chosen him. God! What would I not have given, what sacrifice not made in order to change places with him! My strength, my health abandoned, the knowledge I had but a day to live: nothing would have stopped me from stepping into his shoes to enjoy one instant of triumph, to believe she loved me more than herself. How foolish to think such a thing! For there will never be anyone on earth, no matter how perfect and enchanting, who can possess – one man alone and for always – all of la Pisana's affection and desires. I had some, but what I didn't have I longed for. Gaining the latter, however, I would have lost the first.

For neither Giulio nor any who came before him or after would ever enjoy the esteem and the trust I knew with la Pisana. I alone knew this most intimate, solitary, perhaps holy, part of her soul; I alone, in those few moments when she blessed me with her love, could think of myself as master of her entire being, because I loved her knowing her as she was. Oh, permit me just one reward for a love so long, so patient, so unhappy. Permit me to believe that just as I first tasted the delights of her spirit, so I alone fully enjoyed them. The spectacle of a vast and beautiful natural prospect; a painting finely executed: without true knowledge of nature and of art, they cannot be properly appreciated. And certainly no one can appreciate a spirit's treasures who has not studied that spirit's deepest hiding places at long length and with great love. La Pisana was such a creature; she could be fully known only by one who was born with her, you might say, and grew with her.

Despite my lessons with the Rector, I can assure you that even back then I was neither an exemplary Christian nor a scrupulous young man. The freedom granted me in my childhood, the examples set before me at Fratta, Portogruaro and Padua, meant that the reins controlling my habits were fairly slack. Granted, love is timid in this regard, but I sought every way I could to divert la Pisana from the dangerous path I saw her taking. It was self-serving charity, if you will, but it was an honest effort without any other profit for me. La Pisana was unaware of my efforts; Faustina and Signora Veronica were annoyed. The latter, I suspect, feared I meant to ridicule her free and easy ways, but if that was her fear, why didn't she correct that excessive indulgence of hers with some small amount of severity? Instead, she kept up her foolish coddling, and took revenge by trying to discredit me in every way with la Pisana. In the end I think she concentrated on that poor girl all the bile towards the Countess she'd accumulated in years and years of contempt endured and of silent, quaking servility. She retaliated by ruining the girl with idleness, frivolity and familiarity with all the worst infamy, and it wouldn't be the first time a tutoress took her revenge this way. A strumpet more vulgar and shameless than she (or Faustina) I don't recall ever seeing in any seaport I've visited; but she knew how to behave before the Count and Monsignor, and every evening in the old Countess's chamber would recite her rosary very devoutly, while the invalid from her bed and the little peasant woman who stayed the night with her after Clara's departure, said theirs softly.

With her grandmother la Pisana behaved as she did with everyone else: one week yes and one week no. Only her father, the Clerk and Monsignor were not treated to her tender insults, but they were men of papier mâché, soulless, colourless, without characters of their own, and la Pisana simply didn't think about them. It wouldn't have surprised me if she had also forgotten about her mother and her sister, for distance always acted as a powerful sedative on her feelings. But every two months a letter came from the Countess with a postscript from Clara to remind her of that part of the family that lived in Venice, and because that letter also contained news about young Count Rinaldo (who was nearing the end of his studies), every two months she was also reminded that she had a brother. Her aunt and uncle Frumier were perhaps the only members of the family, far or near, whom la Pisana always remembered and often spoke of. The opportunity to mention a Senator (related to the Doge Manin!) and say, 'He's my uncle' brought her great satisfaction, and she enjoyed it often, even when there was no real necessity. And whenever she seemed upset or unhappy Giulio Del Ponte and Veronica would mention her uncle, the Senator. The magic words would cheer her up and she would immediately revive and begin chattering about Frumier's power and authority, his palazzi, his villas, his gondolas, his silk robes, her aunt's jewels and diamonds. And the more splendid the things she talked about, the more effortlessly she described them, without showing off at all, as if to say such things were so familiar to her that she wasn't in the least impressed. In fact, poor thing, she had never seen a jewel or a palazzo or a villa beyond Casa Frumier at Portogruaro and her mother's diamond cross. Imagination took care of the rest; she was like one of those actresses in a comedy who carry on about their coaches and their treasures without ever having mounted a donkey or sniffed the smell of a *zecchino*.

It always surprised me, however, that despite the great glory she attributed to Casa Frumier, when she appeared in their salon she seemed deflated, awkward, almost dull. Today I can see that having to stand back and let her aunt take first place was a sharp wound to her pride. And that having grown somewhat savage in lonely Fratta and in the company of rude country boys and shameless gossips, she didn't dare to join in the discussions and sulked to think she didn't measure up to the others in wit and style. Hoping to compete using her beauty's charms and splendour, she would then discredit herself anew by fidgeting restlessly and being so self-conscious that she seemed quite vapid. Monsignor di Sant'Andrea, although he had been barbarously abandoned by the Countess, still had a warm affection for her daughter, and he liked to protect her from any malign gossip. He liked to say that she was ever so lively, clever and cultivated, but that for these qualities to come to the fore, a fierce attack of smallpox was needed.

'Oh, but God protect her!' the learned Canon went on. 'Because even the shelves of our libraries are full of cleverness and learning, while a beauty such as she is found neither in Heaven nor on earth, and a man must be made of stone not to be thrilled to the bottom of his heart just to look on her!'

Giulio Del Ponte was a staunch defender of the Canon's views on this, but the Senator's face would cloud ambiguously, watching Del Ponte become too heated in sustaining the point. True, la Pisana was nothing like Clara, but Giulio was far too much like Lucilio, and Frumier had often sought to bring this to the Count's attention. Oh, but it took more than that to get resolve out of the Count! He had laid all his paternal duties on the shoulders of Signora Veronica, but since her endless chatter made his head spin, he addressed his questions to the Captain: 'Oh, Captain! What does your wife have to say about la Pisana? Is she happy with her conduct, her manners, her lessons? Will she soon be competent to look after a household?'

The Captain, well-prompted by Veronica, said yes to everything and then twisted and tortured those poor moustaches of his, so often fingered and badly treated that they had turned from black to grey to white to yellowish. They had taken on the nicest of spun-sugar hue you can imagine, and only his dog Marocco's tail (because it was so old and constantly getting scorched by the fire) boasted a colour anything like it. For that tail alone, Marchetto had volunteered to forgive all the Captain's debts at their dice games, while Andreini and the Chaplain maintained that only the brave Captain and his noble setter could compete with the dawn in the hue of their coats. Now perpetual Castle guests since the Countess had departed, these fellows had grown ever more relaxed and ready to jest, nor was the Chaplain so timid as before. Even the kitchen cats had lost their old wildness and would curl up in the ashes or on the company's feet. One great old tabby, as grave as any state advisor, had become Marocco's closest friend, and they slept together on the same straw with the same fleas, strolled about together, ate their meals together and took part in the same hunt for mice. But in ever such a contained and polite way: you could see they hunted the way gentlemen do, for sport, allowing the servant class of other kitchen cats and kittens to take their prey.

After those brief few days when la Pisana was my faithful friend again, I was not at all happy in that company, to tell the truth. As a little child I had admired them without understanding them; now I understood them perfectly, but marvelled that they could take pleasure in such inanity. In desperation I hid in the chancery, dabbling in the record books and copying out sentences in which, little by little, I tidied up the numerous blunders that flowed from the Clerk's fecund pen. Oh, but my head was in the clouds! At every footstep in the courtyard below I would run to the window to see if la Pisana was going out or coming back from one of her solitary jaunts. I'd become so asinine that even the clatter of a pair of clogs left me unsteady; I kept hearing la Pisana, seeing her everywhere, and however much she avoided meeting me and sulked when she did meet me, I never stopped desiring her.

Signora Veronica liked to mock me for these longings of mine and she would often entertain me with tales of la Pisana's doings at Portogruaro, of Giulio Del Ponte who was besotted with her, and Raimondo Venchieredo, who, barred from seeing her at Fratta or in Casa Frumier, would wait for her on the road or in other haunts she liked to visit. Torn up by jealousy, I would run away from that old telltale, and retrace my steps on those walks I used to take of old. I went out to the Bastion of Attila to see the sunset, soaking up that sense of the infinite that Nature offers us in wide open, solitary places; I studied the sky, the sea, the laguna; I revisited my youth in memory, thinking how all was different now and how many new things the future promised or threatened.

Once in a while I would stop by the Provedoni household in Cordovado, where there was always some peace, some family gaiety, to refresh my soul – when Doretta didn't spoil it by her flirting or affecting to be a great lady. The youngest of the Provedoni brothers, Bruto, Grifone and Mastino, were three good, hard-working young lads, strong as bulls and sweet as sheep. Bradamante and Aquilina, the girls, I found charming in their rough simplicity and the cheerful, ceaseless working of their little hands for the benefit of the whole family. Aquilina was then no more than ten years old, but as watchful, serious and wise as any adult housewife. When you saw her down at the canal at the end of the kitchen garden, rinsing out the laundry in her sleeveless corset with her shirtsleeves rolled up past her elbows, she looked like a grown woman and I would spend hours there beside her pretending to be a boy again, just to enjoy a little peace of mind, at least in my imagination. Brown as a little gypsy, that golden brown that reminds us of splendid Arab women, her body small and strong, wearing two fine, dark eyebrows that met rather mischievously in the centre of her brow, two large, deep grey eyes and a great mass of curly black hair that half-hid her ears and neck, Aquilina was so calm, so sure, she seemed almost manly, in contrast to the somewhat shy hesitancy of her elder sister. Despite her twenty years Bradamante seemed more childish than the other, yet she was a graceful young lady and Signor Antonio liked to say, teasingly, that anyone who wanted to marry her would have to pay him dearly. And both girls were admirably patient with Leopardo and his wife.

Their sister-in-law was arrogant, peevish and perpetually discontent; her husband, constantly goaded by her, was rough and cruel in turn; it would be hard to exaggerate how much his nature had changed under her dominion. He was quite unrecognizable and all wracked their brains to think what potion Doretta had administered to put him under her spell. While he was courting, it was all love, but love, an angel's fan when moved by goodness, turns to Hell's hot coals when clutched by pride and evil. Doretta regretted having settled for that marriage with Leopardo and she wasn't shy about saying so to everyone, even to him, and she made sure he knew that she had stooped to marry him. Raimondo's courtship had made her think that if she had just been patient a bit longer, she might have aspired to a much more distinguished state than wife to a tiny village landowner, daughter-in-law and sister-in-law in a family of hard, frugal, pious peasants. Living at home had become intolerable for her and she often spent entire days at Venchieredo, and if she was asked where she'd been, didn't even deign to reply, but shrugged her shoulders and turned away. So as to cut a fine figure at Portogruaro she had elected Padre Pendola as her confessor. But her frequent confessions did not seem to improve her habits much.

She no longer even used good manners with her father, for irritable temperaments, when they grow annoyed with someone, make everyone pay. She was resentful because Dottor Natalino had consented to her marriage with Leopardo, and when he replied that it was she who had wished it, she snapped back like a viper, shrieking that it was a father's duty to come to the aid of a daughter's immature judgement. If she had said she wanted to throw herself into the well, would he have helped her by giving her the first push? Finally it was the young master Venchieredo who had to calm her rage, and how he did it and how fairly he treated honest Leopardo, I shall leave for my readers to imagine. In the end the whole town was talking about her and yet the Provedoni family bore it with resignation, and her poor husband never watched her desire anything that he didn't pursue like a dragon. From this domestic spectacle I drew my lessons and my comfort; it was all too apparent that happiness is fleeting and relative, if not rare and deceptive. If little of that comfort remained when I then returned to Fratta, at least I had spent a few hours without scratching at my wounds, and one or two of them slowly closed, although the scars went down to the bone, like those walking barometers for whom the twinges in every rib and the creaking of every joint signal a change in the weather.

My autumn holidays continued in that vagabond, melancholy way until one day, thinking I saw a more benign expression than usual on la Pisana's face, I went out behind her past the garden and down to the road to Fossalta, and then stealing up on her, I put my arm in hers and asked if she would have me as her companion. Oh, what made me dare such a thing? She turned on me with eyes that looked ready to devour me, but when she began to vent her fury with some terrible insult, her voice stuck in her throat and she bit her lip, spilling blood onto her chin.

'Pisana,' I said. 'Oh mercy, Pisana! Do not look at me like that.'

She tore her arm violently from mine and ceased to bite her lip, for rage now gave way to words.

'What is this? What do you ask?' she said with scorn. 'We are no longer children, I believe! The time has come for each of us to know his place and I am astonished that you, rather than urge me to forget that, do not bring it to my attention when

I do. You know that I am capricious and impulsive, therefore it is up to you – who are cool and reasoned by nature – to recall who you are and who I am!'

This said, she turned away and began to walk towards the shadows of a stand of willows where Giulio Del Ponte was waiting for her, shotgun on his shoulder. I later learned that they had arranged to meet there and that she'd said those ugly words thinking I had followed her there to spy on her. The pain I felt went right to the bottom of my soul. Back at the Castle, whether dead or alive I no longer knew, I wandered back and forth and up and down the stairs like an unquiet ghost. Without thinking, I entered the old Countess's chamber.

'See if that is Clara,' she said to her nurse, for her eyes were no longer good for anything but to weep the comfortless tears of old age.

Distressed and bitter, I fled upstairs to my old lair, where everything was just as it had been the previous year when I left. After a bad hour there I went into Martino's room next door. My attachment to him (and the unconcern of the others) meant that all his things lay there still untouched. On the floor were some nails left over when the undertaker closed him in his casket; on the table sat a little vial with some dried up cordial inside; on the wall, the dusty, leafless olive branches he had hung there on the last Palm Sunday of his life. I threw myself on the bed (the shape of his corpse was still impressed there) and wept bitterly, recalling my first and probably only friend, calling out his name a thousand times and praying to him to remember me and to come down, body and soul, to comfort me. But my faith wavered, even in this; I did not really hope, I did not believe. Only much later, after many torments and efforts, did a certain vague, confused, yet intrepid belief in the spiritual and the eternal grow in my heart. In those days I would stammer out my prayers in church, but my soul was as dry as a skeleton, my mind shrivelled by the hard air of this world, and my discouraged heart clung to hopes of the void as the only possible place of peace. That discouragement made even the memory of that fine old man (whom despite my desperate invocations I would never see again, and who slept in the grave while I anguished over life) turn mean and bitter.

Little by little the air of death up there began to invade my brain: the tears froze on my lashes, my eyes took on a troubled glaze I was hard put to dispel. The fire of life seemed to be going out of me and I was oppressed by the chill, the phantoms, the terrors of life's last agony. For an instant, approaching death, I believed I was Martino and was astonished to think I had risen from the grave and expected that any moment the gravediggers would come to take me back. This strange and fearful thought widened like the mouth of an abyss; it was no longer a thought but a vision, pure dread. Light from the window struck my leaden eyes – perhaps in that moment the sun emerged from the clouds and filled the room with the day's radiance – and a desire for air, peace and annihilation came over me. Stumbling, I dragged myself towards the balcony, but the crash of a chair I overturned roused me a little from that funereal dream. Otherwise I think I would have fallen from the window and my life would have ended without the long epitaph of these *Confessions*. I put a hand on the table to steady myself and touched something that stuck between my fingers. It was a devotional tract, the one, in fact, that Martino used to browse through every Sunday during Mass, and his glasses were still inside, marking his place. It was almost as if my friend's soul had responded to my pleas and was about to give me his reply from the worn pages of that book; tears welled up in my eyes again and I sat at the table with my head in my hands, sobbing without restraint. And so the peace, if not the light of my spirit came back to me, and gradually I remembered how and why I had come up there, and how grief had made me seek refuge in the memory of a dead man.

Trembling and teary still, but now alert and sure of myself, I sat up and opened the book, turning the pages attentively. They were the usual simple, earnest prayers: divine solace for pious souls; foolish, incomprehensible hieroglyphs for unbelievers. Here and there the pages were interspersed with a few pictures of saints, the odd communion certificate with Latin phrases and the year marked on the front, modest milestones in a long life admirable in its faith, sacrifices and good cheer. Then my eye fell on some pages covered from top to bottom in a minute, irregular script all in capital letters, as those who've only partly learned to write in cursive use. It was Martino's hand and I saw that having reached adulthood capable of scribbling down the odd note, he had taken to keeping a record as best he could of what was in his head, so as to make his accounts to the master of what he'd spent. Those pages seemed to me a treasure and I sought to make sense of them, although it wasn't an easy task. But by studying and restudying, adding something here, subtracting something there, inventing, repairing and gluing together, I managed to make my way through that tangle of letters wandering riotously over the page like a flock of ignorant sheep.

They seemed to be memories or lessons drawn from some dangerous straits of his life he'd come through victoriously, to which he'd added some religious maxims and God's commandments where they seemed pertinent. His style didn't lack a certain rough elegance, like some of our writers of the Trecento or any man who doesn't know how to write but knows how to think better than those who do write.

'When you are very unhappy it is a sign you have some sin on your soul, for a quiet conscience makes a bed wherein your pains may rest. Look and you will see you have neglected some duty or made someone unhappy, but if you make amends for that omission or bad deed, peace will soon return to your heart, for Jesus Christ has said: Blessed are the persecuted.

'Forget the rewards that have come to you from above; seek them below you in the love of the humble. Jesus Christ loved the children, the poor and the lame.

'Don't look at your life as a galley ship to which you are condemned. Galley slaves, the Venetians call their scoundrels. But good men work for their neighbours, and the harder they work, the more they are worth. We must love our neighbours as ourselves.

'Do not rebel against your master; endure his hardness not out of fear, but out of compassion, so as not to increase his sin. Jesus Christ obeyed Herod and Pilate.

'The secret revealed to you by chance is more sacred than that obtained through the trust of others. One is confided to you by man, the other by God. The satisfaction of having guarded it jealously will give you more happiness than any favours or money offered you to betray it. The soul's contentment is worth more than a thousand *zecchini*, I can assure you, and I realize now that my thoughts were right and for the best.

'Living well, one dies better; desiring nothing, one possesses all. Do not covet the goods of others. However, one must not scorn or refuse, so as not to offend anyone.

'If when you have met all your duties you are not yet at peace with yourself, it is a sign you have further duties you're not aware of. Seek them and carry them out and you will be as happy as the human condition permits.

'Despair has always been the greatest folly, because everything has an end. I speak of the things of this life. But the joys of paradise are never-ending, and so is faith in the Lord God. May He help me to obey these rules. Amen.'

In one corner that had remained blank, written in smaller script and at a later time, there were two more precepts: 'When you've become good for nothing because of age or illness, consider every service done you an unbidden gift.

'Do not be suspicious; there is all too much of what is certainly wrong to waste time thinking about what is not certain. The law of the Lord prohibits rash judgements. May He bless me. Amen.'

Let me say that after I had deciphered these words I felt very humbled to have read them, and even somewhat dejected. I, who had always held Martino to be a simple man – a very good man, a good servant, modest, thoughtful and reserved, as such men were once upon a time – and nothing more! I, who next to him considered myself a person of a certain stature (especially in recent years, since I'd begun to have a sprinkling of Latin at my disposal) and who was very pleased with myself for continuing to be his friend, as if mine were a great condescension! I, who had scorned sharing my uncommon wisdom with him for fear, not that being deaf he wouldn't hear me, but that being uncouth and foolish he wouldn't understand me! But look! In four lines put down on a page he taught me more after death than I could teach others in a whole lifetime of study! And further, among his precepts there were some so supremely simple that I did not even understand them, although the words were very clear.

For example, where it was written that we must seek further, unknown duties awaiting us and carry them out (if having met those duties we do know about does not suffice to make us live in peace with ourselves), well, what did the good Martino mean? For this was precisely my own case and I couldn't stop wracking my brains over the matter. Oh, enough! I resigned myself to having to read and reread it and understand it only very abstractly, unable to see how to apply it to my own circumstances. And so I went back and studied the first precept, the one that said that great unhappiness was due to some obligation unfulfilled or some wrong we had done!

'Poor me!' I thought, 'I must have many wrongs on my conscience, because today I feel more miserably unhappy than any man in this world.'

And I swear, I examined my conscience so closely, so scrupulously, that although it was my very first such examination it was not without some merit. My grasp of moral laws was imperfect and I fear I may have excused myself a few times too many, but I also accused myself for things in themselves quite innocent, like the fact that I had never made friends with Fulgenzio's sons and was not very grateful to the Countess. I ascribed the first sin to pride, when it was pure and simple antipathy; the second I blamed on my ungenerous soul, while the blame really belonged to my poor scalp's tenacious memory for having been so unfairly tortured. But what is most important, I did not deceive myself about my greatest sin, my reckless love for la Pisana, which suddenly revealed itself to my conscience in all its bestial savagery. I had loved la Pisana from when I was a tiny child! And intensely! From when I was a tiny child I'd dreamed of a grown man's love with her! Like a boy who thinks with his feet! When I reached the age of reason, still unnaturally naughty, I persisted in that strange idea. Wrong, Signor Carlino!

That was my first stumble, and all the others followed like the twenty-odd letters of the alphabet follow the first. Reason should have warned me that I was la Pisana's cousin or her servant (I say servant because my place at the Castle was with the servants). In neither case should I have attached myself to her, pretending a love outside the order of things. Think for a moment: what is the end of love or what is supposed to be its end? Marriage, certainly: it was something I knew and saw every day. But how could I, Carlino, ever have dreamed of marrying la Pisana? Who was to say? Oh, be silent, you noisy desires pursuing the impossible! The question is not whether such a thing could ever happen in nature, but whether it is customary and would please all those concerned.

And here I had best admit that not only was marriage with la Pisana outside the usual order of things, but neither the Count, the Countess nor anyone else, perhaps not even la Pisana, would have been pleased by it. And therefore? Therefore, to chase that sorcery put me on the wrong path, in danger of straying quite far off course indeed, and certainly not the right way to fulfil my duties of integrity and gratitude.

But what if la Pisana loved me? Ah, there you have another quibble, a mere pretext on the part of inveterate vice, my good Carlino! First of all, even if she did love you, it would be your duty to retreat, for otherwise you'd be profiting from her heedlessness and her infatuation to put her at odds with her parents' wishes. And then, you are poor and she is rich – and let us not stoke the fires of slander! And anyway, she doesn't love you, and so the matter is rather simple.

What? What do you mean she doesn't love me? No, accept it, Carlino! She doesn't love you one bit. She doesn't love you with that blind, intense, unyielding heat that blocks any reflection, removes all distance and merges soul with soul. She doesn't love you, and you know that very well, which is why you fret and trouble yourself so much. She doesn't love you and you came to this room hoping death would comfort you in the face of her cruel words, her contempt. Have no fear, Carlino, if you abandon her she will not suffer a single fever! And you are not even one of those special fellows who would injure her pride. If you were the poetic Giulio Del Ponte or the magnificent lord of Venchieredo you might have to suffer some remorse about leaving her. But you! What the Devil, haven't you understood that here at Fratta your standing with her is no different from that of

Marchetto, Fulgenzio and all the others? You are just one spoke in the wheel of her affections, a beggar waiting for his alms on a Saturday evening. This is all wrong, Carlino! It's no longer a question of duties towards others, but of respect for yourself. Are you a donkey who lowers his eyes and takes the beating or a man who holds his head up and faces the judgement of others? Dust off those knees, Carlino, and stand up. See, you blush with shame; that is a good sign and a bad one at the same time, for it shows you know you have done wrong, but are disgusted and repentant for your error. Go, Carlino, be off; seek a better and more honest road, where there are other passengers whom you can help and show the way; don't lose yourself in those nebulous confines between the possible and the impossible battling your own shadow, or the windmills of Don Quixote. If you're unable to forget la Pisana, you must pretend to forget her and think not of the rest; it will come later. For now, this is your duty towards yourself, towards her, towards all. Stay and you will humiliate yourself, annoy her, and do a disservice to her parents. Away, Carlino, away! Dust your knees and be off!

This advice was the first fruit of Martino's reprimand and it was so bitter that I folded up his pages, put them back in the book, and the book in my pocket. Pale and thoughtful now, I left the room that I had entered so dark and deranged. Of all the things that grieved me, the worst was that I'd been unaware of how worthy Martino was and how wrong my estimate of him: I'd thought of him as an obedient machine, while in fact he was a man, aware and resigned. I shrank so much in my own esteem that I recognized myself no more; the memory of that old servant, dead, buried and already devoured by worms, forced me to bow my head and acknowledge that with all my Latin learning, when it came to the true knowledge of life I knew less than the peasants. In their simple religion, life is courageously seen as temptation or a trial. I had no other words for it than those we use to define the vegetable existence of a plant. I could peck at ideas, yes; and turn the great skein of destinies, births, deaths and transformations over and over. But without an eternity surrounding it, life is but a joke, a laugh, a sigh, a sneeze; the fleeting existence of a creature under the microscope is on a par with ours; the same number of stages define it, from birth to death. Without the spirit above, the body remains dust and becomes dust. Vice and virtue, wisdom and ignorance: these are qualities of another kind of dust, like toughness and fragility, shallowness and depth. I would lay me down to sleep on the metaphysics of the void, while from the heights of Heaven an old servant sang to me of immortal hope!

'Oh, Martino, Martino!' I said. 'The loftiness of your faith is beyond my comprehension, but what I have learned from it is so profound, so virtuous, that all by itself it guarantees your goodness. Old Martino, accept the homage of your unworthy son, even beyond the tomb! He loved you in life, and if he did not prize you very highly then, he venerates you now and accepts your counsel, hoping to be worthy of your valuable lessons.'

The first consequence of this resolution was to lead me away from Fratta. Out and about I went in pursuit of pleasures and amusements, as I had done before. But then I made the brief list of my duties line up before reason and, finding it was very brief, I thought of that dark host of unknown duties that might assail me at any moment, duties that, according to Martino, I might call on to defend me against unhappiness. When the thought flickered across my mind, I sounded the alarm bell in every corner of my soul, but no new sentiment appeared, shouting, 'You must do this and cease doing that!' As for the need to break with la Pisana, I was already in agreement with myself about that, and while I felt the sacrifice would be painful and nearly impossible, I didn't fool myself that it wasn't absolutely necessary. And then, gratitude, charity, study, temperance, honesty: in all these other matters I found myself in order; there were no objections to be made. My only fear was that I hadn't been a zealous enough chancery apprentice, but I resolved I would be so in the future, and on the morrow I began to copy the double of what I'd done before. That blessed morrow was the same on which I was to begin not looking at la Pisana, not seeking her out, not asking about her; but I thought about it so long and hard that I had to put the business off until a later morrow. And I carried on like that for another day, until finally I persuaded myself that my duty was not to murder my love for la

Pisana, but to tire it out with other duties, to distract it, put it to sleep. My own soul was so full of my love for her that it would be something like a suicide, and not wanting to kill off my spirit in a single blow I tore it to pieces and tortured it, shred by shred. Remorse, for that wrong that intellect so sternly condemned, embittered even those remote hopes I still had.

One day, after many hours spent writing in the chancery (but without having received any great benefit from it), I decided to go to Portogruaro to say farewell to Senator Frumier. October was nearing its end and I was soon to be off to Padua. But chance would have it that la Pisana was at luncheon with her uncle that very day, and if I were to swear I didn't know that, you certainly wouldn't believe me. It was Lady Frumier's name day and the group around the table included Giulio Del Ponte, Padre Pendola, Monsignor di Sant'Andrea and the others from the salon. The Senator welcomed me as if I had been invited, and I played dumb, but as I sat down I silently wondered if la Pisana had said nothing to me about the invitation to keep me out of the way. She was sitting very near to Giulio and the glances they exchanged and the confusion of their words made it clear to me that if not an inconvenience, I was certainly an undesired witness. An inconvenience, no, for she would not have pulled back on my account. Even the best side of her soul was unacquainted with any tact, a quality that is often mere custom and sometimes quite hypocritical, but which protects virtue by employing a delicate sense of shame. But where could she have learned such feminine niceties? Her sister Clara, the only one who might have taught her, was always far away in her grandmother's room, and so la Pisana was left alone to express and impose all her whims, and, little by little, had learned not only to let whims have free rein, but never to bother examining them or hiding them when they were ugly and shameful. When instinct takes charge, shame, which derives from reason and conscience, dies.

I was seated next to Padre Pendola, eating little, talking less, observing much, but most of all mortified with rage and jealousy. From time to time Giulio Del Ponte would grow animated, cut into the conversation like a raider, let go a barrage of quips, jokes and epigrams, and then return to his mute dialogue with the young lady beside him, as if to say, 'This is a far sweeter conversation!' You could see that his gaiety wasn't spontaneous; this was no surfeit of wit that couldn't help gushing out. Rather, the thinking went, were he to remain silent, that would create suspicions or threaten the sparkling reputation that had won him the young lady's heart. And, in fact, she only smiled at his smiles and blushed right to her ear lobes, sighed and became confused when he spoke (so nimbly, charmingly, cleverly) and sparked contagious laughter all around. Giulio Del Ponte had guessed what his magic was made of: she liked him because he kindled enthusiasm, gladdened hearts, swept the others along. He might have had three spirits instead of just one: his eyes, his movements, his words and his thoughts were so rich and various that they seemed to create more motion than the single spiritual furnace that lends heat to each of our lives. If you will forgive the comparison with the steam engine, the power of his spirit was that of ninety horses, while the ordinary man has thirty. A great fortune, you'll agree, but woe betide any of these Samsons should Delilah cut off his hair!

Woe, indeed, for the very prize his strength earns him is also destructive; love, which for others makes the fire burn brighter and adds the power of millions of horses, is for him a damper. Love pulls him away from his rightful arena and he loses his primacy, becomes confused with the great mass of other innamorati, any one of whom can outshine him with particular gifts and merits. In a word, love can make a fool sublime, but it makes such splendid, fascinating creatures into fools. Giulio knew that, however, and he defended himself valiantly. He felt love grow like a charmed cloud that clung to his mind and invited dreams of beatitude. He would succumb to the sweet lure for an instant, then good sense shook him awake, reminding him that sleep would bring defeat. No longer was he driven by a surplus of wit and mirth, but by force of will and love's ambition. He had charmed la Pisana and he did not want to lose his conquest. In this he was unfortunate, his temperament being one of those that easily profit from occasions for pleasure, but for whom the chance to love is fatal.

Padre Pendola studied Giulio Del Ponte and la Pisana, then stole a glance at me; two eyes like his don't move without reason, and every time they met mine the slippery chill of his glance touched the bottom of my soul. The rest of the party noticed nothing; they chattered among themselves and drank to the health of Lady Frumier, laughed boisterously at Giulio's banter and, above all, they ate. But when the meal was finished and the company was on its way down to the garden for coffee on the terrace, Padre Pendola took my arm affectionately and asked me to stay behind. His face was lit up with pity, and, dismaying as I found this, it also made me think his nature was better than I'd believed. There's no accounting for it! From one side the magnet attracts iron, from the other it repels it and we don't know why. The magnet's eccentricity works between one man and another, too. I stayed behind because I was curious, to be polite, and also because my eyes wanted not to see.

'Carlino,' said Padre Pendola (we were pacing up and down the hall while the servants cleared the table), 'you are soon to return to Padua, is that right?'

'Yes, Father,' I replied, emitting two deep sighs, as sincere as they were nonsensical.

'It is for the best, Carlino. You aren't happy with your situation here, admit it; uncertainty and idleness are destroying you and spoiling the best years of your youth!'

'It is true, Father. For a while now I have known life's vexations.'

'Good, good! When you go back you will find life ten or twenty times more pleasing. You must simply make the sacrifice of fulfilling your duties.'

Hearing this advice from the mouth of the Reverend came as some surprise, for I didn't at all expect his counsel to agree with that of Martino, and all of a sudden I found myself ready to confide in him.

'I must tell you,' I went on, 'that recently I began to seek, by fulfilling my duties, a refuge against . . . against ennui.'

'And did you find it?'

'I'm not sure. The copy work in the chancery is too material a task and the Clerk is not the best man to make it enjoyable.

It keeps my hands busy, yes; but my thoughts go where they please – and it is the brain, not the hands, that keeps count of time and unhappiness.'

'You speak very well, Carlino, but you know better than I that to be cured one must want the cure deeply. In your case, Carlino, your soul is ailing; if you want to be well, you must go away from here. Now you will say: but the disease travels along with the patient! No, Carlino, that won't do. Trouble nearby is more oppressive than trouble far away. Please, don't blush now. I'm not saying much, this is just the counsel of a good friend, of a father, no more. You have no family, no one who loves you and guides you; I would like to be your spiritual father and allow the light of experience the Lord has granted me to come to your aid. Trust me, try: I ask no more. You must leave this place, not only with your legs, but with your soul. You have already understood how to govern your soul: by industriously carrying out your duties. As you said very well, it is the brain that keeps count of unhappiness, and the heart, I would add, not the hand. And therefore you must keep not only your hand busy, but your mind and your heart.'

'Father,' I stammered, quite moved, 'speak, for I listen with true faith and will try to understand and obey.'

'Hear me, then,' he went on, 'you have no family obligations and the debt of gratitude towards your benefactors is quickly repaid by one whose only assets are affection. On that account your duties will not keep you busy more than a minute, unless it be to press you to study according to your benefactors' intentions. But that is not enough. Study will occupy the mind, but the heart remains idle. The more so because the family that brought you up did not properly guide that heart of yours. No, don't be ashamed, Carlino. How can you expect to be tied by filial love to the Count and the Countess, when they barely know how to make their own children love them as parents? A sense of obligation comes less from the benefits received than the way they are given, and this is true above all for children. So do not be ashamed. That is how things must be. As for trying to force love forth now, that would be the mark of a fine nature, of a sweet and grateful soul, but you will not succeed.

Love springs forth spontaneously; it is not a garden plant. Your heart, Carlino, is as empty of filial affection as that of a foundling. This is a great misfortune that excuses many faults. But let us be clear, my son: it excuses them, but it does not free us from the need to eliminate faults or permit us to grow hardened to them. Early in life the child seeks remedies against such misfortunes instinctively, and a good angel may even make us hit the mark. But often bad luck or childish blindness turn up poisons instead of medicine. And once reason has grown aware, Carlino, we must move the plant and abandon that mistaken, harmful cure for the proper one. You are eighteen years old, my son, both young and a man. Your heart is not equipped for proper, pure and legitimate affection, because until now no one has shown you where it comes from or taught you the necessity. Perhaps I am the first to speak of such duty to you, and how welcome that is, I do not know . . .'

'Go on, Father, go on. Your words are what my thoughts have been seeking, vainly, in these past few days. I believe dawn is breaking in my mind and you may be sure I'll be brave enough not to avert my eyes.'

'Very good, Carlino! Have you ever thought that you are not only a man, but a citizen and a Christian?'

The question, put to me so solemnly by the good father, puzzled me. What being a 'citizen' might mean I had no idea, and as for being a Christian, I had never doubted that I was, for the doctrine had accustomed me to saying so. Perplexed and confused, I replied weakly: 'Yes Father, I know I am a Christian by the grace of God.'

'So the Rector taught you to respond,' said he, 'and I have every reason to think you don't mean to lie. Up until now, Carlino, everyone was a Christian; the question was rather senseless. Religion stood above all disputes, and, for better or worse, the bond of faith (if not the rule of habit, as in the zealous early centuries) held us all together in the great family of the Church. But now, my son, times have changed and to be a Christian does not mean to imitate the others, but rather to begin to do the opposite of what many others do. Behind the general indifference hides the enmity of many, and against those many, the few true believers must fight with every weapon they have so as not to be overwhelmed. Not out of personal pride, you understand, but to prevent the trampling of that faith without which there is no salvation. Carlino, I repeat: you are young, you are a Christian, and as such you live in difficult times, and those you are heading for are even more difficult. But that very difficulty, although a trial for all of us and a wretched problem for you, too, is a great fortune for your own immediate interest and your personal dignity. Think about it, my son: do you want to idle in indifference, without reflecting, without dignity? Or would you rather join the battle of eternity against time, of the spirit against the flesh? The present matters troubling you lead straight to these dilemmas, have no doubt. You are a man of a generous and open nature and you must choose the right cause. Religion means idealism, faith in immortal justice and the triumph of virtue; in short, the rational life and the victory of the spirit. Unbelief means materialism, Epicurean scepticism, the denial of conscience, the anarchy of the passions; a bestial life in all its vile particulars. Choose, Carlino, choose!'

'Oh, I am a Christian!' I said with great ardour. 'I believe in the good and want it to triumph.'

'It is not enough to want,' added Padre Pendola in a small, sad voice. 'Good must be sought and good must be done, in order for it to really triumph. We must give ourselves body and soul to those who sweat, work and fight for that; we must attack our enemies with their own weapons; gather all our constancy to our hearts; arm the hand with might, the mind with prudence, have no fear at all, remain vigilant at our posts; and when we are driven away, return; and when despised, suffer and scheme to come back victorious; and yes, yield if necessary, but only to rise again; bargain, yes, but only to gain time. In short, we must believe in the eternity of the spirit and be ready to sacrifice this brief earthly life to a better, future immortality.'

'Indeed, Father. The horizons you open before me are so vast that I no longer dare to weep over my little misfortunes. I shall broaden my gaze and all those tiny matters that hinder me will vanish. I shall fly, not walk!'

'Really, Carlino? That is how I like to see you, but remember, enthusiasm will not suffice without judgement and constancy. I've shown you the noble duties that lie before you and you are keen to realize their great promise. But along the way you may find you have relapsed into pettiness and vanity. Do not be afraid, Carlino. You are like a traveller who in order to reach Rome must spend many a night in filthy taverns, in the company of coachmen and porters. Endure it all, don't be disgusted by your passing fortunes, raise your sights to your goal and keep them there!'

It's hard to say what I understood. I was certainly dazzled by his resounding words, for they brought to mind those glimmering dreams – humanity, religion, sacrifice, faith – that populate the youthful imagination. I understood that, for better or worse, I was entering a new sphere in which I was but an intelligent atom in a sublime and mysterious composition. With what means would I act? And to what end? I was far from sure, but certainly both means and end far surpassed my amorous concerns and my childish regrets. I had been invited to show I was a Christian; I felt myself a man connected to all humanity, and my stature grew.

'So much for religion,' Padre Pendola broke in. 'As for your condition of citizen, the same rules apply. The acts of every individual fall into place in the great social mechanism when all agree to respect the traditions and the institutions of the *patria*. *Patria*: this is the religion of the citizen and the laws are his creed. And woe to any man who touches them! With our words, our pens, our example, our blood, we hold inviolate the decrees of the *patria*, that wisdom come down to us in twenty, thirty generations. But sad to say, today there is a tireless, secret army of destroyers among us, questioning what the tribunal of the ages has declared true, just and sacrosanct. My son, we must oppose such barbarity at our gates, and bring the same damage on our enemies as they would like to bring on us, by spreading discord and depravity among them. Evil against evil: applied courageously the way a surgeon does. If not, we will certainly fall, friends and enemies alike, under the rule of those heinous men who preach a foolish liberty in order to impose true servitude to reckless, tyrannical, immoral codes! Servitude to passions, our own and those of others; subjection of the soul to earthly, fleeting pleasure. We must fight pride bravely, my son. And therefore we must be humble and obey, obey, obey. May the law of God command, the law of past and present, and not the will of a few fanatics, who claim to reform, but only devour. Do you understand what I mean, my son? So religion and *patria* join forces and prepare a great battlefield for a sacrifice far more worthy than the idolatry of affection or any private interest.'

With one hand, Padre Pendola cast me flat in the mire; with the other he raised me to the stars. I shook off my yoke of sorrow and raised my head. Free, but dismayed.

'I am here,' I said, 'and I hope to cancel the first part of my life and replace it with a purer and more generous existence. What I cannot change, I shall herewith forget, and seek more sacred duties, greater loves . . .'

'Careful with those loves of yours!' Padre Pendola interrupted me. 'You must not use the same words to speak of such different matters. Love is a flash that darts by, a passing meteor. In the new life to which I invite you, you will need faith and zeal, applied with determination and constancy. Our symbols are the cross of sacrifice and the sword of persuasion, and they are far superior to crowns of myrtle or pairs of doves. Persuasion, my son, comes forth from our sacrifice and warms the souls of others the way the sun's heat is absorbed by the seed that germinates. We cannot allow the acrimony and the contradictions of others to block us; persuasion will come if we make way for it with perseverance. When good has triumphed, it is time to pursue evil, but pursue it purposefully and wisely; because, my son, the ranks of the martyrs are sadly not very numerous and to avoid seeing one's own sacrifices squandered, one must get the best value one can.'

'Father,' said I, somewhat cautiously, for I was mystified after that long speech, 'I hope I will understand better when my spirit has been purified of the fog that clouds it. I shall reflect and overcome.'

'You would have overcome already had you thought to fight,' said the Reverend, 'but you were closed up in your shell, Carlino, and did not seek the help of one who could have done much for you. Ideas are not born afresh, they follow a course, my son, and you were wrong to wrap yourself up in your petty passions, without relying on those wise and honest persons who would have led you forward on that path that I now indicate. Last year, for example, I advised you to frequent the Avvocato Ormenta in Padua, an upright, just and generous man who might have turned your mind towards its true ministry and showed you the true purpose of life. Men like him ought to be venerated by the young and taken as examples.'

'Father, on your advice I saw the Avvocato Ormenta quite a few times, but I was distracted by other thoughts. And I seem to remember that his coldness rather alarmed me, and he had a certain air of contempt that wasn't reassuring. I don't recall whether he seemed too old or too different from me, but in any case I didn't go to see him willingly and the room in which he received me was so gloomy, so chilling, as to frighten me.'

'These are the signs of an austere life devoted to the sublime, my son. What yesterday frightened you, will please and charm you tomorrow. Superior things can seem cold; although snow covers the high mountain peaks they are the first to be kissed by the sun, the last to be abandoned. Return to the Avvocato this year and get to know him, and either my judgement is at fault or I shall have done you the great service of indicating a sure guide to the life that awaits you. Now I have planted a small seed in your heart. Let us hope it will grow. The good Avvocato, finding you better disposed, will receive you with more confidence. For that matter I, too, ten months ago, had few hopes of you, I tell you in all honesty, all the more so because today my hopes are great.'

'Oh Father, you confuse me. Why great hopes of me?'

'What, Carlino, don't you know? True, you do not know yourself very well and I don't wish you to become prideful, but I would like you to learn to read your own soul. Your passions are so intense and constant that, raised to a purer sphere where passion becomes adoration, they could shine with divine light! Have you truly decided to shake off your fetters, leave the mire and seek happiness where it is truly found, in fulfilling those most sacred duties that conscience can impose on a man of our times?'

'Yes, Father, I will do so for love of justice.'

'Then trust in us, Carlino. We will assist you and enlighten you. The mists of dawn will slowly be transformed into rays of sunlight. You will thank us, and we, you.'

'Oh, Father, what are you saying?'

'Yes, we will thank you for your great services to the cause of religion and the *patria*, which we defend for the love of humanity and the glory of God. Nature has supplied you with great gifts; use them properly and you will receive gratitude, honours and happiness. I promise you that. If you were a priest, I would say, 'Stay with me: we will fight, pray and win together!' But you are called to another path, also fine and noble. The Avvocato Ormenta will stand in my stead; I shall write to him at length about you, and he will take you as his son, and you may have more occasion to do good in the world than I can ever hope to do among the clergy of a modest diocese. Understand, Carlino: I ask nothing of you but to believe in me, and to try. Above all, I don't want to see you making yourself stupid with boyish dreams. Disdain what must be disdained; break the chain of habit; remember that man is made for men. Be generous, for you are strong.'

Well, what can I say? Let me be sincere: flattery worked where eloquence didn't, or at least it finished the job that eloquence had begun. Tears came to my eyes, I took Padre Pendola's hand and wet it with my weeping, covered it with kisses, promised to be a man, sacrifice myself for the good of other men, obey him, to obey the Avvocato Ormenta, obey everyone and everything except those passions of mine that had so foolishly tyrannized me up till then. I was no longer myself; I seemed to have become an apostle, of whom and for what I could not say. My head was in the clouds and there was nothing on earth I despised so much as my sentiments and my life of previous years. Padre Pendola supported me in this conversion of mine and urged me to pick up the thread of my childish faith, to believe, to pray. The light would come to me and the Avvocato Ormenta would be my candleholder.

We went down to the garden and out onto the terrace, where a pergola covered with vine leaves, already yellowing, shaded the company from the late afternoon sun. The conversation had come to a halt while the sun set in quiet solemnity; the waters of the Lemene gurgled below, green and eddying; the faraway, melancholy ring of some church bells travelled through the air like the last words of the dying day; to the west, the sky was on fire with autumn's splendid colours. My first impression was that I stood in a great temple, God's invisible spirit filling my soul with grave and peaceful reflections. But then my thoughts began to course through my head like blood through the veins after a fast run. My mind flew too high; it no longer recognized the air its wings were beating; it was disturbed by a horror of the infinite. I went to the railing to look at the river, and the water passing by, never coming to a rest, never any variation, made me think of worldly things flowing this way and that into a mysterious abyss. In my memory what Padre Pendola had said to me was like that dream one remembers having seen so clearly, but which has faded to a vague, discoloured confusion. I turned to look for him and saw Giulio and la Pisana whispering to each other. Icarus, I felt the wax melting from my wings and I plunged into the old passions; but pride held me up. Only a little while earlier I had felt myself to be so much older than they; why could I not continue? I looked at la Pisana bravely and smiled with something like pity. But my heart was quivering and the smile, I fear, did not stay long upon my lips.

Just then Padre Pendola, who had been conferring with the Senator, appeared at my side and, almost as if he could see my soul wavering, began to treat me with such exquisite kindness that I was ashamed I had vacillated at all. His words were sweet as honey, compelling as music, merciful as tears, and I was touched, convinced, enamoured. I decided I would make the effort and sacrifice myself to those lofty duties he had spoken of, to be the master of myself for once, and be able to say, 'This is how I want it!'

In the meantime, I was thinking, 'Yes, I shall suffer, but I shall win out and victory enhances one's strength, if only to make one able to suffer in a less cowardly way. Not for nothing did Martino die; not for nothing did Padre Pendola read my heart; both prescribed the same medicine and I shall be courageous and take it strong!'

Padre Pendola went on speaking to me in the soothing tones of a garden waterfall spilling between mossy banks; I couldn't say what he told me, but when we left I had the courage to offer my arm to the Count and to la Pisana to help them up into the carriage, and then took my seat on the box on the pretext it was warm (although, it being an October night, the heat was not very great). Now that I had my own chair in the chancery I was allowed to join the masters in the carriage, and that night I had to engage in something of a battle with the Count so as not to enjoy that precious right. I thought then of that night a few years before when I had discovered that la Pisana was madly in love with Lucilio, and took that same road clinging to the back of the carriage, lost in a maddening whirl of thoughts and dismay. That evening I would have given my life to be able to sit next to her and torture myself with her indifference and greedily savour the wrong she was doing me. How proud I felt to see how much I had changed! Now it was I who voluntarily refused to sit beside her: after so much pining, so much jealousy, so much torment, I had finally got up the courage to run away from her! I don't think I arrived at Fratta any happier or less pale and drawn, however, and had poor Martino still been alive he would certainly have noticed my foul temper. Instead I was met by the Clerk who had a document he wanted me to copy out in haste; not having found me there in the daytime, he rudely fell upon me at night.

Would you believe that I began to work on it immediately and with crazy delight? I saw this as the solemn first step in my redemption, and felt ever so cocky and proud when la Pisana went off to bed and I didn't gaze at the moon or torture myself about her. While I was copying those pages, I did repeat a few words and omit a few others, it is true; and at every dip into the inkwell I said to myself, 'Oh, finally I've succeeded in not thinking about her for half a day!' And I went on thinking like that quite shamelessly and my conscience didn't notice, or pretended not to, like Adelaide's mother.

Padre Pendola spoke to me, instructed me and advised me numerous times in the few days I remained at Fratta. The Rector of Teglio pitched in with his own exhortations and when

I left I felt I was embarking on a Crusade or something like it. Today I can see that I lacked all faith, but I did have curiosity, pride and courage, qualities that can counterfeit faith at least briefly. When the thought of la Pisana came crashing down like a Congreve rocket[5] on my new resolutions meeting in secret council – and one ran this way, the other that – I would whack myself on the breast beneath my cloak and recite a couple of prayers, and with some patience the fire would go out and I could return to being a citizen and a Christian, as Padre Pendola wished. I'm not sure, however, that I should have been able to please the Rector, a Clausedan to his fingernails, who, after waiting in vain for a year had decided the good Padre Pendola was lazy and careless in his handling of diocese affairs. He would have preferred the zeal of St Paul. Padre Pendola instead was navigating below the surface of the water, the better to deceive the fish and the ducks; after he took the reins of the Curia the town clergy was observed to be more outwardly disciplined, more canonical. I wouldn't have liked to know what lay beneath, but gossip, censure and scandals were avoided. With a prudent word here and there and a wink or two, the good father had given the clergy back those dignified appearances that are so important in maintaining authority. Certainly, a Gregory VII[6] would not have stopped there, but the Reverend Father knew what century this was and sought to cure the curable, not risk the patient's life in belated interventions. It was enough for him that some things went unseen and unmentioned; in showing no sympathy for the scruples of the old, the rigid and the incorruptible, he forced them to refrain from their usual insubordination, which had flourished up to then in light of the heedless anarchy of their superiors. The Rector didn't approve of this, but when it came to me, he approved of the holy zeal the secretary had inspired in me, and pressed me to greater heights with his rough, sincere words.

I returned to Padua with all the obsession of the man who has decided to enter a monastery after his love abandons him. As soon as I got there, I ran to see the Avvocato Ormenta, who had already received a letter from Padre Pendola and who welcomed me as the superior welcomes the novice. The worthy fellow who the previous year had seemed suspicious, mocking, a bit cold, now seemed the most open, suave and mellifluous man on earth. His eyes roved ecstatically; his every move was a caress; his every word struck the heart with the greatest conviction. He was happy about everything, indeed he was blissful: about himself, about Padre Pendola, and above all about the precious gift the latter had made him when he entrusted me to his care. He spoke to me of trust, meditation and patience; he invited me to come to luncheon whenever I liked, apart from Wednesday when he fasted (the practice might not suit my youthful stomach). He congratulated me on my young age, which offered me double opportunity to do good. I must study the morals of my fellow students and discuss with him how to correct them and direct them towards better purposes if they seemed errant or mistaken. I would be the channel by which his experience would bring mature wisdom to the impetuous young; would there were many such mediators! But, in fact, there already were quite a few, and the fruit of their action had began to multiply and was evident in the most docile and thoughtful of the young. I was one of the most meritorious, with my sharp mind, my attractive and appealing face, my warm and easy way of talking! I would certainly have my reward: in satisfying my conscience (without doubt the best prize), in earthly accolades and in eternal recompense. The state had need of zealous, shrewd and hard-working magistrates, and the state would find them among us. We must not refuse, for charity towards our neighbours, and the good of the faith and the *patria* demand that modesty be silenced. All men are brothers, but the clever brother must not allow the less clever to act rashly. Love must always be prudent, and sometimes it must be harsh. The hand may strike a blow, and, in fact, it must in certain cases; the heart, of course, remains charitable, indulgent, merciful; it weeps at the sad need to punish in order to improve, to cut down in order to correct. The heart, the heart! To listen to the Avvocato Ormenta, his was so large, so tender, so ardent that he could only err by granting too much love, never too little.

In the meantime, certain things I noticed about the Avvocato rather surprised me. First of all, his damp, dark and practically bare house continued to provoke a feeling of disgust in me, much like the nest of a snake. That a man so open, so honest, should dwell in that gloom, in those grim, sepulchral surroundings! And then, during my visit, his wife, a small, thin, sighing woman of a greenish pallor, came in to ask him something. The Avvocato turned and spoke to her in sharp, ugly tones, more those of a master than a husband, and the woman left the room biting her lip but not daring to reply. So it seemed the gentleman had a double register: the voice he'd used with me the year before and with his wife; and the one he'd used with me a few minutes ago and would continue to use until he had accompanied me to the door. There, I nearly laughed aloud when I saw a messy, filthy, sallow-skinned boy got up like Sant'Antonio playing in a corner of the vestibule with some toys he'd found in the sacristy. The Avvocato introduced me: this was his only son, a small wonder of piety and wisdom who had taken a spontaneous vow to Sant'Antonio and wore his habit, as people sometimes did then and still do today in Padua. That hair of his, shaved at the crown and wild as an abandoned hedgerow all around; those sinister, bleary eyes; his hands smeared with every kind of dirt; his clothing worn and ripped in all its saintliness: it all made a peculiar contrast with the praises the Avvocato sang in his hushed voice. I couldn't help but think this was fatherly illusion; the boy looked about fourteen (he was sixteen, I would later learn) and yet there was nothing about him to justify the praise I'd heard, unless filthiness is equated with saintliness (some very pious souls do make that peculiar equation).

When the door closed behind me, I heard him intoning some canticle in a loud voice and I think I would rather have listened to a dog howling (although sacred music with its solemn, melancholy notes has always moved every fibre of my soul). But devotions lose their sacred nature when they become senseless babble, and teaching them that way to children only leads the young astray, even when the intention is to make good Christians. Spiritual matters must be treated seriously, in my view; otherwise, leave them alone. If it is a disaster to ignore them, it is a sacrilege to mock them.

Following the injunctions of Padre Pendola and the Avvocato Ormenta I now made an effort to overcome my usual reserve.

A small part of my time was devoted to my studies, while various distractions and promises to devote myself to the great and exalted helped to soothe the sharp grief in my soul. It didn't take long to confirm what the good father had told me about my fellow students: most were deeply indifferent to religion, and worse, treated it with scorn, mockery and jesting. They might even have rekindled the faith in me, if my early teachers had ever taken the trouble to light it, but no one had. In this regard, you might say I was born dead, and resuscitation would have required a miracle, something that hadn't happened yet. However, I disliked their foolishness so much that for a while I even thought I did believe, so much did I suffer to see faith so fatuously derided. Youthful generosity misled me about my own opinions; it seemed only right to defend the persecuted and not the aggressors.

I told the Avvocato what I'd seen and he encouraged me to observe more carefully, to investigate how this religious anarchy was tied with political and moral licence, and to identify the ringleaders of the sect, approach them and get them to bare their souls to me, so as to see where to begin to correct, to repair. Above all, he urged me not to call attention to myself, but to blend into the crowd and to say little, limiting myself to asking questions and listening.

'Gentleness brings the lost lambs back to the fold,' the Avvocato said. 'First you must flatter them in order to convince them; we follow them so that later they will happily follow us.'

He never failed to invite me to come often and to stay for luncheon, but while I agreed to the first, I was less willing to partake of the second. One Sunday when he would have me stay to dine with him at all costs, I did; but the company I found there utterly spoiled my appetite. There was a wheezing, balding old lady known as the Marchesa; an ageing meddler, half-policeman, half-priest, who drank heavily and stared at me through his glass; and two large, coarse, very unclean young fellows, who, eating with their hands and gnawing with their teeth next to little Sant'Antonio and that weepy semblance of a mistress of the house, brought on the worst case of melancholy I had ever suffered. In the midst of such elect company, the

Avvocato instead seemed to be in seventh heaven, but I did notice that he never invited the drinker to drink, or the young fellows to eat. All his urging was directed at the Marchesa, who could neither drink nor eat for the cough that wracked her. The Avvocato carved with true mathematical precision and succeeded in getting eight servings from one small roast chicken, a task that in my view exceeds squaring the circle. I had no desire to eat anything at all and passed my portion to one of the young men, who left not even a trace of a bone on the plate.

The Avvocato introduced me to everyone at the table and then drew me aside in a corner to tell me their stories. The Marchesa was the ever so worthy patron of all the pious institutions in town; her wealth was said to amount to eighty thousand *zecchini*, and the Avvocato was her preferred advisor. The elderly fellow, a Venetian, was close friends with the Podestà, who did his bidding and whom he came to flatter whenever he had need of something. The two youths were students from Verona, devoted like myself to the holy cause and full of zeal. It was a great pity they didn't have my cleverness or nice manners, but God had made bread out of stones, and with good will, anything was possible! It seemed to me, however, that if they applied the same zeal to all their works as they did to eating, they would need restraint, not encouragement. I recalled then having seen them once or twice under the portico at the University, neither the most exemplary nor the most modest among the students who met there when not attending lectures.

'Enough,' I said to myself, 'maybe they go there to pursue lost sheep and encourage them to return to the fold.' But I hadn't the slightest desire to make friends with them as the Avvocato urged me to do. The Marchesa's invitation to attend her *conversation* from time to time and spend a few hours far from any danger, among the right sort of God-fearing people, I accepted with a bow. The bow meant, 'Thank you very much, but I'd rather do without your salon!' But the Avvocato hastened to reply for me that I was ever so grateful to the Marchesa and would come to her gatherings as often as my studies permitted. I was very close to saying something irreverent then, so annoyed was I at the way my wishes were being manipulated. But the Avvocato sent me a pacifying glance and whispered, 'The Marchesa adores young people. You must appreciate her fine intentions and forgive her defects, because she can do so much for you!'

Despite all the nice talk, in short, I left the Avvocato's house determined not to take part in his luncheons again, nor in the Marchesa's gatherings. For a couple of days my reward was to find there was more savour to the soup at my college, and with a pound of bread sliced up in it I deemed it a royal banquet. My room was bright with sunlight and I could raise my eyes without meeting the meddler's feline glances. I came across the two students from Verona a few days later in the hallway at the university, but they seemed as reluctant to speak to me as I was to approach them. I asked someone about them and was told they were the most dissolute and drunken of the students. They had been studying medicine for seven years without obtaining their degrees, and as they had no means, they lived by cheating and stealing from the others. I felt sorry for the Avvocato Ormenta that he'd been taken in by such a pair of gluttons, but when I decided to let him know the truth, he was not at all pleased. It was all calumny, he said, and he was astonished I should pay it any heed; I should be thinking about revealing and destroying the vices of the wicked, not the misdemeanours of the good. I began to think the good Avvocato's faith was rather purer than his morals, for if these were misdemeanours, what might be the vices I was meant to battle?

NINE

My friend Amilcare undoes my conversion by Padre Pendola and sends me back to studying philosophy. I travel to Venice where Lucilio continues to plot against the Republic and against the Countess of Fratta's peace and quiet. My heroic abdication in favour of Giulio Del Ponte. A strange turn of events puts the chancery of Fratta in my hands and I begin to perform the relevant services.

Among those whom the Avvocato Ormenta and Padre Pendola would have felt must absolutely be converted was a fellow who appealed to me considerably more than those two young men from Verona, my accomplices. I had begun to make some incursions into the enemy camp on the Avvocato's behalf, and then on my own account, and, in the end, I found the enemy was a great deal less bad than I'd been led to think. And so I began to wonder about the Avvocato's good faith and whether I was happy with the office assigned me. That I should want to dull the pain tormenting me by carrying out the highest of duties was all very well. That I should seek to forget a shameful, disastrous (though very, very ardent) love by training the soul to worship those great ideas, humanity's poetry – in this, too, I could see no wrong. But that my worship of those great ideas should come to nothing but perpetual deceit and indecent spying, that my ever so lofty duties should descend so far into the practical sphere, I was beginning to doubt. I had tested myself as Padre Pendola wished, but I was not very pleased with the result. My mind was distracted, but my soul was far from that ideal peace that compensates all other woes and sorrows. In short, my brain was occupied but not my heart. And that heart, its one-time love obstructed, now empty of all other affection, had become a terrible nuisance with all its useless beating. At first, I'd been confusedly fired up by the ardour of others, but then (because it was false ardour or because there was not much in me to feed the flame) I had cooled so much that I scarcely knew myself. All that prudence, foresight, measure and calculation was ill-suited to a fiery young soul. I aspired to something grander and more vital; I saw I was not made for ascetic ecstasy, and I've already told you that when it came to faith my conviction was weak.

You can imagine how I struggled to strengthen it! But the Avvocato Ormenta, rather than assist me, was forever thwarting me with his ever so earthly scheming. Of course, the purpose of his intrigues was sublime, spiritual and so forth, but I was always losing sight of that, nor did he seem to remember it unless I happened to remind him. In the meantime a student from Treviso, a certain Amilcare Dossi, had become a close friend. He was a young man of strong, bold intelligence, with a heart worth more than gold. We often spent our time together discussing metaphysics and philosophy, for I had stuck my head in those clouds and didn't know how to get it out, while he had been studying these matters for some time and was able to be my guide. I had known him only a few days when I realized that he was exactly the type that Padre Pendola considered a ruthless destroyer of all ideals and noble enthusiasms. Amilcare believed that everything must be put in doubt, reasoned about, discussed. And yet I was astonished to find in him a love of science and a kindness and warmth that seemed to me incompatible with his dry, cold doctrines. I finally confided this to him and he laughed aloud.

'Oh, poor Carlino,' he said, 'you are much behind the times! You wonder at my violent love for those sciences which I then dissect in the manner of the anatomists? The fact is, my dear friend, love of the truth is higher and purer than any other. The truth, however poor and naked it may be, is more lovable and more holy than any sumptuous, dressed-up falsehood. And thus every time I'm able remove some flounce or frill from you, my heart leaps in my breast and a triumphal crown girds my head. Blessed be that philosophy that teaches us that though we be mortal, weak and unhappy, we can be great in equality, liberty and love! This is my fire, Carlino; this is my faith and my belief, every day and every minute! Truth at all costs, equal justice for all, love among men, freedom of opinion and conscience! Who could be happier than one who works with all his might to make of humanity a single harmonious, wise and contented being, so far as the laws of nature permit? Today, moreover, when such ideas grow ever more influential and beat upon the reluctant sphere of fact, today as I watch that fog that hid them from the minds of men disperse, who could be happier than I? This, my friend, is true peace of the soul. Rise to that free and rational faith, and neither bad luck, betrayal nor grief can ever cloud the serenity of your spirit. I stand strong and steady, because I believe and trust in myself and in others!'

Imagine! This profession of faith so answered my needs that I blushed a thousand colours. As I recall, I had not the courage to say a single word, and Amilcare was sure I hadn't understood a word either! But even supposing I did not understand, I did tremble. I was ashamed of myself for having vacillated for so long, and I pitied Padre Pendola and the Avvocato Ormenta (although they weren't in the least need of my pity) and decided I would follow Amilcare in his studies and determine what faith my heart really loved. For the second time now I glimpsed a world of great ideas and noble sentiments and dared to hope that even without la Pisana my soul could make sense of life.

This revolution in my thinking had already taken place when I saw the Avvocato Ormenta again, and, unwilling to behave as if all was well, I nearly picked a fight with him. He was quite unhappy with me, because I had not once visited the Marchesa's salon, although it seemed she was very fond of me. And so we parted rather gruffly, he telling me that the good cause had no use for rationalists and such. I didn't let him hear what was boiling up inside me, but hurried to see Amilcare and told him for the first time of my ties to the Avvocato and of the entire affair, beginning with Padre Pendola's sermons to me and ending with that evening's dispute. As he listened to me he pursed his lips like a man hearing something unpleasant, and then his eyes bore down on my face in a way I shall never forget, as if to say, 'So are you sheep or wolf?' I was so upset that

I nearly repented of having blundered into that long confession. But his suspicion passed in a flash: Amilcare was not one of those souls expert in wickedness who sees evil everywhere; he was a good man and quickly recovered from that momentary uncertainty, and his goodness did him no harm, as so often happens. He told me of the Avvocato's reputation in the city, where he was considered a highly vigilant servant of the State Inquisition.

'Oh, the foul dog!' I exclaimed.

'What is it?' asked Amilcare.

I didn't have the courage to tell him that the fellow might well have used me as the instrument of his knavery, and all courage deserted me when Amilcare told me it was generally believed that the Avvocato was responsible for the arrests of several students the day before, and for several others having been thrown out of their lodgings and many others searched.

'This Padre Pendola of yours must be an Inquisitor in disguise, playing a double game to keep us in the dark,' said Amilcare. 'Venice would have this be the Quattrocento. They live in fear of the century now arriving. But we – by God, no – we will never put our native faith in their service. Good sense is no longer the privilege of one hundred noble families. All want to think now, and he who thinks has the right to act for his own good and for the common good. They have led us on a leash too long. Padre Pendola can retire now: we wish to walk by ourselves.'

When he said these words Amilcare's whole person was transformed: his high, prominent brow, his deep eyes and his fine, flared nostrils sent out flames. He seemed to grow even larger than he already was, and a flush of pride and dignity rushed through his veins.

'Who were the Greeks? Who were the Romans?' he went on. 'People who lived before us, from whose experience we can profit. They were powerful because they were virtuous, and virtuous because they were free. Whether virtue derives from liberty or the other way around, we must put ourselves to the test. The struggle for liberty will provide us real and useful instruction in virtue. How did Lycurgus give Sparta back her might? He gave her laws that would restore the Spartan people's great traditions. We must imitate him! New laws, sound laws, universal laws: they must be clear, strict, permitting no evasion, no privileges! Let us not forget our forebears came from the lines of the Bruti, Cornelii and Scipioni.[1] History repeats itself in ever wider circles; of old disorder a new order is born. The time has come for equality, truth and virtue! Humanity would reign united and we are its heralds!'

I took his hand without speaking, but I was utterly with him in spirit, and my thoughts raced to become one with those great hopes. Justice, truth and virtue: three stars governing all things spiritual. Far from them, all is dark, and every heart trembles and turns wicked. I saw them appear on my horizon like a divine constellation, and all the love in me flowed irresistibly towards them. Another mist dispersed, another wing beat in the heavens, and I had found my religion, and my heart was forever at peace. And yet that mist was like those infinitesimal fractions that grow smaller and smaller but never disappear entirely; that light so far away that just when it seemed about to set the atmosphere on fire, a new piece of sky intervened between it and me. I often spoke to Amilcare of my doubts and he assured me they were due to my poor logic. I, however, believe it was because I apprehended all this in a flash, without asking myself too many questions, that I was able to see the truth. Justice, truth and virtue! Three fine things, three words, three ideas that could captivate a soul and drive it to madness or death: but who would ever bring them down to earth, as Socrates put it?

This was the thorn in my side and it caused me great pain, although I did not yet understand it very clearly. New institutions and new laws will make new men, said Amilcare. But even supposing that was true, who would give us these fine institutions, these excellent laws? Certainly not the foolish and inept governments of the time. Who, then? New people – just, virtuous and wise. And where would they be found? And how would they come to be in charge of public affairs? In fact, I had understood very little then about that muddle I give myself credit for seeing through. But in those times when our minds were still befogged, our lethargy barely shaken and our politics still in their infancy, was there any great man of government able to understand better than I?

And so my love for these principles remained ethereal and sentimental, the love one feels for a woman seen in a dream. I admired Amilcare when he granted that dream the solidity of reality, but I could not do the same. In France, every day brought new developments, and the news from there, coming to us from far away and through the youthful imagination of my companions, relieved my doubts somewhat. I began to wait and hope with the others; meanwhile, I read the philosophers of the Encyclopedia, and Rousseau, above all *The Social Contract* and 'The Profession of Faith of a Savoyard Vicar'. Slowly my mind gave flesh to those fancies, and when I saw them before me, alive and breathing, I threw my arms around Amilcare, shouting, 'Yes, my brother! I finally believe it! We shall be men one day!'

The Avvocato Ormenta, who now saw me rarely, and ever more taciturn and suspicious, had some of his men spy on me, and he learned of my new habits and my friendship with Amilcare, and guessed the rest. In those times events were not going his way and the poor fellow had much to do on many fronts: he must have known he and his party were but ants trying to roll back a great boulder, and even if he didn't know, the fact was that he seemed very distraught. And yet he was not ready to give up hope and he continued to pursue me, hoping to extract from my innocence what he'd previously got from my docility. Having been warned by Amilcare, I spied on the Avvocato in turn, studying his face as a barometer of the times. Whenever I saw it downcast, low and clouded, I would run to celebrate with my friends and we would raise many merry toasts to liberty, equality, the triumph of France, the republic and universal peace. In those days wine came very cheap and the three ducats the Count gave me every month allowed me to take part in my addled companions' fraternal love fests. Politics and the love of mankind were matters a young man such as I could wax enthusiastic about, far more than the Avvocato's worldly, shrewd religion of plots and intrigues. The pure gospel of grace and charity might have had some effect, but by now the die was cast: I became a fanatical, fighting Voltairean. As willing as ever to sermonize, I enjoyed debating with my university companions and being more like them made me judge them less flabby and contemptible. For the truth is, ideas can inflame us, and when opinions are held in common, individual egotism is stifled or absorbed into the whole. Thus the selfishness of the English is useful to the nation, because it is held in common; while elsewhere charity serves no purpose, being erratic and disjointed.

And so we young people made great strides in just a single year, and if the passions, the rancours and the idleness of before still lingered, the winds from the west scoured our minds of petty concerns. Perhaps fear, vice and inertia were still there deep down, but faith soared above them and it was able to do great things. In any event, I was content, and, having got to know Amilcare very well, I began to think that the others were all like him – which was not the case, unfortunately. A very immature judge I was; my errors went to one extreme that year, as they'd gone to the other extreme the year before: those who in another moment I'd have condemned to death, I now judged innocent. Amilcare's belief, his enthusiasm and his free nature led me along; he was light-hearted, gay and bold. Like him, I thought that any sentiment not consecrated to the good of all mankind was a silly sentiment indeed.

I hadn't lived before that, I thought. La Pisana seemed a very insignificant creature, as if I were looking down on her from the great blue heights of a mountain. Often she vanished from my mind altogether, for I had found something to love in her stead. When I was alone, two very different elements in my soul (which, violently stirred together, made one for a time) would begin to divide, each going its separate way. There was my faith in virtue, science and liberty, so fine and ardent; and there was my secret memory of la Pisana that crouched growling and furious in a corner. I had to struggle mightily to keep these two sentiments together; by firing myself up energetically, I usually succeeded. It didn't happen spontaneously without the company and the example of Amilcare, however.

In the meantime, the noise of French arms reverberated at the gates of Italy, and with them great promises of liberty and equality. There was much talk of the Roman Republic and young men cut their hair to look like Brutus.[2] Hope surged across the land as those ideals of ours came closer and more victorious. Amilcare seemed to have gone mad; he went out preaching in the most riotous circles, in caffès and in public squares. The Avvocato Ormenta was ever more sullen and livid; I believe he was even angry at the Marchesa because she persisted in not dying. On my rare visits, I mocked him. One day he spoke to me rather sourly of my friendship with a young man from Treviso, warning me, half in jest it seemed, that if I cared for him I should advise him to be less rash with the insinuations he was making in his speeches. That same evening Amilcare and a number of other students were arrested and taken to Venice under the Inquisitors' orders. I believe I was spared the entertainment because they hoped to frighten me and turn me to the other side. But cowardice, thank heavens, has never stuck to my nature. What happened to my friend made me detest his enemies three times over, and I became bolder than ever in our common cause. And now that his very safety depended on that cause, my impatience knew no restraint.

Time alone sought to calm me. After the first attacks had come a long and inscrutable lull. Alliances were reinforced on the continent; France drew back on herself like a tiger getting ready for a greater leap, but beyond her borders this was seen as a fatal lack of courage. The Serenissima negotiated with everyone, steering carefully among the obstacles; the Inquisitors smiled to themselves to see this storm that had caused such uproar die down; they smiled and kept their claws on those poor devils who had bet on hail and thunderbolts, while everything seemed to point to a season of dead calm. No one spoke of Amilcare and all the others who had gone before him to the prisons, or after; it was rumoured that the French Legation was looking after them and would prevent them from being sacrificed. But suppose the next campaign went badly for France? I shuddered even to think of the consequences.

Then one day I received an envelope sealed in black. The Count sent word that his Clerk had died; and, he went on to say, nearly two years of study was certainly enough, and that while I could take the exam whenever I liked, I should hurry back to him to take charge of the chancery. I cannot quite say what I felt reading that letter, but deep down, I think, I was very pleased that necessity took me back to la Pisana. Without Amilcare and with no hope of seeing him soon, Padua had come to seem a tomb. My hopes dissipated a little more every day, for youthful impatience quickly becomes discouragement. The Avvocato Ormenta had a newly cheerful and triumphant aspect that annoyed me. With the help of a good word from Senator Frumier I sat the second-year exam and finished well; I then quickly prepared to leave Padua, so dazed by events that I could scarcely make sense of myself. It was hard to go, however, without knowing more of what had become of Amilcare, and I hoped that with the Countess and her noble relations as my sponsors in Venice, I might learn something. And so I asked counsel of my few ducats, and found they permitted that brief detour so long as I used them very thriftily. I made a bundle of my things and took them to the boat, then out of politeness went to say farewell to the Avvocato Ormenta.

'Ah, well, bon voyage, my boy,' he said to me. 'It's a pity you didn't stay with us all year, for you are clever and you would have come back to visit me often, and you might have even joined the Marchesa's circle. Give my regards to Padre Pendola, my boy, and trust in those who are older than you. The young are credulous and they will lead you into bad business.

Today I understand what the dear Avvocato meant: he thought I was an old fox, as sly and greedy as himself. But then I understood nothing. At his urging, I was forced to kiss that filthy son of his – still wearing his foul-smelling habit and up to his usual games in the entry hall – on the cheek. This ceremony made me twice as happy to leave Padua, not to mention that I now had the chance to try to make a decent clerk out of a young man of not yet twenty years.

When I got to Venice I wasted no time admiring the domes of San Marco or strolling along the water's edge, but left my bundle at an inn and hurried to Palazzo Frumier. But, good Lord, how the Countess had changed in these last few years!

Her face was darker and more disagreeable, her nose as beaked as that of a hawk, her eyes shone with a greenish light that didn't augur well, and her manner of dress was so dishevelled as to be almost repulsive. There were no pink ribbons or lace on her bonnet and grey hair was strewn messily over her brow. Not even my concern for Amilcare made me want to try to get help from that side, I confess. I pretended I had come to Venice to pay my respects to her, thinking that would be a fine excuse to gain her sympathy, but she was so rude in her reply that my legs felt weak just to hear her, and, keen to leave that room, I was soon downstairs. In the entry hall I took heart once again and thought I would like to see the Contessina Clara and confide in her. Just as I was looking for a servant who could conduct me to her, she appeared, for she had heard of my arrival and did not want to miss seeing me. Her kindness moved me and gave me courage. The poor young woman was just as I had seen her last; perhaps even paler, even graver, and with two red circles around her eyes that spoke of tears or long sleepless nights. Those marks of grief, rather than dissuade me from confiding in her, encouraged my intimacy. I opened my heart to her and told her of my friend, and how I wished to know on what grounds they were keeping him in prison and when he might hope to be released.

The Contessina grew quite disturbed hearing of Amilcare's case, and even more at the probable reason for his arrest, and once or twice seemed ready to interrupt me, but stopped herself with a sigh. In the end she was convinced by my unhappiness and she told me that there was someone in Venice who ought to know a great deal more about this than others, and that I knew him, and that if I went to find Dr Lucilio Vianello he would certainly be able to tell me all I wanted to know about my friend. The poor thing blushed when she said all this to me, and warned me not to tell anyone else, and when I inquired where I might find Dr Lucilio she said she didn't know, but that he would certainly appear from time to time in that great piazza which was then, as today, a meeting place for all Venetians.

I took my leave, thanking her for her great kindness, and, stationing myself in the Piazza, walked up and down, waiting for Signor Lucilio to show his face. No longer tormented by jealousy and full of zeal for Amilcare's welfare, I approached him boldly when I saw him. He didn't recognize me, or pretended not to, but then was very polite and asked me all about my studies and my life, and finally whether I had seen the Countess and her daughter. I told him I had and how I had found them. He told me that the Countess had become a wanton gambler like so many Venetian ladies of the time. Every day she lost large sums at the tables, the moneylenders were at her heels and her only thought was to try to win back what she'd lost, taking ever graver risks. Her temperament had grown ever more sour and she tyrannized her daughter badly; Clara was not allowed to leave the house except to attend Mass at San Zaccaria, where Lucilio saw her once a week. And then she vanished like a shade: she couldn't even stand by a window, because they had given her a room inside the palazzo. As for him being able to enter that house, he had never succeeded, although he had gained quite a professional reputation in Venice and was invited to the most important noble salons. But the Countess was immovable and he had heard from a reliable source that she was negotiating with the nuns of Santa Teresa to have Clara taken in as a novice. Her dowry was the only obstacle, for the Countess was presently only able to pay half the sum required, and the convent would not accept Clara before receiving the full amount. Clara had bowed to her mother's will, and if the sacrifice had not already been carried out it was only because of this disparity of interests. All he could hope for was that she would not obey when they called on her to take vows; that she would not put that insurmountable barrier between herself and the world.

Lucilio told me all this with the forcibly compressed rage of a man powerless against an obstacle he considers both frivolous and foolish, but when he finished he raised his brow and it was obvious he had lost none of his old courage; he continued to hope, and his hopes were no mere dreams. That strong spirit of his would not be content with vain illusions, I knew; the assurance I sensed in him must be well-founded. Seeing him more confident, I finally told him of the reason that brought me to see him, not concealing (and not without a certain self-interest) that it was Clara herself who had told me where to find him. Many vague memories then seemed to swim in his head and he looked at me as if he just now saw me for the first time.

'How long has it been since you've had news of Padre Pendola?' he asked without replying to me directly.

'Oh, a very long time,' said I, surprised at being questioned. 'I don't think the Reverend and I are much in agreement any more, nor is he likely very pleased with me.'

'And did he not give you an introduction to someone in Padua?' said Lucilio, sounding rather absent-minded.

'Yes, indeed, to a certain Avvocato Ormenta, whose nose is quite out of joint with me; a few months ago I learned he is rumoured to be a spy of the Most Serene Inquisitors.'

'Very good, very good, that may be. But do not speak aloud of such things here in Venice. Your friend probably ended up in bad waters just for that reason.'

'Oh yes, quite likely! He talked so loud you could hear him from one end of the city to the other and he made no mystery of his opinions.'

'And as you can see, he was rewarded for his sincerity! But have no fear, he and his companions, I believe, are under the protection of the French Legation and no harm will come to them.'

'Are you very sure? But if France has been invaded by the Allies . . .'

Lucilio cut me off with a laugh and I stared at him, somewhat puzzled.

'Yes, stare at me! I am laughing at your innocence. So you, too, like all the gazetteers of Germany, believe that France is exhausted and riven by discord and will allow the first comer to bring her down? Look me in the face again! I am merely a doctor, but I guarantee you I can see much further than all these great schemers in their gowns and wigs. France is no longer only in France: France is in Switzerland, Holland, Germany, Piedmont, Naples, Rome – and here, where you and I are speaking! She has turned inwards to attract the enemy forces to her, where she will destroy them with a few blows, leaving the way open for her friends, her brothers here! You see, if a moment ago out of habit I advised you to speak softly, now I shout and take no precautions. The fact is, they are afraid now and there is no longer any danger. You can tell the Avvocato Ormenta and Padre Pendola everything I've said to you – it makes no difference to me!'

Lucilio looked at me with such hard and fiery eyes that I felt compelled, against my habit, to lower mine. Perhaps he felt sorry for me then, in my flustered state, for he helped me to stand straight again.

'How old are you?' he asked.

'I shall soon be twenty.'

'Just twenty? Courage then. You were just a child and they thought they could blindfold you, but I hope you will not be taken in, or will mend your ways in good time. Courage, then: confess that your friendship with Amilcare and your concern for him have been suggested by others and are not your own spontaneous sentiments.'

'Who do you imagine could ever make me do such a thing?'

'Who? Padre Pendola, for example, or the Avvocato Ormenta!'

'Them? Rather just the opposite: I believe they were quite displeased by my friendship with that young man, and thanks to him I became disgusted by them and their frivolous, dishonest schemes.'

'Frivolous, their schemes? Not very, my young man. Dishonest they may be, but let us not be hasty in our judgements, because the man defending his bread and butter is a man of many, many rights. Do you think the Reverend Father and the worthy Avvocato would be people of any authority and importance if a fair wind of justice came along and knocked to the ground – yes, to the ground – all the privileges of the nobility and the clergy? They are working for their own interests just as the others are. That's all I can say.'

Lucilio's way of looking at things quite astonished me: open hatred was easier for me to understand than this cold, calculating animosity. My young friend from Treviso seemed to me closer to the truth than the doctor from Fossalta. I was forgetting, however, that in this respect, Lucilio's youth had boiled off and his sentiments had hardened into deep conviction.

'But let us speak of you,' he continued. 'I'd like to believe it was the Contessina Clara and not the Avvocato Ormenta who sent you to me. If that is true, have no fear, for your friend Amilcare is safer in his prison than you or I in this piazza. I would say so even to the Savi, who if they are as sage as their name implies, will discover something for themselves in this opinion of mine. Let me say it again: there are people watching out for him and no harm is going to come to such a valuable young man as he. Meanwhile, try not to let yourself be beguiled by Padre Pendola. For Heaven's sake, Carlino! You were an intelligent boy with a good heart. Don't let yourself be ruined now. I must leave you now to pay a visit to some poor devils living here. What can I tell you? A doctor's best pay is the love of the people. If you are staying in Venice, come to see me at the hospital, where you will always find me before ten in the morning.'

'Thank you,' I said, 'if you do assure me that Amilcare . . .'

'Yes, I assure you that no harm will come to him. What more do you want?'

'Then I thank you and I offer you my respects. I leave Venice today.'

'Give my regards to the Count, the Contessina, the Frumiers and my father, if you see him,' said Lucilio. 'Oh, and give my regards to Fratta and Fossalta! Who knows if those lonely villages will ever see me again!'

He embraced me and left, I believe, with more esteem for me than when we had met. Certainly when I thought about it, it seemed to me that I had told him some not very honourable things about myself, and later I was to learn he had believed I'd sold myself body and soul to Padre Pendola. But the simplicity of my confession had softened that hasty judgement, and my youth gave him hope I was not so very hardened in my views. In any event, once I and my bundle had embarked on the Portogruaro boat, I worked over that discussion with Lucilio in my mind. More strange than admirable to me was the authority I had heard in his words and seen in his bearing. A mere doctor, a young man from the country only recently transplanted to Venice who spoke and judged that way! He seemed to pose as the arbiter of a republic's destiny – if not as arbiter, judge and prophet! Did I sense a touch of comedy in this? Was he teasing me? Had my inexperience been just the opportunity for him to mock me? I nearly repented of having left Amilcare behind with so deficient a guarantee, and although there was certainly nothing I could have done for him myself, I still wondered whether my eagerness to trust Lucilio was caused by cowardice or sheer laziness.

But then I reassured myself with the thought that Lucilio had never been a vain braggart, and that his intelligence and learning so surpassed those of other men as to let me imagine he might be superior to them in foresight and powers. That he was secretly attached to the French Legation was something I had heard muttered around Portogruaro the previous autumn, and now some of his words seemed to confirm the gossip. Perhaps those ties allowed him to know more and see more deeply than others did. In the end, I could think of no reason why he should want to make fun of me.

Such thoughts, combined with that instinctive respect I had for Lucilio and my insignificant hopes of helping Amilcare by any other means, soothed me, and, little by little, I ceased to think about my friend's fate and began to concern myself with my own. As I gradually left the city behind and entered that labyrinth of flood channels, conduits and canals that tie the lower Friuli to Venice, the events of the present year grew dimmer in my mind, and those of years before re-emerged as dazzling and glimmering as dreams. The boat seemed to be carrying me into the past, every dip of the oars taking with them a day of my life, or rather, recovering one from earlier times. Nothing promotes meditation, melancholy and poetry better than a long voyage through the marshes in summer's high pomp. Those vast horizons of lakes, ponds, seas and rivers flooded with all the various colours of light's rainbow; that green thicket of cane and water lilies wherein splendid colours vie with powerful scents to bewitch the senses already exhausted by the heavy, humid air; the scorching, glowing heavens curved above, immense; that perpetual, monotonous quivering of all things animate and inanimate that by the magic of nature transform a wilderness into an ephemeral paradise: all this fills the soul with an inexhaustible thirst for passion – and a hint of the infinite.

Oh yes, the life of the universe experienced in solitude is a majestic spectacle beyond all words! That is why we admire the sea in its eternal battles; the sky with its tempestuous array of clouds; the night in its fecund silences and in its summer luminescence. All this life makes us feel the presence of some existence vaster and deeper than our own. It means we human beings are no longer the critics and the lawmakers, but the eyes, the ears and the thoughts of the world; intelligence is no longer all, but a part; man no longer thinks he can understand and dominate the universe, but feels, palpitates and breathes with it. Thus I gave myself over to a wave of thoughts and dreams and was gently pushed back into blissful memories of childhood. The white-haired man of exile returning to the domestic hearth after years abroad in a strange, difficult land was certainly not more moved and happy than I. Mine was, nevertheless, a state of mind ripe with melancholy, for when past joys break through memory's gloom they are like the night-time visit of a departed loved one and invite rich tears. I recalled, and at the same time I forgot; I dreamed. I recalled the bliss of the child and forgot the sorrows of the adolescent and young man's struggle to find a new way; I dreamed a happy return to Alcina's enchanted shores, from which, once chased away, one tries in vain to return.

Who has not, after some absence, wished to find a lover miraculously changed into a figure of dreams, the ideal creature of our hearts and our poetry? Of such childish games, untrue and unreal, the mind grows enamoured; and love and hope and every other treasure of the soul are squandered dressing up an imagined doll. Of my Pisana in her cradle, I recalled nothing but her long hair, her sweet eyes, her angel's smile; I remembered her charm, intelligence and mercy as a girl; her light, endearing voice; then I watched her grow in pride and beauty and I recalled her generous impulses, her dignified demeanour, her fiery kisses; I felt her arm tremble under mine, saw her breast swell when I gazed at her, saw her look at me!

Oh, who could ever describe how she looked at me and how I recalled (and even now recall) the heavenly language of those two enchanting eyes? How to remember just one of those flashes of love and at the same time the clouds that obscured it? No, her soul, the highest and loveliest part of her lodged in those eyes, was never sullied by wrongdoing. For a human being is not a mechanical device churning out moods and thoughts, but a true blend of the eternal and the temporal, the sublime and the obscene; and life, which is sometimes divided equally between the parts, at other times condenses in one side or the other to transform us into heroes or beasts! A divine side shone in la Pisana's eyes and it was always pure and sinless. Thus that violent, immortal passion that she inspired in me, a passion that no beauty, however great, no sensory charms, however pleasing, could have kept alive in the mind of a man of eighty when she was long in her grave. I loved and forgave that spirit of hers, enslaved and heedless as it was, but always regretful and ready to return to life after its long lethargy.

When I arrived at Portogruaro these fancies of mine came tumbling down, however. Everyone was talking about la Pisana's eccentricities; even her aunt hinted at something and asked me to use my good sense to try to resolve matters, because the Count, although he'd been asked many times, refused to interfere. She had even advised him to place la Pisana in her care, but he had replied that the girl was utterly opposed, and thus he was allowing his daughter to lead him around by the nose, greatly damaging the family reputation.

'Listen to this, Carlino,' she said to me. 'Can you imagine anything worse? Raimondo Venchieredo is always there courting her and she returns the favour with a great fussing and simpering that is quite obscene to behold; but then, when he came one day to ask for her hand in marriage (for she is eighteen and the time has come to think about it), she declared very solemnly that she would never accept him as a husband and they should all leave her alone! Some say that behind all this is a previous love for Giulio Del Ponte, but then no one can understand why she mistreats him and flatters the one she has decided to reject. Not to mention the fact the Giulio is nearly penniless and his health is so poor that he's not expected to see next spring.

'What, is Giulio so ill?' I cried.

'Yes, poor thing,' said Lady Frumier, 'and to tell you the truth it would almost be better if he were to go, so that he doesn't thwart every proper chance to get la Pisana settled, the way Lucilio did with Clara. She at least was calm, reasonable and Christian, and could be prevented from engaging in folly. But this girl? Oh, I don't have many hopes; I fear she wants to bring dishonour on the family.'

I had forgotten all about la Pisana just then at the thought of Giulio, and I say this to my credit: I was desolate at the sad news about his health. The last time I had seen him I had indeed noticed that he wore a gloomy pallor, and his breath came so haltingly it cut his words in half. But I put this down to the trials and troubles that were part and parcel of loving la Pisana, and, to tell the truth, I couldn't help taking a certain barbarous revenge in seeing him suffering so. After Lady Frumier's cruel prognosis, however, all became clearer to me, and I began to fear he might become the first victim of the young lady's hot and heedless nature. His misfortune saddened me, and, even more, the crime that would stain the conscience of his merciless, thoughtless killer. The sins of those I love have always grieved me more than my own suffering, and I believe I would have pardoned la Pisana for loving Giulio if she had only given him back his life and health.

Sadly, I had an opportunity to see that Lady Frumier's concerns were not misplaced. That very evening I saw la Pisana at Portogruaro, and as loving, shy and silent as she was with me (the picture of one who seeks affection and compassion), so she was flattering and provocative with Venchieredo; and indifferent and mocking with poor Giulio. Raimondo, who had now forgotten Clara's rebuff, had been drawn back to Casa Frumier by la Pisana's coquettish ways; perhaps he hoped to get his recompense by seizing an even more appetizing and desirable mouthful. The fact that this was eluding him only fanned his desires, for la Pisana, while she rejected him as a husband, accepted and flattered him as her gallant. To acquire by smuggling that which he'd already pursued by legal means: well, the young hothead would have held himself to be the cleverest and most fortunate of men to achieve that! And la Pisana's behaviour seemed to bode well.

If you had seen the pitiful state of poor Giulio at this point, you can well imagine how mercy for him silenced any thoughts of my own love for the girl. Incredible as that may seem! I detested Venchieredo not on my own account but on behalf of Giulio; I was jealous of la Pisana more on his behalf than on my own; and the spectacle of that young man (so spirited, so clever, so kind) wasted by the hidden cancer of his unhappy passion nearly drove me to penance for all the loathing I'd once felt for him. You think I am too good? Alas, that is how I am made. The schooling I received in patience and abnegation growing up with la Pisana had fostered in me a near-heroic mercy towards the sufferers of this earth. My conduct would later be the proof: perhaps you can fault me for being foolish, but you cannot fail to praise me for courage and generosity.

Venchieredo, meanwhile, was positively bewigged and bedecked with contentment. His face, his manner, his clothing, his words all testified that he was a young man exceptionally well pleased with himself, who wanted nothing and thought of nothing but his own joy, so great and mighty was it. Contentment lit up his face with a rosy glow; it made him light and nimble, his speech fluent and colourful. Everything looked beautiful to him, all was good and delightful. And he was welcomed everywhere, because the spectacle of great happiness charms men, making them think they, too, may one day achieve it. La Pisana was there only for him; she trembled and lowered her eyes at his gaze, smiled at the sound of his voice, followed his every move. As I had seen her behave as a child with Lucilio, now the young lady behaved with Raimondo: the same agitation, the same excitement restrained by neither shame nor fear; she was an enchanting, desirable creature, a thousand times more so now in the full splendour of her beauty at eighteen. I loved her desperately for myself; I loathed her for condemning Giulio to such cruel martyrdom; and I despised her for her wicked flattery of the shameless, frivolous Venchieredo. Some fury to insult her and bring her down overwhelmed me and I was arrogant enough to think that though I still loved her, I would be willing to give her to another in order to save his life.

She, however, went forward blindly as the hangman. Blind! This is all that can excuse her: I believe she saw nothing, was aware of nothing. Her passions were always so extreme that she was never able to see anything beyond them. You only had to watch Giulio's tormented soul wrack that wan, wasted body of his, watch him battle to the point of death against Raimondo's easy, serene supremacy, and tears would come to your eyes. The light of his soul and the glow of his spirit that had once shone on his face were gone and with them all his beauty; even the grandeur of his pallor was marred by brown and greenish spots left by his bile-ridden blood. He looked like a man suffering from pellagra,[3] and his shame at his own appearance stole all courage from his gaze and all assurance from his words. His wit and vivacity, which had already shrunk when love overwhelmed him, battled helplessly with the coffin lid of desperation. At times he flared up like the cemetery will o' the wisp, but the strength of will that briefly ignited him would then decline into greater dejection. It was this that had charmed, this that had brought him love, and without this he would perish: he knew it and he was enraged that the embers of his soul could no longer send out even a funereal flash. To die in a blaze of glory was by now his only hope of love and revenge, but the more he tried, the less his wits, weakened by illness and passion, obeyed him. It was distressing to watch the last gasp of a moribund soul (in the ruins of a body already much like a tomb) striving enviously to recover what had been stolen away by a young, arrogant, reckless power. It was like seeing Lazarus, dying of hunger, ask the rich man for some crumbs from his table and receive only scorn and rebuff.

If only things had gone as they did with Lazarus! Giulio's final joy would have been to vent his just and noble rage, to die with the hope that word of his misfortune would resonate forever in the perjurer's soul. But nothing like that was to be: la Pisana had neither eyes nor ears for him. He was dying one drop at a time, without hope that his cursed death rattle would trouble her smile even for an instant!

When that long evening came to an end my heart was filled with such pity for Giulio that I parted from the Count with some excuse to stay at Portogruaro, and so he departed for Fratta alone with la Pisana, who was much surprised by my peculiar behaviour. Perhaps she thought I was jealous and she sent me a look that signified either encouragement or gratitude, but I was disgusted and, turning my back, quickly left Venchieredo to watch the carriage drive off, while I took Del Ponte by the arm and drew him away from the house. He followed me unwillingly, gasping like a drowning man whose last hope of rescue is failing, his head obstinately turned to observe his fortunate rival's satisfaction.

'Giulio, what has become of you?' I said, shaking him. 'Come back to yourself! Embrace me: you haven't yet even greeted me!'

He stared at me absent-mindedly and then, because we were under cover of darkness on a remote way, he put an arm around my neck without speaking or weeping. It was not how we had parted before. Then he had been happy and triumphant and didn't see how miserable and humiliated I was. He had held out his hand in a farewell gesture, somewhat protective and pitying, but I was neither able nor willing to shake the hand of one who had stolen my soul's riches. How changed we were now that fortune reunited us! Two times disillusioned, I was brave enough to feel more compassion for him than for myself: he who had fallen from victorious unconcern to miserable misfortune, he who had treated me as cruelly the year before as Raimondo now did him.

'Giulio, what has become of you?' I said again, raising his brow to look at him. 'You want to fall ill and you are succeeding, so cruel and ruthless have you become to yourself.'

'I want to fall ill? No, Carlo,' said he in a weak and harrowing voice, 'no, I want to be well, I want to live! I want youth to flower once again in my face and cheerful thoughts to colour my mind; I want my soul to swell like the buds of a rose garden in spring, brimming with pleasing phrases and waggish wit, with hymns glowing with love and poetry! I want sunlight to chase the shades of melancholy from my face, and life's potent rays to revive my dull, withered form. A miracle it will be: a triumph. Because those whose faces display the crude, proud beauty of the flesh must undergo a long and uncertain convalescence if they should lose it; while the man whose face is lit by the flame of the spirit can recapture that beguiling light at any moment. The soul does not depend on medicine's lengthy cures, nor does passion behave in the heavy, stiff way of illness; it destroys and restores; it kills and revives! It is poison and medicament at the same time. I've seen it a hundred times, I've experienced it myself and I shall do so again!'

He spoke with feverish intensity and the words that came to his lips were confused and maimed. He glimpsed his old glory in his mind and he did not want to lose it; but his strength was failing him and his weary, frantic breath tossed about in that tumult of thoughts, hopes and illusions like a mortally wounded warrior in a delirium of glory and high command.

'You must calm down, Giulio,' said I, as moved as I was frightened by his outburst. 'You have more life than you need in that soul of yours: indeed, its overpowering vitality is crushing you, you must hold it in check. I know your illness and I know the remedy. I know you are desperately in love, as one loves that woman who has met our gaze and bewitched our imaginations with the sweetest delights that desire and self-regard can serve up, working together. Now that such love has become torment, what must one do to recover? One must study the causes, look at the roots in ourselves, more than in others. It was a trap, a great blunder, and that's all. Get up again and it will give you a chance to blunder anew, if you are weak enough to stoop to doing so!'

'I understand,' he broke in bitterly. 'I understand what you ask, my friend. Do you think that I, in turn, don't know something of you? I had lost sight of you recently, but from the beginning I knew you loved la Pisana. However, I certainly wasn't going to stand in awe of a lad like you! Now that you are big and rosy and square-built you've come to claim your rights, and you'd rather claim them against one opponent than against two! And so you come to say to me, oh so compassionately, "Stand back, for your own good. Do you see my shoulders? They have the hope and the might to send you to your coffin." Is that not the gist of your reasoning?'

'No, that's not true at all!' I exclaimed, feeling the man's tormented state of mistrust in these unjust suspicions 'It isn't true, Giulio. You know that I'm incapable of such deception and would never lower myself to beg of a rival! Oh, so you did know? Yes, I loved la Pisana when I was a boy, and I don't want to conceal anything from you, I still love her. And that is precisely why it grieves me to see her spurn you so pitilessly.'

'Pitiless? That's what you think, then?' said he, grasping my hand in his agitation.

'Pitiless like one who does not remember, who does not see,' I added.

'So therefore you wish to convince me of the impossible!' he went on. 'You would like me to believe that it troubles you to see your lover being cruel to another! Oh you charlatan, you coward! Is that how you'd like me to see you? And perhaps I'm even being indulgent to call you a charlatan. If that were not the case I would despise you even more and be repelled by your vile pity and your pandering.'

'Be silent, Giulio, be silent!' I said, holding back my indignation and putting a hand over his mouth. 'Yes, it is as you say: it horrifies me to see – not my lover but the woman I love more than my life – torture and kill a soul like yours. I'd like to clear her of that infamy, spare her that remorse! Now understand this, Giulio, and know that I mean it: it is clear to me that I shall always love her, and it would be eternal sorrow for me to love not a foolish, vain thing, not a thoughtless lass, not a seductress, but a fury, an assassin!'

'Love her then, love her!' said Giulio, his voice wracked with sobs. 'Don't you see that I am but a shadow? Your scruples come too late, for she has already killed me and her lips are scarlet with the blood she has let. I still delude myself at times: it is pure vanity, that and hopes of revenge! But then the courage of truth returns and I almost enjoy battling, head to head, the rage that is devouring me. So be it! I'll be avenged for the happiness that awaits you, that awaits all who wait patiently. So be it, if you want to love a base, foul, despicable thing, soulless, heartless and without intelligence. Pursue that foolish, stupid mannequin inebriated by her senses and blinded by her pride! Born woman in cruelty, fatuousness and wantonness; an eternal mannequin in all the rest, even in mercy, which is the saving grace of women but which was denied her by a monstrous trick of nature. Your rights are undeniable, for you were born together in depravity and can love each other shamelessly in your own way, as toads in the swamp or worms in the corpse!'

His voice had come back to life and he walked and spoke like a madman. I could hear his teeth grating as if trying to sharpen their edges on that blasphemy, those curses. But, safe against his words, I let him vent his fury and contempt until he finally achieved the peace that weariness brings. Then I made a last attempt, trusting in the rightness of my intentions (only God can judge whether they were sufficiently good).

'Giulio,' I whispered gravely in his ear, 'so you have judged la Pisana. Now say whether your pride can permit you to love her as you know her.'

'But you love her too?' said he sharply.

'Yes, I love her, because I've always done so from birth, because that love is not a sentiment but a part of my soul, for it was born in me before reason and before pride!'

'And what about in me?' he said, nearly in tears. 'Do you think that two years have not rooted love in me as deeply as twelve or fifteen in you? Do you think love was just a plaything for me? Don't you see I am dying because it has been taken away? Pride, you say? Yes, I am proud. It hurts me to lose what I once possessed and be unable to recover it! Oh, if you knew what agony, what tears, what weakness I would spend now to buy a fleeting glance of beauty, a glimpse of wit, one day, one day only of my thriving past life! If you knew how many hours I stand before the mirror contemplating my lost aspect, my sunken, clouded eyes, my lined and yellowed skin! I am dreadful, Carlo, truly dreadful! I horrify myself. If I were an easy woman, I wouldn't even grant a kiss to an unfortunate fellow that looks like me. A skeleton still upright, but no longer alive or animated! Had I at least the terrible energy of a ghost! I could avenge myself by terrifying, by cursing! But my soul withdraws from me like water from the dry bank, and everything wilts, disappears, dies! All I have left are memories and desires: a dejected mob of silent, rabid thoughts no longer even able to scream and draw sympathy.'

Only then he fell silent, and only then did I, disgusted, sense his profound desperation; and the pity in me was stunned and paralysed. He was more a martyr to pride than to love, and yet something drew me to try every sacrifice to save him. I believe I loved la Pisana so much that I felt I must share her sins and her duty to make amends. Or perhaps I saw in others what I might have become and fear provoked my charity. From time to time, I recalled, I had heard Del Ponte debating the caustic irreligion of Lucilio and a few others in the Senator's inner circle, and I decided it was worth trying this avenue also.

'But Giulio, you at least are a Christian!' I began again after a brief silence. 'You can therefore call on God for comfort, and submit.'

'It is true, I am a Christian,' said he, 'and I submit, and I also give you sufficient proof: I shall not kill myself.'

'No, that's not sufficient: you must also practise other Christian virtues besides submission. You must be charitable to others and to yourself.'

'I am already far too charitable. I haven't slapped her, nor have I ripped apart that sleek, rascally nobleman whose arrogance is crushing me. Does that seem little to you?'

'Take care, Giulio, for your passion makes you partial to yourself and unjust to others. La Pisana is guilty, yes, but as for Venchieredo, as much as . . .'

'Do not speak of him to me! For mercy's sake, do not speak of him, for there are times when I no longer recall even God's commandments!'

'Well then, I shall speak to you of me: don't you think, perhaps, that passion blinds you to duty? A moment ago you should have thanked me, and you insulted me!'

'I insulted you because in truth your behaviour this evening still seems very strange to me. But now I want to believe you and I thank you for your good intentions. Are you content with that?'

'I'd be more content if you would accept my counsel and help yourself to be less unhappy.'

'I shall help myself with my own counsel, and die. I am a Christian, I believe in Paradise, and that is that. I doubt, however, that I can die forgiving. Yes, I doubt that strongly, but the illness will be long and I shall grow weary, and finally be converted by weakness if nothing else. God willing, I shall succeed!'

'No, Giulio, I beg you, don't poison yourself with these gloomy thoughts!'

'You, instead, must see that I am now calm. I am better. Indeed, I believe I am finally well. You couldn't have done better than to remind me of God. I wager I shall sleep tonight – and it is two months since I've enjoyed that good fortune. And I owe it to you: am I unjust to you now? You forgive me, don't you Carlo?'

I embraced him heartily, for those last words, tinged though they still were with some bitterness, had far more effect on me than his previous frenzy. I could feel his heart beating hard against mine, a traveller in a hurry to get somewhere. I kissed his hollowed face, slick with an icy sweat, and watched him go in, coughing many times on his way up the stairs; then I departed with all the discontent of the man who has done a good, but useless, deed.

The next day I left for Fratta before dawn, having done nothing all night but spin the strangest plans and most unlikely hopes around in my head. I spent some hours in the chancery putting affairs in order there with the help of that old sneak Fulgenzio, then went to pay my respects to the Count and Monsignor, the latter plumper and softer than ever; the Count spindled-up like an old parchment burning in the fireplace. But it was getting late and I wanted to hurry to speak to la Pisana; when I had finally finished, I found her coming down the stairs from her grandmother's chamber to take some air in the garden. Faustina and Signora Veronica, who were at her side, slipped off into the kitchen wearing two evil grins, so as to leave her alone with me. I felt my stomach turn, and followed her with a long, hard stare.

'At last we meet,' she said, speaking first.

'What do you mean, at last?' said I. 'I believe we met and exchanged greetings last night.'

'Oh yes, last night, but we were not alone, and, to tell you the truth, I've begun to feel uneasy around people.'

'You are right, we were not alone yesterday; there were many people, among them Raimondo Venchieredo and Giulio Del Ponte.'

I had introduced those names in order to arrive at the matter I wished to discuss with her, but she sensed a grain of jealousy in this, and I think she was grateful.

'Signor Giulio Del Ponte and Signor Raimondo di Venchieredo mean nothing at all to me; they are people like any others, and anyway I no longer hold with making a show of my feelings in public.'

'That would be a very good thing, Pisana, but you do not keep your promise, in fact. Yesterday your feelings for Raimondo were quite clearly visible, and I think Giulio understood them perfectly!'

'Oh I don't let Signor Giulio bother me any more; I've already done enough, and suffered enough, for him!'

'Do you mean that? You suffered for him?'

'Why certainly! There was a time when I was rather fond of him and he became so cocky that he got it in mind to marry me. But you know the way my parents think about this marriage business. It would have been a repeat of that terrible comedy between Clara and Lucilio, and so I had to put some sense in his head, and I didn't mince my words, and to bring him back to reason I started acting a little less bashful with Raimondo. Would you believe that Signor Giulio took offence at this reasonableness of mine – Giulio, who if he really loved me should have encouraged me instead? He began to play the victim, the jealous suitor, and I confess that in spite of everything I even felt sorry for him, but what was I supposed to do? Continue to deceive him and lead him hither and thither? My idea was the better: cut it off at the roots. And so I broke with him and that was that. It was then that Raimondo began to go after me in earnest and I have to say that he would have made a suitable match, but just as everyone was whispering that he was soon to make a formal request, Del Ponte descended on me, all wild-eyed, shouting that if I were to marry Raimondo he would kill himself and worse! Maybe I was too naive, too good, but can I help that? I don't think things through much, and this is my defect, and so to console him, to calm him down and above all to get rid of him, I promised him I would not marry Raimondo. And so it happened that I refused him, although, I swear to you, I quite like him and felt I was making a great sacrifice! I'd say this is friendship! What more could I do?'

'Oh, what the Devil?' I said. 'Giulio told me nothing of this!'

'What? You spoke with Giulio?' said la Pisana.

'Yes, I spoke to him last night. He was looking so terrible that I pitied him for the cruel way you were treating him.'

'I was treating him cruelly?'

'Heavens! You didn't even look at him once!'

'Oh, that's good! He should thank me for that! If I had continued to lead him on, he would only have ended in despair later; it's much better to part as good friends while the disease can still be cured.'

'The disease seems to be less curable than you think. Perhaps you haven't noticed, but he is suffering grievously to see you so infatuated with Venchieredo and so negligent of him. His health is declining day by day; I believe passion is consuming him.'

'And, therefore, what do you advise?'

'Well, it's not easy to say, but it seems to me that if you have promised not to wed Venchieredo, then you ought to break off with him too.'

'And take up with Giulio again?' she said in a nasty tone.

'That, too, if you really think you love him,' said I, making a violent effort to contain myself. 'In any event, once you are separated from Raimondo, Giulio will be less distraught and perhaps even without your love he may begin to recover.'

La Pisana now sat up and brushed her hair back, a wise

smile on her face. As she saw it, the purpose of my entire manoeuvre had simply been to chase the two other pretenders from the field, leaving me full advantage.

'I could try, if you help me,' she said.

'I don't know how I can help you,' said I. 'Yesterday, with no assistance on my part, you were doing a fine job offering up coquetries to Venchieredo. You didn't seem to notice I'd come back from Padua until I came into the hall, and then you only bowed ever so slightly.'

'Oh, that's good! And suppose I wanted to repay you for your coldness?'

'Come, you are a liar! And what were you repaying me for last night? You think I don't know how long you've been indulging this fancy of yours for Venchieredo?'

'But I told you, it was all to discourage Giulio! Do you think I'd refuse him if I really liked him?'

'Just look at how you bring shame on your own virtue! Just a little while ago you boasted of your refusal of him as a great sacrifice!'

La Pisana, dumbstruck, abashed and vexed, was silent. It was the first time her charms did not find a ready dupe in me, and that had made her insist, for she was not a woman to withdraw when she thought she might win.

Yet whether because of my presence, my sermon or her good nature, the fact is that her infatuation with Raimondo suddenly cooled, and poor Giulio found himself the recipient of certain glances from her that seemed infinitely more dear because they'd become so rare. In the end, though, she gave him no more attention than he was due as a participant in the conversation, and little by little her attentions began to concentrate on me. My good fortune was so extreme that I found it quite upsetting. There at Fratta, close to la Pisana, dazed by her beauty and her darting eyes, inflamed by her strange, sparing declarations, sometimes exalted, sometimes crazed with love's delirium, my memory failed me and I became her servant once again: I was all for her. But then at Portogruaro the cadaverish, mocking face of Giulio would appear before me like a wraith and I felt afraid, angry, remorseful. He had the right, it seemed to me, to consider me a traitorous friend. Perhaps la Pisana had understood my heart's innate corruption better than I when she suspected I was trying to make her abandon Venchieredo on my own behalf, rather than his.

And yet that unquenchable thirst, that right we think we have to at least a shadow of happiness, battled fiercely with these scruples of mine. When had I ever been Giulio's friend? Wasn't he the one who had declared war on me by stealing la Pisana's affection, or at any rate her desire, her ardour? What unhappy lover has not opened the door to revenge and then taken advantage of it? In any case, hadn't my intentions towards him been excellent? If destiny would have those intentions end by favouring me, must I confess my guilt or should I not profit by my luck now that I had the occasion? My conscience was not soothed by these arguments.

'You are right,' it said. 'You are right that there is no reason at all why you should be friends with Giulio, but how many things happen without reason? Esteem, similarity of natures, compassion, sympathy: all generate friendship. The truth is, as much as you ought to detest Giulio, that day you arrived from Venice his misery and his torment made you love him and you treated him as a friend, and that alone means you may not tolerate any suspicion that the help you offered him was not sincere. You felt remorse at the pitiful state la Pisana had brought upon him, and you have no remorse for yourself? Shame! Learn something about sophistry from the Avvocato Ormenta. Learn that you cannot be a gentleman merely by seeming one! You wanted la Pisana to give up Venchieredo to save Giulio. Now you must give her up or I shall declare you a coward!'

Those last scolding words from my good lady conscience finally persuaded me. Slowly, by means of a thousand devices and great effort – all painful – I withdrew from la Pisana. She took this from me as humbly as a dog that's been chased away, but that sentence of cowardice hung over me and I silenced my sighs, hid my desires, swallowed my tears and sought solitude far away from her. And then (whether because she knowingly seconded my wishes or to redeem her pride) she stopped seeking me out, and, of course, her coldness, which I had so cleverly provoked with such great persistence, wounded me. Young Venchieredo, briefly jealous of me, was soon cheered not to see me in Casa Frumier. But he was wrong to think he would profit by my disappearance. La Pisana paid no attention either to him or any others, and when she did show any preference it was for Giulio Del Ponte. He gathered those rare tokens of goodwill the way the flower avidly drinks a drop of dew after a month of drought. He quickened with life; all the more so, thinking that it was not my sacrifice nor la Pisana's generosity but his own qualities that brought him affection. It was what I both feared and hoped for. When pity, jealousy, love and pride begin to brawl together, the soul's turmoil is not easy to describe; imagine yourself in my place and you will understand my perpetual contradictions.

Meanwhile, Raimondo, although cheated of his hopes, was not the least convinced he could not oust an enemy as beaten and ill-favoured as Del Ponte. But his arrogant assumption he would win that duel didn't win him la Pisana's favour. Women are like generals who care more for the honour of the flag than for the victory; they will consent to surrender, but they want to be encircled by trenches and threatened by bombs. Only when a fortress is quite insignificant will someone try a sudden attack without previous warnings or siege equipment; and no daughter of Eve is so shameless as to consider herself such a fortress. Having tried nice speeches and been sent away, Raimondo resumed the assault bearing gifts. La Pisana, who was vainer than she was well-mannered, boldly accepted all gifts without even asking who had brought them. And so Raimondo was temporarily contented, and I, galled. Finally, though, the secret satisfaction of my good deed brought me a sad, monotonous peace, not without a certain pleasure. I thought I might even put into practice one of the maxims I'd inherited from Martino: to pay no attention to rewards from above, but seek them among the lowly and humble. Here my duties in the chancery offered me ready occasion.

From the time of the Romans, I'm vain enough to think, justice in the jurisdiction of Fratta had never been administered with such rectitude. A sliver of compassion, some scholarship, some reflection and some good sense came together in sentences so fine that the Count's signature was honoured to make its appearance at the bottom. The patience, the goodness, the justice delivered by the deputy Clerk was praised to the heavens, especially my patience, a quality rare as it is vital for a country judge. I've seen some of these grow enraged because the parties are slow-witted; apply their fists to the one and threaten a beating to the other; all the while expecting from them that moderation, reserve and clear-sightedness that only come with many years of education. You must remember that the ignorant are like children; they require the slow, detailed logic of an elementary-school teacher, not the compressed rhetoric of a university professor. Justice must be bestowed, not imposed; and it is wise to use persuasion to maintain its reputation and its decorum, not make it seem arbitrary with scolding and arrogance. Until the courts change their manners, country people will find the laws little different from the pronouncements of the ancient Sibyls. The sentence is so because they say it is so; and often the man in the right understands it no better than the man in the wrong.

Accustomed to living among rough, unlettered people from birth, I had little trouble assuming such patience; indeed, it came to me freely and I could not do without it. My example served to influence the men of the Commune charged with the smaller cases, for now they were hearing fewer complaints that someone was being neglected in favour of another or that reprisals had been carried out against a third. Old Andreini had died not long before the Clerk, and his son, who replaced him, quickly showed my same zeal for the smooth working of justice. The Chaplain couldn't have been happier; he was no longer being troubled about his friendship with Spaccafumo, and the latter, now inclined to drunkenness, was allowed to visit whomever he pleased so long as he did not disturb the peace on Sundays. He was no longer banished and, although he did not conduct his life very much like other people, no ill was spoken of him, and that was enough to keep me from tormenting him unnecessarily.

A few winters before, he had lost Martinella, who had always provided him with salt and polenta and other necessary foodstuffs, to a runaway chest ailment. Now he travelled farther from the district to provide for himself, but of this we knew nothing and he was like an oyster among oysters. The Chaplain told me that the old smuggler still remembered that night when he had brought me back to the Castle on horseback, and that he always took credit for my accomplishments and considered he was owed the Commune's gratitude. I found Spaccafumo's praise quite flattering, while that of the old Rector of Teglio sent me into raptures. His approval was delivered in such a distinguished and thoughtful way, in the way of the man who has the power to bestow and to withdraw, and, of course, it must be said that the achievements of the disciple always reflect the greater glory of the master. In his eyes I was forever the schoolboy with the protruding ears, the Latin scholar with four mistakes to his every sentence. Even Marchetto got some benefit from my administration, because when his stomach began to grumble at too many long rides, I spared him and his horse by making frequent settlements. The various meddlers and my assistant Fulgenzio moaned, for disputes between other people were a delight to them, but I ignored their complaints and kept a close eye on Fulgenzio, in particular, to make him desist from his old habit of getting two fees for his labours: one from the Count and one from the parties involved. Giulio Del Ponte had warned me not to agitate too much against the fellow, for despite his hunchback and his humble ways, he was rumoured to have the ear of the powerful. Thinking back to the trial against old Venchieredo, those suspicions made a great deal of sense to me, but so did my duty, and I would have scrubbed the snouts of the Most Serene Inquisitors (not to mention one of their filthy little spies) had I caught them openly dishonouring my office.

There was someone else who was quietly sending me to the Devil with all his heart, and this was the steward. My presence and my new authority had badly upset his old habits of stealing and robbing on the sly. When I grew wise to his methods, I absolved him the first time, but it was clear I wouldn't do so in the future, and, knowing this, he was quite bad-tempered about me watching over him. Meanwhile, the Count was delighted to dispense with the clerk's wages and he spoke no more of my taking any exams or of putting me on his payroll. This makeshift arrangement suited him very well. And I was happy enough with all the blessings coming my way for being so impartial, so careful, and above all so relaxed about collecting taxes. Donato, the druggist's son, and Sandro the miller, once my old rivals, became my friends and companions and their high praise of me increased my favour with the little people. In short, I was proving the truth of that old saying that the secret to forgetting one's sorrows and to living well is to perform one's duties most zealously.

Giulio Del Ponte's health, which seemed to improve every day, was the dearest possible recompense for my sacrifice. I considered that miracle to be my own work and I hope I'll be forgiven for my vanity. Raimondo, who had grown very tired indeed of seeing la Pisana wearing the pretty clothes and nice brooches he'd given her without getting even a speck of that tenderness he'd once received, had slipped away. Now, taking advantage of the growing dissension in the Provedoni household, and the fact that old Dottor Natalino was now very aged and helpless, he persuaded Leopardo to move to Venchieredo with his wife Doretta to look after her father. Leopardo, good fellow that he was (and ever more the victim of his wife's vanity) agreed, and soon all were saying that Signor Raimondo was fortunate indeed to live under the same roof with his sweetheart. Only Leopardo didn't believe it, for he was in love with his wife, and even more than in love with her, he was her slave.

So things were arranged, for better and for worse, but Fratta was not the whole world and beyond it, the din, the ruin, the threat of war and revolution were everywhere increasing. The news from Venice was anxiously asked about, commented on, distorted and enlarged to become the material of stormy disputes around the Castle hearth.

The Captain believed that just as two and two make four, the fears were much exaggerated and the Signoria was wise to refrain from extraordinary measures, because the French, no matter how much wind was in their sails, would need three years to get over the Alps and another four to get from Bormida to the River Mincio. He enumerated the lines of defence, enemy forces, captains, fortresses, and, according to him, the war would either come to an end on the other side of the mountains or be handed down to the next generation on this side. Giulio Del Ponte and a couple of others from Portogruaro were not of this opinion; in their view the Allies' strength was far from enough to fully protect the Republic against the French exorbitance, and the latter in two or three months could very well have invaded the mainland states and even the Friuli. The Count and Monsignor were horrified to hear such conjectures, and then it fell to me to dispel the nasty atmosphere left by all these exaggerated and premature fears.

So we drifted along until the spring of 1795. The Republic of Venice had already solemnly recognized the new democratic government of France; the Venetian representative Alvise Querini had made his little speech to the Directory, and, to cement this new friendship, the Republic had expelled the Count of Provence[4] from Verona.

'And they did very well, too,' said the Captain. 'They need to be patient, not go for their purses and their swords immediately. You see? Things are already cooling off over there! The ones who were slaughtering the priests and the monks and the noblemen have now ended up on the scaffold themselves; the crisis is now declining and the Republic has got through it without risking the life of even one man.'

'A terrible error,' replied Giulio. 'The French will have their heels on our necks; they're silent now, but they will be shouting even louder soon. We think we're used to danger, while there is no danger; but soon real danger will come and it will find us asleep or unprepared. God help us. Whatever happens, we won't cut a good figure!'

I was inclined to think like Giulio, all the more so because Lucilio had written to me from Venice that things looked promising and my friend's fate had never been closer to being resolved. But his own fate – the fate of young Dr Vianello – took a terrible turn in those days. Clara was finally sent off to the Convent of Santa Teresa, a fact that we learned in Fratta when the Countess wrote asking that the dowry monies be sent to Venice, saying she had meanwhile had the funds from a moneylender, but he wouldn't hear of long terms for the loan, what with all the troubles going on. The Count sighed and sighed again, but once more he gathered together the funds requested and sent them to his wife. I saw that the family fortunes were heading towards ruin, and that all I could do was try to staunch a few drops from the barrel, while the vent ran out willy-nilly, there being no remedy on that side. I didn't dare to speak to the Count, it was pointless to address Monsignor, a word to the steward would only worsen matters, and la Pisana, to whom I hinted of these things once or twice, replied with a shrug of her shoulders that there was no ordering her mother around and that's how it had always been, that she didn't let it bother her and would somehow find a way to live.

The poor thing seemed to have amended her wild ways considerably. She showed neither annoyance nor pleasure at my distance; she treated me in quite a friendly fashion and she was always pleasant to Giulio, although not as heated as she usually was in her infatuations. She spent most of her day in her grandmother's chamber, determined to make her forget her sister's absence, but the poor woman was by now quite doddering and no longer able to show any gratitude for la Pisana's devotion. Which was all the more meritorious as a result.

When the news that Clara had entered the convent reached the district, Partistagno, who hadn't been seen since the day his solemn request ended in tragicomedy, appeared at the Castle. He ranted and raved and talked a great deal of nonsense, frightening the Count and Monsignor; when he left, he declared he intended to go to Venice to demand justice and free a noble damsel from her family's unconscionable tyranny. As time went on he had become more and more convinced that his merits were quite irresistible, and, despite every reason he had to think the opposite, remained obstinate in his belief that Clara was in love with him and that her family did not wish to concede her for mysterious reasons that he would subsequently reveal. And, in fact, they heard not long afterwards that he had decamped from Lugugnana to Venice, and from Fratta they sought to send word to Venice, but when no further news of the matter came back, they calmed themselves, thinking that Partistagno's terrible threats would probably deflate into idle chatter.

Meanwhile, what I had foreseen for some time now came to pass. The Count's health was worsening day by day and finally he became so ill that before the Countess could be warned of the danger, he died in the arms of the Chaplain, Monsignor Orlando and la Pisana. Dr Sperandio drew eighty *libbre* of blood and recited an extraordinary number of Latin texts to prove the death had taken place according to the laws of nature. But the departed, had he been able to cast an eye around from his casket, might almost have been glad to be dead, for his funeral was quite magnificent. Monsignor wept discreetly and sang the funeral Mass with a voice slightly more nasal than usual. In the first few days la Pisana gave herself over to despair (more than I would have thought possible), but then she suddenly ceased to think about it. And when the Frumiers came to say that her mother wished her to go to Venice, she seemed to have forgotten everything in her great joy to exchange the tedium of Fratta for the entertainments of the capital. Fifteen days later she left, and only when she came to say farewell did it seem that the sorrow of leaving me behind was greater than the pleasures of a new life full of splendid promise. I was grateful for that sorrow of hers, and the fact she let me see it without letting her pride get in the way. Once again I knew she did not have a bad heart. I resigned myself to stay behind.

My presence at Fratta was now quite necessary. The story of the confusion that followed the Count's death is a long one. On all sides, the moneylenders, creditors and claimants appeared. His goods were auctioned off, his stores confiscated, his lands mortgaged: it was a genuine sack. The steward ran off after burning the record books and I was left alone, poor little chick that I was, to try to make sense of things. To make things worse, there were no instructions from Venice, only repeated, insatiable requests for money. The Frumiers were of no practical help, and most likely Padre Pendola was whispering slanders about me, and so they didn't look on me kindly. I was determined to reply to suspicions with deeds, and I sweated and laboured greatly, always thinking how I could favour la Pisana and be of use to those who had, for better or worse, brought me up, so that when young Count Rinaldo came to take the reins at the Castle, the eight thousand ducats of the girls' dowries were secure, the creditors paid or satisfied, income was being produced, and the lands, although reduced by a holding over here and one over there, nonetheless still made up a nice estate. There were still some arrears, but of the kind that need time to be settled. I certainly wasn't the only one to think that a young man of twenty-four just out of college (the Countess would have left him there until he was thirty, had the Count not died) was not the person best suited to handle this operation. Enough! I decided just to keep an eye on things so that I could offer him some counsel. Otherwise I withdrew to the chancery, where, having taken my exams, I soon became Clerk of Fratta.

Giulio Del Ponte, unable to bear the agony of being so far away from her, had followed la Pisana to Venice. I remained all alone at the Castle, consoling myself by thinking of the good I had done and what I could still do; living with my memories, hoping for a better future, reading Martino's memoirs from time to time. My life, if not happy, was tranquil, useful, busy. My virtue lay in being content with this.

TEN

Carlino the Clerk, or The Golden Age. How, at the beginning of 1796, General Bonaparte is viewed by the population of the Castle of Fratta. The democratic Republic at Portogruaro and at the Castle. My amazing dialogue with the Great Liberator. I finally learn for certain that my father is neither dead nor a Turk. The Countess herself invites me to join her in Venice.

Count Rinaldo was a studious, serious young man who paid little attention to his own affairs and even less to the amusements typical of a fellow of his age. He spent long hours in his chamber and with me, in particular, he seldom conversed. It is true that along with the Captain and Signora Veronica I had the honour of dining with him, but he ate little and spoke even less. He said his good afternoons and good evenings to his uncle the Monsignor on entering and leaving the hall, and that was it. Proper, affable and correct when necessary, he gave me no cause to complain about anything and I attributed his unsociable nature to illness or the fear of some organic flaw; and, in fact, his complexion was a rather unhappy colour, like that of a man with a liver ailment.

At this time my days proceeded one after the other, ever serene, ever the same, like the beads of a rosary. Seldom did I visit Casa Frumier at Portogruaro for fear of meeting Padre Pendola, and even less so after the diocese began to mutter that he was a bully in disguise, and the Curia and the Chapter House and the Bishop himself began to resent being led gently by the nose. The excellent Father suffered from terrible fits and I did not wish to be present at such a grievous spectacle. Instead I often went to Cordovado, to the Provedoni household, where I had become great friends with the young people, and where Bradamante and Aquilina warmed the conversation with that feminine magic that makes us men twice as quick and lively when we are in the company of women. At any rate, that is how it has always been with me; beyond those inevitable discussions on fixed subjects, I've never been able to come forth with any real, witty, spontaneous conversation when speaking with men, even when they were friends. I was much more likely to remain silent when I had nothing new or significant to say, and so I probably looked like a fool a thousand times over. But just let there be a woman present! The rosy gates of fantasy immediately opened up and hidden feelings emerged, and fancies and thoughts and laughing confidences met them, smiling like a lady among friends.

Note, however, that I have never been one to fall in love too easily, and while not all women charm me, it has happened with many who were neither young nor beautiful. Let a ray of goodness or a glimmer of the ideal shine from their faces and the rest is achieved by that need inferiors feel to gain the favourable opinion of their superiors. Women, our superiors! Yes, my brothers: accept this strange judgement from the mouth of one who has known many of them. They are superior to us in the constancy of their sacrifice, in their faith, their resignation, they die better than us; in short they are superior to us in the most important things, in the practical science of life, which as you know, is a *race to death*.[1] On this side of the Alps, furthermore, women are also superior, because men do nothing without their inspiration: a glance at our history and our literature will convince you I am right. This works to women's credit, but also to their disgrace, for all those centuries in which nothing good ever happened. Original sin was theirs. But they began to mend their ways in time, and the Apennines will now produce heroes, not mice.

From time to time I would venture forth to Venchieredo to see Leopardo, who was growing more and more stupefied by his wife's frivolity and her despotism. I recall meeting him on the odd Sunday at one of those evening gatherings at the spring. To think it was here that a smile of happiness and love first lit up his face! Now he advanced on Doretta's arm, his head bowed, malicious smiles behind them: the usual solace of the deceived husband. At least he was fortunate enough to notice nothing, for that viper of a woman had enslaved his brain, too. Oh, she was certainly not one of those superior women I spoke of just now! Woe to us when a woman degenerates! As the old proverb says, she is transformed into the Devil. Raimondo, too, sometimes came to the spring. When he bantered and jested with Doretta he did so utterly openly, in a way that would turn your stomach; when he paid her no attention and chased after other country lasses and town coquettes, shameless Doretta didn't hesitate to follow him about, her husband always in tow. And she was so rude, so dismissive of her husband, so openly jealous, that the wits of the company mocked good Leopardo behind his back. The other members of the Provedoni family, when they happened to be present, slunk away in shame, and I myself had to leave, because it moved me to nausea to see confidence so contemptibly betrayed.

Yet it is also true that the spectacle of others' woes consoles us; and that as we go forward in life we seem to grow hardened against sorrow's blows, not out of habit but because at every moment, looking around us, we see others even more unhappy, beleaguered and persecuted than ourselves. Pity for the heartache I saw armed me with patience for that which I felt. La Pisana had promised to write to me from time to time, and I had let her promise, knowing right then how little I could trust her word. And, in fact, several months went by and I heard nothing. Only when summer was upon us did I receive a bizarre, peculiar, scribbled letter, in which her intense affection and humble mode somewhat balanced her past negligence. It might have even consoled someone else, but not me. I knew that volcanic little head of hers, and I knew that once she had exhausted that vein of tenderness and regret, she would return for God only knew how much time to her previous indifference. Some lines from Dante stuck in my head like knives of poison:

> *. . . indi s'apprende*
> *quanto in femmina il foco d'amore dura*
> *se l'occhio o il tatto spesso nol raccende.*[2]

> . . . and thus we learn
> how brief the fire of love in woman abides
> when neither eye nor touch rekindles it.

I had fished that little volume of Dante out of the great sea of notebooks and registers from which Clara had collected her little library many years before. That small, gnawed and worm-eaten book with its mysterious verses, its even more mysterious abbreviations, its plates depicting the damned and other devilry, had not appealed at all to Clara. But I, who had heard it praised and quoted at Portogruaro and at Padua (not always very appropriately) considered it a great treasure, and I began to sink my teeth into it, and for the first time I read the canto of Francesca[3] with considerably more pleasure than fatigue. And at that point I began to fall in love. I kept going and read to the end; then I reread it, rejoicing in what I now understood that had previously seemed unintelligible. In short, I came to venerate Dante as a sort of household god, and swore so much by him that even those lines I've just quoted came to seem articles of faith.

Now, mind you, in those days people were not yet wild about the Trecento; Monti hadn't written his *Bassvilliana*, nor were Varano's *Visioni*[4] popular, except among the learned. You are mocking me already, but do you realize that this religion of Dante, created by me alone – a young man, neither a philologist nor erudite – earned me quite some glory? You would be right to mock. And I will, nevertheless, bask in my glory, for it was not merely the verses or the poetry, but Dante's heart and soul that I loved. And as for his passions, they were great, strong and intellectual, and I liked him for those qualities, by now so rare.

All this has little connection with the proverb 'Out of sight, out of mind', but Dante liked to apply that proverb to the fidelity of women, and I've introduced him here (along with my harebrained studies of some sixty years ago) just as he came to my memory. It is unfortunate, but we often have to put up with such digressions when someone is telling his story. And I shall have real need of your tolerance as I go on, my dear readers; but about this matter of my literary glory you must be doubly indulgent, for I shake it and reshake it, as they say, precisely because I know how insignificant it is. Reading our great authors, I have divined more than I have understood, loved more than I have studied, and, if I must tell the truth, most of those authors set my teeth on edge. Certainly the fault is mine and yet I can only hope that in the future those who write will remember they are capable of speaking, and the purpose of speaking is to make oneself understood. To be understood by many: oh, isn't that perhaps better than to be understood by a few only? In France more books are printed, sold and read than here for no other reason than that the language is universal and the exposition clear. We have two or three dictionaries and the most learned like to rely on the oldest and least-used. As for logic, they use it as a springboard to leap eight or ten times over. Those who like to take it one step at a time end up half a mile behind, and once they have lost sight of the front runner, sit down to wait for another, who will probably never come along. Courage, therefore: I criticize no one, but when you write, consider the fact that many are going to read you. That way our literature can be of more service to national renewal than it has been heretofore.

And la Pisana's letter: where did I leave it? Oh, trust me, I am a wanderer, but over here, over there, in the end I return. La Pisana's letter is still here with the others far in the back of my writing desk, and if I wanted to I could offer you a glimpse or two of her very odd style of expression. But all you need to know is that she gave me news of Clara, still a novice in the convent, and also something of Lucilio, who was much talked about in Venice, because of his fanatical support of the French. If they should retreat, he would probably come to a bad end, it seemed.

But those fanatical Frenchmen had no intention of retreating! The war against them had shrunk; only Austria and Piedmont were still on the field, and, though they were much reduced, they fought with more spirit and greater hopes than before. Nothing new happened before winter, and at that juncture anyone holding a piece of ground maintained it; those who would invent a new war every month had not yet crossed the Alps and snow brought the usual armistice. That winter was the longest and most peaceful of my entire life. My duties in the chancery kept me very busy indeed. Beyond them, the thought of la Pisana was always hammering away at me, but the fact that she was far away, although it made me melancholy, also took the edge off my grief. That I had done my duty continued to give me some satisfaction. Giulio Del Ponte wrote to me a couple of times:

strange, enigmatic letters, those of a man in love, to his friend. It was easy to see from those letters that he was not entirely happy, and that last year's half-measure of happiness had shrunk markedly in Venice, both because of la Pisana's eccentric moods and because his desires were greater. Those letters distressed me on his account, but as for myself, I was somewhat cheered. On the one hand I understood that if I, too, were in Venice, I wouldn't be any happier than I was in Fratta; on the other, well, do you think that a rival's contentment (even when he is a decent man and a friend) is truly uncomplicated, deep down? Here where I did not see Giulio's suffering first hand, I was more inclined to pardon his torturer; that is how things were and I don't wish to pretend to be a saint.

Meanwhile, in our solitude at Fratta, nothing had changed. Young Count Rinaldo was always in his room; the Countess sent a request for funds with every mail coach; the old Countess was confined to her bed under the eye of Signora Veronica and Faustina. Around the hearth, the Captain and Monsignor Orlando bickered every evening about how to stoke the fire. Both wanted to wield the poker, each had his own idea about how the coals should be arranged, and they would end up burning poor Marocco's tail until he took cover under the sink. With every old newspaper that came, the Captain gloated to hear that those damned Frenchmen were stranded between the Alps and the Apennines. He now gave them not four, not six, but a good eight years to cross the mountains.

'And, meanwhile,' he added, 'we can move Schiavonia, fully armed, to the River Mincio, and I'd like to hear how they think that match will end!'

Marchetto, Fulgenzio and the cook made up the audience and they certainly didn't feel they had the right to demolish the Captain's castles in the air; and the Chaplain, when he appeared, helped him to build them up with his naive ignorance. I shook my head and don't really recall what I thought. The Captain's opinions didn't impress me much, precisely because they were his. In the midst of all this we had word one day that a young and quite new general was to command the French Army of the Alps, a certain Napoléon Bonaparte.

'Napoléon! What kind of name is that?' the Chaplain said. 'He must be some sort of schismatic.'

'It must be one of those names that have become fashionable in Paris,' said the Captain. 'One of those names like those in the Provedoni family – Brutus, Alcibiades, Miltiades, Cimon – names of the damned we can only hope will lead their bearers to perdition!'

'Bonaparte, *Buonaparte*,' muttered Monsignor Orlando. 'It sounds quite like one of our own surnames!'

'Oh, now listen! Tricks, tricks, tricks!' the Captain went on. 'They probably put that name out to lead us on, or maybe those big generals are so ashamed of the poor showing they're making that they invented a name, one that no one's ever heard of, a name they can blame everything on. That must be it! And a shameless ruse it is, too! Napoléon Bonaparte! You only have to say it to hear that it's made up, for there's nothing more difficult to invent than a name and a surname that sound natural. Now if they had said Giorgio Sandracca or Giacomo Andreini or Carlo Altoviti: simple names that sound familiar. But no, gentlemen, they had to come up with Napoléon Bonaparte, a name with fraud written all over it!'

General Bonaparte, it was therefore decided at the Castle of Fratta, was an imaginary creature, a spurious name for some old captain reluctant to dishonour himself in a desperate war, dreamed up by the Directory to please Italian ears. But two months later that imaginary creature, having won four battles and forced the King of Sardinia to make peace, entered Milan, cheered and celebrated by the Italian Utopians, as they've been called. In June, with Mantua under siege, all of Italy was in his hands, and everywhere there was a pleading for alliances and a begging for reprieve; and Venice, still deliberating when the time for decision had already passed, clutched at unarmed neutrality for the last time. The French general prevailed with ease. He raided; he invaded; he pillaged the provinces, cities and castles. He broke the armies of Wurmser and d'Alvinzi on the Garda, the Brenta and the Adige; he took Provera near Mantua and in February 1797 the fortress surrendered. At Fratta they were still dubious, but in Venice they were positively shaking;

at San Marco you could just about hear the cannon thundering, and the time for deliberating was clearly up. And yet they kept on hoping that just as they had so far lived by luck, *by accident*, in the memorable words of the Doge Renier, so they would continue to be spared from harm.

The Countess did not feel entirely easy amid all this turmoil, but she didn't think it was advisable to depart for the mainland when the mainlanders were all getting ready to take shelter in Venice. The Frumiers had returned to the capital, to the great dismay of Portogruaro society; the Countess, therefore, wrote to her son that he would do well to join her, too (for a man in the household is always an excellent surety), and she urged him to bring as much money as possible for all emergencies. Count Rinaldo reached Venice, while Napoleon's war was rumbling at the gates of the Friuli, finally convincing Captain Sandracca that the young Corsican general was neither an imaginary creature nor a name in some romance invented by the Directory. The Captain was now as fearful of the real and present French general as he had been scornful of the distant, imaginary one. Suddenly, word went out that the Archduke Charles of Austria was coming down the River Tagliamento with a new army, and the French were heading towards him, and there was going to be a massacre, a sack, a universal cataclysm. Houses were abandoned, castles barricaded against marauders and deserters, church treasures were buried, priests dressed up as peasants or fled into the wild. From Brescia, Verona and Bergamo, the violence, the rapes and the cruelty were bewailed and they were embellished; hatred and terror were mixed in equal measure, but the hatred was more cowardly than the terror.

All fled without restraint, without shame, without any concern for themselves or their families. The Captain and Signora Veronica escaped, I believe, to Lugugnana, where they hid in a fisherman's hut on an island of the laguna. Monsignor went no further than Portogruaro, being less frightened of Bonaparte than of having to fast. Fulgenzio and his sons disappeared; Marchetto, who was ill, had himself taken to the hospital. I had a lot of talking to do to keep Faustina from running off and leaving me alone with the old Countess; only the gardener and the farmer stayed, for, having nothing to lose, they were in no great hurry to hide. But it was no good; all the little rogues of the district, aware of the general fear, grew bolder and began to steal from any place that was solitary or undefended. In any case, I wasn't sure I could trust the gardener or the farmer (and least of all Faustina), so I decided to go to Portogruaro to ask for help before the danger became even greater. I was hoping the Vice-captain would assign me a dozen of those Schiavoni who passed by every day on their way to Venice, and that Monsignor Orlando would supply me with a woman, a nurse to station at his mother's bedside. And so I saddled Marchetto's horse, which had been lazing about the stables for a week, and galloped off to Portogruaro.

In those times, my friends, the news had no steamships or telegraphs to circle the globe in the blink of an eye. News arrived at Fratta on the back of a donkey or in the messenger's sack, and you could often learn of startling novelties happening just three miles from the Castle. When I got to Portogruaro I found no less than the Devil's maelstrom: there were idlers screaming, flocks of peasants jeering, priests discussing, guardsmen sneaking off, and, right in the middle of it all, where the usual standard stood, was one of those famous Liberty Trees,[5] the first I'd ever seen (it didn't even make much of an impression on me right then and there). However, I was young, I'd been to Padua, I'd escaped the wiles of Padre Pendola, I didn't love the State Inquisition one bit, and all that shouting out loud just as they pleased suddenly seemed like great progress. I nearly convinced myself that the usual slackers had become men of Athens and Sparta, and searched the crowd for one of those from the Senator's circle who used to extol the laws of Lycurgus and Draco. But I didn't see a single one. All the shouters were new people. Who knew where they came from? They were people whose very possession of reason would have been questioned the day before, and who were now laying down the law with their hats in the air, dancing around a wooden pole. A new power had bounced up, unarmed but certainly arrogant and sure of itself; its strength came straight from the terror and ineptitude of the fallen. It was the triumph of an unknown

God, a bacchanal of freed slaves who considered themselves men without even knowing it. Whether they had the virtues to be considered men I don't know, but the knowledge they could be and they should be men was already something.

I, too, on horseback as I was, began to roar with all the breath I had in me, and soon was taken to be the ringleader of the revolt. A wild and shirtless mob quickly gathered round me, echoing my shouts and following me as if in a procession. The powers of a horse! I must confess that this halo of popularity played havoc with my brain and I began to take a crazy delight in being followed and cheered by so many people, none of whom knew me, nor I them. My horse was greatly responsible, let me repeat, and perhaps also the blue coat I was wearing; for the people, whatever you say, go mad about great finery, and all those ragged, shirtless men probably thought they'd won the lottery when they came upon a ringleader so well turned out and on horseback to boot. Among the wild country folk looking askance at the Liberty Tree (and who seemed ready to give a beating to its cultivators), there were one or two from the jurisdiction of Fratta who knew me for my impartiality and fairness. Quite certainly they believed I was there to settle matters for the best, and began to shout, 'It's our Clerk! It's Signor Carlino! Long live our Clerk! Long live Signor Carlino!'

The mob of genuine rioters, astonished to find they shared their enthusiasm with that suspicious and rather hostile country rabble, were delighted, if not with the Clerk, with Signor Carlino, and soon they were all shouting together, 'Long live Signor Carlino! Make way for Signor Carlino! Let Signor Carlino speak!'

When it came to conveying my thanks for the honours and riding forward, I was able to handle that quite well, but as for speaking, I would not have known what to say, and, luckily, the great din exonerated me. But then one unfortunate fellow began to hush the crowd and call for silence and beg people to stop and listen to me, who – from the heights of my old nag and inspired by my nice coat – looked like I was ready to tell them some wonderful things. And the first ranks stopped and the second were blocked, and at the back they began to ask what was the matter.

'Signor Carlino wants to speak! Silence! Halt! Listen! Signor Carlino is speaking!'

By now my horse was besieged by a silent, nervous crowd eager to hear me. I felt the spirit of Demosthenes urging me to speak and I opened my lips.

'Shh! Quiet! He's speaking!' The first trial was not very successful. I closed my lips without saying a word.

'Did you hear?'

'What did he say?'

'He said to be quiet!'

'Silence, everyone! Long live Signor Carlino!'

Reassured by such a benign response, I once again opened my mouth and this time actually spoke.

'Citizens,' (this was Amilcare's favourite word) 'citizens, what do you want?'

The question was somewhat loftier than really necessary; in one blow I had swept away the Doge, Senate, Maggior Consiglio, Podesteria and Inquisition, and had sailed into the seat of Providence, one step above any other human authority. The Castle of Fratta and its chancery could no longer be seen from those sublime heights; I had become a ruler, a Washington on horseback high above a brainless, brawling mob.

'What do we want?'

'What did he say?'

'He asked what we want!'

'We want freedom! Long live freedom!'

'Bread! Bread!'

'Polenta! Polenta!'

These cries of bread and polenta brought full agreement between the peasants from the country and the town tradesmen. It seemed San Marco's last prospect was crushed.

'Bread! Bread! Freedom! Polenta! Torture the merchants! Open the granaries! Quiet! Signor Carlino is speaking! Silence!'

It was true; a whirlwind of eloquence spun in my head and I wanted to speak at all costs, so eager were they to hear me.

'Citizens,' I began again in a sonorous voice, 'citizens, the bread of liberty is the most nourishing of all, and everyone has the right to it, for what is man without bread and liberty? I say to you: without bread and without liberty, what is man?'

If I repeated the question to myself it was because I was genuinely unable to answer it. But necessity urged me on and a deeper silence, a wider attention, ordered me to hurry up. In my haste, my logic was less than fine; I wanted a metaphor that would sound striking.

'Man,' said I, 'would be like a mad dog, a dog without a master!'

'Hurrah! Hurrah! Excellent! Polenta ! Polenta! We're mad as dogs! Long live Signor Carlino! Signor Carlino speaks well! Signor Carlino knows all, he sees all!'

Signor Carlino would have been hard put to say how a man without liberty (that is, with at least one master) was like a dog without a master (who, therefore, has the greatest liberty), but this was not the moment to get lost in hair-splitting.

'Citizens,' I broke in, 'you want liberty, and so you shall have it. As for bread and polenta, I cannot provide. If I had them, I would happily invite you all to luncheon. But Providence takes care of everything, and so let us commend ourselves to Providence!'

A long, mixed murmur, suggesting some disparities of opinion, met this proposal of mine. Then came a bedlam of voices, shouts, threats and schemes rather different from my own.

'To the granaries! To the granaries! Let's elect a mayor! No, to the bell tower! Let's get the Bishop down here! No, no, to the Vice-captain! Let's put him in the stocks!'

Those who wanted to go to the Bishop prevailed. Still on my horse, I was dragged and pushed to the gates of the Bishop's Palace.

'Let Signor Carlino speak! Out, Monsignor! Come out, Monsignor the Bishop!'

Evidently my words (although they hadn't been successful in bringing the crowd fully in line with the decrees of Providence) had at least persuaded the rioters to rely on Providence's legitimate representative. Inside the Bishop's palace, however, spirits were far from easy. Priests, canons and church officials all offered their opinions, but nobody had come up with anything really useful. Padre Pendola, whose influence had been faltering for some time, decided the moment had come to secure his position. He decided to try a great *coup de main*, and first waving out of the window to show his confidence, he then courageously opened the doors, went out on the balcony and leaned over the railing. A salvo of shouts and whistles met him. I watched him stammer out a few words, turn pale and hasten inside when the rioters bent over, hands searching the ground for stones to throw at him. Monsignor di Sant'Andrea was sincerely jubilant to see the good Father so humiliated, and, with him, everyone inside the palazzo, in the silence of their hearts, echoed those shouts and whistles from the crowd. The Bishop, who was a saintly fellow, gazed at his secretary compassionately, but precisely because he was a saint, he had already made up his mind to dismiss him. If he did not thank him for his good works right there and then, this, too, was because he was a saint.

His face serene, he turned to Monsignor di Sant'Andrea and asked him to bring him word of what the people rioting outside wanted. I was then staring at the balcony and I watched the canon appear. There were no whistles and no shouts when he came out; just some whispers of 'shut up', a murmur of approval and nothing more.

'My brothers,' he began, 'Monsignor the Bishop would like to know what desires lead you to make such a commotion beneath his windows?'

There followed a long, stupefied silence, because no one, and that included me, knew why we had come. But finally a voice burst out: 'We want to see Monsignor the Bishop!' And then there came a new storm of shouting, 'Out, Monsignor the Bishop! We want Monsignor the Bishop!'

The canon withdrew, and even as he was doing so two parties were already agitating around Monsignor as to whether he should expose himself to the riotous behaviour of that mob. The Bishop sided with the more courageous party, and, parting the ranks of the reluctant with sweet violence, he went out on the balcony, followed by the others. His calm, serene face, dignified manner and the saintliness apparent in his every gesture moved the crowd, and their hatred and abandon were commuted into something like shame. When the uproar that met his appearance had subsided, he addressed us with a calm, severe gaze and a voice of paternal disapproval: 'My sons, what is it that you want from your spiritual father?'

Following this question, there was a silence like that after the canon spoke. But contrition was stronger than wonder, and already some were bending their knees and others raising their arms in prayer, when a voice issued from a thousand mouths as if they were one: 'Your blessing! Your blessing!'

Everyone knelt and I bent my head over my nag's dishevelled mane, and the requested benediction poured over us. And then, even before the Bishop could add some words of peace as he wished, the crowd reversed directions, roaring that we must go to the Vice-captain, and dragged me and my horse over to the Town Hall. Four great Schiavoni sitting at the gate went racing inside to close and bar the shutters. After many requests and consultations the Vice-captain decided to come out on the loggia. The crowd had neither shotguns nor pistols and the worthy official was brave enough to trust them.

'What do I see here, my sons?' he began in a quavering voice. 'Today is a working day. Each of you has a family, as I do myself, and each of you should be looking after his own duties, while instead . . .'

A hurrah for freedom bellowed forth from that wild mob, silencing the voice of the speaker.

'It appears to me that you have already taken your liberty,' he went on in a genuinely humble tone. 'Enjoy it then, my sons. I can take this matter no further.'

'Away with the Schiavoni! Hang the Schiavoni!' many began to shout.

'The French! Long live the French! We want freedom!' others chimed in.

Those French gentlemen then came to my mind for the first time since the disorders began, imposing some clarity on my thoughts. At the same time I thought of Fratta and the reason why I had come to Portogruaro, but the good Vice-captain did not seem to be in a condition to help others or even himself. You could see he had a very great desire to retreat from the loggia and only the continual shouting from the crowd detained him.

'But my good sirs,' he stammered, 'I don't know what use I am to myself or to you standing out here on display under the arbour. I am a just an official, a mere instrument of the Most Excellent Representative, and, in fact, I take orders from him.'

'No, no! You must take orders from us! We have masters no more! Long live freedom! Down with the Representative!'

'Attention, my good sirs! You are not the established authorities! You have no legitimacy!

'Very well, then! We will establish ourselves! We will name an Avogadore! A vote, a vote for the Avogadore! You will obey our Avogadore!

'O Heavens above!' the Vice-captain objected desperately. 'But this is genuine rebellion! It's all very well to elect your Avogadore, but give him time to write to the Representative, who will then communicate with the Most Serene College . . .'

'Down with the College! We want our Avogadore! Stand still right there! Death to the Vice-captain if he dares to move! Let's hold a vote for the Avogadore! A vote!'

The confusion and disarray increased, and with it the noise and the clamour. From this side and that a dozen names were whispered, but the merits of the absent are never as great as the authority of the present. A peasant began to shout, 'Let's name Signor Carlino!' and behind him everyone began to roar 'Here's our people's Avogadore! Long live Signor Carlino! Down with the Vice-captain!'

To tell the truth, my aims on venturing into that crowd hadn't been anywhere near so ambitious, but now that I found myself in such an exalted position, I hadn't the heart to come down from it – even supposing that I could have. They pressed around me, raising the horse's belly almost to their shoulders, waving filthy nose-rags and hats and caps in my face and clapping their hands as if I were an actor who'd played his part well. The Vice-captain glared at me from his loggia the way a big dog on a chain would look at a small, unleashed mongrel, but every time he moved to withdraw, a thousand jailbird faces immediately turned on him, threatening to set fire to the Captaincy House if he didn't obey the new Avogadore.

'Very good, my good sirs. Now if you will be off and just send the Avogadore up here, we shall come to an agreement between us.'

The crowd had been rioting without knowing why and many of the curious had already got their satisfaction, and some of the peasants who'd grown tired of the comedy had headed off for home. I knew not what world I was in or why they'd named me Avogadore or to what purpose the Vice-captain had invited me to consult with him. But I did like this being a person of importance and so I risked all in view of glory.

'Open the gate! Let the Avogadore in!' the mob howled.

'My good sirs,' said the Vice-captain, 'I have a wife and children and I don't wish them to die of fright. I shall open the gate when you have gone. You see that I'm not all on the wrong side. Good pacts, good friends!'

The crowd didn't want to disperse and I, partly because I was tired of sitting on my horse, and partly because I couldn't wait to treat a Vice-captain as my equal, took it upon myself to persuade them.

'Citizens,' I said, 'I thank you. My eternal gratitude! I am moved and honoured by these tokens of your affection and your esteem. Nevertheless, the Vice-captain is not wrong. We must show our trust in him so that he may also trust us. Disperse then and be at ease. Wait for me in the piazza, and, meanwhile, I shall defend your cause.'

'Long live the Avogadore! All right! To the piazza! To the piazza! We want the town granaries opened! We want the chest with the money from the grist tax! The grist tax is the blood of the poor!'

'Yes, be calm, now. Have faith in me! Justice shall be done – but in the meantime stay calm in the piazza and wait for me.'

'To the piazza! To the piazza! Long live Signor Carlino! Long live the Avogadore! Down with San Marco! Long live freedom!'

Shouts echoing behind them, the crowd surged wildly into

the piazza to sack a few baker's shops and greengrocers, but the noise far exceeded their hunger and the damage was slight. A few of the more suspicious stayed behind to see if the Vice-captain would keep his word; meanwhile, I gladly jumped down from my mount, handed over the old nag to one of them and stood waiting for the gate to open. With the greatest of caution a Schiavone corporal cleared a tiny crack and I slipped in sideways. He then replaced all the bars and the chains as if he intended to keep me prisoner. All that rattling of locks and keys made me slightly suspicious, but then I remembered I was an important person, an Avogadore, and I climbed the stairs with my head high and my arms arched at my sides, as if my entire people were in my pockets, ready to defend me. The Vice-captain, now back inside, was waiting for me in a room with a gang of scriveners and guardsmen, who didn't appeal to me one bit. He no longer wore that humble, compliant face he had shown to the crowd just five minutes before. His brow was forbidding, his lip curled, his manner brusque; there was no hint of the victim's greenish pallor, wild gaze and trembling hands. A man of decision now, he stepped forward and asked, 'Pray, what is your name?'

I thanked him silently for having relieved me of the business of asking the first question, for I wouldn't have known what nail to hang myself on. My *amour propre* thus stimulated, I raised my crest like a cockerel.

'My name is Carlo Altoviti, Gentleman of Torcello, Clerk of Fratta, and, most recently, Avogadore of the people of Portogruaro.'

'Avogadore! Avogadore!' sputtered the Vice-captain. 'That's what you call yourself, but I hope you do not take the foolishness of a drunken mob seriously, for that would be very dangerous for you.'

At these words from their boss, his little band of retainers nodded and I felt the blood rise to my head and was on the brink of some reckless remark to show them how little I cared for their bullying. But a high opinion of my dignity held me back and I replied to the Vice-captain that no, I was certainly not worthy of the great honour bestowed on me, but that I had no intention of devaluing myself by appearing even less worthy than I really was. And, therefore, it was up to him to tell me what concessions he was disposed to make so that my client, the people, could take advantage of their newly acquired liberty.

'What concessions? What liberty? I know nothing of that!' the Vice-captain replied. 'No orders have come from Venice and liberty has existed so long in the Most Serene Republic that the people of Portogruaro have no need to invent it today.'

'Oh, not so fast with your liberty in the Serenissima!' said I, for I had already exercised myself in these arguments during my novitiate in Padua. 'If by liberty you mean the free will expressed by the three State Inquisitors I can only agree with you; they can do anything they please. But as for the other subjects of the Most Excellent Signoria, I most humbly enquire in what almanac you learned they can be called free?'

'The State Inquisition is an institution that has proved excellent for many centuries,' said the Vice-captain, and in his uncertain voice you could hear ancient awe struggling against present-day trepidation.

'It proved excellent in the past,' said I, 'but as for the present, we do not agree. The people find it dreadful and by virtue of their sovereign rights they free you forever from the bother of having to serve it.'

'Signor . . . Signor Carlino, I believe,' he continued, 'may I point out to you that no one has so far granted the people of Portogruaro this sovereignty, nor have they done anything to gain it. I remain an official of the Most Serene Signoria and I certainly cannot permit –'

'Come off it!' I broke in. 'What have the officials of the Serenissima not permitted at Verona, Brescia, Padua and everywhere the French have come in?'

'Sham! A mere show, sir!' said the Vice-captain rather incautiously. 'At times one pretends to concede in order to recover more easily later. I know from an excellent source that the nobleman Ottolin has thirty thousand armed men hidden in the Bergamo valleys, and they will let us know whether the return of the Frenchmen resembles their arrival!'

'However, sir,' said I, 'here the question is not what will happen tomorrow, it is to decide whether or not to grant the requests of a free people. To give them back what was extorted from them with that tyrannical grist tax, and then to open up the granaries of the treasury, which, in any case are no longer necessary, because the Schiavoni can return home whenever they please.'

There were murmurs of discontent from all, but the Vice-captain, who had very sensitive ears and had caught the sounds of a new riot building up outside, was more restrained than his fellows.

'I am Vice-captain of the militias and the jails,' said he. 'This gentleman' (he indicated a huge, knobby-faced fellow) 'this gentleman is Treasurer of Customs, and this other gentleman' (he was as long and thin as starvation itself) 'is the Custodian of the Public Granaries. Our duties are invested in us by the Signoria and we certainly recognize no legitimate authority in you, nor do we obey your command without written orders from the Signoria itself.'

'Oh, body and blood!' I shouted. 'So I am Avogadore for nothing?'

They stared at me dumbstruck at such boldness, while I, throwing myself into my part with energy, simply took leave of my senses.

'Sirs, I have promised to protect the interests of the people and I shall protect them. I must also return to Fratta before evening, and before evening I intend to put everything in order. Do you understand, sirs? Otherwise I will turn matters over to the people and leave it to them.'

'I understand,' said the Vice-captain, more obstinate than I had expected. 'But without orders from the Signoria I recognize no superior but the Most Excellent Representative. And as for the people, they will not want to behave too wildly while we are holding you hostage here.'

'What, I, a hostage? An Avogadore?'

'You are no Avogadore. And I am the Vice-captain!'

'Thank you very much! We shall see . . .'

'We shall certainly see, but I would not advise you to be in a hurry. We already know a certain amount about you and how you treat the trusted friends of the Inquisition with little respect.'

'Oh, so you know a certain amount about me! Oh yes, I can imagine. As soon as your trusted friend returns to Fratta I shall have him hanged! That's something else for you to know!'

'On the orders of the Most Excellent Signoria let this person be arrested for lese-majesty!'

At the Vice-captain's quite dramatic outburst, his gang circled around me, as if to prevent me from fleeing. But what was the need for this precaution, I ask myself today, as I did then, when every door was barred and chained? Had I been Pompey[6] I would have thrown the hem of my toga over my head; instead, I crossed my arms over my chest and offered that band of ruffians the supreme spectacle of an Avogadore without a people and without fear. That unforgettable tableau lasted less than a minute, and then a pawing and stamping of horses and a running and shouting of people in the street below drew my jailers' attention. When shouts announcing this new riot grew louder, they all rushed towards the window.

'The French! The French! Long live freedom! Make way for the French!'

Like so many statues who had looked on the Medusa, they stood frozen, one here, one there, around the room. In a single leap I was at the window and I could see a group of light cavalrymen with their lances at the Captaincy House gates, and around them a swirling of madmen, the curious, and fanatics who looked ready to smash one another's heads, so varied were the passions that drove them.

'Long live the French! Make way for the French gentlemen!'

There was no doubt about it: those men on horses were Frenchmen, and they began to beat on the Captaincy House gates with their lances, bellowing and cursing with all the *peste* and *sacrebleu* in their lexicon. From above I shouted that the gates would be opened immediately and my words were greeted with more enthusiastic roars from the crowd.

'Bravo, Signor Avogadore! Keep it up!'

Moved by such appreciation, I bowed and went back inside to make sure the gates would be opened. But no one inside paid me the least attention; they were all running madly from room to room, some flattening themselves inside the empty closets of the archives, others looking for the keys to the jail so as to disguise themselves among the prisoners, while the Schiavoni on sentry duty had taken to their heels by the alleyway door, and so I had to go down and unbolt the gates. It was every man for himself then: as soon as there was room to pass, one damnable sergeant came charging on horseback with his lance, nearly impaling me from end to end, and behind him came the whole crazy platoon, despite the seven steps they had to mount to reach the threshold, and right there in the hall they began wheeling wildly around at a stiff trot, as if they were getting ready to bound up the stairs and ascend to God knows where! The Vice-captain and his underlings, hearing a terrible din downstairs that made the walls shake, commended their souls to the Heavenly Virgin of the Earthquake.

I, meanwhile, sought to make myself understood by the sergeant and tried to persuade him to dismount from his horse if he wished to climb the stairs, as seemed to be his intention. To my great surprise the sergeant replied to me, in good Italian, that he was looking for the Custodian of the Granaries and the Vice-captain, and if they did not appear quickly he would have them hanged from the Liberty Tree. This sentence brought a wild cheer from the people, for the crowd had already invaded the entrance hall, and it was a real inferno in there between the Frenchmen's horses and the shouts of the citizens. The sergeant, having finally understood he could not climb the stairs on horseback and that the Vice-captain was in no hurry to come down, dismounted in one bound and told me to come along to find those officials. When the crowd saw me advance alongside the French officer another roar shook the Captaincy House to its foundations.

'Long live Signor Avogadore!'

Once upstairs, the sergeant and I searched high and low before flushing out the Treasurer of Customs, the Custodian of the Granaries and the Vice-captain, who were squeezed together like three snakes in a corner of the attic. But we had to struggle to save them from the clutches of the people, who had followed us, and only my great authority, backed up by some swearing on the part of the sergeant, brought silence. The sergeant then brusquely demanded a donation of five thousand ducats for the army's marching expenses, and that the granaries be opened in the service of liberty and the French Army. The people here took another opportunity to wish long life to liberty. The three officials shook together in unison like three saplings whipped by the wind, but the Treasurer found his voice and replied that he had no orders and that if force were used . . .

'What do you mean, force?' the sergeant said menacingly. 'Yesterday morning General Bonaparte won a battle at the River Tagliamento; we have shed our blood defending liberty and now a free people would begrudge us some victuals? The five thousand ducats must be disbursed within an hour, and the General orders that the rest of the treasury be put at the people's disposal. As for the granaries, once the camp at Dignano is supplied, they will be left open for the neediest families. Such are the salutary intentions of the French republicans!'

'Long live the French! Down with San Marco! Long live freedom!' shouted the mob, now ransacking the offices, smashing furniture and tossing shelves and papers out of the windows. Those down below howled even louder in their rage at not being able to do the same. I was greatly astonished to see that even fear so close and pressing had not freed the three officials from their ancient and duty-bound terror of the State Inquisition. All three had the same idea, but the Vice-captain was the first to risk opening his mouth.

'Sir,' he stuttered, 'most excellent and worthy Sir, the people, as you say, are free. We . . . we are in no way involved. Where the treasury and the granaries are, everyone knows. Here (he nodded at me), here, in fact is the Most Illustrious Signor Avogadore, named just this morning to the service of the Commune; if you please, ask him. As for ourselves, we resign our powers into the hands . . . into the hands . . .'

He had no idea into what hands to resign, but a fresh shout from the crowd spared him that decision.

'Long live freedom! Long live the French! Long live the Signor Avogadore!'

The sergeant now turned his back on those three wretches, took my arm and led me down the stairs. And while a part of the crowd remained to amuse themselves with their former overlords, making them put on French cockades and shout long live this and long live that, another part joined the platoon of Frenchmen surrounding my very important person as we headed towards the treasury. Along the way I pointed out to the sergeant that I had no keys, but his only reply was a somewhat pitying little smile as he dug his spurs into his horse's belly. Two sappers broke down the doors and the sergeant opened the treasury and put the money there in his case, declaring it amounted to no more than four thousand ducats. He then proceeded to the granaries, once again allowing the people's rage to vent itself on the furniture and the files. In front of the granaries we found a long line of carts, some of them army carts, some requisitioned from farms nearby, guarded by Provençal chasseurs. The barley, wheat and maize meal were put in sacks and loaded on the carts in no time at all. The people were left with the flour dust floating down from the windows, but still they kept on shouting,

'Long live the French! Down with San Marco! Long live freedom!'

When the convoy was ready, the captain in charge, to whom the sergeant had given a report, called me to him with great solemnity and honoured me with a speech in which I was liberally addressed as 'citizen' and 'Avogadore'. He proclaimed me meritorious of my liberty, a saviour of my country and an adoptive son of the French people. The carts then headed off smartly towards San Vito, the light cavalry vanished in a cloud of dust along with the case full of money – and there I stood, speechless, astonished, crestfallen, among a populace that was not very happy and even less satiated. They were still shouting 'Long live the French! Long live freedom!' but by now they had forgotten all about their Avogadore, and this gave me chance to slip away as soon as night began to fall. I had no time to search for my old nag, nor the courage to mount my steed again for some new triumph and I saw that it would be wiser to remain on foot.

On foot, then, and full of remorse for having wasted the day in great foolishness, I took the roads and byways to Fratta once more. A host of political and philosophical considerations – on the instability of human glory and popular favour, on the odd customs of liberty's champions – distracted me from fears that some disaster might have meanwhile befallen the Castle. However, the deserted farms and the traces of pillage I observed on my way did give me some pause and made me involuntarily speed my pace. The closer I got to home, the more I regretted having neglected for so many hours the matter I had set out to deal with. And, sadly, my fears were well founded.

Arriving at Fratta I saw before me a state of utter bedlam. The houses in the village were abandoned, splinters of barrels, carts and household goods were piled up here and there, the remains of scattered fires still smoking, and in the piazza were traces of the worst debauchery you could imagine. Meat, half-raw, half-roasted, pools of spilled wine, upturned sacks of flour, broken pots and plates and glasses strewn about. In their midst grazed the animals, released from their stalls, and twilight lent the scene the outlines of a weird apparition. I rushed into the Castle, shouting at the top of my lungs 'Giacomo! Lorenzo! Faustina!' but my voice was hushed by the silent, empty courtyards and only when I got near the entry hall did I hear the neighing of a horse. It was Marchetto's old nag, which had got loose during the mayhem in Portogruaro and returned home, that one poor animal braver and more loyal than all those other animals who pride themselves on having brains and hearts. A fearful doubt about the old Countess assailed me and I raced across the courtyards and down the corridors, nearly breaking my neck against several columns.

The rays of the moon did not reach inside and so my eyes did not have to confront the signs of that witches' Sabbath, but passing though I smelled the revolting stench. Tripping over broken shutters and smashed furnishings, I climbed the stairs on hands and knees, and when I reached the hall above I nearly lost my senses it was in such disarray. Fear cleared my mind and I reached the old woman's room and threw myself into the shadows inside, shrieking like a madman. Out of the utter darkness came a terrifying sound, a groan both weary and menacing: the pant of a wild beast and the whine of a child come together in a grim, relentless rasping sound.

'Oh, Signora!' I cried. My hair stood on end. 'It is I! Carlino! Say something!'

I could hear the sound of a body struggling to raise itself and my eyes strained from their orbits trying to make out something in that mysterious gloom. I could not even think whether to feel my way forward or go back in search of a lamp; my terrible uncertainty rendered me blank, inert.

'Listen,' said a voice I could scarcely recognize as that of the old Countess, 'listen, Carlino; as there is no priest, I would like to make my confession to you. Know then,' she seemed to hesitate a moment, 'know that my conscience has permitted me to do no wrong and that I have done all the good that I could: I have loved my children, my grandchildren, my relations; I have loved my neighbour and trusted in God. Now I have reached one hundred; one hundred years, Carlino! One hundred years, Carlino, and I die alone, in sorrow and despair!'

I was shaking all over and with the eye of pity peered deep into that soul, come back to life only to know the terror of death.

'Signora!' I shouted, 'Signora, do you not believe in God?'

'I have believed in Him until now,' she said, her voice beginning to expire. In those words I sensed a smile that lacked all hope. Then, not hearing any movement or breathing, I advanced to her bedside and touched an arm already stiffened by death. For a moment I thought I could see her, although the darkness was if anything growing deeper in that funereal room, and I could feel the poisoned darts of her last glances stabbing me mercilessly, and her soul, abandoning its old companion, seemed to hiss a curse at me. A curse on this fleeting, seductive life that wafts us as if by pleasure boat into lovely bays, then tosses us, shipwrecked, against the rocks! A curse on the air that coddles us young, adult and decrepit, then suffocates us as we lie dying. A curse on the family that indulges us and holds us charmed and happy, then scatters far and wide to abandon us at the supreme hour, alone. A curse on peace that transmutes into anguish, faith that turns to blasphemy, charity that becomes ingratitude. A curse . . .

In my grim delirium I swung between rage and stupor; the

thought of that long, sainted life so brutally cut off by dreadful fear overwhelmed me, and I stood for a very long time holding that icy arm, not sure whether I was alive or dead. I finally came to when the room lit up and I saw it was the Chaplain, who was quite amazed to find me there. Behind him, holding a candle, was Spaccafumo. Another time their rumpled clothes, pale faces and sunken eyes, the blood on them, would have horrified me, but now I paid no heed. The priest, approaching the old lady's bed without a word, raised her other arm and then let it drop.

'Those French dogs!' he murmured. 'So she had to die without the comforts of the faith! Oh, and am I to blame, my dear God?'

He looked down at himself, all beaten and bruised after the brutal treatment the soldiers had given him when he insisted on staying at the invalid's side. They had dragged him out and beaten and insulted him, but he had stayed close to the Castle and returned inside as soon as the looters vanished. As for Spaccafumo, even a hundred miles away he could always sense when the Chaplain was in trouble and never failed to rush to his side; he had a sort of second sight, sharpened by gratitude and friendship. I could not then (nor did I wish to later) embitter the good priest's grief more by telling him how the old lady had died. And so I was silent and knelt with them to say the prayer for the dead, in my own case more to comfort the living than to commend the departed. We then arranged the body in a more Christian pose, but the image fixed by death on her misshapen features contrasted horribly with those hands holding a cross in the act of prayer. That silent contrast spinning in my mind, I then departed, leaving the priest and his friend to say the litany for the dead. I wandered over the countryside like a wraith and when I returned to town I heard the terrible tale of those marauding soldiers who had vandalized the whole district before turning on the Castle of Fratta in a drunken fury. The abuses that gang of assassins must have visited on that poor old woman left alone to face them – well, I did not wish to think about them. But what little the Chaplain had seen – the deplorable state of her dead body and the chaos of her room – made it clear what brutal mockery she had endured. I confess that my enthusiasm for the French cooled considerably, but then, when I thought about it, I couldn't believe such atrocities had been committed with premeditation, and, deciding that these must have been the bestial acts of a few soldiers, I determined to ask for justice.

General Bonaparte was reputed to be a true republican and defender of liberty and so I got it in my head to appeal to him; and two days later, when the old Countess's body had been laid to rest in the family tomb with the usual honours, I set out for Udine, where the General Staff of the French Army was stationed. From what I had learned I believed that the guilty soldiers were part of the battalion of riflemen escorting the grain convoy that had left Portogruaro that same day, and so I had some hopes that they would be sought out for exemplary punishment. The admirable virtues of Italy's young liberator were a guarantee of prompt justice, I thought.

At Udine I found the usual disarray. The guests giving orders, the hosts obeying. The Venetian authorities had no backbone, no dignity, no ideas. The people and the local signori were split into many factions, one odder and more wrongheaded than the next. But most of those who a few days before had cheered the Hungarian hussars and the Bohemian dragoons now hailed the French sans-culottes. This was what many centuries of political void had produced: people thought they had been put in this world as spectators, not as actors. Actors get paid and those who sit in their chairs rightly pay those who move about for them.

Commander-in-chief Napoléon Bonaparte (as he was then known) was billeted in Casa Florio. I asked for an interview with him, saying I had some very serious reports to convey about events in the province, and because he was already thick as thieves with the Venetian malcontents I was granted an audience. He did not know what I had come about.

The General was in the hands of his manservant, who was shaving him. In those days he was happy to appear manly and he even sported a certain simplicity in the manner of Cato, and so at first sight I felt quite reassured. He was lean, gaunt and somewhat fretful; his long hair hung lank over his brow, temples and neck, well past the collar of his jacket. He looked, in fact, like that fine portrait that Appiani left us[7] (it hangs at Villa Melzi in Bellagio), a gift from the First Consul and Cisalpine President to the Vice President – and a charming lure from the wolf to the lamb. Except at that time he was even more emaciated and looked as if he had only a few years to live, and, in fact, his great slenderness added a halo of martyrdom to the liberator's glory. He was sacrificing his life for the people's good; who would not sacrifice theirs for him?

'What do you want, citizen?' he said curtly, rubbing his lips with the lace of his towel.

'Citizen General,' said I, bowing only very slightly so as not to offend his republican sensibilities, 'the matters I've come to speak to you about are highly important and extremely sensitive.'

'Go on,' he said, nodding at his servant, who was continuing his work. 'Mercier here knows no more Italian than my horse.'

'Then let me put this simply, a man appealing for justice to one in the heart of the battle for justice and liberty. Three days ago at the Castle of Fratta, some French riflemen committed a horrendous crime. While the main body of the troops was carrying out an unauthorized sack of the public granaries and treasury at Portogruaro, a few stragglers invaded the house of some honourable signori, and they so abused and tortured an infirm old woman of more than one hundred years old who had been left alone there that she died of horror and despair.'

'You see how the Most Serene Signoria exasperates my soldiers!' shouted the General, now jumping to his feet, because the man had finished wiping off his chin. 'They tell the people we are assassins, that we are heretics, and when my soldiers appear everyone flees, abandoning their houses. How can you expect such a reception to encourage humanity and moderation? Oh, I tell you: I shall retrace my steps and clean these bothersome insects out of my way!'

'Citizen General, I do understand that a false reputation may have stood in the way of a warm first reception. But there is a way to prove that reputation wrong, I believe, and if you, with a shining example of justice . . .'

'Oh, I see, you speak to me of justice today, on the eve of a great battle on the Isonzo! We should have had our justice two or three years ago! Now they are reaping what they have sown. But I am comforted to see that the worst damage is not done to them by my soldiers. Bergamo, Brescia and Crema have already freed themselves from San Marco, and soon that foolish, fraudulent oligarchy will finally understand that their real enemies are not the French. The hour of liberty has struck; it is time to stand up and fight or be crushed. The French Republic holds out a hand to all peoples so that they can take back their liberty and exercise their innate and inexpugnable rights! Liberty is more than worth a few sacrifices! There is no way around it.'

'But Citizen General, I do not speak of refusing any useful sacrifice in the cause of liberty. It merely seems to me that the martyrdom of an old Countess . . .'

'I repeat, citizen: who was it that exasperated my soldiers? Who turned the minds of peasants and country priests against them? The Senate and the Inquisition of Venice. Have no doubt that where the real villains are concerned, justice will be done!'

'And yet, wouldn't an example serve to avoid such disorders in the future?

'Examples, citizen, will come from my riflemen on the battlefields. Have no doubt about it! Justice will come to them, too – as long as you don't expect her to kill them all! For they will be in the front line, where their very blood will wash away the shame of their crime and promote the cause of liberty! So evil will evolve into good and the people's cause will be advanced by the very crimes that have disfigured it!'

'Citizen General, I pray you observe . . .'

'Enough, citizen! There is nothing I have not observed. The good of the Republic, in the first place. Do you want to be a hero? Forget these personal quibbles and join us, join those good and stalwart men who in your own country, too, are fighting this long, stubborn, clandestine war against the privileges of imbeciles and the gout-ridden. In another fifteen days you will see me again. By then peace, glory and universal liberty will have erased all memory of these momentary excesses.'

With these words the great Napoleon finished dressing and moved off towards the next room, where some senior officers were waiting for him. It seemed he was neither very pleased about my visit, nor much disposed to give me any more attention, and so I headed slowly down the stairs, considering the tone of our conversation. In truth I didn't understand much, and yet those big words of his – liberty, the people – and that curt, austere manner, fogged my mind and, in the end, my hatred for the Venetian patricians outweighed even that for the French riflemen. The Countess's horrendous fate seemed a mere drop of water next to that sea of beatitude that would overwhelm us if we backed the Republican Army. Citizen Bonaparte was perhaps a bit harsh, a bit insensitive, even somewhat heartless, but I pardoned him, thinking that his great responsibilities demanded it for the moment. And so, little by little, I let peace come to the dead and went back to thinking about the living, and in the letter I sent to Venice to announce the sad event to the family I probably blamed the irresponsible Venetian government and the foolish fears of the people more than I did the invaders' barbarous mayhem.

The Chaplain was astonished to see me return to Fratta empty-handed, yet calmer and happier than when I left. Monsignor and the Captain, who were camped out in the Castle, listened to me with frank terror as I told them of my audience with General Bonaparte.

'Did you really see him?' the Captain asked.

'By Jove if I saw him! He was being shaved, actually.'

'Oh, he shaves his beard?[8] I would have thought he wore it long!'

'That reminds me,' Monsignor jumped in, 'since Mamma's death' (a long sigh) 'I haven't shaved my chin or my head. Faustina!' (She, too, had come back.) 'Put a pan of water on to heat!'

Thus Monsignor Orlando of Fratta endured his private, and the public, grief. I can only say that among all the inhabitants of the castle in that fatal hour, the ones who showed themselves to be most feeling were the animals (and I don't except myself, for my odious oblivion on that terrible day was not erased by remorse that came late and in vain). Besides Marchetto's old nag, who left the brawl in town and came home – as I should have – there was the Captain's dog, old Marocco, who refused to accompany his master on his cowardly flight to Lugugnana. He wandered instead around the empty Castle, sniffing here and there as if in search of a finer soul than his own, but he was not to find it. Instead, some stupid, degenerate Frenchman entertained himself by running him through with his bayonet in the middle of the courtyard. When that bunch of cowards from the Castle got back home, they were so stunned and confused they didn't even smell the stink of the dog's corpse that had been infecting the air for three days. It fell to me to notice it when I returned from Udine and I ordered one of the peasants to bury it in a ditch. But after the man had gone out to do this good deed, he came back to call me, so that I, too, could witness an astonishing thing.

On top of Marocco's already worm-ridden cadaver, his longtime companion the tabby cat had taken up his place and there was no way he could be budged. Caresses, threats, brute force: none of these had the least effect and I was moved to something like veneration for that poor dead creature, who had aroused such deep emotion in a cat. I finally had the cat removed and ordered Marocco to be buried there in the courtyard where he had received his sad proof of loyalty. The man buried him three arm-spans deep and filled the hole with earth, thinking the job was done. But for months and months it was necessary to replace the earth every morning because the faithful cat spent his nights digging it out so that he could rest on the remains of his friend. What could I do? I respected the beast's grief, but I did not have the heart to move those remains, so dear to him and so hard on our sense of smell. I covered them with a stone. And so the cat took up residence on the stone and, day and night, howling and keening and circling around the sepulchre, mourned his friend. There he remained for several months and then he died, and this I know for certain because I didn't fail to inform myself how that tragic friendship ended.

And they say that cats do not have their little piece of soul! As for dogs, their reputation in this regard is well established.

We place their love among the affections of the family; and if they hold the lowest place, they are also the most constant. When the prodigal son came home, I'd wager the first to celebrate his return was the family dog! And when I hear grumbling about that dangerous, useless canine family that competes with human beings for food and sometimes infects them with a fearful, incurable disease, I can only say, 'Respect dogs!' Perhaps today we are on the same plane; perhaps – God forbid! – one day they'll be considered better than us! In the history of humanity, there have been other times like these. We bipeds oscillate between the hero and the hangman, between the angel and Beelzebub. Dogs are always the same; they never change, like the North Star. Loving, patient, devoted: right up until they die. What more could you ask, you who would hesitate to destroy even a tribe of cannibals because they are human?

Meanwhile, I have to confess that my life at Fratta no longer seemed either as peaceful or as commendable as it had a month before. The French had invaded my head; I dreamed of becoming someone of importance, and that seemed to me the best way to regain la Pisana's love. I could think of little but Venice and the fall of San Marco, the new order that would arise, the liberty and equality of peoples. This General Bonaparte was not much older than I. Why should I, too, not suddenly become a winner of battles and saviour of peoples? Ambition, arm in arm with love, was luring me, and I forgot my pity for Giulio Del Ponte and his cruel passion. I neglected my duties in the chancery and spent most of my time polishing my political doctrine with Donato or fencing or target-shooting with Bruto Provedoni. Among the young Provedoni siblings, Bruto was the most fervent defender of the cause of liberty and Bradamante and Aquilina often laughed at us. They had watched the French pass through without, in truth, forming the favourable opinion we held, and we, for our part, would fly into a rage when they tried to break the spell by reminding us of some of the barbarous acts done by those propagators of civilization. Above all I did not want to hear about the torture of the old Countess Badoer. I knew they were right, but did not want to admit it, and that made me feel three times more poisonous.

I have no idea what would have happened had things gone on in that way, but fortune intervened in my favour, despite my mad ambitions and pride.

One fine day (it was near the end of March) there appeared a letter from Venice written in the Countess's hand. I read and reread the signature. No mistake: it really was from her. I couldn't have been more astonished that she had written to me, and even more so that at the top of the page she began with the words 'Dear nephew'. My amazement was such that I almost lost my head, but I had the good sense to hold on and try to understand the rest of the letter. Imagine who had arrived in Venice? My father, no less! Was it not unbelievable? A man thought to be dead, a man who hadn't been heard of for twenty-five years! Reason all but refused to believe it, but my heart, eager for love, said yes, and before I had even finished reading the letter my heart was on its way to Venice. I think it took me almost half a day to read the entire letter, and then, during the journey, I read it over again every once in a while for fear I had misunderstood and got my hopes up in vain.

I gave the chancery over to Fulgenzio's care and left the same day. My heart could not sit still and my head was filled with so many hopes twined with memories, passions, desires, the impossible, that I could not sit still, either. The Countess had advised I should prepare myself to take up the place in society due me as a representative of the patrician house of Altoviti, and she added that my father had not written himself, because he had forgotten the use of the Italian alphabet, and that I should find her not in Casa Frumier but in Casa Perabini in Cannaregio, and finally, she sent her dear nephew her kisses, and those of his cousin Pisana. She and my father made my heart beat a great deal faster than did my aunt.

ELEVEN

How Venice comes to understand that the states of the Serenissima are part of Italy and of the world. On 1 May 1797 I finally join the Great Council with the status of patrician. Plots against the government are fomented by friend and foe alike. The Republic of San Marco falls like Nebuchadnezzar's giant idol and I become secretary of the new Municipality.

The first person I saw and embraced in Venice was la Pisana; the first who spoke to me was the Countess, who, running towards me from the far end of the apartment, began to shout: 'Bravo, my dear Carlino! Bravo! How happy I am to see you! There now, a nice kiss like a real nephew!'

I detached myself very unwillingly from la Pisana's kisses to receive those of the Countess, who looked even more sallow-skinned and hook-nosed than before. But despite the whirlwind of feelings spinning me around I still had enough sense to wonder at such an unexpected reception. I decided I would only be able to understand in time; meanwhile, the Countess sent Rosa out to find my father. That this mission was assigned to the maid surprised me a little and all the more because Rosa, no longer young but still as ill-tempered as ever, obeyed with a great deal of grumbling. Such a job normally belonged to a footman and I wondered just how much of a retinue the Countess had. While I stood there waiting, in fact, I was greatly surprised to see that the rooms were both bare and in terrible disarray: dust and cobwebs made up the decoration; there were a few pieces of furniture, a mirror screwed to the wall, a few emaciated chairs scattered around: it was poverty, in short, at home in a palazzo. What distracted me from such melancholy thoughts was la Pisana's appearance. I had never seen her lovelier, fresher and more animated, no matter how much she sought to hide her splendid charms with all the thousand tricks she'd newly learned in Venice. But whether it was nature's gift or my own blindness, even that artifice, applied to her features, became pure loveliness. However, she seemed even quieter than usual: at times she stared at me soulfully, then lowered her eyes, blushing, and my words seemed to bring voluptuous pleasure to her ears without passing by way of her brain. All this was on my mind while the Countess was drowning me in a flood of chatter of which I understood not one iota, except that the name of my father often came up and it seemed to me that she, too, was very pleased by his miraculous and unexpected return.

'Is she never coming back, that silly Rosa?' the lady grumbled. 'I didn't like to send you out, because I wanted to give you back your papa myself, and to be part of the joy of your reunion. Oh, what a fine papa you have, Carlino!'

La Pisana seemed to blush even more at those words, as if embarrassed by the gaze I kept fixed on her. At last Rosa returned and said that my father would be with us as soon as he had concluded some business in the Piazza. I wanted to go out looking for him to speed the happy moment, but the Countess, insisting I must stay, prevailed. An hour went by, the bell rang, and a hale and hearty little gentleman, lame in one leg and dressed half like a Turk, half like a Christian, came limping into the entry hall. I ran to meet him there and the Countess, running behind me, began to shout, 'Carlino, it's your father! Embrace your father!' and I threw myself into his arms and I shed my first tears of joy ever in the folds of his Armenian cloak. My father was neither very affectionate nor very loquacious towards me. He was quite amazed to learn that a young man with a name like mine should be hidden away in such an obscure cubbyhole as a country clerk's office and promised that once I was inscribed in the Libro d'Oro as his legitimate son I would take my due place on the Maggior Consiglio.

The canny old fellow spoke in such a way that I could not tell if he were serious or in jest and every time he came to the end of a phrase, as if to validate his argument, he would beat the back of his hand on his overcoat pocket, which replied with a attractive tinkle of *zecchini* and *doblas*. At each of these metallic chords, the Countess's yellow face was lit by a rosy glow, like the darkened sky of a storm under the sun's oblique gaze. I watched and listened as if in a dream. This father of mine that had sailed in from Turkey, with riches in one hand and power in the other and a large dose of mischief in both, was beyond all expectations. I couldn't stop staring at those grey eyes of his, a little bloodshot, a little shifty, that for so many years had looked on the Eastern sun; those deep, whimsical lines under his turban, shaped by the corrosive action of God knows what thoughts; those gestures – those of a man of authority or a rude sailor? – that he employed constantly to underscore the halting obscurity of a language more Arabic than Venetian. He was obviously a man accustomed to life; meaning that nothing fazed him; he had little belief and still less faith and, having sacrificed himself for a long time to the prospect of future gain, anything that led to the right end was fine by him. At times, means can thus be a school to despise ends.

At any rate, this was how I judged my father, and I must confess that from the first I enjoyed his company with more curiosity than love. I saw him as one of those old Venetian merchants of Tana[1] or Smyrna, who by dint of their cunning, sharp wits and sharp tongues got the Tartars to forgive or forget they were of a different faith. Turks in Constantinople, Christians in Venice and traders everywhere had made Venice the broker between two worlds back then. There was even a waspish, thin grey beard to link my father's appearance to that of Pantaloon, but he came late on the world's stage. He could have been one of those comic characters still dressed up in their Persian or Mameluke costumes, who, after the curtain has fallen, appear to announce tomorrow's programme. I say this without wishing to diminish his paternal authority.

After he had sat with us for a while, to many exclamations of cordiality and wonder on the Countess's part and a few smothered sighs from la Pisana, my father invited me to come out with him, and he led me to San Zaccaria where he was lodged in an attractive house, decorated in something like the Turkish style with carpets and divans and pipes everywhere. Tables, and some cupboards to put things away, were lacking, but great numbers of armoires, built to contain everything one could desire, made up for them. A dark-skinned mulatto woman, forty years old or more, served coffee from morning until night, and the way she and the master communicated with signs and monosyllables was highly entertaining to watch; I don't believe they spoke in any language of this world, and indeed the Devil probably talks like them on his terrestrial excursions.

My father took off his three-cornered hat and put on a large Moorish cap, lit the pipe, had the coffee served, and pressed me to sit down like him with my legs crossed on the carpet. Thus the future patrician of the Maggior Consiglio busied himself trying to master Baghdad etiquette. He told me he was very grateful to his wife for having left him such a fine inheritance as me, some compensation perhaps for the few pleasures marriage had provided; and he made me understand that he was willing to overlook certain musty old suspicions that had troubled their harmony and brought my mother back to Venice. And, finally, he said he thought I resembled him, especially around the eyes and the nostrils, and that was enough to reconnect him with undying affection to his only son.

I thanked him in my turn for such kindly sentiments towards me and I asked him to pardon me if he found my upbringing defective due to my having been raised an orphan. I didn't want him to know about the rather dishonourable way my aunt and uncle had looked after me, and I think my restraint earned his esteem right from that first meeting. He watched me out of the corner of his eye and, although he seemed to pay little attention to my words, he noted all those other signs that his long experience had taught him he could use to understand men.

And the sentence his experience delivered was quite favourable. At any rate that was the impression I gained, for he grew even more affectionate. He then asked me to tell him about the Contessina Clara and how she had become a nun, and he mentioned Signor Lucilio many times with the greatest respect and marvelled that the Fratta family did not consider themselves honoured to accept him in marriage. Islamic equality tempered his natural aristocracy, or so I thought, and I was confirmed in this opinion when he began to make fun of the way the Most Illustrious Partistagno was trying to push back the new century with his grandfather's sword. I was quite amazed to find that my father knew as much as I of such matters, and also that he would ask another to enlighten him when he was already so well informed. However, it is always best to know things from two mouths instead of just one, and he followed this wise proverb quite faithfully. He then broached the subject of la Pisana and all her suitors in Venice, and her grave error in not saying yes to the richest of them, so as to repair the family dignity and her mother's fortunes.

'Aha!' I thought to myself. 'Aristocracy is making a reappearance!'

Above all, it seemed Giulio Del Ponte was a *saltamartino* as my father called him: a foolish cricket. La Pisana should get him out from under her feet, that jester with his coughing, his grief and his melancholy. Pretty girls should look to handsome young men; in the Levant, the weaklings were sent out to sell peanuts on the streets. All these aphorisms coming from my father excited me and I was just about to confess everything to him. It wasn't compassion for Giulio that held me back, but rather a certain shame at appearing a boy in love before a man of such experience and reason. He continued to watch me out of the corner of his eye, while he was telling me of the Countess's financial dissolution and the ruinous indifference of young Count Rinaldo, who just kept on chasing chimeras in the library, while the chisellers and the cozeners were snatching the last scrapings from their coffers out of his mother's hands. He also confessed to me with a certain malign satisfaction that the Countess had tried to measure the weight of his *doblas*, but he hadn't even let her see the colour of them – and here he slapped his pocket to produce that same jingling of coins.

That meanness didn't go down well with me and I'm almost sure he saw it. But he didn't do me the courtesy of changing the subject; rather, he insisted on it like a man stubbornly convinced that money is the only thing both valued and valuable. While I, instead, would have given half the few ducats in my pocket to the first beggar who asked, and maybe I think that way because I've always had few of them. Poverty taught me to be generous and its precepts remained useful to me when it was no longer my tutor or companion. However, I would soon discover that my father was no miser. That very day he took me to all the finest shops so I could be decked out like a young man from the best San Marco family. Then he showed me my room, which had its own door to the stairway, and left me, promising I would be the second founder of the Altoviti family.

'Our forebears were among the founders of Venice,' he told me before leaving. 'They came from Aquileia; they were Romans from the Metella line. Now that Venice is about to be remade, an Altoviti should have a hand in it. Leave that to me!'

My father's boastful words were full of those airs proverbially put on by the penniless nobility of the island of Torcello, but the Levantine *doblas* did the trick and my right to be inscribed in the Libro d'Oro was quickly recognized. My first appearance as a voting patrician on the Maggior Consiglio took place on 2 April 1797.[2] As for my father, he didn't want to be involved; it seemed he didn't think himself worthy to lead the rebuilding of the line and was content to supply me with the means. Those few days I spent as a gentleman in Venice, entering the best salons, thanks to the Countess of Fratta and the Illustrious Frumiers, provided me with great renown. I wasn't unpleasant to look at, my manners were a cut above the general affectation, I had a discreet level of culture but not so much as to suffocate with pedantry the goodly vivacity nature had granted me. And above all, I believe that rumours of my wealth made me thought an excellent match by all the young ladies in search of a husband, and by all the mothers of such. *Carlino di qua, Carlino di là, tutti mi chiamavano, tutti mi volevano.*[3] Even some young married ladies didn't disdain me; in short, I had only to choose among many varieties of happiness.

For the time being I chose none of them, but the novelty kept me so busy that even la Pisana didn't occupy my mind when she was out of sight. This no doubt vexed her, but she was in a haughty mood and refused to show it, merely venting her annoyance on poor Giulio. I often used to see him in those days and would even have felt pity for him anew if I hadn't been so busy as to have no time at all. The poor fellow was still somewhere between life and death, and with one thing and another, he was reduced to such a state that every fly buzzing around la Pisana made him quiver with terror.

Meanwhile, Italy grew more and more tormented. For more than six months Modena, Bologna and Ferrara had been acting out a servile imitation of France, prodded by France itself: the Cispadane Republic,[4] a mere soap bubble. In the Kingdom of Sardinia, already occupied and reduced to a French military province, Carlo Emanuele succeeded Vittorio Amedeo. All Italy dirtied its trouser knees before Bonaparte's triumphal advance, and he, meanwhile, tricked one and mocked another with alliances, promises, half-measures. The Venetian states on the mainland, astutely provoked by him, revolted noisily against the Lion, and everywhere there were Liberty Trees, how deeply rooted only he knew. And then came the moment when he doubted fortune was on his side, because of the great cloud of enemies before him and because of the distances that separated these new provinces, neither very faithful nor completely duped, from France. Refusing all proposed negotiations, he cast caution to the wind and went all the way to Leoben to impose a peace settlement on Austria.

The Most Serene Signoria had seen the whirlwind of war pass by the way the dying man glimpses the Grim Tyrant in his hazy imagination. Even before that powerful enemy crushed her bit by bit and dishonoured her with deceit and disgrace, Venice had done nothing but humiliate herself, stand by, pray and beg. The Special Provveditore on the mainland, Francesco Battaja, was perhaps the most ardent in his vile servitude, and his anxious toadying was further disgraced by his even more cowardly treachery. When the Venetians humiliated themselves by complaining about the invasion of their cities, the occupation of their castles and fortresses, the popular uprisings, the lootings of their treasuries and the general devastation, Bonaparte responded with mock proposals for an alliance, ironic laments and demands for taxes. Procuratore Francesco Pesaro and Giambattista Corner, Savio of mainland Venice, met with the General in Gorizia to protest the French role in provoking the Bergamo and Brescia revolts, as well as the French pirates hiding out in the recesses of the Gulf of Venice. Bonaparte's reply was such that the two envoys, at the bottom of their report, wrote that only divine intervention could bring about the outcome they desired, for it was not to be hoped for in such merciless conditions. Francesco Pesaro was both upright and a man of foresight, but he lacked constancy and energy, as he would later reveal, and so was unable either to save the Republic or to lend its fall a token of grandeur.

Meanwhile the rioters continued their revolts and the fearful gave them a pretext, and in the Maggior Consiglio we watched a strange spectacle in which cowardice and philosophizing outvoted courage and stability. True philosophy, instead, would have been to find the public welfare in personal dignity, rather than ask it, on bended knee, of a condottiero. I was among the dreamers (and I regret it and am sorry for it), but I was in good faith and I would have gone that way in any case, given my friendship with Amilcare, who was still in prison, and Lucilio, so closely linked to the French ambassador, and my father, more convinced than anyone that Venice was soon to be reformed.

Oh, but it was a hard lesson! To repudiate and scorn the old virtues without having shielded our hearts with new ones; to beg for liberty, while our souls were still so deeply servile! Some rights can be claimed only by those who deserve them; liberty cannot be requested, it must be willed, and those who cravenly request it deserve to be spat on. Bonaparte was right and Venice wrong. Only the hero who is right can also be despicable in his means. The democratic side, which thought of itself as French and was, in fact, French, did not outweigh the others in Venice in number, but in hardiness of spirit, firmness of action and, above all, in powerful backing. Their adversaries represented no side at all; they were but an inert quantity of cowardice and impotence, whose greater numbers gave them no greater force. Nerves obey the soul, arms obey ideas; but where there is neither soul nor ideas, there is lethargy or foolishness.

The Venetian obscurantists were in the lethargic camp. It was the French Legation and not the Senate or College of Savi that governed at the time. Beneath the very eye and to the great annoyance of the Inquisition, the Legation prepared the downfall of Venice's feeble aristocracy, and a great many men of letters and manners gave them a hand. The fearful dungeons became harmless spectres; an order from Ambassador Lallement let prisoners of state walk through those gates that had never swung open before except to corpses and those condemned to death. Dr Lucilio distinguished himself in his fervent devotion to the French cause and perhaps his adult zeal was somehow rooted deep in the mysterious turbulence of his youth. He was, as they used to say, a philosopher, and philosophers made up most of the ringleaders of the secret societies, which were even then burrowing, dark and corrosive, under the cracked veneer of the old society.

Whatever the case, he put all the energy and all the intelligence he had into his liberal gospel, and the patricians who met him in the Piazza shivered like sinners when the Devil comes to them at night. True enough, if one of them fell ill, he didn't hesitate to turn to that demon for a cure. And then the celebrated doctor would take that pulse and study that face with a little grin that vindicated the hatred he'd suffered. 'I despise you so much that I even want to cure you,' he seemed to say. 'I know you are my enemy, but it means nothing to me.' The ladies showed Lucilio such shy and shamefaced respect that they seemed bewitched: respect that at a single glance or sign became more like veneration or submission than love. They used to say he was a master of Mesmer's art and could do miracles; he used that power of his, however, quite sparingly, and there was not one lady who could claim to have intercepted a flash of desire from his eyes. He was as chaste, independent and mysterious as a sorcerer, and perhaps I alone knew the secret of his austerity, for the customs of the day and his reputation as a fine doctor and serious philosopher did not encourage any suspicions that he was utterly possessed by love.

And yet he was, I can assure you; and that love, pervading a soul as large as his, took on the force and grandeur of an irresistible passion. Oh, you will say that he left Clara in peace with her mother, that he never ran riot and tried to climb the balcony or sing her a serenade from a gondola, that he allowed her to enter the convent, and so forth. But his love was not of the ordinary kind: he did not want to steal her away, but to obtain her. Sure of Clara's affection and that she would wait a hundred years without changing her mind or falling into despair, he yearned for that moment, hastened with all the ardour of his deeds and sacrifices, when they would beg him to take her, honoured to have her join with him in marriage. Love and his political faith were all one sentiment – so lively, so forceful, so stubborn – as are all the powers of a strong nature when they are twisted into a single strand. When he chanced upon the arrogant, eagle-nosed face of the Countess or the vague, colourless features of young Count Rinaldo or those charming, somewhat mawkish little faces in Casa Frumier, he would smile to himself. He felt the time would soon come when he would be master and then he'd be able to lay down whatever laws he liked with those ninnies. Their pliant natures and quickness to take fright made it clear he did not have to worry about any troublesome opposition.

But the Countess, for her part, was not idle either; she knew Lucilio better than he imagined and she thought the walls of a convent a weak defence against his audacity. And so she had entrusted her daughter to a certain Madre Redenta Navagero, the saintliest and most astute nun in the convent, so she could strengthen the girl's soul against the Devil's temptations with fresh arguments. And Madre Redenta had indeed gone at it vigorously and, although I wouldn't say she had made great progress, she had swept Clara's head free, if not of Lucilio, of all the other things of this world, certainly. It was no mean feat: many threads had been cut and now there was just the big one, the master cable; but shaking it and sawing it and re-sawing it, she never lost hope she'd be able to cut through that, too, and deliver that blessed soul to the ecstasies of the cloistered life. Clara, though a maid inside the convent, had occasional news of Lucilio, but word came seldom and in the intervals she sought comfort in memory and worship.

However, worship gradually began to take the place of memory, especially when her confessor and Madre Redenta convinced her not to linger much over worldly matters and to pray abundantly, now that prayer was so greatly needed because of the urgent perils facing the Republic and the Church. In the minds of those nuns, nearly all of them patricians, the Republic of San Marco and the Christian religion were one thing, and to hear them talk about France and the French must have been truly hilarious. There was no difference between the word 'Paris' and the word 'Inferno' to them and the oldest nuns shivered in horror to think of the terrible deeds those devils incarnate would commit once they invaded Venice. The younger ones would say, 'There's no need to be frightened! God will assist us!'

And a few of them, the ones who'd taken vows because they were obedient or distracted, sincerely hoped one day they might need that divine assistance. This is not the place to say that it would have been something like the crusaders of Pisa, who arrived when they were no longer needed; but in any case, those who never had a genuine vocation are not really obliged to seek or pretend to have it. Clara, more honest and less sanctimonious, was scandalized by these semi-heresies. As for the French, she agreed with the elder nuns, especially after hearing of her grandmother's dreadful fate, and although some of the story had been withheld from her, she had nonetheless wept for many days and many long nights. In all good faith she believed the French were bestial, heretical, possessed by the Devil, and, during her prayers, after she had asked the Lord to deliver her and the others from all evils, she mentally implored him to free Venice from the French, the greatest evil, as she saw it.

For Venice, if this was not the greatest evil it was certainly the newest and most imminent. All the other old, inveterate evils no longer made themselves felt. This was the open, bloody wound that swelled in the State, sending all its spoiled and stagnant humours to the heart. Every day brought news of a new defection, a new betrayal, a new rebellion. The Doge's bonnet was forever askew, even during the great ceremonies; the Savi lost their heads and called on the ambassador in Paris to buy the secrets of the Directory from some doorkeeper. They even tried to gain Bonaparte's sympathy through a long chain of friends, beginning with a French banker who lived in Venice and who was paid, I believe, several thousand ducats. What props to hold up a wobbling government!

The story of the Republic of Venice is much like the winter season on the stage: a tragedy alone is not enough to occupy the long hours; it must be followed by a farce. And farce there was, though it was not always very funny. Many a young fellow, less because he was a liberal than out of sheer bravado, went wild sending up those brainless old wig-wearers. It is the same with all the greats who have become small, all the powerful in a shambles: all of a sudden they are assailed by curses, abuse and scorn. The broadsides, lampoons and spoofs of those days have in later years been most useful for wrapping up sardines. It's hard to believe how much the authors of those rude, low parodies were celebrated. Giulio Del Ponte, a banterer of quick but crude wit, was delighted to be able to invest that wit at such a high return, and he threw himself into the general tattle. He revelled in the acclaim and it must be said that his little treatises were better than the rest and sometimes hit the mark with force, brio and pertinence. La Pisana, seeing him so admired and even feared, sent him a few of those glances she once favoured him with, and for those he would risk a beating on the street and even a scolding from the Countess.

I, too, annoyed my aunt with my democratic fancies, but my father's *doblas* kept her happy enough and she often laboured – elbow to her daughter's ribs – to get her to be more polite to me. That elbowing and my constant distraction irritated la Pisana and her mind wandered from me; and yet there was always that fugitive glance from her, that half-hidden blush, which would have been encouraging had I observed them properly. Giulio Del Ponte did see them and became yellow with bile, but he sought compensation in vanity, running to his friends, who flattered him day and night as the Persius Flaccus, the Juvenal, the Aristophanes of his time. Only Dr Lucilio, as much as he shared his views, warned him clearly of the danger of attacking high government officials not out of deep conviction or devotion to the public good, but out of conceit and frivolity.

'What do you know of it?' Giulio replied. 'May I not have

the citizen's proper virtues just as you pretend to have? Or must I borrow all my ideas from presumption and unease?'

Lucilio shook his head at Giulio's thoughts, so swollen with vanity and fluttering with foolishness. But perhaps he felt a secret compassion for that slender, ravaged person, his many gifts already exhausted. For the doctor could read both body and mind. And there in Giulio he had observed the symptoms of a fatal passion; and he knew that, though it was dormant, that passion was forever lodged in him and woe to him should it be reborn with all its dreadful violence. No fear of this touched Giulio, however, for now that he thought he was worth something he felt he might punish la Pisana with indifference, should she reject him. He had to repent, though, for the weathervane was ready to point elsewhere, and so he was forced to double his charm and attention to make himself pleasing. It was me he sought to outshine above all, because he had sensed in her behaviour towards me some wisp of a desire unsatisfied, some memory of love that was not yet cold. I didn't find it so easy to let him upstage me, especially after the acclaim I'd grown used to in Venice. And so hard feelings and mutual resentment grew up between us and often exploded, even in front of la Pisana, in nasty remarks and abuse. Giulio would accuse me of being an aristocrat, a San Marco-lover; I, in turn, would madly extol liberty and equality; la Pisana, too, took a heated part in these discussions and soon became the wildest and most incorrigible free-thinker, just like us. I don't think disputes like this – in which all are in agreement and each competes with the other to express the same plans and hopes – can easily be repeated today. The French were the chosen theme of our discussions; without them, we could see no progress. Giulio sang their praises in verse, I in prose, and la Pisana used her imagination to summon up scores of knights of liberty, the flames of heroism glowing on their brows. She had even gone to meet her sister in the convent and convinced the nuns that their hatred of the French was mistaken.

One day we heard that the French had entered Verona, considered until then the city most reluctant to embrace the new. The peasant militias had dispersed; the troops that had taken Bergamo and Brescia had retired to Padua and Vicenza. There was great revelry among the backers of France. But several days later came the shock of the tremendous Veronese Easter uprising,[5] with all its disgraceful atrocities against the French. Bonaparte protested angrily and warned of all-out war. Senators, Savi, Counsellors and all Venice began to think that what had long endured might also come to an end. They put their heads together to procure supplies for the Serenissima. As for defence, they gave it little thought, because, to tell the truth, no one believed in it. Finally, General Baraguay d'Hilliers surrounded the estuary with his camp and communications were cut off. Francesco Donà and Lunardo Giustinian, sent to meet Bonaparte, revealed that the General demanded a new, broader and more liberal form of government in the Republic of Venice. He also insisted that the Admiral of the Port and the State Inquisitors be consigned to him to face charges for hostile acts against a French ship trying to enter the Lido port.

The Savi understood the warning and put themselves at the humble service of the General, 'beard and wig', as they say in Venice. They decided the Maggior Consiglio deliberated too slowly to meet the demands of the day and improvised a sort of requiem power, a college of undertakers for the moribund Republic, made up of all the members of the Signoria, the Advisory Savi, the three chiefs of the Council of Ten and the three Avogadori of the Commune: forty-one members in all, with the Most Serene Doge at the head, under the convenient name of the Conference. Meanwhile, rumour had it that sixteen thousand conspirators with daggers drawn had already crept into Venice to carry out the Slaughter of the Innocents among the nobles. Imagine what a comfort for the Conference! I remember – trying to sound as worldly as I could – asking Lucilio how true he thought that rumour was.

'Come, Carlino!' he replied with a shrug of his shoulders. 'Do you think the French are so mad as to hire sixteen thousand real conspirators when they can obtain the same effect by having imaginary ones appear? Believe me, there is not even a pinprick of truth in all this, and yet it might as well be true, for there is no need to kill these patricians! They are already good and dead!'

The Conference met for the first time on the evening of 30 April in the Doge's private apartments. His remarks opened with the words *The gravity and severe constraints of the present circumstances*,[6] but the idiocy of the comments that followed, although pointing to some 'severe constraints', was not at all in keeping with the gravity of the circumstances. Once again it was suggested that they try to gain Bonaparte's sympathy through his close friend Haller. It was Cavaliere Dolfin who resuscitated this impressive piece of advice. Procuratore Antonio Cappello (whom I had met in Casa Frumier) stood up to deride its foolishness, and Pesaro joined him in asking that they confine the discussion to their defence capabilities and nothing more. In truth, the intentions of the French were as clear as they could be and it was pointless to invoke vague chimeras. But the Savi made sure the thread of the discussion was lost and, in the midst of things, a message from Admiral Tommaso Condulmer was delivered to the effect that the French were advancing on the laguna using rafts perched on floating barrels. The consternation was immediate and nearly universal: some tried to flee, others proposed negotiations or, better, surrender. It was then that the Most Serene Doge Lodovico Manin, pacing up and down the room and tugging his breeches up over his belly, pronounced those memorable words: *Tonight we won't be safe, even in our own beds*.

Most of the council, Procuratore Cappello assured me, were His Serenity's equals in morale and courage. It was swiftly decided to call upon the Maggior Consiglio; two deputies would be assigned to negotiate a new form of government with Bonaparte. Pesaro, furious about this cowardly deliberation, spoke with tears in his eyes about the already certain ruin of his native land and declared he would depart from Venice that very night and take refuge among the Swiss. This, however, he did not do; he took the post coach to Vienna instead, I believe. Really, I haven't the heart to try to cloak with miserable national pride the buffoonish cowardice of such scenes. They contain a great, severe lesson. You must be men if you wish to be citizens; trust in your own virtue, if you have any, not in that of others which may fail you, and not in the indulgence or sense of justice of the victor, for he is no longer constrained by fear or laws.

On the first of May, wearing my gown and my wig, I entered the Maggior Consiglio arm in arm with the Gentleman Agostino Frumier, the Senator's second-born son. The first-born, who sided with Pesaro, refused to join us. Attendance was slight that day, just over six hundred voting, the number below which no deliberation was valid. The old members were pale-faced, not from grief but from terror; the young sought to appear proud and sure, but many knew privately they would be forced to do harm to themselves and their gaiety was insincere. The decree granting the negotiators the authority to reform the Republic at their discretion was read out, along with the promise to Bonaparte that all those arrested for political crimes from the day the French Army had arrived in Italy be released from prison. In that last clause I recognized the influence of Dr Lucilio and thought of Amilcare and I was perhaps the only one there to rejoice with a certain decorum.

I was, however, a goose-brain not to see the treachery in that promise and to approve it for strictly personal reasons. The decree passed with just seven dissenting votes and there were another fourteen of the *non sinceri*, the 'undecided', who, neither approving nor rejecting the measure, maintained that the time was not right. As soon as word of the vote reached the street, the backers of the French, who were already rioting, went running to the jail. And out came the jailbirds along with the good men; the depraved, as well as the true believers – and the tale of those sixteen thousand conspirators came far closer to being true.

Now, the patricians were convinced they had shown supreme courage in ignoring the General's demand to consign the Admiral of the Lido and the State Inquisitors to the French. But Bonaparte turned the tables on them, declaring he would not receive Donà and Giustinian as the envoys of the Maggior Consiglio if those four officials were not first imprisoned and punished. And so the most humble Maggior Consiglio bowed down once again (this time by a vote of seven hundred, not five hundred as before) and the Captain of the Port and the three

Inquisitors were jailed that very day for the strange crime of having been less disloyal to the laws of their country than the others were. Francesco Battaja, the traitor, was among the Avogadori of the Commune charged with carrying out that outrageous decree. But even this was not enough for either the impatient reformers or the weak-kneed, terrorized nobles. The Conference now served up another decree ordering Condulmer not to use force against the French military, but to try to persuade them to hold off invading the Serenissima until the Schiavone troops had time to depart, and so avoid any unpleasant consequences. In short, they wanted to cut their fingernails so as not to mistakenly scratch the fellow getting ready to strangle them. If this was not the most wondrous meekness – indeed a meekness unique in all the world – I do defy sheep to come up with better. My father had come back from Turkey just in time to allow poor me to participate in this vile nonsense without knowing it. On the other hand, what difference does knowing make? Dr Lucilio was smeared worse than I in that ugly tar. Woe befalls the wise man out of touch with his times; buoyed up by confidence in his own doctrines, he quickly rises to inhabit the clouds, and if he does not lose faith immediately by virtue of his judgement, he will lose it by virtue of his experience.

Amilcare, meanwhile, had been released from prison and I took up my old friendship with him. He was another man possessed, for he saw the French as the world's liberators, and up to there perhaps his reasoning held, but it slipped when he believed them to be the liberators of Venice. I don't say that Amilcare didn't help to excite me and persuade me, too, for his ardour wasn't constrained like that of Lucilio but swelled with all the exuberance of youth. Now, guess who was liberated from the claws of the Inquisition along with Amilcare? The lord of Venchieredo. You probably weren't expecting that, because his crime was certainly not to favour the French. But I'm convinced that either he had dealings with them in prison or he was pardoned by mistake or his sentence was about to finish. Whatever the case, Lucilio gave me his news, adding mysteriously that from the Rocca d'Anfo Venchieredo had hastened to Milan where General Bonaparte was stationed and where the fate of the Republic of Venice was under diplomatic negotiation.

One evening (we were already racing at high speed towards the abyss of 12 May)[7] my father called me to his chambers, saying he had important things to tell me and that I should listen very carefully and think matters over well, because now my fortunes and the glory of the family depended on my abilities.

'Tomorrow,' he said, 'there will be a revolution in Venice.'

I started in surprise, because the Maggior Consiglio was so docile, so acquiescent, and negotiations were still under way in Milan and I didn't see how there was any need of revolution.

'Yes,' he went on, 'don't be astonished, for tonight everything will become clear. In the meantime I want to put you on the right path so you don't lose your way at the crucial moment. My son, do you know what a democratic republic is?'

'Why, certainly!' said I with all the naive enthusiasm of a young man of twenty-four. 'A democratic republic is ideal justice in perfect harmony with practical existence, the reign not of one man or another, but of the free, collective views of a whole society. He who thinks correctly has the right to govern and will govern well. That is the motto of the democratic republic.'

'Very good, very good, Carlino,' my father muttered. 'That is a fine scientific notion, which you can lay aside so that Signor Giulio may use it to make himself charming with some little verse of his. But a government of all, sought by just a few, imposed by even fewer and created by a Corsican general – a free government of people who do not wish to and do not know how to be free – well, do you have any idea what direction such a thing might take?'

I looked around quite puzzled, because in such matters I was accustomed to do my arithmetic without thinking about human beings; I would add and subtract, multiply and divide as if it were all gold, but in the end, rather than find myself before a neat, liquid sum of *zecchini*, I might very well end up with some worthless little *soldi* and *quattrini*. As I say, I hadn't thought about such things and therefore I was confused by my father's question.

'Listen to me,' he went on patiently like the teacher starting over from the beginning again, 'these things that you embellish with dreams and illusions, I have foreseen for many years, just as they are taking place. I do not understand your fancies in truth, nor do I pretend to, but I do see in them a good dose of youth and inexperience. If you had spent some time dealing with a pasha or the Grand Vizier I believe you would spew less philosophy, but you would see better and further. The Mamelukes' plump guile teaches us to recognize the slender, subtle guile of the Christian. Believe me, for I have known it. And I didn't know it for nothing, because I was working to further my own ends, and I would still be doing so, had I not, returning to Venice, remembered you. And then, you know, I thought, "By Allah! Providence has sent you the ball at just the right moment! You were old and suddenly you can grow younger by forty years with a wave of the hand. Be bold, Bey. Give your place to the younger horse and you will get to the post first." In short, Carlino, I took you as my certain and legitimate son and I wanted you to inherit my hopes before I die. Are you the man to take on this task? That is what we shall soon see.'

'Speak, Father,' I said, when the pause after that long, half-Mohammedan peroration continued.

'Speak? Speak? It's not as simple as you think. These are things that must be understood without words. However, seeing your ignorance, I shall try to explain myself. First, you should know that I have a certain amount of credit, a certain amount of influence, with these Frenchified young fellows and with the French themselves, who now control Italy's future. Covert influence, not so very immediate influence, if you will, but nevertheless, influence. And this is crowned by several million piastres whose gleaming rays nicely reflect my glory. Carlino, I leave this all to you, I hand it over to you, so long as you assure me a divan, a pipe and ten cups of coffee a day. I hand it over to you for the greater lustre of Casa Altoviti. There's no help for it. This is my *idée fixe*: to have a doge in the family! And I assure you that we shall succeed if you will leave it all to me!'

'What, I . . . the Doge?' my voice was flat and I could hardly breathe. 'You want me to become Doge just like that?'

'Oh excellent, Carlino, you grasp things quicker than I could have hoped. The Doge's job is about to become far more profitable and far less irksome and dangerous. You will bring in the ducats and I will make them bear fruit. Six years and we shall buy the entire island of Torcello and the Altoviti family will become a dynasty.'

'But Father mine, whatever are you saying?' I can assure you that I thought he was one step from utter madness.

'Oh,' he went on, 'I don't see why you are surprised. Under the new order that will stick us together, those who are deserving will be in charge of those who are not. So it will work in the abstract. But concretely, given such habits and customs as we have here, do you not think the richest and the cleverest will be judged the most deserving? Every era has its lucky souls, my son, and we would be idiots not to act on our own behalf . . .'

'Heavens, how all looks ugly and corrupt to you! And what a sad role you assign me, who had set out to fight for liberty and justice!'

'Excellent, Carlino! But there is no other road but mine to set out from. For if you remain among the crowd I defy you to fight. You will only be crushed. If the true and the good are to triumph you must be at the front – even elbow your way there, it matters not. Just think how harmful it would be if the dissolute and the ne'er-do-well were to claim those places at the front! Therefore, my son, you must take your place, so that the others may take theirs – and may your intentions excuse your methods. I don't say you will become Doge tomorrow or the day after, but if you will be somewhat patient, the medlars will ripen quicker than you think! Meanwhile, I wanted you to be forewarned so that you can do as your friends urge and not abstain out of false modesty. Do you think you are an upright man with good, firm intentions? Don't you think the public business should be directed by one who loves his country and does not make deals with the enemy?'

'Oh, yes, Father, I do think so.'

'Courage then, Carlino! Tonight Signor Lucilio will speak to you more clearly and you will know, comprehend and decide. Stay by his side. Do not waver, do not draw back. He who has a conscience and a heart must step forward with generosity and courage, not for his own vanity but for the good of all.'

'Have no fear, Father. I shall step forward.'

'For now, it's enough that you let yourself be pushed. In any event, we understand one another. You will be backed by the nobles and you have the democrats' favour. Your luck cannot fail. I go now to Monsieur Villetard[8] to put the final clauses in order. We shall see each other this evening.'

I was so astonished and puzzled after this exchange that I didn't know which wall to beat my head on. The worst was that I understood almost nothing. I was to take the lead, perhaps even the highest seat in the Republic? What did this madness mean? My father had come back with yet more tales from the *Thousand and One Nights* when he returned from the East, it seemed. And those remarks of his about revolution, about clauses and all that: what did they signify? Monsieur Villetard was the young secretary of the French Legation, but on what authority did my dear father deal with him on matters of state? The more I thought about it, the more my thoughts went spinning into the clouds. I wouldn't have come down at all had Lucilio not arrived to give me back my bearings. He invited me to follow him to a place where matters of the utmost importance for the public good were being discussed; in the street we met some others, unknown to me, who were waiting for him, and together we made our way towards one of the most deserted alleys in the city, behind the Arsenale bridge. After a long, brisk, silent walk, we entered a dark and empty hall and climbed the stairs by the dubious light of an oil lamp. No one opened the door to us, no one showed us in; we were like a company of ghosts haunting the dreams of some scoundrel.

We finally arrived in a bare, damp room and were granted less miserly illumination; by the light of four candles on a table I was able to see all of those assembled and more or less distinguish their features. There were about thirty of us altogether, most of us young, including Amilcare and Giulio Del Ponte, the first looking fiery and impatient; the second, very pale and dishearteningly lethargic. There was Agostino Frumier and also Vittorio Barzoni,[9] a large, impetuous young man enamoured of Plutarch and his heroes, the one who later wrote a pamphlet against the French called *The Romans in Greece*. Among the older members of this assembly I recognized Francesco Battaja, the grocer Zorzi, old General Salimbeni, someone from the family Giuliani da Desenzano, the most honest and liberal of the Venetian patriarchs Vidiman, and a certain Dandolo,[10] who had a reputation as a firebrand in the most rebellious circles. The others were unknown to me, although some of them looked familiar. They were all clustered intently around a reddish, scurfy little man who spoke in a low voice and said little, waving his arms around like a ballet dancer. Dr Lucilio paced the room, silent and thoughtful, and all made way for him respectfully, as if waiting for his orders. For a moment Battaja tried to take centre stage in a loud voice, but the others paid him no attention; one slipped off this way, one that; one cleared his throat and another coughed into his handkerchief; in short, nobody lined up behind him and he stood there like a crow after it has finished crowing.

I listened for a long time without understanding anything, either what I'd heard before coming or the abbreviated remarks of Amilcare and Giulio. Finally another old fellow – yellowed, bewigged and frightened-looking – hurried into the room. Lucilio went to meet him at the door and the whole company gathered round in a circle as if to hear some great and long-awaited news.

'It is the deputy Savio for the week!' whispered Amilcare in my ear. 'Now we shall see whether they are ready to capitulate with good grace.'

I pretended to understand and studied the wig-wearer with greater attention; he didn't seem at all easy about having to convince that large band surrounding him. Battaja stepped up to him to question him, but Lucilio cut him off and everyone fell silent, waiting to hear what he would say.

'Signor Procuratore,' he began, 'I believe you are aware of the Serenissima's deplorable condition, now that all the provinces of the mainland have raised the standard of true liberty. You know how helpless the government is since the first Schiavone regiments departed and how difficult it has been to restrain the fury of the people.'

'Yes . . . yes, sir, I know all that,' the Savio stammered.

'I've considered it my duty to inform the Most Excellent Procuratore of the sad state of the Republic,' added Battaja.

Lucilio, paying no attention to him, resumed speaking.

'Signor Procuratore, you are aware of the terms of the treaty that will shortly be signed between the Maggior Consiglio, now moribund, and the Directory of France!'

That cruel reminder gouged two big tears from the eyes of the Procuratore, tears which, if they didn't hint at courage, were not without a certain resigned and melancholy dignity. They made crooked paths though the powder sprinkled over his face, now even yellower and less beautiful than before.

'Signor Procuratore,' said Lucilio once again, 'I am but a simple citizen, but I seek the good, the genuine good of all citizens. I believe it would be an act of patriotism and a proof of independence to go halfway towards the excellent intentions of the other side and thus spare Venice the many internal disorders that will certainly complicate the situation if the treaty's conclusion is delayed. Any sort of ambition is alien to me and you will understand this by the role I intend to play in the future administration. Monsieur Villetard' (he nodded towards the nervous, reddish fellow) 'has been good enough to write up the conditions, which state that once the old government institutions have been abolished, a French presidium will enter the city to guard the founding of real liberty in Venice for the very first time. They include the usual articles': (he took a document from the table and began to read) 'raising of a tree of liberty; proclamation of democracy based on representatives chosen by the people; a provisional administration of twenty-four Venetians, headed by ex-Doge Manin and Giovanni Spada; free access to four thousand French allies in Venice; Venetian fleet to be recalled; the mainland cities, Dalmatia and the islands to be invited to unite with the *patria*; definitive disbandment of the Schiavone regiments; the arrest of the Bourbon accomplice Monsieur d'Entragues[11] and the consignment of his papers to the Directory via the French Legation. All known and approved by the people's unanimous consent. Yesterday, in fact, the Doge himself publicly declared he was ready to lay down his ring and bonnet and put the government in the hands of the democrats. We are asking less than he is disposed to grant. We want him to remain as the head of the new government, as a guarantee of stability and independence for the future Republic, is that not so, Monsieur Villetard?'

The little fellow assented with a great waving of hands and many grimaces. Lucilio now turned back to the Savio and handed him the document he had just read.

'Here, Signor Procuratore,' he said, 'here lies the destiny of the *patria*. It is up to you to make sure that the Most Serene Doge and the other noble colleagues . . . otherwise, God protect Venice! I have done all I humanly could to save her.'

Tears in his eyes, the Procuratore replied:

'I am truly grateful to you illustrious gentlemen for your kind regard' (at the mention of that excommunicated title 'gentlemen' the incorruptible citizens shuddered). 'The most Serene Doge and his colleagues, perpetual servants of the Republic, are ready to sacrifice themselves for its welfare' (sacrifice themselves meant 'survive') 'in as much as the loyalty of the remaining Schiavoni is beginning to waver and we would not be at all surprised to see them join our enemies . . .' (here the Procuratore saw that he had made a blunder and began to cough until he turned as scarlet as his robes) 'that is, to see them join our friends, who . . . who wish to save us at any cost. Therefore, I promise that these conditions' (he held up the document as if he had a viper in his hand) 'will be most heartily accepted by the Most Serene Signoria, that the Maggior Consiglio will ratify our excellent agreement, and that soon we shall all form a single family of happy and equal citizens.'

Here the Procuratore's voice expired in his throat like a sob, but his final words were drowned out by a volley of applause. The poor man blushed, in shame most likely, and then he quickly asked for someone from the distinguished gathering to accompany him to present the document to the Most Serene. Tommaso Zorzi was chosen by unanimous vote: a grocer, paired with a procuratore, ordering a doge to abdicate!

Two centuries before, the entire Council of Ten had appeared before Foscari[12] to demand he give back the Doge's ring and horned bonnet. All Venice, silent and trembling, waited at the palazzo gate to learn whether he would obey or refuse. The grand old Doge chose to obey and died of grief: it was the last, solemn, terrible act of a mysterious drama. How times have changed! Doge Manin's abdication could be a scene in one of Goldoni's comedies and it wouldn't seem any less dignified.

Meanwhile, the Procuratore and Zorzi left, and so did Villetard, Battaja and a few other patricians, foolish traitors; and there were only we few left, the best, the flower of Venetian democracy. Dandolo had the most to say, and I, certainly, understood the least. Lucilio had resumed his pacing, his silence, his thought. Suddenly he turned towards us with a troubled face and said, almost as if he were thinking aloud, 'I fear we are going to fail!'

'What?' said Dandolo. 'You think we are going to fail just when everything smiles on our ambitions? Now that the very jailers of liberty are themselves taking up the chisel to break off our chains? Now that a world redeemed by justice is preparing a place for us – a worthy, honourable and independent place – at the great banquet of the peoples; now that Italy's liberator, the man who has tamed tyranny, holds out a hand to lift us from the abjection into which we'd fallen?'

'I am a doctor,' said Lucilio in a calm voice. 'Diagnosing illness is my profession. I fear that our high purposes have not yet taken root among the people.'

'Citizen, do not lose hope in virtue, like Brutus!' The roaring voice came from a callow, almost beardless youth with stormy features. 'Brutus lost hope dying; we are about to be born.'

A Levantine from the island of Zante,[13] this lad was the son of a surgeon with the Venetian fleet who had taken up residence in Venice when his father died. His views were still somewhat malleable, for it was whispered that only a few months before he had got it in his head to become a priest, but whatever the case, rather than a priest he had become a tragic poet and one of his tragedies, *Tieste*, performed the previous January at the Teatro di Sant'Angelo, had been all the rage for seven nights running. This angry young man who roared was Ugo Foscolo. Giulio Del Ponte, who hadn't said a word all evening, roused himself at that roar and, out of the corner of his eye, darted him a glance like a stab from a stiletto. His envy of Foscolo was the worst kind: envy of intelligence, colder and more ferocious than all others – but poor Giulio knew he was outdone and could only try to make up for it by adding poison to his own rancour. The young lion of Zante didn't even bother to look at this flea biting his ear, or, if he did whack him with his paw, it was more out of boredom than anything else. At heart, he was a young man of considerable presumption and I don't know whether the glory accorded to the poet of the *Sepulchres* ever really measured up to the desires and hopes of the author of *Tieste*.

But back then he was not so much a literary man as the oddest and most comical example of a citizen you'd ever seen: a real, growling, indomitable, republican bear-cub; a model of civic virtue who would happily have shown himself off to universal admiration; a man who admired himself just as sincerely as he despised others, who took the great principle of equality so much in earnest that he might have written a letter advising (on a perfectly equal basis) the Emperor of all the Russias and been quite irked when the imperial ears paid no heed. He was a man of hope, despite his lugubrious tirades and his periods of despair, for temperaments like his, blooming with life and passion, do not easily resign themselves to apathy or death. Struggle is a necessity for them and without hope there can be no struggle. Giulio Del Ponte was not the only one who started when Foscolo cited the Roman example; Lucilio gave him a smile between the tolerant and the pitying, but he said nothing directly.

'Who among you,' Lucilio now asked, 'was watching Villetard while I read out his conditions to the Procuratore?'

'I was watching him,' said a tall, thick-set man I knew to be Spada, the one they meant to put alongside Manin in the new government. 'He looks like a traitor to me!'

'Very good, Citizen Spada,' said Lucilio, 'although he believes he is nothing more than a good servant of his country, a wise and fortunate minister. It has been some time since glory took the place of liberty on the French flag.'

'And what are we supposed to do about it?'

'Nothing,' said Lucilio, 'there is nothing we can do. I only wish, for any who are yet unaware and before the formal command arrives from Milan, to declare our ambitions in carrying out this revolution. They are thus: that scepticism is an excellent virtue, especially for the weak, but I fear it will not suffice. It would be better if the French were our assistants, not the executors: this is what I mean. We want to change by ourselves, not be changed by others, as if we had lost the faculty of movement. The French will come here because they can and because they so desire, but let them find the job finished, so that they do not hover over us like masters!'

'Let the French come to spare us from civil war and Sulla's proscriptions,'[14] said Foscolo.

Barzoni, who hadn't said a word, raised his head and sent a withering glance towards the rash orator.

'Well said,' Lucilio went on, addressing Foscolo, 'but you should have added, "Let them come to spare us another century like those past, only different in appearance. Let them come to shake us, to frighten us, to shame us, to rouse, by the fear of their tyranny, our majestic liberty!" That's what you should have added! Whether we shall be strong enough to take them as models and not as masters, we shall know in a few months' time. Villetard doubts it and he fears it and that makes me think that those above him desire otherwise!'

'What does it matter?' Amilcare interrupted. 'We respect what you have to say, citizen Vianello, but our wrists will not stand to be bound and we laugh at Villetard and those above him, just as we laugh at San Marco, at the Schiavone troops and at Procuratore Pesaro.'

Lucilio banished such thoughts – too melancholy, perhaps, or come too late – from his mind and turned towards me with an almost paternal air.

'Citizen Altoviti,' he said, 'your father has done much for the cause of liberty and a reward is due him, which he would prefer to concede to you. We should have taken no notice of the matter had your nature and your conduct not given us hope you would continue the family example. You are one of the youngest members of the Maggior Consiglio and one of the few, indeed the very few, who voted for liberty not because you were a coward, but from higher principles. I therefore now inform you that you have been chosen as first secretary of the new government.'

His words were met by a murmur of wonder among the young people present.

'Yes,' continued Lucilio, 'the man who spent some millions in Constantinople to turn Turkey away from France's European enemies; the man who gave many years of his own life in the far-away East to weave together this great act, which perhaps will make us free and will certainly make us men; the man responsible for all this, would like as much for his son! I say this, I can say this, because when we have achieved our victory I intend to return to my hospital, my patients and my bloodletting!'

Unanimous applause broke out among the entire company and ten pairs of arms battled to embrace Dr Vianello. In the midst of the wild enthusiasm, I slipped away and stood thinking in a corner, that 'first secretary' crushing my chest like a millstone. The discussion broadened and there was talk of the fleet, of Dalmatia, of the best way to gain General Bonaparte's backing for the new government institutions. Much breath was wasted until midnight, when Zorzi returned, looking every bit as eminent as a shopkeeper who has just overthrown a thirteen-century-old government.

'Is it done?' the company asked.

'It is done,' said Zorzi. 'The Doge asked me to go to Villetard to obtain his conditions in writing; the Most Serene didn't know we already had them in hand. Tomorrow the Maggior Consiglio will be asked to immediately adopt a democratic system for the new provisional government of Venice devised by us.'

'Long live liberty!' everyone shouted.

And then there was such a roar of joy and enthusiasm that I, too, felt a streak of fire run through my veins. If at that moment they had ordered me to believe Rome could be resurrected by the Camilluses and the Manliuses, I wouldn't have found it at all strange! The group then dispersed and, although it was very late, Venetian etiquette permitted Giulio and myself to stop in at the Countess's. I was quite beyond myself without having any idea why; so the loyal horse must feel when the trumpets sound. Giulio was unhappy about the too-modest role he had played in the evening's gathering, although it was not as if he weren't used to such company. Both he and Foscolo were accused of being mixed up in sedition (and Foscolo's mother was said to have advised her son to go to his death before revealing the names of his companions). The Spartan mother, it seemed, was back in fashion.

In any case that evening la Pisana had eyes only for me, but I was so deep in thought about the new government, the Maggior Consiglio meeting of the morrow and my father's plans for me, that I didn't respond. I did look at her, but only because she was listening closely to what I had to say and this behaviour of mine didn't please her one bit. As for Giulio, so dull and unhappy, she barely tolerated him and his weary gallantry earned him not a quarter of what it cost him. The Countess, however, rewarded him with a deluge of questions on the day's events, but the good man of letters wasn't keen to reply and seemed more willing to be considered an ingrate than be a martyr to ennui. The shrewd old lady was trimming her sails as the bad weather got worse, and by now, to hear her talk, she was practically a sans-culotte. God alone knows how much hatred and bile was smouldering inside her.

'What do you think, Signor Giulio? Will these Frenchmen come? Are they going to abolish loans issued against feudal earnings? And the patricians, can they count on getting a pension or a position? Can San Marco be sure he'll still be on the flag?'

Giulio sighed, yawned, ground his teeth and twisted from side to side, but the Countess, relentless, was determined to extract some answer from him, although I think he'd have had a tooth extracted with better grace. In the meantime I could not resist showing off my future glories to la Pisana and I let it be known that there would be a nice place in the future government for me.

'Oh really, Carlino?' she said to me very quietly. 'But didn't we agree that equality must be instated?'

I shrugged my shoulders. So, you want to philosophize with women! Was I silent with disdain or because I didn't know what to say? Whatever the case, that evening ambition outran love and when I parted from la Pisana I couldn't even have told you what colour her eyes were. Absently, I left Giulio in Calle Frezzeria and continued on alone, leaping with impatience along the Riva degli Schiavoni.

I will always remember that night of 11 May! So lovely, so warm, so peaceful, it seemed a night made for nothing but love talk, solitary meditation or cheerful serenades. And instead, under such great calm of heaven and earth, under the lyric spell of life and spring, a great republic was disintegrating like a body rotting with scurvy. A great queen fourteen centuries old was dying and there were no tears, no dignity, no funeral services. Her children slept, indifferent, or shook with fear; while she, a shadow torn with shame, floated down the Grand Canal in a ghostly Bucintoro,[15] and, little by little, the water rose and ship and ghost disappeared into that liquid grave. Had it only been like that! Instead, for months, that dead shade lay exposed to the world's abuse, maimed and disfigured. Her old spouse, the sea, refused her ashes and a French corporal tossed them to the four winds, a fatal gift to any who dared to collect them. There was a moment then when I raised my eyes without thinking to the Doge's Palace and saw that the moon had left a fine glimmer of poetry on its long balconies and great, strange windows. For the last time a thousand heads covered with old seafarers' hoods or warlike helmets thrust their empty, ghostly faces out of that façade and there came a moaning from the sea like a lament. I can assure you I shivered, although I detested the aristocracy and hoped that liberty and equality would triumph at its extinction.

There's no way around it: to watch great things slip into the shadows of the past and disappear forever is terribly, inexpressibly sad. But the greater these human things are, the more they resist the destroying breath of time, until that small shock comes and turns the corpse to dust, abolishing the appearance and even the memory of life. Who noticed when the Western Roman Empire fell with Romulus Augustulus?[16] It had already fallen when Diocletian abdicated.[17] Who in 1806 noticed the end of the Holy Roman Empire? It had vanished from the people's sight with the abdication of Charles V.[18] Who grieved, when the French entered Venice, for the ruin of a great republic, heir to Roman civilization and wisdom and bulwark of Christianity throughout the Middle Ages? She herself had drawn back from the world's attention after Foscari abdicated. Abdications mark the downfall of a state, because a captain neither abandons, nor is forced to abandon, the helm of a ship fitted out for his every manoeuvre with an expert and disciplined crew. Despair, prostration, indifference, mistrust come before the shipwreck and the sinking.

And so I looked up at the Doge's Palace and shivered. Would that great proud, mysterious edifice be destroyed now that its last animating spirit was dispersed? The hard, eternal marble seemed to promise not memories, but remorse. I could see, meanwhile, further down the Riva, a crowd of loyal Schiavoni, embarking, silent and sorrowful, their grief consoling only moribund Venice. A sharper fear invaded my soul then. With the French in our midst, this new liberty, this fine equality, this impartial justice began to stick in my throat. Lucilio had been right to say we should have our revolution before Bonaparte sent his orders and instructions from Milan, but in any case the French would quickly arrive from nearby Mestre, and, once they were there, who knew what would come next? To banish such fears I called up Amilcare's noble self-regard. 'By Jove,' I thought, 'we are men like any others and this new fire of liberty inspiring us will produce the necessary miracles. Europe cannot be ungrateful; her own interests don't permit it. With our substance and our goodwill we shall return to being us, and help should not be far away from leeward or from windward.'

Thus reassured, I turned towards home, where my Father told me he was most pleased at the place reserved for me in the future Municipality, and that I must take care to conduct myself well and follow his counsel if I wanted to rise higher. I don't recall what I said to him; I know I went to bed and did not close an eye all night. It must have been a quarter to nine when I heard the bells ring for the Maggior Consiglio and headed out towards the great staircase of the Doge's Palace. As much as the nobles of Venice were in a hurry to commit their great matricide, the pleasures of bed didn't permit them to begin more than a quarter of an hour earlier than usual. There were five hundred and thirty-seven of them: an insufficient number, because the statute declared that any resolution discussed in a gathering of less than six hundred was illegitimate and null. Most of them were quivering with impatience and fear, in a hurry to finish, go home and remove those robes, now the dangerous insignia of a fallen reign. Some boasted confidence and happiness: these were the traitors. Others sparkled with real contentment, with a generous pride for that sacrifice that, cancelling them from the Libro d'Oro, made them citizens and free. Among these were Agostino Frumier and myself, side by side, holding hands.

In one corner of the stairway apart from the rest stood a group of about twenty patricians wrapped in their robes, silent and rigid. There were some venerable ancients who hadn't attended the Council for years but came that day to cast their last, impotent vote in honour of the *patria*, and a few young fellows and one or two honest men inspired by the noble sentiments of a father, a father-in-law, a forebear. In the midst of them I was quite surprised to see Senator Frumier and his eldest son Alfonso; I knew they worshiped San Marco, but I didn't know they were so courageous. They were all squeezed together in a tight little circle, neither surly with contempt nor livid with hatred, but as mild and firm as martyrs. God bless their faith in the *patria*! Its last ray glowed majestically, albeit without hope. They were not aristocrats, not rulers, not inquisitors: they were the descendants of Zeno and Dandolo,[19] reminding us of their ancestors' glory, their virtues, their sacrifices, for the last time. When I looked at them then I was hostile, stunned; I think of them now with wonder and emotion. I at least can laugh at those false tales that have been told; I know the last Maggior Consiglio pronounced no curse on human nature.

The entire hall was a single murmur, a single indistinct buzz; only in that one remote corner did sorrow and silence prevail. Outside, the populace was rioting; the ships, now disarmed, were coming in; the last remnants of the Schiavoni were departing; the guards, against all precedent, were protecting the doors of the palace. All bleak omens. Oh, death's slumber is very cold indeed if the heroes, the Doges, the captains of the Ancient Republic didn't wake then, if they didn't come out of their graves!

Pale, trembling, the Doge stood up before the sovereign Maggior Consiglio he represented and proposed a uniquely vile plan. He had read Villetard's conditions (aimed to meet the desires of the Directory and placate the wrath of General Bonaparte) and he approved them out of ignorance and incompetence, unaware that what Villetard, a traitor through and through, had promised no one intended to honour. And Bonaparte even less than the others! Doge Lodovico Manin stammered out a few words: they must accept these conditions; it was useless to resist and, furthermore, it was impossible; General Bonaparte was a magnanimous man; the advised reforms, if carried out, offered the promise of a better future. He then boldly proposed that they abolish their old institutions and establish a democracy. In his day Marin Faliero was beheaded[20] for half such a crime! But Lodovico Marin babbled on, dishonouring himself, the Maggior Consiglio and the *patria*, and not a single man dared rip off his doge's mantle and crush his cowardly head on that floor where ministers sent by kings and legates by popes had bowed their heads! Even I pitied him; I who saw nothing but the triumph of liberty and equality in the humiliation of a doge.

Suddenly, some rifle volleys exploded outside and the Doge, alarmed, made to come down the steps from his throne, but a mob of frightened patricians crowded around him, shouting 'The resolution! To the vote!' Outside came roars from the people; inside, the confusion and dismay mounted. It was the Schiavoni, rebelling! (The last of them were just leaving and they had, in fact, saluted ungrateful Venice with those shots.) It was the sixteen thousand conspirators! (Lucilio's dream.) It was the people longing to wallow in the blood of the nobles! (The people not only preferred obedience to those nobles, but, threatened with hard servitude, they loved obedience and clung to it.) In short, amidst the shouting, the shoving, the haste and the fear, the vote took place. Five hundred and twelve votes approved the resolution that had not yet been read, stipulating that the nobility would abdicate in favour of a Provisional Democratic

Government (so long as it should meet General Bonaparte's wishes). Because of the grave domestic danger, it had been decided not to await the General's supreme requirements but to stipulate the terms immediately. Just twenty votes opposed this vile rush and five were 'undecided'.

Oh, I shall never forget that spectacle: the faces I saw then in that throng of quivering, shameful, humiliated sheep, I still see today, sixty years later, with deep dismay. I still recall the twisted, cadaverish look of some, the lost, drunken appearance of others, and the anguished haste of the many, who, I believe, would have gladly thrown themselves out of the windows in order to depart the scene of their cowardice as quickly as possible. The Doge hurried towards his chambers, disposing of his regalia along the way and ordering that his banners be taken down from the walls, and many gathered around him, as if to ignore their own disgrace in the face of even greater disgrace. Those who went out into the Piazza took care to discard the wigs and robes of the patrician order. We alone, the few deluded lovers of liberty in that servile sheepfold (there were five or six of us) ran to the windows and down the stairs, shouting 'Long live liberty!' But that sacred cry was quickly profaned by those who glimpsed in it a guarantee of safety. The traitors and the cowards soon mixed with us and the noise and the shouts grew louder, and I thought that pure enthusiasm had turned those pitiful men into heroes and ran out into the Piazza, tossing my wig in the air and shouting at the top of my lungs 'Long live liberty!'

General Salimbeni, standing there along with some other conspirators, had begun to roar at the crowd, provoking the people to jubilation and riot. But then the mob turned furiously on him, forcing him to shout 'Long live San Marco!' That new cry stifled the previous one, and many believed that the old Republic had come safely through the terrible trial of the vote. 'Long live the Republic! Long live San Marco!': the entire piazza packed with people shouted as if with one voice, and banners were raised on three flagpoles and the great Evangelist's image was carried about in triumph, and a threatening wave from the mob spread out towards the houses of those patricians who were said to have plotted to call in the French. In the midst of this crowd, troubled, confused and divided from my companions, I met my father and Lucilio, who, if less confused than I, were more disheartened. They took me with them towards Calle Frezzeria. Those few patricians who had voted for the independence and stability of their country passed close by us still wearing their wigs, gowns trailing. The crowd made way for them, without insulting them, but without acclaiming them either.

'Do you see that?' Lucilio whispered in my ear. 'The people are shouting "Long live San Marco!" and they haven't got the courage to carry one of those last, deserving masters left to them in triumph and make him Doge! Servile! They are servile! Eternally servile!'

My father had no time for quibbles; he simply picked up his pace, for he was in a hurry to get to his rooms where he could safely reflect on the positive and the negative sides of the situation. From the new Municipality came a proclamation depicting the patricians' vile complicity as a free and spontaneous gesture to the spirit of the times, justice and the welfare of all, bringing peace once again to the good Venetian people. Just as a mouse's tooth is enough to send a worm-eaten ship to the bottom, so the intrigues of a minor secretary from Paris, four or five traitors and a few republicans had been enough to topple a political edifice that had stood up to Suleiman and the League of Cambrai.[21] It was a revolution without grandeur because it was without purpose; something demagogues should study and learn from whenever chance puts the destiny of their country in their hands. Four days later, Venetian boats brought French troops to the city, and Venice, which a few days before had been defended by eleven thousand Schiavoni, eight hundred pieces of artillery and two hundred warships, consigned herself voluntarily and in chains to the rough mercy of four thousand mercenaries led by Baraguay d'Hilliers. The Municipality paid them court before a silent, contemptuous crowd. As secretary, I took my share of those tacit insults, but la Pisana's enthusiasm and my father's urging emboldened me to bear anything in the cause of liberty. If I pitied the ignorant, I didn't mean to pity the poor.

My courage, however, was slightly weakened by the replies

from the mainland provinces to our invitation to join the new government. While the authorities wavered, the French generals laughed at us. And Venice was left to herself with her counterfeit liberty. Meanwhile, Istria and Dalmatia were occupied by Austria, according to the secret treaty of Leoben. This, too, was disheartening. France, using the Venetian fleet, was seizing our possessions in Albania and the Ionian, and was threatening worse. Poor secretary that I was, I wasn't able to put together all these contradictions and make sense of them. I sighed, I worked, I hoped for the best. In the meantime, let us note the error that made Venice fall, dishonoured and unlamented, after fourteen glorious and worthy centuries of life. No one, I believe, had ever before then noticed or properly defined the cause of her ruin. Venice was no longer anything more than a city, but she wanted to be a people. In modern times, only people live and fight, and if they fall, they fall strong and with honour, for they are certain they will rise again.

TWELVE

In which, after a moving farewell to carefree youth, I begin to live and reason in all seriousness – but unfortunately the wind is not in my favour. Right from the beginning it is apparent that the promises of guests who would be hosts can be trusted only at our peril, but the guests, at least, had the merit of warning us. In the meantime, Clara becomes a nun, la Pisana marries His Excellency Navagero, and I continue copying out records. Venice falls a second time in punishment for the first, and our patriots withdraw, fuming, to the Cisalpine territory. I remain, it seems, to keep my father company.

Farewell fresh and carefree youth, eternal joy of the ancient gods of Olympus, heavenly but fleeting gift to us mortals! Farewell dewy dawns glistening with smiles and vows, clouded only by too brightly coloured illusions! Farewell mellow sunsets idly watched from the shady bank of a stream or from a lover's flowered balcony! Farewell chaste moon, inspirer of vague melancholy and poetic loves, you who innocently play with the curly heads of children and dote upon the pensive eyes of youth! The dawn of life comes and goes like the dawn of a single day and heaven's nocturnal tears dissolve into restless, roiling humours in nature's immensity. No more ease, but work; no more beauty, but deeds; no more quiet and fancy, but truth and struggle. The sun wakes us to serious thoughts, laborious tasks, enduring and vain hopes; then disappears at nightfall, providing us a brief and much desired oblivion. The moon ascends the starry curve of heaven and tosses on sleepless nights a vaporous azure veil spun of light, gloom, memory, grief. The years go by, ever more dour and sullen, like masters unhappy with their servants; old and frail they seem, white-haired, the tracks they leave are ever lighter, like the footsteps of a shadow that grows huge as sunset nears. Farewell shining entrance halls, enchanted gardens, life's harmonious preludes! Farewell green fields with your wandering paths, meditative retreats, infinite beauty, light, liberty and trill of songbirds! Farewell to childhood's tiny nest, to great working houses that seemed as large to us children as the world to adults, where the work of others was our delight, where a guardian angel watched over our dreams and cosseted us with a thousand enchanting fancies!

Content without effort, happy without knowing it: the schoolmaster's frown or the tutor's reproof were the only lines our future wore on her brow! The universe ended at the courtyard wall, and inside, if we did not enjoy utter beatitude, our desires at least were contained and injustice took on such a childish cast that a day later one would laugh at it as a joke. The elderly servants; the grave, stately priest; those mysterious, surly relatives; the noisy, talkative maids; the meddlesome boys and bright, brash, beguiling young ladies appeared before us as if through a magic lantern. One shrank from the cats that scuttled under the credenza, patted the aged hunting dog beside the fire, admired the coachman as he curried the horses without fear of getting a kick. In my case, there was the spit to be turned, it is true, but I forgive even the spit and would happily go back to turning it to regain the naive happiness of those blessed evenings on Martino's lap or next to la Pisana's little bed.

O melancholy, precious shadows of those I loved, you live in me; loyal even in old age, you don't flee my cold breast and frozen countenance. You hover over me like a cloud of thoughts and affection, dispersing far, far away in the bright rainbow of my youth. Time is not time, except for the man awaiting his profits; for me time was never anything but memory, desire, love, hope. Youth stays alive in the human mind; the old man happily gathers up the memories of his younger self. But must it come to nothing, that ever-growing wealth of thoughts and affection? Comprehension is a great sea of which we are the streams and rivers. O boundless, bottomless Ocean, I fearlessly entrust my tired life to your mindful waves. Time is not time but eternity for those who consider themselves immortal.

And so they came to an end, those delicious years I lived in the old world: the world of powdered wigs and *buli* and feudal jurisdictions. I emerged from them the secretary of a democratic government with nothing to govern, my hair shorn in a Brutus cut, my head in a rounded cap with raised side wings, the shoulders of my jacket padded like two mortadellas from Bologna, wearing long trousers and boots with heels so intimidating you could hear me coming from one end of the palazzo to the other. Imagine the leap from those sleek, soft slippers worn by the gentlemen of old! It was the greatest revolution that had ever come to Venice. As for the rest, water flowed downhill as always, except that our French friends wracked their brains daily to see what they could pluck from us. Paintings, medals, manuscripts, statues, the four horses of San Marco: all took the road for Paris. We can console ourselves that science had not yet invented ways to move buildings and transport towers and cupolas or Venice would have been left as it was when Attila's first successors came through.

By now Bergamo and Crema had been occupied to round out the Cisalpine Republic; from other provinces deputies came to meet in Bassano to determine which side to back. That clever fox Berthier[1] presided, making sure nothing significant happened; I communicated the Municipality's wishes to Bassano and received the replies. Dr Lucilio, who, although he didn't seem so, continued to be the moving force behind the new government, didn't want to give up that last anchor, and he, too, manoeuvred stubbornly. It seemed we were close to reaching agreement, when wily Berthier suddenly declared than an accord was out of the question and that was that! Venice was left alone with her oysters; the provinces, with their presidents and French generals. From Padua, General Victor[2] rudely squawked that no one should pay the least attention to the Venetians, a race of rotten and incorrigible aristocrats. Bernadotte,[3] more honest, forbade any deputies from Udine to participate in that silly comedy in Bassano. In those sad times, cruelty was all but merciful and certainly better than hypocrisy.

I, however, pressed onwards, blindfold on my eyes and pen in hand, believing I was following in the footsteps of Cincinnatus.[4]

My father shook his head, but I paid him no heed; I thought the will or the presumption of a few hotheads would be enough to separate this freedom of ours (still an infant, but already quite decrepit) from its mother. One evening I went out to look for the Countess of Fratta at her usual lodgings and was told she had moved and was to be found at the Zattere, on the other side of town. I trotted over there and climbed a broken, worm-eaten staircase to find myself in a damp, dark apartment with hardly any furnishings. La Pisana came to meet me in the entryway; my astonishment grew and I followed her into the sitting room, as if in a dream. And a pitiful one it was, too!

The Countess was slumped in an armchair of peeling black morocco leather; a little oil lamp sputtered on a tottering table propped against the wall. The floorboards were crooked, the ceiling beams half-plastered: these were real rented rooms, without furniture or curtains. The walls were bare and pocked, the doors and window-frames so ill-fitting that the miserable lamp flame was always just about to expire. Next to the Countess, on a straw-backed chair, sat a dull, white, puffy-looking old man; he wore the finery of the patrician, but his stubborn, heavy cough belied his elegant clothes. The Countess, seeing the amazement and distress on my face, countered with a smile of great good cheer to head me off.

'You see, Carlino?' said she, her gaiety somewhat forced. 'Do you see what a provident mother I am? The revolution has ruined us and I am forced to tighten my belt on behalf of my dear children!' With this she glanced at la Pisana, who was sitting next to her, facing the old gentleman, her eyes down and her hands in her pockets.

'May I present my cousin, the Gentleman Mauro Navagero? A generous cousin prepared to join his lineage with ours,' she went on. 'In short, as of this morning, he is betrothed to our Pisana!'

In that instant I think I saw all the stars in the firmament, as if a great stone had fallen on me and crushed me; a moment's blindness followed that flare of stars and then I could once again see and hear, although I was unable to make any sense of the faces around me or the roaring in my ears. I suppose the

Countess must have been expounding on the great merits of this alliance, for neither the gentleman, with his cough, nor la Pisana, so deeply embarrassed, were saying much. I confess that my love of liberty, my ambition and all those other strange ideas that my own good nature and my father's tricks had put in my head, went scurrying off like a dog scalded by boiling water. La Pisana was left all alone and regal in my mind; and I regretted, I repented, I despaired that I had neglected her so long, and understood I was too weak or too depraved to find happiness in great abstractions. Blessed is that state where private attachments prepare for civic virtue; where domestic and moral education prepare a man to be a citizen and a hero! But I had come forth from another breeding ground and my attachments were in conflict among themselves, alas, the way the last century's customs conflict with present aspirations. It is a malady that still affects the young today and although we lament its consequences, we don't seem able to prevent it.

When I finally dared to look at la Pisana, it was as if some impediment turned me away again: this was the cold and peevish gaze of the gamy, well-aged fiancé, which flickered from la Pisana's face to my own with miserly unease. There are certain looks that you can feel before you see them, and that of His Excellency Navagero went right to the soul without troubling the optic nerve. It troubled *me*, however, and as a last, desperate resort I turned towards the Countess's stingy, scrawny face. She looked so radiantly happy that I became enraged and utterly lost my composure. The fool who picks a quarrel in a circle where all are against him is in a better position than I. And la Pisana, with her half-mocking reserve, annoyed me more than all the others. I was just about to get up and escape, go somewhere else to vent my heartache, when my father came thumping in. Even more sprightly and strange than usual, he seemed to be informed about all that had surprised and dismayed me, for he congratulated Navagero on his good fortune and turned to the young lady with one of those looks more eloquent than any language.

It was too much for me. To see my father join the ranks of my enemies and lap up my misfortune like so much manna filled me with a fury so great I no longer thought of leaving.

I felt something like the heroism of Horatio at the bridge, alone against all Tuscany.[5] I settled back in my chair in proud defiance of the Countess's nervous laugh, la Pisana's indifference, Navagero's jealousy and my father's cruelty. When it was time to leave I saw too late that my knees barely held me up and anyone watching me walk alongside my father and Navagero would have thought us three happy drunkards in different stages of inebriation. Unable to listen to their remarks, I went to bed for the first time with no thoughts of that golden cap the future democratic Doge of Venice would wear.

A thousand strange and dreadful designs spun such arabesques in my head that I could not contain them. I would challenge Navagero to a duel with sword and rapier, stick him like a frog, deliver my solemn curse to la Pisana and throw myself in the canal (through a convenient window). Or, once I had killed him, I would take her in my arms and carry her off on a Smyrna pirate ship to live with me in the desert among the ruins of Palmyra or in the sands of Arabia. Such were my least adventurous Pindaric flights: I versified without metre, without accents, without rhyme; nothing was difficult or impossible, and if I'd had a hippogryph in my stables or all Croesus' gold in my pockets, I couldn't have been freer or built more magnificent castles in the air. With these dreams, I fell asleep and kept on dreaming; and, waking early, picked up the thread of what I'd dreamed the day before.

Amilcare soon inquired why I was so lost in thought and perhaps I told him more than I would have liked. Shame! A secretary of the Municipality losing himself in such idiocies! Did I not blush to be jealous of a worn-out, drooling old aristocrat; to go swooning like a fool after a ninny who would have wed a satyr just to be married? That was obvious; what kind of bargain did I wish to lend myself to? Better to wait and be a man, to give myself to my country and the creed of liberty, especially now that there was so much need!

My friend spoke from the heart and he convinced me. It made no sense to trail after la Pisana like an ass, when the concerns of government demanded all my time and attention. I pulled myself together, spared Navagero's life and altered that speech I'd planned to perform before la Pisana before drowning myself or taking off for Arabia into a silent apostrophe: 'Take him, you perjurer! You are unworthy of me!' That I had any right to deliver such a sentence, I rather doubt. First, the young lady had never sworn her love to me, and second, my compassionate retreat in favour of Giulio Del Ponte and the neglect of her that followed must certainly have made her think I'd lost all desire to make her mine. I, however, knew very well that I'd never desired more, but my strange, cockeyed temperament obliged me to be frank with her about her intimate affairs. When I decided to break with her I was firmly convinced I was a victim and this authorized me to go on being infatuated, where my heroic intentions or Navagero's patience might not have. Young Count Rinaldo, who rarely appeared in his mother's chambers, showed some annoyance at seeing me play the turtle-dove to his sister. He too, poor thing, went at me like all the others did, but it didn't change my mind a bit, for I was convinced that I was utterly taken up by my role as secretary and was blissfully ignoring la Pisana and her marriage.

The affairs of the house of Fratta were ever more strained. The Countess continued to gamble compulsively and when her money ran out she would pawn something with the Monte di Pietà. The young Count's beloved philosophy and la Pisana's carefree nature in no way interfered, and their view, I believe, was that His Excellency Navagero had been chosen to mend all those holes. What quite amazed me was that the Countess and my father still saw each other frequently, although the latter hadn't loosened his purse strings one bit and had raised a thousand obstacles to the Countess's designs to marry la Pisana to me. I understood vaguely that my father didn't favour that plan, and he, without ever speaking to me about it, guessed my preferences and went to work to deflect them. But how had he been able to oppose the Countess's ambitions while remaining in her graces? I set about trying to discover how; and what did I find but that he had been the broker for the marriage with Navagero and thus I owed my misfortune primarily to him? As for me, the wily old trader had high aspirations: he thought it would be nice to have an extremely rich young damsel from the

Contarini family for a daughter-in-law, and he never failed to give me a whack so that I could pick her out in the crowd among the many young ladies who (less haughty now) wouldn't have declined to add my name to their own. Every actor on the stage of this world has his lucky beneficiary and now I would have mine too. Citizen Carletto Altoviti, ex-Gentleman of Torcello, secretary of the Municipality, favourite of Dr Lucilio and renowned in Piazza San Marco for his fine clothes, his self-possession and above all for his father's millions, was not a man to toss aside in a corner.

I, however, my pride humbled somewhat by la Pisana's betrayal, felt slightly deflated; and despite Amilcare's urging, had trouble keeping myself aloft in the exalted heights of liberty and glory. Those heights had begun to darken and threaten great storms all around. That the ground should give way under our feet – that was all we needed! Nevertheless, I was an honourable man and did not neglect my duties at the Municipal Hall. It was just that I preferred being eaten up by rage at la Pisana's side, to the hints, inside that hall, of the future Doge's majesty my father foresaw for me.

Around this time, when Venice had already begun to behave like a servant of France and the future was looking ever more melancholy, Dr Lucilio appeared one day at the Countess of Fratta's apartments. She had been dreading this visit for a month, yet no longer had the courage to refuse him. The doctor sat down before the Countess in his usual way, neither humble nor arrogant, and made a formal request for Clara's hand. The Countess pretended to be greatly surprised and shocked and replied that her daughter was soon to take vows and had no intention of venturing out among the worldly perils she so prudently avoided. The lady then reminded him that Signor Partistagno had first rights and had never ceased trumpeting his complaints all over Venice about the sacrifice that had been imposed on Clara, and that he would certainly not permit her to leave the convent and marry someone else. Lucilio replied in the clearest of terms that Clara had promised herself to him before any other; that she hadn't yet taken her vows; that the laws of democracy meant that nothing could stand in the way of their union any more; that Clara was now of age; and that as for Partistagno, he could only laugh at him and his whining, which had been the joke of every circle and club in Venice for the past year. The Countess, tight-lipped and wearing a nasty smile, said that since he had mentioned Clara being of age, he could go to her directly, and she complimented him for being so firm of purpose (if perhaps a bit slow to make up his mind) and wished him the very best of luck.

'Madam,' said Lucilio, 'I am firm of purpose, as you say, and I have been so for many years, although I would sooner turn the world upside down on behalf of my purposes than merely violate good manners or beg a favour on bended knee. Now that circumstances have made us equals, I do not hesitate to ask what can only be readily granted. I consider myself fortunate that you do not wish to pit maternal authority against my sweetest, most stubborn hopes.'

'Certainly, just as you please!' the Countess said quickly. She spoke as if she were in awe of Lucilio, but perhaps she was merely thinking about Madre Redenta, to whom she had entrusted the thorny problem of defending Clara's soul from the Devil's clutches. The Reverend Madre had been keeping watch for some time now, and Dr Lucilio, when he took his leave from the Countess, didn't realize that his task had scarcely begun. I wouldn't say that he was very confident, however. He had been procrastinating for days, because he wanted to see his faction (and the preference for democracy) victorious in Venice. And then when he sensed, perhaps before any of the others, that the tide was moving against them, he hastened to cash in the last assets fortune had provided and satisfy his heart's ultimate vow. He saw those fine dreams of liberty, glory and public prosperity dissolving and hoped to save himself by clinging to domestic happiness. So he was thinking as he headed towards the convent of Santa Teresa, told the nun at the door his name and asked that the Contessina Clara of Fratta be called to the parlour. The doorkeeper disappeared inside the convent, but soon returned to say that the noble young lady wished to know the reason for his visit and would reply to his request without withdrawing from her meditations. Lucilio, surprised and angry, sensed, however, some nunnish trick in this reply and so he reiterated that it was necessary, indeed indispensable, for him to speak to Clara and that the young lady herself knew that, and no one in the world could deny him that meeting. And so the doorkeeper once again went inside and a few moments later appeared, sour-faced, to say that Clara would soon be down in the company of her Superior.

That Superior stuck in Lucilio's craw, but he was not a man to be intimidated by a nun. He waited somewhat uneasily, measuring out the red and white marble floor of the convent parlour in long strides. He had been pacing up and down like that for quite some time when Madre Redenta and Clara came in: the first with her crooked neck, her downcast eyes, her hands crossed over her stomach, the moustaches on her upper lip bristling; the other, calm and serene as always, her beauty grown somewhat listless in the cloister, so that her soul shone purer and more ardent than ever, like a star through melting fog. It had been years since the two lovers had been in such proximity, but they betrayed no signs of great emotion; their force, their love, was so deeply rooted in their hearts as to show but a pale reflection on their faces. Madre Redenta was spying through the thick brush of her lowered eyebrows in hopes she wouldn't be observed. Her ears were so finely tuned that she could have heard a fly settle at the other end of the room.

'Clara,' began Lucilio in a voice perhaps more agitated than he might have wished, 'I come after a long absence to remind you what you promised me, and I believe that for you, as for myself, these many years have been but a day's wait. No obstacle now stands in the way of our hearts' desire; and so today, no longer heedless and impatient as we were in youth, but with the strong judgement and firm purpose of maturity, I ask you to say the word and renew that vow of happiness you once made before Heaven. Parental will, legal tyranny, social convention: none of them can now obstruct your liberty or my happiness. I offer you a heart filled with but one love; lit by a flame that will never die; tested and retested by labour, patience and misfortunes. Clara, look me in the face. When will you be mine?'

The young lady quivered from head to foot, but only for an

instant; then her hand, pale as could be against her novice's black habit, came to rest on her breast. She turned towards Lucilio with a long, enigmatic gaze that seemed to bore through everything in search of help from the heavens.

'Lucilio,' she said, pressing that hand hard upon her heart, 'I swore before God that I loved you and I swore to myself to make you as happy as I possibly could. All this is true: I often think of it and I make every effort to be certain my vows are realized to the fullest extent that God will permit.'

'Which is to say?' Lucilio burst out nervously.

Here Madre Redenta dared to raise her lashes, looking as terrorized as if she'd seen Beelzebub's horns. But Clara's calm tranquillized her and she once again withdrew behind downcast eyes.

'Let me tell you all, Lucilio,' Clara went on. 'Let me tell you all and you will judge. I entered this house of peace to entrust my soul to God and Providence, and I found affection, thoughts and consolation here that now make me look with horror on the world outside. Oh no, Lucilio, I do not scorn you! But our souls were not made to find happiness in this century of vice and perdition. We must resign ourselves and find happiness above!'

'What are you saying? What are these words I hear that rend my heart, yet come from your lips with such melodic sweetness? Clara, I beg you, come to your senses! Think of me! Look me in the face! I clasp my hands in prayer and repeat: think of me!'

'Oh, I do think of you! I think of you all too much, Lucilio, for I am too tangled up in the things of this world to offer myself pure and simple up to God. But what do you want of me, Lucilio? What do you want? Our Republic has fallen into the hands of foreigners without religion or faith. There is no more good, no more hope, except in Heaven for souls who fear God. How can one trust in earthly prospects, Lucilio? How can one found a family in a society that no longer respects God or the Church?'

'Enough, Clara, enough! Do not mock my grief, my anger! Think about what you are saying, Clara; remember you must answer for my soul to that God you adore and whom you hope to serve better by committing such a terrible crime. The Republic has fallen? Religion is in peril? What does all of this have to do with that promise you made me? Remember, Clara, that the first and most exalted precept of the Gospel commands you to love your neighbour. Now, as your neighbour and nothing more than your neighbour, I ask you to remember your vow to me and not try to gain credit with God by betraying it! God abhors and condemns such betrayal; God refuses sacrifices that cost blood and tears to others! If you must sacrifice yourself, then sacrifice yourself to me! If I am not to be happiness, then accept me as martyrdom!'

Madre Redenta coughed noisily to spoil the effect of Lucilio's speech, uttered so desperately, so imploringly, that it wounded the soul. But Clara turned to her and reassured her with a look, and then, with a heavenward glance, she approached Lucilio and laid a chaste hand on his shoulder. Shrewd as he was, the poor fellow understood everything from that glance and that hand; and, heart-broken, saw that he could not follow that saintly, sorrowful soul escaping him all the way to Heaven.

'But why, Clara? Why?' he went on, without waiting for her to explain the dreadful meaning of her gestures. 'Why do you want to murder me when you could bring me back to life? How can you forget that holy, eternal, indissoluble love you swore to me?'

'Oh, I still promise you that love, holier, more eternal and indissoluble than ever,' she replied. 'Let our wedding be in Heaven, for on earth it is forbidden to God's faithful. I swear to you, Lucilio! I love you. I love no one but you! I have purified and sanctified my love for you, but I cannot tear it from my viscera without dying. So you see how true, how stubborn, is my vocation! I shall always love you. I shall live with you forever, our souls and our prayers commingling. But more than this, you have no right to ask, Lucilio. I cannot give you more, because God forbids me!'

'And so God bids you to kill me!' Lucilio's voice rose in a howl.

Here Madre Redenta broke in, urging him to be more temperate, because the sisters were at prayer and loud voices might bother them. Clara bowed her head; the poor thing was weeping, yet she did not relent or waver in her conviction. Although she was enduring the greatest torture, her companion's stratagems had utterly bewitched her. By now her soul resided in heaven and she looked on things below only from those infinite heights. She would have given her life to pay for some venial sin of his, but she would also have killed him to assure his eternal salvation. Trembling, half-senseless, she drew near him, then recovered herself.

'Lucilio, do you love me?' she said. 'Well, then, run from me! We shall meet in a better place than this, you can be sure. I shall pray for you, fast and wear sackcloth and pray for you . . .'

'This is blasphemy!' Lucilio shouted. 'You, pray for me? The hangman who intercedes for his victim? Such prayers can only be abhorrent to God!'

'Lucilio,' said Clara mildly, 'we are all sinners, but when –'

Madre Redenta interrupted, giving her a timely elbow in the side.

'Humility, humility, my daughter. There is no need to speak to or instruct others when there is no special reason to do so.'

Lucilio shot the old woman a glance worthy of a lion behind the bars of his cage.

'No, no,' said he bitterly, 'please do instruct me, for I am a great novice in this sphere and I will certainly die of heartbreak before I learn.'

'And I? Do you think I burn to live a long life?' said Clara ruefully. 'There is no mercy I ask of the Virgin more insistently than to die quickly and ascend to Heaven to look after you!'

'And I scorn those prayers of yours!' Lucilio had begun to roar. 'I want you! I want my happiness, my own good!'

'Do be calm! Have pity on me! There is no good in this world; this I know, alas! It is already being rumoured that all religious orders will be abolished and the convents torn down!'

'Yes, yes, and these rumours will come true: that I swear to you! I myself shall make sure that when it comes to these tombs of the living, not one stone rests upon a stone!'

'Silence, Lucilio, I beg you to be silent,' said Clara with an anxious glance at her Superior, who was squirming in her chair, perhaps with secret satisfaction. 'Convert to fear of God and the true faith, beyond which there is no good! Do not commit these sins of heresy: they are mortal sins before God. Do not offend those saintly souls who wed their Creator on this earth so that he may be more clement to their exiled brothers!'

'Hypocrite souls,' said Lucilio through clenched teeth. 'False, depraved souls who try to ensnare and crush other weak and simple souls!'

'No, my dear Doctor, you must not vilify us so foolishly,' said Madre Redenta, her voice dry and nasal. 'Those hypocrite souls who will sacrifice an entire life to shore up and save the weak are the last ones left defending morality and the faith against worldly perversity. It is to their credit if so many weak souls become strong enough to place all their hopes in God, and to consider a mere vow an unsurmountable barrier dividing them from the wicked and the unbelievers. It is true,' she added, lowering her head, 'that we are linked to them by the spiritual bond of prayer, which we'd like to hope will save one or two from the Devil's claws.'

'Oh, the wicked and the unbelievers will very soon be rattling off your vows,' said Lucilio in a booming voice. 'Society is the work of God and those who withdraw from it are either petty cowards, apathetic souls or remorseful criminals. As for you,' here he addressed himself to Clara, 'as for you who have perverted your conscience into something bestial, as for you who would ascend to heaven by treading on the corpse of someone who loves you – who sees not but for you, lives not but for you, thinks not but of you – oh, may wrath and curses come down on your head!'

'Enough, Lucilio,' said Clara solemnly. 'Do you want to know all? Well, I shall tell you! Those vows that I intend to swear before God's altar on Sunday, I've already sworn in my heart before the very same God on that fatal night when the enemies of God, the faith and Venice entered the city. There were eight of us ready to offer our liberty and our lives to keep that plague at bay and if those foul villains are forced to drop the prey they so basely snatched, perhaps God will have smiled on our sacrifice!'

Madre Redenta grinned faintly behind her wimple. Lucilio, no longer in the grip of his fury, began to head towards the door, but then retraced his steps back to Clara, as if he were incapable of leaving her like that.

'Clara,' he said again, 'I shall not beg you any more; I see it is useless. But I shall offer you the spectacle of so much misery that remorse will pursue you all the way into your cloistered peace and silence. Oh, you do not know, you have never known, how much I have loved you! You have never seen the bottom of those deep abysses of my soul so full of you; you have never lost yourself, as I have lost myself, in you. You impose these sacrifices on yourself with a thousand tricks of the mind, yet you will not accept sacrifices prompted by spontaneous affection and sentiments! Clara, I leave you to God – but will God want you? Is He permitted adultery by those holy commandments that sum up all our duties?'

I don't know whether Lucilio, so saying, intended to capitulate or make one last try. In any case, he and Clara were like two fencers out of range, two litigants each speaking a language unknown to the other. Madre Redenta, looking down modestly, thus quietly prevailed over that tireless mover who had toppled a fourteen-century-old government and changed the face of much of the earth. Why did she take such pleasure in this? First of all, because there is no pride like the pride of the humble; then, because she could avenge her own unhappiness this way; and, finally, because she wanted to keep her promise to the Countess. After so many years of slow and patient toil, she could now admire her own efforts in Clara's constancy and she wouldn't have traded that moment for the richest abbacy in the order.

As for Lucilio – after so many years of striving and perseverance, now that he had overcome every impediment and felled every obstacle – to find himself repelled by a young lady's devout scruples, unable to conquer that soul he knew still belonged to him, was lunacy beyond all measure. All the greatest efforts of heart and soul had brought him to a place where he could neither advance nor retreat, and he began to doubt himself, after such a long series of triumphs. The self-assurance he once had possessed made his defeat most desperate. And yet I don't think he gave up, for he was made of that stuff that never gives up except when broken by death. Love, however, turned to rage, hatred, fury in him, and those bitter parting words to Clara were animated, I think, by pride alone. Love had sunk deep within his soul and sparked a blaze of all those passions that once had served him obediently, almost rationally. Clara said nothing to the insults he hurled at her, but her silence was more eloquent than speech, and Lucilio attacked that silence with a hail of curses, like the crazed bull blocked from leaving the ring that splits its skull against the fence.

If his rage scandalized Madre Redenta, Clara responded with great compassion. Then his will got the better of his furies, and it was strong and proud enough to persuade him to go, aiming a last glance of mercy and defiance at the young lady. Let me repeat that it was his pride, perhaps more than his love, that was wounded; even in those terrible moments, in fact, he was able to retreat with honour. Where I might have foolishly died of a broken heart, he forced himself to live, insisting that he was the only master of his own passions and his own life. Whether that was really true, I cannot say. I recall seeing him in those days, and although I was very busy with my own affairs, I nonetheless detected a tremendous distress, which he took pains to try to conceal under his usual austere self-possession. But bit by bit the man he had been won out; the proud Titan recovered from his brief defeat, strong, invincible and ready to face Venice's misfortunes, perhaps even stronger and more invincible for all the desperation in his heart. Clara solemnly made her vows and Lucilio kept his rage and anguish at that fatal loss all to himself.

Not long afterwards la Pisana married Navagero, and Giulio Del Ponte followed them to the altar wearing a smile of hope. He didn't love her as I did. And so I alone was left to make a spectacle of my rage and heartbreak. I could find no peace, nor think about the future without wincing, and yet, even in my wildest grief I never cursed la Pisana; all my curses were reserved for the Countess, who had humiliated her daughter with that monstrous marriage in order to enjoy the ease and wealth of Casa Navagero. Later I would learn that even the tricks used to make a nun of Clara involved matters of money.

The Countess had only paid half of her daughter's dowry to the convent, guaranteeing the rest with her jewellery. But the coffers were empty and her jewels were glittering down at the Monte di Pietà, and she was afraid that if Clara married she would have asked for an accounting of what was owed her. So many troubles caused by the woman's wild itch for the tables playing *bassetta* and Pharaoh! Count Rinaldo saved himself from ruin and from Navagero's disreputable patronage by accepting a very modest post in the government accounting department. A silver ducat per day and the Marciana Library took care of all his earthly needs. But I saw even him walking with bowed head and wary eyes, and I would bet he wasn't the only one to suffer from those low customs and base times.

I say this with shame; the times were really base. Everyone knew where matters were heading and everyone pretended not to know, so as to avoid despair. Barzoni alone among the literati dared to criticize the French with that book I've already referred to, *The Romans in Greece*. But his erudition dressed up as a pamphlet, his strained analogies, pointed to a feeble temperament, an emasculated literature. There was much whispering about the book and its anonymous author; but people read it behind closed doors with only a candle for a witness, always ready to toss it on the fire and appear in the caffès the following day declaring that Lucullus's depredations and Flaminius's cunning generosity were in no way similar to Bonaparte's liberal and open-handed rule. In truth he stole our shirts to pay tribute to France's liberty; we future servants must be as naked as the helots of Sparta.

He had already reconstituted the Cisalpine Republic around Milan: more a threat than a promise to the still-provisional Municipality of Venice. When d'Entragues, the Bourbon minister so vilely handed over by the old Signoria, was freed, the General gained a reputation as a gentleman among the monarchists. They were hoping for a Monk;[6] clever, weren't they? Meanwhile, the incorrigible republicans, the stormers of the Bastille, the Liberty Tree lovers, the Brutuses, the Curtiuses and the Timoleons, were giving him nasty looks, muttering accusations of arrogance, deception and tyranny. The Municipality, after its humiliation at Bassano, saw the ground giving way under its feet and made a foolish error: asking the new Lombard Republic to incorporate the Venetian states. But the governors of Lombardy replied with hard, arrogant words: fratricide, you might have called it, had Bonaparte's unspoken wishes not meant it was plain servility. In any event the names of those who signed that sheet denying aid to an unfortunate and tottering sister city, will be forever infamous. Better to go down together than save oneself and not extend a hand to a friend begging pitifully for help.

Like the others I had put my hopes in the General. I thought perhaps the monuments and ruins testifying to our past greatness would sway him from that cruel indifference he'd already begun to show towards us. But instead of the General (held back by remorse or shame) we had only a visit from his wife, the beautiful Joséphine. She appeared in Piazza San Marco with all the pomp of a Doge's wife, and if her Creole features lacked majesty, they certainly were splendid. All Venice was at her feet; those who had flattered Bonaparte's friend, the banker Haller, hoping to prolong the agony of the old Republic, now flattered the wife of the people's agent, in hopes our miscarriage of liberty would not be killed before it was born. I, too, paraded around in my glorious Secretary's sash, courting our Parisian Aspasia.[7] I watched her lovely mouth smile at our Venetian gallantry, heard her soft voice pronouncing French almost as if it were an Italian dialect, and I, who had studied a little French in those days of universal Frenchification, stammered out my *oui* and my *n'est-ce pas* to some of the aides-de-camp accompanying her. Whether it was a trick of beauty, a show of goodwill or simply our tenacious illusions, our hopes were somewhat revived by the visit of that woman. Even my father no longer shook his head, but pushed me forward to be seen in the front lines of her admirers.

'Women, my son, women are everything,' he told me. 'Who knows? Perhaps Heaven has sent her. From tiny seeds great trees come forth. Nothing would surprise me.'

But Dr Lucilio, friendly as he was with the French minister, had more than anyone else been admitted to the lovely visitor's confidence, and he did not join in the general rapture, it seemed to me. In Joséphine he saw not the woman but the wife, and from her he deduced the husband. What she foretold about our destiny, which lay in the husband's hands, was not very encouraging. Lucilio's deep despair was further confirmed and he seemed even more sombre and cryptic than usual in those days, while the others were all dancing about as if this were the eve of the millennium. Officials of the Municipality, bosses of the people, ex-Senators, ex-nobles, mature ladies, young maidens, abbés and gondoliers: they all crowded around the wife of the great military man. Beauty can achieve much in Venice; it can achieve all when quickened inside by some other sentiment, as we would soon have proof. The woman makes the man, but enthusiasm can make a woman, even when she was brought up as but a doll. Often, while I was trailing after Mme de Beauharnais[8] or waiting in her antechamber, la Pisana and her thoroughly mature husband passed by so close she grazed my elbow. I shivered all over, as if a basin of cold water had been poured down my back, but I didn't forget my dignity and my father's counsel and drew myself up self-confidently to attract the attention of our illustrious guest.

And, in fact, she noticed me and I saw her ask His Excellency Cappello, on whose arm she was leaning, about me. They whispered together and she smiled at me and held out her hand, which I kissed with great respect. So the wives of our liberators were treated then: with lips devout and bended knee. True, that hand was so plump and perfect, so soft, that you might forget it belonged to a citizen; many an empress would have liked a pair like that, nor did Catherine the Great ever have such, no matter how much soap and orange water her distillers supplied. And so I became – after that kiss, I mean – an important personage and la Pisana bestowed on me a glance that certainly wasn't indifferent. His Excellency Navagero's look was even less indifferent than his wife's; he would probably have liked to see me disappear altogether.

At just the right moment, Giulio Del Ponte came to my aid. He seemed to be trailing the lucky couple, and I turned, unhappy, to talk with him. I don't recall what we spoke about, except that we fell upon the subject of la Pisana and her marriage. Giulio had been blessed with not even one per cent of the happiness he'd dreamed of on their wedding day; I studied him now and he looked cadaverous, a lover at the end of his rope. The malaise had returned and it was gnawing away at a body frail by nature and already corroded by previous trials. I felt no sympathy, however, for I had understood the nature of his love and considered it unworthy of my respect or pity. It astonishes me today to think that with my careless upbringing I had such principled judgement in moral matters. (Was that judgement mostly to the detriment of others, perhaps, and far more indulgent when it came to myself?) Whatever the case, I didn't share Giulio's suffering this time, but left him to his own despair and anguish, all the more so because I could no longer concede la Pisana to him, nor make that unwelcome wraith of a husband disappear. The old man's leery, green-eyed jealousy was poor Giulio's prime torment and yet there was another, far worse.

'Do you see?' he murmured in my ear with an angry squeal of teeth. 'Do you see that eager little officer who's always one step behind la Pisana, who leaps from her side to that of her husband, then draws near the lovely De Beauharnais, bowing and pressing her little finger so charmingly? Well, that is citizen Ascanio Minato of Ajaccio, half-Italian, half-French, one of Bonaparte's compatriots and General Baraguay d'Hilliers's aide-de-camp, billeted at Palazzo Navagero by order of the Municipality. As you can see, he's a fine-looking young man: dark, lively and tall; brimming with wit, self-assurance and good health; as brave, they say, as any bandit and a better swordsman than Don Quixote. And, furthermore, he wears the soldier's uniform, which women prefer even to courage. Old Navagero, who won't have any Venetian suitors and swains around the house, has had to bow and accept this overseas intruder. The poor thing's afraid, and to allay suspicions he's an aristocrat or a French-hater, he'd be ready to . . . Oh, enough! There is such a thing as the heroism of fear and it suits that babyish, decrepit old face, mottled yellow and red like parrot-grass.[9] The young lady grows more French every day; she can already chirp out half the dictionary like a Parisienne and I fear that the most interesting words have already entered her conversation. The Corsican officer, needless to say, does not deign to speak Italian. And I speak nothing but Italian! The Lord help us! But one day all will see who these liberators are! They've struck the *Pax tibi Marce* from the Lion's Book[10] and written in the Rights of Man. We'll get what we deserve, for having wished them on us! And it will be a thousand times worse for those who play along with them! You wait and see!'

Until now I had let that flood of eloquence rush by unimpeded, but when he began to howl out his cruel desires and augur a great and public disaster to avenge his own very private wrong I felt a storm of indignation blow up in me and came forth with a tirade that turned him to stone.

'And you can tolerate watching her?' said I with scorn and wonder. He stood there like stone as I spoke, except that every breath cost him effort – effort that stone at least need not make. Giulio's tale of la Pisana's new misadventure cost me a pang, too, but his cynical rant had so horrified me that I assure you there was no place in my heart for any regrets. I went on, scolding and badgering him about his obscene hopes, and I assured him that the most cowardly are not those who tolerate, but those who take satisfaction in the baseness of others and their country's ruin. I grew so heated that we were left alone before I knew it; the company had followed Mme de Beauharnais to the treasure room of San Marco, where a magnificent cameo necklace was to be taken out to give her as a present. When we went ahead to join them they had already gone out to the Piazza and were on their way to the Palazzo del Governo. Imagine my astonishment when I saw Raimondo Venchieredo among those paying court to the lady; and, mingled in the crowd, Leopardo Provedoni and his wife, they too drawn by curiosity into the procession. The ceremonies of the day were over now and, leaving Del Ponte to his ire, I approached the couple and received a hearty welcome with many an 'Oh!' of wonder and delight, as is common when fellow townsmen or old friends meet in a distant city.

Doretta had eyes only for Raimondo; he, in turn, had disappeared into the palazzo along with the most fanatical of the courtiers; Leopardo gripped my hand without having the heart to smile. However, when he had accompanied his wife home –

two little rooms near Ponte Storto – and was alone with me, he recovered some of his aplomb and told me why and how they had come to Venice. It seemed that Old Venchieredo was very close to General Bonaparte in Milan and he had gone with him to Montebello for a secret meeting with the Austrians, and then had raced from Milan to Gorizia, from Gorizia to Vienna and from Vienna to Milan, and shortly thereafter back to Vienna. Returning from this last journey and on the way back to Lombardy he had stopped at Venchieredo to see his son, bidding him to go to Venice right away, for there were soon to be great changes with which his fortunes would prosper. As Signor Raimondo did not wish to be parted from his secretary, Leopardo and Doretta had also had to move house and so they found themselves in Venice. Leopardo was not at all pleased about the matter and had it not been for his wife's pleas they would have stayed in Friuli. Telling his tale, the poor fellow blushed and stammered and only with great effort kept himself from losing control. When I saw this I changed the subject and asked him about the news from home and what had become of friends and acquaintances.

As we conversed and walked along the alleyways and by the canals, his glum spirits dissipated and he nearly forgot his own troubles, but I suffered for him, knowing the moment would come when, sadly, he would recall them once again. In the meantime, he confirmed what I had heard about the sorry state of the family at Fratta. The Captain and Monsignor did nothing but stir up the fire and eat great meals; now that the old servants were either dead or had been dismissed, they'd been replaced by a band of thieves who were busy stealing what little remained. No pot or pan was big enough to provide luncheon for Monsignor. Faustina had married Venchieredo's *bulo* Gaetano, who'd recently been let out of jail, and when she left she had walked off with most of the household linen and sold it. The Captain and Monsignor not only fought over the poker but also the nightshirts; Signora Veronica mistreated them both; and the silliest thing was that old Sandracca would at times get bitten by jealousy, and this provided a third argument for great battles between himself and the Canon.

Otherwise, Fulgenzio, the old sacristan, was raking it in. Right after my departure he had bought a piece of land near Portovecchio from the Frumiers and he topped up his earnings by playing the market after he had pre-paid the masters their share. For example, there was wheat in the barn and from Venice they were demanding money; if wheat was selling cheap, he pretended to buy it with that sum he sent to Venice, and then, when his supplies rose in price, he sold them and paid himself a nice wage. If the price of grain kept falling, he abandoned his phony contract and turned the purchase price into a loan, from which he deducted seven, eight or even twelve per cent. So he satisfied his conscience, while making most immoderate profits from the exercise of his duties.

His sons were neither sacristans nor doorkeepers; Domenico was apprenticed to a notary in Portogruaro and Girolamo was studying theology at the seminary. And, sooner or later, they said in town, Fulgenzio would become the lord of Fratta or something like it. Andreini, who had been asked by Count Rinaldo to keep an eye on Castle business overall while the young lord was gone, was so lax in his supervision you might have thought he was part of the pilfering. The Chaplain, poor fellow, was afraid of Fulgenzio and largely averted his eyes. The Rector of Teglio, who was no favourite in the parish for his austere and rigid ways, had too many problems of his own to stick his nose in the affairs of others. The Diocese, after the arrival of the French and the departure of Padre Pendola (who, according to Leopardo, was also in Venice), had reverted to dividing and subdividing in sects and gangs. They felt entitled, for the accord that had been patched together by Padre Pendola's clever machinations was made of inferior stuff.

'Padre Pendola in Venice!' I muttered. 'What can he have come here to do? This is neither the place nor the season for him, it seems to me!'

Leopardo sighed at my words, adding in a low voice that, alas, the signs were clear: if there is one thing that attracts a crow it is carrion. We reached the Piazza as he said this and he raised his eyes and saw that miraculous edifice that is the Doge's Palace. Two tears ran slowly down his cheeks.

'No, we shall not think of that!' he said, shaking my arm with Herculean force. 'We'll think about that later!' He then began to tell me about matters at home: his sister Bradamante had married Donato from Fossalta; and Bruto, his brother, along with Sandro, the miller, taken by a fit of heroism, had joined a French regiment. I was quite surprised by this news, but I foresaw that Sandro would acquit himself well and the facts did not prove me wrong. Bruto, I thought, was too wild to make a perfect soldier; he'd be a tough fighter, but as for 'to the right' and 'to the left', I had little hope for him. Leopardo also spoke of how the decision had grieved their father; the poor man had lost the use of his mind and his legs, and chance and God's will now directed the affairs of the Commune. There was, in any case, the same muddle everywhere – that interregnum between governments; those three or four jurisdictions at once coalescing and then battling; one of them aged, weak and impotent; the others tyrannical, their power arbitrary and military – all this oppressed the people so much that they all prayed together that a single master would come to chase away those three or four who harried them, but were unable or unwilling to defend them. Municipalities, communes, legal congregations, feudal tyrants, the French military government: where was one to turn to obtain even a crumb of justice?

With this continual to and fro of governors, justice was bound to become personal; every day there was violence, there were brawls and murder; the gallows were working overtime, and even so the knives were always busy. Only where the French command was headquartered was there good humour and perpetual celebration; the officers flaunted the riches stolen in the countryside and small towns; the rabble wallowed in every kind of abundance; the ladies, as was the fashion, flirted with the tidy, well-washed Frenchmen. What better way to become a patriot and a liberal than by making love? It happened everywhere, as it did in Venice: you began by putting on a hostile face and you ended up embracing, the best of friends. Shared vices are whoremongers to every sort of baseness, and there were many, even without la Pisana's rash temperament and decrepit husband, who made do with some little lieutenant to get through those uneasy, provisional times. I know, these are weaknesses and defects inherited from parents and grandparents, but we mustn't excuse them because they are inherited; scrofula, too, is inherited and it's by no means a pretty thing. As for democracy and devotion to reason, they were the opportunistic products of fear and vanity. Those who danced around the Liberty Tree would celebrate the next year's Carnival at the Ridotto gambling tables, despite the Treaty of Campo Formio,[11] and would later soil their knees before the god of Austerlitz.

I don't think the world will ever see a popular celebration so grotesque and funereal as when the Liberty Tree was planted in Piazza San Marco. Behind four drunkards and twenty silly women leaping about, you could hear the French swords scraping on the pavement, and the officials of the Municipality (I among them) stood stiff and silent on their loggia like those ancient corpses just dug up that need but a single breath of air to disperse into dust. Leopardo came with me to that event and he gnawed at his lips like a man with rabies. On a loggia facing us his wife sat next to Raimondo, showing off all the Venetian coquetry she had been able to add to her own in one week of practice.

The days passed, melancholy, monotonous, stifling. My father had returned, stolid as a Turk; he spoke only to his maid, in grunts and monosyllables; he rarely thumped his sack of *doblas* and didn't annoy me any more with his panegyrics about the young Contarini girl. The Frumiers were holed up in their palazzo as if they feared plague in the air; only Agostino ventured out now and again to the caffè, where he loudly declaimed his Jacobin creed. He was one of those who believed the French rule would be permanent and he hoped to reacquire, for love or money, at least a few degrees of his lost eminence. Lucilio moved like a shade from house to house, a doctor who no longer cared either for his own life or that of others, who visited his patients more out of habit than from any conviction he was serving the good of humanity. Leopardo grew gloomier and more taciturn; idleness was eating away at his spirit; he didn't let his misery be seen, he merely allowed himself to die from it little by little. Raimondo and Doretta were blind to him; they brazenly played out their jealousies in public. At times he would thrust his hand beneath his shirt and draw it out, his nails coloured with blood. And yet his clouded, handsome, marble brow showed no trace of anything. His only respite came when he poured out to me, not his grief, but his piercing memories of lost happiness. Then for a moment he would break his monkish vow of silence and words burst like a song from his innocent, ardent lips, memories tinged with great sorrow and bitter pleasure, but without a trace of hatred or rancour.

The one who was (and had always been) truly disturbed was Giulio Del Ponte. The illness that had once brought him near death when he watched la Pisana flirt with Venchieredo had returned in a far more violent guise. And this time he seemed weaker and more defeated, while his competitor was three times handsomer, more carefree and sure of his victory. I never visited Casa Navagero (it would have caused me too much anguish), but I had news from Agostino Frumier. It seemed that wretched Giulio was determined to pursue la Pisana, while every day she disdained him more. His corpse was battling with his living flesh in a fearful struggle that prolonged his pain and death throes and denied him death's patience. His face, ravaged by consumption and distorted by suffering and rage, was horrible to behold; his spirit whipped him, helpless and furious, into a perpetual spin of lurid thoughts, and if he struggled to show some wit, his eyes, his mouth, his voice all belied him. Winded, breathless, he was plagued by hopeless thoughts that twisted his words. His ire at finding he did not amuse la Pisana tormented him and cast a pall of death on his face.

The jovial Corsican officer mocked this shade who had barged in on their pleasure with his protruding bones, his wild hair and his trembling hands. La Pisana ignored him, or if she did see him, found him so sour she had no wish to look twice. Once, he had amused her with his vitality and his enchanting wit; now that these were gone she no longer recognized the Giulio of the old days. And even had he remained himself, the handsome officer would likely have outshone him; in any case she didn't care about him any more or love him at all, and maybe she had never loved him, and lastly, I don't wish to enter into such conjectures, for when faced with a matter so arcane and chaotic as love and a temperament so hasty, changeable and indefinite as that of la Pisana, I could never come up with a prediction worthy of an almanac.

Sometimes Giulio left Casa Navagero with his hands on his head and a storm of jealousy and hurt pride in his heart. Then, among the shadows of night, on the bank of the farthest, most silent canal, he would seek that peace that always escaped him the way clouds flee the man climbing the mountain. And there, under the moon's pale gaze, cooled by a fresh sea breeze, to the distant murmur of the Adriatic, he would pull himself up from his despondency by sheer force of imagination. From the figures that danced in his head, an ultimate riot of life and youth came forth. In his eyes he was a genius who had written the *Iliad* or a general who had won a battle or a saint who had smitten the worldly and felt deserving of Heaven. Love, glory, riches, happiness: for him they were too little. Such fleeting earthly treasures were low and contemptible, he felt; he was grander than they; he scorned them as the rewards of low, crawling beings. He would raise his head haughtily, gaze at the heavens as if he were their equal and say to himself, 'Whatever I wish, I shall do! My soul is mighty enough to raise the world! It was not Archimedes but I who discovered the leverage point: my pride and will!'

Pathetic illusions! Touch one, and it disintegrates between your fingers like a butterfly's wing. Each of us, at least once in our lives, has believed we could accomplish the impossible with ease, that our frail faculties were all-powerful. When those youthful beliefs are proved wrong, yet something strong, something healthy, remains, then we may look forward to our hour of rest, if not of joy, in life. Real desperation hits only when, having understood how weak we are, we cannot find a place to hang our hopes or pride. Then our souls, gone astray, make us stagger like drunkards and fall flat: in the middle of life's journey, unable to raise ourselves again. There are no more lips to smile at us, no more inviting eyes, no smell of roses, no charming views, no glimmers of light to convince us to go forward. Only darkness ahead, at our sides, above. And behind us, relentless memory (a mirror of all the good that has abandoned us and the ills that are mounting) steals our strength of will and power of movement.

So Giulio was left after those nights of delirium: miserable and abject for having seen how vain his dreams of grandeur were. Like Nero, I believe he would have chopped off mankind's head to obtain not a smile of love but a glance of desire from la Pisana, to see his hated rival's arrogant certainty undone, his lips quiver with fury. Such a high price to put on a mere glance, when only moments before he had behaved as if the world were beneath his feet! What humiliation! And he could not even turn to death as a last resort. No, he couldn't! A glorious, tear-stained, long-lamented death would have been as welcome to him as a friend; but now the Corsican's triumph and la Pisana's indifference would follow him to his grave. The man who knows there is life in him can well give in to death, but Giulio, although he dared not confess it to himself, smelled the horrid scent of worms in his overheated and infirm flesh. He struggled desperately on life's sea, but he was growing weak; the water rose from his breast to his throat, now his cheeks were full, now his chin vanished into the abyss of nothingness and darkness, where there was no more pride, no more hope, just nothingness, nothingness, eternal nothingness. He shook himself from this tormented dream with disgust or something more like wretchedness; he knew he was afraid and the fear stemmed from his own worthlessness.

'Oh, life, life! Give me another year, another month, a day of that life of mine once so full, so sure, so vital. Enough to kindle the flame of love, enjoy the bliss of pride and pleasure, and die on a bed of roses, envied and mourned. Give me just one day of my youthful vigour, so that I can inscribe in words of fire a curse to burn the eyes of all who dare read it, so that I will be notorious down the centuries, like Belshazzar and his *mene, mene, tekel, upharsin.*[12] Oh let me die, but may I, with the last howl of my tortured soul, forever destroy the impudent cheer of those who never shed a tear for my sorrows! If I am forbidden the happiness of love, the gods' joyous cup, may I have at least Herostratus' immortality,[13] and the hubris of Hell!'

So the miserable Giulio raved on, pen clutched in one agitated hand, searching his grim imagination for those terrible, infernal words that could preserve his martyr's existence in memory and take his revenge by inflicting anguish. Out of a frenetic whirl of butchered, battling ideas, of flickering chameleon pictures and mute raging passions came but two mediocre, almost cowardly thoughts: fury at the happiness of others and a horror of death! If only he had been able to impress on his thoughts that stamp of excruciating truth against which a man measures himself in horror, unable to avoid admiring the lugubrious prophet who fills him with dread and desperation! But even this was denied him by the shaky ground of his fear. The soul's energies must all work together to bring forth an honest image of the truth; Giulio dissipated his in endless, colourless whims. This was not the wise man's meditation, but the delirium of the sick. Mere chemical combination drove out any spiritual toil: so the small man's pride is punished.

'Oh, to have to die like this, seeing the stars in one's mind expire one by one! Feeling the matter of which we are made dissolve, atom by atom, unable to let go of the serene, radiant (but now disfigured) soul that not long ago floated on air and soared to the heavens! Oh, to have to die like a rat in a barn or a frog in a marsh, without leaving any permanent trace of one's passage! To die at twenty-eight, greedy for life, avid for the future, mad with pride, replete only with pain and humiliation! To abandon life without a dream, without belief, without an embrace; with only the fear and rage that one has to abandon it! Why were we brought forth? Why did they raise us and get us used to living, as if we were to be eternal? Why did the nursemaid, teaching us our first word, not say 'death'? Why did they not accustom us to stare this hidden enemy in the face, to pound it with questions, this enemy that attacks so swiftly, to show us that our virtues are merely another form of depravity? Where are the comforts of wisdom, the illusions of glory, the consolations of love? All has been tossed overboard to escape shipwreck, and when the voracious swell opens its jaws only the helmsman is left, clinging naked and helpless to the highest mast. Struggle and tears are in vain, as are prayers and curses. Destiny is inescapable and the wild noise of the waves drowns out the nearby shouts of the furious, the moans of the terrified. Below is nothingness; all around, darkness; above, mystery. What does the philosopher say? Do not think of it, do not think of it! But how are we not to think of it? My mind has but this one thought, my nerves send to my brain but this one image; all other thoughts and images are dead to me. I am halfway into the great kingdom of the shadows and the rest of me will soon be there. My love of mankind, my faith in liberty and justice, have vanished from my soul, ghosts dreamed up to deceive ghosts. When the foundation collapses, how will the walls stand up? What is fixed and solid in a man, if man can evaporate like the morning mist? When the heat of sentiments has gone cold, our words come forth like wind through a crack in the wall: vanity, all is vanity!'

And yet Giulio, in defiance of this sad soliloquy, took up his pen to write a patriotic anthem, a republican philippic, something to leave a halo of glory around his imminent end. Then he was ashamed of what he had written and threw it on the fire. As badly as we may express those sentiments that are foremost in our minds, far worse is the case with those that are faded and obscured. Giulio thought about himself too much, he was too wrapped up in contemplation of his own destiny to properly understand the hopes and feelings of all mankind. Such things he had, I won't say learned, but found in books, and they had lodged in his brain like fashionable chimeras and nothing more. Crushed by his urgent, personal passions, he could not draw from those ideas that sincere enthusiasm that alone warms a work of art. Barzonis' erudite declamations and young Foscolo's Greek pedantry, so crudely satirized by Giulio, had more fire in them than all his political ideas, a warmed-over broth from Rousseau and Voltaire lacking any powers of persuasion. He knew it and worried his pen with his teeth and threw himself, exhausted, on the bed. A deep, obstinate cough drained his long nights; bathed in sweat, aching on every side, his face shrunken in fear, he pressed on his breast and opened his weary lungs, convincing himself that death was still far off.

In those very moments Ascanio and la Pisana stood at a balcony over the Grand Canal, chirping of love in all the tender *mots* the French language can provide, while His Excellency

Navagero, alarmed by the officer's nasty glances, dozed (or pretended to doze) in an armchair. I didn't have the courage to enter that house, but, passing along the Canal Grande in my gondola late one night, I saw the two lovers lit up like a picture in the window frame. Poor Giulio! Poor Carlino! Providence, seen from the long perspective, governs all with justice. Wherever there are two happy creatures, two unfortunates stand opposite, like shadows in a painting. If my misfortune was the lesser, it was also true that I deserved it less than Giulio. Misfortune avenges all, but sanctifies nothing, especially not pride, envy and lust. He chose to consume himself in those three ugly passions and that was his error; we pity him, which is a long way from glorifying him. His cross was a gallows; Christ alone was able to transform it into an altar.

Summer was nearly over. The proud Dalmatians of Perast,[14] grieving, had already burned the last standard of San Marco. The Republic of Venice was dead; the last vestiges still floated on the distant horizons of the Levant coasts. Carlo Vidiman, governor of Corfu (brother of the wisest and best officer of the Municipality), expired of grief, tormented by the French who had landed there to play the master. The people, disgusted by the weakness of the Venetians, refused to serve the servants; better the French themselves or anything but the limp ineptitude of a hundred patricians. Respected for many centuries for its might, then venerated for its prudence, then tolerated out of habit, Venice was now held in contempt, as always happens where undeserved deference has been too long enjoyed. In the Municipality, all opinions were tinged with despair and none could agree; Dandolo and Giuliani urged a universal republic, the latter without the least concern for our suspicious allies. Vidiman counselled moderation, for history had taught him that if a new government is to survive, change must be cautious and slow. They shouted at each other in the hall of the Maggior Consiglio, where a simple word from a patrician had once decided the fates of Italy. The one who suffered the worst vexation was me, who had to draw up reports based on hours of interminable chatter and pointless, undignified bouts of mutual recrimination. At last the great announcement, which had been circulating in the shape of fear, burst out in words of real and certain anguish. Under the Treaty of Campo Formio, France was allowing Austria to occupy Venice, the states of the Levant, and those of the mainland as far as the River Adige. For itself, France was taking the Low Countries of Austria, and the Cisalpine Republic would annex the provinces of Venetian Lombardy. The words and the treaty were as underhanded as those who wrote them.

Venice woke in horror from her lethargy, like those moribund souls who come to their right minds at death's very door. The officers of the Municipality sent envoys to the Directory and to Bonaparte, asking to be allowed to defend themselves. Their request was perfectly in keeping with the wording of the treaty, which 'permitted' the occupation of Venice. What could be more ingenuous than asking your executioner for weapons to defend yourself against him? The officers of the Municipality knew they were powerless; they merely sought to delude themselves to the end. Bonaparte threw the envoys in jail; those bound for Paris didn't arrive in time to act out their parts. One fine morning that teary old crocodile Villetard appeared in full session to announce that Venice must sacrifice herself for the good of all Europe, and that this necessity broke his heart, but it must be endured with great courage; that the Cisalpine Republic offered a homeland, citizenship and even territory to build a new Venice for all those who wished to escape the new dominion, and that monies from the treasury and the sale of public assets would soften their exile with a certain comfort. The ever so proud Italian character instantly revealed itself at this last proposal. Weak, divided, credulous, boasting, incompetent, yes – but venal, no, never! All the assembled rose in a shout of indignation, refusing the ignoble offer, refusing to confirm what the French Republic had agreed in its facile, barbarous pact, putting the matter before the people, letting the people decide between servitude and liberty. The people voted, en masse, collected, silent, and they voted for freedom. The Municipality was dissolved and many went into exile, from which some, among them Vidiman, never returned. Villetard wrote to Milan and Bonaparte replied, detached, mocking, but furious. The subject who allows himself to be crushed, yet does not obey, is greatly provoking to a ruler.

Sérurier[15] appeared in those days, the true gravedigger of the Republic. He dismantled ships, sent cannon, rope, frigates and battleships to Toulon; made one last raid on the public treasury, churches and picture galleries; scraped the gilt off Bucintoro, feasted and drank on what was left, and insured himself in perpetuity against any regrets for having left the city's new masters even one penny's worth. Thus was the sworn alliance respected; thus the promised protection, and the sacrifices imposed and ignobly (more than generously, perhaps) agreed to. So they behaved towards Venice, which had defended Christianity against Mohammedan barbarity for so many centuries. But those swine did not read history; rather, they were writing terrible chapters of history to come.

The very evening that the Municipality gave up its authority, all those who had remained friends of liberty and firm enemies of treason, met at the usual place behind the Arsenale bridge. Our numbers were fewer than usual; some shied away in fear, others had already left Venice for various destinations. The meeting served more to console one another and clasp hands than for any deliberations. Agostino Frumier did not appear, although an hour previously he had promised, under his breath, that he would come; Barzoni was absent: he had quarrelled in public with Villetard, then set sail for Malta, where he said he intended to publish an anti-French paper; I didn't see Giulio Del Ponte and thought I knew why. Lucilio, as always, paced up and down the room, his face composed, a storm in his heart. Amilcare ranted and waved his hands against the Directory, against Bonaparte, against all. 'We must live in order to avenge ourselves,' he said. Ugo Foscolo sat in a corner, the opening lines of his *Last Letters of Jacopo Ortis*[16] inscribed on his brow. As for myself, I have no idea what lay in my heart. I felt nothing. I suffered without comprehending. I heard that most of us were inclined to seek refuge in Cisalpine territory, where there would always be some hope for Venice; and I, too, thought this was the proper course, an honourable and active exile conducted in a fraternal country that was already almost Italian. That prickly pride that would refuse hospitality offered in the name of France was far from fitting in such a moment of supreme need.

We agreed to convene in Milan, where – in the government, in the army, by word of mouth, by pen or by hand – we hoped to work for the public welfare. In those days the ups and downs of fortune came so hot on one another that hope sprang forth from desperation, wilder and more confident than ever. In any case, we wished to show an example of Venetian dignity and constancy to counter those terrible changes that events were hurling at us. We all left one by one to put our affairs in order or to collect a few things before going abroad. One ran to embrace his mother, his sister, his lover; one squeezed his innocent children to his breast; one spent that last night on the Riva contemplating the Doge's Palace, the domes of San Marco, the Procurators' offices (those venerable, sullied expressions of the ancient queen of the seas). Tears flowed from faithful eyes, the last to be freely shed and gloriously commemorated.

I had stayed on alone with Dr Lucilio, not having the energy to move, when a clatter was heard on the stairs and Giulio Del Ponte, his face as pale and grey as death, burst into the room. Lucilio, who had not said much up to this point, turned to him sharply, asking what was the matter and why had he come so late. Giulio said nothing; his gaze was frozen, his tongue stuck to his palate; he seemed unaware a reply was expected. With one hand Lucilio tossed back his black hair (a strand of silver glistening here and there), gripped the young man's arm and drew him forcefully into the lantern light.

'Giulio, I'll tell you what the trouble is!' said he in a low but certain tone. 'You are dying of sorrow all your own, now when it is only permissible to die for the sorrows of all! Rather than surrender ignobly to the consumption devouring you, you must rise courageously to martyrdom! I am a physician, Giulio; I do not wish to deceive you. A passion made of rage, pride and ambition is slowly consuming you; its bite is poisonous, incurable. Without a doubt you will succumb. But do you not think the soul can escape the ills of the body and mark out for itself a great and glorious end?'

Puzzled, Giulio rubbed his eyes, his cheeks, his brow. He was shivering all over and coughing now and then, unable to say a word.

'Do you imagine' continued Lucilio, 'that under this hard, frozen skin of mine exist no torments such that I would prefer inferno or the tomb to the toil of living? Well, but I do not wish to die weeping for myself, grieving for myself, caring only for myself, like a sheep to the slaughter. When our limbs have lost their strength, the soul flees from them so much freer, stronger and more blissfully! Giulio, allow your body to die, but save an immortal intelligence from baseness and misery!'

I stood astonished, watching the two of them, Lucilio seeming to infuse the other with courage and energy. At the doctor's words and touch, Giulio drew himself up and his eyes came back to life; a shadow of shame fell across his brow, but his spirit, revived by great sentiment, suffused his coming death in a sublime glow. He neither coughed nor trembled, and where illness had made him sweat, he was now heated by enthusiasm. His words were still broken and confused, but only because he was impatient to repent and serve. It was a genuine miracle.

'You are right,' Giulio said at last, in a deep, calm voice. 'I have been a coward until now, but I shall no longer be one. I must certainly die, but I shall die a brave man and my spirit will survive my body's ruin! I'm grateful to you, Lucilio! I came here by chance, out of habit, in despair; I was desolate, demoralized, ailing; I shall leave with you, healed, dignified, certain. Wherever we must go, I am ready!'

'We shall leave tomorrow for Milan,' said Lucilio, 'and we shall find a rifle for each of us there. No one asks a soldier if he is ill or well, but whether he is brave and bold! This I can assure you, Giulio: you will not die trembling with fear and longing to live. Together we will leave this spineless, deluded century and take happy refuge in eternity's bosom!'

'Oh, yes,' said I. 'I, too, will go with you!' I clutched the doctor's hand and embraced Giulio like a brother. So surprised and moved was I that no fate seemed kinder than to die beside such comrades.

'No, for now you must not leave,' said Lucilio softly. 'Your father has other plans; consult with him, as is your duty. As for my own father, I learned this very day that he has died. As you can see, I am now all alone, naked of those affections that enclose so much of our lives within domestic walls. My horizons are opening out: from the Alps to Sicily, all is one home to me. I live in it with a single sentiment that will never die, not even when I do.'

As Lucilio said these words, the memory of the convent of Santa Teresa flashed across his vision like a thunderbolt, yet it did not disturb the calm tone of his voice or leave any trace of melancholy on his face. All worries vanished before the superb assurance a soul enjoys knowing it holds some part of the eternal. We parted then; our farewells austere, without tears or regrets. The names of Clara and la Pisana were not pronounced in our parting speeches. And yet I am certain that all three of us, Lucilio included, felt malevolent love tearing at our innards. The two of them headed towards the hospital, with plans to set out in the morning at dawn; I hurried off to find my father. I did not know what his intentions were, for Lucilio had told me nothing; now I was in haste to learn of them, and so unload my private sorrows on to some great and useful sacrifice, following Giulio's example.

THIRTEEN

A Venetian Jacopo Ortis, a Venetian Machiavelli. I finally get to know my mother twenty years after her death. Venice between two lives. A Greek family at San Zaccaria. My father in Constantinople. Spiro and Aglaura Apostulos.

My father was not at home and the old Mohammedan servant, with many negative signs and hand gestures, persuaded me she meant to say she had no idea when he would return. I was debating with myself whether to wait for him when she handed me a note, waving her arms around to suggest it was of great moment. I thought it might be a message from my father, but then I saw it was written by Leopardo.

'I did not find you at home and so I am leaving you these few lines. I need your help right away for a service that three hours hence you will no longer be able to provide.' There was no further explanation.

Trying as best I could to make the old woman understand that I would be back soon, I grabbed my hat and hurried off to Ponte Storto. What could I do? The note said nothing and when I had left Leopardo that same morning, he'd been grave and taciturn as usual, but quite sane and reasonable. And yet my heart told me to expect disaster and I longed for winged feet to get there faster. The door to his house was open and a lamp was lying on the ground before the stairs. I raced up into Leopardo's room and found him sitting in a chair, his face as serious as usual, but much more pallid. He was staring fixedly at the lamp, but when I came in he turned his eyes to me and greeted me silently. 'Thank you,' he seemed to say, 'you've come in time.' Taken aback by his manner and his silence, I asked him very uneasily what the matter was and what I could do to help him.

'Nothing,' said he, closing his mouth with difficulty, like a man speaking on the verge of sleep. 'I'd like you to keep me company. Pardon me if I don't say much; I have some stomach pains.'

'Good Lord, then let us call a doctor!' I exclaimed. I knew that Leopardo was not a man to complain about trifles and the fact that he'd summoned me at night suggested he feared the worst.

'The doctor,' he said with a pained smile. 'Carlino, I must tell you that an hour ago I swallowed two grains of mercury salts.'

I let out a groan of horror, but he covered his ears and continued,

'Oh, do be quiet, Carlino! My wife is sleeping there in the next room. It would be a pity to trouble her, all the more because she is expecting and this new state of hers makes her irritable.'

'For Heaven's sake, Leopardo, let me go!' He was clutching my wrist with all his might. 'We may still be in time: a good emetic, some deathbed antidote, something! Let me go, let me go!'

'Carlino, it is pointless. The only thing I will accept from you is one last hour of company, as I said. Accept it, for I am even more accepting, more willing to be gone. The emetic and the doctor will arrive half an hour too late; I've studied the necessary chapter on toxicology for a week. You see, I'm already at the second stage of symptoms! I can feel my eyes bulging from my head. Let us hope that the priest the concierge went to look for arrives soon! I am a Christian and I want to die by the rules.'

'No, Leopardo, I beg you! Let me at least try! I cannot allow you to die like this!'

'It is my wish, Carlino. If you are my friend you must grant me this favour. Sit down beside me and we will end it conversing, like Socrates.'

I could see now that such terrible calm left no room for hope and so I sat down beside him, cursing the sad circumstance that so meanly stole from me one of the bravest men I had ever known. That business of sending for the priest pointed to the suicidal brain's supreme disorder, for he could not be unaware that the church considered his act a mortal sin. He seemed to guess my thoughts, for he began to rebut them without me ever taking the trouble to say anything.

'It's true isn't it, Carlino, that this desire of mine to confess surprises you? What can I say? For many months I happily forgot that God forbids suicide and just now I've remembered; being close to death does indeed aid memory wonderfully. But luckily, it's too late! Too late: the Lord will punish me for this long distraction, but I hope he will not be too severe with me and that I will get by with a stint in Purgatory. I have suffered so much, Carlino; I've suffered so much in this life!'

'Oh damnation, damnation to those who pushed you to such a dreadful fate! Leopardo, I will avenge you, I swear I will!'

'Be silent, my friend; do not wake my sleeping wife. Meanwhile, I beg you to forgive, as I do. In fact, I nominate you my executor of forgiveness, so that no one will be harmed by my death. And I advise you not to let it be known it was by my own hand. It would be a great scandal and others might suffer distress or remorse. Say that it was an aneurism, a fulminating apoplexy or what you will. I will work things out with the priest and so hope to die in peace, leaving peace behind me.'

'Oh Leopardo! That a heart such as yours should expire like this! With all your goodness, your strength, your fortitude!'

'You are right; just two years ago I would never have dreamed of such a foolish thing. But now I've done it and there's nothing more to say. The sorrow, the humiliation, the disenchantment accumulated inside here,' he said, putting a hand on his chest, 'and one day the pot overflowed, and farewell judgement! This is how I must express it in order to gain God's forgiveness.'

Now I saw, or rather guessed, the lengthy tortures imposed on that poor heart, so honest and candid; the anguish that a soul so open and loyal and so ignobly betrayed had endured. How delicate he was, determined to see nothing and to die without imposing even the punishment of remorse on his murderers! I said nothing of this, respecting the dying man's astonishing discretion. Leopardo began to speak again, in a deeper, wearier voice; his limbs were going stiff and, little by little, his flesh took on an ashy colour.

'Do you see, my friend? Until yesterday I often thought of death, but defended myself bravely. I had my native land to love and hoped one day to serve it and to forget about the rest.

But now that illusion, too, has vanished; that was the blow that decided me.'

'Oh no, Leopardo; all is not lost! If that is how you think, you must get well, come back to us. We shall carry our native land in our hearts wherever we go; we shall teach and propagate the sacred creed. We are young and better times will come to us; let me . . .'

I had got to my feet, but he held me by the arm with a convulsive force and I had to sit down again. A faint, melancholy smile hovered on that countenance already almost undone by death; never had the soul's beauty obtained a greater triumph over bodily imperfection. If the body was no longer lovely, the soul glowed in all its splendour from his cadaverous face.

'Stay with me, please,' he said, making a great effort. 'In any case, it is too late. Preserve your pure faith, my friend: this is my counsel, for it is, if nothing else, a powerful incentive to carry out fine and honourable deeds. As for myself, I go without regrets. I am sure I would have waited in vain. I am tired, tired, tired!'

With these words his limbs relaxed and his head, sagging, came to rest on my shoulder. I tried to move and call for help, but he came to himself just enough to see my intentions and forbid me.

'Haven't you understood?' he said weakly. 'I want only you and the priest.'

I did understand, alas, and I beamed a glance full of hatred and disgust towards the door, behind which Doretta slept her placid sleep. Then I put an arm under Leopardo's neck and, seeing that the spasms seemed to diminish in that position, I made an effort to hold his head up that way. His weight on my arm grew and I was shaking all over with weariness or perhaps grief, when the concierge came back with the priest. She had knocked on the parish priest's door in vain and so she had returned with one she'd met by chance. He had been reluctant to come at first, but had agreed when she told him it was a fulminating apoplexy, as Leopardo had described his ailment. Imagine my amazement when I lifted my eyes and recognized . . .

Padre Pendola! The good Father gave a start no less than my own and for a moment we stood there, surprise blocking any motion at all. In that silence, Leopardo raised his eyes with great effort, but as soon as he had seen the face of the priest he leaped up as if he had been stung by a viper. Padre Pendola withdrew a few steps and the frightened concierge let the lantern fall from her hand.

'I don't want him! He must leave! He must leave at once!' shouted Leopardo, writhing in my arms like a man possessed.

The Reverend had the greatest desire to take this advice, but he was ashamed before the woman and wanted at least to salvage the honour of the cloth. This turned out to be easier than he had feared, because Leopardo's rage quickly subsided and he went back to being as gentle as a lamb. The good Father drew near with an angelic smile and began to comfort his immortal soul in a tiny, rather sincere-sounding voice.

'Reverend Father, I pray you, leave me!' Leopardo's hiss was grim and threatening.

'But my most beloved son, think of your soul. Remember that you have only a few minutes to live and that I, however unworthy a minister of our Lord, can –'

'Better no one than you, Father,' Leopardo cut him off.

The concierge, not very happy with this spectacle, had left the room to look after her own affairs, and so the prudent Pendola decided it was unwise to insist. He waved his holy blessing and headed off to where he had come from. As he was going out of the door, Leopardo spoke up.

'From the brink of the tomb, one last reminder, Father, one last spiritual reminder to you who are charged with looking after the souls of others. You see how I die: peaceful, cheerful, serene. Well, to die like this, one must live as I have lived. You, I'm afraid, will long for such a fate in vain; you will remember me at the supreme moment and you will pass into the other world quaking and fearful, feeling the claws of the Devil in your flesh. Good night, Father. At dawn I shall sleep more peacefully than you!'

Padre Pendola was already gone, making a sign of horror and pity behind him, and I wager that on the way down the stairs he made many more signs of great joy at having got away so cheaply. Leopardo gave him no more thought, but begged me to go find another confessor. I left him to the care of the concierge, went out and rang so loud at the parish priest's door that he was roused from his bed and I took him to the dying man. During my absence Leopardo had grown so much worse that had I seen him anywhere else I would not have recognized him. Still, the arrival of the priest comforted him greatly and I left them alone for a moment. When I returned I found him in his death throes, but even calmer and more serene than before.

'Well then, my son, do you truly repent of the grave sin you have committed?' the confessor asked. 'Do you admit that you lost faith in Providence and that you wanted to destroy God's work by force and that no creature is permitted to make himself the judge of divine will?'

'Yes, yes, Father,' replied Leopardo (with a slight hint of irony he was unable to suppress and which perhaps I alone perceived, for the dying man himself was unaware of it).

'And have you done everything in your power to inhibit the consequences of your crime?' the priest now asked.

'There is nothing to be done,' the dying man whispered. 'There was no more time. Father, two grains of mercury salts are too potent a dose!'

'Well then, the absolution I impart will be confirmed by the Lord.' And he began to recite prayers for the dying. Now Leopardo's moribund veins began to freeze and his limbs went slack and his lips grew dry and his eyes rolled back dreadfully, and still his spirit reigned unmoved over that tempest of death raging below. They seemed to be two different beings, the one observing the sufferings of the other with all the detachment of an inquisitor. The priest now administered last rites and Leopardo composed himself to await death with the grave piety of a true Christian. Peace had returned to his person, that solemn peace that precedes death, and I could admire what greatness religion can bring to a noble, manly soul, and for the first time I envied those sublime beliefs forever denied me. The death of the old Countess Badoer had discredited them, but Leopardo's death made them seem worthy again. It must be said, though, that his mettle was such that he would have passed the test with faith or without it.

Soon he was assailed by sharp, new pains, but they were the last; his breath came faster and shallower; his eyes half-closed as if he were contemplating an enchanting vision; and his hand rose to caress some of those angels who were coming to meet him. The golden dreams of his youth shimmered before him in delirium's vague twilight: his best hopes and his most splendid dreams took on the visible shape of reality, the recompense for a virtuous, unstained life – or portents of heaven. From time to time he fixed his gaze on me, smiling and seeming to know me; then he took his hand in mine and put it to his heart, that heart that, although it was now scarcely beating, still brimmed with courage and love. Once he made as if to rise and I almost thought I saw him suspended in the air in a wonderful posture of prophecy and inspiration. He proudly said the name of Venice, then fell back exhausted and returned to his fantasies.

When he was near the end, I saw him open his mouth in a smile like nothing I had seen for some time on that broad, majestic face. He put a hand in his shirt and took out a scapular, on which he pressed his lips a number of times. Each kiss was slower and less energetic, until he took his lips away and sent his soul up to God, and his last breath came out of his breast so deep and full it seemed to say, 'Here I am at last, happy and free!' That piece of cloth to which he'd consecrated his last breath fell into my hand as his grip loosened and I took it as a token, a sacred inheritance, and knelt before him as before God. I've never again seen a death like that; the priest shook holy water over the body and went off, drying his eyes, assuring me that Leopardo would be given a proper burial and never mind that the rules forbade it. His death was so saintly that the letter of the law could be stretched. When I was alone I let my grief burst forth; I kissed and kissed again that holy martyr's face, wetting it with my tears, contemplating his smile at length, half in love with the superhuman peace he emanated. I learned more about virtue from half an hour with a dead man than in all my dealing with the living.

The lamp was down to its last flickers and the first light of day shone through the shutters when I remembered that it was my job to tell Doretta of her husband's death. The very thought filled me with disgust. Nevertheless, I steeled myself to knock on the door, when I heard a rustle of steps behind it; the door opened slowly and the pale, somewhat suspicious figure of Raimondo Venchieredo appeared before me. My shout was so loud it echoed through the house and I lunged towards Leopardo to embrace him, as if to protect or console him for that posthumous insult. At first Raimondo understood nothing, merely stammering out some words, including 'gondola' and 'Fusina', in a hurry to leave. Later I would learn that he had sent Leopardo to Fusina with orders to remain there all day, awaiting his father, who was supposed to come there to receive a very important message. And Leopardo had, in fact, departed at sundown, but halfway to his destination realized he had forgotten the letter and so he had returned at about three o'clock in the morning. He had seen Raimondo furtively enter his house and Doretta's room; the rest is easily imagined. He had, however, procured the mercury salts from a grocer early that morning, after having witnessed the meeting of the Municipality in which Villetard pronounced his death sentence on Venice. It seemed this final outrage against his honour merely set in motion a decision already matured for various motives. The letter to Venchieredo in Padre Pendola's hand was found in the drawer of the table in front of him.

I did not know all of this back then, but I guessed something like it. However, I could not bear to see Raimondo go off like that without knowing anything of the tragedy of which he had been the cause. I hurried after him to the door, grabbed him by the shoulders and dragged him, trembling, on bended knee before Leopardo's corpse.

'Look, you traitor! Look!' I said to him.

He looked, frightened, and only then did he see the mortal pallor of those inanimate remains. When he understood, he let out a scream that was sharper and more terrible than my own and fell down as if struck by a thunderbolt. That second shout brought the concierge into the room, along with Doretta and everyone else in the house. Raimondo had come to, but could barely stand up, Doretta was tearing out her hair and I couldn't say whether she was shrieking or weeping; the others observed the lugubrious spectacle fearfully, whispering questions one to another about what had happened. It fell to me to tell the lie, and it wasn't difficult, for I wanted to honour my friend's wishes scrupulously. But I could not avoid, in blaming his death on a fulminating apoplexy, letting my tone of voice say otherwise. Raimondo and Doretta understood and endured the shame that criminals feel before my unbending gaze. I left the house, with plans to return the following day to accompany my friend to his last resting place. What my heart felt, what my thoughts were, I do not wish to confess today. Several times I stared at the deep, roiling waters of the canal with unspeakable longing, but my father expected me and other sorts of martyrdom awaited me on the way to Milan and the hard punishment of exile.

My father, in fact, had been waiting for an hour and had grown impatient not seeing me return. I apologized, telling him the atrocious tale, and he cut me off, exclaiming, 'Madness! Madness! Life is a treasure and one must use it well to the last penny.' His placid acceptance rather nauseated me and I felt no desire to do as he wished, as Lucilio had persuaded me I should the evening before. But my father, not even waiting for me to grow annoyed, launched into the subject.

'Carlino, tell me the truth, how much money do you need per year?'

'I was born with a good pair of arms,' said I coldly. 'I can look after myself.'

'You, too, are mad! Mad!' said he. 'I was also born with arms and have made them work wonderfully, but I've never turned down help from a friend. Take this, however, you will, but I am your father and I have the right to advise you, and even, if necessary, to issue orders. Don't look at me so haughtily! There's no need! I feel for you: you are young, you lost your head. I, too, spent all day yesterday not knowing if you were alive or dead; I suffered, too, you see, as much as any man in the world, seeing all my hopes overturned by the very ones I'd trusted to carry them out. I too wept; yes, I wept with rage to find myself mocked, derided and repaid for seven years of service with ingratitude and betrayal. Today, however, I scoff at all that! I have a great idea in mind; it will occupy me for months, perhaps for many years; I hope to succeed better than at the first trial, and then we'll meet again. A man, you see, is rather a weak animal; he is future kin to nothing, but he is not nothing! And so long as he is not nothing he can be the first link in a chain on which everything hangs. Listen to me, Carlino! I am your father and I respect you and love you very much. You must accept the counsels of my experience; you must preserve yourself for that future that I will work to create for you and our country. Remember that you are not alone, that you have powerless, needy refugee friends, and there will be times when you are happy to have bread to share with them. In this pouch are many millions that I consecrate to a great campaign for justice and revenge. They were to be yours, but no longer. You see, I speak openly and candidly. Do me the same courtesy, therefore, and tell me how much you need to live on comfortably for a year.'

I bowed to my father's pressing logic and told him that three hundred ducats would be more than enough.

'Bravo, my son!' he replied. 'You are a great gentleman. Here is a letter of introduction to the Apostulos House in San Zaccaria, which you will present this very day to their representative. You will find good people there, generous and loyal people: an old man who is a pearl among honest merchants and who will be another me for you; a young man just back from Greece who is worth twenty of our Venetians; a young lady you will love as a sister; a mother who will love you as a mother does. Trust in them; you will have my news from them, because I plan to sail before noon; I do not want to witness this infamous day. The house for which I paid two thousand ducats is yours; I have already drafted the deed. In the desk are some papers that belonged to your mother. They are yours by inheritance and by law. As for your future, I give you no advice, for you do not need it. Others still put their faith in the French and are emigrating to Cisalpina. Keep your own interests in mind and never stop thinking of Venice: don't let yourself be blinded by good fortune or wealth or glory. Glory will come when you regain your native land; good fortune and wealth are valuable only when backed by liberty and justice.

'Have no fear, Father,' said I, quite moved by this advice, expressed in leaps and bounds more Moorish than Venetian, but no less generous for that. 'I shall never stop thinking of Venice. But why can I not depart with you and be a part of your plans, a companion of your labours?'

'The truth, my son? You are not enough of a Turk to approve of all my methods. I am like a surgeon who when he works does not wish to have snuffling, silly women around him. I don't say this to insult you, but I repeat: you are not enough of a Turk. That speaks well of you, but for me it would mean forfeiting that freedom of movement that speeds along the things of this world. And a man of sixty years, Carlino, is in a hurry, a great hurry. What is more, there are not enough strong and right-thinking young men in these lands. It is best you remain here, for we must learn to take charge of things ourselves. Here and there, matters are growing complicated. In Ancona, in Naples, they are already on the boil, and when the fire spreads, those who set it may get burned, and then it will be your turn – that is, ours. That is why I ask you to stay and let me go where old age is favoured over youth, where money outweighs bodily strength and courage.'

'My dear Father, what can I say? I shall stay! But may I at least know where you are going?'

'I go to the East, to the East to make an agreement with the Turks, for I don't seem to be understood here. Soon, even if you don't hear talk of me, you will hear talk of the Turks. Then you will be able to say I had a hand in it. I cannot say more, for these are all still ghosts of plans.'

My father then went out to confirm the departure time with the captain of a tartan ready to sail for the Levant. I went with him, but learned little more, except that he was going straight to Constantinople, where he might remain briefly or at length, depending on the circumstances. His thoughts were certainly neither petty nor base, but enlarged his person and lent him an authority I hadn't seen before. He wore the usual hat and the usual Armenian-style breeches, but a new fire flashed from under his greying brow. Around nine he boarded ship with his trusty maid and a small trunk. Not a sigh, not a farewell to anyone; he set out quite willingly on that road to exile with all the boldness of a young man who sees certain victory before him. He kissed me as if we would meet again on the morrow, reminded me to go see Apostulos, then went below deck while I returned to the gondola that had brought us to the ship.

Oh, how alone, abandoned, miserable I felt when I trod the stones of the Piazzetta once more. My sad soul raced towards la Pisana, but the thought of Giulio and the Corsican officer blocked it midstream. I began to grieve for Leopardo and honoured his memory with those mourning thoughts that make up an elegy for a friend. I wept and raved on for a while, until, to distract myself, I recalled the letter and turned towards San Zaccaria to meet the Greek merchant. I found a large, grey-haired, mustachioed fellow of few words who honoured my father's signature and asked me how I would like to be paid. I said I only wanted to take the interest year to year and would happily leave the capital in such good hands. The old man then uttered a sort of grunt and a younger fellow appeared to whom he handed the letter, adding some words in Greek that I could not understand. He then told me that this was his son and that I should go with him to the cash desk, where the sum would be delivered however I wished. Gruff and surly as the old shopkeeper was, his son Spiridone was likeable and courteous in proportion. Tall and lean, with a very ardent modern Greek profile, olive-toned skin and two eyes like thunderbolts, he won my affection from the first. I sensed a great soul beneath those appearances and I loved him right off, as was my habit. He counted out three hundred and fifty shiny new ducats and asked me, smiling, to pardon his father's gruff welcome, adding that I should not be alarmed, because the old man had spoken of me quite favourably that very morning and I was welcome in their house, where I would find the peace and intimacy of a family. I thanked him for his kindly words, adding that this would be a delightful pleasure, should some unusual circumstance keep me in Venice. And so we parted; bosom friends, it seemed, from the very start.

I took my meal that noon (with what pleasure you can imagine) in a low tavern where some porters and gondoliers were bickering over the departure of the French and the arrival of the Austrians. I could not but lament the sorry state of a people who had enjoyed fourteen centuries of liberty without having developed the least hint of judgement or any self-sufficiency. The blame, perhaps, lay in the fact that theirs was not real liberty; accustomed as they were to oligarchic rule, they saw no reason to disdain military control or foreign domination. For them it was all one, all servitude: the only matter they discussed was the master's mood and their wages – no more. Anyone speaking of larger matters was a sour note in that concert, and they were even afraid to listen, for the State Inquisition had trained them well. When I recall Venice as it was then, it astonishes me that a single generation changed it so much and I can only bless Providence's unexpected assistance or the fleet, mysterious twists and turns of human nature.

Returning home, I was hard hit by solitude, fear and despondency. Finding my father's pipe, still full of ashes, on the carpet sent tears streaming down my face. Ashes: that's how everything ends, I thought; and my heart was seized by an involuntary fear that the pipe was an omen. In such a state of mind, poor Leopardo drew me to him with irresistible force and I spent the rest of the day by the bed where some merciful neighbours had laid him out. The concierge told me that the widow had departed with her things, leaving eight ducats to pay for the funeral. Before she left, she told her she did not have the heart to stay another hour under the same roof with the remains of the man she had loved so dearly.

'Oh, and the lady seemed to be very cross,' the concierge continued, 'because that handsome young cavaliere who was here this morning did not come to fetch her, and she was quite irritated with my girl because she let one of her caps fall to the floor. You tell me: are these the signs of terrible grief?'

I said nothing, begging the woman not to trouble herself on my account, and when she kept on chattering and supposing things I turned unceremoniously towards the bed where Leopardo lay. She left me alone then, and I was able to sink into the dark abyss of my thoughts. The *memento homo* of the first day of Lent says it well: dust thou art and unto dust shalt thou return. Small and great, good and bad, ignorant and wise: we are all alike, in the end as in the beginning. So the eyes say, but what about the mind? The mind is too bold, too proud, too limitless to be satisfied with palpable reasons. Are not the marvellous, supreme deeds inspired by the Gospels themselves legitimate offspring of the doctrine of Christ's soul? So there is a divinity, an eternity in us that does not end in ashes. Didn't silent, cold Leopardo live in me; didn't the scalding memory of his noble, stalwart nature still warm my heart? So a spiritual life passes from being to being. The philosophers may find comforts that are sounder and deeper, but I am content with this: to believe that the good is not evil, nor my life a flash in the pan.

With this melancholy solace in mind, I took from my pocket the scapular that had fallen from Leopardo's hand into mine the day before, and from a little cavity closed with a button drew out an image of the Virgin and a few dried flowers. A great horizon opened before me far, far away, of poetry, youth and love; and between that horizon and me danced the abyss of death, but my thoughts could leap over without repugnance.

Ghosts hold no terrors for one whose love is eternal. I thought of Leopardo's fine, simple words; I saw the spring at Venchieredo and the charming nymph with one foot in the pool and the other rippling the surface of the water; I heard the nightingale sing its prelude and a concert of love coming forth from two souls, like two instruments, one repeating the notes of the other. I saw a blaze of joy and hope spread out beneath that thick bower of alders and willows. Then, from those far-away, imagined prospects, my thoughts returned to the real things around me and I looked, trembling, on that corpse that slept beside me. Here was another kind of joy, so very different! After the light, gloom; after expectations, the void; after everything, nothing: yet between nothing and everything, between the void and expectations, between gloom and light, how much happened, what thundering tempests and streaks of lightning! Let the captain be armed with endurance to find a port in those wild, agitated seas, let him raise his eyes to the heavens to fix the stars shining beyond the tempest's doleful veil. Ships pass, sometimes calm and graceful as swans on a lake, sometimes beaten and driven like flocks of pelicans battling the winds against them; menacing waves rise to the heavens, plunge to the earth, nearly disembowelling it, then spread out gracious and sparkling under the sun, like a silky mantle on the shoulders of a queen. The air goes grey and suffocating; the sky fills with clouds, squalls, thunder; it grows black like the image of nothingness in the darkest hour of the night, and grey like a witch's tossed mane in morning's transparent whiteness. Then a sweet-smelling breeze whisks away these horrid apparitions like mere imagined spectres; the curve of the heavens turns calm, serene and blue, with no fear and no memory of those airy monsters. Yet a hundred million miles above these ephemeral battles the stars reign eternal on their thrones of light; at times the eye loses sight of them, but the heart can always sense their benevolent rays and feel their mysterious heat. O life, O inscrutable mystery, O sea without end, O desert of fleeting oases, O caravans always in motion and never arriving! To gain solace from you I must launch my thoughts beyond you; I see the stars grow larger in the eyes of coming generations; I watch the small, modest seed of my hopes, germinated with such persistence, fertilized by so much blood and tears, grow into a gigantic tree that fills the air with its branches and shelters my children's happier families in its shade! Shall I not always live in you, great soul and humankind's absolute intelligence? Such are a young man's thoughts at his friend's deathbed; so the old find comfort in the boldness of youth. Justice, honour and *patria* live in my heart, forever.

Overcome by weariness, I slept a few hours on that same bed where Leopardo slept for eternity, and my sleep was as deep and peaceful as a baby's on its mother's breast. Death in such a guise, there so near to me, had nothing fearful or disgusting about it; it was more like a severe, cold friend who would always be loyal. It was time for the last rites; I laid him on his bier and went with him through silent waters to the island of San Michele. I envy the Venetian dead this posthumous voyage; if the dead still sense life faintly, as Poe,[1] the

American, believes, then the gentle sway of the gondola must lull their sleepy senses very sweetly. On that narrow, deserted shore populated only by crosses and sea birds, a few shovelsful of earth separated me for ever from those beloved remains. I did not weep, for I was turned to ice inside like Dante's Ugolino;[2] the same boat that had brought the bier carried me back and the living man returning was no more living than the dead man who had remained.

Back in the city I noticed the crowds were moving to and fro and the French garrison was busier than usual. I heard from someone that the imperial commissioners had arrived for the handing-over ceremony; they had been seen entering the government palace and people had come out to watch them emerge. I don't know why I stayed to watch; perhaps I wanted a new sorrow to distract me from my grief. Not long thereafter the commissioners appeared with a great clatter of swords and show of plumes. They were laughing and talking loudly with the French officers at their sides; and laughing and joking in this way they boarded a barge sumptuously decked out by Sérurier to return them to their camp. Only one remained in Venice: this was no less than the lord of Venchieredo! Half an hour later I saw him walking through the Piazza, arm in arm with Padre Pendola, no longer dressed with sword and plumes but wearing a black coat in the French style. Raimondo and Partistagno (whom I now saw in Venice for the first time) followed him, looking triumphant. The fact that Partistagno had joined such a bad breed distressed me quite a bit, not so much for him, but because it showed how the scheming can exploit the ignorant. The blade does not think, but it is still a deadly instrument in an experienced hand. In the end I ran home, for I knew I would not hold up long, and I confess that at that moment I was incapable of any firm judgement. I had fallen into that mindless prostration in which one lacks the nerve and the will even to leap from the window, and a thunderbolt striking or a beam falling on one's head would seem like a gift from heaven. Only then did I recall those papers belonging to my mother that I was to find in the desk, the miserable inheritance left by an unlucky lady to an even more unlucky orphan. Uneasily, I opened the drawer and, untying an old pasteboard folder, began to rummage through the dusty yellow pages they contained.

The first I came upon were love letters, somewhat Venetianate in style and full of spelling errors. They had been written by a nobleman who is probably long dead and buried with the ghosts of his lovers; his name did not appear, but passages here and there in the correspondence attested to the nobility of his house. If I read you a sample you'd see how a man courted a marriageable young lady in the middle of the last century. Apparently, the most important matters were not committed to paper; rather, the lover took special care to show off his fine qualities and to describe his reactions to the young lady's good graces. His language was far from exquisite, but what it lacked in delicacy was made up for in ardour; his letters shone with that sincerity and propriety you'd only find today in letters that boys away at school write to their relatives at Christmas.

However – believe me – those letters were not much in keeping with my mood that day. I moved on. There were letters from teachers and friends at the convent, more insipid than the first. I continued. What followed was my father's entire amorous correspondence. There was much that was quite bizarre, but he seemed to be as much in love as a man could be. The last of his letters fixed the day and the hour of the elopement that led my parents to conceive me in the Levant.

The corollary to those letters was a diary in my mother's hand, written in many cities of the Levant and Asia Minor. There the story began. My mother's happiness had lasted halfway through the sea voyage. Storms and seasickness completed the voyage; then came misery and quarrels during their first land travels; and finally illness, fatigue and even hunger had damped considerably the first flames of love. She continued, however, by the side of her husband, patiently tolerating his eccentricities, his indifference and above all his jealousy, which seemed quite peculiar. For weeks on end he would be away from wherever he had settled his wife and she would be put in the hands of some poor family of Turks, where she had to work as a servant or scullery maid to earn her keep. My father, meanwhile, travelled around to the harems and summerhouses of rich Mohammedans, trading in hatpins, small mirrors and other knick-knacks which he sold at unbelievable prices – or so my mother, who had been reduced to almost nothing, wrote. One fine day his jealousy emerged more violently than ever in connection with her pregnancy. The man accused was an exuberant *fellah* living nearby and my mother wrote fiery words against her husband's injustice. She seemed to think he deliberately sought to make her weary of that life, to finish her off or perhaps force her to flee. Now her pride began to reassert itself, and from her laments and desperation emerged the noblewoman whose honour had been offended. In those notes, scribbled down on paper day after day in a furious hand, she grew more and more exasperated, until finally came a blank page upon which was written nothing but the words: 'I have decided!'

So the diary ended, but it was accompanied by a letter she had written to my father, once she had decided. I cannot do less than offer those few lines, which serve better to explain my mother's nature. Oh, it is hard! Why am I unable to speak of her at length? Why, in my life, is my childhood love of my mother but a distant gleam of vague memories? That is the fate of an orphan. I'm eighty years old, but it still grieves me that my memory contains no portrait of my mother. Lips that cannot recall the taste of her kisses dry quickly in contact with the malign air of this world.

'My dear husband,' (so her letter of farewell to my father began) 'I wanted to love you, wanted to trust in you, wanted to follow you to the ends of the earth against the wishes of my family, who depicted you as a heartless, brainless scoundrel. Was I right or wrong? Your conscience alone will tell. As for myself, I know that I can no longer bear these suspicions that dishonour me, and that the child growing in my womb cannot be imposed by force on a father who refuses him. I was a vain and frivolous woman, and your love made me pay dearly for my faults. Now I must resign myself to full penitence. In all, I have no more than twenty ducats, and with these I must do my best to return to Venice, where I will find nothing but shame and contempt. But once I have given the child over to relatives who will not have the heart to disown him, let God do with me what he will! You will be away another eight days, and when you return, you will not find me. Of this I'm sure. Everything else is in God's hands!'

The letter came from Baghdad. From Baghdad to Venice, across four thousands miles of desert and sea, in stifling heat and with little knowledge of languages, drained and exhausted by hunger and nerves: so I imagine my poor mother. Leaving the house of a brutal, suspicious husband with twenty ducats in her pockets; heading off on a wearying, perilous voyage towards home and shame and rejection. A loving, unappreciated wife who would be counted among the loose women and lucky if one of her relatives was generous enough to take in her baby. Oh, Lord! And it was on my account that she had suffered such disgrace, endured such hardship! I felt something like remorse that I had been born, that a long, long life devoted to comforting that saintly soul and bringing her joy would barely be enough to appease my heart's sorrow. I had never even contemplated her face, her smile, her gaze, nor sucked a single drop of her milk! I had sent her on the road to perdition by being born and left her there, alone and comfortless. I was close to detesting my father and thanked God that he had departed and that it would be a long time between my reading of those pages and the moment I once again laid eyes on him. Otherwise I wouldn't have been able to say where the battle of affections in me might have led. I could not contain my curses, my vilification.

Oh, did I weep that day! And happily indulge that outburst of filial love to lighten the infinite burden of my grief with tears! And in that anguish that poured from my heart in howls and weeping were mysteriously united the *patria* betrayed, the friend who had chosen to die, and the false and unfaithful lover, and the shade of my mother, her face worn by suffering! Oh, how I hurled myself, enraged and terrible, against those who had tried to defame her memory and make me despise her with slander! Yes, I wanted it to be slander at any cost, for accusations against the helpless dead are always slander – mindless, shameless accusations hurled against a tomb. Those who had believed them in good faith had exaggerated my mother's guilt: did they know of her sacrifice, her suffering, her tears, the long martyrdom that had likely consumed her strength and dissolved her reason? I clawed at my breast and tore at my hair, unable to avenge myself on those evil cowards, and my childhood silence before those furtive critics gnawed at me like a crime. Why had I not unmasked them with all the courage innocence bestows, all the vehemence of a child insulted in the memory of his mother? Why didn't my little eyes flash with contempt, my heart refuse to accept charity – a crust of bread, a cubbyhole for a bed – paid for with disgrace? Shame rose to my face and I would have given my blood, my very life, to relive one of those days and avenge my ignominy. But it was too late. Patience, awe and something like hypocrisy – the three deadly sins of the beggar – had been instilled in me while I sucked at the breast, you might say. I had grown up docile. My temperament, made soft by submission, needed only a pretext to comply, a master to obey. Now I understood the dangers of running after the opinions and the wishes of others and resolved for the first time to be myself and none other but myself. Did I succeed in my resolve? Sometimes I did; more often I did not. Reason is not always at hand to tug in the opposite direction from instinct; at times reason is an innocent accomplice; at times, reason maliciously sides with the strong. And so we imagine we are strong when, in fact, we are cowards, all the more so because we are sheltered from the world's contempt. There is no way out, no hope. The compendium and theme of an entire life is contained in the temperament of youth, and I shall never tire of saying, 'Oh, you saviours of the people. Oh, you minds turned towards the future, you hearts burning with love and belief: mind the innocent, look after the young!' In them is faith, humanity and our country.

I had now finished reading the inheritance left me by my mother. But between her last letter and the envelope, I found a page with some lines on it, written recently, it appeared. Indeed, it was dated just two days previously and was in my father's hand. I cannot conceal the fact that I looked at those lines with something like loathing; they seemed about to burn my fingers. But when I calmed down, I read:

'My son. I might have hidden from you forever all that you

have read here of your mother; be grateful then to me for having raised her in your esteem, even at the cost of your regard for me. I saw you were in need of comfort and I wanted to provide it, although the price for me was high. I married your mother for love, I don't deny it; but I don't think I am made for that sort of passion, and love disappeared very quickly from my head. My departure for the Levant, my work and my travels all had a very noble goal; I wanted to make some millions and then I would achieve that goal. A wife, I confess, was a serious obstacle. My mood soured; the cruelty with which I exploited myself, reducing my needs to the bare minimum, was seen by her as intended to make her suffer. My continued absences and my preoccupation with that grand design lodged in my mind, became the occasion to quarrel and engage in constant battles. By the end she was happy to spend her time in any sort of Turkish or heathen company, so long as it was not my own. Often, returning home, I would hear her shrill Venetian laughter behind the shutters; when I appeared, so did the anger, the laments, the tears. There was above all that one *fellah* whose presence made her quickly forget her distant, surly husband.

'What happened then is what often happens in natures that are neither very generous nor perfectly honest. I grew jealous, but perhaps deep down I knew that jealousy was a way to give my wife so much trouble that she would be forced to leave me. I swear to you I was impatiently awaiting some desperate scene, a demand from her to return to Venice at once. I certainly didn't expect her to run away. She was timid, delicate, the sort who tends to talk rather than act. Her sudden departure surprised me and upset me, but I was then in Persia and returned only a month later, when it was no longer possible even to try to find her. My head was ever more full of that business of growing rich and any worries that assailed me I considered my enemies. To salve my bad conscience I persuaded myself that my jealousy was not without cause and that I was not responsible for her being with child. I grew to like this convenient belief so much that I no longer gave any thought to her or to the child she had borne.

'I knew that for better or worse she had reached Venice and, pleased about that (and to be finally free of a tie that weighed on me), I devoted myself even more tenaciously to my affairs. It was only when I was returning home with those hard-driven millions (my tenacity coined in gleaming *zecchini* and fat *doblas*) that I had the leisure to look among the papers your mother had left me. Forty-two days at sea gave me the time to think about these matters at length. Once I landed in Venice I was quite pleased to meet you and all my suspicions about your birth began to dissipate. But what can I say? I was having trouble convincing myself. I felt I could do no right, like one of those silly fools who, having concealed a crime for twenty years, runs to a judge to confess and have himself hanged. It amazes me – it will always amaze me – that my Levantine morals could permit such unhealthy contrition. It is true that I was used to treating the Turks and the Armenians like beasts, bartering with them and killing them without any qualms. But I had never put my claws into Christian flesh, and your mother – may God bless her and whatever her sister the Countess may say – was more Christian than most of us.

'Perhaps self-interest also led me to reconsider my unfair suspicions. The resurrection of Casa Altoviti gradually came to be associated in my mind with the resurrection of Venice, and I hoped, as the saying goes, to kill two birds with one stone. I had laboured, in Constantinople, to convince Turkey to break off with the Russians and the Austrians. Having succeeded at keeping them at least at bay, I had some credit with the French, who were then considered, from afar, the world's trailblazers. In favour with the French; assisted by some inside conspirators, who were well ahead of me in their oriental intrigues; astute as I am, with my pockets full of millions, I hoped to move in such a way as to hold the fate of the Republic in my hands. Does that frighten you? Do you know I almost had it: all but the Republic. It was just that I found I was a bit old – and here, perhaps I may take some credit. I could say that to have admitted I was old as soon as I met you was a fine gesture that led me to try to repair the wrongs I had done. Whatever the case, I happily leave the hidden motives behind my deeds obscure (a mere flash in that glimmer of conscience that I have left) and don't seek to assign myself dubious virtues. I saw you, embraced you, took you for my true and legitimate son, loved you with all my heart, placed all my ambitions in you. Your intimacy with me lent strength and kindness to those feelings, and these lines I now write seem to me the proof I really am your father.

'Now that I am about to return to that perilous, adventurous life of mine, in pursuit of that dream that slipped away from me just when I thought I had it in my hand, now, as I embark on a voyage that may end in death, I wish to hide nothing at all so far as our ties of blood are concerned. I must extract a terrible vengeance and I shall use all those means that fortune grants me; but you are still part of my hopes, and once I have achieved the justice I seek, the honours and the rewards will be yours. This is why I asked you to stay, beyond the reasons I told you then. You must stay before the eyes of your fellow citizens and gain their affection and esteem. Remain, remain, my son! The fire of youth burns bright from Venice to Naples and he who hopes to use it for his own profit may find he gets burned at the last minute. At any rate, this is what I hope. If it were up to me to choose where you should go, I would say Ancona or Milan, but you will be the better judge according to the circumstances. Meanwhile, you have taken the measure of these prattling Frenchmen; turn their arts against them; use them for your own advantage, as they used us for their own benefit alone. Keep Venice in mind; Venice, where only Venetians ruled.

'Now you know all and you can judge me as you will. If I did not make this confession aloud, it was only because I am the father and you the son. I did not wish to defend myself, but to tell a story; and you see that I have philosophized more than necessary in order to spell out the bad as well as the good sentiments. So judge me now, but take my sincerity into account and don't forget that if your mother were alive today, she would be happy to see a loving, indulgent son in you.'

Once I had read this long letter, so unlike my father's usual sombre manner, in which his nature was revealed with all his goodness, his failures and his unusual acumen, I sat for a while lost in thought. At length it occurred to me to raise my mind to holy and eternal things and there, carved in indelible letters,

I found that commandment that is truly worthy of God: *Honour thy father and thy mother*. A double affection that cannot be divided: to honour my mother meant that I must pardon him, whom she would certainly have pardoned, seeing him so afflicted, so remorseful about his troubled, devious ways. Must I also confess it? My father's harsh, wild (but also tough and honest) nature exerted a certain power over me; the small are always inclined to admire the great, and when duty is involved, that admiration can exceed all bounds. I meditated on it, then freely gave my heart to him who alone could demand it with blood's sacred rights. What those new plans were that took him back to the Levant I did not even try to guess. I simply put my trust in him and waited to see something great come forth one day; and though he had been tricked, as we were, by the very same illusions, I considered him so superior in his vision, tenacity and force of will that I could not imagine him deluded and defeated for a second time. I was young in those days and even grief had not suppressed my hopes, which ploughed on confidently despite all discouragement, fear and anguish.

Now that this moment of useful introspection had returned me to myself, I dined on a piece of bread found atop a cupboard and went out in the dark of night to see whether Agostino Frumier was still in Venice and plan my departure with him. The truth was that a deeper and more shameful need to speak out hid behind this pretext to delay leaving, and although directed towards Casa Frumier I soon found myself walking unawares all the way to Campo di Santa Maria Zobenigo, where Palazzo Navagero stood. When I got there I regretted it, but could not stop myself from spying through the windows, nor even from boarding the ferry, so as to peer in from the Grand Canal. But all the shutters were closed and I could not even guess whether the apartments inside were lighted or dark. Like a beaten dog, I slowly, reluctantly headed off for Casa Frumier, where I was told that His Excellency Agostino Frumier was in the country. A week before, no servant would have risked pronouncing that honorific, but now the nobility was once more showing its face. I didn't pay much attention, although I disliked the ready opportunism (something I would later have ample time to grow accustomed to).

'In the country!' I exclaimed, somewhat incredulous.

'Yes, in the country near Treviso,' said the servant. 'He left word he will return next week.'

'And the Nobleman Alfonso?' I asked.

'He went to bed two hours ago.'

'And the Senator?'

'Asleep, they are all asleep.'

'Good night,' I concluded.

And with those words I put to rest all the concerns and fears that had been needling me. The best, most civil and judicious part of the Venetian patriciate would pretend to be asleep. And the others? God free me from them! What is certain is that the following week, when the imperial government was seated in Venice, that infallible citizen, that Swiss-lover, that Atilius Regulus of the fallen Republic, Francesco Pesaro swore his allegiance. I write this here, so that names, at least, do not disguise things. I went on strolling in the moonlight. Shipyard watchmen, municipal guards and French soldiers were elbow to elbow in the alleyways, avoiding each other like the plague, each pursuing his own aims. The French wanted to load as many Venetian assets as they could aboard the ships sailing for Toulon. To console us, their commanders said, 'Rest assured! It is a strategic move! We shall soon return!' Meanwhile, in spite of what wasn't going to happen, they laid us so low that few would have wanted them to come back. The people – insulted, betrayed and thoroughly despoiled – withdrew to their houses to weep and their temples to pray, and where once they prayed God to keep the Devil away, now they prayed He would send the French to the Devil. The common folk surrendered to the lesser evil, but can we expect more from the man who feels first and reasons after? They hoped at least to regain some of their lost goods, for if liberty is precious, so are work, peace and abundance for the labouring man. It's a grave mistake to expect equal views from people at different stages of culture, just as it is a great and ruinous error for politicians to build their projects upon that faulty expectation.

From Casa Frumier I went to Casa Apostulos, for solitude was forcing me to think and I had no great wish to do so. When

I got there I found enough company to spend a couple of hours and I wager I never dreamed I could spend them so pleasantly. The old Greek banker was still in his study and beside a Spanish brazier sat his elderly wife, a true matron with a nice pair of spectacles on her nose and a *Lives of the Saints* open on her lap. There was also a pretty young lady in brown, graceful and Greek from the roots of her hair to her splendid Mani sandals, embroidering an altar cloth. Finally, there was the appealing Spiro, who was studying his fingernails. The last two jumped to their feet at my arrival, while the old woman gave me a dignified look over her spectacles. The young man then presented me to his mother and his sister Aglaura, and I sat down to talk.

A meeting among Greeks does not take place without a pipe and they offered me one that went right out of the door, and since I had mastered this very important art of modern life upon coming to Venice, I managed to acquit myself without too much disgrace. However, I had little desire to smoke and my distraction sent not a few puffs down the wrong way.

'What do you think of Venice? What have you been up to today?' asked Spiro, to get the conversation under way.

'To my eyes, Venice is a tomb where the gravediggers are rifling the corpse,' said I. And then, to describe what I had been up to, I told him of the friend who had died and of the last, painful offices I had performed for him.

'I heard about that in the Piazza,' said Spiro. 'They say he poisoned himself out of patriotic despair.'

'His soul was certainly capable of such exalted despair,' said I, without actually assenting.

'But do you think such a thing is an act of genuine courage?' he asked me.

'I don't know,' I told him. 'Those who do not kill themselves say this is not courage, but saying so is in their interest, and, furthermore, they have never tried. My belief is that to live deeply, as well as to die of one's own accord, demands a strong carapace of courage.'

'It may even be courage,' said Spiro, 'but a courage that is blind and not very clever. As I see it, genuine courage reasons about the usefulness of its sacrifices. For example, a stone that falls from high in the mountains and breaks into splinters in the valley far below: I do not call that courage. It is obedience to the laws of physics; it is necessity.'

'And, therefore, you believe that a man who takes his own life bends slavishly to the physical necessity that brings him down?'

'I don't know if I believe that, but I do think that a man who kills himself pointlessly today is not truly strong and courageous, when he might usefully sacrifice himself tomorrow. When all of mankind is free and happy, then there shall be no doubt about the heroism of taking one's life. You may quote me the case of Sardanapalus and I will tell you that Camillus was stronger and bolder than Sardanapalus.'[3]

The old woman closed her *Saints*, while dark-eyed Aglaura was looking daggers at her brother, hand on her embroidery. I studied the young lady covertly, because her resolute, somewhat superior attitude piqued my curiosity. But then her mother intervened to divert the conversation from that tragic topic and Aglaura went quietly back to her embroidery, her needle threaded with silk going in and out of the pretty crimson cloth. And so we spoke of the news on everyone's lips: the coming departure of the French, the arrival of the imperial forces, the peace so gloriously hoped for, so despotically imposed. In short, we spoke of everything and the two women joined in without any display of vanity or foolishness, with that tactful discretion that Venetian ladies rarely employ (and even less so back then). Aglaura seemed fiercely opposed to the French and lost no occasion to call them assassins, liars and merchants of human flesh. But I was to learn that the looming Austrian rule had caused her lover to flee, scalding the Greek blood in her tender veins with grief and fury and rousing her to stormy pronouncements. Just the day before, when she was about to kill herself, her brother had saved her from that violent act by tossing a vial of arsenic, all prepared and ready, into the canal – and now she was shooting him nasty looks, but in her heart (perhaps out of respect for her mother if nothing else) she wasn't unhappy that he had stopped her. And so, if her head remained full of fierce intentions, at least that of suicide no longer bothered her.

At midnight I bade farewell to the Apostulos and went back home, Spiro and Aglaura and the *Lives of the Saints* turning over and over in my head: everything, in short, but that decision that I had to make about my future. In the meantime I wrote to those who had gone abroad to Tuscany and Cisalpina about Leopardo's tragedy delaying me. When, many years later, I read *The Last Letters of Jacopo Ortis* there was no way I could be persuaded that Foscolo hadn't borrowed from my friend's sad story some of the lines and colours of his own gloomy portrait. However, I do remember that I dreamed more of la Pisana than of Leopardo that night – and that may say something about my duplicity.

FOURTEEN

In which we learn that Armida is no fictive character and that Rinaldo[1] *may appear many centuries after the Crusades. Some constables put me back on the path of conscience, but during my travels I fall prey to another sorceress. What next?*

The following day, I'm not ashamed to say, I spent the entire morning hovering around Santa Maria Zobenigo, rather worried to see the shutters of Palazzo Navagero still closed. It's true that I crossed paths a couple of times with the young lieutenant of Ajaccio (who seemed to be very preoccupied), but this was no great comfort, however much his evident unease and bad temper seemed to bode well for me. I returned to my lair in a sour mood, thinking that although the French were leaving, the seed sown by wandering officers would remain, and that in addition to that obstacle of la Pisana's husband I might also have to deal with this other atrocity. In that moment no acquaintance with the encyclopedists or mad passion for liberty could have excused her infatuation for that stripling in uniform she'd hit me with. I locked myself in my house and then in my room, to gnaw away at a mouldy crust of bread as if it were Lent; in three days I was as thin as a rail, but not even hunger made me relent. On the surface of my brain was a great ocean of patriotic indignation, grand designs and elegies for the dead; underneath swam the petty thoughts of a sixteen year old, mean and suspicious as any lookout boy. To leave la Pisana behind, God only knew for how long, without seeing her, speaking to her, advising her about the dangers all around her, distressed me so much that I would have risked my life to stay.

Thoughts of the genuine risks I would incur in staying on after the French had left helped to bolster me against my conscience, which from time to time reminded me of the friends awaiting me in Milan. I also felt the pangs of a coming conflict, however. My father's words rang in my ears; I caught sight of Lucilio's sharp, fiery gaze, far, far away. Mercy! I think the fear of that gaze alone got me scrabbling to pack my trunk, but just as I was dusting it off and had lit a lamp in the long, dark room, I heard a great clanging of the bell.

'Who can that be?' I thought.

The Inquisitors' *buli*, the French police, some Austrian scouts – my imagination was spinning. I decided to go downstairs rather than pull the cord, and, from the cracks of the door, I let out a thundering: 'Who goes there?'

A trembling female voice replied: 'It's me. Open up, Carlino!'

Why she should be trembling I did not know, but I hurried to open with such anxiety in my breast that I couldn't stop fumbling. La Pisana, dressed in black, her lovely eyes red with tears and indignation, hair unbound with only a silk shawl over her head, threw herself in my arms, begging me to save her. Thinking that someone had insulted her on the street I was about to leap outside and retaliate, but she took my arm and led me to the stairs and up to the drawing room, as if she knew every corner of my house – although as far as I knew she had never been there. When we were seated next to each other on my father's Turkish divan and her tearful gasps had subsided, I asked what her confusion, her trembling, her sudden appearance meant.

'What does it mean?' she hissed in a sharp little voice, honed on her teeth as it left her lips. 'I'll tell you what it means! I've left my husband. I'm fed up with my mother. My relatives don't want me. I've come to stay with you!'

'Oh, God have mercy on me!'

I really did say that; I remember it as if it were today and I also remember that la Pisana was in no way offended and did not give up even a minuscule part of her resolve. As for myself, this sudden turn of events put me in a pitiful state of confusion, greater than any joy or fear for the moment. It seemed I had been flung outside the very air I was used to breathe and I felt a throttling round my throat; it was a few minutes before

I returned to my senses and asked la Pisana what lucky star made me useful to her in some way.

'Well, you know that at times I am too sincere, at other times a liar and by habit closed and reserved,' she said. 'Today I can conceal nothing: my very soul is on the tip of my tongue and, happily for you, you will get to know me very well. I married to spite you and to please my mother; but such revenge, such sacrifice, quickly pales. I am made so that I cannot love, even for twenty-four hours, a husband who is old, infirm and jealous. I allowed Signor Giulio to court me by your intercession, but I was quite annoyed at you, and just imagine how I felt about your protégé! And what is more, my soul was bursting with love of country and yearning for liberty, while my wheezing, coughing husband preached calm and moderation; he said we didn't know how things would turn out. Well, as you can imagine, we just grew closer and closer! At first I was happy enough to watch my mother enjoy the delicacies served at Casa Navagero and lose her son-in-law's money at the *bassetta* table, but then I began to feel ashamed of what I'd previously enjoyed, and what with my husband, my mother and all the other greyheads, quacks and big-beards crowding me, I began to feel like a lamb in the midst of wolves. I was so bored, Carlino, so bored, that a hundred times I sat down to write you a letter, throwing aside all my pride; but I held back – I held back – out of fear you would refuse me.'

'And now what do you think?' said I. 'Me, refuse you? How could you even imagine it?'

As you can see, while la Pisana was speaking, I had found the thread to escape the labyrinth and this was to love her: to love her more than anything, without looking for imperfections, without distilling my heart's eternal vow through the apparatus of reason.

'Oh yes, I feared you would refuse me, for I hadn't given you the assurance of any kind of exemplary behaviour. Now I want to give you that assurance by showing you all my defects and even disgust you with them, if I may.'

I shook my head, smiling at this new fear of hers, and she,

rearranging her hair on her head and securing some loose pin to her waist, went on.

'During those days a French officer, a certain Ascanio Minato, was billeted in my husband's house.'

'I know this Minato,' said I.

'Oh, you know him? Well, you can't say that he isn't a handsome young fellow; he looks quite manly and good-hearted, although when put to the test I found he was deceitful and disloyal; a liar, a goose-brain and a chicken-heart.'

I heard her out quite gracelessly, her string of abuse confirming all too well, I felt, what Giulio Del Ponte had told me that day when we were in the company of Mme de Beauharnais. La Pisana was unembarrassed to confess her own licentiousness so shamelessly, nor was she aware of the pain her unwelcome sincerity was costing me. I bit my lips and gnawed my fingernails, berating Providence I hadn't been made deaf like Martino.

'Yes,' she went on, 'I regret and am ashamed of that small amount of trust I placed in him. I thought the Corsicans were brave and bold, but I see that Rousseau was wrong to expect great strength and civic wisdom from that stock!'

'Rousseau! Rousseau!' I muttered to myself.

Her tirades and citations annoyed me. I wanted to get to the conclusion and know everything without so many quoted phrases. I flailed about on the cushions and stamped my feet, like a lad who's tired of the sermon.

'What did I ask of him? What did I want of him?' la Pisana began again even more energetically. 'Supernatural feats, impossible acts or base ones? I asked nothing but to make himself a benefactor of humanity, my country's Timoleon![2] I wanted him to be the idol, the father, the saviour of an entire people, and along with that I promised him my heart, all that he wanted from me! What a blackguard, what a coward! He used to kneel before me and swear (lying) that he loved me more than life itself, more than his God! What was he thinking? That I would give myself to the first comer who had nice eyes and gleaming epaulettes? Well, all he got from me was the mark of a woman's slap on his face. Where the men are deficient, we women must take charge.'

'Calm yourself, Pisana! Calm down!' I said, still unsure whether I had understood correctly. 'Tell me the story from the beginning; tell me how you came to be so angry with M. Minato. What did he want from you and what did you, in turn, expect from him?'

'What did he want? He wanted to make love to me under the eyes of my jealous husband, who would pretend to sleep because he feared the French bluster. What did I expect from him? I expected him to arouse his fellows in arms to a solemn act of justice, to oppose the wrong-headed concessions made by the Directory and Bonaparte, and unite with us to defend Venice against those who will now, without firing a shot, become our masters. All that any one of us – even the imbecile, even the greatest coward – would consider his duty without any persuasion beyond his upright conscience and a hatred of unjust, unfair rule! But when a man loves a woman and she proposes this noble task, must he not do even more? Must he not adopt that woman's country and repudiate his own, so shamefully guilty of such misdeeds? When the woman he swears to love so entreats, must not any Frenchman take off his helmet like Coriolanus, declare eternal war and furiously attack the Medea[3] who devours her own children? *Patria*: what does it mean without humanity, without honour? Manlius Torquatus condemned his son to death; Brutus killed his own father.[4] Here are the models for anyone brave and strong enough to imitate them!'

I confess I am neither brave nor strong enough to produce a tirade as violent as la Pisana's, but I was brave and quick enough to understand it, and while I was admiring her proud, fine temperament, I felt sorry I'd misjudged her words at first. I had thought her accusations against the lazy, tepid republican were aimed at the timid or unfaithful lover. Thus we can blunder when we fail to look at the overall temperament and concentrate too much on one aspect.

'Tell me,' said I, 'how this volcanic explosion against him and everyone else came to be?'

'It came to be because time was growing short, because for days he had been leading me on with smiles and deeds that weren't at all convincing; maybe he hoped I would drape myself in a toga like a Roman to seduce him and finally grant him everything just to hear his mawkish talk! Well, now he knows! And I am very pleased that this bastard Italian now knows what a real Italian woman is made of! Yesterday, as you know, the imperial commissioners arrived to discuss how the hand-over will take place. I realized I had little time and began to press, so much that he got all heated up – and what do you think he had the gall to propose to me? He invited me to abandon Navagero and depart with him when the French garrison left Venice!

'"Oh yes," I said to him, "I'll come with you when you have stood in the public square and declared my country free; when you have led your soldiers to ambush, conquer and rout these usurpers who think they can come in without firing a shot! Do that and I'll be your wife, lover, maid: whatever you want!" And I would have done what I said; I think I'm capable. My love, perhaps not; but I would certainly give my everything to the man who vindicated us so nobly! I would give my all with the martyr's blind enthusiasm, if not with a lover's pleasure! And do you want to know what he replied? He twisted his upper lip naughtily, then regained his composure and, putting out a hand to touch me (I drew back), he stammered out weakly, "You're such an adorable hothead!" Oh, if you had seen me then! All my strength converged on these five fingers and I delivered such a thundering slap to his cheek that my mother, my husband, the servants and the maids came running from the other room. My charming officer was roaring like a lion. The liar! The chicken-hearted liar! His hand went flying to his sword, but he thought better of it when he saw my woman's breast bold and firm before him. And so he ran from the room, his arms flailing defiantly, making furious eyes.

'"Oh, what have you done? Oh mercy! You will be the ruin of this house! We must tolerate the lesser evil to avoid worse!" That was how my mother and my husband repaid me; and my husband, in particular, disgusted me. And he was the one who was jealous!

'"So I bring bad fortune to this house?" I shouted. "Well then, I shall change house and leave you in peace!" And I ran out then and there (no one tried to stop me), grabbed a shawl from my room and went to look for my brother. They didn't know where he was; they thought he had left Venice! And so I went to my aunt and uncle Frumier at their palazzo. They were all asleep and had left word that no one was to be let in, not man or woman, relation or friend. Where else could I turn? Carlino, there was no one left but you!' (Oh, many thanks for the compliment!) 'I regretted not having come to you first.' (Well, at least that!) 'At the Frumiers' gate I learned you were still in Venice and where you lived, and now here I am at your mercy, heedless and fearless, because if I must speak the truth, I have never really loved anyone but you, and if you no longer want me because of my quirks and foolishness, then the blame, the harm, the unhappiness are all mine. And yet some of it will touch you, too, because in view of our long friendship, whether it is convenient or not, agreeable or not, I now intend to plant myself at your side and never leave. And if your father still wants to marry you to the Contarini girl, let him do as he pleases, but the bride had better be willing to swallow the bitter pill of having a sister-in-law – at least that! – underfoot.'

That said, la Pisana began to bounce up and down on the divan as if to state it was at least partly hers. Having heard her two minutes before and watching her now, I was hard-pressed to believe she was the same person. The wild republican, the Greek and Roman philosopher, had become a fickle, imperious young lady – indeed, you might have thought Ascanio's slap was truly undeserved. And yet those two women, so different although blended into one, thought, spoke and acted with equal sincerity, each in her own time. I'm quite sure the first would have despised the second, while the second recalled nothing of the first; and so they lived together in excellent harmony, like sun and moon. But the strangest of all was me: in love with both of them and unable to decide which I preferred. I loved the one for her abundant vitality, her high sentiments, her eloquent speech; the other stole my heart with her tenderness, intimacy and beauty. In short, however you looked at it, I was madly in love, and in my place any one of my readers would have been so too. Just those two brown eyes with their bluish whites, so pitifully, fearfully entreating: they alone would have won the case. Without even counting the rest, of which there was enough to make a dozen Dalmatian maids[5] beautiful.

On the other hand, if I was overawed by la Pisana's stage show, there was also a consoling side to it. Much reading, greedily consumed and jumbled together in that voluble, impetuous brain, had gone into it; a fire was going to break out and there would be nothing left but the little spark of grandeur that had ignited it; and with this I would live in sweet accord – old, old friend that she was to me. And what is more, I knew from that rush of eloquence and classic pomp I'd heard from her that now she wouldn't open her mouth for a while. That's what they used to say when she was a child, and often, on a restless, furious Sunday, Faustina would mutter to herself: 'Today the young lady's tongue is sharp and her blood is hot! The better for us, for she'll leave us in peace the rest of the week!' And that was, in fact, what happened. I was never wrong, in the years to come, to apply Faustina's reasoning.

And so I told la Pisana that she was most welcome in my house and (having first pointed out the dangerous step she was taking and the damage to her reputation that could result, and seeing that she was nevertheless determined) I simply went on to say that she was now her own mistress, and mine, and mistress of all my affairs. I knew her much too well to think she would change her mind because of my objections, and perhaps I loved her too much to try, but that is more a qualm than a confession. Having accepted this plan of hers wholesale and without many scruples, it now had to be put in practice, and here many difficulties arose about the details. First, how could I become a sort of guardian to her, uncertain as I was about whether I would remain in Venice – in fact, certain that my honour demanded I go away soon as promised? What would her family, and above all His Excellency Navagero, her elderly jealous husband, have to say? Wouldn't they find some pretext for having me banished? Was it my job to second the insults and abuse la Pisana was aiming at them? And that was not all: there was the ultimate misgiving, the biggest predicament, the capital stumbling block. How was I, in the eyes of the world and in the long term, to justify even to my own conscience a life so closely bound together with the beautiful young woman I loved and whom I had every reason to think loved me? Was I supposed to say that we were thus evading boredom while waiting for her husband to die? That was a darn worse than the hole, as the saying goes!

While all these pointlessly wearying difficulties leapt to mind, la Pisana was enjoying herself and her newfound liberty, singing and dancing and caring not a fig what anyone might have to say about it. She had me show her the entire house from the cellar to the attic, and found the carpets and divans and even the pipes to her taste, and assured me we could live there like princes, showing not the least concern for modesty or appearances. As you know, when a woman is not dismayed by certain . . . things, it's not our business to be dismayed. Rather than bigoted foolishness it would be an offence to her delicate sentiments, and the confessor who suggests sins to his penitent deserves no praise. Suddenly, just as I was admiring her breezy, uninhibited good cheer, uncertain whether to ascribe it to love for me, to relaxed manners or to pure levity of mind, she came to a halt with her arms crossed in the middle of the room, raised her eyes, somewhat disturbed, to mine and said, 'And your father?'

Only then did I remember that she knew nothing of his departure, and marvelled three times over that she had so frankly come to settle with me, while at the same time her feminine modesty suddenly seemed more apparent. When a father is involved, two young people are safer from temptation and from their neighbours' gossip. Besides this thought another leapt to mind: that she might be afraid at finding me alone and would retreat from her excessive intimacy. A minute ago I'd been slightly dismayed that she seemed unconcerned about her honour and social propriety, now I'd have rather she was as shameless as a hussy if it meant she was happy to be with me. You see how we're made! In any event my immense desire to have her with me didn't extend so far as to put lies in my mouth. I thus told her quite straightforwardly that my father had left and that I was living there all alone without even a maid to sweep away the cobwebs.

'All the better,' she said, leaping up and clapping her hands. 'I was somewhat afraid of your father, and who knows whether he would have approved of me.'

But after this explosion of joy, she suddenly grew pensive and said nothing more. She pursed her lips as if she were about to cry and her pretty cheeks grew pale.

'What's the matter, Pisana?' I said. 'What troubles you and makes you put on that scowl? Are you afraid of me or of being alone with me?'

'Nothing is the matter,' said she annoyed, more at herself than at anyone else, it seemed to me.

Now she circled the room a couple of times, staring at her toes. I waited for my sentence, quaking like an innocent who has a distinct fear of being found guilty, and yet her hesitation was sweet balm to me, for it seemed to say I was loved just as I desired. Until then, her absolute assurance and superb confidence had a fraternal flavour that wasn't to my taste.

'Where shall I sleep?' she asked all of a sudden, with a quavering voice and a faint blush on her face that made her a hundred times more beautiful. With the first of those four words she looked at me directly, I recall, but the rest came out more softly, her eyes wandering here and there.

'On my heart!' I wanted to say. 'On my heart, where you slept so many times as a child and never complained!' But la Pisana seemed so dear to me in that gesture of love mixed with shame, of boldness and reserve, that I had to respect her for her virtue and held back any breath of desire so as not to tarnish her fineness. I even went so far as to forget the intimacy I'd had with her in other times and imagine that if I dared to touch her now it would be for the first time. I was like a talented violinist who takes on the most arduous passages for the pleasure of mastering them, sure of his ability, but always pleased to prove it.

'Pisana,' said I calmly and with exemplary modesty, 'you are the mistress here, as I said from the beginning. You honour me with your trust and I must show I am worthy of it. Every room has its chain on the door and this is the key to the gate. You may lock me out in the alley if you wish and I will not complain.'

Her only reply was to throw her arms around my neck, and

in that sudden gesture I recognized my Pisana of long ago. I had, however, the tact and shrewdness not to take advantage of her, and gave her time to recollect herself and correct her heart's overwhelming naivety with words.

'We are like brother and sister, no?' she added, her tongue getting muddled in her words, then trying to right matters with a cough. 'We get on well, don't we, like in those blessed days at Fratta?'

It was my turn then to feel a quiver run through my veins, and la Pisana looked away and didn't know what to say, and finally I saw (just in time) that we had gone too far ahead for that first evening and that it was best to separate.

'You see,' I said, making an effort, conducting her to my father's room, 'here you will be safe and as free as you like. I shall make up your bed instantly!'

'Just imagine if I'll let you make up my bed! That is a woman's job and belongs to us by right; in fact, I'd like to make up yours as well; and tomorrow, given that the coffee pot is here (there was one in every corner of my father's room), I intend to bring you coffee.'

A small battle of politeness ensued, distracting us from temptation, and, content that I had stopped there, I retired happily to sleep (or not to sleep) another night in the company of my desires: troublesome company indeed when you have no hope they will abandon you, but full of delicate pleasures and poetic joys when you think they may be met. Correctly or incorrectly, I thought I belonged to this second case. And (amazing!) I was right, as the following night would confirm.

This might be the place to reply to a delicate question that few of my female readers (but many of the men) would like to ask. At this point, how did la Pisana's virtue stand up? Up until now I have spoken of her without much respect, emphasizing her defects and insisting a hundred times over that she was more inclined to the bad than to the good. But inclinations are not everything. How many steps down this stair of evil had she come in fact? Had she really come down with her whole person, as imagination (and perhaps even desire) descended? It might seem to be the case, but there is a big difference between smelling a rose and plucking it and placing it in one's bosom. A gardener, no matter how jealous of his flowers, will never stop you from smelling them, but should you make a move to touch them, well, then he will turn ugly and hurry you out of the hot-house! The question is a delicate one, but the duty to reply is even more ticklish. As you can imagine, I don't like to shell out guarantees for anyone, but in la Pisana's case I firmly believe she went to her husband if not entirely chaste, then as a virgin bride, and so he left her for the necessary reasons of old age. Whether it was her own doing or her early mischief illuminated her, whether fortune or Providence had a hand in it, I can only say I have good reason to believe this. With her temperament, the examples before her, the liberty she enjoyed, the upbringing she had, the company of Veronica and Faustina – well, it was no small miracle. There's no denying it.

For women, religion is the strongest check, for it controls the most powerful and elevated sentiments. Honour is by no means sufficient, for it is guided by our own judgement and imposed by ourselves alone. The power of religion instead lies in a place inaccessible to human judgement. It commands us not to do: for that is the will of the all-powerful and the all-seeing, the punisher and rewarder of human deeds according to their intrinsic value. There is no escape from this justice, no way to evade its rules, no human obligations or duties or circumstances that make licit what they forbid absolutely and forever. La Pisana, bereft of this assistance and with a very imperfect notion of honour, was fortunate indeed that she went no further than the premeditation of sin, without committing it. I don't mean to give her great credit for this, for – I repeat – it seemed to me more a miracle than anything else, but I must get the facts straight here and also satisfy the curiosity of my readers. You'll pardon me for treating the matter at such length, but the times I recall here were very different from our own. Although, it is true, the difference was often more in the varnish than the substance.

It was not yet eight o'clock the following morning when la Pisana arrived in my room with coffee. From the first day, she said, she intended to assume the habits of a good and diligent housewife. The night's passionate dreams that had made me forget all my troubles; the dim room, shaded from the sun already high in the sky by oriental-style curtains of blue; the memories of us that surged forth from her every gaze, every word, every act; the enchanting beauty of her smiling face, on which the roses were just beginning to glow under the dew of sleep: it all made me want to join again that chain so long left suspended. I had but a single kiss from her lips, I swear; a single kiss, and even that sweetness was mixed with bitter coffee. And they say there was no virtue in the past century! There certainly was, but it demanded twice the effort for the lack of any proper upbringing. I can assure you that St Anthony in the desert deserves less credit for resisting the Devil's temptations than I for lifting my lips from the cup before I had slaked my thirst. Still, I was certain and determined I would slake it one day or another, and perhaps this means my virtue was really a refined sort of gluttony.

As soon as I got up it was time to consider how to live; that is, how to find a woman to look after the cooking and household tasks. We couldn't live on coffee alone, especially considering the love devouring us. For the first time in my life I busied myself with great pleasure in these petty household matters.

I knew a goodwife or two in the nearby Campo, and, asking around, turned up a maid who (at least to look at her) would serve all on her own to guard the house against Turks and Uscocks.[6] Ugly as sin, so tall and lean she resembled a grenadier after a four-month campaign, she had grey eyes and hair and a red kerchief twisted around her head in the style of the snakes of Medusa. She squinted slightly and was somewhat bearded, with a hard nasal voice that spoke neither Venetian nor Slav, but some bastard language between the two. Mother Nature had given her every ugly stamp of loyalty; I've often noticed that loyalty and beauty tend to quarrel and rarely settle down to a peaceful life together. I was sure that anyone who came to the door and met that marvel would have gone to the house of the Devil rather than take a single step over the threshold, so charming and pretty was she! Of course, I gave her firm orders to tell anyone and everyone that the masters were away from Venice, for I had many good reasons to remain hidden. Happiness is sufficient all by itself, for as soon as other men notice you have it, they can't help but go after you and try to spoil it. And so, once I had posted my Cerberus in the kitchen and taken care of our safety and our victuals, I returned to la Pisana and forgot everything else.

Perhaps this was not the moment; perhaps, God forgive me, other duties awaited me and it was not the time to loll like Rinaldo in Armida's garden,[7] but know that I did myself no violence to forget all the rest, but rather forgot it so spontaneously that when later I was recalled to public life it seemed an entirely new world to me. If there are ever any excuses for becoming delirious with love and drunk on pleasure, I can certainly lay claim to them. However, I don't wish to conceal my wrongs and will confess I am a sinner. That heedless month of joy and pleasure, which was lived while my country was being humiliated and was robbed from exile's decorous penury, marked me with eternal remorse. What a distance there is between the shabby supplication of an excuse and innocence's proud independence! How many lies was I forced to tell to hide my cowardly, clandestine happiness from others' eyes! No, I cannot ever be indulgent towards myself or excuse even a single moment of my oblivion, for honour demands we remember always and deeply. La Pisana, poor thing, wept sadly when she finally saw that all her efforts to make me happy only succeeded in interposing a few light-hearted flashes in the gloom of discontent that kept spreading, and made me ashamed of myself. Oh, why did she not favour me with that powerful, inspirational love that had so dismayed Ascanio Minato's flirtatious little soul? Why did she ask for kisses, caresses, pleasure, from me, rather than impose some great sacrifice, some desperate and exalted mission? I would have died a hero, not lived a swine.

Alas, our sentiments obey a law that guides them forever along the path on which they began. That strange passion for the lieutenant from Ajaccio, born more of fury than of love, fed by manly thoughts of the country's ruin and the danger to our liberty, came close to grandeur because it was lit by holy ardour. My love, so many years old, so rich with feelings and memories (but innocent of any thought) was condemned to idle on that bed of pleasure where it was born. I was ashamed that I did not inspire in la Pisana what a ha'penny gallant had inspired, and once I understood our love's original sin, I could not enjoy it as much as she would have liked.

Nevertheless, the days passed, brief, unwitting, feverish. I saw no way to leave, nor had the will or the courage to do so. I might instead have tried on la Pisana that miracle she had tried on the young Corsican: to raise her soul to those heights where love becomes a reason for great deeds and noble enterprises. But she had not granted me her heart with thoughts of parting, and as for making her the companion of my life, my exile and my poverty, I did not think I had the right. And so I avoided any decision, waiting for events to counsel me, my personal torments somewhat compensated by the happiness that lit up her beaming, beautiful face. Seeing how her mood had changed and softened in those few, charmed days, I could only marvel: never a complaint, never a nasty look, never a tantrum or an act of vanity. It seemed she had decided to reverse the low opinion of her that I had formed before. A girl fresh from the convent in the care of a loving mother could not have been more serene, more amiable, more innocent. To anything outside our love, anything that could not be tied to it, she paid no attention. The tales she told me of her past life and other things all tended to confirm her eternal, fervent – if mixed and strange – love for me. She spoke of how her mother had urged her to put on a big smile for this or that of her suitors, in the hopes of hooking a good match.

'But what can I say?' she said. 'The more wonderful, handsome and charming they were, the more they bored me. Whenever I gave the least sign of kindness or approval, it was always towards the ugliest and puniest of them, to my great surprise and that of all around me, and they thought this eccentricity of mine was some exquisite art of flirtation. In fact, I flattered those who seemed to me too hapless to flatter themselves, and if that kindness of mine was insulting, God forgive me, but I couldn't do otherwise.'

She also revealed certain family secrets I would much rather not have known about, they disgusted me so much. Her mother the Countess gambled desperately and refused to face up to penury, and so she was always begging money here and there; and when she got in real straits, she would work up some sleight of hand with Rosa, her old maid, to empty the pockets of friends and acquaintances. Because they had grown tired of being importuned, Rosa had the idea of putting la Pisana forward, to move the most devout admirers of her beauty to pity with tales of her financial straits. And so the unwitting Pisana had been living on filthy and despicable alms. When she finally understood, she had thrown Rosa out of the house, despite the Countess's silent indifference. This was one of the things that had convinced her to accept Navagero's hand, for she was ashamed to be exposed to such infamy by her own mother. I then asked why she hadn't relied instead on the Frumiers, but she told me that they, too, were in difficulty, and that though they might have made some sacrifices to rescue her from starvation, they had no intention of ruining themselves to feed the Countess's insatiable vice. I marvelled at how far this passion of hers for gaming had gone.

'Oh, I don't marvel!' said la Pisana. 'She is always so sure she will win that she is certain it would be wrong not to play, and then the best part is that she always pretends she has won and that it is my brother and I who have consumed her immense winnings! And I never have anything to wear but homespun, and I've always let her have the interest from my eight thousand ducats. My brother eats and clothes himself like a friar and I have to keep him on four *soldi* a day. But she is so convinced she's right that it's pointless to discuss it with her, and I pity her, poor thing, because she is used to having her meals put before her, and there's no way to get to the truth when you pay no attention to what comes in and what goes out. And by the way, she's not alone in this passion of hers; all the Venetian ladies are possessed by it now, and the best houses are going to ruin at the gambling tables. It's beyond me! They're all being ruined, and nobody ever fills up the coffers!'

'The reason,' said I, 'lies in that old proverb: the Devil's flour does not make good bread. The woman who risks her children's fortunes at Pharaoh will certainly not become so provident as to invest her earnings at five per cent tomorrow. They'll be spent on foolishness and the only increase will be in the losses. But your mother is more inexcusable than the others, because she wasn't ashamed to endanger her daughter's reputation to satisfy her whims!'

'Oh, no,' la Pisana exclaimed, 'I pity her for that, too! It was that greedy Rosa who put her up to it, and I suspect she herself took half what they got. And, of course, because Mother had first asked in her own name, she could now ask in mine. She's not my mother for nothing!'

'You know, Pisana, you are really much too good. I don't want you to get used to thinking this way or everything will be excused, everything pardoned, and the confines between good and bad will disappear. Indulgence is a fine thing, but both where she is concerned and also where others are concerned, it must be administered with great caution. Let us pardon her wrongs, yes, when they are pardonable, but let us call them wrongs. If they are put in the same pack of cards as what's right, all bets are off!'

La Pisana smiled and said that I was too strict, and teasingly added that if she excused everything, it was because others always excused her for her failings. Just then she hadn't even one, if not perhaps to make herself loved too much, which was more my failing than hers – and here I put a hand on her mouth and said, 'Oh, please! Don't punish me now for my unjust strictness of long ago!'

After a few weeks of this sweet domesticity, I decided it was time to go to Casa Apostulos and get some news of my father. My conscience nagged me that I had forgotten him for too long, and I hoped to make up for this with a haste that, considering how little time had passed, was certainly pointless. But when we want to persuade ourselves we are not in the wrong, reason is of no avail. As I was going out, la Pisana asked me to accompany her to the convent of Santa Teresa to visit her sister. I agreed and out we went, arm in arm, I with a hat over my eyes and she with a veil down to her chin, looking around us suspiciously to avoid, if possible, being stopped by acquaintances. And, in fact, I saw

Raimondo di Venchieredo and Partistagno in the distance, but was able to get round the corner in time, and, leaving la Pisana at the convent doorstep, turned towards the house of the Greek bankers. As you can well imagine, my father had not yet reached Constantinople or sent word in such a brief time. They were all quite astonished to see me still in Venice, especially Spiro, and I told them, my face reddening, that I had been detained by some extremely serious business and that my interests demanded I remain, despite the great risk, because I was the object of suspicions. I didn't dare say who might have such suspicions, because I didn't know for sure who ruled Venice and although I imagined that the French were gone, I wasn't certain.

Aglaura then asked where I intended to go after my business was finished and I said, stammering, probably Milan. The young lady cast her eyes down and shivered, and her brother sent her a withering sideways glance. With so much on my mind, I didn't think about what this pantomime could mean and bade them farewell with assurances we would see each other again before I left. Back on the street I was now more fearful of being seen, and, in truth, I was ashamed as well as afraid. I was very keen that I should not be observed, for the perfect freedom from any annoyance we had enjoyed up until then convinced me that her family did not know I was in Venice. Otherwise, wouldn't they have thought to look for her at my home? I didn't realize then that the scene between la Pisana and Lieutenant Minato had caused such an uproar that neither Navagero nor the Countess wanted to pursue the matter for fear of compromising themselves. Turning into an alleyway, I found myself face to face with Agostino Frumier, looking more fresh-faced and ruddy than ever. By mutual consent we each pretended not to recognize the other, but he was as amazed to see me as I was amazed to see him, and I was the more ashamed.

When I finally reached the convent, the paving stones were scorching my feet and at every step I regretted not having waited until nightfall to take that walk. I decided I must open my heart to la Pisana as soon as possible and make her see that the drunken happiness she provided me came entirely at the expense of my honour, and that respect for my country, loyalty to my friends and the bond of my word all pressed me to leave. Immersed in these thoughts, I entered the convent parlour without thinking that the good sister might be surprised to see her sibling in my company; but la Pisana hadn't thought about it and neither had I.

It was the first time I'd seen Clara since she had taken her vows. I found her pitifully pale and haggard, as transparent as one of those alabaster vases in which a tiny lamp is put to burn, and somewhat bent as if from long hours of obedience and prayer. The indulgent smile on her lips of years past had been replaced by cold, monastic rigour; you could see she had achieved that isolation from worldly things so dear to Madre Redenta, and that she not only despised and dismissed the world, but no longer understood it. In fact, she didn't wonder at all about my intimacy with la Pisana, as I had feared, but served up some wise counsel, never mentioning the past except with distaste, and only once relaxing her fixed, pursed expression, when I mentioned her excellent grandmother. So many thoughts in that half-smile! But she soon repented, resuming the coldness that was her soul's obligatory vestment, like the black habit that always clothed her limbs. I guessed that Lucilio flashed across her mind in that moment and she had fled, terrified, from the memory. Where was Lucilio now? What was he doing? The fearful question must have pierced her soul from time to time via the deep, invisible auger of remorse. Indeed, it cost her some effort to return to her severe, marbled self; her eyes were not so fixed nor her voice so calm and monotonous as before.

'Alas,' she suddenly said, 'I promised my dear grandmother a hundred Masses for her soul, but I've not yet been able to carry out my vow. It is the only thorn piercing my heart!'

La Pisana, with her usual careless generosity, said right off that she herself could remove that thorn, that she would help her, that she herself would have those Masses celebrated according to Clara's intentions.

'Oh thank you, thank you, my sister in Christ!' said Clara. 'Bring me the chits from that priest who celebrates them and you will have earned a high place in my prayers and even greater credit with God himself.'

I did not feel at ease with such talk and was much surprised to see how smoothly la Pisana could tune her feelings to those of others. But she was so generous and such an exquisite teller of lies that I really should have been surprised had she done otherwise. After we had taken our leave of Clara, I was once again seized by the fear of being seen together and suggested to la Pisana that we return home separately, each by a different route. And so we did and I had reason to be glad about it, because when I had gone a hundred paces I came across Venchieredo and Partistagno once again and this time they followed hard on my heels and never let up. The path I led them on through those tangled labyrinths of Venice I could never repeat, but I tired before they did, unhappy to leave la Pisana alone so long. And so I decided to turn towards home, but to my great astonishment what did I find but la Pisana at the door, where she'd apparently arrived some time before and stood making friendly chatter with Rosa, the very maid who'd had her begging from her suitors? She seemed quite unperturbed by my appearance, but bade Rosa farewell politely, inviting her to visit, and then entered the house, scolding me because I'd been so slow. Out of the corner of my eye I could see Venchieredo and Partistagno watching us from nearby, whereon I slammed the door and climbed the stairs morosely.

Upstairs, I couldn't think how to begin to alert la Pisana to her thoughtless behaviour, but finally I decided to speak plainly, perhaps encouraged by my sour mood. And so I told her I'd been amazed to see her in close confabulation with that shameless woman who had caused her unpardonable offence, and that I couldn't understand why she had stopped in the doorway to gossip, given all the reasons we had to avoid being seen. She replied she had stopped to talk without thinking, and, as for Rosa, she had felt sorry for her, seeing her in rags, her face drawn with hunger. In truth, she had asked her to come and visit just for that reason, hoping to be able to help her in some way, and, further, if the woman regretted her wrongs la Pisana was obliged to forgive her; and, in fact, she forgave her, because Rosa herself had insisted she never intended to do her harm and had always worked for the good and followed the Signora

Contessa's suggestions. La Pisana seemed so convinced of this last point that she almost regretted having chased Rosa away and took on her conscience all the troubles the woman claimed to have suffered for her scornful severity. In vain I disagreed, arguing that certain wrongs could never be excused and that one's honour is perhaps the only thing one has the right and duty to defend, even at the cost of one's life and that of others. La Pisana said she didn't agree, that in such matters one had to rely on feelings and that her feelings advised her to redress the ills involuntarily imposed on that poor woman. Furthermore, she begged me to give her a hand in this good deed, by offering Rosa a room in the house. At this request, I began to shout and then she began to shout and weep. In the end we agreed that I would pay Rosa's rent at her present lodgings and only after I had made this promise did la Pisana agree not to bring her into the house.

It was the first time our love had failed and our temperaments bristled one against the other. I went to bed with great foreboding and Raimondo's mocking, curious glances stuck in my throat[8] all night. The morning brought another skirmish. La Pisana said she wanted to go out and arrange for the hundred Masses for her sister. Well, you can imagine how much this new bee in her bonnet appealed to me, starved as I was of money! For obvious reasons of gallantry I hadn't told her that my father had departed with all his wealth, leaving me no more than a small income. With our domestic expenses, the maid's wages and la Pisana's purchases (for she had come to me with not much more than her slip), the better part of what was to last me a year had already slipped through my fingers. However, I was loath to let her know about my poverty and cast about for a hundred other reasons not to celebrate those Masses. La Pisana simply wouldn't listen. She had promised; it was for her sister's peace of mind; and if I loved her, that was that, I had better do what she asked! So then I told her loud and clear how things stood.

'Is that all?' she replied, with a lovely smile. 'There's no problem. First we must meet any obligations and then we shall starve if there is nothing left for us.'

'Oh, it's all very well for you to talk of starving.' I added. 'I'd like to see how you manage when you can't stand up!'

'I may fall down if I cannot stand, but no one will ever say I grew fat on what served the good of others.'

'Remember that after one hundred Masses I shall have few lire indeed.'

'Oh yes, you are right, Carlino! I must not sacrifice you for one of my whims! Better that I should leave. I shall go and stay with Rosa and live by sewing and embroidering . . .'

'Oh, what is this now?' I shouted, quite indignant. 'I would rather flay the skin from my back than leave you to such a fate!'

'Then, Carlino, we are agreed. Grant me all I ask and let Providence take care of the rest.'

'You know, Pisana, you really astonish me! I've never seen you so trusting in Providence as now when Providence seems not to have the least thought of you.'

'If only that were true! I should be so happy if virtue grew in me when needed. However, let me tell you that I've begun to have faith in Providence; I feel its courage and its strength. There's always some devotion at the bottom of our womanly hearts: which is to say, I throw myself into God's arms! I can assure you that if we are stripped of everything, you will not find two arms that work more valiantly than mine to earn a living for both of us.'

I shook my head, having little faith in courage so far from being tested, but no matter how little I believed, I still had to pay for the one hundred Masses and Rosa's rent, and finally I saw my love happy, now that there was nothing more than some twenty ducats to face the future. Meanwhile, though, not far away, others were looking after my affairs assiduously, working discreetly to assist me. They aimed to toss me from the frying pan into the fire, and they succeeded. But since I should have been on that fire a month already, I can thank them for salving my conscience.

It seemed that the scene staged by la Pisana with the Corsican officer had caused an uproar across Venice, as I said, and her disappearance from her husband's house added some mystery to the tale, and many strange and grave things were reported that sound quite mad in the telling. Someone saw her dressed in white, wandering under the arcades in the Piazza at dead of night; another said he had met her in a deserted alleyway with a dagger in one hand and a torch in the other, like Discordia the goddess of strife; according to the boatmen, she wandered the laguna all night, alone on a gondola without oars, leaving behind her a phosphorescent trail on the silent waters. From time to time, some splashes were heard near this mysterious apparition; these were the enemies of Venice she had magically torn from sleep's silence and tossed into the deep. This imaginative chatter, to which popular credulity added some poetic refinements every day, did not much please the new provisional government established by the imperial powers after Sérurier's departure. It was a sign that sympathy was scarce. The people had better be cured of these poetic tics!

And so an energetic search was under way for la Pisana, but so far they hadn't found her and certainly no one suspected that she was staying with me, for in those days it was thought I was far from Venice. Our gypsy maid was quite incorruptible; when a couple of guardsman in disguise came to ask about the masters of the house, she replied they had been away from Venice for a long time, and so we weren't bothered again. Knowing my father had left for the Levant, they imagined I had gone with him or with those other ne'er-do-wells who'd gone to find a *patria* in the peaceful cities of Tuscany or the riotous provinces of the Cisalpine Republic.

Raimondo Venchieredo's discovery put the constables on my tracks. He mentioned it to his father as a mere curiosity, and the old fox understood it could bring him a nice profit, and so, after consulting with Padre Pendola, he decided to earn some credit with the authorities by telling them I was a dangerous conspirator hiding out in Venice, ready to carry out God knows what desperate acts. That I was living with that wild and impetuous lady who had the idlers and the people so busy talking, strengthened his accusation. And so one fine morning, while I was peacefully sipping my coffee thinking how I might stretch out my last seven or eight ducats as far as possible, I heard a furious rapping on the door and a tumult of voices shouting, responding, back and forth from window to alley and from alley to window. As I tuned my ear to that commotion I heard a great bang like a door being torn off its hinges by force, then another blow, louder than the first, and a shouting and hammering that went on and on. La Pisana and I were just about to go out and see what was happening when our gypsy ran into the room with her nose bleeding, her dress torn to ribbons and a huge hearth shovel in hand. It was the one my father used to perfume the house as they do in Constantinople.

'Master!' she shouted, breathless. 'I took one of them prisoner and he's locked in the kitchen with his face flattened like a cake. But there are twelve more outside. It's every man for himself! They've come to arrest you for crimes against the State . . .!'

La Pisana didn't let her go on, but ran to close the door; then, looking out of the window that gave on to the canal, began to urge me to think of myself, to run away and save myself, that this was what mattered most. I had no idea what to do, and a leap from the window looked like the best way out. In an instant, the act followed the thought. I hurled myself out, without looking where or how I would fall, certain that, earth or water, I would meet something. I met instead a gondola, in which, during my flight, I had glimpsed the face of Raimondo Venchieredo, who had been spying in through our window. The blow with which I hit the bottom of the boat nearly dislocated my shoulder, but the somersaults of youth and my gymnastics with Marchetto had accustomed my bones to such havoc. Like a cat I bounced up fast and ran to the prow to jump to the far bank, but was halted by an involuntary movement: Raimondo, just emerging from the cabin, who froze, terrified by the falling body that had made the gondola rock under his feet.

'So it's you, you old rogue!' said I, furious. 'Here, take your wages for spying!'

And I gave him a back-handed slap so hard he went rolling over the rowlock, which very nearly put out his eyes. Meanwhile, I had leapt to the bank and was waving goodbye to la Pisana, who was watching from the balcony and urging me to hurry up and flee. My gypsy saviour was still there with her hearth shovel in front of the battered door, her bellicose presence holding off the twelve constables, none of whom wished to follow their chief into the house and meet the bad end that maybe he had met. Had they paid more attention, they would have heard him howling; closed up in the kitchen, his face battered by that terrible shovel, he was wailing out the high note in his bass register like a little pig on the way to market. I saw all this in a flash and, before Raimondo could recover or the constables find me, I had disappeared down a nearby alleyway. In that great confusion of events and ideas it was providential that I thought to take refuge with the Apostulos. But I did, and arrived safely without any troubles greater than that hazardous leap from the window. My friends were happy indeed to see me safe and sound after so great a risk, but I could certainly not speak of victory yet, for so long as I wasn't beyond the laguna or rather beyond the provinces this side of the Adige, my liberty was sorely threatened.

'Where do you think you will go?' the old banker asked me.

'Oh . . . Milan,' said I, not really understanding much of what was being said.

'You are still determined to go to Milan?' Aglaura now asked.

'It seems the best gamble,' I said, 'and my closest friends are there and have been expecting me for some time now.'

While we spoke, Spiro had hurried to the office to dismiss the clerks, and Aglaura seemed just about to make further enquiries when he came back. Her face changed then and she stood and listened as if uninterested, but every time her brother looked away she observed me attentively, and I heard her sigh when her father said that I would be able to leave the following morning, disguised as a Greek and with the passport of one of their representatives.

'No sooner,' he added, 'because the police always tend to be wary and clever at first and you would easily fall into their clutches. Tomorrow, however, they won't be as careful, because they'll think you've already left the city; and because it's a feast day the customs men will be busy going through the pockets of all the country folk who come to town.'

His wife, who had also appeared to celebrate my safe arrival, nodded her agreement. When I got to Padua, Spiro went on to say, I would do better to remove my disguise and take back roads to the border; my Greek dress would be too noticeable. I said yes to everything and turned to another matter, that of money. With the seven ducats I had in my pocket I couldn't dream of making it to Milan. I would need a fair sum; and since even an advance on the interest for a year wouldn't be enough, and because I also wanted to leave some means of subsistence to la Pisana, I proposed to old Apostulos that he give me a thousand ducats, and from the other capital pay out the interest yearly to the noble Contessina Pisana of Fratta, Lady Navagero. The Greek was very happy to do so, and I made out a receipt and a proxy order and advised la Pisana by letter of my intentions, adding a document giving her the use and benefit of my house. I had no idea how long I might be away and it seemed best to make plans for the long term. I didn't worry that la Pisana might be offended by these arrangements of mine, because our love was not the kind that suffers humiliation because of a trifle. If you have it, you give it: that is the rule among neighbours. All the more so, then, for two lovers, who are not mere neighbours, but between them one thing!

Once this business had been disposed of it was time to dispose my stomach to endure the hardships of my first day of exile. By now it was evening; in twenty-four hours I had taken nothing but a coffee; and yet I was no more hungry than if I had just got up from a wedding banquet. What can I say? There on the table to the left and the right were great bottles of Cyprus wine and I put my faith in them, and while the others ate and urged me to eat, I began to drink, in despair.

I drank so much I understood nothing of the great discussion that took place after supper, except that it seemed to me that when I was briefly alone with the women, Aglaura whispered some words in my ear and went on pressing my knee and knocking my foot under the table when Spiro and her father returned. Out of courtesy, she had been seated next to me. All this was beyond my comprehension; for better or worse I dragged myself to the bed assigned me and slept so swinishly that I could hear myself snoring. But when they woke me in the morning it was quite another matter! It was the calm that comes after the storm, the pain that follows befuddlement. Until then I had stubbornly held on to my hopes, as the consumptive does, but now I came up against brute necessity and could neither retreat nor hope any more. I can't even say I had the force to get out of bed, put on my new Greek outfit and bid my hosts farewell. My body performed these moves with an automaton's silly obedience, and as for my soul, I was sure I had left it in the Cyprus wine.

Spiro came along with me to the Riva del Carbone, where the boat departed, and promised me that he would get me news of my father as quickly as it arrived, shook my hand and left. I stood there for a moment at the bridge looking at Venice, grimly contemplating the dark waters of the Grand Canal, where the mirrored palaces of admirals and doges seemed to sink into the abyss. I felt something being torn out of me, my very viscera, and stood motionless, lost, utterly lifeless, like a man facing a calamity that can end only in death. I didn't even notice when the transport left; and I was still seeing Palazzo Foscari and the Rialto Bridge when we were already beyond the laguna. But when we came to the customs house and I heard a voice with an accent that certainly wasn't Venetian order us to stop, I emerged from my imaginary anguish into the grip of a real and profound grief. All the misfortunes of my country then appeared before my eyes, mixed with my own, and one by one each stabbed its dagger in my heart!

We were just casting off from the customs house landing when a fast caique approached and begged us to wait. The helmsman halted and I was astonished to see young Apostulos appear a moment later on the deck. He approached me somewhat nervously, looking right and left, and said, his words a bit of a jumble, that he had hurried to catch up with me in order to give me the names of some other friends of his in Milan who might be helpful. His consideration quite surprised me, although it was customary in such circumstances to supply the traveller with letters of introduction; nevertheless I thanked him and he left me to search for the captain, to ask him to look after me, he said. On that pretext he went down into the cabin and I saw him whisper something in the captain's ear, in fact, and the captain shook his head and gestured, as if to say, be my guest, look around wherever you like. Spiro went to the back of the cabin, saw some boatmen sleeping wrapped up in their cloaks and came back with a look of studied indifference on his face.

'What the deuce! You have a very fine boat here!' said he, his hawk eyes peering into everything from bow to stern, his nose poking into every cupboard and corner, somewhat to the irritation of the helmsman who was waiting to get under way again.

'Can I be off?' he asked the captain, hoping to hurry the importunate visitor.

'Wait until I get down,' said Spiro, jumping from the transport to the caique and waving goodbye to me, somewhat abstracted. I knew that he had not caught up with us and inspected the boat so thoroughly just for the reason he'd told me, but I was too upset to let my imagination roam, and so he quickly fled from my mind. I turned to watch Venice disappearing in the bluish haze of the laguna, looking ever more like a stage curtain blanched by the dust and smoke of the footlights.

O Venice, O ancient font of wisdom and liberty! Although by then your spirit was murkier, more emaciated, than your countenance; it was vanishing into the past's blind obscurity, where even life's track dissolves and all that is left are memories (but these are only ghosts) and hope, the long slumber of sleepers. Did I love you when you were tottering, dying? I don't know, don't want to say. But when I saw you wrapped in your shroud, admired you beautiful and majestic in the arms of death, when I felt your heart was cold and your last breath spent, then a tempest of grief, remorse and despair stirred up my deepest passions! I felt the exile's rage, the orphan's desolation, the murderer's torment. Matricide! Murder! So the mournful echoes of the Doge's Palace ring. You could have let your dying mother rest in peace on the standards of Lepanto[9] and the Morea; instead, you wrenched her rudely from her venerable bed; laid her on the hard stone; drunkenly, cowardly danced around her; handed her enemies the cord to strangle her! There are those supreme moments in the life of a people when the worthless become traitors, when they commandeer courage and wisdom. Were you powerless to save her? Why did you not confess it to the world? Why have you confused yourselves with her executioners? Why did some of you, horrified by the shameful bargain, then hold out your hands and accept the buyer's alms? In his virtue, Pesaro was alone; but he was the first and the vilest of all when it came to humiliating himself. And he had many, too many, imitators.

Mine is not an accusation but a reckoning; not an attack but a confession. I confess what I should have done and did not, what I could have done and didn't want to see; the deeds I committed out of thoughtlessness, but will despise forever as vile crimes. Bonaparte and the Directory betrayed us, it is true; but only the spineless let themselves be betrayed that way. Bonaparte treated Venice like the lady who mistakes servitude for love, who kisses the hand that beats her. First he neglected her, then he insulted her, then he enjoyed himself deceiving her and mocking her, finally he threw her under his feet and kicked her like a slattern, said to her contemptuously, 'Go and get yourself another master!'

Can anyone who has not experienced it understand the deep gloom such thoughts provoked in me? And when I compared it to the blithe, carefree happiness that had delayed me those few days, my dejection, my distress, if anything, grew worse. There it was. I had touched the very zenith of my desires, had pressed in my arms – amorous, happy and beautiful – the first and only woman I had ever loved, she who from my earliest years I'd imagined as my life's consolation and remedy against all sorrow, and she had filled me, inebriated me with all the pleasures a man can ever have in mortal life! And what did all this leave me clenching in my hand? Remorse! Intoxicated but not satiated, ashamed but unrepentant, I had abandoned love's ways for that of exile, but if the police hadn't bothered to warn me I might have stayed to profane Venice's funeral with my shameless pleasures. Even my soul's nutriment had turned to poison and I was forced to despise that which I desired to possess all the more ardently.

Pallid, agitated, upset; having touched no food or drink; neither looking at my travelling companions nor answering their questions; tossed here and there by the boatmen's careless elbows, I finally reached Padua. I got down, hardly knowing where I was, nor recognizing the banks of that canal where I had so often walked with Amilcare. Enquiring where a tavern might be, I was told of one to the right of old Porta Codalunga (where a few years ago the gasometer was built). I headed off with my bundle under my arm, followed by some little scamps who admired my oriental garb. When I got there I asked for a room and something to eat. Then I changed my clothes, took some food (refused the wine) and, when I had paid the modest bill, went out of the tavern, remarking loudly that I hoped the town rascals would pay me no attention in those clothes. Then I made as if I were on my way, but when I got to the gate I stepped aside and hurried down a little lane that I seemed to remember led to the road for Vicenza.

On my way out of the tavern I'd noticed a fellow who seemed to be trailing me and I wanted to learn whether I was right. And, in fact, looking sideways, I continued to see a shadow that followed mine, slowing its pace, hastening and pausing along with me. Now, heading down the lane, I could hear a light, cautious step accompanying me and had no further doubt: the fellow was there for me. My thoughts immediately went to Venchieredo, to Padre Pendola, to Avvocato Ormenta and their informers, although I did not know yet that the estimable Ormenta was in the government under Pendola's protection. I felt, however, that frankness was the best tactic and so when I had led my little hunting dog right out into the countryside, I turned around swiftly and made to grab him if I could and give him a taste of my own unpleasant company. But to my great surprise he neither moved nor took fright, but lowered the hood of the sailor's cloak wrapped around him to show me his face. Now I, too, let down the better part of my ire and simply reminded him that it was not permissible to trail a gentleman in that way. While I was speaking and he, looking rather uncertain and uneasy, watched, I thought I saw the traces of someone I knew in his face. I quickly reviewed all my Padua friends, but no one seemed the least like him, and yet I couldn't help feeling I had seen this person very recently and his memory was very, very vivid in my mind.

'So you really don't recognize me?' he said, putting the palm of his hand to his face, in a voice that immediately made things clear.

'Aglaura! Aglaura!' I exclaimed. 'My eyes do not deceive me?'

'Yes, it is Aglaura, and I have been following you from Venice. I travelled with you in the same boat and ate at the same tavern, and would not have had the courage to reveal myself if you hadn't been suspicious and turned on me first.'

'And so,' said I, quite stunned by this surprise, 'and so it was you Spiro was looking for this morning?'

'Yes, he was looking for me. When he came back home and didn't find me (because in the meantime I had boarded the Padua boat, after having changed my clothes at the home of our washerwoman) he suspected the very thing he had feared for some time. Yes, I had gone out with the maid, but then she returned saying I had asked her to leave me alone in church, and so his suspicions grew. Luckily, he was in a hurry and didn't have time to determine whether the maid's tale was true or not, and so when he asked the boat captain whether there were women aboard and he said no, Spiro believed I really had stayed to pray, hoping that prayer would give me the strength to resist the temptations that had been assailing me. Poor Spiro! He loves me, but he doesn't understand me, doesn't feel for me! Instead of taking my part, he'll carry out my father's curses!'

Her words, the timbre of her voice and the tenor of her gaze convinced me that poor Aglaura was in love with me, and that her grief at my departure had led her into desperate pursuit. I was full of gratitude and sympathy. If la Pisana had stayed with Navagero or run away with Lieutenant Minato, I believe I'd have fallen in love with Aglaura out of simple gratitude. But now I am tired of writing, and in any case I'd like to end this chapter leaving you uncertain what will happen next.

FIFTEEN

Travels may turn out well, even though they begin badly. We arrive in Milan on the day of the celebrations for the Federation of the Cisalpine Republic. I begin to see matters clearly, but also perhaps to put too much faith in the things of this world. Cisalpine soldiers and Ettore Carafa's Parthenopean Legion. I rapidly become an officer in this last.

Forgive my discourtesy for having broken off so rudely, but the fault is not really mine. A man's life (haphazardly told, as best he can) offers no good occasions to be neatly subdivided, and so I've taken the habit of writing a chapter every day and ending it whenever sleep makes the pen fall from my hand. Last night sleep arrived just as I most needed all my sentiments alert and clear, and so I decided it was best to suspend my tale until today. Now, you only have to turn the page and read a few more lines.

Young Aglaura in her sailor's garb was as pretty as a picture by Giorgione. There was a certain combination of strong and soft about her, of boldness and modesty, that would have made even a hermit in the desert of Thebes fall in love. I didn't, however, succumb to these enchanting gifts, but, making a supreme effort, tried to get her see her folly and think of her parents, her brother, her moral and religious duties, and even persuade her that it wasn't love she felt but a momentary agitation that would cool in a couple of days – and finally (if I had to) tell her quite candidly that my heart was already taken and any effort to conquer it was pointless. You see how heroic I was! Luckily I was not a professional at this and the young lady's directness spared me the ridicule of tilting at windmills, à la Don Quixote.

'Don't condemn me!' she continued what she'd said before, silencing me with a wave of her hand. 'First you must hear me out! Emilio is my intended. When we first met he had no thoughts of intrigues and matters of State. It was I who urged him on that path, I who procured him that exile: stripped of everything, without family or friends, in ill health, he suffers in a distant, foreign land, perhaps unto death. Now you may judge me: was it not my duty to sacrifice all, in order to redress the harm I had done? It's clear, is it not? Spiro was wrong to hold me back. It isn't just love that makes me flee my home, it is mercy, religion, duty! Let all else fail, but do not let this terrible remorse grip my heart forever!'

I stood there as dumb as Pinchbeck,[1] as they say, but I managed to keep a smile on my face (although shame rose to my cheeks for the blunder I'd been about to make) and found some non-committal words that temporarily concealed my mistake. Above all, I was embarrassed to hear of this Signor Emilio (stripped of everything, ailing, interesting) that Aglaura called her intended and about whom I'd never heard a word spoken by her parents. She probably supposed that Spiro had mentioned him, and, in fact, she went on talking as if I knew him as well as she did.

'Last week,' she said, 'I couldn't stop thinking of killing myself, but when I first saw you and heard you meant to go to Milan, another idea, less tragic for me and a consolation to the others, entered my head. Why not follow you? Emilio, too, was in Milan. Long silence had deprived me of any knowledge of him. If I killed myself I would know no more, nor bring him any comfort, but if I joined him and stayed at his side always, who knows? Perhaps I could soften the hardships I'd brought on him with my liberal folly. And so I decided I would go with you, for even the thought of undertaking the voyage alone quite frightened me. Imagine! I'm so unused to putting a foot outside the house! It wasn't courage I lacked but practice; how many pitfalls might there be waiting for me? But with a true and trusted friend by my side, I could safely go to the ends of the earth. This decided, I pondered a second question. Should I tell you of my plans or follow you without your knowledge until our mutual circumstances obliged you to take me along whether you wished to or not? Sincerity inclined me to the first course, but fear you would refuse me and a concern for secrecy urged the second.

'Still, the greatest obstacle to be overcome was my brother. Between us we make up a single soul; thoughts are born in him and take colour in me; we are two lutes of which one repeats, spontaneously, somewhat uncertainly, notes played on the strings of the other. And, in fact, he saw my plan the very first time you came to the house. I don't say that he guessed I had thought about going with you, but he read in my eyes my desire to flee to Milan. It was enough to make that flight impossible, or anyway very difficult; I know the immense love my brother feels for me, that he would rather die than part from me. What could I do? At times I think this love of his is excessive for a brother; but that is how he is made and you'll agree it's a happy defect. You cannot imagine the tricks I adopted to rid him of his suspicions, the fibs I served up looking utterly innocent, the many extra embraces, the care and love I devoted to all things familial! Only someone who believes that God and her conscience call her to penance for her sins could do the same and then confess it without dying of shame and heartbreak. My old parents and Spiro himself were fooled. See, the thought makes me weep even now! But it is God's will and may His will be done! They were all fooled, as I said, and this morning, when I said my prayers with Mamma and bid Papa good day, no one can have suspected I meant to disappear half an hour later, dress myself as a sailor and travel the Earth with you, repenting of my sins! I'm committed now; I've taken the great step. If God gave me the strength to dissemble so thoroughly, and the cleverness to deceive such wise and loving guardians, it means He approves of and defends my conduct. And He will repair the ills that my disappearance may cause!

'As for my parents, I am not really worried. Whether because of my sex or my scarce merits (or the fact that they are old and somewhat self-absorbed), I have never seen them love me more than tepidly. At times my mother seems to regret having neglected me and smothers me with embraces meant to be maternal, but a bit too self-conscious. My father doesn't bother with such things, but simply forgets about me for days on end and treats me as if I had just turned up today and might leave tomorrow. We females, in fact, are only a fleeting possession for our fathers, a plaything for a few years; they think of us as belonging to somebody else, if I'm not mistaken, and certainly my father never suggested he thought I was his. And thus I'm not greatly concerned about them; they will not be very troubled as long as they know I am alive.

'But I do feel very uneasy about Spiro! His temperament is proud and rash; his heart knows neither patience nor measure. Who knows what havoc he may cause! I can only hope his love and respect for our parents will restrain him somewhat. In any event I shall write to him and try to calm him, and pray to Heaven that we may be reunited.'

As she spoke she had already begun to walk in the direction I'd been going before I stopped to confront her, and I was walking along beside her, unthinking. But when she finished talking I came to a halt and said, 'Aglaura, where are we going?'

'To Milan, where you are going,' said she.

Her self-assurance confused me, I confess, and all those clever arguments I'd intended to pull out to dissuade her from her reckless plan sat idle in my pockets. I saw there was no persuading her and my thoughts wandered to my father's remarks, that in the Apostulos' daughter I would find a sister and love her as such. Was he so prophetic? It seemed so, and in any event I had decided not to abandon the girl but to help her with my counsel, to stay with her and offer those fraternal offices she deserved because of our fathers' long-standing friendship. If not siblings, we were, therefore, some kind of cousins and so I put my heart at rest, prepared to let circumstances be my guide and to use all means to get Aglaura back to the bosom of her family. In the meantime, I kept to my plan, which was to walk until I reached a village nearby, then take a cart up into the foothills, and then, from cart to cart, and town to town, slipping between the cities and the mountains, reach Lake Garda and be deposited by boat on the Brescia shore. However, before I put part one of this plan into action, I solemnly questioned the young lady as to whether Emilio was really her intended and whether she knew for certain he was ill in Milan.

'You ask if Emilio is my fiancé? You don't know Emilio Tornoni? Do you mean that Spiro has never spoken of him?'

'Not that I recall,' said I.

'That's very strange,' said she between her teeth.

Then, without making matters any more puzzling, she told me a brief tale. Even before Spiro had returned from Greece (where he'd been living with an aunt for fifteen years), Emilio, a handsome young man from one of the best Istrian families, she said, an officer of the Arsenal in Venice, had asked for her hand in marriage. Her brother's return and other vicissitudes that had made it necessary for him to come back from Greece, had at first delayed the marriage, and then when the revolution came everything was uncertain, and finally Emilio had to flee with all the rest because of that wicked Treaty of Campo Formio; and she continued to insist that she was uniquely responsible for all these troubles, because she had fired him up and distracted him from his naval duties and lured him into that bacchanal of ephemeral liberty. I disagreed with her, pointing out that a man is always responsible for his own actions and also for his misfortunes if he lets a woman lead him around by the nose. But Aglaura couldn't be persuaded of this and continued to insist she must find her fiancé and somehow repay him for all she had made him suffer. She had no doubts he was both ailing and in Milan, because in his last letter he had told her he would remain there, and, having received no subsequent word, she was convinced he was either dead or gravely ill. When he wrote, the poor exile had very likely been feeling the first symptoms of that illness that now confined him to the plague-infested bed of some hospital. Aglaura's imagination was so vivid she could almost see him lying neglected by some mercenary nurse, in despair that he must die without at least a kiss from his beloved.

While we talked we reached a village and were able to obtain a little cart that dragged us as far as the town of Cittadella. You would laugh if I told you how philosophically Aglaura accepted the discomforts and fatigue of our army-style transport. At night we would sleep in some slovenly country tavern, where often there was just one room and just one bed. True enough, this was often large enough to sleep a regiment, but modesty, as you know, cannot permit certain risks. As soon as we entered the room we would put out the light and she would undress and lie on the bed. I would curl up as best I could on a table or in some straw-backed chair. It would have been hard indeed had I been accustomed to soft mattresses and Venetian featherbeds all my life! A couple of nights and my bones would have been ground down. But luckily these bones of mine still recalled my cubbyhole at Fratta and its relentlessly lumpy straw, for they stood up to the trial courageously and were able to endure the mad jolts and thumps of another hard cart the next day.

And so, arduously, bumping along, and, I must say, laughing, we traversed the provinces of Vicenza and Verona and on the fourth day arrived at Bardolino on the banks of the blue Benacus.[2] Despite all my woes, my fears and the distractions caused by my companion, I thought of Virgil and saluted the great lake that, thundering like the sea, sometimes swells its waves and lifts them towards the skies.[3] Far away in the haze was Sirmione, queen of the lake, jewel of islands and peninsulas, as Catullus, sweet lover of Lesbia, wrote.[4] I saw the melancholy green olive groves and pictured the poet of Latin graces wandering in their shade with sweet verses on his lips. Under the moonlight I ruminated happily over my classical education, thanking the old Rector of Teglio with all my heart for having shown me a font of such pure pleasure, of comfort so simple and so potent. Orphaned of parents and *patria*; catapulted here and there by mysterious destiny, obliged to act as guardian to a girl not joined to me by ties of family or love, I could nevertheless find a gleam of happiness in the poetic imaginations of men who had lived eighteen centuries before me. O blessed poetry: harmonious, enduring echo of what we perceive as great and beautiful! Resplendent virgin dawn of human reason; fiery, cloud-streaked sunset of the divine, in a mind inspired by genius! Poetry travels on roads eternal, inviting the generations of the earth, one by one, to her side; every step we take on her exalted way reveals greater horizons of virtue, delight, beauty! Let the anatomists bend to examine and cut up her cadaver; thought and sentiment, wrapped in the spirit's mystical fire, will escape their knives.

We took a walk along the crest of the hill, while our host prepared our supper, a small trout and a few sardines. I meditated on Virgil, Catullus, poetry; I thought of Venice, la Pisana, Leopardo, Lucilio, Giulio Del Ponte, Amilcare; and all of them, dead, alive, dying, loves of my heart, quivered sweetly in my muddled thoughts. Aglaura was beside me, wrapped in her cloak, her brow tense with melancholy imaginings. The moon lit up one-half of her face and, outlining her delicate profile, enhanced her Greek beauty three times over. The muse of tragedy, she seemed to me, when she first came, pensive and severe, to Aeschylus' fancy. All of a sudden, after a sharp climb in the road, we came to the edge of a bluff that hung precipitously over the lake. The rock face, dark and cave-like, was gloomily blanched by the moon on a few outcrops; below, the water lay black, deep and silent, the heavens reflected in it without illuminating it, as happens when the light comes straight down, not sideways. I stopped to contemplate that bleak and solemn spectacle, worthy of a pen more masterful or bolder than my own. Aglaura leaned over the steep, sharp slope and for a moment seemed absorbed in some very gloomy calculations.

My thoughts, meanwhile, drifted to peaceful horizons, green meadows, the shimmering sea coast near Fratta; I saw the Bastion of Attila and that vast, wondrous panorama that had made me bow my head before the great deity that orders the universe. How many flowers of a thousand shapes, a thousand colours, does Nature hold in her lap, ready to scatter them far and wide over the many faces of the earth? A long, deep sigh from my companion brought me out of my reverie, and I saw her bend forward and fall headlong into the abyss that loomed at her feet. The scream that emerged from my throat was so harrowing that it chilled even me; fear made the hair stand up on my head and I, too, felt attracted by the whirling delirium of the void. The thought of casting an eye on those depths and perhaps glimpsing the bleeding, inanimate remains of poor Aglaura was horrifying. Just then I thought I heard, beneath me and not far away, a feeble lament. I leaned over the edge of the bluff, listened carefully, and heard a louder moan. It was she, no doubt about it, still alive. Striving to the utmost to see, I finally made out the shape of a bush and next to it a black thing like a body that seemed to be hanging on it.

Impatient to help and to stave off the imminent danger of a branch breaking or a root coming unstuck, I boldly let myself down the almost vertical rock face. I slid rapidly down on my face, my knees, my elbows, but the very act of sliding and a few tufts of grass I clung to in passing broke my sheer vertical fall. By some miracle I arrived safe and sound (or at least with legs unbroken and vertebrae still lined up correctly) at the dog cherry patch that had broken her fall. But there was no time to marvel at miracles; I pulled her out of the thorny bush in which the skirts of her cloak had become entangled and laid her, only half-alive, on the slope. Without any water or any help in that thicket as dense as a huge eagle's nest, there was nothing I could do but wait until she revived or watch her die. I'd heard it said that breath can help those who've fainted after a blow to the head, come back to their senses, and I began to blow on her eyes and her face, watching her every movement anxiously. She finally opened her eyes and I let out a sigh, as if someone had lifted a great weight from my breast.

'Alas, I am still alive,' she murmured. 'It is a real sign that God wants it so.'

'Aglaura, Aglaura,' I said in a pleading, loving, whisper. 'So you really have no faith in me? So my protection and my company have done nothing but make your life a torment?'

'You,' she said softly, 'you are the dearest and most trusted friend I have; for you I would condemn myself to live, if necessary, twice the years that fate has allotted me. But what value can my life have for the good of others?'

'Oh, great value, Aglaura! First, for your parents, then for your brother, who loves you and adores you (and you alone know how much!) and then because there is a heart in this world authorized to love and possess yours. You love, Aglaura, and so you have lost the right to kill yourself, assuming that a person ever has that right.'

'Yes, it is true, I do love!' she replied in a tone of voice that might have been due to her laboured breathing or perhaps to bitter irony. 'I love!' she repeated, this time with greater sincerity. 'And I must live to love; you are right, my friend! Give me your arm and we shall go back home.'

I pointed out that from where we were we could go neither up nor down without danger, and that in any case it would be unwise to try after her long fainting spell.

'Oh, I'm more Greek than Venetian,' she said, drawing herself up proudly. 'I fainted because my wind was blocked, not out of grief or fear, believe me. As for getting out of here, if there's no going up, we can always go down. Didn't you see how masterfully we came down just now?'

My knees had something to say about that mastery (and she had simply plunged), but these were not experiments to perform twice. I made no objection, however, fearing she would judge me more Venetian than Greek.

'Down there along the lake,' she went on, 'there is a strip of sand that continues, I believe, all the way to the port of Bardolino. Once we get our feet on it, we are sure of the road back.'

'The best part will be getting our feet on it,' said I.

'Watch,' she said, 'and follow me.'

With these words she grabbed a knotty, flexible branch extending from the rock, then let go of it and I watched her slide down as I had done not long before. A minute later and her feet were resting on the soft, damp sand, where the waves came whispering in and expired. Well, I certainly didn't wish to look less daring than a woman, so I took the leap and, after a second round of bashing and flaying, arrived at her side, unable to believe it had cost me so little. I thanked Heaven with a sigh so great that the air itself must have felt its weight. My companion, however, was skipping along merrily, as if she'd just emerged from a ball or the theatre. And to think that just a quarter of an hour before she had hurled herself down from the height of two bell towers! Women! Will we ever count the hundred thousand elements (ever new, ever changing, ever in discord) of which you're made? I had never seen Aglaura so happy, so sparkling, as just after she played that desperate card on me. It was only when I tried to make her talk sense that she became slightly vexed, but her cheerful mood was quickly back, brasher and bolder than before.

'Do you really want to know? I'm mad – and that's all there is to it!'

And thus she had the last word and we spoke no more of it. So cheerful, carefree and talkative was she that she even communicated some of her good humour to me as we walked back. If my knees remembered a great deal, my mind, for that half hour, forgot everything.

'What makes me unhappy is to think we'll be eating cold trout and warmed-up sardines!' she said teasingly as we approached the doorstep.

To tell the truth, as much as I had revived, my thoughts weren't clear enough to isolate trout and sardines. I smiled weakly at this regret of hers, however, and promised her a frittata if the fish didn't appeal.

'Yes, indeed, a frittata, and I want to flip it myself!' said Aglaura.

Sappho flipping the frittata after her deadly leap from the Leucadian rock: very much a new character in the great drama of human affairs! Well, I can assure you she was no grotesque poetic fiction but a creature of flesh and blood like you and me. And, of course, Aglaura, who decided she didn't like the trout, was soon in the kitchen beating eggs. The poor trout, I suspect, was shamelessly slandered so she could satisfy this whim that had possessed her. My mouth was agape in admiration. Kneeling before the hearth, the handle of the pan in one hand, the cover in the other to shield her face from the heat, she could have been the cabin boy of some Levantine ship preparing luncheon. The frittata came out very well and even the trout retaliated for the abuse doled out to it by proving quite edible. The sardines then did their best to slip in where the trout had gone. Finally, there was nothing left on the plates but fish bones, and ever since I've been convinced that nothing whets the appetite like having tried to kill yourself an hour before.

Aglaura thought no more about it and I was beginning to regard that ugly incident as a dream or a prank, and my stomach was working so willingly I could hardly believe it, so soon after that frantic anxiety. Even today, I confess, that furious appetite seems magical, if it wasn't Aglaura herself who bewitched me. Every sardine I swallowed was a dark thought that vanished and a happy, positive one appearing. Gnawing at the tail of the last one I was dreaming of the happiness I'd enjoy with la Pisana on that enchanted shore, in some time of peace, love and harmony.

'Who knows?' I thought, swallowing the last bite. I had a remarkable faith (to say the least) in my lucky star after the tempest of that afternoon! But then, extremes meet, as the proverb says. Bertoldo[5] was right to think fair weather was coming when it rained.

That was the jolliest, most pleasant evening I spent with Aglaura during our travels, but much of the contentment was probably due to finding ourselves safe and sound after such great perils. As I accompanied her to her room (for even at the end of the last century the Bardolino tavern had pretensions as an inn) I couldn't stop myself from saying, 'You won't frighten me like that again, Aglaura, will you?'

'Certainly not, and I swear to it,' she said, pressing my hand.

And, in fact, the next morning when we crossed the lake, and the following days as we travelled through the newborn departments of the Cisalpine Republic, she was so composed, so serene, that I could only marvel. Several times I risked touching upon that crazy plunge of hers, but she always scolded me, saying she had already confessed a hundred times that she was mad and that I shouldn't worry because she wouldn't sink into that particular madness again. And so, quite happy, we arrived in Milan, where the great hero Bonaparte and a dozen Lombardy bunglers were at work improvising a flimsy copy of the French Republic, one and indivisible.

It was the twenty-first of November[6] and a huge, festive crowd surged from street to street, on to Corso di Porta Orientale and beyond it to the Lazzaretto Green,[7] now baptized Federation Green. The artillery thundered, thousands of tricolor flags flew; it was all festive pealing and shouting, hats flying, heads, handkerchiefs and arms waving in that cheerful, rowdy, not very calm or dignified crowd. Neither Aglaura nor I wanted to close ourselves up inside, while, in the light of day and the free air of the heavens, the proper Italian government of the Cisalpine Republic was about to be inaugurated. I stowed my bundle away and we went out and joined the throng, she still wearing her masculine guise, pleased to have arrived in time for that solemn event. When we saw the Archbishop blessing flags between God's altar and that of the *patria* amidst a numberless, quivering crowd, before the new government's popular representatives under the glorious supervision of Buonaparte (who was seated on a special throne) I confess that all reservations flew from my head. Before me was a living people, and whether the French or the Turks had awakened them, I found nothing to complain about.

Those faces, breasts, shouts were full of enthusiasm, of great and auspicious omens; that unity imposed on various provinces wrested from foreign domination to make up one independence, one liberty – it all made further, greater hopes possible. When Gian Galeazzo Serbelloni, President of the new Directory, swore on the memory of Curtius, Cato and Scaevola, patriots all, that he would uphold the Directory, the constitution and the laws with his life if need be, those ancient Roman names were perfectly attuned to the solemnity of the occasion. We may laugh today, with hindsight, but back then our faith in them was immense; the republican virtues and industrious liberties of the Middle Ages seemed tiny by comparison, and we tried ardently to connect to the great shade of the republic abolished by Caesar.

In the midst of that carnival of liberty I thought of Venice and a tear came to my eye, but the great drama before me drove out those memories. The speeches and the slogans that day were so pregnant with possibility that the prospects Villetard had hinted at in Venice no longer seemed either false or lies. The Venetians present that day in Milan wept with excitement, not grief, and it seemed impossible that France, having granted liberty to territories long enslaved and quite indifferent, would then deny it to those who'd always had it, and who had showed to the last how dear it was to them. Bonaparte was newly admired and loved by all; at the most, it was whispered that the French Directory had tied his hands (the usual excuse employed by thieves and swindlers of public gratitude). Even I began to think that the Treaty of Campo Formio was merely a temporary concession in order to take back more than had been conceded. Seeing the work of these Frenchmen and the civility of the Cisalpine government close up, I was no longer surprised that Amilcare could write to me, now cured of his Brutus aspirations, and that Giulio Del Ponte and Lucilio had signed up in the new Lombard Legion, from which future armies would come.

I searched the ranks of the militias assembled on the Lazzaretto Green, hoping to catch sight of these friends, and I even thought I saw them, although they were far away and I couldn't be sure. The one I did recognize was Sandro, my friend the miller, in command of a French platoon and wearing great plumes on his head and gold and tassels on his shoulders. It seemed impossible they had decorated him so splendidly in so little time, but it really was Sandro – or if it wasn't the resemblance was awfully deceptive. I then asked Aglaura if she had happened to spot Signor Emilio, but she replied very dryly that she hadn't. She seemed to be quite caught up in the celebrations and her cries and clapping of hands made such an impression on people close to her that they had formed a knot around her.

'Aglaura, Aglaura,' I whispered. 'Remember that you are a woman!'

'Woman or man, what does it matter?' said she loudly. 'Lovers of liberty are not divided by sex. They are all heroes!'

'Bravo! Brava! Well said! A man! Or a woman! Long live the Republic! Long live Bonaparte! Long live strong women!'

I had to drag her off or they would have carried her about in triumph, which she would have accepted quite happily, I'm sure. The fire that lit her eyes recalled the ravings of Pythia.[8] With some effort I moved her to another corner where a great female crowd had gathered, as noisy as ever filled a market. It was a true republic, or rather it was an anarchy of frivolous and flighty heads. In my opinion, there's no creature who talks as much nonsense as a political woman. You be the judge, based on what I heard then!

'Ladies,' said one, 'don't you think they'd have done better to dress our Directory in red? That green colour with the silver embroidery makes them look like the old governor's Master of Ceremonies.'

'Oh, silence, you fool!' replied her companion. 'Republican sobriety wears dark colours.'

'And you call that sobriety?' said a third. 'You should see what two young French officers did to my niece!'

'Bah, it's all slander! They were probably noblemen in disguise! Down with the nobles! Long live equality!'

'Long live, long live; but meanwhile they say those gentlemen of the Directory are almost all aristocrats.'

'They were, they were, my dear, but they've been *purified*.'

'What the Devil? How did they do that?'

'You don't know? Haven't you ever seen the painting of the Purification in the church of San Calimero? They take two turtledoves and two pigeons to church.'[9]

'And that's all?'

'The other part's done by the priest: all I care about is that they're purified; the ceremony doesn't interest me much. Hey! Lucrezia! Lucrezia! Over there, your brother! He looks so handsome with his gun on his shoulder and that cockade on his hat!'

'Oh, I can see him! If he wasn't my brother I'd fall right in love with him! You know he's sworn to kill all kings, all princes and even the Pope?'

'Oh yes? Good man, by Jove! He'll keep his promise!'

I myself had seen him smash a constable's face after the fellow stepped on his foot at the tavern. Long live the Republic!

All those tireless throats now joined in rapturous unison: 'Long live the Republic!' 'Long live Bonaparte!' 'Long live the Cisalpine Republic!'

'Well now,' said the one who wanted to dress the Directory in scarlet to her companions. 'Can you tell me where and what is this Republic? I don't see it. Maybe it's like Maria Theresa,[10] who was always in Vienna and only sent her *sous-chef* here!'

'Down with the Governor!' shouted another, purifying her ears of those abject memories her companion had recalled. She then proceeded to spell out what this Republic was, assuring her it was like a mistress who doesn't meddle, who lives and lets live and doesn't make the poor work for the profit of the rich.

'You see,' she went on, 'the Republic exists, but no one has ever seen it and so nobody's in awe of it, and everyone can shout and run around and make a racket in its place, as if there were no one there.'

'What do you mean there's no one there?' said Lucrezia, her voice throaty and harsh from loud screaming. 'Don't you see the French and the Cisalpini?'

'As I was saying,' the first continued, 'what does it mean, this Cisalpine Republic?'

'Oh mercy me, it's just a name like Teresina, Giuseppina or any other.'

'No, no, I'll tell you what it means!' said Lucrezia. 'You don't know anything!'

'What do you mean I don't know anything? And you? Right, you're a genuine learned lady!'

'Oh, you ninny! Can't you see I know what I'm talking about? I danced around the tree as the Spirit of Liberty and my brother's in the Republican Legion!'

I was all ears awaiting this definition of the Republic that was struggling to come out, and paying scant attention to the delegates from Mantua and the Legations, not yet joined with the Cisalpini, who were holding forth just then before the Directory, offering fine new proof of Italian concord.

'Well then, now, just what is this Cisalpine Republic?' I asked a woman who looked to me the silliest and most garrulous.

'What is it? What does it mean?' Lucrezia shouted proudly. 'It means that there's the Cisalpine and that the Republic will preserve it. He said it and he swore it, our Serbelloni, and General Bonaparte agrees with him.'

'I can't abide that General Bonaparte; he's as gaunt as the side of a penny and his hair is as lank as nails.'

'Oh, it's nothing, my dear! You'll see better! It's the continuous heat of battle that has left his cheeks and his hair looking like that. You'll see my brother when he comes back from the war. I'll bet he won't be able to get his breeches back on!'

'Lucrezia, that's an insult to your sister-in-law! You mustn't say these things!'

And here began another battle royal, because such disrespectful jesting was out of place at this solemn moment. The two began to tear at each other's hair and the others took hold of them, trying to calm them down. A French corporal appeared and restored order with the butt of his rifle. The one who'd asserted that it was not no one, but the Cisalpini and the French who were there, was proved perfectly right. The French, above all, were certainly there. On close inspection you could see they had established the government, chosen the Directory, nominated the members of the congregations, secretaries and ministers, and even reserved the right to elect the members of the two legislative councils. But the people, new to such zealous energy, were busy trying to live up to it. They had taken a great leap from weak and spineless obedience to strong and active obedience, and the rest would come later. Bonaparte was the guarantee of that.

I must confess that I, too, fully shared the common illusions, and I wouldn't even call them illusions were it not for the downfall that came after. There were, after all, great and excellent reasons to hope. And, in fact, it was a grand day, well worthy of being honoured by posterity. It marked the first real revival of national life and thought, and Napoleon (whom I then trusted and in whom I later lost faith) will always have part of my gratitude for having hastened it along. Venice had to fall; he hurried it, and dishonoured the fall. Shame! But sometime or other Machiavelli's great dream[11] had to leave the ghost world and actively shape events. Bonaparte performed the metamorphosis and it was a real accomplishment, real glory. And if it were only by chance, if he acted then only with future ambitions in view, still, chance and his ambitions conspired for a moment with the welfare of the Italian nation, and imposed the first steps of our revival. Napoleon – his arrogance, his mistakes, his tyranny – was fatal for the old Venetian Republic, but useful to Italy. Let me pluck from my heart the petty irritations, petty hatreds, petty preferences. Liar, unjust, autocrat: we welcomed him.

Now, if I was this excited, you can just imagine Aglaura, who, I don't have to tell you because you've already seen it, had a head full of enthusiasm for republicanism and liberty! That enthusiasm, I thought, must have been responsible for the fact that she'd taken little trouble to find her Emilio that day. In the evening, when we had taken two little rooms in a very humble hostel on Corso di Porta Romana, I brought up the matter.

'It is you,' she said, 'who thinks I took no trouble. In fact, this morning I did nothing but look around for him, and if I didn't find him it's certainly not my fault. But don't you have many Venetian friends here in Milan that you intend to search out this evening? Well then, go out and find them and I shall know something through them. In the meantime I will adjust these women's clothes you bought me. I thank you, you know, my friend! I swear I shall be eternally grateful. But above all, if you should meet Spiro, play dumb on my account. It wouldn't surprise me at all if he had got to Milan before us.'

I promised to do as she asked, but on my part I begged her to keep her word and send her parents news. She promised she would and I went out, first stopping at the post to see whether there were letters for us. There were four: three of them for me, and two of these from la Pisana. One told of what had happened after I fled; the other was all sighs, laments and tears for my absence and yearning to embrace me soon. I was shocked by what I read. His Excellency Navagero had thrown his cousin the Countess out of his house, and she had gone to live with her son, who had regained his post with the government accounting department. Old Venchieredo had made quite an uproar about my departure, and shouted and stormed that he would get them to impound everything I owned, but when the only thing he could find was a poor little house, his zeal cooled and he forgot about the house and so la Pisana was still there. It also seemed that Raimondo had stepped in to limit his father's revenge, for the clever young fellow had not forgotten la Pisana's coquetry and now seemed to be taking it very seriously. Or at least that was what I suspected, for she herself had written to tell me that one day la Doretta had paid her an unexpected call. That was certainly Raimondo's work; he was seeking a way in by means of his lady friend. Doretta did his bidding without question and he felt free to toss aside his instrument as soon as his objective was reached. I wasn't at all pleased that la Pisana should become familiar with those ruffians and I decided to write and advise her to stay away from them. Although she always laughed and joked about them, you can't predict everything. And with that brain of hers!

'Enough!' I thought to myself. 'The French had better light the fuse quickly or things will soon turn sour. That crazy girl needs great and present love if she is to keep on loving. I'm not keen on prolonging this distance between us much longer.'

Two other surprising pieces of news were that Partistagno was still carrying on about Clara, and that Padre Pendola had now been appointed canon of San Marco. The first, recently promoted to Captain in the Imperial Army cavalry (by virtue of his famous uncle the baron's influence, I imagine), had gone about clinking his spurs day and night in front of the convent, until Madre Redenta asked for a sentry to back up the nun at the gate. And day and night the sentry was busy presenting arms to the terrible Partistagno, who never ceased riding back and forth in front of the convent. He was convinced that the Countess had forced Clara to become a nun, because she envied and hated his family. And wild as he was in his thirst for revenge, he had hit upon the dangerous plan of buying up the mortgages on the Fratta lands and then sending out scores of petitions and executive orders to attack the last remains of that unhappy estate. Partistagno himself, of course, wasn't capable of such diabolical cleverness, but behind him you could spot the cloven hoof of old Venchieredo, who, after his prison term, had sworn eternal hatred towards the House of Fratta, down to the last generation.

His assaults and those of Partistagno, along with Fulgenzio's thievery and Count Rinaldo's crowning lack of interest had made a profitable concern into a losing one, and the only thing you could bet on now was bankruptcy. Abandoned by all, the Castle was falling into ruin and only Monsignor's room still had windows and doors. Elsewhere, farmers and factors and assorted ne'er-do-wells had carried off almost everything: one selling the windowpanes, another the door knobs, another the pavement stones and the ceiling beams. The poor Captain's door had been ripped off, and now Signora Veronica had such bad coughs and colds that his marital cross had grown fifty times heavier. Marchetto had left the Castle and, no longer bailiff, was now the parish sacristan. A strange new role! But *buli* were no longer in fashion and there was no choice but to become a saint. Worst of all was that the Countess, no longer receiving money from her properties, now got nothing but dunning letters. She had no idea where to turn and if it hadn't been for the scant interest from la Pisana's dowry, she wouldn't have had bread on her table. But she continued to gamble it away and Rinaldo's meagre salary often went directly into the bottomless pockets of some hardened sharp.

The news from Fratta, la Pisana told me, came from her Cisterna aunt and uncle, who had gone to live in Venice, hoping to profit from the family's favour with the Austrians to place their children in some career. From one side and the other, many hands were stretched out towards the public purse. What was the point of staying in the middle, where there wasn't the remotest chance of any rewards? I confess I've seen few of such miracles in my life, and almost none among grown men. Disdain for honours and for wealth belongs to youth. And may youth hold fast to this blessed gift, which all by itself makes possible great purposes and generous deeds.

The other letter was from old Apostulos, informing me of his daughter's flight and the measures taken everywhere but in Milan to find her. In Milan, the task was assigned to me. I should ask around, search for her, find her and either send her back to Venice or keep her with me, as she wished. He certainly didn't intend to exert his paternal rights over this rebellious, fugitive daughter. Let her do as she pleased; he didn't disown her, for the mad don't deserve that, but he wished to stand aside. In a postscript he added that he had ordered careful searches in other mainland cities and there his correspondents had orders to bring the guilty party back right away. In my case, he was more lenient; if I thought that her aberration could be cured better in Milan than in Venice, I should act accordingly. These last words were underscored, but their meaning was obscure to me. I thought I might ask Aglaura to enlighten me as to whether perhaps he was alluding to marriage with Emilio, but I couldn't understand why Apostulos was being so mysterious. My strange fate was that each side thought me the confidant of the other, and everyone spoke to me in hints and half-words that I understood no better than Arabic. Meanwhile there was still no news from my father, but they didn't think I would hear anything before Christmas, and in general the reports from the Levant were good.

With all these thoughts, news, complications and mysteries swimming in my head, I stopped in a caffè to enquire where the Cisalpine Legion barracks might be. At Santa Vicenzina, they told me, next to Piazza d'Armi. With that, I knew less than before, but by asking, turning back, asking again and walking some more, I got there at last. Discipline wasn't very strict; you could go in and out at will and the noise, confusion and disorder couldn't have been greater. The officers were peacocking around in their new stripes, getting ready to conquer some lovely lasses before they went into battle, where they would terrify their enemies. The sergeants and the foot soldiers were bickering among themselves, because the first considered themselves superior by rank, while the second considered themselves their equals (republicanism brings up the last). Try as we must, this muddle of equality and subordination is going to be difficult to straighten out, especially among us Italians, where there isn't a goose-brain who doesn't hold dear to Virgil's 'Thou alone shall rule the people' and Dante's 'Any peasant, taking sides, can be a Marcellus.'[12] Perhaps this is merely one of the strengths of the Italian character, become a flaw because of changed circumstances. Arrogance suits the lion in the desert very well, but it is problematic for the beast in a cage. However, you may say, maybe what was can be refashioned, and by shaping and reshaping, through education and habit, much can be obtained. I, too, will say I also hope so, especially if we do not worship ourselves too much, and for the rest I'd rather rely on the prickly presumption of the Italian than on the fawning obedience of the drunken Slav. Here, there is room for a long disquisition on the views of those who think civilization will be perfected by the Slavs, who are said to work harder than the Germans, while we, poor bastards of Rome, have no claim but to a first draft (a bit idealized, a bit false), but also a bit ours, it seems. It would be a waste of time, though, to write volumes against those critics of the Latin races; it's enough to open those already printed. Italy is the world's past and France, whatever they say, is the present. And the future? We may even leave it to the Slavs and the Kalmuks, if it makes them happy. Personally, I don't expect that future will come to pass.

All this, however, is no excuse whatsoever for the slovenly and insubordinate state of the Cisalpine Legion. Leaving aside their principles, the notorious Cernide of Ravignano were certainly superior in terms of discipline and order. What would Captain Sandracca have said, that great military mastermind who argued that in a proper regiment one soldier should resemble another more than two brothers, such was discipline's great assimilating power? Well, the man who could find two Lombard legionaries whose beards were clipped the same would deserve a prize as big as the Duomo of Milan, I reckon. In terms of beard fashions, the models ranged from Adam to the Babylonians, from the Ostrogoths to Frederick II's grenadiers.

A filthy, scowling soldier was rabidly polishing his colleague's boots for the price of half a pitcher, and I enquired of him about Dr Lucilio Vianello, Amilcare Dossi and Giulio Del Ponte.

'They're in the first company, turn left,' that helot of equality replied.

I turned left and repeated my question to another, even more filthy soldier who was cleaning the barrel of a rifle with oil and wadding.

'What the deuce, I know all three of them, God flay them!' he replied. 'Vianello is the doctor of this very company, the one who's going to finish us all off on the orders of the French, who are tired of us. Did you know, Citizen, that they have closed the Hall of Public Instruction?'

'I know nothing,' said I, 'but where might I . . .?'

'Now just wait. As I was saying, Vianello is our doctor, Dossi is sub-lieutenant, and Del Ponte, Corporal Del Ponte, is a real dead drunk who can't stand on his two feet and lays all the work on me. See, this is his musket that I have to rub up! After that party this morning! Making us stand as straight as sticks for ten hours, smelling the wind, which smelled of winter, pretty much. What the deuce? We signed up to go to war and wipe out kings and aristocrats, we did! Not to pay court to the Directory and carry a candle for them in the procession! If that's what they want, then they should go and call the Archduke's lackeys. It's a scandal. All day long I haven't drunk more than a third of a flask of Canneto wine. What, do they expect us to be republicans for nothing? Citizen, would you honour me with a small loan to buy a pint? Giacomo Dalla Porta, head of the line in the first company of the Cisalpine Legion, at your command.'

I gave it to him (as a loan, of course): one Milan *lira*, on the agreement that he take me without further comment to one of the three men I'd named. He threw down the gun, the oil and the wadding and began to hop along like a clown with that *lira* between thumb and index finger, his other hand flattened over his nose, and raced downstairs in search of the tavern-keeper.

'Oh yes, trust in republican honesty!' I thought, an old man grumbling. I had forgotten that where there's printed money and a festival on the green you could not count on reforming everyone's habits, and in any case there will always be, in every republic on earth, those who prefer drinking wine to assisting others.

In a hallway I finally found another soldier, quite spruced up, composed and almost elegant, who replied to my salute with a courtly bow, or nearly, and addressed me as 'Citizen' just as he would have called me 'Count' or 'Excellency' four months before. Such were his courtesy and fine speech: he must have been some marquis beguiled by a love of liberty who had become a friar of this new religion by signing up as a Cisalpine legionary. Elegant, casual martyrs of whom there are many in all revolutions and anyone who speaks ill of them is quite wrong, because with a dash of patience they can become heroes.

(And quite a few of them have recently earned their place on our saint's calendar: Luciano Manara,[13] for example, Milanese like the anonymous marquis to whom I spoke.) This latter, to make a long story short, very graciously led me to Dr Lucilio's room, and there we said farewell with such civility we were like two prime ministers after a conference.

I entered. Words cannot describe the doctor's surprise, congratulations and warm embraces, and those of Giulio, who was with him. I really don't think they would have been more delighted to see a brother, and from that I deduced that they did care for me, at least a little. I did, however, feel some remorse holding Giulio to my heart and kissing him. You might say my lips were still warm from those of la Pisana, the woman he, too, had loved and who had maybe, with her heedlessness and coquetry, lit that feverish fire in his veins that was consuming him. Still, he had left her for a worthier, more fortunate love, and I found him, although pale and gaunt, certainly not worse than he had been in Venice, despite the hard life of the barracks. Lucilio reassured me that his illness had not grown worse and that good humour, moderate and regular duties and simple food might even bring some improvement in the long run. Giulio smiled like a man who perhaps believed, but didn't feel he had to hope; he had become a soldier in order to die, not to get well, and had grown so accustomed to the idea that he held on to it cheerfully and like Anacreon[14] crowned himself with roses, one foot in the grave.

I asked about their hopes, their duties, their lives. All was well. There were great and impatient hopes for the revolution that was boiling in Rome, Genoa, Piedmont, Naples, and for the trend towards unity growing out of the coming annexation of Bologna, Modena and even Pesaro and Rimini to the Cisalpine Republic.

'At Massa we will reach the Mediterranean,' said Lucilio. 'How can they stop us from reaching the Adriatic in Venice?'

'And the French?' I asked.

'The French are of great help, for alone we're not able to manage. Certainly, we have to keep our eyes open and not fall for tall tales like those of that fool Villetard, and above all we must hang on to our liberty by our fingernails and not let go for all the gold in the world.'

These were pretty much my own ideas, but from the heat of his voice and his lively manner I could easily see that the morning's solemn ceremony had warmed even Lucilio's diffident fancy, and that he was not, in that moment, the dispassionate doctor of a few months before. I liked him better that way, but he was also less infallible, and, although his vision of things agreed with my own, I didn't yet want to trust his opinion blindly. I thus raised a few questions about the ignorance and lack of experience of the people, saying I doubted they were prepared for the educated civility of the republican order and mentioning the insubordination I myself had observed in the newly created army.

'Two objections to which I reply with one argument,' said Lucilio. 'What do we need to train disciplined soldiers? Discipline. What do we need to shape true, virtuous and honest republicans? The Republic. Neither soldiers nor republicans are spontaneously born; we are all born men; that is, beings to be brought up well or badly, future lackeys or future Catos, depending on whether we end up in corrupt or honest hands. In any event, you will admit that if the Republic is unable to make perfect republicans, tyranny will be even more able and willing to make them!'

'Who knows?' said I. 'After all, Brutus' Rome came forth from that of Tarquinius!'[15]

'Oh, I wouldn't worry about that, Carlino; we've never lacked for Tarquins in four or five centuries of madness and oppression! We ought to be well trained. Tell me something about yourself, instead. Why did you linger in Venice until now? How were you able to survive there?'

Once again I brought out my excuses, Leopardo's death and my father's affairs left half-finished, and then finally got up my courage and, glancing quickly at Giulio, mentioned la Pisana. Both of them then fired questions at me about that flap with the French officer, of which some news had spread even to Milan. I told the story in detail: la Pisana's troubles and the risks she had run; how I'd been forced to remain there to protect her and comfort her. I dwelt at length on my escape, hoping to impress them with the dangers I'd faced staying in Venice, dangers I'd rather not have faced if grave necessity hadn't forced me. In short, I privately declared myself guilty of that careless delay, but didn't give anyone else the material to accuse me. And not wishing to dwell on that sore point, I went on about the changing of the guard at Venice, Sérurier's final days of plundering and the new government in which, it seemed, Venchieredo had some influence.

'Confound it! Didn't you know?' said Lucilio. 'He was courier between the imperial command in Gorizia and the Directory in Paris.'

'Or rather, Bonaparte in Milan,' said Giulio.

'As you wish; it's the same. Bonaparte could not undo what plans the Directory had already hatched. Venchieredo was well rewarded, but I fear (or hope) things will turn sour for him, because he's too eager to serve and servants end up being harmed or mocked.'

'By the way,' I said, 'what do you know of Sandro from Fratta? I saw him this morning at the celebrations with so many constellations on him he looked like the Zodiac!'

'He's now Captain Alessandro Giorgi of the Foot Chasseurs,' said Lucilio. 'He distinguished himself putting down peasant revolts outside Genoa, and now he's advancing. He was made lieutenant and then captain in the space of a month; in his company, between getting shot, getting killed and great hardship, only four men are still alive. One of them had to become captain: the others were two cobblers and a drover; so, as was his due, the miller was chosen! When you meet him you'll see how he swells with pride! He's a good, honest lad who stands up for everyone he meets and he won't hesitate to stand up for you, too.'

'Many thanks,' said I. 'I'll be grateful to accept.'

'Not now,' said Lucilio. 'Your place is here with us and Amilcare.'

They then gave me news of Amilcare, telling me that he was prouder and wilder than ever, and that he kept up morale in their company with such expedients as only he knew how to extract from the worst situations. With no income beyond their wages, their pockets were often empty, but Amilcare was clever about finding ways of making money and economizing until their next payday. Amilcare made me think of Bruto Provedoni, who was supposed to have enlisted along with Sandro and about whom I'd heard nothing. It seemed he was fighting skirmishes in Liguria and Piedmont, for, although the King was a good friend and loyal servant of the Directory, the French kept the resistance simmering, so as to have a pretext to strike whenever it suited them. Meanwhile, they had prodded the revarnished Ligurian Republic to declare war on the King and forbidden him to defend himself. The poor King didn't know where to turn: a precipice on all sides! Luckily Piedmont, so bellicose and loyal, was nothing like sleepy Venice, or some similar infamy would have resulted. Infamy there was – but all on the side of the French.

This seemed a good point to ask about Emilio Tornoni, and so I did, pretending I knew him. He had gone off to Rome with a pretty Milanese countess, probably to join the revolution, said Giulio with a crooked smile. Their scornful manner aroused my suspicions, but I could get no more out of them. Not long afterwards that hothead Amilcare returned and there were more kisses, more astonishment. He'd become as dark as an Arab, with a voice like musketry rat-a-tat-tat; and he explained he'd grown hoarse trying to teach the recruits to march. This taking a step (by itself quite simple), well, the tacticians had made it into the most arduous exercise in the world and apparently, before Frederick II, battles were conducted without marching or marching very badly, and it wasn't too far-fetched to think that a hundred years from now they'd be teaching soldiers the three-step and the polka march! The afternoon never seemed to end, we had so much to tell; but at a certain point we had gone out on the ramparts and when the drums sounded Lucilio reminded the other two it was time to retire.

'Yes, indeed,' said Amilcare shrugging his shoulders. 'My view is, an officer must obey the drums.'

'I'm ill, and down as being in the hospital,' said Giulio.

I was sure Lucilio would remind them of their duty, because

I was eager to rejoin Aglaura and take her the letter and news of Emilio, but the two conscripts paid no attention to the doctor's words and so I had to enjoy their company until after nine o'clock. And then they insisted on coming along with me to my lodgings, and when I didn't invite them up and they saw a light at the window and a shadow like that of a woman on the curtain, they began to joke and come to a thousand conclusions and congratulate me on my good fortune. Crazy Amilcare made such a ruckus that I kept fearing that at any moment Aglaura would come out on to the balcony. When, finally, God so willed it, Lucilio persuaded them to leave and I was able to go up and console the young lady for having been left alone for so long. I gave her the letter and saw her sigh and nearly weep reading it, but she made an effort not to be seen.

'If I may ask, who writes to you?' I said.

It was her brother Spiro, she told me. But she quickly fended off any other questions, only telling me that he was very well and believed her to be with me in Milan. Why, if he loved her so very much, did he not come to join her? Here was the question that remained a mystery to me, but later I would learn that Spiro had been thrown in prison as an accomplice to my escape. And the letter, in fact, was sent from prison and that was why Aglaura was tearful. She then asked if I had received letters from Venice and, when I said yes, asked for news. I handed her the letter from her father and the one from la Pisana in which she told of events in Venice. She read them without comment, until she came to a point in which Raimondo Venchieredo and Doretta were named, upon which she started in surprise and repeated the name Doretta, as if to be sure of it.

'What is it?' said I.

'Oh, nothing! Just that I, too, know this lady, at least secondhand, and I was astonished to find her name in a letter addressed to you. Had I known that Venchieredo comes from your parts I wouldn't have been so surprised.'

'And how do you know the Venchieredo family?'

'Oh, I know them . . . because I know them! No, let me explain. They were corresponding, about business matters I suppose, with Emilio.'

'By the way, I must give you sad news.'

'What?'

'Signor Emilio Tornoni has left for Rome.' (I was prudently silent about the countess.)

'I knew that, but he will be back,' said Aglaura, rather defiantly. 'I would ask you to find out tomorrow whether M. Ascanio Minato, aide-de-camp to General Baraguay d'Hilliers, and M. d'Hauteville, secretary to General Berthier, are here in Milan. They are persons who wish to have any news of Emilio that I might receive.'

'At your service.'

'And tell me, did you learn nothing else about him?'

'Nothing!'

'Nothing, nothing . . . nothing at all?'

'Nothing, I tell you.' I was almost impressed by the young lady, hearing her speak so casually of aides and generals, but I didn't want her to know about that unspoken contempt I'd sensed in Lucilio and Del Ponte when I'd mentioned Tornoni. I knew how much the enamoured like to hear their true loves disparaged.

'Aglaura,' said I after a moment of silence, 'you are quite the mystery, and you'll agree that my goodwill and discretion are . . .'

'They are matchless,' she said.

'No, that was not what I meant, but rather that they merit a tiny pinch of trust on your part.'

'That is true, my friend. Ask and I shall reply.'

'Oh, if you sit there so stiff and serious like a queen, words fail me. Come, be cheerful and simple as you were the first time I saw you. That's it, that's how I like you. Now, tell me then how it is you are so familiar with the names and surnames of the French General Staff? Just now you seemed to be a commanding general deploying his troops for battle!'

'That is all you wish to know?'

'That's all; for now my curiosity ends here.'

'Well, those gentlemen are Emilio's close friends; that's why I know them.'

'M. Minato, too?'

'He more than the others, but he is more gentlemanly than the rest; that is to say, less of a scoundrel than those other bandits.'

'Easy, Aglaura! You're not the young lady you were this morning! Now you insult those you praised to the sky before.'

'I? I praised the Republic to the skies, not those who made it. Even the ass may bear precious stones, and bandits at home may be heroes outside, but they are butcher-heroes, not . . .'

'Tell me now, does Spiro write to say he'll come and get you or that you are to go to Venice?'

'Why do you ask? Are you tired of me?'

'Have a good night, Aglaura. We'll talk tomorrow. You're not well disposed today.'

And so I retired to my little room behind hers and went to bed thinking of la Pisana: the straitened circumstances tormenting her and the dangers she faced being alone. Above all, her reconciliation with Rosa and those visits from Doretta concerned me. Raimondo would come next, for I knew he was the great ram who would slip in through the gap made by the ewes. In my mind I went to work on the long letter I would write the following day, and from thoughts of la Pisana I shifted to those of Aglaura, less anxious, but more obscure. Could anyone find a flicker of clarity in that little whirlwind of a head? I certainly couldn't. From Padua to Milan she had whisked me along from revelation to revelation, less like a girl busy living her life, than a writer of French romances composing a great epic. Her words and her actions came together, drew apart, leapt over one another in events, counter-events and surprises worthy of one of Pindar's odes badly patched together by a scholiast.[16] I dreamed about them all night, observed her for a good part of the morning and went out with the letter to Pisana in my pocket, without having made any progress. Inside that letter was another for old Apostulos in which I told him of Aglaura's behaviour and put myself at his service in all that concerned her. I also asked him to lend la Pisana any money she needed as if she were myself. I posted this without saying anything to the young lady, because my conscience was at stake and I wanted to avoid scenes. To play her father was fine, but not to play the villain on her behalf.

At midday I met Lucilio at the Caffè del Duomo, then the

fashionable place to meet, where we'd made an appointment. He said he was sorry he'd been unable to enrol me in the Cisalpine Legion, but there wasn't a single vacancy. Rather than allow someone like myself to remain idle he'd have taken suggestions from the Devil, he said, and I could rejoice, for an excellent idea had come to him.

'I'm going to take you to your general,' he said. 'General, commander, captain, fellow-soldier, anything you like! He's one of those men who are too far above everyone else to bother to show it; there's no way you can think he has only one soul, for his enormous activity must wear out a dozen a day. And yet he's able to admire the calm and even sympathize with the lazy. In the field he could win a battle all by himself, I'd wager, so long as his eyes (seat of his most extraordinary powers) were not harmed. He's Neapolitan and in Naples they would say he exercises *la jettatura*, the evil eye, as we call it, not to be confused with the nasty cross-eye of the old Clerk of Fratta.'

'And who is this *rara avis*?' I asked.

'You'll see, and if you don't like him, I'll have myself struck off the rolls of the Christians.'

With these words he dragged me from the caffè and marched me past the Porta Nuova canal towards the ramparts. We entered a huge house with a courtyard full of horses, stable boys, trainers, saddles and harnesses, like a cavalry barracks. Soldiers, sergeants and orderlies were running up and down the stairs as if this were the headquarters of the General Staff. In the entry hall were more soldiers; more weapons were on display or stacked in heaps in the corners, and there was a small warehouse of tunics, shoulder straps and soldiers' boots to one side.

'What's this?' I said. 'The Arsenal, maybe?'

Lucilio kept going, undeterred, as if he were at home here. Without even announcing himself, he pushed past an aide, who was counting the ceiling beams, into the last room, opened the door and went in, dragging me by the hand, to meet the strange master of that military academy.

He was a young man, about thirty years old, the living picture of one of those Orsini, those Colonna, those Medici for whom life was an endless series of battles, pillage, duels and prison. His name was Ettore Carafa,[17] a noble name made even more illustrious by the bearer's independence and his love of liberty and country. He had long been imprisoned in Naples's notorious Castel Sant'Elmo, had fled to Rome and from there to Milan to build up, at his own expense, a legion that would liberate Naples. He was one of those men who must act at any cost, in company or alone, and his large spirit shone in his broad, open face. A small scar surrounded by a pale halo cut through one eyebrow, like a mark of misfortune on a bold man's great hopes. He rose from the bunk where he was resting, held out a hand to Lucilio and remarked on the fine officer accompanying him.

'Not much of an officer,' I said to him. 'I know the military arts only by name.'

'Are you brave enough to be killed defending your country and your honour?' asked Carafa.

'I'd give not one but one hundred lives for those noble causes,' I replied.

'Very well, my friend, I permit you to consider yourself a perfect soldier from now on.'

'A soldier, yes, but an officer?' intervened Lucilio.

'Let me be the judge of that! Can you ride a horse, load a rifle and handle a sword?'

'Yes, I know something of all of these,' I said. (I owed this to Marchetto and thanked him then, just as not long before I had thanked the Rector for his instruction in the classics.)

'Good, then you are also an officer. In a legion like my own, which will wage war in feints and skirmishes, a good eye and a firm will are worth more than any training. Come back here at the last post call. I will assign you your company and, rest assured, in three months we shall have taken the Kingdom of Naples.'

I might have been listening to Robert Guiscard[18] or one of Ariosto's knights, but he was quite serious, as I would later learn. I hesitated to ask if I might sleep outside the barracks, but finally I did ask and he told me, smiling, that it was an officer's privilege.

'I understand,' he said, 'you've promised your nights to another colonel.'

I hesitated, then didn't deny it, and Lucilio smiled, too. The truth was I couldn't leave Aglaura alone, but heaven only knew whether I enjoyed standing guard over her. I was very happy indeed with Signor Ettore Carafa, though, and would be doubly happy later on. I shall always remember fondly that frugal, tough, martial life. Drill with my company in the morning, then luncheon and a long chat with Amilcare, Giulio and Lucilio; the afternoon and evening with Aglaura, who was still waiting for Emilio and didn't want to return to Venice. In between, a bittersweet letter from la Pisana. And thus we arrived at the revolution in Rome, which was to launch Carafa's military operations in the Bourbon Kingdom.

SIXTEEN

Wherein the most amazing family drama imaginable takes place. A digression on the affairs of Rome, and on Foscolo, Parini and other personages of the Cisalpine Republic. I gain a sister and bequeath a wife to Spiro Apostulos. To Mantua, Florence and Rome. Skirmishes at the border of Naples. Ettore Carafa's nymph Egeria.[1] *I regain la Pisana in a wager, although I am not terribly pleased at first.*

On 15 February 1798 in the Campo Vaccino five notaries drew up the act of liberty for the people of Rome.[2] Standing by as their liberator was Berthier, the same who had stood by as traitor to the Venetian Republic at the Congress of Bassano. The Pope was closed up in his palace among priests and Swiss guards, and when he refused to give up his temporal authority he was removed by force and sent off to Tuscany. The sole example of Italian inflexibility in those days of constant vacillation and fearfulness, and it was Pius VI! As little a Christian as I was, I do remember admiring the old man's determination, and when I compared it to the doddering weakness of Doge Manin, the contrast between two of Italy's oldest governments was painful. Rome, already depleted after the Treaty of Tolentino,[3] was stripped of all power by the republicans. The murdered General Duphot[4] (his killing was the pretext for war) was celebrated with funeral orations, splendid light shows – and a sack of all the churches. Crates heavy with precious stones went off to France, while the army, left empty-handed, rioted against General Massena, Berthier's successor. The countryside, too, was in revolt and ripe with murder: in short, one of those great social dramas that could only happen today in southern Italy and Spain was under way.

In Milan, now that Carafa's legion was ready and drilled, we were merely waiting for the French commander to say the word so that we could set off ourselves. I was in a nice muddle, however. Aglaura wanted to come with me, because she liked the idea of travelling to Rome, while I neither wanted to forbid her, nor to expose her to the dangers of that long march in such perilous times. And so I wrote to Venice, but there was no reply. Even la Pisana had not sent me any news for a while. The expedition to Rome seemed to bode very ill. Yet from day to day I continued to hope; and while Carafa tormented the French to get that blessed consent, forever delayed, I consoled myself with the thought that another day meant more time to entertain vague hopes. My three friends had already left for Rome along with a part of the Lombardy Legion. I was all alone, with no other company but splendid Captain Alessandro.

The worst was that (whether from Venice or from Milan) word had spread that I was living with a beautiful Greek girl and there was endless jesting about this among my fellow soldiers. Imagine how pleased I felt about the kind of reputation this lent me! I can assure you I'd have given a hand (like Muzio Scevola)[5] to have Emilio tire of the countess and come back to claim Aglaura. Not that she weighed on me very much, for I had grown used to her and she acted as my housekeeper with admirable patience, but it annoyed me that the happiness I appeared to have actually belonged to another.

My friendship with Foscolo, renewed when he spent some time in Milan, offered some distraction. I found his fiery, fevered eloquence bewitching; once I listened for more than two hours while he cursed and maligned everyone: the Venetians, the French, the Austrians, kings, democrats, the Cisalpini, deploring tyranny and abuse in all. What he saw around him were the very excesses of his own spirit. And those times in Milan made a worthy theatre for him. The best and bravest men of Italy had collected there and our ancient nation, which wouldn't have paid them much heed scattered here and there, rightly basked in that illustrious council. Aldini, Paradisi, Rasori, Gioia, Fontana, Gianni, both Pindemonte brothers:[6] names that could fire up Foscolo's powerful rhetoric. Through him I also met the poets Monti and Parini: one the harmonious singer of praises; the other the sober, elegant censor. Parini – grave, serene, affable – remains impressed in my memory. If his nearly lame feet carried him forward very slowly, fire still flashed from that old man's soul. The letter in which Jacopo Ortis recounts his dialogue with Parini offers a lively historical memory of the times; I can testify to that. I myself saw the ageing abbé and the young hothead sitting together under a tree out beyond Porta Orientale. I would join them and we would mourn lost *things*, so much less grave than people, alas. Who said it better than Parini (when asked to shout 'Long live the Republic and death to the tyrants!') who replied 'Long live the Republic and death to no one!' Who better than Foscolo when he ended his self-portrait: 'Only death can give me peace and repose.' I was no more than a humble sub-lieutenant in the Parthenopean Legion, but in my heart (I say this proudly) I felt the equal of those great men and made myself part of their company.

Foscolo, too, had become an officer in the Cisalpine Army. In those days officers sprang up like armed men from Cadmus' teeth. Doctors, men of the law and of letters all carried swords; the toga made way for arms. Young men from the best families came forward; resolve, zeal and emulation made up for the lack of time. Despite passing disorders and republican insubordination, the core of the new army had already been formed. Carafa feared that the French generals wanted to delay and wear us out until his legion finally joined the Cisalpini. A Neapolitan first and foremost (hot and vindictive as they are), he not surprisingly got carried away with that suspicion. I think he would have declared war on the French had they given him even the tiniest excuse. At last he got the long-awaited consent. On the first of March the legion was to proceed to Rome and join the Franco-Cisalpine Army for future operations.

There was no more time to hope good fortune would rescue me. Aglaura was still in my hands and I had to leave without news of la Pisana and my father. If honour and love of country and liberty had not been so strong in me, I would very likely have done something stupid. Meanwhile, up in the clouds, the ice storm that was soon to descend on my head was stirring and I was aware of nothing.

In despair at the long silence from la Pisana and old Apostulos, I had written to Agostino Frumier, asking him, as my long-ago friend, to give me news of those dear to me. I said nothing of this letter to anyone, because not only Lucilio but the other Venetians were angry at Frumier and considered him a deserter of their cause. I posted the letter, nonetheless, because I didn't know who else to turn to, and, after waiting and waiting and giving up all hope, the reply came. But now guess who wrote to me? Raimondo Venchieredo.

The Frumiers, uneasy about carrying on a correspondence with a banished man, had passed the job to him. Raimondo wrote that everyone in Venice was amazed to learn I had not had news from la Pisana for such a long time, and he most of all. They all thought she was in Milan with my consent, agreement and our mutual profit, and he had delayed writing to me because he believed any news was superfluous to my peace of mind, and my agitation nothing but a ruse to fool my aunt the Countess, Count Rinaldo and old Navagero. They had all come to terms with what she'd done, in any case, but I should tell la Pisana that even if he had also come to terms there would still be plenty of time for him to take his revenge. And so the letter abruptly broke off and once again my brain was busy trying to spin a tale out of someone else's hints. Why was Raimondo so angry at la Pisana? What did her disappearance from Venice mean? Was it really true? Was she living in Milan without a word to me? I couldn't believe she was. What means did she have to undertake these travels and the expenses of room and board? It was true that she owned a diamond or two, and perhaps she had turned to the Apostulos family. But Raimondo had said nothing about them. What had become of them? Could Spiro still be wasting away in prison? Why, then, didn't his father write?

In short, the news from Venice merely added another thorn to those already in my side and made me very unwilling to leave. Even Carafa now seemed less impatient; that is, he didn't seem so irritated as before by my ill-concealed desire to delay. One day, I recall, he took me aside, just the two of us, and subjected me to a strange line of questioning. Who was that pretty Greek girl who lived with me? Why were we living together?

(I didn't know myself!) Had I other lovers, and where, and who? Well, I felt like some young fellow just back from his first year of university being questioned by his father confessor. I answered truthfully, but with a fib here and there, above all when it came to Aglaura. All by themselves things were so tangled up that I needed far less than that surprise inquisition to make a complete mess of them!

'So, therefore, you love a young lady from Venice and yet live in Milan with this beautiful Greek?'

'Unfortunately, yes.'

'I find that somewhat hard to believe, it is so unusual. In fact, I don't believe you. I do not believe you! Farewell, Carlino!'

He went off in the best of spirits, as if disbelief in my reply was worth a boundless fortune to him. I'd grown used to Signor Ettore's ways, however, and concluded he was simply pleased because he always liked a laugh. While I, now that Amilcare had left, had no wish to laugh at all, and if anyone smoothed my brow at all it was Aglaura, so vivaciously stubborn. She did owe me that little compensation for all the fury and unease she'd made me suffer since we met in Padua.

One evening just before we were due to leave, I was sitting with her in our rooms at Porta Romana, where two trunks and the empty drawers and wardrobes reminded us of the travels we were about to undertake – as if we weren't reminded all too much by the fears that both of us felt without wishing to share them with one another. For several days now I'd been cross at Aglaura; her obstinate wish to follow me to Rome although she had no news of her family made me suspect her good faith. I was just about ready to toss the bomb and tell her that the man for whom she seemed ready to sacrifice everything, even her sacrosanct filial duties, was perfectly dishonest and unfaithful, when something about her humble, pained glance made me soften. From the judge I was set to be, I felt myself little by little turn contrite. My anguish had grown monstrous and needed an outlet. That glance from Aglaura was an invitation I could not resist and so I told her of my suspicions about la Pisana; her long, cruel silence; her departure from Venice without telling me.

'Oh, it is hard!' I exclaimed. 'But, alas, it would be madness to delude myself! She has returned to what she's always been. Distance has caused her love to die of monotony. She's taken up with someone else, a rich man, maybe, or some dissolute fellow who will shower her with pleasures for a year or two, then . . . Oh, Aglaura! To despise the only soul I love more than life itself is a torment greater than a man can bear!'

Now Aglaura clutched furiously at the hand I'd raised to the heavens when I said these words. Her eyes were aflame, her nostrils wide and in the lamp's pale light two angry tears reflected the sinister fire of her gaze.

'Yes!' she shouted wildly. 'In my name, too, curse the vile and the traitors! Let that hand you raise to God steal a sheaf of his thunderbolts and hurl them down upon their heads!'

I saw I had touched a secret, bloody wound in her heart, and the sympathy between my grief and hers opened my own heart even further. I felt I'd found a friend in her, or rather, a true sister, and I let the tears that had been building in me so long come forth. Her indignant mood softened, we embraced like siblings, weeping together, pouring out tears, the poor comfort of the wretched.

Just then the door flew open and a figure hidden in a cloak dusted with snow came into the room. He let out a shout, threw back his mantle and we both recognized the pale features of Spiro.

'So, have I come too late?' he asked in a tone of voice I shall never forget.

I was the first to throw myself in his arms.

'Oh, I'm so happy to see you!' I babbled, covering his cheeks with kisses. 'I've been hoping you would come for such a long time! Spiro, brother Spiro!'

Pushing me away, he unbuttoned his collar roughly, as if he were suffocating, and said nothing beyond a deep growl.

'Spiro, please, what is it?' Aglaura said timidly, her arms around his neck.

Feeling those hands, hearing that voice, he shook all over and the sweat ran cold on his face. He glared at me no less fiercely than a tiger at someone murdering her pups, then with a great shrug of his shoulders he pushed us both back against the bed and stood alone and hostile in the middle of the room. He looked like the Angel of Death, who has travelled across Hell to punish some wrong. And we, in fear and anguish, stood before him, bowed and silent like wrongdoers. Our very posture deceived him; it made him think that what he feared was so, when it was not.

'Listen to me, Aglaura,' he began in a voice that sought to be calm but still betrayed the wild and strident wail of the storm. 'Listen, for you know how much I love you. I was just about to follow you here, when prison stopped me. Every day, every minute in jail I pondered how to escape and find you, to save you from the abyss you've fallen into! And finally, I succeeded. A fishing boat took me to Ravenna and from there I decided to come to Milan, for my heart told me you were here. But then, when I got to Bologna, I heard from some Venetians that Emilio Tornoni had come through there from Milan with a lady and they were on their way to Rome. You can imagine that I didn't want to waste time thoroughly checking the dates and details. What I had guessed was pretty much confirmed, and so I raced down to Rome and got there when the Republic had already been proclaimed!

'Now Aglaura, I want you to know this: your Emilio was vile and faithless, as I always said, although you refused to hear. He betrayed you for a noble Milanese strumpet! He betrayed Venice for the French, and he betrayed all and sundry for the imperial *zecchini* that Venchieredo brought him from Gorizia! He went to Rome for no other reason but to betray! On the recommendation of a certain priest in Venice, he got into the good graces of some cardinals, in order to get the Pope on his side, claiming he was a powerful friend of Berthier. Meanwhile, he was deceiving Berthier, skimming off for himself much of the spoils of Rome. Outraged, the people seized him while he was leading the sack of a church, and both the French and the Romans were delighted. He was solemnly hanged on the Capitoline Hill. The day before, his sweetheart had sailed for Ancona with her very good friend Ascanio Minato!'

During this furious tirade from Spiro, Aglaura turned all colours. By the time he had finished she had already regained her customary gravity.

'Very well,' said she, a firm eye fixed on Spiro. 'Very well, then, justice has been done. God took it upon Himself and didn't allow me to dirty my hands. Blessed be God's mercy.'

'Oh, so it is true?' said Spiro bitterly, stabbing me with fierce, cruel eyes. 'And you are shameless enough to confess it to me! You love him no more? Fear me, Aglaura, for a single word from me can punish your insolence!'

'Fear you?' said Aglaura, calmer than ever. 'There are but two things I fear: my conscience and God. Soon I shall no longer fear anyone.'

'And what do you plan to do?' asked Spiro in a threatening tone.

'Kill myself,' she said, cold and disdainful.

'No, by all the saints in Heaven!' I interrupted. 'You swore to me and you must keep your word.'

'You are right, Carlino, I will not kill myself,' she said. 'But as you are unhappy and so am I, let us make common cause. Let us marry and may God take care of the rest.'

I thought the ceiling had fallen on my head, so loud was the howl that escaped from Spiro's innards. He rushed forward, eyes closed and arms straight out. I think that if he had struck us we'd have been annihilated. I threw myself in front of Aglaura to shield her bodily from his wild fury. His delirium subsided; his face lit up with hellish rage. He opened his mouth to speak, but his voice died in his throat. I could see there was great punishment and torment in him, and I gathered all my strength to understand. But he stopped himself and when he looked at us again it was with pity mixed with scorn.

'And if . . . ,' he began, as if replying to an unspoken question that went no further, and then his features relaxed, his face went paler, his limbs stopped trembling; in short what had seemed to be a beast became a man again. All these particulars remained perfectly fixed in my mind, for that night I did nothing but turn them around and around in my head, trying to infer what terrible, mysterious passions stirred in Spiro's soul.

I couldn't believe that a brother's indignation could explode with such bestial violence.

Having recovered his (at least apparent) composure, he sat down with us and we were all too aware of the effort he was making, although we dared not refer to it. He studied both of us furtively, and from time to time pity, defeat and vestigial rage alternated on his unquiet face. He told us then that the reason we'd had no letters from his father was that the old man had departed suddenly for Albania and Greece and hadn't yet returned.

'And so,' he went on, 'so, Aglaura, you don't want to come back with me to Venice, where I am alone, unhappy, without prospects?'

'No, Spiro, I cannot come with you,' she replied, head bowed before the young man's fierce eyes.

Spiro stared at me again and if his look didn't devour me it was only because looks can't. Then he turned back to Aglaura.

'What prospects have you now, Aglaura? I beg you, tell me! I have the right to know in the end! I am your brother!'

Those last words came hissing out between his teeth and were hard to understand.

'Tell me if you have ties of affection or duty,' he said. 'I swear that I will help you to make them good.'

This also came out with a hiss, even more tormented and diabolical than before.

'No, I have none,' replied Aglaura weakly.

'And why not come with me, then?' said Spiro, stiffening in front of her like a master before a slave.

'I fear you know why!' said Aglaura, letting the words fall one by one on Spiro's fury, which was ready to explode again. And, in fact, her words did calm him again.

He cast a long interrogating look around the room and left, saying he would see us tomorrow, when one way or another all would be settled. But then, however much I begged Aglaura to explain some parts of that conversation that I had not understood, I couldn't get a word out of her. She wept, she tore at her hair, but she wouldn't open her heart to me, not even one syllable. Half-indignant, half-pitying her, I withdrew to my little room, but I was quite unable to lie down and torturous imaginings kept me awake past midnight. At that point I heard a knock at my door and, thinking it was someone bringing orders from my captain, I bid him come in, somewhat annoyed. My room faced on the stair and I had forgotten to lock the door. To my great astonishment, instead of a soldier, Spiro came in. He had changed so much in those few hours, though, that he didn't seem himself.

Begging me humbly to forgive his rabid outburst of before, he implored me by all I held sacred to help him obtain Aglaura's forgiveness, too. I felt I was losing my grasp of reason, and then I lost it, when he began to shout that he loved her and could hold back no more.

'You love her?' I said. 'Well, that sounds perfectly logical! Are you not of the same blood, the same parents? Love each other, then, and may God bless you!'

'You don't understand, Carlo,' said Spiro. 'Very well, now you shall! Aglaura is not my sister. She is your mother's daughter: you are her brother!'

A sudden flash then exploded in my mind's darkness, but just as I was about to question him more about this extraordinary development, Aglaura, who had heard Spiro say those words in a loud voice, came flying into the room, right into my arms, weeping with joy.

'I knew it!' she said. 'I knew it and I dared not think it!'

Puzzled, confused, not knowing what to think, but deeply, deeply moved, I pressed Aglaura's tearful face to my breast. Later I would ask for explanations and proof; just now I felt the supreme comfort of finding a twin soul, when I had wandered the earth forlorn, an orphan. Spiro watched in silent contentment, his rage abandoned, sharing our happiness. When we had concluded our sweet embrace, he explained that my mother had sent Aglaura to her own father from the hospital where she'd given birth to her, then died a few days later. My father, when he learned of the birth, had written to Apostulos from Constantinople, asking him to look after the child (for she was his wife's daughter), but to raise her as if she were his own, so she would not be ashamed of her birth. Who would have thought my father a man of such tenderness, such delicacy? I blessed him with all my heart, reflecting that the roughest, coarsest stones are often diamonds. Spiro then related his mother's few, cautious words from which he had guessed the mystery of Aglaura's birth (even before he had left for Greece). For fifteen years fancies swirled in his head and when he came back he fell in love the instant he saw her. But her invincible love for Emilio (against whom he'd vowed eternal hatred without even having met him) barred the way. His hatred turned to rage and his love grew tender with compassion when he learned of the young man's infamy and betrayal, of which some hint must also have reached Aglaura.

'Oh yes, certainly,' Aglaura leaped in. 'Why do you think I left Venice if not to punish him for betraying our native land?'

'Then why did you always forbid me to find fault with him?'

'Why?' said Aglaura in a tiny voice. 'I was afraid of you – you, my brother!'

'Oh, it is true!' poor Spiro shouted. 'I was a brute! But does a man command his own eyes at every moment? How could I treat you as my sister when I knew you were not, when I had nursed a love, nourished by distance, for fifteen years? Forgive these eyes of mine, Aglaura! If they sometimes sinned, it was not because I willed it!'

'Oh, I forgive you! Spiro, had I really felt I was your sister I would have fled from your gaze in any case. Allow me to think the misdeed was neither mine nor yours, or at least divided between us two.'

Somewhat naively I then asked Spiro why he hadn't revealed his sweet secret three hours before and whether he had enjoyed playing the ferocious Orestes. He didn't know what to say, but finally he forced himself, explaining that when he had heard of Emilio's new love and learned that the lady who'd gone with him to Rome was not Aglaura, he'd been tormented by monstrous suspicions.

'When I first arrived here and found you in one another's arms, those suspicions overwhelmed my reason! My God! What a terrible misfortune! I say misfortune because you were not to blame, and yet there are accidents that leave us with eternal remorse like the most terrible crimes. You understand now, Carlo. I was mad!'

I shivered to think what he had felt.

'And yet you revealed nothing!' said I.

'Oh, there was a moment, a moment when I was about to tell all! I thought I'd get my revenge that way!'

'But you held back?'

'Mercy, Carlo, and fairness held me back! If the wrong had already been done, why punish innocents? Better that I should go away and take my despair and jealousy elsewhere, leaving you happiness, rather than irreparable remorse.'

'Oh, Spiro, how generous you are!' I said. 'You deserve not merely love and gratitude but admiration!'

Aglaura wept hot tears, clutching my arm with one hand and, I think, peering at Spiro through the fingers of the other.

'You must tell me now where you have been for all these hours,' I said to Spiro.

'At first I was outdoors, breathing the free air and begging God for inspiration, and then I followed my heart's counsel and returned to this inn to question the owners. It didn't take much, Carlo. It didn't take much for me to see the truth! That fog of despair around me melted; and yet even before I'd been unable to believe God would permit such evil to take place in the guise of innocence. And then, when I heard of the life you conducted here, like brother and sister; simple, modest, discreet! When I heard of your fine respect for Aglaura, I was certain of your innocence and I wept and cursed my stupid haste and swore I wouldn't let the night pass without extracting the knife I'd plunged in your heart. Ah, I beg you, Carlo . . . Aglaura . . . if my great affection is worth nothing to you, have pity on me, forgive me, keep a tiny corner if no more in your memory for me, and if my presence recalls to you some vexed memory . . .'

Without a word I turned to Aglaura, for I myself felt quite inadequate to Spiro's great generosity. She understood me, and perhaps her own heart, and took the young man's hand and put it in my own, so that we were all three united as one, and said, 'Enough, Spiro. This is our reply: we shall be a single family!'

The rest of that night was spent in friendly, cheerful talk, in studying the papers Spiro had brought from Venice, where his father had left them, which offered evident proof that Aglaura had been born of my poor mother in the hospital in Venice. The father's name did not appear and, as you can imagine, none of us dreamed of pointing out this unfortunate lacuna. We behaved as if the father were an unnecessary bit-actor in the mystery of generation, and, knowing something of my mother's many troubles in the last stage of her life, I even pitied her; but neither filial piety nor respect for myself and my father's name suggested I should bring that story to light. And so I took Aglaura as my sister quite wholeheartedly and thanked the heavens for that precious and unexpected gift, even more welcome now that my friendship with Spiro had evolved into family ties. It was not entirely easy for Aglaura to stop thinking of death, hatred and revenge and begin contemplating peace, love and marriage, but with my help and Spiro's, she did. Among other things, she saw that all would be right if she did so, and women are capable of marrying to make everyone happy – so long as the expedient pleases them first of all.

In those times a wedding entailed few formalities. Interpreting Spiro's tacit wishes, I busied myself making sure that before the legion departed I had the pleasure of seeing him Aglaura's husband. We then left Milan all together, because Signor Ettore had kindly given me a permit to accompany them as far as Mantua; from there I would meet the legion in Florence, by way of Ferrara. That fleeting meteorite of family happiness helped light up my grim outlook, which was beginning to weigh on me, and this despite the fact that Spiro had brought some news of my father that if not direct, was at least credible. He was said to have arrived safe and sound in Constantinople and to be quite busy with the project that concerned him (which, however, unexpected obstacles had delayed). He was well, would send news and would return when the task was done. Old Apostulos's departure for Greece perhaps meshed with my father's machinations in Turkey, but I saw that Spiro didn't know or couldn't say more and so I changed the subject, urging him merely to let me have any news from my father as quickly as possible and wherever I was.

Aglaura, who chose to think that because we shared a mother we shared a father, gave me her word it would be done, and that she would do everything in her power to send word often, because it meant a great deal to her, too, to have such an excellent father. We parted in Mantua the very day that city at last obtained permission to join the Cisalpine Republic and the sorrow of our farewells was lost in the joy of universal rejoicing. I had found a sister; I thought I was on the way to finding a country, too; and it was good to be alive, even if love was lost to me forever. In the meantime we agreed we'd meet again in Venice: republicans, free and happy. They went over the horizon in a horse and cart on the road to Verona and I walked back into town the mile I'd gone out with them. That clutch of buildings, towers, cupolas surrounded by the waters of the River Mincio made me think of Venice. What can I say? I didn't smile, but sighed; the past still had far more power over me than the future, and the future itself would clearly be what it would be, something quite different from the beloved creature of my imagination.

Nevertheless, the celebrations in that Italian city (already a great city in herself, with her own courts, laws and privileges), which was joining the others to be free or slave, happy or unhappy, filled me with hopes. The sort of hopes that are sure to grow, and when we are dead will grow in the breasts of our children and grandchildren until they've become real everywhere. Now the house of Gonzaga was no more than a memory. May the Gonzagas rest in peace, as long as they don't play that joke Lazarus did; but they never will, for where would they find a Martha[7] to pray for them? In any case they kept Mantegna in their pay, got Giulio Romano to paint the vault of the Gods, freed Tasso from the madhouse and won (or lost) the Battle of Fornovo in the person of Francesco II.[8] It was time they were laid to rest along with the others: the Visconti, Sforza, Torriani, Bentivoglio, Doria, Colonna, Varano and so on. They were lucky to be the last, but I fear they slept on their feet for quite a while and those who came after were hard-pressed to follow.

In any event I left Mantua in better spirits than I could ever have imagined. My rather slim purse (those thousand ducats had suffered considerably during my long stay with Aglaura in Milan) and a certain soldierly simplicity permitted me no better than a wooden cart down to Bologna: one of those vehicles that give the patient the illusion he's sitting in a carriage with all the discomfort of a stiff trot on a miller's horse. The carriages I'd taken to Vicenza and beyond were nothing like these: they were gondolas compared to these grinders. And so I arrived in Bologna with my nerves all twisted and sore, and decided to cross the Apennines on foot in order to straighten them out.

Oh, what a beguiling walk, what scenes of Paradise! I think that if I'd been happy within, I'd have said to the Lord, like St Peter, 'Please, let us make our tabernacles here.'[9] Later I heard that the wind is too strong in those saddlebacks of mountains, but at the time, although it was barely spring, there was such a peace, a warmth, a wealth of colours and shapes in that corner of the world that it was obvious the road led to Florence and Rome. When I got to Pratolino, where the eye descends on Tuscany below, my enthusiasm was beyond measure and I think if I had known the metre and the words, I'd have improvised a canticle to match that of Moses.[10] How beautiful you are, my country! How grand in every part! When I seek you with my eyes – bay-lined shores of the sea, endless green of the plains, fresh and woody waves of the hills, azure peaks of the Apennines and snowy white caps of the Alps – you are everywhere a smile, an enchanting fatality! When I seek your spirit and glory in the eternal pages of history, in the eloquent grandeur of ancient remains, in the living gratitude of our people, you seem majestic, wise, a queen! When I seek you inside us, around us, you hide your face at times in shame, but then purpose revives you and I know that of all the nations of this world, you alone will never die!

In those times, Italy was, you might say, taking the first steps of its third life,[11] steps as unaware and shaky as the first paces of a little babe. In Tuscany, as in Piedmont, we had the strange discrepancy of a prince who ruled and a French general who commanded. They looked something like the kings of Bithynia, Cappadocia and Pergamo with Sulla, Lucullus and other such fine gentlemen at their heels. They died leaving their estates to the Roman people, but neither Lucullus nor Sulla nor the French generals of sixty years ago were shy about taking legacies for themselves.

In Florence I found Carafa, but not the rest of the legion, which had gone by way of Ancona, because the Grand Duke insisted Tuscany was neutral. Signor Ettore seemed to be brooding; I was convinced he was thinking about his soldiers, but he was annoyed that I had even mentioned them. He was cursing women ferociously, saying it was real foolishness on our part to agree to be born from such demons.

'What the Devil, Captain, and how would you like to be born?' I asked.

'From Vesuvius, Etna, from the whirling deeps of the sea,' he said. 'Certainly not from these little monsters with their viperish powers who take their revenge for childbirth by stealing life from us drop by drop!'

'Captain, are you so unhappy in love?'

'I certainly am! I have a lover who loves me and doesn't love me; that is, she loved me and let me love her as I wished for a week, and now she wants to love me in her way, which is the strangest and most intolerable way on earth.'

'What way is that, Captain?'

'Like the date palms, which make love the one in Sicily and the other in Barbary.'

I laughed a little at this comparison, but the truth was, when the matter at hand was love's woes, I had very little desire to laugh. And yet, because I didn't consider Signor Ettore a great master in such affairs, and because I was very fond of him, I took the liberty of offering some advice.

'Insult her pride,' I said to him. 'Invent a rival.'

'We shall see,' he said. 'In the meantime, you join the others in Ancona. When we get to Rome I'll be able to tell you whether your advice was sound, although it seems to me an old ruse worn out by long use.'

'Old wisdom, new fruit,' I replied, and went off to get a wholesale view of Florence before leaving for the Marches. I liked everything about Florence except the Arno, which seemed a very small river for one with such a great name. However, justice demands it be noted that all rivers suffer, some more, some less, by comparison with the reputation that fame assigns them. In my experience only the Thames lives up to its promise, and even there I was dismayed to see it flow upstream at the slightest breeze. For such an immense river, its meekness was quite repugnant. Yet how many large men are like the Thames! And how many women are like London; that is (forgive me!), they're happy to rely on a river that's vast and has a great deal of water but a doubtful current! There was the smooth-talking native of Padua who used to sing to his sweetheart a famous gondolier's song:

Come, you are like London
A kiss of Love!

He would never have dreamed I'd have to struggle so hard one day to parse the erratic moral of his couplet.[12]

From the Arno to the Adriatic was three days; from Ancona to Rome, ten, because I was travelling with the legion and as the men were not used to long marches we had to begin cautiously. And so I had the time to reflect that the first enemies a new army meets on its path are chickens and priests. Threats, reprimands and punishment were useless. Chickens meant musket-shots; and priests, pranks and ribaldry. The men would kill the chickens, eat them in the house of the priest and drink his wine; but nothing more; and if the priests were men of the law, easygoing, and had a dusting of political sense we would part the best of friends. One of these priests was able to incline the entire legion towards Pius VI. True, in those days Cardinal Chiaramonti had reconciled religion and republic in his famous homily,[13] and it was possible to incline towards everything at once. The older I get, the more I think that every religion is far better off staying away from politics, for it doesn't serve. Oil will never mix with vinegar, nor sentiment with reason, without something false and silly coming forth.

And finally we arrived in Rome. I can't tell you how much I'd desired it. Rome alone, I thought, would allow me to forget la Pisana; yet as much as I was counting on that oblivion, I was still puzzling about what could have happened to her, constructing theories, inventing and exaggerating fears, giving shape and life to the most monstrous apparitions. Her Cisterna cousins, recently arrived in Venice; the colourless Agostino Frumier; the sneering Raimondo Venchieredo: one after another they came forward as rivals. But all such thoughts disappeared when Aglaura and Spiro wrote to say that la Pisana had left Venice and her family knew nothing and seemed to care little. The Countess was eating up the interest on the eight thousand ducats, and that was enough for her. Count Rinaldo went from his office to the library and from the library to his supper and his bed without any thought that other men inhabited the earth. Both miserable, most miserable; but not inclined to concern themselves with others.

You will agree that if not heroism, it showed at least great staying power on my part to remain there putting up stakes and commanding my troops on Monte Pincio, when I'd rather have run off and searched the world for my love! I loved her, you see, more than I love myself, and as I'm not selling trick phrases here but make it my business to tell the truth, that is to say a lot. Nonetheless, I found the courage to put my country first, and if I had to make an effort to include Naples in that whole, Rome helped me to pass the test. Rome is the Gordian knot of our destinies; the grand, many-shaped symbol of our stock; our ark of salvation, whose light at once reveals the twisted and confused dreams of the Italians. Do you wish to know if a certain political order, a certain plan for progress and civilization, will endure and bring fruit to our nation? Name Rome: the stone that will distinguish brass from gold. Rome, that she-wolf who nourishes us from her teats, and all who do not drink her milk know nothing. I don't deny that aiming too much at Rome sometimes made us neglect closer and more accessible goals, goals we might have used as stepping stones to greater conquests. But still, aiming too high was never as harmful or dishonourable as not aiming at all, and no period of Italian history was as confused and nonsensical as when the *département du Tibre*[14] was monstrously subsumed into the Empire of France.

Once in Rome, my sorrow enjoyed the same fate as any small

thing overwhelmed by a large one. It was stunned, stifled, nearly forgotten. What is the sorrow of one man compared to the grief of an entire nation? Contemplating the blasted remains of the great fall, I found a kind of weary peace of mind, a melancholy without bitterness. The ostentation and the odds and ends of the centuries of Christianity looked like mere artifice and cleverness to me. Only in the catacombs did I find a spirit of faith and martyrdom that raised Christianity to the heights of the pagan tombs. When I bent, shivering, inside those holy places of blood and sacrifice, where torture, flagellation, insults, massacre and death, joyously suffered for an idea I admired but did not understand, those terrible burdens I thought I could not bear shrank in my mind. Emulating the great, the small are redeemed.

If life in the ancient Rome of consuls and martyrs was somewhat comforting, the Rome of those times filled me with acrimony and something like dread. The Pope had departed, neither derided nor praised, for when he had been forced to do without much of the ceremony and magnificence he was accustomed to, the people no longer thought of him. It was his splendid court and rites (rather than his virtuous, saintly life) that made the prince of Christianity superior. A muddle of things venerable because of their age were falsely defamed and foul things raised to the heavens and splendidly decorated; there were superstitious fools and vile betrayers, pillage and hunger, gluttons and the starving, friars chased from their monasteries, monks tossed out of their hermitages, cardinals pursued by cavalry and cavalry murdered by brigands. Everything was in turmoil; all was heading towards perdition. Everyone's clouded, mistaken judgement served to determine good and evil: priestly resistance, French authority, popular licence, private crimes were all mixed up together. Great and honourable names were put forward to cover the perfidy of the small; changes took place that neither convinced nor improved, led by rapacious men with shady ambitions. The French cursed the Italian traitors, the people of Trastevere rebelled to the cry of 'Long Live the Virgin Mary!' and blood flowed in the woods and the marshes and the caves. Both city and country armed with equal fury, but deep in the bowels of the *Culiseo* (as the Romans called their monument), up in their mountain eyries, in the arms of their wives and at the feet of their aged parents, the rebels were chased down. Murat[15] murdered, shot and hanged; the survivors were sent to the galleys, and some called them martyrs and others criminals.

Nothing sows greater discord and future rebellion than when the gallows becomes an altar. Four commissioners of the French Directory came to revive the ancient offices of consul, senate, tribune and quaestor, using them to disguise new and servile, rather than republican, purposes, because of the haste in which they were imposed. The five consuls were replaced every time General Berthier changed his mind; but nonetheless the Roman Republic (a weighty name to bear) was treated on a par with the Cisalpine Republic. A medal was coined with the words in Latin 'Berthier, Restorer of Rome' on one side, and 'Gaul, Saviour of the Human Race' on the other. We knew what to think of the first side; of the second: may God make it so!

In such a state of disarray (or rather dismantling and collapse) of the public good, just how the Romans could become a nation organized in a civil way and according to their own needs, I do not know. And, therefore, I don't have the heart to condemn those who took part, with results that certainly fell short of their ambitions. There are certain moral and economic disorders in the life of a people, born of many centuries of corruption, idleness and servitude, that won't be cured just because the patient himself has become aware of them (just as the ailing do not get well simply by knowing they are ill and wishing for health). Bold and wise doctors are needed to act bravely and impose quiet, trust and patience. To heal the wounds of a gangrenous and immoral despotism there is nothing better than vigorous, upright, absolute rule. And if this view puts some noses out of joint, history replies triumphant with its truly philosophical and insuperable argument: necessity. One may certainly detest the absolute ruler, but one must endure him, as punishment and expiation. The legislators of the last century who undertook to give a constitution to the Romans after Pius VI was hurried off, were faced with the heaviest weight political shoulders ever tried to lift, I believe. They collapsed under it, but who could have stayed upright? Perhaps Caesar, with thirty legions and no other legal frills.

After the entire countryside rebelled, the army, then mostly billeted in Rome, was spread out in patrols, garrisons and reinforcements in all the small cities and other walled towns of the papal territories. I spent a few days with Lucilio, Amilcare and Giulio visiting the beautiful things of Rome and its surroundings, but when the army was redeployed Giulio and Amilcare were sent to Spoleto, while Lucilio and I remained at Castel Sant'Angelo. My legion was still awaiting our captain, who was slow to arrive from Florence, but perhaps he hesitated because the few French forces and King Ferdinand's[16] huge internal fortifications left little grounds for hope of a Neapolitan war just now. To idle his days away in an armchair (as is the soldier's destiny in times of peace), a caffè in Florence was as good as any in Rome. At any rate, that was how I explained Carafa's delay.

Meanwhile, Lucilio and I continued to enjoy Rome's beautiful antiquities and I set myself to study history by means of the monuments. It was the only distraction I knew from my misery at receiving no news from Venice. My sister and brother-in-law wrote, and even my father wrote to me, via the Apostulos, urging me to continue to hope and prepare myself, but these communications were of little help, for no one was able to tell me anything about la Pisana, not even rumours or speculation. Instead, I heard that they were planning to appraise her inheritance, a sign they feared or hoped she was dead, and I cannot tell you how much this news (in which I sensed the Countess's cruel greed) enraged me.

And what is more, political disenchantment began to set in. The changes imposed on the Cisalpine constitution by Trouvé,[17] French ambassador to Milan, backed up by French bayonets, made it clear that the liberty granted to the Italian republics was a base alloy. Peace with Austria in hand, the French wanted to keep a firm hand on the course of affairs. Roughly, tyrannically, they changed the statutes, then changed them again. And soon the best and most illuminated minds parted company with that government serving another mad and capricious government, and some of them stopped obeying and began to think for themselves. There were many of such independent minds in the Cisalpine Army, including men like Lahoz, Pino and Teulliet.[18] We underlings seconded the views of our superiors, as usually happens, and a blind hatred, a deep suspicion of the French prepared the way for a new Austro-Russian invasion.

When God willed it, Carafa arrived from Florence: severe, irate and prickly as never before. He was always rubbing that scar in his eyebrow, and this was a very bad sign. Worse was that he had decided, if it was not possible to attack Naples, to move near the border of the kingdom; and so he transferred his legion and me with it from Castel Sant'Angelo in Rome to Velletri. This is a rural town like many you see in the countryside around Rome: picturesque from the outside, terrible, filthy and foul-smelling within; by day full of ducks and carts, herds of oxen and horses moving in and out; the night-time animated by the lowing of cows, the crowing of cocks and the bells of the convents. Just the place to cure a poor fellow who's ill with too many beautiful places and large horizons. Carafa was billeted outside the town in a convent that had been sacked by French republicans, to which he'd sent ahead from Rome the necessary to make the place comfortable and habitable, if not splendid. There were just a few guards defending it and a pair of little, mule-drawn country field guns. No one was permitted to enter his private rooms except his servant, who was said to be a sorcerer. The shepherd girls in the nearby pastures who delivered milk to the convent said they'd seen a beautiful *signora* at the window; Signor Ettore's lady-love, we presumed. Other soldiers who'd been in his service longer than I (who had always thought of him as temperate, a man who didn't have time for such foolishness) didn't believe it, and they said the woman was probably a witch or some Neapolitan princess he meant to bring in to replace Queen Maria Carolina.

Places can cast a great spell on the imagination and Velletri and its surroundings will fill any healthy mind with fables and witchcraft (just as the meadows around Lodi up north inspire thoughts of cheese and heavy cream). I may have been the only one to hold myself aloof from those Gothic fancies, for I knew that after a long period of abstinence one tastes the forbidden with that special gluttony that follows a fast. As an example I offer Amilcare, who insisted he had never tasted wine before he was twenty; from the age of twenty onwards no one drank as much as he. Perhaps the same sort of thing had happened to Carafa. Therefore, I believed his was a genuine, noble love rather than some consequence of witchcraft, and this was the source of frequent quarrels and even wagers between myself and my companions.

After I parted from Lucilio, I had become so contrary and intractable that it took little to get my goat and I used to accuse those who saw miracles and magic everywhere of being simpletons and hare-brains. I, in turn, was reproached for being all talk and no action, and so I had to show it wasn't true. The continual hammering I felt within; the boredom of our sluggish, bestial existence: it all conspired to make me despise inaction and I was pleased to have found a motive to do something, even if something only quite silly. The Captain had forbidden, on pain of death, any officers or soldiers not in his guard to approach the convent where he'd established his headquarters. It was close to the border with Naples, and the new Neapolitan Army (even the priests and the nuns had been taxed to support it) was massing every day in the nearby Abruzzi. Skirmishes might be set off; indeed, one already had been; more because the soldiers were impatient than because their leaders had ordered an attack. Carafa didn't want the legion in those parts, fearing the men would become involved in some pointless incident.

However, this cautious approach was greatly at odds with his usual boldness and the truth was that he didn't want any prying eyes around the convent. I swore to my companions that I would go and have a look, whatever might happen, and one Sunday evening was chosen for the great test.

My plan was this: to raise the alarm among the guards, circle the walls and enter the garden where the fence was broken, while everyone was clustered round where they expected the enemy to attack. It was a feast day and the main body of the troops was scattered among the low taverns of Velletri, so no great ruckus was likely to ensue. My trick would be revealed, but I would have done my business before the officers assembled their troops.

Carafa, who would certainly come outside to give orders, wouldn't see me, and anyone else in the convent, whoever they might be, had never seen me before. The only danger (rather great, to tell the truth) was that I might be discovered when I left the convent, but I could always say I'd come in to escape an attack by the Neapolitans. Whether they believed me or not made little difference, and even if I had to pay with my skin for this trick, I'd made a promise and intended to keep it.

And so, just before sunset, seeing a great cloud of dust rise between the convent and the mountains (herds of cattle descending, it seemed likely), I and some of my companions in the wager, pretending to have been surprised in a nearby tavern, ran to the first guard post, shouting that the Neapolitans were coming and they should sound the alarm, while we raced up to Velletri to warn the others. The small garrison was quickly assembled, for Carafa, preparing for such an eventuality, had set up an ambush on the left side of the road, leaving but a sentry or two around the convent, with the idea that his men could always withdraw, while the main body of the legion coming down from Velletri would trap the enemy between two lines of fire. And so, while he ordered his men into ranks atop hills crowned with cypress and along roads lined with laurels, and waited for the field guns to be mounted with that foresight and attention that was peculiar only to him, my companions and I, greatly amused by all the excitement, made a quick jog into the countryside and around to the back of the convent, where the garden bordered on the nearby marshland. While they watched, I scaled the wall easily and crossed the garden, where the cabbages gone to seed and the orchard burned by the sun suggested the banned Capuchins were enduring a long Lent. When I reached the convent itself, I searched the doors and windows to find a way in, but it was more difficult than I'd imagined. The windows had very solid grills and the hard maple doors would have resisted a catapult. There I was, but as they say in Rome, I couldn't see the Pope.

Then I spotted a wooden ladder among some trees, probably used by the gardener to pick the peaches, and it occurred to me that the windows upstairs were probably not as jealously guarded as those below. I moved the ladder and went up. And, in fact, the first window I tried was merely closed, but neither locked nor barred. I opened it slowly, saw there was a wardrobe inside that Signor Ettore had made into a gun closet, and put a leg over the sill. But just as I was about to put the other leg in, a clattering, a trembling, a shouting nearby left me poised astride the window sill. Above the same wall I myself had scaled, I saw a three-cornered hat appear, then another and another. Men in a very great hurry they were; ready to break their heads falling from the wall into the garden rather than remain on the far side. One of them reached the top and began to descend when something like a rifle shot rang out and he threw out his arms and fell to the ground like a real dead man. Those who had already got over were now running through the cabbages and I recognized them for my companions, but right away other hats began to appear above the wall, and behind them, no end of other heads, arms and legs. One jumped down and another ten climbed up: it was a real invasion, a plague of locusts darkening the air.

'The Neapolitans! The Neapolitans!' shouted my companions, who had reached the convent and were climbing up the ladder I was sitting on top of.

'Slow down, be careful!' I said. 'Otherwise you will all kill yourselves without waiting for them to do the job.'

Indeed, the ladder, with one man on each rung was creaking like a pear tree too heavy with pears. I had prudently drawn both legs inside, and felt I was doing more than my share in keeping the others supplied with good advice.

'One at a time! Keep away from one other! Don't shake the ladder so much!'

All of a sudden there was a squeak here and a squeak there, an explosion like four or five thunderbolts colliding and such a banging that the window glass beside me was shattered. Seven of my colleagues bounced into the room; one was left outside, dead (and luckily he was dead and not injured), and adding the other who was killed scaling the wall, we had the right number, for there had been exactly ten of us. What the Devil? There was no doubt about it: those had been rifle shots and they'd hit their targets! It was the first time I had ever smelled gunpowder. The effect on me? A fit of laughter, like someone who's got away scot free. However, I wouldn't swear I felt no fear at all: allow me to boast of my candour, at least. Still, if I was afraid, I was not so afraid that I didn't go back to the window and make a certain, very expressive gesture towards those Neapolitan string beans who were looking up at us, but couldn't pursue us, because we had cleverly pulled up the ladder. That hand play of mine was the magic touch that put the fire in my companions, but our enemies weren't fooling either and they began to play a tune with their muskets that crushed all desire to stand on the balcony and look up at the sky. Meanwhile, we supplied ourselves with guns, knives and pistols in that weapons closet so conveniently at hand and returned their salutes very politely, and while they shot holes in our hats, we shot them in the heads and stomachs. Whether they liked the exchange, I don't know. But we did have some worries as that comedy continued. Where had these Neapolitans come from? Did our Captain know nothing of them? Might they have been marching up the marshes even as we were sounding the false alarm towards the mountains?

This was, in fact, just what had happened; and I (and the entire legion) stood to pay a high price for that crazy jest, that silly act of bravado taking on the appearance of treason. In the meantime, the shots aimed down continued to meet with greater fortune than the shots aimed up, until we thought we saw the enemy fire slacken. Some of us were getting ready to celebrate victory and perhaps finish off those obstinate few who hadn't yet withdrawn and were darting among the trees in the orchard, when from beneath our feet came a roar like an underground explosion, and then footsteps on the ground floor, followed by shouts, howls, curses and religious invocations, according to the pious custom of the Neapolitans when they go to war. We were all terrorized, for while the sharpshooters had been keeping us at bay, the main body of our assailants had knocked down a door with a small mine. Now they had invaded the convent and at ten of them to one of us, resistance would be futile. At this point, my conscience heavy with remorse for this ill-fated adventure,

I stood up bravely to lead my companions. A few words, a ready example, and I knew they would follow me, and their duty.

'Friends, if it costs our lives, we must not surrender the upper floor! Think of your honour and that of the Legion!' With these words I leapt out of the wardrobe and began to build a barricade at the door to the stairs with armoires, tables and other furniture we could scrape together. The Neapolitans came confidently up, but when they saw some musket bores pointing out of the chinks in the barricade, they fell back on one another.

'Be brave, my friends!' I said. 'Help cannot be far away.' And indeed, I couldn't believe that when Signor Ettore heard the shots he hadn't sent someone out to see what was going on. I never imagined that the Neapolitan Army's first move would be planned for that very day, and that the Captain was then very busy trying to send off their advance guard so that the Legion could arrive from Velletri. In any event, we fought so valiantly behind our double oak door that the enemy desisted in their plan to mount the stairs. We soon became aware, however, that they had desisted in favour of another, more dangerous plan: to light a fire under our feet. The smoke, filtering through the cracks in the attic floor, filled the hallway where we were huddled and took our breath away; soon the beams began to crackle and flames began to appear between the red-hot bricks.

We fled into the adjacent rooms just as that floor collapsed with a frightful crash. But those other rooms were no safer; the fire had spread in seconds, because the barn full of hay was right below us. We had to get out or resign ourselves to being roasted alive. Pistols in hand and knives between their teeth, my companions leapt from the windows, scattering the few enemy soldiers there, who were watching the fire, and made it safely to the hills. Only one tripped while jumping and broke a leg (the leap down from that side was quite a long one) and those murderers were at him in an instant like wolves at a lamb; and if I told you of the tortures and the torments they made him suffer I'd be called a liar, for you wouldn't believe a human creature could be so brutally assaulted and so quickly. I withdrew in horror and yet a superhuman force ordered me not to flee, but kept me inside those walls engulfed in flames. Others were blocked inside there, I knew not who; but it was enough to make me, the innocent cause of that massacre, sacrifice myself in the distant hope I might save them. Running like a madman through the long corridors, I went from door to door among the innumerable cells and the cloister's large apartments. The air was growing hotter and hotter, like an oven in which the flames are constantly stoked. Everywhere emptiness and silence; and yet the shouts from outside and a distant rattle of gun shots made those anguished moments even more terrible.

Having decided I wouldn't leave until I was certain not one living soul remained in that inferno, I ventured to cross the floor that had all but collapsed under our feet. There were a few smoldering beams left, and on the wall side, a sort of vault covering the stair below. This I ran across and began to rove wildly through that other wing of the building. Here I came to a closed door that certainly wouldn't have resisted two arms like mine, fortified by desperation. However, I first shouted nervously, 'Open up! Open up!'

In reply came a shriek that sounded like that of a woman, and then a pistol shot emerged from a hole in the door, whizzed past my temple and embedded itself in the wall behind me.

'Friend! Friend!' I shouted. But new shrieks drowned my voice and a second shot came through the door, grazing my arm and making the blood spurt out.

I threw my shoulder against that door, determined to save them in spite of themselves if they were friends and get myself killed if they were foe. The door fell to pieces and, smoked and bloody, my clothing burned and shredded, I pitched myself into that room like one of the damned. In my haste I overturned a woman running back and forth inside with her hands raised to the heavens or tearing at her hair, as if possessed by fear. Another woman ran past me, apparently ready to save herself by leaping from the window, but I was quickly behind her and got my arms around her just as her body tumbled over the window sill. The flames from below were singeing her hair, two or three rifle shots greeted our appearance at the window and I lifted her up to remove her from that dangerous position, saying I was a friend, had come to save her, that she must not be afraid or we were lost. Her face, lit up with supreme desolation, turned towards me suddenly. I felt as if I'd been struck by a bullet in the breast.

It was la Pisana! La Pisana, my God! Who could put words to the tempest the sight of her raised in my heart? Who could enumerate each and every one of those passions that overwhelmed me? Love, love was the first, the mightiest, the one that redoubled my courage and purpose and made me invincibly bold!

I lifted her to my shoulders and off we went through the flames, past the tottering attic floors, the ruined walls and collapsing vaults. I came down at the front gate, where the flames had left a way through, but on both sides I could feel the burning air sear my throat. One last effort! Let it never be said that I fell with so much weighing on me! Let it never be said that I abandoned to the flames those lovely limbs I'd so often admired as a perfect work of nature, that enchanting face from which her generous spirit flashed like lightning through the clouds! I would have crossed a volcano without loosening by a hair my grip on that precious, failing body. If she were dead, I too would die, so as to be able to think in my supreme moment, 'I have perished for her, and with her.' The fears, suspicions, jealousies and revenge that had swollen my heart were dispersed in an instant and only love was left, love that is reborn from the ashes like the phoenix, love so strong it scorns even death.

La Pisana in my arms, desperation in my heart, terrible menace in my eyes: waving my sword demonically I scattered a line of foes who were warming themselves carelessly by the smoking convent. Among them, I recall, was a priest who was praying and haranguing the soldiers. He was the prior who had led the Soldiers of the Holy Faith[19] to take that awful revenge; according to him, the enemies of religion had been roasted in their own fat. Meanwhile, the last of these – not an enemy of religion, but of the fanatics who arm it – was miraculously escaping their fury. If God was watching over Velletri in that moment, He was surely on our side.

Still running, I reached the hill where Carafa had deployed

his soldiers in ambush, and there the outcome of the fighting had been quite different. There we met the wildest of the legionaries, who had pushed the Neapolitans back to the mountain gorge and then returned to attack those who had set fire to the convent. Ettore himself, who had only just then received word of what was happening at his back, raced off, leading his men, unsure whether he would get there in time but certain that his defence (or his revenge) would be devastating. I hid among the laurel trees until he passed, but then mercy overcame me and, stopping a corporal who was following him with a fresh platoon collected from Velletri, I asked him to tell Carafa that she (he knew whom) was already safe in town. I had only walked a few steps further when I met a couple of my soldiers and asked them to carry la Pisana, for I was exhausted and it was all I could do just to keep up with them as they climbed the hill to Velletri.

When we arrived, I laid her on my bed, summoned a nearby barber to open her vein and let some blood and, while I waited for her to come to her senses, I withdrew to a loggia overlooking the countryside so as to spare her the shock of finding herself there with me. In the distance the convent was burning like a huge pyre, the smoky, reddish flames outlined against the darkening sky; and in their dismal glow I could see the legionaries' bayonets flashing as they drove off the Neapolitans. The battle was over, but the liberators' first advance to the borders of the Roman Republic was not auspicious.

When I came back inside, la Pisana was already sitting on the bed and seemed more self-possessed than I had expected. Indeed, she was the first to speak, which quite surprised me, because she was often quite stingy with her words, even in far less difficult moments.

'Carlo,' she said, 'why didn't you leave me where you found me? I would have died a heroine and they'd have buried me in the new Pantheon in Rome.'

I stared at her dumbly, for although the words sounded mad, she seemed the soul of reason and I felt I must treat her so.

'Had I left you there, I'd also have been obliged to stay!' said I, my voice gone feeble with emotion. 'I swear, Pisana, that when I first recognized you, my greatest desire was to kill you and die myself!'

'Oh, why didn't you?' she screamed so wildly that I couldn't help but see her anguish was sincere.

'I didn't . . . I didn't, because I love you!' said I, head bowed as if confessing something shameful.

She was in no way abashed by my discomfort, but raised her eyes proudly like an offended virgin.

'Oh, yes, you love me!' she spat out. 'Oh, villain! Deceiver! Traitor! May the heavens hear your lies and send them down your throat as molten lead! You abused me as if I were a slave; you cheated me as if I were a fool; you planned just how you would betray me, by my side, and in my arms. Oh, lucky you! Lucky, for a man has stepped between us. Taking revenge out of my hands and leaving me with a shame that torments me every day, every minute. Otherwise I'd have planted a dagger straight in the breast of your whore, annihilating you both with a single blow! Go! Leave me now! Enjoy my humiliation and your triumph. You saved my life! How good you are! In ten years' time you'll have a crown on your brow, but I shall obstinately refuse the dregs of that dishonourable chalice I'm supposed to drink. I'll defy that foolish love I so rabidly accepted! For six months now I've mocked him; now I shall ridicule him. Vengeance for vengeance! A dagger from his hand will bring me death – and eternal remorse to your craven heart!'

To hear myself vilified by the woman who had betrayed me so horrendously, when I had trusted her so deeply, loved her so constantly, and had even proved it by risking my life to save hers (even though how and where I found her should have poisoned my affection with rage); to find her haughty and irate, while I awaited her hesitant and humble: it was a blow that cut me to the heart. My ire smote even God, for permitting an innocent to be so brazenly mistreated, for permitting vice armed with thunderbolts to hurl them down from his throne of shame.

'Pisana!' I shouted, breaking into sobs, 'Pisana, stop! I will not and cannot listen any more. Your words are viler and more obscene than your betrayal! Oh, it is not your place, not your place at all to accuse me! Even as you confess the most heinous crime a lover can commit, you cruelly gorge yourself on my tears, you gloat on my suffering, you pretend to be outraged and insulted and threaten me with terrible revenge – though less appalling than that you've already committed against me! Be silent, Pisana. Not another word or I shall forswear all that is still just and holy in this world; I will tear my honour from my breast and throw it to the dogs. Yes, I shall forswear even that false honour that suffers in shame, rather than explode like a volcano at such brazen slander.'

La Pisana thrust her head in her hands and began to weep, then suddenly she leapt from the bed where they'd laid her, dressed as she was, and said she wanted to leave the room. I held her back.

'Where do you intend to go now?'

'I want to go to Signor Ettore Carafa. Take me to him immediately.'

'The Captain is very busy right now pursuing the Neapolitans and it will not be easy to find him. In any case, he has been notified that you are safe and he cannot but come to you as soon as he can.'

These last words were seasoned with a nice dose of irony and she stiffened and said, prophetically: 'Woe to him or woe to you!'

'Woe to no one,' said I sternly. 'Woe to no one, alas! I would be very happy to kill someone!'

'Why not kill me?' she said very simply.

'Because . . . because you are too lovely, and because I recall you were also good once.'

'Silence, Carlo! Do you think Signor Ettore will come soon?'

'Didn't I tell you? As soon as he can.'

She was silent then for a long time, and by the shadowy light of the moon from the loggia I saw many and various thoughts cross her face. Now it was dark, now glowing, now stormy as a clouded sky, now calm and serene as the sea in summer. Now she bowed as if in prayer, now she clenched her fist as if she held a knife and was stabbing a despised breast over and over. Her dress was torn, dusty and blood-stained; her hair tangled and scorched; her features marked by the terrible events of the day.

Where she rested her elbows on the table, even the wood seemed scorched and bloody. She looked like a black prophetess from the underworld, meditating on the fearful mysteries of the hellish sights she'd seen. I dared not disturb her silence, needing to collect myself as well, before hearing the revelations of that grim prophetess. Thoughts of her peregrinations, and that of her heart, after my departure, flashed through my fearful mind, but I had a horror of them; for the moment they seemed to demand more strength than I possessed. If someone had said to me, 'If you are willing to become an idiot, I shall convince you of her innocence,' I would have accepted the bargain.

About an hour later, Signor Ettore Carafa appeared, alone and scowling. He wore no hat, having lost his in the fray, and his scabbard was empty of his sword, for he had broken it on the cranium of some cavalryman after sawing halfway through his helmet. His scar was so white it was almost incandescent. He bid us good day and, placing himself between us, waited for one of us to speak. At once la Pisana, quite irate and commanding, ordered him to repeat the tale of my liaison with the beautiful Greek girl, just as he had told it to her. And Carafa, after asking my permission, calmly reported what he had heard of that affair in Milanese circles, and spoke of the girl's beauty and how jealously I kept her hidden from the others.

'And there you are, Pisana,' he concluded. 'That is the story I told you when you arrived in Milan and came to me to ask about my officer Carlo Altoviti and that mysterious romance of his everyone was talking about. What I told you was merely what everyone was saying, and as for the hero of that story, it's not as if his honour looked immaculate! Was I wrong? I don't think so. In any case, I need answer to no one!'

La Pisana seemed quite pleased by Carafa's rather lenient tirade, and turned to me the way the judge does towards the guilty man after an irreprehensible witness has testified.

'Pisana, why do you look at me like that?' I said.

'Why? Because I detest you, because I despise you, because I want to bring down more shame on you than I've already done by throwing myself into the arms of another . . .!'

I was horrified by her cynicism, and she saw it and twisted

back and forth like a scorpion thrown on the fire. She was sorry to have shown herself for what she was: crazed and diabolical in her rage.

'Yes, look at me,' she said. 'Can I not love a different man every day, when you swore you loved me, even as you were preparing to steal away with Aglaura?'

'You are mad!' I shouted. Running to my trunk I took out several letters from my sister and threw them on the table before her. 'A lamp!' I ordered and when one was brought to the door I held it near la Pisana and said to her, 'Read these.'

Luck was on my side, in that she didn't know I was unaware the girl was my sister when we fled from Venice, and I sensed it was better not to say more, so as not to complicate an already painful and difficult tale with more details. She read two or three of those letters and passed them to Ettore, saying, 'You read these, too.' And while he quickly skimmed through them, making faces of astonishment and displeasure, la Pisana kept repeating through clenched teeth, 'I've been betrayed! It was a plot! Those villains! I will annihilate them all!'

'No, Pisana, no one betrayed you,' I said. 'Rather, you betrayed me! Yes, you. Don't try to defend yourself. Don't rage against me! Oh, if you had really loved me I could have been a liar, evil, malicious and you would still love me. Do you know why I say this, Pisana? Because that is what I myself feel. Because no matter what you've become – and I'm ashamed to say this – I still love you, I still adore you. Oh, have no fear! I shall go away and you will never see me again! Just let me have my revenge this once: know that you have brought eternal grief on that man you could have provided with joy, comfort and happiness for an entire lifetime.'

Carafa, who had now read through some of the letters, handed them back to me and said, 'Forgive me. I was deceived by gossip, but I did not intend to deceive.'

Such a plea in the words of such a man moved me so that I could barely hold back tears, for I could see the great effort Signor Ettore was making to force out that apology. His seething pride was forced to bow before will's absolute might. La Pisana wept and a double shame prevented her from looking either at Signor Ettore or at me. Taking pity (whether on me or on her, I'm not sure), he asked to speak to me outside the room. There he described his first meeting with la Pisana, who, knowing I was an officer in his service, had come to him to learn certain facts. She was mad with jealousy, he said, and he was enamoured at first sight. In short, he thought I was wildly in love with my Greek lady friend and so did not think it wrong to take advantage of that good fortune that had fallen into his hands; for love, as much as he desired it, had rarely penetrated his soldier's hard breast. And so he made it his business to turn la Pisana's fury to his own advantage and in the early days he had even succeeded.

'But then,' he went on, 'she lost all wish to return to those first euphoric days. She followed me to Milan, Florence, Rome, always silent, proud and cold, enjoying my mad passion for her, but answering my pleas and threats with these sour words: "Oh, I have avenged myself all too well!" And I suffered, Carlo. How I suffered! I swear that you, too, have been avenged! I begged, I pleaded, I wept, made vows to God and the saints; I no longer knew myself. I even stooped to bribery, tempting her maid, a Venetian woman always at her side, with gold.'

'Who is that? What is her name?' I asked.

'Rosa, she's called,' he said, 'and she's the squalid sort who would have sold her sister for ten *carlini*. But today she had a horrible punishment for her crimes: I saw her body reduced to charcoal among the ruins of the convent. Well, not even her sordid intercession had any effect, and now my humiliation was complete. And so I took la Pisana away from Rome to this lonely place, thinking I would even use force if necessary to bring her back to me. Vain thoughts, Carlo! Force falls to its knees before her gaze! I saw that some supreme determination, some invincible passion, held her back from me forever, after that one moment of shock in which she'd almost involuntarily granted me her favour. This is the whole truth, as much as it doesn't flatter me; make your own judgement and act accordingly. By tomorrow evening my headquarters will be in Frascati, for General Championnet[20] has ordered a full retreat along the line. Discuss matters with la Pisana. My house will always be open to her, for I never forget another's favours or my own promises.'

With these words, Carafa shook my hand rather reservedly and departed, quickly regaining his proud warrior's scowl. Thrusting his chest out and tossing back his hair, he discarded all boyishness and clothed himself in Hercules' lion's skin.

I returned to la Pisana's side and waited for her to question me, saying not a word.

'Where has Signor Carafa gone?' she asked, genuinely concerned.

'To order a retreat to Frascati,' I said.

'Leaving me here? Without even telling me where he's going?'

'He asked me to tell you. He fails in none of his duties as a gentleman, you see, nor does he refuse to meet those obligations he contracted with you.'

'Obligations? To me? I am astonished. His only obligation would be to return what he has stolen, but these things cannot be returned. I shall not be the first woman to make herself respected without a knight and his naked sword at her side. Please call my maid!'

'Have you forgotten where we left her? She fell victim to the fire.'

'Who? Rosa? Rosa is dead? Oh, poor me! Oh, sorry me! I was the one who let her die that way! I forgot her just at the moment when I should have taken most care! Oh, curses on me, the blood of an innocent forever on my conscience!'

I struggled to explain to her that because she had fainted in the midst of that chaos and was needful of my help to escape, she could hardly have given a thought to Rosa or anyone else. She went on wailing and sighing and talking on and on, without, however, another word about following Carafa or going off by herself. My feelings for her were so tender that I would not have refused to turn humble and sweet again, if she had shown me she desired it.

'Carlino,' she said to me suddenly, 'when you left Venice you didn't know Aglaura was your sister, for otherwise you'd have told me.'

'No, I didn't know,' I said, seeing no reason to lie further.

'And yet you lived together as brother and sister only?'

'There was no other way.'

'And how long did this innocent life together go on?'

'For many months, certainly.'

La Pisana thought about that for a moment, and then said, 'If I were to sleep on this chair, would you mind, Carlo?'

I said that she could even rest on the bed and that I had another place where I would try to sleep downstairs. She seemed very pleased with this arrangement, but waited until I had gone downstairs before taking over the bed. And then (for out of curiosity I had stopped to listen) I heard her bolt the door very quietly, making not a sound. The previous year in Venice she wouldn't have done that, but the care she had taken not to be heard made me understand she was ashamed.

The following day we spoke no more of the previous; and this was easy for la Pisana, who always forgot everything, and difficult for me, unable to shape my present out of anything but memories of the past. She asked me what kind of a vehicle we would take, as if we'd been travelling together for several years, and when we had settled into a cart, her natural festiveness made the trip to Frascati brief. Love was no longer in question; it was replaced by friendship between sister and brother, full of sympathy and things unspoken. Note that I refer to speech and manners; as for what was boiling underneath, I couldn't honestly say, and sometimes I believe I betrayed some annoyance at how placidly I'd accepted that tacit, cold compromise. La Pisana seemed overjoyed to be, I wouldn't say loved, but endured by me: she was so innocent, so obedient, so loving that only a daughter could have been sweeter. This was, I think, her silent way of asking my forgiveness – but hadn't she already obtained it? Alas, I often forgave and forgot wrongs that were quite unforgivable with the same ease I condemned in her! In any event, I maintained my dignity, and in Spoleto, in Nepi, Acquapendente, Perugia and everywhere else Championnet moved the army to gather its bits and pieces and prepare to retaliate, we played the part of siblings in arms who'd had a happy childhood together, going at it with almost unhealthy enthusiasm.

In the meantime, Ferdinand and his Austrian commander

Baron Mack[21] made their triumphal entry into Rome. The French had prudently withdrawn and the illustrious baron claimed victory on behalf of his complicated strategy. The Roman Republic collapsed like a house of playing cards and a provisional government was established under the King's protection. Mack, meanwhile, wasn't sitting on his hands, but hatching ever more complicated plans to chase Championnet out of the papal states and perhaps out of Italy altogether. General Naselli landed at Livorno and General Roger de Damas at Orbetello,[22] while Mack, having divided his army into five corps, advanced on both sides of the Tiber. Without great difficulty, Championnet (from behind, from the front, from right and from left) battered, broke up and dispersed the Neapolitan troops. Baron Mack, hoist by his own petard, had to flee. His king went before him back to Caserta and Naples, and the Roman Republic, after seventeen days of catalepsy, re-awoke to its paltry life. Championnet proudly pushed back the borders of the kingdom, with Rusca[23] in command of the Cisalpini and Carafa at the head of the Parthenopean Legion skirmishing at the front. The threat of revolution now snarled at the gates of Naples.

SEVENTEEN

The epic events of Naples, 1799. The Parthenopean Republic and the expedition to Puglia. The French abandon the Kingdom of Naples, Cardinal Ruffo invades with his brigands, Turks, Russians and Englishmen. I find my father once again, but only to see him die; then I myself fall prisoner. La Pisana comes to free me and while the finest, most unselfish Italian blood is being spilled on the scaffold, we two, along with Lucilio, embark for Genoa, the last, quivering bastion of liberty.

Armed on the battlefield, the people of Naples had been dispersed by a handful of Frenchmen, because of Baron Mack's convoluted ignorance. Abandoned by the King, the Queen and Acton (ruin of the kingdom),[1] and betrayed by Viceroy Pignatelli into a hasty and humiliating armistice,[2] that same people now rose up without arms and without orders in a vast city open on all sides and defended Naples for two days, despite the victors' growing self-assurance. They then withdrew to their lairs, defeated but not discouraged, and when Championnet entered Naples, triumphant, on 22 January 1799, he felt the volcanic soil rumble under his feet. A new Parthenopean Republic was born, notable for the honesty, courage and wisdom of its leaders; pitiful in its anarchy and the ruthless, perverse passions that destroyed it; ill-fated and exemplary in its tragic end.

The new government was not even properly seated when Cardinal Ruffo[3] and his bands of followers arrived in Calabria from Sicily, posing a grave threat to republican authority in that far corner of Italy. Some places welcomed him as a liberator; others treated him as a murderer and defended themselves – or were captured, burned and demolished. Gangs of brigands led by men called Mammone, Sciarpa and Fra Diavolo[4] followed in the Cardinal's wake. Seven Corsicans, one of them pretending to be Prince of Naples, had been enough to make trouble across much of the Abruzzi, but the French fought back energetically and solemnly hanged a few of them as examples. This was no war between men; it was wild beasts tearing each other apart.

Naples waited for the new government to consolidate, for the people to acquire republican sentiments, to be taught the democratic gospel (translated into dialect by a Capuchin friar) and to witness the miracle of San Gennaro the democrat.[5] But from afar the Russian Army of Suvorov and the Austrians under Kray[6] were approaching Italy, while Nelson's fleet, victorious at Aboukir, and the Russian and Ottoman fleets, masters of the Ionian, ploughed across the Mediterranean. Bonaparte the conqueror was undercutting himself in far skirmishes with the Bedouins and Mamelukes; with him, fortune had deserted the French flag and only courage now defended it in those foreign lands he had so rapidly possessed. A few months later, what had been feared took place. MacDonald[7] (replacing Championnet) was called to northern Italy, where the Austro-Russians had invaded. Small garrisons were left at Castel Sant'Elmo, Capua and Gaeta, but he had to fight his way out, for rebellion had now spread to the border with the Roman State.

I met Lucilio, Amilcare and Giulio Del Ponte often during that chaotic war, but always for brief intervals, for our men were rather adept at fighting in the mountains and in ambushes, and they were constantly being deployed left and right, on the Adriatic and the Tyrrhenian. I had left la Pisana with the Princess of Santacroce, sister of a Roman prince who had died not long before, defending the Republic against Mack, and so I was unworried on her behalf. Carafa treated me very fondly and seemed to place great trust in me. I had no other yearning, no other passion, than to see the cause of liberty, to which I'd dedicated myself body and soul, victorious. When the French left it was a great blow for the Neapolitan republicans. They had accomplished much, but could not do without French backing. Lucilio, Amilcare and Del Ponte did not want to depart and asked to join the legion of volunteers then being enrolled by General Schipani[8] to fight Cardinal Ruffo in Calabria. Poor

Giulio, after so many marches, so much effort, could barely walk. He had gone into a hundred skirmishes, ten battles, begging for charity in a bullet that never came. He was growing weaker by the day and feared he might die on some flea-ridden straw pallet in a military hospital. His two friends tried to comfort him as best they could. Amilcare's zeal had turned to rabid fury and Lucilio's great faith had become stoic resignation. If such sentiments can provide comfort, then any desperado can offer an example of patience and moderation before putting his head in the noose.

It was in those days that Ettore Carafa's column was sent to Puglia to fight the rebellion that was gaining ground there, too. I went off, having kissed my friends and la Pisana, perhaps for the last time. Only Lucilio knew of her presence in Naples; Giulio suspected, but dared not speak of her; Amilcare had other things on his mind. All he could think about was Ruffo, Mammone and Sciarpa, strangling and murdering them in his mind's eye. As for la Pisana, that was the first kiss from me she'd endured since we met in Velletri, and although she tried to remain cool and composed, when our lips touched both responded with passion and, when I straightened up, I was trembling all over and her face was streaked with tears.

'See you again!' she shouted after me from afar, looking confident.

My reply was a shrug of resignation, and I was off. A few days later the Princess of Santacroce, forwarding some letters to me that had arrived in Naples, wrote to me that after my departure a fit of despair had driven la Pisana close to death. She had torn and scratched her breast and face in a fury, screaming she could not live without my forgiveness. The good Princess tactfully gave no hint she knew what forgiveness the poor girl referred to, and, not wanting to be less thoughtful, I wrote directly to la Pisana asking her pardon for my cool and distant manner of recent months, saying I knew that pretence of fraternal affection amounted to an insult, and I offered in repair all my love – more tender, more vehement, more devoted than ever. So I hoped to bring her peace of mind, even at the cost of my pride; and because I seemed unaware of what the Princess had confided to me, my pleas appeared spontaneous. I later learned that my act of kindness had given great comfort to la Pisana, and that she always praised me to her protectress as the dearest, most magnanimous man on earth. Had the Princess said those nice things to me to bring about our reconciliation, I would still be grateful. One must not be too prideful towards women; when dealing with them, male honesty, strength and courage must adopt the softness of the female nature. One can be all too kind and good without risking servility or cowardice.

In the meantime I had arrived in Puglia quite content with myself and my affairs. From Venice came very good news: Aglaura was with child; old Apostulos had returned safely from his travels; my father was on his way back. And as for this last, whose activities concerned me the most just then, great things, great hopes, were hinted at. I'd been puzzling over that news for some time now, but apart from a few half-phrases from Lucilio, had learned little. It seemed, now that republics had been created from Milan to Naples, that they wanted (or some hoped) to be rid of the French and govern by themselves. They therefore wanted to induce the Ottoman Porte to join forces with Russia and attack France in the Mediterranean. Powers so far away, it was felt, would not try to take control directly, but rather could be persuaded to oppose the influence of nearer powers contemplating permanent rule. I suspected my father was already involved in that Turko-Russian alliance[9] that had shocked the world for being so sudden and monstrous. But what they hoped to gain, now that the French seemed more ready to withdraw than to tyrannize us, I really could not say. In my own poor judgement, it seemed to me that if our independence must be propped up by the Turks and the Russians, it was not very solid. But there were those whose illusions went far beyond this: General Lahoz, who joined the insurgents, died a miserable death near Ancona. We, meanwhile, stopped in Puglia, where we watched Turkish and Russian ships from the newly conquered ports of Zante and Corfu aim towards the Apulian beaches.

Ettore Carafa was not a man of half measures. When he arrived at his estates in Andria, where the peasants and townsmen were backing Ruffo, he spoke to them quite politely of peace and moderation. When they didn't listen, he drew his sword and ordered the assault – and an assault by Carafa meant certain victory. Invulnerable as Achilles, he was always at the head of the legion; an expert soldier with sword, musket and cannon alike, he behaved like one of his men, then resumed his role as Captain without arrogantly flaunting his rank. Lately, his warrior's toughness had been tempered by a touch of sadness; his men loved him for it and I admired and pitied him. But he was one of those men who find comfort and a haven against all misfortune in their political creed, one of those natures of fire and steel who make no distinction between God and *patria* and never think of themselves when the public good and the defence of liberty gird their hero's loins. There was something barbarous in his greatness; he did not believe an enemy's courage was honoured by pardoning him and saving his life, for example. He judged others as he preferred to be judged and executed the defeated in those cases where he would rather have been killed than kept alive to adorn a victory. These fierce, old-fashioned virtues and his name, powerful and renowned throughout those lands, meant he quickly subdued the province. He ruled with absolute power, and had the government in Naples had five military men his equal, neither Ruffo nor Mammone would have destroyed the last remnants of the Parthenopean Republic at Marigliano at the gates of Naples.

Instead, the government became stupidly jealous of Carafa. Oh, just the moment for jealousy it was! As if Rome had feared Fabius when he alone remained to defend her against Carthage! They said Puglia had been pacified and that better use of his services could be made by sending him to the Abruzzi, where there was very important work to do. Obedient, a bit ingenuous, Ettore was a true republican; he didn't spot the ambiguity behind these nice words and headed off for the Abruzzi. However, sensing that Puglia might not remain as loyal and secure when he was gone, he decided that Francesco Martelli, another officer, and I, should remain there at the head of a small commando to put down the minor revolts that were likely to arise. That such a man put great trust in me: well, it is not without tears of pride and gratitude that I recall it. May his noble, blessed soul have that prize that he did not obtain below, although he so deeply deserved it!

Martelli was a young Neapolitan who had left wife, children and business behind to defend liberty with his sword. Both of us men-of-the-law turned soldiers, both of us quiet but determined, we had been great friends since our days together at Velletri. He was one of those who had bet against me when I went to the convent to spy on Carafa (the loser was to offer a supper and ball for all the officers in the Legion) and since no one had settled the wager, he had the wild idea of paying it off for the others while we were there in Puglia thinking of anything but suppers and balls. One evening, returning with our fifty men after chasing some brigands pretending to be royalists who had plundered a nearby farm, I found the Castle of Andria all lit up and the great hall readied for dancing. Some decent imitations of damsels and maidens from the nearby towns, hoping for some entertainment, were happy to forget for this once that we were godless republicans.

With a princely sweep of his hand, Martelli indicated the ballroom: 'Here's the payment for our debt of Velletri, and you shall have supper, too! Who knows what awaits us: tomorrow we may be dead, and so I want to put things right.'

Dead or not on the morrow, that evening we danced and danced, and my beloved Friuli often came to mind, and those glorious country feast days at San Paolo, Cordovado and Rivignano, where we danced until we lost our senses, and our shoes. When it comes to dancing, the Neapolitans and the Pugliesi are no less possessed; from top to bottom of this poor country of ours we are not so different from one another as some would have us think. Indeed, some of the similarities are so odd they cannot be matched in any other nation. A Friuli peasant, for example, is every bit as stingy and hardheaded as a Genoese merchant, and a Venetian gondolier employs the same Attic style as a fine Florentine gentleman; both the broker from Verona and the baron from Naples excel in bluster, while the constable from Modena and the priest from Rome are both masters of guile and cunning. Piedmontese officers and Milanese men of letters are equally superior and bossy; the water-sellers of Naples and the doctors of Bologna vie for who is most long-winded. The Calabrian brigand is as brave as an Aosta rifleman; the Neapolitan *lazzarone* as patient and superstitious as any Chioggia fisherman.

And the women. Oh the women are alike from the Alps to ancient Lilibeo[10] in far Sicily! They are cut from the mould of true woman: not marionette-woman, not excise-tax-woman, not man-woman, as you find in France, in England and in Germany. The foreigners may say what they will, but where do their poets come to seek – to beg – a sip of love? They come to us, because only in Italy do women know how to inspire and sustain love. And if they complain about our brothels, we shall reply . . . No, we will not reply at all, for great prostitution does not excuse the small.

The task Martelli and I were charged with was not easy. The country folk were ignorant and a little wild; the barons were ferocious and unbending, worse than Robespierre when republicans, utterly hypocritical if followers of Cardinal Ruffo; the priests were boorish and superstitious and made me think of the Chaplain of Fratta, and worse; our enemies were astute and not at all fussy how they went after us. Still, the authority of Carafa, in whose name we operated, and the example of Trani (which had been sacked and burned for repeated riots) put some respect in the population, and the republican government was quietly tolerated along the Adriatic coast. In the less barbarous towns and where some education had been imparted in the middle classes, people were afraid of Ruffo's bands, and the massacres at Gravina and Altamura led by the Cardinal worried them more than any excesses by the French. It was in those days that I discovered that strange circumstance whereby in the Kingdom of Naples the greatest civility and the highest education was confined to a very few men, most of them noblemen or local gentry, while the common people were left to rot in abjection, ignorance and superstition. The cause was a jealous form of absolute rule, almost despotic in the oriental style, which kept the most illuminated minds at a distance (thus pushing them to extreme theories) and curried favour with the vicious, fanatical mob. Liberal men of the church like Monsignore di Sant'Andrea and philosopher-patricians like Frumier existed by the hundreds in the towns of Puglia, and the republican side was largely made up of them. But these were times of battle and the brigands overwhelmed the cultivated.

One day we heard that the allied fleets of Russia and Turkey had been sighted off Puglia. We had no precise orders for such an event, but Carafa had told us not to be alarmed, because any landing would be made up of few men. And so we hurried off to Bisceglie, where they seemed to be concentrating their scattered ships, and there, with the spirited population at our side and some cannon we found in the castle, we went about arming the beach. We had spread the word that the ships were loaded with Albanian and Saracen gangs ready to invade the territory and put it to fire and sword. And as the Turkish nation has long been hated in those parts, the people backed us fully. All was thus ready to fend off an attack at Bisceglie, when a messenger from Molfetta, seven miles away, came galloping in to say that ships were attempting a landing there, and the townspeople were struggling mightily to rebuff them. Our defence at Bisceglie in good order, Martelli and I decided we had better go to Molfetta, where no preparations had been made for an enemy landing. We doubted we could hold out for long, yet felt we would rather lose our lives but do our best for the Republic.

Saddling what horses we could find, we raced off towards Molfetta, leaving most of our people behind at Bisceglie. I don't know what it was that day, but I felt my strength and resolve shrink: perhaps it was the certainty we were defeated and were fighting now for honour alone. Such premonitions take a while to sink in. Martelli, more pessimistic than I but stronger, urged me not to lose heart and to cling to that miraculous conviction in our cause that up until now had been better than an army at keeping the Puglia countryside loyal to us. I told him not to worry, that I would fight to the last, but that despite myself, a supreme weariness was weakening my spirit. About a mile from Molfetta we began to see smoke and hear muskets firing. Out at sea, some boats were trying to come to port, but they were being pushed away by high waves. In town, the chaos was complete. The Turks and Albanians, who had landed in small boats, were sacking and killing with such cruelty these might have been the days of old sultan Bayezid.[11]

I seethed with fury at the barbarians who had allowed this beautiful part of Italy to fall to such monsters, and with Martelli and our companions, decided to exact a tremendous revenge. Every man we met was sliced by our swords, trampled by our horses and torn limb from limb by the desperate crowd at our back. At the piazza, where most of them had retreated to their boats to return to sea, the slaughter was long and terrible. It was the one time I ever took savage enjoyment in seeing blood spill from the veins of my fellow men, in watching their bloodied bodies heaped together, gasping and injuring one another in their death throes. The crowd was howling wildly, lusting for blood; some of the boldest had already reached the boats, and now there was no escape. The last of the raiders impaled himself on my bayonet and immediately a hundred angry hands reached for that dreadful trophy.

Molfetta was saved. The descendants of Suleiman learned, to their cost, that one cannot turn back history unharmed, and that Mehmed the Conqueror (if you will pardon my chronology) is as remote from them as Trajan is from us. In the meantime, the streets were swarming with people on their way to church to give thanks to the Virgin. And so the names of captains Altoviti and Martelli, along with the Blessed Virgin of the Garrison, were raised to the heavens by a thousand voices.

We had left orders at Bisceglie that we be informed immediately of any news, and when no one appeared, wanting to give our people a much-needed rest, we retired to an inn until dawn. We did fear, should the sea calm, that the Turks and Russians might land anew to take revenge for their lost boats; but there was such a mad sirocco blowing that any precautions just then seemed superfluous. Our men received word of this brief respite with great jubilation, and their festivities with the sailors and women of the town quickly erased all memory of the day's labours and dangers. Martelli had gone out on the pier with some knowledgeable local person to observe the weather and set up the sentry posts. Alone and somewhat melancholy, I sat in the hall of the inn, my elbows on the table, staring at the little lamp before a portrait of the Virgin of Loreto on the wall facing me, and gazing out into the courtyard where our men were dancing the tarantella under the leaves of a great vine. Twenty paces from that piazza where the blood was still flowing and twenty or thirty corpses awaited burial, life had resumed its cheerful Southern course as if nothing had happened. That ephemeral victory had left me with no animosity and no joy. Inwardly, I cursed that perverse instinct that makes us live happy today rather than fearful for the morrow; and I envied the heedless ones who danced and drank without a thought in the world for past or future.

From one sad thought to another, I was musing there when an old, bent, almost ragged priest approached me timidly and asked if I were Captain Altoviti. I said yes rather roughly, because experience had left me less than tender towards the Neapolitan clergy (and these were times when a priest's collar was no great recommendation to a republican). The old man did not flinch at my harsh words, but, drawing near, told me he had some very important news to impart: that a person with whom I had sacred family ties wished to see me before dying. I leapt to my feet, thinking immediately of some madness on the part of la Pisana, and because I was inclined to see calamity everywhere just then, my mind raced to the most gruesome and irreparable. I worried that if she had learned I was alone in Puglia, she might have had the crazy idea of trying to join me and been mortally hurt in the massacre at Molfetta. I grabbed the priest by the arm, therefore, and dragged him out of the inn, warning that if he meant to make a fool of me I wouldn't stand for it. Once out in the darkness of a deserted street, he whispered, 'Captain, it is your father.'

I let him go no further.

'My father! What do you know of my father?'

'I saved him in the midst of those madmen who assaulted us today,' said the priest. 'A small, gaunt man, who, when he heard the name of the captain, began to twist about on the bed where I'd laid him, and asked about you and swore he was your father and said he would not die happy unless you came to see him.'

'My father!' Stammering, half out of my mind, running so fast the old priest's legs could barely keep up: well, you can imagine I could make no sense of it all.

After hurrying along for some minutes we came to a door between two columns, like that of a monastery. The old priest opened it and took a lamp burning in the entryway and led me to a room from which I heard the groans of a dying man. Dazed by astonishment and grief, I fell with a shriek on the bed where my father lay, his throat cut, stubbornly fighting death.

'Oh, my father! My father!' I said. I had neither the breath nor the brains to say another word. The blow had been so unexpected and so terrible it had stolen my last gasp of courage.

Now he tried to raise himself on an elbow, and even succeeded, and began to search with his hand for something at his waist. With the help of the priest he drew from under his wide Albanian breeches a long leather purse, telling me, with some difficulty, that it contained all he could give me of his fortune, and that for the rest I must make enquiries with the Grand Vizier. He was about to say a name when blood gushed from his throat and he fell back on the pillows struggling for breath.

'In the name of God, Father!' I said. 'Think of living! You must not die! Not now, when I've been abandoned by all!'

'Carlo,' he began again, his voice weak but clear, as if that last surge of blood had eased him. 'Carlo, no one is abandoned here below, so long as there are others he does not forsake. You lose your father, but you have a sister, unknown to you till now . . .'

'Oh no, Father, I know her and I love her. It is Aglaura!'

'So you know her and you love her? Very good. I die with more serenity than I thought possible. Now listen, my son, there is one last thing I want to leave you in legacy. Never, never, never, no matter how men and the times may change, allow a noble, great, eternal cause to depend on the interests and greed of others. You see, I have wasted my wealth, my talents, my life on that foolish idea, and now I see . . . now I'm certain I've failed and can no longer make amends. Oh, the Turks! The Turks! But do not blame me, my son, for having put my hopes in the Turks. I believed I could use the Turks to drive out the

French, and make them leave us alone. What a fool I was! A fool! Today, today, I saw what the Turks were aiming at!'

With these words he fell into a violent delirium; in vain I tried to calm him and hold him up so that his wound would hurt him less, but he went on ranting and howling that everyone was a Turk. The old priest then told me that my father had received that terrible scimitar wound to the throat when he had tried to stop the Turks from slaughtering the town's miserable inhabitants, and that the townspeople would certainly have cut him to pieces right there in the square if the priest, who had witnessed the entire scene from the bell-tower window, had not dragged him inside. I thanked the old man for his Christian mercy and asked him in a low voice whether there was not a doctor or surgeon in town to whom we might turn. The dying man roused himself at these words and shook his head.

'No, no,' he said after a pause, his voice a whisper. 'Remember the Turks! What do we want a doctor for? Remember Venice, and may you one day see her great again, mistress of herself and the sea, a forest of ships around her and a halo of glory. My son, may Heaven bless you!'

So he died.

His death was not the sort that leaves one stunned and afraid to resume life; it was an example, a consolation, an invitation. Respectfully, I closed my father's bright eyes; his spirit was so strong and energetic that his deceased remains still seemed to pulse with life. I kissed his brow, and whether I prayed or not I do not know, but my lips murmured some words I have never again repeated. I would have remained at length with him, his last thoughts teeming inside me, but the very sight of him reminded me of those noble duties to which he'd been a heedless martyr, perhaps mistaken at times, but always firm and resolute.

'Father,' I thought, 'you know I deprive myself of seeing you to your grave so as to attend to our Republic, now in desperate health!'

A smile of agreement seemed to hover on his lips. I left the room, my heart in pieces. With some effort I got the old priest to take a few *doblas* for the funeral and a Mass. Back at the inn, Martelli had already ordered our men to prepare to leave and they were very worried when I hadn't appeared. Dawn was playing with the sea, white fingers showering all the colours of the rainbow on the water, but yesterday's sirocco had roughed up the waves and there was not a single ship to be seen. Church bells were calling the fishermen to first Mass; the women on their doorsteps talked about the horrors they'd endured; here and there a ship's boy, up early, sang as he hoisted the sails. Nothing in that land, those heavens, that life seemed to be in accord with the grief of a man who had just closed his father's eyes.

'Where have you been? What happened?' said Martelli, bending over his horse's mane.

I leapt on my horse and, driving my spurs in his belly, rode off at a gallop without replying. For a while we were followed by the cheers of the inhabitants come out to bid us farewell. We galloped on like that for a couple of miles, until the thunder of a nearby cannon brought us to a halt. Everyone had an opinion about what it meant, but then one of our men came racing up without a gun or a hat, his horse exhausted, to resolve the mystery. A ship flying a white flag had entered the port at Bisceglie. They weren't Turks but Russians, led by His Majesty Ferdinand's general, Chevalier Micheroux,[12] who asked permission to land, he said, merely to oust the remaining French from Capua and Gaeta. The people began to cheer. They tossed away their guns and waved their handkerchiefs. One thousand four hundred Russians disembarked and headed straight for Foggia, where they could surprise everyone at the fair and so terrorize the whole province. Martelli and I exchanged a look. To get to Foggia before the Russians and ready the city's defences was the obvious plan.

And so we headed off towards Ruvo and Andria, but when we got to the castle of Andria we were surrounded by a riotous armed mob. It was one of Ruffo's bands sent to join up with Micheroux and his Russians. Slow to see we had fallen into this hornet's nest, we had to battle our way out. Martelli was able to escape with seventeen of our men; ten were killed and eight, including myself, who were more or less badly injured, were set aside to adorn the gallows on some feast day. So it was written in Ruffo's military code under the heading 'Prisoners'.

The gang that held me prisoner was led by the famous Mammone, the worst and most bestial man I've ever met, who wore scores of medals on his hat like the dear departed Louis XI. Forced to walk behind them, barefoot and the butt of all their insults, I wandered across that very Puglia where five or six days before I had nearly been the master. I must confess I didn't enjoy this life much, and with irons on hand and foot that stopped me from escaping, the only hope I entertained was to be hanged quickly. One evening, however, when we were approaching the estate of Andria, seat of my former powers, a shepherd approached as if to insult me as the others did, and after having loudly pronounced the most shameless oaths that Neapolitan fancy could invent, said so quietly that only I heard him, 'Take heart, master! In the castle they are thinking of you!'

I thought I recognized him as one of Carafa's most trusted tenants, and when I raised my eyes to the castle, I was amazed to see the windows lit up, for just a few days before I'd left it locked and empty and its master was still in the Abruzzi: in fact, he was reported to be under siege by rioters in Pescara. Having nothing better to do, therefore, that night I began to nourish hopes. Around midnight one of the brigands came to release me from the barn where they had confined me, showed the guards an order from their captain, unlocked the irons on my hands and feet and ordered me to follow him. When we reached a poor hut a stone's throw from the castle, he handed me over to a smallish and somewhat mysteriously cloaked fellow, who said nothing but a clipped 'Very good!' The brigand went back where he had come from and I remained with this new master. I was undecided whether to stay or run off when a second person (it was quickly evident she was a woman) appeared from behind the cloak and threw herself on me with the warmest of kisses. I felt, rather than saw, it was la Pisana. The man in the cloak was impatient with this scene and warned us we had little time to lose. I knew his voice, too, and murmured, even more touched than I was astonished, 'Lucilio!'

'Be quiet!' he said, and led us to a dark corner behind the hut where three fine fast horses were waiting impatiently. We took our mounts, and, although I had neither eaten nor drunk anything since noon, those eight leagues we covered in two hours went by in a flash. The roads were terrible, the darkness total; la Pisana, her horse squeezed between ours, leaning sometimes to the right and sometimes to the left, was prevented from falling only by our shoulders that held her up in turn. It was her first time on a horse and she even had the courage to laugh from time to time!

'I suppose you'll tell me by what sorcery you convinced Signor Mammone of all this?' Lucilio asked her. From what I could see he knew not much more than I did of the story.

'The deuce!' replied la Pisana, when her jolting horse permitted. 'He told me I was very beautiful and I promised all he asked; indeed, I swore to it by all the medals on his hat. At two o'clock in the morning he was to go to Andria to be paid the price of his generosity! Ha!' This noble falsehood made her laugh shamelessly.

'Oh, so that is why you were so keen to leave before two o'clock. Now I see!'

It was now my turn to ask for explanations. I learned that la Pisana and Lucilio, who had set out to join me under Carafa's powerful protection, had met a runaway from Martelli's band who told them I was being held prisoner. When they heard that Mammone was supposed to reach Andria the next day, they went ahead to meet him, and there la Pisana, encouraged in part by the Bible, had deployed Judith's wiles to save me from hanging. Between Mammone and Holofernes,[13] I don't know who was better fooled! At daybreak we came to the first sentry post at the republican camp of Schipani, where Giulio and Amilcare were surprised and pleased to hear about the dangers I'd so luckily survived. Infinite joys, embraces, congratulations followed, but in the midst of it all there was grief in their hearts, for the Republic's fall was near and inevitable; and I, too, was grieving, for the tragic death of my father. I spoke first to Lucilio. He listened more in sorrow than surprise. 'Unhappily,' he said, 'it had to end that way. I, too, made such errors. I, too, regret the time, the talents, the lives so pointlessly wasted. My prophecy is this: something similar will soon happen near Ancona!'

I had no idea what he meant, but I remembered his words

religiously. And they came to mind several months later when the Cisalpine General Lahoz, deserting the French side because they had broken their vows of liberty to Italy, turned to the Romagna rebels and the Austrians to be rid of the Republic's last bastion in the region: the fortress of Ancona. Killed by his own brothers, who were loyal to the Frenchman Monnier, Lahoz spoke eloquently of his devotion to Italy as he lay dying. And yet he died in territory that was not Italian, among non-Italians. And with him went the spirit of that secret society[14] that from Bologna had swept the country, promoting Italian independence from all the various powers disputing it. Rather than back one to defeat the other, those patriots urged we back no one and be ready to die.

We reached Naples along with Schipani's column, pushed back to the capital by Ruffo's growing mobs. Disorder, fear and unrest were at their height. Garrisons were nonetheless stationed in castles and fortifications, and although there was no war, many heroes died. Francesco Martelli was assigned to defend the Torre di Vigliena and, determined to die rather than surrender, wrote me a letter entrusting his wife and children to my care. Giulio Del Ponte, ever more feeble and in fact almost gone, begged to be assigned the same dangerous position as Martelli. When he left Naples on that desperate mission, la Pisana kissed him on the lips, a true farewell kiss. Giulio smiled weakly and gave me a long, resigned look of envy. Two days later the commanders of the Torre di Vigliena, under fire from Ruffo, the King's regulars and brigands, unable to hold out further, lit the fuse and blew themselves up along with a hundred of the enemy. When their shattered corpses fell in shreds on the smoking ground, the mountains were still echoing the men's final shouts: 'Long live liberty! Long live Italy!'

In those anarchic last days we lost sight of Amilcare, and only a few months later did we learn he had ended his life as a real brigand in the Sannio Mountains: not an unusual fate for the strong and impetuous when the times and governments were contrary.

A few days later the Russians, the English and Ruffo's rabble-rousers entered Naples, courtesy of the French commander of

Sant'Elmo and his spineless surrender. Nelson then annulled the terms under which the King had earlier capitulated, arguing that a king did not capitulate to rebellious subjects. The murders and martyrdom now began. It was a real heroic epic, a tragedy that had no parallel in history apart from the massacre of the Pythagorean school[15] in that very same Magna Graecia. Mario Pagano, Vincenzo Russo, Domenico Cirillo, three leading lights of Italian science, as simple and as great as the ancients. They died bravely on the scaffold. Eleonora Fonseca, a woman. She drank a coffee before mounting the stairs and recited Virgil's words: *Some day, perhaps, remembering even this will be a pleasure*. General Francesco Federici, Admiral Francesco Caracciolo:[16] the pride of the Neapolitan nobility, the finest in letters, arts and sciences in that distinguished part of Italy, were condemned to die by the executioner's hand. And the English, and Nelson, did their part.

Finally, there was Ettore Carafa. He had defended the fortress of Pescara to the end. Consigned by the republicans themselves to the King, he was taken to Naples under the promise he would not be harmed. They condemned him to death. The day he was to die, Lucilio, la Pisana and I stole away from the Portuguese vessel on which we'd taken refuge and were lucky enough to be able to see him pass by. He looked at la Pisana, then at me, then at Lucilio, and then at la Pisana once again, and smiled! Oh, blessed are we feeble human beings, when, with just one such smile, we redeem a century of abject submission!

La Pisana and I bowed our heads in tears; Lucilio watched him die. He wanted to be beheaded lying on his back, to see the blade's edge or perhaps the heavens or perhaps that one woman he had loved as unhappily as he had his country. Nothing bound us to Naples any more. Having entrusted Martelli's widow and his children to the Princess of Santacroce, and supplied with a small income from what my father had left me, we sailed for Genoa, the last remaining bastion of Italian liberty.

After the glorious fall of Naples, the surrender of Ancona and the victories of Kray and Suvorov in Lombardy, the rest of Italy was under the control of the anti-French confederates as the year 1800 began.

EIGHTEEN

The year 1800 arrives. The misadventures of a cat and my amorous delight during the siege of Genoa. Love forsakes me and I am visited by ambition. But I quickly recover from the bureaucratic plague, and when Napoleon is crowned Emperor and King, I leave my post in Bologna and gladly return to poverty.

Our century (pardon me, I say 'ours' in the name of all of you; as for myself, I have some rights to the previous one, but as for this one, I hold on to it only by my fingertips), whether, in short, it be our century or yours, it has had a very strange birth. A demonstration, perhaps, that when you seek novelty at any cost you will never fail to find it. The Ottocento has overturned every system, all that reasoning that had wearied brains for fifty years before; and while still employing the same men, pursued perfectly opposite ends. Many were the empiricists, who, hiding paradox under clouds of syllogism, converted it into perfect dialectical accord; but not being a juggler myself, I continued to hold to my views. Something is done; something is undone; but in the undoing what was done can never be furthered. To the contrary.

And so, the year that came to an end with republican martyrs and anti-French victories was followed by another that put paid to those things, too, at the Battle of Marengo,[1] and offered Bonaparte, just back from Egypt, the reins of Europe. The thirty-year-old First Consul was no longer that general of twenty-six who had received me while he was being shaved; he was already drafting court protocol in his head. Pardon me for interrupting this latter part of my tale with the gaudy first steps of consular ambition (which will end, as usual, in a miserable account of a few, ordinary boyish feats). But I'm drawn by the light and I must gaze at it, even if it means losing my eyesight.

You may also have noticed I was in a hurry to escape the sorrowful outcome of my Neapolitan adventure. Every time I recall those grim but noble memories, my spirit flies so high it nearly leaps them in one bound. Those months were so different from the ones that came before and after that they seem no more than a day, a single moment. I can scarcely believe that someone who slumbered ten years in a kitchen, waiting for the occasional shout or slap, watching the cheese being grated, could have lived a year of so many sublime and varied sensations. I tend to think it was a dream, a year unfolded in a minute. In any event, for me Naples remains a magical, mysterious land where the things of this world do not plod along but gallop, don't fit together but straddle each other; where the sun brings forth fruit in a day, when elsewhere a month would barely suffice for a flower. Told without dates, the tale of the Parthenopean Republic would seem, I think, to unfold over many years, when, in fact, it was just a few months. Men fill up time and great deeds expand it. The century in which Dante was born is longer than the four hundred years that then elapsed before the war of the Spanish succession.

Certainly, among all the little republics across Italy that teemed under the fertile influence of France – Cispadane, Cisalpine, Ligurian, Anconian, Roman, Parthenopean – the last was most resplendent in republican virtues and deeds. The Cisalpine Republic had greater consequences, because it lasted longer, was more stable and, perhaps, had greater or more balanced culture among its people, but who would say, reading about it, that the Cisalpine order lasted longer than the Parthenopean? Perhaps history finds the great, thundering catastrophes the most pleasing.

Meanwhile, we had reached Genoa; la Pisana and I rather worse the wear for seasickness (and therefore cured of any other worries); Lucilio, very glum and thoughtful, as if he had begun to despair, but was trying not to. Strength grew in him according to need; he had a real Roman spirit, made to command even from the lowest rank, a fatal gift common among Italians and responsible for many of our misfortunes and a few of our most tragic acts of heroism. Now, secret societies are refuges for men of proud natures and imperious talents, men unwilling or unable to act in the narrow spaces governments assign them. For some time now I had known that Lucilio belonged (perhaps as far back as his days at university) to some secret society of Illuminati or Freemasons, but over the years I'd watched his philosophical interests give way to politics, as his role in Cisalpine circles and then in Ancona attested. Lucilio was an avid follower of political events and even sometimes predicted them with astounding accuracy. Whether he had prior knowledge or was a prophet, I don't know, but I tend to think the latter. He never spoke of any news he had received, nor was it very easy for us to receive letters with fresh news. No news – fresh or salted – came to Genoa, and the last word from Venice had come from an Austrian prisoner who the month before had been billeted in the house of la Pisana's husband, perhaps in the very same room as Lieutenant Minato.

News of the Lieutenant was one of the unpleasant novelties I found in Genoa, along with hunger. The day after we arrived, the English fleet commenced a very harsh blockade and in just a few weeks they reduced us to hunting cats. I had, however, one great comfort: the protection of my friend Alessandro Giorgi, Sandro the miller. He, too, was in Genoa, no longer captain, but colonel. In those times the living advanced quickly. Colonel Giorgi, not yet twenty-seven years old, had survived to become chief of his regiment and give orders left and right in a booming miller's voice. He didn't know the meaning of fear and would throw himself into the fray without ever losing sight of the men he commanded: these were his merits. He wrote passably, made some spelling errors and had been acquainted with Marshal Vauban and Frederick II[2] for no more than a month, and by name only: these were his defects. Apparently, his merits counted for more, if he had become colonel in two and a half years, but his greatest merit of all was the massacre of his entire battalion, which as I said, had made him captain by necessity. I met him one day when the food stocks were growing impoverished and those with food were inclined to hoard it. La Pisana was unwell and I had been unable to find a pound of meat for broth.

'Hello, Carlino,' said he. 'How goes it?'

'Well, I'm still alive,' I said, 'but I don't know about tomorrow or the day after. La Pisana's not well and things are going from bad to worse.'

'What? The Contessina is ill? What the Devil! Can I get you eight or nine regimental doctors? The regiments are gone, but the doctors have survived, proof of their fine learning.'

'Thank you, thank you, but I have doctor Vianello and he will suffice.'

'Of course he will. I merely meant another consultation, another opinion.'

'No, we know what the illness is: a lack of air and nourishment.'

'That's all? Oh, leave things to me! Tomorrow I'm on guard at Polcevera Creek and I can get her more fresh air there in an hour than she'd get in a day at Fratta.'

'Oh, certainly, at Polcevera, with those fennel bulbs Melas keeps aiming at you!'

'Ah, it's true. I forgot she is a countess and the bombs might annoy her. Well then, there's nothing to be done, she'll have to walk on the roofs.'

'If she had the strength and the will, the roofs would do fine, but she's a weak thing nourished on lettuce broth and doesn't have the energy.'

'Poor thing! However, I can come to your aid. As you can see, I've still got some fat on me, I believe!'

'Oh yes, you might be the Chaplain of the Portogruaro Cathedral!'

'Chaplain, my backside! Do you think you get muscles like this by singing in the choir?' he said, flexing an arm and nearly bursting a seam. 'You see, I've taken care of myself, thanks to my foresight. I slaughtered my two horses, had them salted and so I eat four pounds of meat a day. Afterwards, who can say? But if you'd like to be part of this plenty . . .'

'Oh, I'd be delighted, although it would pain me to deprive you. But salted horsemeat won't do for la Pisana.'

'Well then, I have another idea. My landlady is as stingy as you find in Genoa and eats nothing but boiled herbs from her courtyard, which she calls by the fine name of a garden. Even before the siege I don't think she ate any better; life for her is but one long blockade. But picture this: on her knees she keeps an old Angora cat so fat and tender it would be considered a great treat in Milan.'

'It's the Angora cat, then!' I said. 'La Pisana doesn't much like live cats, so far as I know, but she'll like a dead one. We'll make sure she thinks it's chicken broth, not cat. I'll get a handful of feathers and leave some around the house.'

'If I can help you with the feathers . . .'

'Oh, thank you, Alessandro, but as I recall the pillows on my bed are full of them. Rather, how will you get the cat off the lady's knees?' Here the good colonel stuck his chin in his collar and rubbed it up and down like a tomcat on the prowl. 'Yes, by Diana, how – if the lady is so enamoured of her cat?'

'Carlino, it's my bad luck that she's even more enamoured of me than of the cat. She's always after me, driving me crazy!'

'She must be ugly if it annoys you so much.'

'Ugly, my friend? She's terrifying! Can a miser be beautiful? She reminds me of Signora Sandracca with a few less teeth.'

I gave a start of horror.

'Oh, don't you worry! You won't have to see her. I'll keep that pleasure for myself. Out of respect for you and the Contessina, I'd risk even worse. I hope, though, to get away with nothing more than a good scare. Every morning she knocks on my door and asks if I've slept well, turning the key as if to come in. I always pretend I don't notice this little itch of hers, and every night I lock up with a chain. I'd sooner forget to take off my boots than to take that security measure. Tomorrow, however, I'll deliberately forget; the lady will come in and, in the meantime, my men will make short shrift of the cat.'

'An excellent plan, by Jove! With such a marvellous imagination you will soon be a general. I thank you, and do not forget that my cousin's health depends upon your cat.'

The following day Alessandro came to find me in my room around noon; he was livid and scowling.

'What has happened?' I said, getting up to meet him.

'That foul harpy!' said the colonel. 'Who would ever have

thought she'd come to knock on my door with that stupid cat of hers under her arm?'

'And so?'

'And so I had to endure a half-hour of conversation with her that left my insides in a terrible state, and I'll bet I'm as white with bile as when I used to work in the flour mill! Oh, how can I get her to part from that diabolical cat? You tell me, if you have any ideas!'

'Well, suppose you made as if to embrace her?'

Poor Alessandro looked as if I'd given him some carrion to smell.

'I fear it is the only way,' he said, 'but if the cat doesn't move, if it's slow to leave us?'

'What the Devil? A captain of your stature and you lack the means to draw out the battle?'

At these words of mine, Alessandro assumed a grave and dignified look. I could not understand why, until suddenly it came to me in a flash.

'Oh, I'm sorry, you know,' said I. 'I used the word captain in the etymological sense of capo, head; the way Julius Caesar, Hannibal, Alexander the Great and Frederick II are called captains! But I do not forget the rank you now hold!'

At these words and especially at the mention of Frederick II, the colonel's face brightened.

'Very well,' said he happily, patting his cheeks. 'I'll flatter the old harpy a bit. But wait, now that I think of it, what will the maid say?'

'And what has the maid to do with it?'

'Oh, she has to do with it, good heavens! She has to do with it, because I have . . .'

'Is she young and pretty, the maid?'

'Fresh, by God, and firm as a nice little apple that's not too ripe. With some padding all around like our own country girls, and lips that have no equal in all Genoa.'

'Ah, then I understand what you have to do with it, and she, too. The consequences of consequences! Well, you could send the maid out to buy, let's see, some Tripoli powder[3] to polish your spurs.'

'No, no, my friend; that would make the doorkeeper's daughter jealous!'

'But my dear Alessandro, are you such a lady's man? It seems that for the fair sex there are impulses more compelling than hunger!'

'It's just by chance, Carlo! Although, when you look around at all these siege victims, well, my colour, the flesh on my bones, can't help but make an impression. And then, between Genoese and Friulians there's no choice but to communicate by signs; our dialects are so incomprehensible to one another that if you ask for bread you're likely to get stoned.'

'Oh, that's good! Woe if you had to do without your salted horse meat! Perhaps you could give the maid something to iron?'

'Yes, yes, I understand. I'll take care of it! Tomorrow you shall have your cat and broth for a fortnight.'

'I'm counting on it, you know! Because all I could find today was half a pigeon and it cost me dear. And tomorrow we have nothing at all.'

The brave colonel left me, indicating he would not fail, and probably gave great thought to how he could flatter the woman, but not *too* much, and snatch the cat from her bosom. It was not yet ten the following morning when one of Alessandro's men brought me the famous beast. It weighed no less than was reputed: I'd never seen, not even in the kitchen of Fratta, a cat so large.

'And the colonel?' I asked, my thoughts elsewhere.

'I left him in his room with all the women of the house, shouting,' said the soldier. 'But he can stand up to the Russians; a few skirts won't frighten him.'

A quarter of an hour later I had already handed the beast over to the cook with orders to obtain the most broth possible, disguising the feline flavour with onions and celery, when Alessandro appeared before me, shaken and in disorder. He looked like Orestes pursued by the Furies, as played by Salvini.[4] He threw himself on a chair, grumbling and moaning that he would rather go out and conquer an ox on the field against the Austrians, the Russians and all the rest, than chase another cat. I feared I might laugh, but held back so as not to offend him.

'Just hear what happened to me!' he said, tossing aside his

hat. 'My plan was to send the doorkeeper's daughter out of the house, and then send the maid out after her, while the landlady came to my room and I played the cat trick on her. My men would have full rein to capture the beast however they could, and when the doorkeeper's daughter and the maid came back they would rescue me from their mistress. Instead, what do you think happened? The doorkeeper's daughter and the maid met each other on the stairs and began to quarrel. I had tossed the cat to the floor when I clutched the woman in a sort of embrace, but could move neither backwards nor forwards with that cursed cat between my feet and the old lady at my neck! Stamping a foot here and a foot there, I finally got the cat to run away. But just then the doorkeeper's daughter and the maid came in, scratching at each other, and saw me wrestling with the landlady. One shrieked, the other screamed; they roused the whole quarter, I reckon. The old lady was red with rage, not shame, and I was pale with terror. I began to shout that it was nothing, that I was just allowing the old lady to try on my sword. The maid threw herself at her mistress, threatening to gouge out her eyes if she didn't pay her wages, that this was no way to keep her promises, that the French officer's services were all due to her. In the meantime we could hear the last howls of the cat downstairs as my man cut its throat with the landlady's scissors, which were found all covered with blood. Oh yes, I must dress down that fool for being so stupid!

'Well, you can imagine what a brawl! The old lady, who had let go of me, wanted to grab me again; the maid had me by the neck; the doorkeeper's daughter by the jacket: everybody wanted her part. Tired of them clutching at me, I raised my voice so loud that all three were struck dumb and I was finally able to move. I hurried out of the door, grabbed my hat and raced here, but I swear to God, if I'd faced a triple charge of Cossacks I wouldn't be more out of breath!'

I comforted the young colonel on his trials and sent him to see la Pisana to receive the thanks we owed him, but we had to call the cat a turkey, so the perils he'd risked capturing it seemed somewhat less impressive. In any case, thanks to the clever Piedmontese cook, the broth pleased the young lady. It tasted insipid for being turkey, but as even the birds were suffering from starvation, no one bothered too much about it. Perhaps such tales sound frivolous after our epic adventures in Naples, but every season has its fruits and our stay in Genoa tended towards the comic right from the start. Lucilio alone gave up none of his usual seriousness; he chewed his chicory roots gravely as if they were game croquettes or chicken sausages.

Another time the miller-colonel, looking less ruddy and jovial than usual, came round to see me. I thought it was the salted horse meat that was growing scarce, but he told me he had something else entirely on his mind and would take me to a place where I, too, might feel I didn't want to joke any more. The attraction of guessing games was wearing thin, in truth, but as much as I pressed Alessandro, he would tell me nothing but that tomorrow I would see. The next day he took me to the military hospital. There we saw poor Bruto Provedoni, who was finally getting up after a long recovery – on a wooden leg! It was a dreadful shock. Alessandro himself had known nothing of his friend's calamity, and, having heard nothing for a long, long time, had feared the worst. He had gone searching the hospitals for one of his men, who had disappeared and was reported injured, and instead had encountered his friend. Of the three of us, Bruto was the least dismayed, it seemed. He laughed, sang and tried to walk and dance on his wooden leg, the most grotesque antics you could imagine. His only comment was that he was sorry to have lost the leg before the blockade, because in times of hunger he would have eaten it very happily! I was pleased to have found him, thinking I might somehow be of use. And, in fact, he spent his entire convalescence with la Pisana, myself and Lucilio, thus avoiding the tedium and inconveniences of the hospital.

In Genoa I also saw Ugo Foscolo again, now an officer in the Lombard Legion, and it was the last time we were together as old friends. He was already beginning to comport himself as a man of genius, withdrawing from friendships, particularly with men, so as to be more admired, and writing odes to his lady friends in the high classic style of Anacreon and Horace. This serves to show that we didn't spend all our time dying of hunger, and that even a diet of chicory doesn't extinguish the poetic urge or blunt youth's good humour.

In the long run, though, the poetic urge began to wither and good humour was fading. One bean was going for three soldi; an ounce of bread cost four francs; if you wanted something beyond beans and bread, you'd be ruined in a week. I had no more than twenty thousand lire in coin and Austrian bonds, but this was not the place to trade the latter, and thus all my wealth amounted to no more than a hundred *doblas*. Looking after la Pisana's vacillating health and feeding her something beyond mice and sugar candy easily cost one *dobla* a day. In the end, I was lucky to be able to rely on Alessandro's salted horse meat. Salt horse one day, salt horse the next, and soon there was nothing left but the bones, however, and we had to do like everyone else: eat rotten fish, boiled hay (when there was grass) and sweets, of which there was an abundance in Genoa for they were an important item of trade there. Fevers and rashes completed our comforts, yet in our own house, health began to improve just as everyone else was sickening.

The sweets agreed with la Pisana; her cheeks regained their pretty roses and her wild, extravagant humour came back, replacing the tame normality during her illness that had made me fear the worst. I was cheered to see there was no damage, that her organs were untouched; indeed, I was so cheered that I began to be frightened. There were times when she would leap up and bite like a viper or begin to sulk and keep it up for an entire day. Everything had to be done her way; she would shift from obstinate silence to wild volubility in an instant. Cancelling from my memory all the years in between, she took me back to our tempestuous childhood games at Fratta. When I closed my eyes, I saw myself not as the veteran of a long and bitter war, but on the banks of our ditches by the meadows, drilling holes in snail shells and polishing up pebbles. I became as childish as any great-grandfather, and I was not yet a father, nor in a hurry to become one. Now this was a matter of dispute between us: she wanted a child at all costs, and I (no matter how much I worked myself up explaining that in that place and time a baby would be the worst obstacle imaginable) always ended up playing my pipe. Otherwise the hue and cry would have brought the ceiling down on my head. The usual disputes, battles and jealousies ensued, all for that blessed baby; and yet I can assure you that if Providence didn't provide it, I wasn't to blame, nor was I sorry.

Until then I had always admired la Pisana for never being jealous of me, although my admiration was somewhat mixed with irony, if you will, because her assurance seemed to be due either to her coolness in love or great confidence in her own merits. Now, however, I had nothing to complain of. I didn't dare to look out of the window but she turned on me with a scowl. She wouldn't say why, but she'd let me see. Opposite us there dwelt two dressmakers, a woman who took in ironing, the wife of a shipyard worker and a midwife. She insisted I was enamoured of the whole rude lot of them (not the best proof of my good taste), especially the midwife, who was uglier than a sin forsworn. In vain I kept my eyes at home, like San Luigi;[5] I was only pretending and she told me so with a sarcastic smile worse than any impertinent words. She was fed up with being a good wife to me, she said, and she began to go out and wander around for half the day, although the city offered no opportunities for pleasant strolls. Everywhere there was a smell of hospitals and death, and the coffins were coming out of the windows, and the sick were carried on human backs, and the rubbish tipped out to steal some kitchen leavings from the worms.

One day she insisted I take her all the way up to the forts to meet my companions. When I didn't show great enthusiasm she accused me of being spineless; it wasn't enough that I should do nothing, I wanted to deprive those who were doing something of that small comfort that a visit from some good souls would provide. It was best to go, and I did. Had she demanded I take her to Ott's[6] fortified camp or among the Monferrato mobs led by Azzeretto (threatening Genoa's finances more than the Genoese) I'm sure I would have agreed, I'd been so reduced to numbskull and husband.

Another time we were returning from a visit to Colonel Alessandro at the fort of Quezza, one of the most exposed. The bombs were raining down as we raised glasses of Malaga to

Bonaparte's luck and General Massena's stamina. Soon la Pisana was weaving about like a *vivandière* and I would have liked to give her a slap, but she was so very beautiful I'd have hated to spoil her looks, no matter how foolish and wild she was. As we left the fort Alessandro warned us to look out for the nice fireworks, and, in fact, Ott's bombs made such lovely arcs and curves that if they hadn't made a thump falling and a roar exploding it would have been good fun. I began to walk faster, not so much for myself, I assure you, but to remove la Pisana from harm, but she took it badly and began to mutter that I was useless, and got my back up by praising Alessandro to the skies, with his fine army manners and his not so refined wisecracks and vulgarity. But la Pisana loved typical specimens; a Neapolitan *lazzarone* without rags and without *maccheroni* wouldn't have appealed to her, and neither did a miller-colonel who didn't swear and deliver pinches. I defended myself with dignified silence, but she put my silence down to envy. Finally, I exploded in fury and began to rail and shout that if I were a woman I'd have admired Monsignor her uncle rather than that ignorant peasant of a colonel!

Now we began to fight in earnest. She accused me of ingratitude and I accused her of being much too tolerant of Alessandro and his filthy manners. We ended up back at home, sitting in the dark, me on one chair, she on another, facing the wall. When Lucilio returned home not long afterwards we were both asleep, a sign that the storm had barely roused our bilious humours, despite the furious words. To provoke me, la Pisana went on for a long time praising and extolling the fine behaviour and the extraordinary courage of Colonel Alessandro, insisting that a miller who had become an expert soldier in such brief time must be exceptionally intelligent, and that she had always had a soft spot for the young man and had seen he was superior to the others when he was just a child. Those memories of days past made me furiously jealous (for back then little Sandro had often been my more fortunate rival) and when I saw her enjoying these recollections, my suspicions became grossly inflamed.

And so, jealous, wearied by hunger, facing a future that did not look hopeful, we did our best to annoy each other in every way possible. But let the handsome Alessandro puff out his chest at her flattery and she would take fright. Then it was my turn to point out that it was unkind of her to be too fastidious; that an imperfect upbringing demanded sympathy and that a few silly remarks from a good and courageous soldier must not be confused with the scurrilous allusions made by some foul-mouthed young gentleman. Alessandro, loathed by me when la Pisana was courting him, and defended by me when she disdained him, was like an acrobat on the wire before he had got his balance, half-coming, half-going. When, however, la Pisana treated the poor colonel particularly unfairly, I had the means to make her relent: I would remind her of that fine turkey broth he had provided. She had been wanting more of it for some time now, because the sweets were beginning to cloy. And so she began pursuing him again with the most delicious flattery imaginable and Alessandro's breast swelled with pride. But when I began to hint about why she was being so friendly, his face darkened and he complained that his landlady had no more cats and it was a good thing, too, for God only knew what might happen the second time.

The siege intensified, food grew ever more scarce, and no one was fighting any more for causes like liberty or independence. What did General Masséna want?[7] To make of Genoa a second Pompeii, peopled by cadavers rather than skeletons? To distance the enemy from our walls with the fear of pestilence, rather than with arms? Everyone was complaining. The general alone knew that whatever the cost he meant to delay the surrender, by a month, by a day. Bonaparte, in that lapse of time, would gather the last republican sparks in France and ignite Europe a second time. By force of hardship, suffering, fortitude and cruelty, we made it to the beginning of June, when Bonaparte came down like a thunderbolt to disturb the tranquil squabbling between Melas and Suchet,[8] and Italian hopes were reawakened in Milan.

The fall of Genoa was termed an accord and not a surrender, and Masséna's eight thousand men moved conveniently out to swell Suchet's forces. The new conquerors of Liguria made no mention of restoring the old governors, as they didn't in Piedmont. Not the time to think about restorations! His army's scattered forces were pulled together by Melas in forced marches to the banks of the Bormida, just in front of that point where Napoleon, before leaving Paris, had put his finger on the map and said, 'I'll break them here!' The First Consul hurried out of Milan, crossed the River Po, celebrated victory at Montebello and pushed the enemy towards Alessandria. It was a very strange position for both armies, for each had its own territory behind the enemy.

The exiles from Genoa, under the accord, were to be taken by English ships to Antibes. I was among them, along with la Pisana, Lucilio and Bruto Provedoni. It was a terrible voyage and it cost me my last *doble*. At Marseilles I was happy indeed to find a moneylender who would change my Austrian bonds at thirty per cent. We had already heard the news of the victory at Marengo and all together we set out on the road back to Italy. We were very hopeful; we hoped for even more than had been regained – and what had been regained was almost a miracle. But no one dreamed that Melas would lose heart at the first defeat, and as the war continued our hopes expanded until far in the distance we thought we could see Venice restored to liberty or part of the Cisalpine Republic.

Along the way we heard of the surrender of Alessandria, with Melas withdrawing behind the Po and the Mincio, and the French reoccupying Piedmont, Lombardy, Liguria, the duchies, Tuscany and the Legations. Pius VII, newly elected pope in Venice and lately returned to Rome and a magnificent welcome by his Neapolitan allies, had thought he would have to regain his territories from the tenacious hands of friends,[9] when instead he had to accept his enemies' mercy and sign a concordat with France on 15 July. In those days the First Consul presented himself as protector of order, peace and religion, and the good Chiaramonti, now pope, didn't hesitate to believe him.

Provisional assemblies were springing up everywhere in this new climate of order, peace and religion. Lucilio and the old democrats frowned on them, but Bonaparte knew how to cajole and intoxicate the people, flatter the powerful and reward his soldiers lavishly; and no republican annoyance could argue with such blandishments. I myself, loyal to my old principles, put my faith in the new, for I could not believe that men could change so much in so little time. And so I was disappointed when Lucilio refused an important post offered him by the new government, and I willingly took a position as auditor with the military tribunal. From there – honest administrators being in short supply – I moved to Ferrara to become Secretary of Finance. I didn't mind at all having to earn my bread honourably, for I had left twelve thousand lire to a bank in Naples for Martelli's widow, spent my *doblas* in Genoa, exchanged my bonds in Marseilles, and now all the monies left me by my father before he died had been consumed. Colonel Giorgi was always saying that he could get me appointed major in the Engineers or the Artillery, but living as I was with la Pisana, a military career made no sense and civilian employment suited me better. And indeed, we found a very nice place to live in Ferrara. Bruto Provedoni had travelled there with us on his way to Venice and the Friuli, and he promised he would write at length about all that we wished to know; and, happy to have escaped that tempest that had engulfed people greater and cleverer than ourselves, we settled down to await those unexpected events that would finish putting our lives in perfect order.

His Excellency Navagero's death, which could not be far away, was of particular interest to me. Poor fellow! Not that I wished him ill, but as he had lived some seventy rather happy years, he could certainly permit us a little happiness, too. Without intending to, I think I grew more moderate myself during that temperate second republican period; my heedless, drunken, delirious love, so much in tune with the rash and ardent passions of revolution, was now quite at odds with the sober, legal, measured views emerging. The concordat with the Holy See put thoughts of marriage in my head, in spite of myself. La Pisana gave me no hint of her hopes or intentions. Now that our life was back to normal, she was back to her usual unbalanced moods: long taciturn periods interrupted by sudden outbursts of chatter or laughing; her usual love, seasoned with anger, jealousy and negligence.

Ascanio Minato, who had become a captain and left the

fickle countess he'd stolen from Emilio, was now posted to the garrison in Ferrara. In Genoa he had tried to approach la Pisana without success, but she had paid him no attention in those busy days. In Ferrara, however, she was thrilled to be able to relieve the domestic tedium a little; and so, in the end, I was forced to allow the talented young officer into my home. I disliked him for many reasons: because of what he'd done in the past, on behalf of my own pride, on behalf of Giulio's memory, for his brash behaviour and speech, for his affected French manners, so silly and vulgar in a Corsican. But I took care not to betray any of this in la Pisana's presence, knowing that nothing is more dangerous than a contrary opinion, especially in one who can't resist contradiction. And so I was quite composed and well-behaved, as befitting a public official and the master of the house, but I kept my eyes open and Signor Minato rarely had the courage to meet them with his own.

The news from Aglaura and Spiro in Venice was more varied than it was good. A second child had been born, but their mother had died and they were deeply sad; their business prospered, but the men in charge of public affairs seemed to be squalid. Old Venchieredo bossed everyone about quite shamelessly, with that arrogant foreigner's manner and language of his. According to Spiro – who had been forced to go and beg him to free one of his compatriots sent to Kotor with the republicans captured in mainland Venice – these foreign masters were but a step above our own stewards and farm-bosses. The Avvocato Ormenta was always at Venchieredo's side, distinguishing himself mostly with hidden fraud, rather than open extortion. Behind them was Padre Pendola, who, chased out of Portogruaro and in discredit with the Venetian Curia, had nevertheless built up a following among the less educated clergy. Some considered him a martyr; others, a scoundrel. Old Frumier and his wife had both died, a month apart from one another. Alfonso had passed up marriage to join the Order of Malta and nobody knew if he was dead or alive, but there were rumours he was courting a certain Lady Dolfin, fifteen years older than he and once the wife of a Correggitore at Portogruaro. I remembered her and reminded la Pisana and we both laughed.

Agostino had petitioned for a post in the new government, for he had no other means of support, having lost all his wealth at the death of his parents. They made him a customs inspector, and he, the fervent republican, was humbled. He thought he might regain something by marrying well and there had been some flirtation with that Contarini girl my father had wanted to palm off on me with promises I'd have a dowry and become Doge. His aunt, the Countess of Fratta, tried to get some sparks going, but she was motivated less by love for her nephew than by hopes of a large commission, for her passion for gaming hadn't waned and the family estate continued to shrink, now amounting to some hundred plots around the Castle, mortgaged against her daughters' dowries. Clara, after Madre Redenta's death, had become the leading light of the convent and they wanted to make her Abbess. She, therefore, had less and less interest in worldly affairs, either good or bad. Count Rinaldo slaved away at his accounts and in the libraries. Raimondo Venchieredo had offered to help him get a better post in the administration, but he had stubbornly refused. Grimy, down at heel, he took his ducat and left at the end of the day, and although his mother often took the ducat, he was unwilling to bow and scrape any more than strictly necessary, I think.

From Aglaura I had some news of Doretta, who, as I've said, had dealt with her before when she arranged through Venchieredo to deliver Emilio's letters after his departure for Milan. The wretched woman, now abandoned by Venchieredo, had lost all restraint and with each new lover sank deeper into Venice's most fetid and infamous slums.

'And you trusted her!' I said to la Pisana.

She confessed then that it had been Doretta who told her I had fled with Aglaura, the fool harlot thus serving Raimondo's aims against her own interests.

'What can I say?' she added. 'You know that when you're annoyed with someone, bad words make a greater impression than good. And, frankly, Raimondo himself depicted you as a rogue who had stayed in Venice after the others and then run away to Milan, because you were involved in foul-smelling, filthy matters.'

'Oh, scoundrel!' I said. 'That's what Raimondo told you? He'll have to take it up with me!'

'However, I didn't much believe him,' she went on, 'and even if I did believe him, he didn't get much profit from it, because he was trying to take me away from you, but all he did was hasten my departure for Milan!'

'Enough! Enough!' I said, for I didn't like hearing about this part of our life. 'Let's see what Bruto Provedoni writes from Cordovado.'

We now read the long-awaited letter from the war veteran. I could, as I've done up to now, summarize the contents, but my modest skills as a writer wouldn't do them justice. Here I must leave the field to a better man: see how a noble spirit bears adversity, observing the things of this world from on high, without ever giving up his role in them or his compassion. I keep this letter still among the things most dear to me, in that reliquary of memory that begins with a lock of la Pisana's hair, and concludes with my son's sword, just arrived from America with the long-delayed news of his death. Poor Giulio! He was born for greatness – but it had to be great misfortune. But let us return to where we set out and read together what Bruto Provedoni wrote to me in Ferrara, just back in his village with one leg less and many an additional worry:

'My dearest Carlino! I mean to write at length, for there is much I want to tell you, and coming back has left me with so many sad impressions that I fear I can never recount them all. I am so unused to holding a pen in my hand, however, that often I must put aside my thoughts and limit myself to those material things I can best express. But I don't feel I owe you any deference and I shall allow my soul to speak in its own way. And if it doesn't express itself properly, you will understand anyway and I'm sure you'll forgive my ignorance, for my intentions are good.

'Oh, Carlino, if you could see this place! You wouldn't know it any more. What has become of the fairs, the gatherings, the feast days that used to cheer us in our youth from time to time? Where are all those families that once provided dignity to our territories, kept alive the old traditions of hospitality, Christian patience and religion? What sorcerer has silenced all the clamour, the contests between one village and another, the disputes and the fights when some fellow stared at a pretty girl or the parish priest was elected or someone asserted his rights? Four years have passed and they might be fifty. There has been no famine here, but everyone complains he is starving; no soldiers were called up and no pestilence arrived as it did in Piedmont and in France, but the countryside is deserted and the houses empty of the best workers. Some went to Austria, some to the Cisalpine Republic, some went to Venice to find fortune, some are hidden away on the most distant plots of land. Political differences have undone families; war's sorrows, suffering and exploitation have killed the old and aged the strong. No one marries any more and rarely do the church bells ring for a baptism. When the bell tolls, you can be sure someone is dying. The vigour of our people, expressed for better or worse in household crafts and village trades, is completely exhausted. Penniless, defenceless, hopeless, each man thinks only of himself and what he needs today; each one hastens to build a refuge against his neighbours' deceit and his superior's aggression. With public affairs and the law so unsteady, men shrink from making contracts; they speculate about the good will of others, but never trust in it.

'As you know, the gentry's old jurisdictions have been abolished and now Venchieredo and Fratta are but villages, governed like Teglio and Bagnara by the prefect of Portogruaro. Prefect, so they call the new magistrate who administers justice, and while the innovation may be useful and in keeping with the times, the peasants don't believe in it. I'm far too ignorant to understand why, but I suppose they don't expect anything good from men who have done them so much damage with the war. What is certain is that the corrupt have profited in the meantime, while good men continue to be exploited and impoverished, not having the courage to take something for themselves in the general disarray. The wicked know the good: they know they can rely on them and they skin them alive. The contracts offered provide no damages or escape clauses; the good leap innocently into the net and are mercilessly trapped. The stewards of the large families, the moneylenders, the grain-brokers, the men in the communes who furnish military supplies: this is the riff-raff that prospers while the rest of us decline. These people, servants and peasants not long ago, are more arrogant than their former masters and, bereft of good upbringing and gentlemen's manners, don't even try to give their villainy the appearance of honour. They have lost all pretence of good and evil; they want to be respected, obeyed and served, merely because they are rich.

'Oh, Carlino! For now, the revolution brings us more bad than good. I fear that in a few years time we shall have proudly installed an aristocracy of money, one that will make us long for aristocrats of birth! But I say *for now* and I stand by that: if men have seen how vain it is for rights to be based on the worth of a grandfather or some other ancestor, they will soon see how monstrous it is for power to be based not on any merits of past or present, but only on money, which is indistinguishable from force itself. That a man with money may keep it and spend it and make use of it: very well. But when money serves to buy an authority that can only derive from knowledge and virtue: this I can never accept. It's a barbarous flaw of which human nature must cure itself at any cost.

'If you could see the Castle of Fratta now! The walls are still standing, the tower still rises above the leaves of the willows and poplars around the moat. But as for the rest: desolation! No one comes and goes, no dogs bark or horses neigh; there's no Germano polishing muskets on the bridge, no Clerk emerging behind the Count, no townsmen lining up to doff their hats at the young countesses. All is empty, silent, in ruins. The drawbridge lies rotting; the moat is stuffed with cartloads of rubbish and bricks from the gardener's house, which collapsed. Grass grows in the courtyards; the windows not only lack shutters, but the frames and windowsills are coming to pieces under the dripping rain. They say that some creditors or maybe just thieves have sold the very roof beams of the attic; I know nothing, but I can see that a big piece of the roof is missing and that the rain and snow come in, damaging the apartments, as you can imagine. Marchetto, who's now sacristan at Teglio and who has become as silly as a capon, still goes to the Castle once in a while, out of habit. He tells me that Signora Veronica is dead; that Monsignor Orlando and the Captain have only the Chaplain's maid Giustina to rely on, and she looks after them and cooks them luncheon and supper. Monsignor sighs because he can no longer drink wine; the Captain complains because he promised his Veronica on her deathbed not to take another wife, and now the druggist's widow at Fossalta, who is mad, would like to marry him, I can't imagine why. In the winter they go to bed at five and Monsignor takes refuge in sleep. Among all his old friends only the Chaplain remains and even seems to cling to him more tightly with every new disaster. Monsignor di Sant'Andrea and the Rector of Teglio are both dead. In short, as I said before, I left a town and returned to a cemetery – and I haven't told you everything yet.

'As for how these gentlemen survive, they live on the tributes (you might as well say alms) of those four tenants they have left, because all the real earnings go to Venice. The stewards and the factors and the brokers have triumphed, filling their pockets at the expense of fools. Fulgenzio had already bought the Frumiers' house at Portogruaro and was greedily carving it up like a real gentleman when I left. His son Domenico is a notary and got a post in Venice; the other said first Mass just yesterday and will be a clerk in the Curia. Don Girolamo, as he's called, is a nice little priest and when all is said and done I prefer him to his brother and his father, although he, too, is a shrewd fox.

'Now, Carlino, I come to the worst calamities; I call them the worst because they affect me the most and I have kept them for last because if I'd started out telling you about them I might never have moved on to the rest. My father followed my mother's example (she died a month before I signed up to fight with Sandro Giorgi). He died, poor thing, in young Aquilina's arms, because his other children were all at odds with him and didn't believe he was dying. Bradamante was in bed giving birth and couldn't help her sister in those last offices of mercy. I don't like to speak ill of my brothers, but the eldest, knowing nothing, and the younger ones, vandals that they were, have wrought havoc on the house. Carry this away, drag that away, wear out, sell, lend: and the rooms are empty. Leone, who has moved to

San Vito with his family and works as the land steward, decided to let the house, apart from three rooms used by Aquilina and Mastino (Grifone, who's a master builder, has gone off to work in Illyria). Three months later Mastino was offered a post as a copyist in Udine and went off, leaving his fourteen-year-old sister all by herself in those three rooms. True, she is quite grown up for her age and I was very pleased to hear the priest praise her conduct, but a brother who goes off like that is a man whose fraternal love is all in his heels!

'Now I'd heard of some of these calamities by letter, others I'd worried about, but to tell the truth, Carlino, seeing them at first hand was just terrible, worse than I'd ever imagined. It may be that finding myself so crippled and helpless made my sorrow more bitter; it was already quite bitter by itself. But another blow was waiting for me on my arrival and it just knocked me to the ground. Dottor Natalino, I'd heard from Aquilina among others, had died a few months previously. And one evening, guess who came to see me? My sister-in-law, that trollop Doretta. She had some scribbler with her, a scrawny young fellow who claimed to be the son of one Avvocato Ormenta of Venice, and who came with her to reclaim her dowry and Leopardo's inheritance. Now, what do you say to that? How tender! The dowry that no one ever paid us! The inheritance of a man who, you might say, she murdered! But she had a piece of paper in Leopardo's hand written eight months after their marriage and attesting he owed her money, and she complained of her poverty (and the scrawny fellow warned me quietly that without the money her reputation was at stake), and so, hoping to rescue her from the bad path she was on and out of respect for our name and my brother's memory, I did everything I could to pay her. I sold my stake in the lands left us by my father, gave her the money and off she went with God (the young man looking eager to rid her of the weight of that heavy bag).

'Some time later I heard that the money served her as a dowry to join a home for reformed women that had recently opened in Venice to look after priests of Christian heart and good intentions, but not of noble families. She stayed there a month and then ran away, possessed by the Devil, they said;

and now I fear she's in an even worse state than before, for the gift of the dowry was irrevocable and, in any case, it was not enough to make her independent for life.

'Now you know our situation and some of that of the town, too. I act as father to Aquilina; I look after those ten fields that still belong to her; and earn something for myself giving penmanship lessons in town and to a few good families who prefer to disguise their kindly charity thus. Sundays, our brother-in-law Donato comes to collect us with a cart and we go to Fossalta to see Bradamante, who already has three little ones, the eldest hopping about like a crane and the youngest still at the breast. Despite the wooden leg, the older boy and I take part in great exploits and I'm teaching the second to walk (she's a girl and something of a lazybones for her age).

'I have no idea whether this state of affairs is permanent, whether these are just setbacks before better luck arrives or a lull before worse disasters strike. I know I've done my duty and I always will, and if any of my decisions was hasty, it was because I felt called to it and I've never regretted those decisions. Yes, things could have certainly gone better, but I wouldn't trade my poverty or even my wooden leg for all the wealth, the ease and the brazen good health of some scoundrel. Isn't that right, Carlino? I know you agree, so I speak from the heart. In any case my hopes don't all reside under my own roof tiles: some venture out in search of you; some retrace my own steps and refuse to quietly accept the hard results of the wars we've seen. Our First Consul has won at Marengo, but we, too, can offer him some nice battlefields, and he already knows them and they were auspicious. Oh, if we could see that! I'd dance a great jig on my wooden leg! I'd kiss you all: you, la Pisana, Dr Lucilio. By the way, is it true that the doctor has remained in Milan? For his part, Sandro Giorgi and his regiment have been sent to fight in Germany. If the war continues he will certainly do well, and so I hope, for along with a failing or two, he has a heart – a heart that would cut itself in pieces for other people. Oh, but will I never stop nattering on to you? Hold me dear, then, write to me, remember me to la Pisana and do what you can to bring us all together again.'

My fine friend, who apologized for not knowing how to write! When the heart feels something, who pays heed to words? Who needs style, when another soul delicately touches our own? I'm not ashamed to say I wept over that letter, not the sentences per se, which perhaps would move no one, but precisely that good and merciful effort *not* to move, that sensitive, painstaking care not to reveal one's own grief to others, so that the pleasure of news from a friend would not be poisoned by the sorrow of knowing him unhappy. His father's death, the family's dispersal, his brothers' unkindness: I was sure that these blows one after the other must have hurt Bruto far more than he wanted to show. I imagined him with Aquilina, that sweet, graceful girl, so grave and loving, who even as a child had the kindest and most compassionate woman's heart you could desire! Her innocence, her heavenly smiles would soothe Bruto's pains, they would compensate him for taking care of her, and certainly two creatures reunited after so much strife would find fraternal love an idyll of peace and happiness.

La Pisana was with me in those humble hopes. A romantic creature, she adored tragedy's powerful contradictions and proud intensity, but she also appreciated the rosy innocence and peace of the pastoral idyll. Pursuing Bruto and Aquilina in our own imaginations, we saw the tranquil meadows between Cordovado and Fratta, the lovely streams darting though a countryside bright with flowers, the sweet-smelling thickets of juniper and honeysuckle, the pretty spring at Venchieredo with its shady paths and mossy banks! We wished them all this; we basked in it ourselves. If only there were not that wooden leg playing havoc with every fine romance one could wish for Bruto. In towns like ours such a defect is unpardonable; the crippled hero is worth far less than the healthy scoundrel. Women of the city can be more indulgent, although they may not be the greatest admirers of heroism. But had Bruto no wooden leg, would he have returned to Cordovado? Where was Amilcare, where were Giulio Del Ponte, Lucilio, Alessandro Giorgi? Where, in the end, was I (if less drawn by a brave temperament into dangerous ventures)? Refugees, exiles, dead, roving here and there like slaves driven to work fields that were not our own, no roof over our heads, no family, no country of our own in our country's very lands! For who could be sure that the *patria* a conqueror conceded so wilfully would not be wilfully withdrawn? Already in France there were rumours of a new government order; the Consul, it seemed, did not sit on a curule chair, but on a higher throne. Bruto was already excluded from that arena where we were jousting away without knowing what prize we might earn. At least he had returned to his paternal home and the place of his childhood and had a sister to love and protect. His destiny, already written, was perhaps not glorious or grand, but it was peaceful, safe and full of affection. His hopes would take flight with ours and fall with ours, with no remorse for having wasted time in idleness, no regrets for having struggled in vain pursuing a chimera.

In short, there I was, envying the fate of a young soldier who had come home without a leg and, rather than meet the arms of his father, found only a grave. And I was not the most unfortunate! Middling in my hopes, my desires, my passions, I found that when my private means began to run out, public means came to my aid. To obtain the post of secretary in a new and important branch of the public administration like the department of Finance – at twenty-six, without protectors, without bribery, in a foreign land – was no small or contemptible fortune, and I knew it. Here, I expect I'll come in for some teasing and recrimination. But I confess without any shame: my instincts were always those of the quiet snail, whenever the whirlwinds didn't carry me off. Acting, working, slogging away: all this I did happily to build a family, a country, my share of happiness. But when my objectives no longer seemed near or possible, desire led me back to my garden, my hedgerows, where at least the wind did not blow too wildly, and where I could bring up my children in view of better and happier times. I didn't have Amilcare's blind, implacable fury, ever driving forward, never turning back; or Lucilio's tireless obstinacy, seeking a second path when the first was closed, and then another, always aiming at some noble and lofty end, but also, perhaps, after four years of toil, finding himself further away and less certain than he had been at the start.

For myself, I believed in the great high road of moral improvement, social harmony and education, to which we must always return whenever shortcuts lead us astray. A road I would have happily taken, and left only if called by some urgent demand. Instead, fate had me beating a path left and right across the countryside. The year before, a useless hungry mouth in Genoa; now secretary in Ferrara: the hieroglyphs my auspices spelled out were so mismatched that putting them together beggared good sense.

But, luckily, la Pisana often diverted me from my foolish thoughts. Her feminine reprisals with Captain Minato; her extravagant ways, which set Ferrara's moribund society aflutter for a month: for those few hours I had free from the thresher of work, she kept me busy. To go from additions, subtractions and graduated tables of taxes to the strategic calculations of a jealous lover was no easy task. Indeed, I had to call on all the flexibility of the spirit and the ready reactions I'd acquired in fifteen or more years of practice. There were days when la Pisana spent all her time thinking about me, policing me as if I were a bad boy planning to run away; and I could either pretend not to be aware of her suspicions or put on a scowl, but there was nothing I felt less like doing when I might have been resting from my labours or gathering my energies for the future. Was there ever a lover or a husband who worked so hard to take charge of his woman without letting her feel the weight of the reins as I did during that time in Ferrara? The papal dandies, the neat, clean little French officers all said, 'What a good-natured fellow!' although they probably wished I were less under their feet (and even if I had trodden on them or been nasty, they wouldn't have retaliated). I was, in short, a genuine inconvenience; and the worst thing was that they could not complain or make me out to be some silly tax-collecting Othello.

The news that the Countess of Fratta was ill brought these bouts of joust and defence to an abrupt end. Count Rinaldo so informed la Pisana without adding any further comment; he merely wrote that because Clara could not leave the convent, his mother was alone, looked after by a not-very-helpful scullery maid, and that he, knowing that la Pisana was in Ferrara, had felt it was his duty to set aside all reservations and let her know of this grave misfortune. La Pisana looked at me, and I, without a second's thought, said, 'You must go!' But I can assure you it cost me dearly to say so, and it was a sacrifice to public opinion, which otherwise would have held me responsible for perverting a young lady in her due respects to her mother. La Pisana, however, took my suggestion all the wrong way, and, even though I believe that if I had remained silent she would have said the same, she now began to sulk, saying that I was already tired of her and that I was just looking for any kind of excuse to get rid of her. A solemn injustice to me, you will agree. With a shrug of my shoulders I replied that the way I saw it, she was always chasing after obscure pretexts to annoy me and she should instead be grateful I was the first to suggest she make a voyage that was in every way displeasing and inconvenient for me. Apart from the fact that I'd be left alone, there was also the problem (rather pressing in those days) of money. I liked to live well and la Pisana had not the slightest idea how to balance accounts and never gave the least thought to her own purse or that of any others; she simply went on spending wildly, even posting little debts here and there in the shops.

In any event, she wanted to quarrel with me and she succeeded. I've never understood this tendency of hers to torture me when we were about to part, considering how much she cared for me – because, I assure you, she would have let herself be torn limb from limb for me. I guess unhappiness about having to leave spoiled her mood, and in her usual thoughtless way she took it out on me. At times she grew red-eyed and followed me around the house like a little girl behind her mother, and then if I gave her a loving look and a kind word her face would darken and she would turn her back and pay me no attention. To you this may sound like ordinary childishness, but I write of it to show the continual suspicion I endured because of her contrary soul, and also because her nature was so unusual it would make a story all by itself.

And so, several days later, when I had scraped together the money needed, I took her in a carriage as far as Pontelagoscuro and from there she caught the boat to Venice. The docks on the

Po marked the border between the Venetian provinces occupied by the Austrians and the Cisalpine Republic, and so I could accompany her no further. A week later I heard from her that her mother was now out of danger, but that the convalescence was likely to be long and we must resign ourselves to a separation of a few months. I wasn't at all happy about that, but in light of the other good news she sent, I tried to console myself. Aglaura and Spiro were living happily with their two little children who were a delight to behold; their business was prospering and they offered their help to her and to me in every way possible. Her brother the Count, despite the coolness of his letter, had treated her very fondly and there was one other piece of news of interest to both of us. His Excellency Navagero had been lying abed for a month, completely paralysed and reduced to imbecility. She wrote to me of her husband's sad condition in the most compassionate words you could imagine, but the care she took to describe his (indeed) sad and desperate state, suggested she was quite resigned to the fact that the final blow might come within days. My solitude was therefore less onerous and I threw myself heavily into my work to blunt the pain.

In those very days the Assembly of Lyons met to remodel the Cisalpine Republic, which came out baptized 'Italian Republic' and was now reordered under the new designs of First Consul Bonaparte, who was elected President for ten years. The Vice-President, who would govern personally, was Francesco Melzi,[10] a liberal and man of large and patriotic sentiments, but whose grandeur and noble origins were not to the taste of the most ardent democrats. From Milan, Lucilio wrote to me of these developments with a certain cold rage that said far more than he dared to. Evidently, he expected me to refuse to serve a government from which all true republicans had distanced themselves. I was leaning his way, not so much on behalf of the republic per se, but because the republican cause was by now the only thing still driving my hopes for Venice and inclining me to continue in my duties. But then something happened to change my mind. I was named nothing less than Intendente of Bologna, which is to say Prefect of Finance.

Now, whether the new government saw me as a man of order

and moderation along their own lines or whether they wished to reward me for my last few months of hard and fruitful labours, I don't know, and the appointment came as a great surprise. Perhaps the post demanded someone diligent, meticulous and tireless and they thought a young man might be better suited than a seasoned public servant. In any event I was carried away by such crazy ambition that for two or three months I never thought of Lucilio and scarcely even of la Pisana. The Ministry of Finance seemed ready to fall into my hands, and once I had reached those heights, who knew? It is easy to change office once you are inside the great room where decisions are made! I thought of my father's old hopes for me and they no longer seemed strange or irrational. Only that ten-year presidency of Bonaparte gave me pause and, rash as I was, I did not, I confess, even dream of replacing *him*. Too big a man to budge, he seemed to me. As for the others, I'd appoint Prina, an able administrator,[11] and Melzi and I would see eye to eye. I'd heard there were tensions between him and the First Consul, because of his thoroughly Italian tendency to take charge and his inclination to govern Italy independently from France. I would use all my talents and my cleverness to profit from that, keeping in mind that my ambitions were aimed at enlarging the Italian Republic to include Venice. If my madness had an excuse, this was it.

Installed in Bologna with these grand objectives in mind, I became a most eloquent and bountiful Intendente, hoping to pave the way to future greatness. I later learned, however, that my swelled head led them to call me, in their biting Bolognese vernacular, Intendente Blowhard. After a few months of prideful bliss and hard work to put order in the public finances (something quite unusual in the former papal legations) I began to feel I was not yet in paradise and to hope that la Pisana's return would make up what I felt was lacking. Not two or three but six months had passed since she left me in Ferrara and not only had she not come back, but now that I had moved to Bologna her letters had grown scarce. It was lucky I had my head in the clouds or I should have beaten it against the walls. La Pisana had a particular way with her correspondence; she never replied immediately to letters she received, but set them aside and wrote back three, four, even eight days later, when, no longer recalling what she had read, her replies ventured out into entirely new territory and one was always playing blind man's buff. Many, many times I wrote that I was tired of being alone, that I could think of nothing but her, that if she meant to return, she must at least tell me the reason for her great delay. Nothing! It was a foolish quest. She would write back saying she loved me more than ever, that I must not forget her, that she was bored in Venice, that her mother was now quite well and that she would come as soon as circumstances permitted.

I would write back by return post asking what were these circumstances and did she need money; and if there was some pressing reason why she could not come, would she please tell me because I would then ask for a passport and come to keep her company for as long as I could get leave. I never failed to ask about the inestimable health of His Excellency Navagero, who I imagined must have gone to the Devil some time back, but la Pisana did not even reply to say which world he was in. Her neglect of what she knew was of the greatest interest to me finally began to prick at the magnificent Intendente's pride. To fully realize my grandeur, to put all four wheels on my victory chariot, I needed a wife and this I could only hope for with Navagero's death. I could hardly believe that this useless nobleman didn't hurry up and die to please such a distinguished Intendente as myself. And if it was la Pisana who delayed giving me the news, well, she'd have to answer to me! I'd make her suffer for at least a year over the hand of the future Minister of Finance. And then? Oh, I'd never be able to hold out longer, not even in my own mind. I'd elevate her to my throne, as Ahasuerus made the humble Esther the Queen of Persia, and I would say, 'You loved me when I was small, I repay you now that I am great!'

It would be a master stroke and I congratulated myself, walking up and down the room, stroking my chin and savouring in my mouth the sweet words I would reply to la Pisana's fiery thanks. My underlings coming in with folders of papers to sign would hesitate in the doorway and then retreat, reporting that Intendente Blowhard was blustering away and looked quite mad.

Still, they had less reason to complain of me in those days

than in many others and, on the whole, because I worked hard and was patient and indulgent, they had begun to be fond of me despite my Blowhard nickname. The Bolognese are the kindest, the fairest and the sharpest-tongued in all of Italy, and even when they are friends, and very good friends, you must allow them to speak ill and make fun of you at least twice a month. Without such an outlet they would die and you would lose helpful and devoted friends, and the world would be short of cheerful, sparkling wits. As for the women of Bologna, they are the most light-hearted and uninhibited you could hope for; government by the priests not having succeeded in making them cold and shrewish. If the latter behaviour used to be common in Verona, Modena and other cities of strict and pious manners, the blame must lie more with the nuns, the mothers and the husbands, than with the priests. The Catholic religion is neither scolding, severe nor unyielding; in fact, it is among the Protestants that you will find the strict and bad-tempered. I don't know whether these vices of theirs are compensated by other delightful virtues; I merely observe, note this down impartially, and move on. The other day a rabbi assured me that his religion is the most philosophical of all and I heard him out, although, however much a philosopher the rabbi was, I might have said to him: 'Master, all the philosophers, be they Mohammedan, Brahmin, Christian or Jew, find their own religion more philosophical than the others. Just as the blind man calls red the loudest of the colours. Religion is something felt and believed; philosophy is argued and examined: let us not confuse one thing with another!'

To finish up speaking of Bologna, I can say that both then and now life there was cheerful and sumptuous with plenty of good friends and festive gatherings. The city gives way unobtrusively to the countryside and the countryside to the city: fine houses, lovely gardens, all that one needs, without that provincial frippery that says, 'You had better respect me because I'm very expensive and must last a long time!' Bologna is busy and vital; the Bolognese are lively enough to measure up to anyone's wit and chatter; they are ready to please those good women (who are so ready and companionable); quick to run here and there to satisfy everyone's wishes. In Bologna you will eat more in one year than in two in Venice, three in Rome, five in Turin and twenty in Genoa. Although in Venice you eat less because of the sirocco, while in Milan, more, thanks to the cooks. As for Florence, Naples and Palermo, the first is too affected to want its guests to stuff their bellies, while in the other two the contemplative life nourishes through the pores without wearying the jaws. The very air is impregnated with volatile citron oil and lush fig pollen.

What does this matter of eating have to do with all the rest? A great deal, because digestion works in accord with hard work and good humour. A ready and lively conversation that touches on all the feelings like a hand on a keyboard, that exerts the mind and the tongue to run and jump here and there wherever they are called, that excites and over-excites your intellectual life, will prepare you better for your meal than all the absinthes and vermouths on earth. They did well to invent vermouth[12] in Turin, where men speak and laugh very little, except in Parliament; and in any case when they invented it, they did not yet have their Albertine Statute.[13] Nowadays there is more activity, but of the kind that stimulates deeds, not appetite. Excellent for the hopeful and for the vermouth-makers!

Although my babbling on here might suggest otherwise, la Pisana showed no sign she intended to come back to me, and, little by little, Bologna lost its ability to stimulate my appetite. For an Intendente of twenty-eight years, a faraway love is not a tragedy to joke about. For a month or two it was bearable, but after eight or nine months, almost a year! I had taken none of the three monastic vows and I had to keep the most indecent of them. Confound it! I can see you all now, laughing at how stupid I was. But I don't wish to deny anything. In those days I loved la Pisana so much that other women seemed, to say the least, men. Pretty, pleasing, elegant little men, let me say with all due respect, but still men; and there was nothing foolish or hypocritical about this, it was pure love. And so I'm not ashamed to confess that I often behaved like Joseph with Potiphar's wife[14] in those days, while during the later separation from la Pisana I was, you might say, subject to various distractions. It was not that I loved her less, but differently; and whatever the Platonists may say, I bore the second separation in far better spirits than the first.

At that time, however, I was in a mad hurry to be with her again, and, unable to get any clear reply from her, I turned to Aglaura, begging her, if she had any sisterly love in her, to inform me without mystery and without sugar-coating what my cousin was up to. Until then my sister had always avoided explicit replies to my inquiries on the matter, getting by with 'I think' and 'I don't know'. But this time, seeing from the tenor of my letter that I was distraught and ready to do something crazy, she replied that she had held back because la Pisana herself had asked her, but now she saw I was in turmoil and she wanted to be frank with me. For the past six months, she told me, la Pisana had been living in her husband's house very busy nursing him and did not seem inclined to leave him. I should be reassured that she loved me as always and that her life in Venice was really that of a nurse.

Oh, to have got my claws into His Excellency Navagero! He wouldn't have needed a nurse for long! What made that putrid carcass think he could rob me of my share of life? How was it just that a young woman such as his wife . . . that word 'wife' brought me to a halt for a moment, for it occurred to me that vows sworn at the foot of the altar might, in the event, count for something. But such scruples were quickly brushed away.

'Oh, yes,' said I, 'very just indeed that his wife should be bound to him like a living person stuck to a corpse! Out of the question! By Bacchus, I'll detach her and end this monstrous torture. After all, even supposing we forget the rule that charity begins at home, is it not nature's rule that he should die and not I? Not to mention the fact that I shall really die, while he may be capable of dragging on this way for years and years, that imbecile!'

I took up my magnificent Intendente's pen and wrote such an impressive letter that it was worthy of a king furious with his queen. The substance of it was that if she didn't come immediately to revive me, my glory, my destiny and I would soon be several arm-spans underground. This letter of mine went unanswered for a couple of weeks, until, in fact, I was about to go not underground but to Venice, when suddenly la Pisana appeared. She was irritable, as women are when they've been made to do things someone else's way, and before I got either a greeting or a kiss she made me promise to allow her to depart when she wished. Then, seeing that her remarks had stolen half my pleasure at her arrival, she threw her arms around my neck – and goodbye, Signor Intendente! I was very impatient to have her see all the benefits connected with my new office: the sumptuous apartment, doormen aplenty, tobacco, oil and wood all paid for by the State. I was smoking like my poor old father, so as not to deny myself even one of my privileges, and I took my meals with oil three times a week, as religiously as a Carthusian monk. But I had also set aside a nice sum to allow her to show herself off nicely in Bolognese society and, as I saw it, this was such proof of my love that she should have fainted dead away before me. Instead, she scarcely seemed to notice; for in order to understand what my efforts had meant, she'd have had to be capable of them herself, and the blessed thing had more holes in her hands and her pockets than a Roman beggar in his jacket. Hearing of those four hundred *scudi*, she merely flashed two big, round eyes; apparently the mere mention of such a large sum of money was something she was no longer used to. In fact, it was not as large as it seemed. Dresses, hats, necklaces, excursions, refreshments: soon my expenses were nicely back in line with my salary and the *scudi* didn't tarry in my pocket more than a fortnight.

Entertaining herself, high and low, la Pisana quickly revealed to me a new side of her character. She became the merriest, most loquacious little lady in Bologna, able to keep four, six, eight partners busy; never sulking, never tiring, never sinking into some private observation or thought or distraction and forgetting the others, but so good at distributing a word here and a smile there that there was always something for everyone and never too much for anyone. I could trust her; the trials and troubles of Ferrara were finished. Meanwhile, everyone was talking about the Intendente's cousin, some said his wife; some, his mistress; and there were those who wanted to marry her, and those who would have liked to seduce her or steal her away from me. She saw it all and laughed politely, and if she dispensed her charm all around, she saved her love all for me. Other women quickly take to women of this kind, because the men grow tired of making great exertions for nothing and finally they court merely out of habit, while conducting their true love affairs somewhere else.

A month later my Pisana, in demand among the women and adored by the men, would walk the streets of Bologna as if celebrating some victory, and even the little scamps would run after her, shouting, 'It's the pretty Venetian lady! She's the Intendente's wife!' I wouldn't like to say whether she was vain about this good fortune of hers, but she certainly knew how to make me aware of it as graciously as you could imagine. My role, of course, was to love her (and rightly so) in proportion to all that desire buzzing around her.

And so, amidst this life of continual pleasures and domestic happiness, she no longer spoke of going away. When letters from Venice arrived, she scarcely cast an eye on them, and if the writer turned the page, she certainly didn't, but just stopped reading halfway. I, however, read them from start to finish, but was careful not to let her know how urgently her mother or her husband sometimes begged her to return. Navagero seemed neither very jealous nor very close to death and he wrote of me with a great show of friendship, as if I were a close and very dear relative, and of their future years as a great land of plenty that would never end.

'That deathbed monster!' I would groan. 'He's been resuscitated!' And I would hover on the edge of jealousy myself for all the time that la Pisana had lived with him. But she would fall over laughing at my silly anxieties and I would laugh, too, but still I intercepted her letters and, once she'd tossed them aside, I took care that she never saw them again. Her forgetfulness was a great help to me in this. As for her long stay in Venice, here is the story, or rather the story as she told it to me in bits and pieces as her mood willed. Her mother, convalescing, had begged her to pay a visit to her dying husband if only for the sake of convention, saying Navagero would be most pleased. La Pisana had agreed to go and the poor man's condition, his financial straits (his one-time opulence was much reduced), the negligent state in which he lived, had moved her and convinced her to stay on with him, as he evidently wished. She was all goodness and, as much as I complained of the bad consequences for me, I could only praise her from the bottom of my heart and love her even more.

I was very cautious, however, about trying to force these confessions from her and never insisted for more than an instant, for I was dreadfully afraid that if I went after her too hard, I would revive all that pity of hers and make her want to leave. I was fair enough to praise her, selfish enough to keep her from acts of heroic virtue, and, as it happened (la Pisana being a good and compassionate creature, but also very, very heedless), I was able to keep her in parties, song and laughter for almost six months. Still, I watched with worry the number and the urgency of the letters increase, but when nothing untoward happened I grew used to them and thought my beatitude would never end. From Minister of Finance and Vice-President and President of the Republic, I had modestly and peaceably come down to my present post, and if others were to accomplish those nice things that whirled around my head, I would have been quite happy to stay put.

Poor mortals, how fleeting is our happiness! It was the establishment of the mail-coach service between Padua and Bologna that did me in. Count Rinaldo, whose weak stomach would not have permitted him to travel over water even as far as Ferrara or Ravenna, was quite delighted to take the coach, and suddenly he was underfoot in Bologna, even though no one had invited him; and he wanted to be taken to see the Madonna di Monte and the Montagnola and San Petronio[15] and then, in recompense for all this, on the third day he departed, taking la Pisana. The sight of her brother had reawakened all her compassion and begun to prick her conscience and, oh no, it wasn't she who had accepted his invitation, she was the first to suggest she keep him company on his return. That assassin said nothing; he didn't even say he had come expressly for her. He preferred to leave me with the innocent illusion that he had trotted out from Venice to Bologna because he was curious to see San Petronio. But I had seen it in his eyes the first time

I looked on him; and it infuriated me to watch him succeed in his intent without troubling to say a word. An unwashed, bleary-eyed library rat, more able in woman-diplomacy than a young, handsome lover, an Intendente at that? So it seemed. I was left to sigh and gnaw at my fingers.

Back to my work, then. I threw myself into it, if for no other reason than to distract myself from my woes. And by working hard and forgetting as much as I could, I gradually became another man, and you will decide whether better or worse. The fumes of poetry were evaporating from my head and I began to feel the weight of my thirty years about to hit me. I prolonged my stay at the dining table happily and divided the love that dwells in the soul from that which titillates the body. Pardon me; I believe I said I became another man, but I believe I was becoming a beast. When his mind loses its youthfulness, a man can only fall from the human state to some other, lower, animal condition. That reason that distinguishes us from the brutes is not the one that calculates our own gain, procures us ease and evades toil, but the one that bases its judgements on the soul's great hopes and wondrous imagination. Even a dog knows how to find the choicest mouthful and dig out a bed in the straw before sleeping in it; if that is reason, then let us give dogs diplomas as men.

What is more, a short-sighted life of mechanical toil had an excuse once, when there was one great intelligence thinking for us, whose will was so much superior to all of ours that only a few ideas were needed to produce great deeds. Today, instead, ideas prosper, but of deeds, whether black or white, there are none: all because of that great misfortune that those with heads do not have arms. Once upon a time Napoleon's arms opened across Italy (and halfway across Europe) to shake and rouse the dormant life forces. We merely had to obey and miraculous activity flowed evenly out from the nation's old order. I don't like to make forecasts, but if things had gone on like that for twenty years, we might have grown accustomed to living, and intellectual energy would have come forth from material, as when the ill recover. The enthusiasm for life that animated half the world back then could make you dizzy. Justice was one and equal for all; everyone took part according to his capacities in the great movements of society; it wasn't ordered, it happened. We wanted an army and an army appeared in just a few years, as if by magic spell. From populations grown feeble with idleness and corrupt with lack of order, legions of brave, sober, obedient soldiers were conscripted. Habits were remade by force and anything could be obtained with order and with discipline. The first time I saw our conscripts lined up in ranks in the piazza I thought I was seeing things; I didn't believe so much could be done, that a mere law could tame the rustic herd and urban rabble, who had never before taken up arms except to pillage the countryside and rob travellers.

From such beginnings I expected miracles and, convinced we were in good hands, I didn't ask where were heading, merely admired our progress. To see, one day, my Venice under her own arms and wise with new experience, take up her place among the Italian peoples at the great congress of nations: this was my vow and faith. It was among the future deeds the Revolution's rule maker had promised, or so I thought when the Cisalpine Republic became Italian, hinting at other, exalted developments to come. When Lucilio wrote to say things were going from bad to worse, that if we surrendered all judgement hoping for a liberator we would merely obtain a master, I laughed at his fears (half-mad, half-ingrate, I said to myself), tossed his letter on the fire and went back to my labours as Intendente. I think I even enjoyed la Pisana's absence, because the peace and solitude favoured my work, and my hopes to make my mark and advance. Long live Signor Ludro![16]

So passed quite a few months, all work and faith in the future, no thoughts of myself and never a glance outside the picture I'd placed before me. Today I can see this was not a life to awaken capacities or invigorate the spirit; one ceases to be a man and becomes a cog. And we know what becomes of the cog that is not oiled on the first of the month.

Was it misfortune or good fortune? I don't know, but the proclamation of the French Empire[17] unfogged my eyes a little. I looked around and saw I was no longer my own master and that my work meshed with other things that were being carried out above and below me to the sound of the drumbeat. Woe to him who tried to exit: he was nothing. If everyone was in my situation, as I suspected, then Lucilio's fears were not far from the truth. I now undertook a hard examination of conscience, studying my past life and comparing it to the present. I found a difference, a contradiction that frightened me. The principles and hopes that drove my actions were no longer the same: once I was a poor, tired workman, but also intelligent and free; now I was a thing of wood, nicely varnished and stroked; bending unthinkingly, methodically, like a machine. As much as I didn't want to make any hasty decision, I certainly didn't intend to go one more step down that ladder of servility.

When word came that the Republic had been transformed into a Kingdom of Italy I took my few things and the few *scudi* I had left and went straight to Milan to resign. I met four or five colleagues come on the same mission and each of us thought we'd find a hundred and make a great stand. They thanked us very much, laughed in our faces and took down our names in an ugly book that didn't bode well for our futures. Napoleon came to Milan and put the Iron Crown[18] on his head, saying, 'God granted it to me and woe to the man who touches it!' Penniless, alone, I sat in the old rooms near Porta Romana, saying in turn, 'God has granted me a conscience and no one shall buy it!' Napoleon's enemies found enough zeal and strength to touch and take that fatal crown from his head; but neither Australia nor California has yet dug up enough gold to pay for my conscience.

That time, I was stronger and more far-sighted.

NINETEEN

How millers and countesses protect me in 1805. I pardon Napoleon for some of his errors when he unites Venice with the Kingdom of Italy. I repent very late for an old venial sin, which nearly causes me to die, but la Pisana revives me and takes me back to Friuli. I become a husband, an organist and a land-agent. Meanwhile, the old actors vanish from the scene. Napoleon is twice defeated and the years go by, mute and disheartened, until 1820.

Lucilio had gone into exile in London; he had friends everywhere and, in any case, a doctor is at home wherever he goes. La Pisana had kept me at bay with her promises to join me, but when I gave up my post I didn't even have the courage to call on her and ask her to share my poverty. I was loathe to ask Spiro and Aglaura for money; they punctually sent me my three hundred ducats every Christmas, but I had spent two years' income paying off my debts in Ferrara. And so for the first time in my life I had no roof over my head or anything to eat and very little means of procuring either. A thousand different schemes turned in my head, each of which required a nice pile of *scudi* just to begin, and as I had no more than a dozen of those *scudi*, I had to make do with schemes. Every day I plotted how to live on less. I believe I could have made that last *scudo* last a hundred years if, on the day that Napoleon left for Germany,[1] one of those famous pickpockets who work the streets of Milan by pious tradition hadn't robbed me of it.

The Emperor, grown fat, was on his way to victory at Austerlitz; I recalled him lean and resplendent with the glory of Arcole and of Rivoli. By Jove, I wouldn't have traded the Little Corporal for His Majesty! As I watched him depart among a cheering Milanese throng I wept with rage. They were noble tears, though, of which I am proud. 'What could I not do if I were that man?' I said to myself and that thought, and the list of the great things I could have accomplished moved me deeply. Indeed, he was at the height of his power then. He had just left Albion resounding with his roars from across the narrow Channel and was threatening the necks of two emperors with his omnipotent claws. Caesar's youthful genius and Augustus' maturity came together to exalt his destiny beyond human imagination. He was truly the new Charlemagne and he knew it. For my part, though, I was proud to pass by him without bending my knee. 'You are a giant, but not a God,' I said. 'I've taken your measure and find my faith much greater and nobler than you!' It was no small statement for a man who thought he had but a *scudo* in his pocket – and hadn't even that.

Providing for my supper was the great challenge; no man could have been in a worse fix, I think. Taking advantage of the discretion of some friends as I was leaving Bologna, I had converted every pin, ring and other not strictly necessary thing into ready money. However, when I made a new inventory I was able to find many more superfluous items in my wardrobe, and I tied these into a bundle and took them to the rag man, pocketing four *scudi*, which seemed a million. The illusion lasted no more than a week and then I had to dig into things I needed: linen, shoes, collars, coats. It all went to the rag man and we even struck up a kind of friendship. His shop was at the corner of Tre Re, near the post office, and I would stop to talk to him on the way from my lodgings toward Piazza del Duomo.

Finally, I came to the end of all my things. As much as I had scanned the heavens in the meantime trying to think how to get myself out of this urgent predicament, not a single idea had come to me. One morning I met Colonel Giorgi coming from Boulogne in France; he, too, on his way to Germany and hoping to become a general quickly.

'Join the army administration,' he said, 'I promise I'll get you a good post and you'll become rich in no time.'

'What does one do in the army?' I said.

'In the army we conquer Europe, we court the most beautiful women in the world, we get paid very well, we spread a lot of glory all around and we march on.'

'Yes, but on whose behalf do you conquer Europe?'

'How should I know? Do you think it makes sense to ask?'

'My dear Alessandro, I shall not join the army, not even as a broom-pusher.'

'What a shame! And I was hoping to make something of you!'

'Perhaps I wouldn't have measured up, Alessandro! You had better concentrate on looking after yourself. You'll become a general sooner.'

'Just two more battles to rid me of a couple of old men and I'll be one by right. My allies are the Russian and Austrian bullets; that's the way to live in harmony with everyone. But you, now, are you really so bothered by us poor soldiers?'

'No Alessandro; I admire you, but I'm not capable of imitating you.'

'Oh, I see. You do need a certain toughness of the muscles, yes. Tell me, do you have news of Bruto Provedoni?'

'Excellent, if I may say. He is living with his sister of eighteen or nineteen, Aquilina, do you remember? He acts as a father to her; he's building up a small dowry and he earns his living giving lessons in town. Recently, with what he inherited from his brother Grifone, who died in Ljubljana when he fell from a roof, Bruto bought the house from his other siblings for himself and his sister. Now he no longer has to put up with being squeezed into his own house with spiteful, raggedy tenants. If he can just arrange a decent marriage for Aquilina I don't think there will be a happier man in the world.'

'You see how it is with us soldiers? We can be happy even without legs!'

'Very good, Alessandro; but I have no wish at all to lose my legs. They're a capital to be invested wisely or held on to.'

'So I can't help you in any way? You know, I could come up with thirty *scudi* or so; but not more, you see, because I'm not the thriftiest soldier, between gaming and women and what not, the pay tends to go. But wait, now that I think of it: would you be willing to try the civil service?'

The good Colonel could not see beyond the army; he had forgotten that just a quarter of an hour before I'd told him the tale of my entire career in the Department of Finance and my resignation as Intendente. Perhaps he believed that Finance was nothing more than a sub-office of the army, providing them with meals, clothing and enough funds to withstand assaults from the Pharaoh and *bassetta* tables. When I said I'd be happy with any employment that wasn't public, he made a face like a man forced to withdraw the better part of his esteem and yet his eminent kindness did not waver.

'I have a landlady in Milan,' he began.

'Oh yes, like the one you had in Genoa.'

'No, anything but! That one was as stingy as a druggist, while this other is more splendid than a minister. I had to steal a cat from that one; this one, if I wanted to, I could get her to give me a diamond every day. She's as rich as Croesus and she's been around in her time, but now that she's got a nice inheritance she's settled down and is considered a real lady; there's no peach bloom on her cheeks, but she's still attractive and can be charming, above all at the theatre when she gets a little excited. Well! She's taken such a huge fancy to me that every time I pass through Milan she wants me to stay with her; she even told me in confidence that if she were twenty years old instead of thirty, she'd like to go off to war with me.'

'And what has this lady to do with me?'

'Oh, the Devil! Everything! She's very well connected at the highest levels and can put in a useful word for you in connection with that post you want. And if a private job suits you better, I believe her estate is grand enough to offer work to you as well.'

'Remember, I don't want to steal anybody else's bread, and if I eat it, I want to earn it by my own toil.'

'Oh, don't worry, you needn't have any qualms on that score. You're probably thinking of our great farms in Friuli, where so often the steward gets rich behind the master's back without lifting a finger. Well, my friend, they know a thing or two in Milan! They pay well, but they want to be served well; the accountant gets fat but the master doesn't want to grow thin as a result. I know how these things work here!'

The plan didn't displease me and, although I had no great faith in all-powerful letters of recommendation or in the good Colonel's splendid lady, I was aware that I could do little alone and might as well try relying on the help of others. I went home to brush my coat for the meeting, which was to take place on the morrow. I, too, had recourse to the splendour of my landlady for a dab of polish to shine up my boots and I laid out on a chair the last shirt remaining to me, apart from the one on my back. Its whiteness was delightful and consoled me for the meagreness of the rest.

The next morning the colonel's orderly came to tell me that the lady was very pleased to meet me, but preferred I present myself in the evening, for her day was going to be a busy one. I looked at my boots and my shirt, sorry not to have stayed in bed to preserve their original freshness until the solemn moment. But then I thought: in the evening the fine points matter less, and anyway an ex-Intendente ought to possess reserves of liveliness and culture sufficient to make a lady forget the overwhelming modesty of his attire, and so I told the man that I would come to the house about eight, and not much later I went out. It was breakfast time, but I let it pass without feeling in my pockets, in heroic deference to the coming hour of luncheon. When this arrived I put a hand in and pulled out four *soldi*, worth altogether some fifteen centimes of a franc. I hadn't known I was so poor, in truth; squaring the circle looked like a far easier problem than getting luncheon out of such a miserable sum. But then I hadn't been Intendente for nothing: who better than I knew how to balance income with expenses? And so, clinging to my courage, I tried. One *soldo* of bread; two of something savoury, and one of aquavit, to fill my stomach and prepare it for the evening visit. Oh Lord, but what was one *soldo* of bread to a man who hadn't touched food for twenty-four hours? I recounted: two *soldi* of bread, one of pecorino and the same of *racagna*, as the Lombards call their aquavit. Then I decided that one *soldo* of pecorino was a preconception, an aristocratic notion of dividing bread from what went with it. Better three *soldi* of bread.

And so I boldly entered a baker's shop, bought my three *soldi* worth of buns and finished them off in four bites. I noticed, somewhat baffled, that I didn't feel the slightest hint of thirst and so, betraying the *racagna*, I got myself another bun and put it where the others were. After this brief diversion, my teeth were still very restless, and as they gathered up the last crumbs that had escaped, were whining among themselves in alarm, 'Is the party already finished?'

'Finished!' said I, and my stomach felt even more alarmed than my teeth. I then permitted myself a fair trick of the imagination that I'd often used before to fool my appetite: I reviewed all those friends from whom I could have asked luncheon, had they been in Milan. The Abbé Parini, dead six years (and a light eater himself); Lucilio, in exile; Ugo Foscolo, Professor of Eloquence at Pavia – of all my old acquaintances, I couldn't find a one. My landlady, when she'd given me the boot polish the night before, had hooked her big nose in a certain way that meant, 'Away with you and your bad jokes!'

There was still Colonel Giorgi, but I confess I felt ashamed, just as I think I would have been ashamed before the others had they been in Milan, and should have preferred to die of hunger rather than let Ugo Foscolo buy me a coffee and cream. Still, it was a consolation to be able to think while starvation gnawed; and when I had exhausted that pastime I was unhappier than before; and felt even worse, passing through Piazza Mercanti, when I saw it was just five o'clock. 'Another three hours!' I feared I might not make it to the hour of the visit still alive, or cut a very famished figure. Therefore, I tried to distract myself with another ploy, thinking of all those people from whom I could have loans, gifts, aid, at will. Spiro, my brother-in-law; my friends in Bologna; Colonel Giorgi's thirty *scudi*; the Grand Vizier . . . By Jove! Whether it was the hunger or something, or a special favour from Providence, I paused to think about the Grand Vizier that day. I remembered I did indeed have a bill of exchange for a very large sum, signed in an Arabic hieroglyphic I couldn't understand at all. But the house of Apostulos had many agents in Constantinople and some influence with the Armenian bankers who were fleecing the Sultan of the time. And so I raced to my rooms with no thoughts of my appetite, wrote a letter to Spiro, enclosed the bill and happily took it to the post.

On my way back through Piazza Mercanti, the clock was striking a quarter to eight and I headed off to my appointment. But I'd left the hopes connected to the Grand Vizier at the post and now that the solemn and fatal moment neared, hunger made itself felt again. Do you know what I dared to think of then? I thought of the rich Bolognese meals of the previous year and felt happier than I did now on an empty stomach. I comforted myself thinking that I was alone and that chance had spared la Pisana having to share my misery. Chance? I could not let that word by. Chance, more often than not when you study it, is manufactured by men; and therefore I worried, not wrongly, that forgetfulness, reserve and perhaps some other sweetheart had cooled la Pisana's ardour for me.

'But can I honestly complain?' my thoughts went on. 'If she loves me less, is that not fair? What was I doing all last year?'

What can I say? It all seemed very fair and reasonable, but my suspicion that la Pisana had forgotten me, abandoned me forever, hammered at least as hard as did the hunger. This was no longer the furious, jealous frenzy of the past, but a bitter despair that left me with no wish to live. Beaten by these various types of pain, I went upstairs, where I found the Colonel at home reading the weekly reports of his captains, smoking the way I used to smoke when I was Intendente and watering his throat from time to time with good Brescia anisette.

'Excellent, Carlo,' he said, offering me a chair. 'Pour yourself a glass; I'm nearly finished.'

I thanked him and sat down, glancing around the room to see if there was some bread or cake or some other substance to marry with the anisette in restoring my stomach's peace. There was nothing whatsoever. I poured myself a brimming glass of that healing liqueur and tossed it back and I could feel a new spirit entering me. But we know what happens when an old spirit and a new begin to wrestle, above all on an empty stomach. What happened was that my head began to reel and when I got up to follow the Colonel I was as merry and loquacious as I had been dull and surly when I sat down. My soldier friend took this as a good omen, and as we climbed the stairs he urged me on: women of middle age with little time to lose like their men merry, quick and bold, he said. Really! I was so merry I nearly stubbed my nose on the top step, and worse; in my case, along with those other qualities, I always develop one – frankness – that usually leads to my first blunder. When the footman opened the door and the Colonel led me into the entryway, I was dancing and weaving so that I hardly seemed to touch the floor.

'Who would ever think,' said I in a very loud voice, 'who would ever think that I am absolutely swooning with hunger?'

The footman turned to stare at me in wonder, however much the rules of his job forbade it. Alessandro elbowed me in the side.

'Daft, you are!' said my friend. 'You and your pranks.'

'Oh, I swear this is no prank, but . . . oh, oh, ouch!'

The Colonel had given me such a pinch that I could not continue our dispute, but had to break off with this triple interjection. This time the footman turned to stare at me with full justification.

'Nothing, nothing,' said the Colonel. 'I stepped on one of his corns!'

It was a fine reply on the wing and it didn't seem the moment to defend my foot's virginity, because we had just then entered the signora's room. By now the Colonel had understood the danger, but the ball was on and we must dance, and a veteran of Marengo does not know the meaning of retreat.

In a dead, reddish light that filtered down from lamps hanging from the ceiling and shaded with red silk, I saw – or thought I saw – the goddess. She was reclining on one of those curule chairs that Parisian taste has dug up from Republican Roman custom, as popular under the reign of Augustus as they are under Napoleon. Her short, revealing robe was draped around a body that was dubiously firm, but certainly very opulent: an abundant half of her bosom was bare. I didn't look at her with much pleasure, but felt rather an itch in my teeth, an urge to devour. Through the anisette fumes I spied flesh and all I had left was that barbarous flicker of good sense that cannibals possess. The lady seemed to be very pleased with the good impression she'd made on me and she asked the Colonel whether I was the young man looking for employment. The Colonel hastened to say yes and did his best to distract the lady's attention from me. Instead, she seemed ever more captivated by my fine bearing and, ignoring the Colonel, kept observing and addressing her remarks to me.

'Carlo Altoviti, I believe,' said the lady, making a most gracious effort of memory.

I bowed, becoming so red I felt I would explode. It was stomach cramps.

'I believe I've seen that name, if I'm not mistaken, in the rolls of high government officials last year,' she said.

I exhaled heavily in memory of the blowhard I was reputed to be in Bologna and stood up straight, my chest puffed out, while the Colonel replied that indeed I had served as Intendente of Finance in Bologna.

'And I'm to understand,' said the lady in a low voice, leaning towards me, 'the new government . . . the rules . . . in short, you have resigned!'

'Yes,' said I with great self-importance, without having understood a word.

Now the room began to fill up with counts and countesses, princes and abbés, one by one announced in the footman's resounding voice. A great deluge of *Dons* was drumming in my ears and if I may say so quite impartially, that clipped, nasal Milanese dialect does nothing to clear a drunken man's mind. Soon the Colonel approached the Countess (for so was the mistress of the house) to take our leave, for I could not hold out much longer. She whispered in his ear that everything was all arranged and that I should go by myself to the counting house the next day, where they would assign me a job and tell me the conditions of my employment. I thanked her with a bow, dragging my feet so that a dozen of those stiff, silent dons turned to look at me in wonder. I then clicked my heels smartly at the Colonel's side and headed out of the room. The fresh air did me good, for it quickly cleared my brain, and among the things I felt was some shame at the state I realized I was in and the bad impression I feared I'd made in the lady's salon. However, I still had a fair streak of frankness in me and began to complain about how hungry I was.

'That's your problem?' said the Colonel. 'Let us go to Rebecchino and there you will get what you want.' I don't, in truth, recall whether he said Rebecchino, but I believe so and that even back then that grand Milanese trattoria was already in existence.

I let him take me there and stuffed my belly without drawing breath or saying a word, and as my stomach slowly settled down my head did, too. My shame was mounting as the moment of payment drew near and I was just getting ready to play out the penniless man's usual comedy – feel in my pockets with great surprise, reproach myself for being so deucedly careless as to have lost or forgotten my purse – when a more honest shame held me back. I blushed to think I'd been more truthful in my drunken state than now, and confessed my poverty fairly and squarely to Alessandro. He was furious that I'd hidden it from him up until then and insisted I take those thirty *scudi* of his (twenty-eight after the meal was paid); and made me promise to come to him for anything else I needed, for although he might only have a little, he would help me with all his heart.

'In the meantime, tomorrow I must leave for Germany without fail,' he said, 'but I depart with the hope these few *scudi* will suffice until you get your first pay, which will come to you soon, perhaps even tomorrow. Chin up, Carlino, and don't forget me. This evening I must meet with the captains of my regiment to give them some orders, but tomorrow, before I go, I will come by and embrace you.'

What a fine Alessandro he was! There was a mixture of soldierly roughness and feminine kindness in him that touched me; he lacked the so-called civic virtues of that time (I wouldn't know what to call them now), but his many other virtues were so superabundant that he could be excused. At dawn the next morning, when I was still asleep, he was there to kiss me goodbye. I wept, unsure I would ever see him again; he wept at my pig-headed wish to remain an obscure pen-pusher in Milan when I could come along with him and become a general without much effort. Few hearts were the equal of his and yet he heartily wished death on all his colleagues, so as to put a higher rank on his hat and have three hundred more francs a month.

Such is brotherly love as taught – or rather imposed – on even good and merciful souls by the Napoleonic government!

When the time was right I dressed as nicely as I could and went to the Countess Migliana's counting house. A fat, round, clean-shaven fellow of patriarchal appearance and manners received me, you might say, with open arms: he was the chief accountant and secretary of the lady. The first thing he did was take me to the cash box, where sixty gleaming new *scudi* were handed over to me, my salary for the first three months. He then conducted me to a desk where I saw many crumpled, torn and greasy volumes, and in the middle one large book, which you could at least touch without dirtying yourself. He told me I would be master of the household, the Countess's major-domo, for the time being, until a post more suited to my qualities arose. Indeed, to come down from Intendente of Bologna to the administrator of a cupboard was no small plunge, but despite my patrician Venetian origins in the ancient Roman nobility of Torcello, pride has rarely been a defect of mine, especially not when need speaks louder. I tend to share the view of Plutarch, who supervised the street-sweepers of his home town of Chaeronea, they say, with the same dignity as if he were presiding over the Olympic Games.

My post meant I was to dwell in the palazzo and live close at hand with the Countess. I wasn't sure whether I liked that or not, but at least I hoped to rid the lady of the bad impression she must have gained of me the day before. I found, instead, that she was very pleased with me and with my noble and polite manners; in truth, I was very surprised to learn this, never imagining that the ladies and gentlemen of Milan appreciated drunkards so much! She treated me more as an equal than as a mistress to her major-domo, a delicacy on her part that reconciled me to my new condition and made me write grateful, enthusiastic letters about her to Aglaura, Lucilio, Bruto Provedoni, the Colonel and la Pisana. I hoped to avenge myself thus on la Pisana for neglecting me and to try to provoke a little jealousy in her. I hadn't yet been duly enlightened by that bizarre retaliation she'd taken for my imagined infidelity. After five or six days, however, I realized that la Pisana would not be entirely wrong to be jealous of the Countess. The lady behaved towards me in such a way that either I was a great fool or I was being invited into confidences that are not generally part of a major-domo's duties. What can I say? I won't try to excuse myself or hide the truth: I sinned.

The Countess's salon was one of the most crowded in Milan, but despite the lady's cheerful temperament, the conversation never seemed carefree or animated. A certain mistrust, a certain Spanish hauteur, kept the gentlemen's lips tight and their brows grave. And then, it seemed to me, young people were scarce and the few who did come were pitifully dull and dim-witted. If our country's hopes resided in them, you could only make the sign of the cross and put your faith in God. Even the Countess, who in intimate discussion or in the bosom of the family was very lively and even somewhat reckless, became unsmiling and ill-at-ease in her salon, looking at you in a dull, severe way and moving her lips as if she were more ready to bite than to speak or to smile. I understood nothing, and least of all then, when Italy's ups and downs had instilled in me a ferocious will to live.

But two weeks later I did understand something. A guest from Venice was announced and there, to my great astonishment and after many years, was the Avvocato Ormenta. He didn't recognize me, because my age and changed appearance meant I no longer resembled the student at Padua; I pretended not to know him, because I had no wish to take up with him again for any reason. It seemed he had come to Milan to ask the Countess's protection for himself and his family, and, in fact, during those days there was a greater to and fro than usual of French generals and high Italian dignitaries. Several ministers of the new kingdom had spent hours closeted with the Avvocato and I sought in vain to learn why one of the leading advisors of the Austrian government in Venice should be involved in the affairs of the French government in Italy. This, too, I was soon to understand. The clever Avvocato had foreseen the battle of Austerlitz and its consequences and, by passing from Darius' camp to that of Alexander, he hoped to make up for some of the damages the Austrian defeat would cost him. If it should surprise you to find a feminine hand in such important intrigues, history says this: women never interfere so much in matters of State as in times of military rule. Greek mythology was well aware of this when it mixed Venus and Mars in its tales.

The first reports of the victory at Austerlitz reached Milan just before Christmas and caused a great stir. The impression grew when we learned of the Treaty of Pressburg, signed on Santo Stefano,[2] under which the Kingdom of Italy extended its borders to the River Isonzo. For a moment I forgot about the problem of liberty and simply rejoiced at the thought I would see Venice, la Pisana, my sister, Spiro and their children, and all those dear places where I'd tarried in childhood and which were still so much a part of me. I wouldn't like to repeat to you the letters that la Pisana wrote me then or I might bring a great heap of envy on me. How her deep yearnings corresponded to her neglect of me during the past months was difficult to understand, but my elation in the present won out over all else. No thoughts beyond this, I went up to the Countess with a tear in my eye and declared that after the Treaty of Pressburg . . .

'What's this? What difference does the Treaty of Pressburg make?' the lady shouted, her eyes narrowing viperishly.

'The difference is that I can no longer be Intendente or major-domo.'

'Oh, you are a rogue! And this is how you tell me? I've been a fine woman to put my . . . my confidence in you! Get out from under my feet and may I never lay eyes on you again!'

But I was so beside myself with happiness that her scolding felt like a caress, and it was only later, thinking it over, that I understood how indecent it was of me to take leave of her in that way. When a favour has been accepted, it must never be forgotten; and the man who does forget deserves a kick in the behind. If the Countess was not more unkindly to me, I know now that the indulgence was all hers, and therefore I never had the heart to join her detractors when I heard the bad things said about her that you will shortly hear.

La Pisana welcomed me to Venice with all the noisy joy she was capable of in her moments of enthusiasm. I had asked that a small apartment be left free in my house and she wanted to stay with me at all costs; that impulse did seem strange, considering the tenderness and care she had recently devoted to her husband. Stranger still was that old Navagero, desperate about his wife's decision to leave and the excellent nursing he was about to lose, sent word to me in secret begging me to go and live with him, that he would be very pleased to see me. This went well beyond ordinary Venetian permissiveness and I understood that the apoplexy had drained him of all his jealous humours. However, I did not wish to accept the gentleman's kind invitation and I told la Pisana of my qualms, asking her to remain with her husband against her wishes. What it lost in ease, our love would gain in zest and freshness. Spiro and Aglaura also wanted me to stay with them, but I had stuck my head in my little house at San Zaccaria and I did not want to move from there.

And there I lived, heedless of everything and blessedly happy until the spring, staying as far away as I could from the Countess of Fratta and her son, and enjoying the best hours of the day in the company of my Pisana. Her compassion for that doddering old carcass Navagero was so extreme that it sometimes piqued my jealousy. Quite often it would happen that after we'd had some dull and unwelcome visitor and were finally alone for a moment, she would rush off to change her husband's bandage or pour out his potion. This excess of zeal annoyed me and I could not help muttering some fervent prayer to the heavens that the poor sick fellow be admitted to the glories of Paradise. There's no way around it. Women are lovers, wives, mothers, sisters, but above all they are nurses. No dog of a man is so filthy, contemptible and repellent that should he fall ill and have no one to help him, he will not find some woman to be his merciful, caring guardian angel. A woman may lose all honour, religion, shame; she may neglect her most sacred duties and the sweetest and most natural of her affections, but she will never lose her instincts of pity and devotion when her neighbour is suffering. Had woman not taken her necessary place in creation as progenitor of men, our ills and infirmities would as necessarily have demanded her as our solace. And then in Italy we have so many maladies that our women are, you might say, busy from birth to death ministering either to our souls or bodies.

Blessed are their fingers glazed with balsam and honey. Blessed their lips that spout the fire that burns and heals.

My other acquaintances in Venice paid little attention to me, except for Venchieredo, who tried in every way he could to gain my confidence, but I kept my distance with all the caution my excellent memory suggested. Of the Frumier family, the Knight of Malta seemed to have been buried alive; while the other, who had married the Contarini girl and risen in the department of Finance, had got himself named secretary. Ambition drove him on to a career that his new wealth would have made it easy to renounce; that goose-head believed that now he could put his signature on a report, he could look down on the Horses of San Marco and Men of the Hours on the piazza clock tower. It also came as some surprise to me to learn that he, as well as Venchieredo, Ormenta and various others who'd been employed by the late government were also tolerated by the new, either in their old offices or in new ones that were quite important and sensitive. However, as I had nothing to share with either the outgoing or the incoming, I didn't torture my brain to determine why. What did bother me at times was that many of my friends (and those of Lucilio and Amilcare, and of Spiro Apostulos, as well as my brother-in-law himself) treated me somewhat coolly. I didn't feel I had any less reason to deserve their friendship and didn't even mention the matter to them, but I did say something to Aglaura and she avoided the question, saying that Spiro was very occupied with his business and had no time for parties and ceremonies.

One day in the Piazza I saw a face I never met without a certain unease: Captain Minato, I mean. I tried to slip away, but he stopped me thirty yards away with an 'Oh!' of surprise and pleasure, and it fell to me to politely down a great long draught of his Corsican nonsense.

'Oh, I say!' said he. 'I've just been to Milan and I must congratulate you. You, too, were there, just in time to inherit one of my beauties.'

'What beauties are these you refer to?'

'Confound it, is the Countess Migliana not a beauty? Ever since I made her travel back from Rome and Ancona she's seemed a little wilted, but if you didn't know her before, you'd say she still looks quite splendid.'

'Who? The Countess Migliana is not . . .'

'Yes, she's Emilio Tornoni's friend, and my little trophy of '96! So many years have passed!'

'Yes, they have! Impossible! You're telling tales! Your adventuress had another name and she possessed neither the fortune nor the social connections of the Countess Migliana!'

'Oh, when it comes to names, I can assure you that the Countess has never borne the same one for more than a month, out of the most delicate consideration for each one of her lovers. As for her wealth, you yourself must know that she only began to receive her inheritance a few years ago. In any event society is much too shrewd to deny entrance to those who can pay, and well. You've seen the sort of people who surround the Countess now, at least in the hours she receives. Well, they are the ones who, for the price of a fresh hand of varnish or some nice alms for pious causes, agree to draw a veil over the past and take the lost lamb into the great bosom of the aristocracy. What do they call it in Milan? The Biscottesque aristocracy!'[3]

'And therefore?' I said.

'And therefore you might well say that, having been majordomo in her house . . . I don't know quite how to put this . . . you didn't find the lost lamb so loyal to the fold as not to wander from time to time into some solitary pasture, some wanton pastime, and . . .'

'Sir, you have no right to demolish a lady's honour or –'

'Sir, you have no right to prevent me from talking when everyone is doing so.'

'You come from Milan, but here in Venice –'

'Here in Venice, sir, they are talking even more than in Milan!'

'What? I hope this is but your imagination!'

'The news, from what they say, arrived with the Avvocato Ormenta, who praised your love affair as an opportune conversion to the cause of the Holy Faith.'

'The Avvocato Ormenta, you say?'

'Yes, yes, Ormenta! Don't you know him?'

'Alas, I do.' Here I began to ponder why, having so forgotten me that he didn't even recognize me, he should now take the trouble to spread such unpleasant chatter about me. It did not occur to me that he, in turn, might have thought I did not recognize *him*, and that when my name sounded from time to time on the Countess's lips it helped make a certainty of his suspicion that I looked something like young Carlo. People of his ilk seek only to spread distrust and discord: this was evidently the reason for the malicious slander. As for the rest, I hadn't the least interest in knowing more, but now quite convinced that Minato had done me a great service in opening my eyes to these falsehoods going around, I took my leave of him with less relief than usual and went back to la Pisana to gnaw at my anger somewhat less bitterly.

That day I found a visitor with my lady I had not expected: Raimondo Venchieredo. After all the words we'd exchanged about him, after all the evil thoughts I'd had about his intentions towards la Pisana, after the plots he'd spun to trap her using Doretta and Rosa, I was very, very surprised to find her in his company. And what is more, she knew the enmity between myself and Raimondo was still hot, and that alone was reason to keep him away. The clever fellow decided it was best to get out of my way quickly, and disappeared after a deep bow, impertinent as could be. As soon as he was gone we began to bicker.

'Why do you receive such types?'

'I receive whomever I like!'

'No signora, you do not!'

'We shall see who orders me around!'

'I do not order, I pray you!'

'Prayer suits those who have the right to pray.'

'I believe I've acquired that right after many years of penitence!'

'A rich penitence it was!'

'What do you mean by that?'

'I know what I mean – and I say no more!'

We went on like that for a while in one of those monosyllabic squabbles that are dialogues in the form of bites and scratches, but I could get no more from her.

I stormed off in a fury, but as angry as I was I found her even colder and more sullen when I returned. Not only wouldn't she explain herself, but she avoided any argument that might lead to declarations of love, and as for love itself, she scorned it as if it were sacrilege. The third or fourth time we met, things grew worse; once again I found Raimondo in her rooms, playing with her little dog – and the dog began to bark at me! The first time I endured it, but the second I utterly lost control (I could see that from the smug and mocking look on Raimondo's face) and ran down the stairs, pursued by the howls of that filthy little dog. Oh, these beasts are barbarously frank! In the name of their master they make and withdraw declarations of love as precise as a hair's breadth. And I was so wild with rage that, for me, mistress and dog were one thing to wrap up together and toss in the laguna. And you say I pride myself on my mild and accommodating nature! What an impetuous hothead would have done in my place, I do not know.

The one point that did seem clear was that la Pisana had betrayed me and that she was infatuated with Raimondo Venchieredo. That he was the cause of my woes I could not say for sure, but I wanted to believe it and unload the scathing hatred I felt on someone. To exasperate my delirium, I had a letter from Lucilio so cold and enigmatic that I nearly tore it up. Did all my friends and enemies mean to take me to the brink of despair? And this blow came from Lucilio, the friend whose judgement I placed above all others, the one who kept my conscience in order and helped me preserve the strength and constancy that sometimes failed me: it was a blow that knocked my very sense of misfortune out of me. What had I not done, what would I not do, to keep Lucilio's esteem? And now, without telling me whys and wherefores, without questioning me or asking me to justify myself, he seemed to have withdrawn that esteem. What dreadful crimes had I committed? What treachery, cowardice, murder, had earned me such a sentence? My mind was too disordered to grasp it. I wracked my brain, I sighed, I wept with rage and humiliation; shame bowed my head, a shame I knew I didn't deserve. But temperaments like mine, too sensitive, react this way: we suffer the unjust accusation as if it were guilt itself. Brazen virtue is not in my nature.

In such moments Aglaura was capable of soothing my sorrows with indescribable sweetness. For the first time I saw how good is that calm, devoted affection that doesn't draw back when we err, or change direction with opinions. My good sister and her little children always smiled on me, no matter how cruel and hostile society was. Wordlessly, they defended me before Spiro, for how could he turn that grim and twisted face on a man forever being kissed and embraced by his own wife and children?

The more my old friends' trust shrank, the more I was pursued with a thousand courtesies by the Avvocato Ormenta, his son, old Venchieredo, Padre Pendola and their confederates. The Reverend Padre had become the spiritual director of that home for reformed women administered by the Avvocato, and every time our paths crossed there were broad smiles and a great doffing of hats that turned my stomach, because it seemed to say, 'You're one of us again! Very good! We thank you!' It was all I could do to dodge them and spare myself all that salaaming, but people saw them, including some who were suspicious of me, and the slander took off and there was no way I could rid myself of it, like those boggy quicksands where, once you fall in, you may kick as much as you like but you will keep on sinking deeper. I was ready to give up: as much as I never relent against certain enemies and clearly defined trials, I'm unable to face the hidden trick or the mysterious trap. I yearned for a living death, that vegetative state that briefly prolongs the body's decay after it has smothered the soul's prospects. Nothing around me seemed worth a day measured out in sighs and sobs; I was nothing and good at nothing; why, then, think of others and have my heart broken more? If I didn't contemplate killing myself, I sank down voluntarily and let myself be crushed by the weight rolling over me. I had all the suicide's weariness and none of his fury.

In such a discouraged state we are often weak and credulous before the attentions, however interested or malign, of others.

Faced with a good man, we're tempted to say, 'Look out, the depraved are better than you!' A childish vendetta, a moment of puerile pleasure that does us perpetual harm. The Ormentas, father and son, redoubled their attentions and courtesies; apparently I had some credit with them, or their faction had grown so impoverished they would go to any length and expense to gain a convert. They surrounded me with enticers and procurers; I remained unshakeable. Worthless I might be, but not to them. My friends' injustice was killing me, but I would never agree to point the tip of a finger against them. Beyond those misled, unjust friends of mine stood eternal justice: ever present, never misleading, never misled.

Burning inside me, the belief I might resist offered me a sliver of courage, a dash of force. I looked at myself again to see if having been forsaken by all, betrayed in love, without friendships, had truly left me as worthless and powerless as I thought. In a flash my memory filled up with all the pleasures, the toil, the pains, of my youth: I watched that spark of faith that had guided me for so many years to a distant, honest goal come alight; I saw a path edged with thorns, but eased by the shining heavens and a comforting breeze of hope, that crossed the abyss of death airy and straight as a ray of light and then climbed to join the sun, intelligence and ordering force of the universe. My belief became enthusiasm; my weakness, strength; my solitude, boundless. I saw that the opinions of others were nothing next to the armour of my conscience, true seat of all my punishment and recompense. The world has a thousand eyes, ears and tongues, but only conscience has virtue, courage, faith.

When I emerged, I was a man through and through. From that indestructible fortress that was my conscience I looked out proudly on those whose silent contempt I had endured. I thought of Lucilio and for the first time had the courage to say, 'Prophet, you are mistaken! Wise man, you are wrong!' Only those who have known the sublime joy of the innocent man persecuted can appreciate how much gladness this courage gave me. Above all I was glad for that honest instinct that – however pinched and desperate I had been – had made me reject the lure of the false and the depraved. The weak man who weeps and wails when they drag him to the scaffold, but refuses to betray his friends and gain a pardon: I believe he is more admirable than the strong man who gives himself over to the hangman with a smile on his face. Tremble, but triumph: even the craven can hear this command. To tremble is of the body. Triumph belongs to the soul, which bows the body under the will's might. Tremble, but triumph. After two victories you'll tremble no more; you will watch the thunderbolt flash, unblinking.

So I did. I trembled at length; I wept, despite myself, at the friends who'd forsaken me; I tore at my breast; my heart beat fast, as if impatient to be done with its labours. I despaired of my love, who, after a thousand sweet words, after I'd followed her, laughing and winsome, along the flowering paths and capricious ups and downs of youth, had abandoned me alone, widowed, heartbroken on those very few steps through the dark wood of real, hard, militant life. Oh, my dear Pisana! So many tears I shed for you! Tears that once would have shamed me as weak and feminine, but in which I now glory as proof of a constancy that gave me some trace of grandeur and virtue! You were like the wave that comes and goes at the sandy foot of the rocks. Strong as that rock I waited for you, not scorning your affronts, accepting your kisses and embraces with modesty. Heaven made you as fickle as the moon and me as steady as the sun; but as the two revolve their lights meet, they reflect one another, they merge. In the great peace of the elements, sun and moon lie together eternally gleaming and harmonious. Pindaric flights! These are Pindaric flights. But not for nothing was the swallow given its wings, the lightning its flash, the human mind its supreme quickness of thought.

Yes, I wept and suffered greatly then, but my conscience was at peace and my faith pure. I wept and suffered for others; in myself I felt no sin or guilt. But one of nature's great injustices towards us is that conscience, no matter how much at peace, cannot boldly fight off undeserved imputations; blame from others acts as punishment on us. Discouragement, pain, humiliation, long battles between a mild and sensitive nature and a furious, adverse destiny: all this deeply shook my health. I learned then how true it is that our passions contain the germs of so many illnesses that afflict humanity. The doctors called it inflammation of the veins or congestion of the liver; I knew very well what it was, but said nothing, knowing my condition was incurable. From afar I watched my hour approach, minute by minute, beat by beat of my pulse. My smile was resigned, the man who had no hopes but in eternity and to eternity commended his innocent soul. Forgive me, O peevish moralists, if you think I was too indulgent with myself. But all by myself I had made up a rule quite different from yours, a rule, alas, that in your books stank of heresy: that anything that caused no ill to others did not count as wrongdoing by me, and that if I did wrong, I would repent, facing without fear that justice that never dies, which reasons not by words, but by actions. Although you surrounded my bed with chains, phantoms and demons, I assure you I saw nothing but benign ghosts veiled by a blue haze of heavenly melancholy, angels with sad smiles, far horizons in which the spirit dissolves like the cloud that disperses bit by bit; lightly, lustrously filling up all the ether's infinite spaces.

I had never before seen death so close, or rather, I had never contemplated it so calmly. I did not find it ugly, fearful or distressing. Today, so many years later, death is closer and more certain. I see that same face shadowed by a cloud of hope and melancholy; a wraith both mysterious and merciful; a mother, courageous and uncompromising, who murmurs the fatal consolation in our ears. We will wait or atone or repose; but the agitated, vain struggles of life will be no more. There in the lap of eternal truth, if you are guilty, you will fear; if innocent, hope and sleep. What sleep was never compensated by dreams? Life repeats itself always. One night's sleep rests and restores a man; one man's death is an instant of sleep within humanity.

And so I approached death, Aglaura and her grieving comfort on one side; Spiro on the other, no longer able to maintain his hard suspicions before a dying man's utter serenity. Before the shadows of the tomb, no one is deluded or foolish; we all gain enough lucidity so that all the wrongs and virtues of a life flash by in an instant. Gaze on that eternal night, calm and sure, and you will find in yourself the image of God: He who does not fear eternal punishment or the whirling maelstrom of chaos or the unimaginable abyss of the void. I should say I must have had a rather eloquent self-defence written on my brow, for Spiro, just to look at me, burst into tears – and he certainly didn't have a weakling's frail nerves; and his Greek temperament was more inclined to the judge's rigour than the guilty man's shame and penitence. That was my first reward for my resolve. That my peaceful aspect, calm voice and clear gaze alone could win over that creature of fire and steel was a real triumph. He neither asked my pardon nor did I give it, but we understood each other without a word; our hands met and the surety of death clinched our return to friendship.

The doctors said little in my presence, but I knew by their silence and their various opinions that they despaired of me. I tried to use my last days as best I could, showing Spiro and my sister the experience of my life and how my sentiments had been shaped; and how affection, friendship, love of virtue and of *patria* had burst forth in me chaotically and then with time became purified and edified my soul. I saw things so clearly then that I was, you might say, a generation ahead of myself, and with all due modesty, the germs of Cesare Balbo's and Massimo d'Azeglio's[4] ideas were already there in my thoughts. Aglaura wept, Spiro bowed his head, the children stared at me, puzzled, and asked their mother why Uncle's voice was so weak, why he always wanted to sleep and never left his bed.

'Your turn to keep watch will come, children,' I said with a smile, and then to Spiro: 'Have no fear, for what I see now, many will soon see, and, in the end, all. Concord in thought leads to concord in deeds. The truth does not go down like the sun, but rises towards the eternal noonday. Every clairvoyant spirit that flies up there shines its prophetic light on a hundred other spirits.'

My words did not bring peace to Spiro; he felt my pulse and looked me anxiously in the eyes, seeking for that hidden cause of my illness that had escaped the doctors.

One day when we were alone he finally got up his courage and said to me: 'Carlo, tell me the truth! Are you unable to get well – or don't you wish to?'

'I cannot, no. I cannot!' I said.

Just at that moment Aglaura came rushing into the room to say that someone – someone very dear to me in the past – wanted to see me at all costs.

'Let her come in, let her come in,' I murmured, half-dismayed at the sudden wave of relief I felt. I could see through walls and read the mind of that dear soul who'd come to see me, and I think I was afraid of this almost superhuman flash of clairvoyance and worried I might expire at the abrupt resurgence of so much life.

Now la Pisana came in, her eyes fixed on me and me alone. She threw her arms around my neck without tears and without words; her laboured breathing and her wild, dazed eyes told me everything. Oh, there are moments in a life that memory recalls and will ever recall as if they were eternal, but can neither examine nor describe. If you could enter into the gossamer, airy little flame of a fire that is going out and imagine how it feels when a great rush of spirit floods in and brings it to life, perhaps you would understand the miracle that took place in my being. For a moment I was breathless with happiness, then my momentary drowsiness gave way and life came seething forth and I felt a blend of hot and cold run, healthy and sensuous, through my nerves and veins.

La Pisana refused to leave my bedside; thus she asked my forgiveness, and obtained it immediately and fully. What do I mean 'obtained'? A glance would have been enough! I now understood the true cause of my illness, which my pride had probably hidden from me. I felt life begin to come back and sent the doctors away, refusing their silly potions. La Pisana did not sleep at night, never left my room even for an instant, allowed no other hand but hers to touch my limbs, my clothes, my bed. In three days she became so pale and drawn she looked more ill than I did. So as not to see her suffer long, I focused all my will on getting well, shortening the course of my illness by several weeks; when the time came to convalesce I was in perfect health. Spiro and Aglaura were quite amazed: la Pisana seemed to expect no less, such was the power and sincerity of her love. Was there anything I wouldn't have forgiven her? Once again, it was like the other times. Lips were silent, hearts spoke: she gave me back my life and the chance to love her more. I was in her debt: her simplicity, tenderness and infinite love meant a great deal more than one day's thoughtless betrayal.

'Carlo,' she said to me one day when I was well enough to go out, 'the air of Venice doesn't suit you; you need to be in the country. Would you like to go and visit Monsignor my uncle at Fratta?'

What could I say to a proposal that so nicely responded to my most ardent desires? To go with la Pisana to revisit the haunts of our childish happiness would be Paradise in my eyes. I had a small sum of money set aside from the rent of my house over the past four years; living in the country would improve my finances: everything concurred to make the plan not only appealing but opportune. I also knew that Raimondo Venchieredo had remained in Venice, and I knew, too, of the low and dirty methods he had used to alert la Pisana to my affair with the Countess Migliana and turn la Pisana's vexation to his advantage. I had forgiven la Pisana, but not him, and I was sure I'd be overcome with rage were I to meet him. Two days went by and la Pisana didn't say anything about leaving, but I could see she was wrapped up in other thoughts and she seemed to be preparing for a long absence. Finally she appeared at my house with her trunk and said, 'Cousin, I'm ready. My husband isn't well yet, but his illness is now stable and the doctors tell me he may live many years. My sister, who comes out of the convent tomorrow—'

'What?' I exclaimed. 'Clara is leaving the order?'

'Didn't you know? Her convent has been suppressed; she's been given a pension and comes out tomorrow. Of course, she hasn't the least intention of renouncing her vows and she'll continue to fast her three Lents a year. But meanwhile she's agree to nurse my husband. I convinced her that Monsignor my uncle needs me, and my mother, who gets her own quid pro quo from my departure, has backed the plan with all her might.

'And what is your mother's quid pro quo in these travels of ours?'

'I've granted her not only the income, but the property of my dowry.'

'That's madness! What's left for you?'

'For me, there are the two lire a day my husband insists on giving me, despite his financial straits. In the country I can live like a great lady on that.'

'Pardon me, Pisana, but the sacrifice you've made for your mother seems to me both foolish and pointless. What good will it bring her to own the dowry as well as the income?'

'What good? I have no idea. Probably she'd like to spend it. It isn't up to me to do the accounts. My mother explained to me her sad situation; how her old age constantly requires new comforts, new expenses; the debts forever harassing her; and I also saw what those little whims of hers cost and I didn't want her to be forced to sell her mattress for two games of *tresette*. And so I said, "If that is what you want, so be it! But allow me to leave, because I need a breath of fresh air and to see our countryside again." "Go, go then, and may Heaven bless you, my dear daughter," my mother said. I think she was quite relieved to see me go, because I'd no longer be there to persuade Rinaldo to buy a new hat or a coat that was somewhat less indecent every once in a while, and so she would have a few more *zecchini* for herself. And so I went to a notary and the deed was drawn up and signed. But when I was just about to give it to my mother, you'll never guess what I asked her in return?'

'Oh, let's see. You asked for exclusive rights to Navagero's estate or that she give up all her claims on Fratta?'

'Nothing like that, Carlo. For some time now I've been itching with an indiscreet curiosity put in my head by that old gossip Faustina – you remember her. And so I asked my mother if she would swear to me, hand on heart, that I was not the daughter of Monsignor di Sant'Andrea.'

'Oh, to Hades with you! You crazy woman! And what did the Countess say?'

'She said what you said. She called me vulgar and crazy and refused to say anything. Oh, Carlo! Eight thousand ducats of mine gone and I didn't get a whit out of them, not even enough to satisfy my curiosity!'

This incident will give you an idea of la Pisana's temperament and upbringing, and also tell you something about Venetian customs in the past century. Here is a daughter, stealing the bread from her own mouth in majestic sacrifice, giving up her only property to permit her mother her vices, and what does she ask in return? An ugly confession and the dubious pleasure of satisfying a foolish curiosity. I say no more. To light up an entire painting we need open only a small window.

'And so,' I said to her, 'you are left with but two sorry, paltry lire a day, thanks to Navagero's miserable munificence. And if the old lunatic changes his mind you go straight to the poor house!'

'Oh, please!' said la Pisana. 'I'm young and strong, and anyway I'll be with you and you can count the cost of keeping me as my wages.'

Such an arrangement was very much in keeping with la Pisana's way of thinking and quite acceptable to me, only I would need some profession to increase my poor income until Navagero's coveted death put us on a more solid footing. For now, I wouldn't think about it; the important thing was to go away and recover my health completely. I had a hundred ducats in my bag; la Pisana insisted on giving me another two hundred she'd got from selling some of her jewellery, and with this great sum we happily prepared to leave.

Before departing from Venice I was lucky enough to see old Apostulos, now back from Greece, for the last time. He had become involved in one of the schemes of the day to liberate his country under the aegis of the so-called Phanariots,[5] the Greeks of Constantinople, and had been travelling far and wide on the pretext of business. Spiro, who leaned towards the younger faction (which would later become the main one and bring about the final war of independence), obeyed his father unwillingly in those second-rate plots, in which greedy half-Turkish Greek princes were always looking to make profits for themselves; and there was a certain coolness between father and son. Old Apostulos gave me news of my Grand Vizier. He'd been strangled, following that convenient system then popular in the Porte (as opposed to the European way, a thousand times more costly, of forcing them to step aside). His successor was willing to honour my bills of exchange, but since my credit amounted to seven million piastres and His Highness's treasury was not well-stocked just now, he preferred to pay me in a few years' time. And so, prospective millionaire with three hundred ducats in my pocket, I boarded the boat for Portogruaro with la Pisana and we arrived there on the second day, having broken a good many tow-ropes and lost a great deal of time changing the horses and scraping the sandy banks of the Lemene.

It was a long, happy trip. La Pisana, if I'm not mistaken, was twenty-eight years old and looked twenty, but in her heart she felt no more than fifteen. I, veteran of the Parthenopean War and ex-Intendente of Bologna, grew ever more boyish the closer I got to the Friuli. When we landed at Portogruaro I believe I was about to turn somersaults the way I used to do in the Frumiers' garden when I still had my milk teeth. Our elation was, however, mixed with some sorrow. Our old acquaintances were nearly all dead; among those of our own age or younger, very few were left in town. Fulgenzio, now doddering and dimwitted, was afraid of his own sons and had fallen under the spell of a clever, greedy maidservant who tyrannized him and whose avarice had enabled her to amass a tidy sum. Dottor Domenico fumed, but with all his great learnedness couldn't free his father from the witch's claws. Don Girolamo, who taught in the seminary and was a distinguished specimen of the lowland clergy, accepted the situation philosophically. His view was that they must wait patiently until the Lord touched his father's heart, but Domenico, who was in a hurry to get his hands on his purse, was not soothed by his brother's priestly consolations.

Fulgenzio departed this world a few days after we returned to the Friuli. Death came with a dreadful delirium in which he felt demons tearing his soul from his breast, and he clutched his housekeeper's hand so hard that she was just about to forgo the inheritance and leave him to the gravediggers. But greed made her hold fast. So much so that when her master died they had to tear her arm away from his frenzied fingernails. When the will was read, we learned she'd landed a fine sum of money in addition to what she'd stolen. The will also provided for numerous Masses and donations to churches and convents, and these good works were crowned by the imposing sum Fulgenzio left to build a sumptuous bell tower beside the Fratta church.

Thus he meant to apply the last coat of whitewash to his conscience and settle his accounts with God. There was no mention of any restitution to the House of Fratta; the impoverished heirs of the old lords would consider themselves lucky to be able to gaze on the new bell tower. Don Girolamo was content with his not entirely small share left over after all those bequests, but Dottor Domenico jumped in with protests and lawsuits. The will proved incontestable. Everyone had his share, and stones and mortar began to accumulate in the square, ready to give the desired shape of a bell tower to the posthumous benevolence of the dead sacristan.

Another strange piece of news we had at Portogruaro concerned the recent marriage of Captain Sandracca and the widow of the druggist of Fossalta: the lady, and her income of seven hundred lire. The Captain, disturbed by the vow of celibacy he had made to the late Signora Veronica, but even more by the penury crushing him, had resolved the matter by composing a nice little speech in his head that he intended to deliver to his first wife, should they meet in some back street of the other world. A promise extorted from a poor fellow in a moment of true desperation was neither valid nor in any way binding, he would argue, and in any case, pity for her husband ought to win out over some trifling posthumous jealousy. His heart still belonged to her, he assured her, and the only thing he really loved about the lady-druggist was her seven hundred lire. He flattered himself that Signora Veronica would be deeply moved by these arguments and would cease being cross about what only seemed to be infidelity. Had he married an unwed girl, the harm would have been irreparable, but with a widow it was all much simpler. She would go back to her first husband, and he to his first wife, and they'd have no troubles or worries *per omnia saecula saeculorum*. For ever and ever. And so the Captain savoured those seven hundred lire and entertained hopes of a generous pardon.

Meanwhile, we had made our entrance into the ruins of the old jurisdiction of Fratta. Even from afar, the sight filled our hearts with grief. The Castle looked as if it had just been sacked by a demonic band of Turks and was inhabited only by the wind and a few sad owls. Captain Sandracca met us very hesitantly, unsure whether we had come as friend or foe. Monsignor Orlando, instead, was as serene and unruffled as if we had just returned from an hour's stroll. His noble collar had more than doubled in size, and he walked dragging his legs behind him and praising his health to the skies (apart from that cursed sirocco that troubled his knees). It was the sirocco of his eighty years, which now I suffer from myself, and it blows from Christmas to Easter and from Easter to Christmas, insistently, and mocking all the almanacs.

While la Pisana, sweet and silly, made a fuss over her uncle and teased him about how long he and his sirocco would last, I slowly reacquainted myself with the old rooms of the Castle. When nightfall came, at every door and every turn in the corridor I thought I saw the dark ghost of the Count or the Clerk before me or the ruddy, open face of Martino. Instead, it was the swallows coming in and out of the windows with the first bits of straw, first beaks full of mud for their nests; the bats flickering by on their heavy, uncertain wings; a scornful owl hooting in the masters' old bedchamber. I wandered here and there, letting my legs guide me, and my legs, true to old habit, brought me to my little dog-hole near the friars' room. I don't know how I got there unharmed, across the ruined attics, through long corridors where beams and plaster that had fallen down from the granaries occasionally barred my way and threatened to send me to the floor below.

A swallow had built its nest right on the beam where Martino used to pin his olive branch on Palm Sunday. After peace came innocence. I recalled Martino's little book found in that room so many years ago, that gave me back my grip on life and my sense of duty when I was desperate. I recalled the night, even further back, when la Pisana had climbed the stairs to find me, defying for the first time the Countess's scolding and smacking. Oh, that lock of hair, which I kept with me always! I'd thought of it as a sort of talisman of my love and I had not been wrong. Pleasure mixed with tears; despair and beatitude; servility and domination; contradictions and extremes: all that had been promised had been delivered, and it was all chaotically tied up in my destiny. So much pain, so much happiness, so much hope, so much life stemming from that day! How much more trouble and travail awaited me before I set foot on those dusty, broken floors again? Would man or the elements bring down that ancient dwelling that Fulgenzio and other birds of prey had vandalized? Would some future owner come to rebuild those crumbling walls, plaster them and scrape away the signs of age that spoke to me so powerfully? Such is the destiny of men and of things: health and vigour can disguise a mean spirit and a hard heart.

When I went downstairs again my eyes were red and my mind possessed by strange ghosts, but la Pisana's laughter and Monsignor's round, serene face smoothed my brow. I kept on waiting to be asked if I'd learned the second part of the *Confiteor*. The good canon instead complained that the gifts he got were much less abundant than before, and those rogues of tenants, rather than bringing him their nicest capons, as they knew they should, came with pullet hens and cockerels so scrawny they slipped out of the chicken coop.

'And they call them capons!' he said with a sigh. 'But when I wake at night I can hear them crowing to put St Peter to shame!'

Soon Sandracca came in with the Chaplain, the two of them looking so old, my God, they were shades of their former selves. Veneranda, Donato's mother and the Captain's new bride, also came in. She had enough flesh on her to compete with the Canon and it didn't look like seven hundred lire would be enough to keep her plump. Although it is true that fat people sometimes eat more sparingly than thin. She took out a slice of lard and six eggs: the makings of an omelette, our supper. She also made a show, somewhat tight-lipped, of preparing two beds, but we already knew what conveniences there were in the Castle and that if we stayed, the two sweethearts would have to sleep in the hen coop. We took pity on them and the six eggs, therefore, and got back in our pony cart to ask Bruto Provedoni for hospitality, as we'd agreed before leaving Portogruaro.

I won't even try here to describe Bruto and Aquilina's festive welcome, nor the fine cordiality with which those two simple people made their house our own. All had been arranged by letter and we found two rooms at our disposition, for which, along with our meals, we exchanged but a modest sum. It was not payment, but a sharing of our slender means to defend ourselves against real need, pressing on us from all sides. Aquilina leapt about as happy as a madwoman and however much la Pisana tried to help her in the house those first few days, everything was always taken care of. Bruto went out in the morning to give his lessons and when he came back at midday we would amuse ourselves together working, laughing, reading and strolling, the days sailing by like butterflies on the wings of a spring breeze. I've forgotten to tell you that while I was friends with Amilcare in Padua, I learned to pound on the spinet. My ear was quite good and this allowed me to acquire some skill as a tuner; and now, in Cordovado, I recalled this art I'd learned and, as the proverb says, providentially set aside. Bruto put out the word I was the most reliable tuning fork anywhere, and here and there a rector called on me to tune an organ. With some help from the town blacksmith and some brazenness on my own part, I acquitted myself with honour. My fame then spread throughout the entire district and there wasn't an organ, harpsichord or guitar that didn't get pinched by my hands and made to play properly. My role as clerk had made me popular once and my name had not been forgotten. In the countryside it does a good clerk no harm to be thought a man of harmony, and by dint of breaking, stretching and torturing strings, I believe I did accomplish something in the end.

I finally reached the height of my glory appearing as an organist at a few fairs and events. At first I'd clashed quite often with the stern *Kyrie* and *Gloria* singers, but then I learned the part and enjoyed hearing them sing at the top of their lungs, no longer turning to cast looks of reproach and pity on the capricious organist. And now I've told you this, too. I went from major-domo to organist, and keep in mind that this sequence of professions is rather rare indeed. However, I worked hard to earn my bread, and what with Bruto, penmanship master; la Pisana, seamstress and dressmaker; Aquilina, cook; and Carlino, your organist, I can assure you that in the evenings we put on some brilliant and very funny comedies. We mocked each other in turn and we were happy; and peace and happiness restored to me thrice the health I'd had before.

From time to time I went to Fratta and took the Captain and his dog out hunting. The Captain didn't like to go beyond those ten square yards of marsh he seemed to have on lease, where the ducks and waterfowl were very careful never to set foot. His dog had the bad habit of sniffing too high off the ground and of pointing at trees, so it looked like he was hunting peaches rather than game. But by dint of shouting at him I taught him to put his nose down, and if I didn't shoot twenty-four snipe in a morning like Leopardo's grandfather, I often put a dozen in my sack. Five I gave to the Captain and Monsignor, and the rest I kept for us; and the spit went round and I was often tempted to take up the job of turnspit, but then I remembered I had been Intendente and resumed my air of majesty.

Our hosts were becoming dearer to me every day. Bruto was now a brother, and as for Aquilina, whether to call her sister or daughter, I'm not sure. The poor thing was terribly fond of me and followed me everywhere, and would do nothing without first knowing whether I approved. She saw with my eyes, heard with my ears, thought with my mind. I, in turn, tried to repay this great affection by being useful; when we were idle, I taught her some French and how to write correctly in Italian. Between master and pupil the most comical little wars would sometimes break out, and la Pisana and Bruto would leap into the fray in great style. I loved that girl so much that I felt a real paternity bump[6] sprouting on my head, and could think of nothing else but how to see her settled and find a good young man who would make her happy. We talked at length about this while she was busy with household duties, but she didn't seem inclined to accept our ideas. Pretty as she was, somewhat strange and unruly but good and sensible as a lamb, she didn't lack admirers. But she kept her distance, and at the spring or in the town square she was happier to be with us than join the swarm of girls and their swains.

La Pisana urged her to enjoy herself and have fun, but when she saw Aquilina's pretty face grow fretful at her encouragement, she would take her in her arms and cover her with kisses.

They were more than two sisters. La Pisana loved her so much I was jealous; and if Aquilina called her, she would always break away from me and run to her, even growing very sulky if I tried to detain her. What this new eccentricity of hers was, I couldn't make out; but perhaps later I understood better – as much as one could understand a temperament as obscure and enigmatic as la Pisana's.

After a few months of this simple, peaceful, industrious life, Fratta family matters called me back to Venice. My purpose was to get Count Rinaldo to agree to sell some uncultivable low-lands over towards Caorle, which a wealthy gentleman from those parts wanted to acquire so that he could carry out a great land reclamation project. But the Count, usually so unworried, so detached, was not at all keen about the sale and would not agree to it, despite the evident advantages for himself. He was one of those indolent and fanciful creatures who exhaust all their activity in plans and dreams; castles in air relieving them of any need to build something solid on earth. He dreamed the family fortune could be restored by cultivating those swamps one day, and all the gold in the world would not persuade him that he could do without those great fields for the exercise of his imagination.

When I arrived in Venice I found that things had changed greatly. The initial jubilation at joining the Kingdom of Italy had little by little settled into a calmer appreciation of the bene-fits for Venice. France weighed on us like any other rule; the form was perhaps less absolute, but the substance was identical. Laws, initiative, activity: they all came from Paris, like ladies' hats and veils today. Conscription literally castrated the people; taxes and duties milked our wealth; material progress did not make up for the moral stagnation that made minds sluggish. The old noble governing class was either laid low by inertia or tucked away in the meanest, pettiest jobs of the public adminis-tration. Citizens, a new and still unruly class, were poor at managing things for lack of training. Business languished and no one looked after the naval yards, reducing Venice to a small provincial city. Poverty and humiliation were apparent every-where, no matter how the Viceroy struggled to cover them with the imperial mantle's glorious pomp. The Ormentas and the Venchieredos were still in the government; they couldn't be thrown out, because they were the only ones who knew how things worked. That French and foreign dignitaries gave them orders merely wounded local pride, without correcting the crooked and obscure way in which public affairs were conducted. In Milan, where, for better or worse, they'd come forth from a republic, public spirit still meant something. Venice had endured conquest after conquest; lackeys followed lackeys, venal and indifferent, except to what the master would pay for.

These signs of neglect and apathy left me discouraged and I saw that Lucilio hadn't been entirely wrong to go to London; that good sense was on his side, in fact. But as much as I had tried to resume our correspondence, he no longer replied to my letters. I finally tired of knocking where I wasn't wanted and contented myself with getting news of him second-hand, from some acquaintance in Portogruaro or from rumours in town. I heard he'd become a famous doctor in London, highly esteemed among the English aristocracy. He had great hopes that England would oust the tyrant Bonaparte from France and that Italy would achieve its liberty. His views hadn't remained just and moderate for long, and his frantic need to do and undo had led him off course once again.

In any event, I remained in Venice no more than a month, always hoping to get the desired signature from Count Rinaldo, but all I was able to extort from him was permission to sell a few fields detached from the main body of the swamps. The rest he wanted to save for the family's future redemption. The few thousand lire from the sale served only to provide the Countess a larger stake at the gambling table. It is certainly true that death takes the best and leaves the rest: she who'd been the ruin of the family had no apparent intention of leaving us, while that nuisance of a husband Navagero seemed determined he would not allow his wife to become a widow.

I'd hoped to take Aglaura and her children back with me to the Friuli, but the death of her mother-in-law detained her. This was unfortunate, because the country air would have been beneficial for all those ailments that had begun to trouble her.

Spiro, who was as strong as a peasant, found it hard to believe his wife was delicate. But the fact was that not having taken care of herself straight away with a rest or a change of scene had caused her health to decline, and Spiro only understood this when it was too late. He was always saying to her that if she wished she could join her father in Greece, but she was a tender mother and did not want to subject her somewhat delicate small children to such a long and dangerous voyage. She replied with a smile that she would stay in Venice and that if her native air didn't bring back her health, no other air would. I reproached Spiro for being too much the merchant, his mind on nothing but bills of exchange and the price of coffee that kept rising because of the English smugglers. He merely shook his head without saying anything and I never understood what he meant by that inscrutable gesture.

In the end I departed for the Friuli alone; and the amusements, the excursions, the fine days of peace, of walking, of the country I'd dreamed so much about with Aglaura and her children, all these remained one of those prospects that I shall hasten to make good in the other world.

Back in Cordovado, I found the friendship, the intimacy, the – something more, if only there were some other more expressive word – between la Pisana and Aquilina had grown considerably. La Pisana's love now came to me only by means of the other. The girl would say, 'Pay heed to Signor Carlo! Signor Carlo wants you! Signor Carlo needs this or that!' and only then would la Pisana look after me; otherwise it was as if I didn't exist, a total eclipse. Aquilina stood before me and la Pisana saw only her. Even in those circumstances when thoughts do not stray very far, I would find la Pisana's mind was occupied with Aquilina. Had these been the days of Sappho, I'd have thought this was some perverse witchcraft. What can I say? I could make no sense of it: at times Aquilina seemed positively hateful to me, and la Pisana, at the very least, crazy.

And now I come to a point in my life that is always very difficult to explain to others, because I've never been able to make perfect sense of it myself, to wit: my marriage. One day la Pisana called me up to our rooms and without beating about the bush, said: 'Carlo, I see I've come to be a problem for you; you can no longer care for me even a hundredth part of what you once did. You need secure affection to give you peace, contentment and family. I'm giving you your freedom; I want you to be happy.'

'What are you saying? What is this nonsense of yours?' I exclaimed.

'I say what is in my heart and I've been thinking it over for a long time. I say it and I repeat: you do not really care for me. You keep on loving me out of habit or out of kindness, but I cannot go on forcing you; and, to make amends, I must put you on the path of true happiness.'

'The path of happiness, Pisana? But we've already walked a long way together on that path. We merely have to link arms and the roses will bloom under our feet and contentment will burst forth in any corner of the world.'

'You see, you don't understand me, or perhaps you don't understand yourself. That is what makes me wild. Carlo, you're no longer a thoughtless and inexperienced young man; the days when you could enjoy a happiness that may come to an end tomorrow are finished. You must take a wife!'

'God willing, my dear heart! Oh, Heaven forgive me my foolish yearning, but when your husband shall have left the world of infirmity for that of eternal health, my first act will be to join your fate and mine in a sacred religious vow.'

'Now Carlo, don't lose yourself in such fancies. My husband does not intend to die for now and you must not waste the best years of your manhood. I would make you quite an inadequate wife; you can see that I'm not made to bear children. And what kind of a wife would that be? No, Carlo, don't delude yourself: to be happy you must choose marriage.'

'Oh stop, Pisana! Do you mean to say you don't love me any more?'

'I mean to say I love you more than I love myself. Therefore, you must listen to me and do what I advise.'

'I shall do nothing but what my heart commands.'

'Well then, your heart has spoken. And you will marry her.'

'I'll marry her? But you are raving! You don't know what you're talking about!'

'Oh, yes, I tell you; you will marry . . . Aquilina!'

'Aquilina? Oh, enough! Have you lost your mind?'

'I am very much in my right mind. Aquilina is in love with you. You like her. It's suitable in every way. You will marry her!'

'Pisana, Pisana, don't you see you are hurting me?'

'I see the good I'm doing you, and even if I wished to sacrifice myself for your good, no one could stop me.'

'I will stop you! I have rights over you that you must not forget.'

'Carlo, I have the courage to live without you. You can measure my strength by the shamelessness of that confession. Aquilina would die. Now, *you* choose. I've already made up my mind.'

'But no, Pisana, think again! You exaggerate. You are imagining. Aquilina's affection for me is tender, calm, sisterly. She will be delighted by our happiness.'

'Silence, Carlo: trust my woman's knowledge. Her youth will be poisoned if she sees our happiness.'

'Then let us go away, back to Venice.'

'Go if you have the courage. I do not. I love Aquilina. I want her to be happy. You, too, will be happy to marry her, and I myself will join your hands together and bless your wedding.'

'Oh, I would die! I would detest her and feel my very entrails rebel against her, and not even my worst enemy would be as abominable to hold in my arms.'

'Abominable? Aquilina! Carlo, any more such vile insults and I will leave you and you'll never lay eyes on me again! The angels command us to love and you are not so perverse that you abhor what descends from on high, the most beautiful incarnation of divine thought. Look, Carlo, open your eyes: look at the crime you are committing. You have been blind up to now and haven't noticed her martyrdom, nor my remorse. Until now, I've connived with you, but I swear I won't do so any more. I won't murder with my own hands an innocent creature who loves me as a daughter, although . . . Oh, Carlo, her heroism surpasses imagination itself! Never a hint of anger, never a look of envy, but a weary resignation, a love to make you weep! No, I repeat, I will not repay the kindness we've received in this house with murder, and you will follow me in this act of charity. Carlo, once you were good and generous! Once you loved me and if I'd urged you to some brave and lofty venture you would not have made me waste so many words!'

What can I say? First I was silent, then I wept, begged, tore my hair. It was useless. She was unrelenting; no matter if we both died! She kept on telling me to observe and that if I wasn't persuaded of what she said and didn't agree to what she asked, then I was a despicable creature, unable to love and incapable of any other feeling. From that moment on she denied me any glance or smile of love, and forbade me to enter her room. She was all for Aquilina; there was nothing for me.

And as much as I wanted to deceive myself, I was forced to see that her suspicions about the young girl's love for me were not wrong. By what sorcery, I hadn't noticed and could not say, but now I was enraged at my stupidity, my ingenuousness. I even tried to turn some of that rage against Aquilina, but I couldn't do it. After she guessed what had happened between la Pisana and myself, she turned so pleading, so humble that I lost all courage. She seemed to be asking my pardon for the trouble she'd involuntarily caused, and sometimes I saw her trying to get la Pisana to make it up to me. She even tried to avoid me or pretend she was irritated at me, so that I wouldn't see what was in her heart and we could all live together in harmony once again. Bruto, who until then had been blissfully enjoying the jolly life we were leading, was distressed to see those first signs of trouble and dissension, and although he didn't understand much, he suffered for it. He even said something to me, but I drew back coolly, shrugging my shoulders, and this was a further cause for suspicion and distrust. Meanwhile, Aquilina's health was failing and her brother was concerned; doctors were called in and they spun great speculations and guessed nothing. La Pisana pressed me harder; I softened. Finally, I don't know how, I let a 'yes' escape my lips.

Bruto was quite astounded at the proposal put to him by la Pisana, but, following repeated assurances from her that all between us was finished and we had agreed upon it, and that Aquilina was pining for me, he was persuaded. He spoke to the girl, who at first refused to believe him and then fainted in relief. But when we met, she was breathless and said nothing; the poor thing guessed that I had come forward dragged by force and she didn't have the courage to ask such a sacrifice of me. Would you believe it? Her behaviour touched me, so that I immediately felt la Pisana's abnegation in myself. I felt I was saving the life of an angelic creature at the cost of my own, and this valorous deed gave me all the serenity and contentment of real virtue. Aquilina was incredulous: at first she had been reluctant to believe what la Pisana had told her, which was that we two had never loved each other except as good cousins, but then when she saw me calm, affectionate and even sometimes happy, she began to do so. At last she no longer tried to contain the joy in her soul and it was my turn to be grateful to her, if only out of pity.

To see that innocent being blossom like a rose watered by the dew, grow lovelier and more smiling at every glance and every word from me was a spectacle that made me fall in love, if not with her, then with a miraculous act of charity. La Pisana couldn't contain her delight at this happy outcome and sometimes her joy warmed me into virtuous emulation, while other times it sent a dagger of jealousy through my heart. Oh, what a mad whirlwind of affections is contained within the heart's little walls! Once again I showed that extreme malleability that gave a bizarre twist to so many of the actions of my life, however much my peaceful, thoughtful nature shunned the bizarre. It was she who led me by the nose who contributed that extravagance; although on this occasion I don't know whether I did well to allow myself to be led or would have done better to follow my own intuition and say no. Certainly my sentiments (and I say this without any pride) were supremely generous then, and it astonishes me, although I do not regret it. To regret a deed so lofty, so good, however much harm it causes us, is always a vile thing to do.

I had better tell you this quickly. The wedding was set for Easter 1807. La Pisana had the wit to get Monsignor, her uncle, to invite her to come and keep house for him. I stayed with Bruto and Aquilina and the marriage was celebrated (contrary to what I wished, and at la Pisana's request) with great ceremony. Aquilina, poor thing, was in seventh heaven, and I forced myself to enjoy her delight, and I believe I didn't spoil it, at least. There were moments when I looked back and was surprised at where I'd arrived, and understood neither why nor how, but the current carried me along and if there was ever a time when I believed in fate that was certainly it.

In short, I married Aquilina. Monsignor Orlando of Fratta blessed our union; la Pisana was godmother. I felt a great desire to weep inside, but my melancholy was not without some sweetness. The wedding luncheon was not overly joyous, but not much food was left on the plates. Monsignor ate as if he were twenty years old; I, sitting next to him and somewhat stunned by all the startling changes that had come my way, asked him about his health I don't know how many times during the meal. Between one mouthful and another, he said: 'My health would be a wonder if it were not for this blessed sirocco! It wasn't like this once! You remember, don't you Carlo?'

In fact, it hadn't rained for a month and in all Italy Monsignor alone detected sirocco. The wedding guests included Donato, his wife and children, the Captain with Signora Veneranda, and the Chaplain of Fratta. Another guest (you may have forgotten about him) was Spaccafumo, who in all the chaos of events and governments one after the other had continued to administer justice in his own way, but every year he spent a month or so in prison and in time had become an old drunkard. His exploits were now more verbal than real, and bad little boys would tease him and get him to repeat the most extravagant nonsense in the market square. He lived on alms (as it were) and despite all Bruto's invitations to sit at the table, he couldn't be budged from the kitchen, where he enjoyed the wedding with the cats and dogs and scullery maids. In the evening there was dancing and everyone was more interested in having a good time than thinking of the bride and bridegroom, and it was great fun. Marchetto, now a sacristan who resembled the Devil in priest's garb, despite his age was scraping away at a bass viol with all the fury of a bailiff, and his legs could barely keep up with him. La Pisana tried to steal away silently that evening, but I saw she was about to leave and our eyes met and exchanged, I believe, a last kiss. Aquilina, talking to her sister Bradamante, was distracted for a moment.

'What is it?' Bradamante asked.

'Nothing, nothing,' said the new bride, who looked faint. 'Don't you think it is stifling hot in here?'

I heard those words, although she had spoken very quietly, and after that I could think of nothing else but to fulfil the new duties imposed on me. The rest of the evening I was kind and loving to Aquilina. And then? And then I understood that in certain sacrifices Providence (perhaps rewarding virtue) can add a goodly dose of pleasure. My wife's innocence and charm won the case and I decided I would always be a good husband. 'What's done is done,' I thought, 'so let us do what must be done well.'

I don't think Aquilina noticed, not even during those first days, the effort I made to be more ardent than I felt. And, little by little, I became accustomed to caring for her in the new way that I must, and it didn't cost me so much effort, and if I sighed thinking of the past, I also found that even without much philosophy I could content myself with the present. Good deeds are a great distraction. Making my wife happy kept me quite busy and I soon found I was a better husband than I'd ever dared to hope.

La Pisana witnessed this change in me. Convinced that her great, but too ready, sacrifice on behalf of Aquilina could only be due to a distinct cooling of her feelings for me, I didn't bother to conceal how easy it was for me to fulfil my part of the sacrifice, easier than I'd ever hoped. I thought that if she saw I wasn't unhappy, she'd feel less remorse about having used violence to impose her will on mine. That was how she understood matters at first, but the days passed and her face was ever less sunny on her frequent visits, and little by little the admiration in her eyes at my performance turned to suspicion and vexation. She thinks I'm not attentive enough to Aquilina, I said to myself; and so I redoubled my zeal and good will, but she went on being very sulky, and even with my wife she was not as affectionate as before. One morning, when Bruto and Aquilina were out for some reason or other, she turned up in great agitation. Without even letting me say a 'Good day' she silenced me with a wave of her hand.

'Be quiet,' she said. 'I'm in a hurry. You two are now in love and have no need of me. I am going back to Venice.'

I tried to reply, but she didn't give me the time. On her way out she shouted to me to give her greetings to my wife and brother-in-law, then she leapt into the horse and cart in which she'd come with the Chaplain of Fratta and, run as I could behind her, I wasn't able to catch up. When I got to the Castle an hour later, she had already left on the gardener's cart, whether on the road to Portogruaro or to Pordenone, no one could say. I was in a great fix to explain her hasty departure to Bruto and Aquilina, but then I had the wit to make up a story that the Countess had suddenly been taken ill and they believed that without any trouble. And so, neither happy nor able to forget, but at peace and willing, I went back to my life as organist and husband. Aglaura and Spiro wrote, astonished at my sudden conversion, and I replied, joking, that it was God's work, but often one writes what one does not feel.

The months went by, easy, industrious, serene like those autumn skies that light up nature without warming her. All mine, Aquilina every day put on new charms to please me and I was so grateful for her nobly offered love that I grew more and more attached to her and my regrets grew ever scarcer. There were times when my heart still wandered, but when the mind made comparisons, I confess I found Aquilina the most perfect and lovable of all the women I'd ever known. And in the long run the mind has some influence on the affections of a man of thirty-four. When I saw she was with child, when I held that sturdy, rosy little soldier in my arms and felt moved to my fatherly innards, I saw I owed that delight to her and scarcely knew who I was any more; I nearly blessed la Pisana for having forced me into that bizarre, misguided marriage. However, my memory was still alive.

I made sure to have frequent news from Venice and when I learned that la Pisana was living, along with Clara, in her husband's house and did nothing but look after his health, I abandoned certain rash judgements I'd made after she left

Fratta. If she were angry at me, she wouldn't have shown it like that. I had practical experience of la Pisana's revenge. And even from afar, I was still useful to her. I had improved the administration of those few farms that still belonged to the Castle, as well as the collection of rents. The family's income had increased by thirty per cent. Monsignor could sit down to a capon that wasn't a cockerel, and Count Rinaldo, social rustic though he was, thanked me for looking after their interests so effectively and without being asked.

You will be amazed and annoyed to learn that my life, once so volatile and disorderly, now adopted such a peaceful, monotonous course. But I recount, I do not invent; and in any case this is a common phenomenon in Italian lives, which are like a great river, quiet, slow and swampy, interrupted here and there by abrupt and noisy rapids. Where the people do not play a permanent part in government, but seize it by force from time to time, such reversals, such metamorphoses, must necessarily occur, for the life of the people is no more than the sum of many individual lives. And so I turned the spit for several years, was a student and something of a conspirator; then I was a peaceful clerk, then a Venetian patrician in the Maggior Consiglio and secretary of the Municipality; from heedless lover I suddenly turned soldier; from soldier to layabout once again; then Intendente, then major-domo; and now I was married and played the organ.

It is for you to say if in these perpetual ups and downs I rose or fell. For my part, I know that I went through thirty-four years: years in which I lived all for myself. Then, family ties and precise material duties took over my feelings. I was no longer the colt frolicking about the marshes, jumping ditches and boring through thickets, but a harnessed horse solemnly pulling the cardinal's carriage or the gravel cart. But have no fear; there will be no shortage of upheavals and disorders to free the horse and put him back on his crazy path across the world. Only now am I finally sure I won't run any more; for, as I say, I have the octogenarian's sirocco in my legs like Monsignor.

While every day I was becoming more a man of the house and the country (and my little Luciano, already trotting around the courtyard, was joined by a second boy we named Donato in honour of the uncle who served as his godfather), Napoleon's martial triumphs were thundering around the world. He defeated Prussia at Jena, Austria at Wagram; he married into old dynasties,[7] and now, master of Europe, he closed off the continent from England and threatened the semi-Asiatic empire of the Tsar. Italy, crushed in his fist to be nibbled at will, had, however, raised the flag of unity in Milan. And we grew accustomed to fix on that and see Napoleon more as an enemy than a protector, because his ambition was vast and careless of history and people. But when the sword he'd given us fell to the ground, who would dare to take it up? No one thought of that. They thought they were strong, not understanding that strength belonged to the colossus and would fail with him. Of a hundred who plotted, only one was thinking; the other ninety-nine would collapse in the final trial. I saw none of this, but I guessed. Spiro's letters, meanwhile, were becoming more fiery and cryptic and I understood that some lofty idea was fermenting in the Greek merchant's soul. The poet Rigas[8] founded the patriotic association Eteria; in return he was betrayed by Christians, his natural allies, and put to the stake by the Turks. A second independence plot in favour of the Greeks developed in Italy under Napoleon. The new Charlemagne, they hoped, would be matched by a new Byzantium. They were dreams, but they rekindled the cinders, never extinguished, of volcanic Greece, and in the mountains of the Mani they sang:

> A gun, a sword, if nothing else a sling-shot: our weapons are these.
> I can already see the Turkish chieftains at my feet; they call me lord and master.
> I've stolen their guns, their swords, their pistols.
> Oh Greeks, lift your humbled brows! Take up your guns, your swords, your slingshots. Soon our oppressors will call us lords and masters.

The fire spread among the savage hordes of Albanians and the shepherd tribes of Montenegro, where it is an insult to say,

'Your men died in their beds!' Ali Pasha of Tepelena[9] used cruelty and treachery to prevail; the exiles inspired all of Greece to terrible revenge. Their strength was still invisible, but it was the true and invincible strength of a nation that has pondered its adversities for a long time and stored up insults and abuse, waiting patiently for its moment of reprisal. For the last time, Old Apostulos sailed for the Morea. Hopes of bringing Greece back to life under the Phanariots had faded, and he turned to war and blood with the greed of the lion that has seen its prey snatched away just as it sat down to eat. He met his death at Chios and Spiro gave me this sad news, adding that his father's last wishes would inspire everything he now did. He was forever inviting me to move to Venice with my family, where, he said, there was no shortage of decorous ways to support myself, nor of chances to be of service to myself and to us all. But I was content with what I had and did not want to risk myself and above all my family in uncertain enterprises. Bruto, reading passages of those letters from my brother-in-law, bit his lip and pounded his wooden leg furiously. I looked at Aquilina and little Donato at her breast and could not tear myself away from that peaceful scene.

The great war of the modern giants came. Napoleon entered Germany with five hundred thousand men. To Dresden he summoned emperors and kings, who were more vassals than allies, and then said, 'Let them wait.' Why, he wanted the Tsar to explain, was his friendship so tepid? The mystical Alexander called holy Russia to arms, a war of the people against a war of ambition, and that wretched Cossack cavalry, as Napoleon called it, became the scourge and the terror of the invincible army. He reached Moscow, ever victorious; then fled, beaten by fire, ice – the elements, in short – not by men. Blood from the veins of forty thousand Italians darkened the snows of Russia, allowing the remains of the Grande Armée to withdraw. But when this immense disaster was announced, the bulletin concluded with the words, 'His Majesty's health has never been better.' What fine consolation to the widows, the orphans, the mothers deprived of their children! He went to Paris to raise new armies, stir up new enthusiasm with his presence, new courage with new lies. But France did not believe him, Germany rose up;, his allies betrayed him. He failed again at Leipzig,[10] abdicated from the Empire of France and the Kingdom of Italy and retired to the island of Elba.

And then we saw what the Kingdom of Italy was without Napoleon and what happens when people are led by institutions, even vigorous ones, without liberty. There was universal panic and confusion, upheaval, conflict among various monstrous hopes, all vain. In Milan, a minister was brutally murdered; the old powers were struck down; men wallowed in the freedom of the present, giving no thought to the future. And the future was to be what the others wanted, despite the respectful and sensible demands of the provisional Regency, despite the nice speeches of the foreign ambassadors. The people didn't exist. They weren't there.

Whether I was dismayed by these events, which shook me out of my torpor as a father and realized the fears I'd long harboured, I'm not the man to say. From this account of my life, you already know me rather well. I sighed for myself, wept in despair for my country, then, studying the tender features of my children, I felt comforted and caught sight of a flicker of hope. We were born, as it were, eighteen years before; and we'd had the school of adversity to educate us, and the life of a people isn't measured by the life of individuals. If we sons had paid for the sins of our fathers, our sons might harvest the shoots propagated by our blood and tears. Fathers and sons are a single soul, a nation that never perishes. And so I dedicated myself to moral regeneration, not to the Viceroy Beauharnais, Tsar Alexander, Lord Bentinck or General Bellegarde.

So the years passed as quickly as months do in youth, although you mustn't think they passed as quickly as it seems in the telling. The longer it takes to recount something, the quicker it often moves in reality. The days in Cordovado were peaceful, serene, even sweet if you will, but I wouldn't say they went by unusually swiftly. La Pisana's letters were rare at first, but grew steadily more frequent as the political turmoil raged; it was as if she knew how much I must be suffering and wanted to comfort me with her words. She wrote of the squawking and cackling of the Venchieredos, the Ormentas and Padre Pendola and his faithful; of the excellent posts gained by her Cisterna cousins, especially Augusto, who overnight was named government secretary; and of Agostino Frumier, who, wanting to retire from public service, and rich as he was, hadn't been ashamed to request that part of a pension he had a right to.

Squalor and graft, as you can see, were widespread and it couldn't have been otherwise, because austerity was a quality of the best. Old Venchieredo, scorned because he worked too hard, had lost much of his influence and had fallen from the highest rungs down to Director of Street-Sweeping. He sighed about it, but to no avail. To serve too well is to serve badly. He hadn't been clever enough. Partistagno, come back to Venice as Colonel of the Uhlans, had married a Moravian baroness, because she was the spitting image of his favourite horse, he said. His rancour against the House of Fratta was undiminished, and when he learned that Clara had left the convent and lived in Palazzo Navagero, he would often peacock around in high uniform out front, hoping to catch her eye and get her to say, 'Oh, what a shame I didn't accept that one at any cost!' But Clara, grown nearsighted poring over the Office of Our Lady, could not see as far as the alleyway and she couldn't tell the difference between the magnificent, spectacular Colonel Partistagno and one of those beggars who tie up the gondolas.

There were some who said that Alessandro Giorgi had gone from the Italian army to the Austrian, keeping the rank of general, which he'd gained in Moscow, but I didn't believe it. And, in fact, a few months later I had news from Brazil, where he had gone into exile and had found a good position. He didn't fail to offer me the protection of Emperor Dom Pedro,[11] and inform me that there were numerous Countess Miglianas in Rio de Janiero who could do much better than make me majordomo. Most likely he had forgotten I was an organist, married and with children, although he had seen me with my little family when he marched through with Prince Eugène on the way to Hungary in 1809. Despite his forty years, the good general was still rather heedless and libertine.

The wan years that followed were but a mournful cemetery.

The first to go was the Chaplain of Fratta; then it was Spaccafumo's turn; then Marchetto the bailiff, sacristan and bass viol player, who was struck by lightning while tolling the bells during a thunderstorm. To this day, the parishioners there worship him as a martyr. In the year of the famine and the one after, death ravaged the poor and the tolling was perpetual. Signora Veneranda also departed (not on account of the famine), leaving the Captain a widower for the second time, but with seven hundred lire at his disposal, which freed him from the problem of finding a third wife. In those years we, too, had to tighten our belts considerably, for there were no families ready to pay a tutor for their children or rectors wanting to repair their organs. It was the expenses of that year, in fact, that first began to unbalance our accounts and when the imbalance grew worse it led to those new developments you'll duly hear of.

I don't recall exactly when, but sometime in those days Count Rinaldo travelled to the Friuli. He came for money and, finding none, he sold the most ruined parts of the Castle to a builder. I watched it being demolished and it was like attending the funeral of a friend. The Count himself couldn't bear to look at the remains and, having pocketed his few *quattrini*, went back to Venice. His mother's illness was now a matter of serious concern. As soon as the courtyards were cleared of great stones split with a pickaxe and all the mountains of rubble left over from the demolition, Monsignor began to find the sirocco even more troublesome than before. One morning he fainted during the Mass, and after that he never left his room. I went to see him on the next to last day of his life and asked him how he was and he gave me the usual lament. That pesky old sirocco again! However, he did eat for two, even while in bed, and when his last hour came, his breviary sat on one side and half a roast chicken on the other. Giustina asked him, 'Won't you eat, Monsignor?'

'I'm not hungry any more,' he said, his voice somewhat more feeble than usual.

So died Monsignor Orlando of Fratta, smiling and eating as he lived, his appetite appeased at least. His sister-in-law, who followed him a few months later, raved on to the very end about gaming hands and Tarot cards, and died with a head full of fabulous winnings, her coffers empty and all she owned at the Monte di Pietà. The Cisterna branch had to lend Count Rinaldo a few ducats to bury her, for neither Clara nor la Pisana had a penny to their names, and His Excellency Navagero went on and on about how poor he was. Everyone was leaving us, but Navagero was a hard nut. My most ardent vows of previous years had evidently not received the Good Lord's blessings. La Pisana informed me of her mother's death in the saddest of terms, and she also told me, in confidence, of a quite unexpected visit she had received. One evening, while she and Clara were in the palazzo chapel saying the rosary (and that I wouldn't have expected from la Pisana), they were told a stranger had come to the door asking urgently to see them. He was small and lean, they were told, had a fine beard, eyes that sparkled despite his age (which must be at least fifty) and a forehead that was quite high – in fact, without any hair at all. Who could it be?

They went to the drawing room and there la Pisana recognized, more by the voice than by the person, Lucilio Vianello. He had come aboard an English ship; he knew that Clara had left the convent and had come one last time to ask her to honour her vow to him. He was so gloomy and menacing, la Pisana said, that she found him frightening; Clara told him quite bluntly that there was nothing between them any more, that she was married to God and would certainly continue to pray for his soul.

'In that moment, I can assure you,' wrote la Pisana, 'fury and indignation made him seem a man of twenty. Then suddenly he took on death's ashen colours and turned at least eighty. Bent, shaky, murmuring strange words, he left the room. Clara made the sign of the cross and, sounding very composed, invited me to take up my rosary again. I said I had to warm some broth for my husband, and did so, for that scene had made me feel awful. I would never have believed such passion could hide under that icy guise: surviving immaculate all the vicissitudes, upsets and revolutions of a life that's been little less than legendary. Do you remember him in Naples, in Genoa? Didn't he seem to have entirely forgotten Clara? Did he ever ask us for news of her? Never! I do think that to make our final judgements we must wait until men die. And you, too, Carlo: avoid judging me until I have joined my poor mother.'

There followed the usual salutations and some even more affectionate than usual greetings for Aquilina, Bruto and my boys, who were now growing up, poor things, full of courage and goodwill. She also asked me to put a little gravestone for Monsignor Orlando in the cemetery of Fratta, but I had already thought about this some months before and found that Don Girolamo, whatever his notary brother thought, had preceded me in this pious deed. The stone bore an inscription whose elegant falsehoods can be forgiven, for anyway no one in town understood them. One of our townsmen who knew how to read had succeeded in translating the words up to the point where it was written that the Reverend Canon had died *octuagenarius*, which, according to him meant on the *octua* of the month of *genarius*. But there were protests at this, for many pointed out he hadn't died on the eighth of January, but on the fifteenth.

'Oh, as if it matters!' the good man said. 'Do you really expect stone-carvers to concern themselves with such minutiae? A day more, a day less, the important thing is that he's dead, so you can plant the stone on top of him.'

I wrote to la Pisana to let her know that her kind wish had already been carried out some time ago and praised Don Girolamo, adding that if he wasn't Vincent de Paul or Francis of Assisi, he did know how to ask pardon from the poor of Portogruaro for what his father had stolen. 'They are not all like Padre Pendola,' I wrote. She replied that there were some good stories going around about the reverend father. Ever since the Pope had repealed the ban on the Jesuits, Pendola had been working hard to reinstall them in Venice. His new home for reformed women was not prospering and he hoped to get the agreement of the few sisters remaining and a licence from their superiors to turn the home into a seminary. However, the government seemed far from enthusiastic about the idea and it was said that the Avvocato Ormenta, who was pressing for it, was about to be dismissed.

From this report I could see all the manoeuvring that was

going on, and how those fine priests who had founded the home had been nothing but obedient puppets in Padre Pendola's hands. But prosperity and plenty would not last long for him, either, and, in fact, he died without seeing the Society of Jesus return to Venice. In the long run, whether good or evil, all must go. There was no shortage of epitaphs and travesties, panegyrics and indictments for the good father; some wanted to canonize him, some to toss his corpse in the water. When he was dying he had begged those looking after him to allow him to be forgotten; he said he was an unworthy servant of the Lord. Little did he know how quickly they would obey him. After a week he was no longer spoken of and all that remained of so much ambition was a rotting old carcass wrapped in a shroud and nailed inside four pine boards. They hadn't even polished his coffin, as they do for dead men of distinction! How ungrateful. In the end, I think, the Curia was quite content to be free of that dangerously shrewd advocate of God's glory and his own interests.

The old actors were leaving the stage. Enter the new. Demetrios Apostulos, Spiro's eldest son, was twenty; Theodoros, his second, was turning eighteen. My two sons were ten and twelve. Donato had three boys between sixteen and twenty-two, three very sturdy young lads indeed, and, luckily for them, they hadn't been of age at the last Napoleonic conscriptions. They continued to sign up the young men, year after year, in spite of all the thundering proclamations of the Holy Alliance,[12] but it wasn't difficult to find a substitute, and with peace looking quite enduring, many shirkers were happy to accept the well-fed ease of the army. The younger generation hinted to their elders that we should retire and they might even have hinted quite boldly, as if they were disgusted with us, and they wouldn't have been wrong. Instead, they admired us as the movers and witnesses of great enterprises, generous attempts, incredible portents; they seemed to say, 'Direct me, so that I don't fail where you did!' But more than direction was needed; drive was needed and we no longer had it; harmony was needed and it had been abolished.

In 1819 Europe was in the grip of that nervous unease that overtakes the body after an all-out, exhausting march of several hours. There were no clear ideas, no good and universal sentiments, unless in some individual separated from the rest by disdain or despair. Even where the people had risen up against France out of national pride, ingratitude on the part of the powerful and distrust among the little people left everything in disarray. They thought they were taking part in a great project of liberty, when they hadn't made sure that the interests of a few weren't served at the expense of the many. This happened above all in Germany. Here, instead, people were discontent with the past, which hadn't brought that generous inheritance they'd hoped for, and discontent with the present, because it seemed a cruel mockery. Most did no more than try to get by, build their nests, stock their pantries. Experience had destroyed any unity of opinion and even the few who understood how matters stood saw no future or had greatly inflated hopes. Those few who couldn't do without hopes, even at the risk of fruitless endeavour, turned to Spain, where something like liberalism flourished. Excluded from public life, a talent for command (indestructible in men who are thinking, working beings) led them towards the secret societies. From Calabria the Carbonari[13] spread across Italy, collaborating with the democrats in France and the progressives in Spain. The old Latin races, rejuvenated by new dreams and sentiments, threw themselves into the battle of the times with typical enthusiasm. Across the sea the Greeks – less advanced but readier for independence, fortified by united opinion and the people's consent – responded. When Ali Pasha took his revenge it was a desperate call for liberty to the Greeks (although they had once been his enemies) and it resounded from the ruins of Parga to the melodious shores of Skyros.[14] The Holy Alliance had laid an iceberg on the heart of Europe, but fire flared at the extremities and the Earth's viscera rumbled in menace.

Towards the end of 1820, when we'd become quite a bit more impoverished and Spiro gave me hope I might be able to settle my famous credits from Constantinople, I decided to go to Venice to have a talk with him. At the end of July the Carbonari had contrived a revolution in Naples and were able to impose a very broad constitution, but King Ferdinand had already gone to the Congress of the Allies in Troppau,[15] where he betrayed the liberal principles he'd agreed to in Naples. They were arming down there against the storm gathering in the North. I would need to go to the Kingdom of the Two Sicilies to find my father's death certificate, Spiro told me, without which the Turks would not settle the note. I'd need to find witnesses and get them to recall circumstances long forgotten, and such business could not be done by letter. This was my reason for obtaining a passport; but I was also charged with other matters delicate enough not to be mentioned aloud. My family I entrusted to Spiro, who promised to go and visit them during my absence. I departed with no regrets, for what I knew about Neapolitan affairs told me I was obliged to help out where I could, and now that others' eyes were upon me I didn't want to betray their trust for private reasons, although I think I was more pessimistic than most about the rosy hopes of the day.

Among other things I saw la Pisana in Venice, as you might expect. In fact, I marvelled at her. When I looked at myself in the mirror from time to time, I could see my forty-five years were easily legible on my face, but when I met her now she looked younger than when we'd parted. She was slightly rounder and thus her warmth looked sweeter, but she had the same languid, fiery, sensual eyes; the same fresh oval of a face; the same soft white neck; the same nimble, graceful manner. It was quite a struggle for her to conform with Clara's monastic severity and quite hard for her to convince me they led a saintly life together, for I saw the same Pisana as ever . . . Oh, enough! If I hadn't taken a wife . . .

Her good health was all the more astonishing because the two of them had to earn their keep with their own hands, as it were, as the few *quattrini* that slipped from the crabbed claws of old Navagero were not enough to pay the doctors and the medicines. The gentleman, during my brief visit with him, praised his wife loudly, but I don't think he was very pleased to see me, being afraid I might carry her off.

'Believe me, Signor Carlo,' he said, 'if my nurse were to run away, I'd die the day after.'

'Old fellow, you know we women care more about sick people than about lovers,' said la Pisana.

The invalid squeezed her hand and mine, and I left, promising we'd see each other soon on my return to Venice. La Pisana, however, was quite cool and contained when we said our farewells, as behoves a saint.

The evening before I left I saw Colonel Partistagno in the Piazza with his wife, and, in fact, he was right: the Baroness really did look like a horse, her arms, legs and chin were so long. Nevertheless, Raimondo Venchieredo was pursuing her. He saw me in passing, as I withdrew to the darkest corner of the Caffè Suttil to put my nose in the *Gazzetta*. He had aged and was livid and decayed as an old rake, and I don't think he was wallowing in splendour, because both his father and Ormenta had been dismissed at half pay. Those two old wrecks were ending their thieving, underhand lives rather badly, but the Avvocato was the more fortunate of the two, because his son was in Rome on a diplomatic mission, he said, and he was awaiting great developments. I certainly didn't weep to leave such riff-raff behind me in Venice, but I was pained to see Aglaura ever more enervated and melancholy on my departure. Poor thing! Where was the handsome young sailor who once accompanied me from Padua to Milan in the days of the Cisapline Republic?

TWENTY

Sicilians at General Guglielmo Pepe's[1] camp in the Abruzzi. I become acquainted with prison and very nearly with the scaffold, but thanks to la Pisana I lose no more than my eyesight. The miracles of love delivered by a nurse. Refugee Italians in London and soldiers in Greece. I regain my sight with the help of Lucilio, but soon thereafter I lose la Pisana and return home with only my memories still alive.

Oh, poor Adriatic! When will the great Roman fleets of Brindisi, the swift liburnians of Illyria and the galleys of Venice ride your waves again? Today, your tides beat stormy on two shores all but deserted: the marshes and thickets of Puglia and Albania's lonely heights. Venice is but an inn; Trieste, a shop: not enough to console those shores for having been abandoned. When dawn comes to burnish your billowing mane, no issue appears but ruins and memories.

The weather was serene when we sailed from Malamocco, port of Venice. It didn't feel like winter and even less so on the high seas, where bare trees and white snows can't be seen. The tepid west wind played with the tips of the waves, bringing the hot sighs of Africa to dry Dalamatia. Where was Salona now, Diocletian's retreat, or Hippo, Augustine's bishop's seat? Memories, memories, amid these restless waves that haven't changed in centuries, this air ever sweet and perfumed, this land, insatiable and fertile. The East slowly produced a civilization that amazed us, although it was degenerate; the North, for three hundred years, has cavorted in puerile arrogance, thinking itself adult when perhaps it is not yet even born. Twice Italy has surpassed the East and preceded the North; twice she was mistress and queen of the world: prolific, powerful, calamitous. She ponders it still, and despite Lamartine's funeral laments and the mistrust of pessimists, one day she'll overtake those one pace ahead of her, but who believe themselves to be a thousand miles ahead. One pace, no more, I tell you; but it is a long one.

Near Ancona, the sirocco rose to annoy us and obstruct our progress. Our snug Chioggia ship resisted, but the wind was stronger than her sails and we had to lower them. Anchoring here, tying up there, it took us four weeks to reach Manfredonia, where I was to disembark. When I arrived at Molfetta it was already February and the provincial militias were heading towards the Abruzzi to fight the foreign invasion, alongside General Guglielmo Pepe. The greater part of the enemy awaited us on the Roman road and the regular army under Carrascosa's[2] command was camped on the western coast between Gaeta and the Apennines. I took care of my business in just a few days. The old priest was dead, but he had recorded my father's demise among the deceased of 1799. I obtained a proper death certificate and hurried off to General Pepe's camp as per my instructions.

The young general received me quite courteously. He had the greatest confidence in his flocks of volunteers, with whom he felt sure he could put down the diversionary force the enemy had positioned there. It never occurred to him that Nugent[3] would attack with his entire army. Still trusting the papal forces, he had decided to strengthen his position by sending an advance guard to Rieti in the Papal State. He was working out this bold plan when I was announced and gave him my letter of introduction. He received me very politely and told me of his plans, arguing that at the worst, the King's return would settle matters without any foreign intervention. I then conveyed to him what I'd been asked to, and he was very pleased and said that we could consider it if the enemy failed to negotiate and engaged, and he was able to push them back beyond the Po River as he hoped. He further told me there was a Milanese gentleman at the camp who'd come with a proposal like mine and that he'd introduce us.

We met at table, but I was distressed to recognize this gentleman as one of the most faithful visitors to the Countess Migliana's salon, which didn't please me at all. He said little, but stared and muttered a great deal, as was the habit in Casa Migliana. He stayed another day and then disappeared when the danger mounted and we didn't hear of him again, except when he was seen a few days later in Rome with the young Ormenta, to whom he supposedly had appealed solely to get a return pass to Lombardy. Many believed this, but I did not, and, in fact, he emerged as someone quite disreputable during the trials of later years. Although he knew little, he used that little to save himself and leave others in the lurch.

There were also some Sicilians at the camp who had come to look after Sicilian affairs (which couldn't have been more outrageously different from those of Naples) and they were ardent, courteous, exquisitely brought-up young men. Sicily is the Tuscany of southern Italy and it marries very badly with rough, boasting, brawling Naples. There will always be resentments where there is no equality and, say what you will about our system of Municipalities, you must admit that Marseilles in France would grumble about being ruled by Lyons, just as Edinburgh grumbled for centuries about submitting to London, and perhaps still grumbles today. And this despite the fact that London surpasses every other city of the United Kingdom, far more than Rome does other cities on our peninsula. But Rome is backed by traditions, history, the glory and the majesty that make it the capital not only of Italy but of the world, and no place is so brazen as to be ashamed to obey Rome.

In Sicily, however, two provinces had demanded they be freed from Neapolitan rule, and an army led by Florestano Pepe[4] had been sent to calm them down. And this, too, was an error: to divide their forces and engage in tussles about supremacy, when elsewhere the question was: were they to be or not to be? If, while Carrascosa with his regulars was guarding the Capua road, Florestano's army had backed the unruly militias of his brother Guglielmo, we might not have had the routs at Rieti and Antrodoco (a blot against the Neapolitan army, which wasn't responsible for them, and the inevitable outcome of such a battle involving regular soldiers, trained cavalry and rag-tag bands of shepherds and brigands).

The Sicilians in camp defended their native land. It wasn't

arrogance or foolishness, they said; it was the Calderari – the secret society founded by the Minister of Police himself to combat the influence of the Carbonari – who were responsible for that untimely outburst of Palermitan pride. But secret societies protected by governments[5] are but phantoms: either they come to nothing or they mutate into violent bands that end by attacking government itself. And, in fact, the Minister of Police Canosa[6] was removed because his nasty hounds became too visible. A party that governs by the light of day does not need to command in shadow, mystery and intrigue. We replied, therefore, that if the Calderari had taken hold in Palermo it was because the ground was shaky. But those spirited young Sicilians would not hear of that and they, in turn, put forward some information that if it were true, proved Sicily must be brought to heel immediately.

The General was polite, but it was a day for action and he was more concerned with the news from the Marche than with Sicilian affairs. Just after luncheon we learned that a company of Uhlans had passed by the evening before and, according to the peasants, the entire army was behind them. The General then understood the clever plan of the imperial forces: to feign an approach to Naples by the Capua road, so that our defences would mass there, and then come around to attack us through the unguarded passes of the Abruzzi. However, he was still unsure whether those peasant reports might not be exaggerated, as they always were; mistaking a few companies of scouts on foot and horseback for thousands of soldiers. He hoped to concentrate the scattered guards behind Rieti and to give Carrascosa at least time to position himself between Naples and the enemy at the backs of Pepe's militiamen. The General wanted to send someone to Rieti immediately and I and the Sicilians came forward. He thanked us and offered us a cavalry escort, asking that we communicate with him as soon as we could. Meanwhile, he would send out messengers to all the commanders ordering them to draw back along the road from Rieti to Aquila with their men.

What we had feared was true, alas. Nugent had deployed his whole army along the borders of the Abruzzi and a large cavalry corps bore down on Rieti. Pepe was so advised within two hours, but it was already too late for him to deal with such an emergency. He only had time to move in where the danger was greatest. The imperial horses had already begun their assault and our irregulars, armed with carbines, were not equipped to resist a cavalry charge. The fields were swept clean, the roads ran with blood, terror spread, fed by surprise, the vast number of assailants and the meagre defence. There was no artillery and the light cavalry didn't amount to four hundred in all, I would guess; the others were all spread out in various positions. After two hours of fighting, Rieti was lost and Pepe had to retreat.

But as soon as he had withdrawn and collected his men and reinforcements arrived, he saw that Rieti was the key to the battle and that once it was lost, there was no other hope. He convened a council of war and the opinion was that they couldn't regain the city with so many imperial cannon already installed in the piazza. But the General could not be swayed from his daring, irrevocable decision. He shouted out that only those who wished to need follow him, but he would not leave the Abruzzi border without making a last stand at Rieti. His honour and his duty so commanded. Most of the volunteers bravely answered this desperate appeal, the young Sicilians and I leading them.

Thoughts of my wife and children flashed through my head for an instant, but only to convince me that a father's first duty is to be a brave and bold example. For a mere organist from Cordovado, you'll agree, this wasn't bad. In that moment death looked so grand and glorious as to require a life much, much longer than mine, with thrice the sorrows and adversities. In all my many years, the occasions to live well have been rare, it is true, but occasions to die well were never lacking, and this, too, allows me to leave this world without regrets.

Our attack was strong and sudden, but there were too few of us and when the cannon thundered they made a dreadful hole in our ranks. Just one of those brave Sicilians was left alive and he was taken prisoner at the mouth of a howitzer. We returned for a second strike, but few of us still had our courage and we were met by a hail of bullets; we broke ranks, the men scattered and many wounded and dead were left on the ground, where they shook under the hooves of the enemy cavalry running riot. The General, almost alone, was able to flee to Aquila where the rest of the army was camped, but he was quite discouraged about this first disaster and about those who had fallen at Rieti. I was badly wounded in the shoulder, but used all my art to hide myself and crawl into a thicket. However, some imperial riflemen found me and, when they learned I was not a Neapolitan, took me to headquarters to be questioned. Advancing along with the Imperial Army, I thus learned about the routs of Aquila and Antrodoco.

In March I was taken to Naples, lodged in Castel Sant'Elmo and sent before a military tribunal that would weigh my crime. They determined I was guilty of high treason for having voluntarily fought on behalf of a constitutional government that was not my own. And given that my shoulder wound had healed, one fine morning they read me out my death sentence. I had not sent word home, thinking it is always better to delay informing others of irrevocable disaster, and I prepared to die with fair resignation, although unhappy I wouldn't know how this squalid chapter of history had ended. They also came to offer me a pardon if I would say who had sent me there and why I'd come; but these brute questions had already been answered by my father's death certificate, signed and sealed at Molfetta and found on my person. I replied that I had come for no other reason but this; that I had merely gone to give my regards to General Pepe and was drawn into that nasty incident by bad luck. It was as if I hadn't spoken, but, nevertheless, I took the opportunity to ask those kind gentlemen to send the death certificate to my family, along with my own, so that the Ottoman Porte's nasty distrust might at least be allayed to my wife's advantage.

Those gentlemen snickered at these remarks of mine, thinking perhaps I was trying to prove myself mad, but, flashing them the nicest of smiles, I urged them to be good enough to trust my reason, and then I asked them once again to do me that favour. I even gave one of them Spiro Apostulos's address in Venice and that of Aquilina Provedoni Altoviti in the town of Cordovado in the Friuli. This persuaded them I wasn't in jest and they promised to do as I asked. I also inquired when I would leave prison for the ceremony, for I'd been rotting in there for three months and it seemed a good bargain to obtain a breath of fresh air in return for my life. But when I learned that the execution would take place in two days' time in the castle moat I was quite annoyed. To have to die in Naples without getting to see it again! You have to admit that was harsh.

Once they'd left me, though, I sought comfort where I could. These last days, I said to myself, must not be frittered away in foolishness and vain desires; it was better to be serious about death and show my executioners, at least, what a noble spirit looked like. A fine example speaks with the mouths of many and is always to the good. The hangman causes more damage by talking about such examples than he provides benefits by hanging people.

The next day, having slept, I admit, rather restlessly, I heard steps in the corridor that didn't belong to either guards or jailers. When they opened the door I expected to see the priest or some servant of the executioner come to shave my head or measure my neck. But it was nothing like that. Three very tall, very black figures entered, one of whom had a paper tucked under his arm. He unfolded it slowly and began to read in a pompous, nasal voice. It sounded like Fulgenzio reading the Epistles, and the memory wasn't pleasant. I was so sure I must die on the morrow, so busy staring at those three tenebrous giants, that I didn't bother to listen to what they were saying. Then my attention was caught by one word: *pardon*.

'What?' I said, all jitters.

'The death sentence is therefore commuted to forced labour for life in the Ponza prison,' the clerk's big talking nose continued.

I finally understood what it was about, and I'm not sure I was cheered, because I've always thought there was very little difference between death and prison. And in the following days I had reason to believe that any advantage was on the side of the gallows. On the island of Ponza, and above all in the prison for life where my free will was confined, you could not say the comforts of life abounded. A long, narrow room furnished with wooden planks to sleep on; water and bean soup; many,

many Neapolitan thieves and Calabrian brigands, and, into the bargain, legions of insects of every type and breed, more than Job himself endured when he lay on the dunghill. Whether someone was stealing or the food was simply scarce and of Pythagorean frugality,[7] the fact was we were starving. The guards said the air of Ponza fattened you up, but I found the beans emaciating and I hate to think what would have become of me had I stayed there more than a month. How Augustus' daughter and granddaughter survived ten years there I don't know; probably they had something more succulent to go with the bean soup. Luckily, as I say, I was there but a month. Then I was sent to Gaeta, where the company was better and so was the food, but my sight began to suffer.

I had a little cage, all plastered white, that looked out over the sea, and the sun shining in the sky and reflected by the water sent such a glare inside that my eyes were failing. I made complaint after complaint: all in vain. Perhaps it was considered admissible to deprive of his eyes a man who'd been granted his life, but why hadn't they claimed that privilege in the act of pardon? In three months I became almost blind; I saw things in blue, green and red, but never in their natural colours, and my grasp of proportion was distorted, so that my little cage seemed a huge hall and my hand an elephant's foot. The jailers looked like real rhinoceroses.

In the fourth month I began to see my little piece of world through a fog; in the fifth, darkness fell, and of the colours I had once seen all that was left was a dark red, a mixture of dust and blood. Now came an order to transfer me to Castel Sant'Elmo in Naples; then the usual clerks appeared to read out the usual hocus pocus. I'd been pardoned! If I never again saw the world in its true colours, at least I could walk about and smell it as much as I liked! I would visit my village, my children, my wife . . . But not so fast. I had been pardoned, yes, but I was banished from Italy and you could be sure that meant that neither France nor Spain would open her arms to me. What clemency was this that sent a poor blind man out to beg alms? God alone knew. I did have the consolation of knowing I'd been pardoned thanks to the Princess Santacroce's intercession and would be permitted to meet her before sailing from the port of Naples.

The Princess had surely aged considerably, but she wore that look of goodness that gives a woman eternal youth. She received me very warmly and, although I couldn't see her, I could have sworn she was no more than thirty, as she was at the time of the Parthenopean Republic. She told me she'd worked very hard to get me pardoned and released, but had been unable to achieve this sooner. She also said there was another person to whom I was even more indebted than to herself, someone I knew very well, who would come forward once informed about my health and whether my eyesight was really so poor as they said. Exactly who I thought that unknown, compassionate soul might be, I don't recall, but I was impatient to see – as much as I could.

'My Lady,' I said, 'sadly, I left the clear light of my eyes at Capua and now am condemned to live in perpetual twilight. The features of those I love are hidden from me forever; it is only in my imagination that I am blessed with your dear, serene face!'

I could tell that the Princess's smile was sad, as if she felt she gained by not being seen.

'Well, then,' she said, opening the door to a little side room, 'please come in Signora Pisana, for Signor Carlo has real need of you.'

As much as my heart might have sensed it, I went almost mad with joy then. La Pisana, my good angel: every time fate seemed to have abandoned me, she was there, defying fate for me. She threw herself furiously into my arms, but withdrew just as I closed them to press her to my heart. Taking my hands, she gave me her cheek to kiss. In that moment, I forgot everything and my soul was alive in that kiss alone.

'Carlo,' she began, her voice breaking with emotion, 'I came to Naples seven months ago with your wife's permission, or I should say, at her request. The Princess had sent an urgent letter to Venice asking whether that Carlo Altoviti imprisoned at Castel Sant'Elmo and accused of high treason was the same she'd met twenty years before. She wrote to me, not knowing anyone else in your family. Well, you can guess how we felt about this news: I, who had been waiting for a letter from you for three months and feared you had become involved, by desire or by chance, in the Neapolitan revolution! I wanted to leave immediately, but practical matters held me back. I confided in your brother-in-law Apostulos, explaining that I could try to help you through an influential protector in Naples. He wanted to come with me, but the health of his wife, your sister, was declining and he was forced to stay. And so he gave me money for the journey – you know how we are always short – but before I left I asked him another favour: to go and see your wife, tell her all and ask her permission to act on your behalf. Aquilina, poor thing, was very distressed to hear about this new catastrophe, but by God, she was willing! Famine all around, two boys who are mere lads, her brother all but powerless – and she wanted to leave everything and come to suffer and die with us. Spiro dissuaded her, arguing that her presence brought us no advantage, while staying there would greatly help her children. She was convinced, happy to know I would do everything I could to save you, and trusting in my influential connections. I came here; and you owe all the clemency you received to the Princess's gracious intervention, but since God had also afflicted you with this other misery that she cannot allay, here I am, proud of the trust your wife has placed in me, ready to be your friend, your guide if you will let me, and, in any event, your nurse.'

'Pisana, you are too modest,' the Princess said. 'Your petitions in Naples did every bit as much as my own. If I was able to bend wills, you convinced hearts.'

'Oh, you are both my greatest benefactors!' I said. 'My life can never be long enough to prove my gratitude, if only in words.'

'All these formalities!' said the Princess. 'Now let us turn to something useful. Tomorrow you leave on a long journey and we must reflect, so you lack nothing you need.'

In fact, that excellent lady, although she was not very wealthy, had prepared me a trunk full of everything I might need, and there was nothing I wanted but a way, any way, to show her my gratitude. In the meantime she had also been busy looking after poor Martelli's children, for the widow had died not long after her husband's heroic sacrifice. Both boys had received a fine education; the first was a highly esteemed engineer and the other was second in command of a merchant ship.

Before we left I had the pleasure of meeting the elder and I found he was the spitting image of his father. He, too, had taken part in the recent events and been put on trial, but had been able to free himself. The city esteemed him even more now for the admirable firmness he'd shown at every step of the way. The next day I left Naples's enchanted shores rather sadly, although they had twice proved fatal for me. My eyes could not say farewell, but my heart beat time to a sorrowful hymn of parting. I knew I'd never see those shores and if I didn't die for them, they were anyway dead to me.

The following month we were in London. England was the only country where I was then permitted to live and our dire situation forced us into terrible privation. The high cost of food, expensive lodging, my eye ailment, which grew steadily worse, the indigence looming without any hope of escape: we felt nothing but anguish in the present and fears that the future would be even more disastrous. La Pisana, poor thing, was nothing more (or less) than a sister of charity. She looked after me night and day and studied English with the idea she could then teach Italian and provide for me. Meanwhile, we were spending more than we had and, despite doctors and cures, I was now completely blind. Just when we were expecting some help from Venice, Aglaura wrote to say that she could send very little, because Spiro had taken their two sons and all their assets and sailed for Mani when the first cries of rebellion were raised there. She herself had thought it her duty to encourage him and the only reason she hadn't gone along was that her health was very poor; and so she had stayed in Venice with her hardships and her pains, content to think that these were valid sacrifices on behalf of a holy cause and a great, oppressed people.

Pleased as I was by their generosity, this meant my last hope of getting some charity from that side was nil. As for my credits with the Porte, nothing could be done about them now that Spiro and his compatriots had declared war on the Turks. The only other place to turn was Cordovado, but that demanded a delicate touch, more deceptive than sincere, in describing our needs. Aquilina and Bruto would have let the blood from their veins to help us, and so to prevent them from ruining themselves and my children, we tended not to tell them anything but good news. They knew nothing of our great privation or of my blindness, and so, to account for la Pisana's long absence and my handwriting (as abominable as that of any blind man who struggles to write), I led them to think I was very busy and she gainfully employed as a governess with an important family and in no hurry to return to Venice, because with Clara there to assist Navagero, she was more of a hindrance than a help.

Meanwhile, she tried in every way she could to earn some profits from her stitching, and although at first she hadn't wanted to share my lodging, as my infirmity grew along with our need, she was forced to. We lived together as brother and sister, unmindful of those times when sweeter ties had joined us, and if I accidentally recalled them, la Pisana was very quick to make a joke of it or change the subject.

Alas, our every hope was disappointed. La Pisana had learned English with miraculous speed and spoke it fairly correctly, but the desired lessons didn't come, and, hard as she tried, she could find no one but some miserable shopkeeper's children to whom to teach Italian and French. She then tried to help out with lacemaking (Venetian ladies were highly skilled in the art back then), but although this brought decent earnings it was too fatiguing to do very much. I spent my long hours thanking her for what she did, and I don't think I ever suffered a worse torment than having to accept those costly sacrifices to preserve a life as worthless as my own. La Pisana laughed at my great speeches about devotion and gratitude, and tried to convince me that what seemed to me to cost her a great deal was but very little trouble to her. But her dry voice and bony hand told me all too well that the work and the hardships were consuming her. I, instead, put on fat like a horse kept in the stall and this was not the least of my worries. I feared I must seem insensible to all her proofs of heroic friendship.

'Friendship! Friendship!' she was obsessed (as we Venetians say) by that word, although I found it hard to believe la Pisana could stay within the bounds of such a tepid sentiment. I don't know if I feared or was flattered to think that memories of our past explained her present sacrifices. But she mocked me so sweetly when I lapsed into even the most distant allusion to all that, that I was ashamed of my suspicions and felt they revealed my egotism or my little faith that her heroic deeds were disinterested. In any case, her perpetual, heated speeches about Aquilina and my sons and the happiness I would find in their arms one day, were enough to persuade me otherwise. As far as I was concerned the Pisana of the past seemed to be dead and buried. And so the months passed and day and night were the same to me. I'd lost all hope of regaining my sight and never left the room except on Sunday, for a stroll on la Pisana's arm. She wearied herself dreadfully, however much she tried to make me think otherwise; and she was often out all morning, from what she said, running from house to house for the numerous lessons she was giving. I guessed she must have taken a job in a shop, but never imagined what I was later to learn.

'Pisana,' I once asked, 'why aren't you wearing your silk dress? It's Sunday.' I could tell by the rustle.

She said she'd taken it to be adjusted, but I knew she'd given it up for money, because a neighbour who'd helped her sell it had told me so.

Another day it was her shawl that was missing and I knew it because it was cold and her teeth chattered. She assured me she was wearing it and had me touch some wool she said was the shawl. But I knew the soft weave of that cashmere and she couldn't fool me by putting a merino cape in my hand. The shawl had taken the same trip as the silk dress. At times I felt it was a comfort to be blind, so as not to have to witness our poverty, forgetting that my blindness was the very cause of it. Then I would sink into despair, knowing I was so impotent as to owe my daily bread to a woman's mercy.

Aquilina, despite our protests we were quite comfortable, sent as much money as she could, but it was only a drop in a great bucket of need. Every day, she wrote, she set aside something in order to come to London, and that meanwhile many enquiries had been made in Venice to obtain a pardon so that I could return home. My head sank, for by now I felt quite hopeless, but la Pisana snapped at me, saying I was a fool to be so disheartened and that we were lucky to be able to survive honestly without having to work too hard. Sometimes, trying to shake me out of my apathy, she stung me quite hard with that strange, malicious humour of hers that I remembered from the past. But a moment later she would be kind and patient, as if her temperament had suddenly changed or was bent by her will. In short: there may be children who cost their mothers dearly, lovers who give their all for their mistresses, husbands who receive the highest proof of love from their wives, but the man who owes a greater debt to a woman than I to la Pisana would be very, very hard to find. No mother, no lover, no wife could have done more. If her conduct was also judged wild and eccentric, if they called her mad (as some of her Venetian acquaintances did) for her heedless generosity, well then I bless madness, and I would knock down the altar of wisdom and erect one far more holy and well-deserved to lunacy.

Sadly, though, it has been decided that few are mad and the many, sane. And in these times of ours, those who think first of being generous, and only then of their interests and what is the rule, are locked up in the hospital. If the brain answered the heart and the body, too, obeyed the heart rather than the head, do you think we'd have a second chance? Oh no, our history would finish with a magnificent 'The End' and we'd be busy, at the most, writing some glorious appendix. We must, alas, change course: our national renewal must be based not on ideals but on a concord of interests, something that will prove an excellent capital, giving sure, fat dividends. This, too, can be achieved, but what a difference from those lofty, unselfish impulses we had at first!

A poor blind man and a woman until then accustomed to all the comforts of the leisured Venetian nobility: just think what it was like for them to live in that vast, stifling, busy vortex that is London. Political refugees enjoyed no particular favour, nor was I considered any sort of fascinating menagerie animal. We even had to pay for the water we drank, and, apart from the meagre assistance sent from home, la Pisana had to provide for everything. But what, in London, are the three or four hundred ducats I could count on for a year in Venice or Cordovado! Penury! Especially with my infirmity, which la Pisana was always trying to cure by consulting the most renowned doctors, even though I had lost all faith in medicine and reproached her for a luxury I considered worthless.

She was absent more and more from home and for longer periods, and I became gloomy and suspicious, and she, contesting me, grew angry and our quarrels and disagreements mounted. It was up to me to back down and remain silent, for I owed her so much, but there were times when I felt I had the right to know what was on her mind, and, of course, whatever is denied us always seems the one desirable thing in the world. I would stubbornly try to convince her and she would, in turn, become nervous, and these quarrels of ours didn't always end in a friendly fashion. She would often storm out of the room, stamping her feet and growling about my distrust of her, but she never accused me of meanness or ingratitude. Not that I didn't give her the occasion. But then, while she was gone, I had time to repent and prepare myself for her return.

'Carlo,' she would say to me, 'will you be good to me now? If so, I'll stay; if not, I'll go out and come back later. I cannot bear it when you doubt me and think that what I don't tell you is something sinister and important, because it isn't true.'

I pretended I believed her and that I had no interest in that part of her life that she hid from me so mysteriously, but my imagination went on working and at times it was not far from the truth. Oh my God! It filled me with horror even to think of it! But I didn't let my mind linger on certain thoughts, for I didn't have the right. I did everything I could to convince myself that she was hiding nothing from me and that lessons took up all that time she spent outside the house. However, little by little, she ceased to tell me that yes, she was very well, and that she had no nostalgia for the florid years of her youth. I could hear her breathing heavily after coming up the stairs and coughing a lot, and sometimes, without being aware of it, she sighed so deeply that pity stung my heart.

As the second year of our exile began, she fell gravely ill and the despair, the torment, that this poor blind man suffered I cannot tell you: it astonishes me that I survived it. What was worse, I had to stifle all my misery so as not to weigh on her, and yet she still comforted me ever so sweetly in my hidden grief. On the verge of death, she spoke only of getting better; a deadly fever coursed through her veins and she fretted about my infirmities as if her own were trivial. She would go out next week, she kept saying, adding up the meagre credit she had accumulated here or there to cover our biggest expenses and make up for her lost income: anything to make me forget her illness and convince me she was almost well again. Still, I spent my days and nights at her bedside, feeling her pulse from time to time, listening to her heavy, laboured breathing.

Oh, what wouldn't I have given for a glimmer of my sight to judge how much to believe of her merciful falsehoods! With what dread did I follow the doctor down to the landing, imploring him to tell me the truth! I sometimes thought she must be right behind us, preventing the doctor from telling me the danger she was in. And when I refused to calm myself, she had the nerve to become irate and insist I believe her and not torment myself with imaginary fears. Oh, I was not fooled by her ruses! My heart warned me of the calamity threatening us, and in any case the potions the doctor ordered were not those prescribed for a passing ailment. We were utterly impoverished and I had to sell our linen and clothing, but I would have sold myself to give her a moment's relief.

At last, God had mercy on her, and on me. Her illness was tamed, if not beaten; the fever wracking her wasted body abated and, little by little, her strength returned. She got up from her bed and right away she wanted to dismiss the servant to reduce our expenses and look after the house herself. I fought as hard as I could, but her will was indomitable. Illness, disaster, persuasion, orders: none of them had ever moved her. The first few days she went out, I, too was unmoveable and went along with her, but then she grew so vexed at me that I had to give in and let her go out alone.

'Now Pisana,' I said to her, 'I thought I understood that you intend to go here and there to collect those little sums owed you for your lessons. Let us go, then. I'll accompany you wherever you like.'

'A blind man!' she said. 'A fine escort! Oh, wouldn't I just love to make myself ridiculous going around like that? And what would they think? No, no, Carlo. The English are terribly proper. Let me say it again: I won't be seen unless I am alone.'

And so, grumbling and not at all convinced of what she was telling me, I had to let her have her way. Once again there were long absences and I waited, half-paralysed with fear that she wouldn't return. And sometimes she came back so weary that no matter how hard she tried she couldn't conceal her exhaustion from me. I chided her gently, but then I had to remain silent, because even the slightest reproof made her so irate that she nearly had convulsions.

London, as you know, is a large city; but mountains stand still and men, moving about, come together. And so it happened that one morning, la Pisana met Lucilio, whom I had supposed was in London, but hadn't wanted to turn to because he'd been so unjustly cool to me in the past. They met and she told him about what had happened to me and to her, and why we were in London without any resources. My situation seemed to convince him that those accusations about me he once held to be true were false. He came to see me and was more friendly than perhaps he had ever been before. It was a nice way of asking my pardon for that long injustice and I couldn't have expected more from someone as proud as Lucilio. I was very comforted, and took our meeting as a promise from Providence that our fates were soon to change for the better. And this happy conviction looked even more true when all of a sudden our affairs seemed to take a very good turn.

My hope returned when Lucilio examined my eyes very carefully and told me they were covered by cataracts and that in a few months I could undergo an operation he was sure would succeed wonderfully. Oh what a great gift is sight! Only those who have lost it appreciate it properly. Lucilio then asked about me and my family and how things stood, and when all was explained he gave me hope that he would bring Aquilina and my sons to London and set us up with an eye to the future and not merely to present expenses. He had a large clientele of lords with whom he was in turn quite influential, and the protests that had recently been heard in Parliament about what had been decided at the Congress of Verona[8] were, I believe, inspired by him.

I was hesitant, both because of the great expenses involved, for which my purse was certainly unprepared, and then, I must confess, I was almost ashamed to show my eagerness to have my family near, lest it seem an affront to la Pisana's great, unique devotion. When we were alone for a moment, I told the doctor my qualms.

'No, no,' said he dolefully, 'you need your family and you should be aware that they will be of great service to the Countess Pisana, too.'

I wanted a better explanation of this enigma, but he dodged my question, saying that caring for a blind man was a heavy burden for a lady accustomed to the soft Venetian life and that the help of another woman would lighten her load considerably.

'Tell me the truth, Lucilio,' I said, 'does la Pisana's health not come into your thinking at all?'

'It does, yes . . . because it could fail.'

'Well then, now that we're on the subject, do you find it good?'

'My God, can one ever say whether health is good or bad? Nature has her secrets and not even doctors are privileged to know them. Now look, I've grown old in this profession and yet only yesterday morning I left a man who seemed to be getting better and that evening he was dead. These are the slaps that Nature administers to anyone who tries to pry into her and violate her mysterious virginity. Believe me, Carlo, science has got nowhere with her, we've merely kissed her on the cheek.'

'Oh, so you don't even believe in science! What do you believe in then?'

'I believe in the future of science, at least so long as some comet or cooling of the Earth's crust doesn't come to destroy centuries of work. I believe in the enthusiasm of those souls who, whenever they may intervene in our social order, will anticipate the triumphs of science by several millennia, the way the poet, with his bold intuition, may anticipate the discoveries of the mathematician with his sums.'

'And thus, Lucilio, you're still pursing your old dreams, hoping to spark that great enthusiasm with your secret plots and dark machinations!'

'No, don't condemn so foolishly what you don't understand. I'm not running after phantoms; I am meeting a need. Carlo, plots are not always secret, nor machinations dark. Touch this scar,' here he bared his breast near his throat. 'I got this a year ago at Novara. Nothing came of it, but the scar has remained.'

'And look at this, which I got at Rieti,' said I, rolling up my sleeve and showing him my arm.

Lucilio threw his arms around my neck with more feeling than I'd ever expected to see in him.

'Oh, blessed are the souls who see the truth and follow it, even when not driven by some overwhelming force,' he said. 'Blessed are the men for whom sacrifice is no pleasure, but who offer themselves anyway: noble, elective victims. They are the truly great.'

'Do not flatter me,' I said. 'I went to Naples out of vanity, you might say, and yet I feel a certain remorse for having sacrificed the interests of my family to my petty pride.'

'No, I swear to you, you've sacrificed nothing. Your family will join you here. You'll see the fair light of day again and the dear faces of your loved ones. It is true that London's sun is not that of Venice, but its melancholy hues suit the teary eyes of an exile perfectly.'

'And do you give me hope that by then la Pisana will be perfectly well?'

'Perfectly,' said the doctor, a quiver in his voice.

I shook all over, thinking I had heard – what? – a death sentence, but he went on coolly talking to me about la Pisana's illness and about the course it would take and the proper treatment and inevitable recovery, until the memory of that funereal 'perfectly' vanished.

The good doctor did all he could to help us, and from then on, thanks to him, we lacked nothing. I was much ashamed to live like that, on charity, but he told la Pisana he was obliged to his future sister-in-law and would not permit anyone else to assume those duties.

'What?' exclaimed la Pisana, 'you still have it in your head that you will marry my sister? But don't you see that she is even older in spirit than she is in body and, what is more, a nun right down to her toes?'

'I am incorrigible,' the doctor replied. 'What I tried at twenty and did not succeed at, I tried again at thirty, forty, fifty, and I will try again at sixty, which is not far away. My life is meant to be a trial, a hard and obstinate trial, for that is how I'm made, and bless the others if they imitate me. One must hammer to get the nail in.'

'But you will never get the obstinacy out of a nun.'

'Well then, let us not speak of it; let us speak instead of Aquilina and the two boys who should soon be arriving. Do you have news of their travels?'

'I had a letter yesterday from Brussels,' I broke in. 'Bruto has come with them, he and his trusty wooden leg. I confess I don't know how to thank you for the great expenses you have undertaken.'

'Thank me? You know, don't you, that a hundred pounds is what I make for writing out a prescription? I merely have to prolong some lord's noble gout for a couple of days and I earn enough to allow you all to travel across Europe. Do you know Lord Byron, the poet?[9] He offered me ten thousand guineas to lengthen his lame leg by an inch. Although I think I might have succeeded with a method of my own invention, I didn't need money then, and didn't want to waste my time straightening legs in the House of Lords. And so I laughed in the great poet's face and told him I was needed at the hospital.'

'And he?'

'He was delighted by my wit and retaliated by writing the finest sonnet ever composed in English, addressed to me. Let me tell you that behind the stormy mask of a Don Juan or a Manfred burns a pure flame that will set the world ablaze one of these days. Byron is too large a man to be a poet in books and rhymes alone. He will make a poem of his very life.'

'God willing!' I said. 'Poetry is the spirit's true happiness, the only one.'

'Well said,' Lucilio replied and I swelled with pride as he repeated my words. 'Poetry is true happiness of the spirit. Beyond it lies pleasure, but not genuine contentment.'

'And therefore I'm a poetess, because I am happy?' said la Pisana, her voice quite cheerful, but weak.

'You are Corinna, you are Sappho!' said Lucilio. 'But muttering odes or sonnets is not enough for you, you create them with your deeds, you lend your actions poetic loftiness. Before they were poets, Achilles and Rinaldo were heroes.'

La Pisana began to laugh, but in such a heartfelt way you couldn't suspect false modesty.

'Oh, I'm a pallid Corinna, a scrawny Sappho!' said she, still laughing. 'I feel I've become almost English, for I look like a horse, although perhaps I've gained a more aristocratic style.'

'You have gained in every respect,' said Lucilio, ever more heated. 'Your soul shining through the pallor of your face makes you look younger; it will prevent you from ever growing old! A man could swear you are but twenty-five and no one would doubt him.'

'Oh, yes, especially now that the poor old Rector who baptized me is dead. It's very sad, don't you think, to find ourselves ringed and shadowed by tombs. The first ranks are already almost gone. Now we ourselves are the first ranks.'

'But we are not afraid of the end, you can be certain of that. Neither you nor I nor Carlo has a compulsion to live. Our three temperaments are very different, but they are much alike in being humble and obedient before Nature. And this although my own character demands I use my life ruthlessly and spend it well, squeezing every drop from it, as they do with the grape seeds, which, once the wine has been pressed from the grapes, are crushed again to extract oil.'

'And will you have gained something?'

'Oh, yes. To have made my every talent bear fruit and to have offered an example to those who are to come.'

I nodded my agreement, for I'd always liked that notion of providing an example and considered it a good bargain, and

I had more faith in it than in books. La Pisana, in turn, confessed that in everything she'd done she'd never considered the glory of having imitators, but had simply given herself over to the sentiments transporting her.

'At least you've never allowed another to wither your spirit,' added Lucilio sadly.

I was filled with tenderness for him, that tough, tenacious soul who'd borne a wound for forty years with no thought of healing it or forgetting. A man of extreme pride, who wanted to feel pain in order to show he could bear it, and to be able to accuse others of betrayal and cruelty. This great physician revered by the dukes and peers of London had never repudiated the little doctor of Fossalta; he never admitted he had been modest, but insisted he had always been in some way great; and steely old age gave a hand to blazing youth, compensating all pain, lending him the invincible might of a sure conscience.

In those few days before our travellers arrived, la Pisana was colder to me than usual, but every once in a while the odd gesture of tenderness escaped her, and then she would stubbornly try to show me, with a thousand discourtesies, that it was a mere whim or even a way to mock me.

'Poor Carlo,' she would say sometimes, 'what would have become of you if pity hadn't moved me to look after you? How lucky you were that my old husband was such a bore and made me want to leave Venice, for thus I've been of some use to you, and soon you'll be able to kiss your dear ones again.'

She had never spoken to me so crudely and there was little hint of kindness in her as she spelled out the list of benefits I owed exclusively to her pity for me. It hurt me bitterly, but it also persuaded me that there was no trace of love for me in her and that this heroic compassion of hers was merely freakish eccentricity.

Finally came the day when I could clasp my sons to my breast, kiss their fresh, round faces and refresh myself with the pure sentiments of their young hearts. Good Aquilina, who had proved a brave and loving mother in bringing them up, had her share of my embraces, too, and I joyfully threw myself into Bruto's friendly arms. And yet I could not see their faces! For the first time I was pierced by dumb rage against my destiny, for it seemed that fiery will alone should be enough to relight my eyes, so intense was my desire. Lucilio soothed the pain a bit, telling me that soon he would attempt the operation, and by postponing the pleasures of sight until then, he gave me reason to enjoy right away all the others that my unhappy condition permitted.

For the rest of that day and the next there was no end of questions, enquiries, reminiscences about this or that person, about the tiniest things, the most trivial matters. Of Alfonso Frumier they knew nothing; about Agostino it was said in Venice that he was hungry for ribbons and crosses and was decorated like a little altar with them, but he also had a lot of children: to one he'd assigned the future office of minister; to another, general, patriarch, pope, and so on. His Excellency Navagero was neither dead nor alive, as usual, and Clara was always at his bedside, except when she had to recite the Hours, and then, even if he died, she couldn't be disturbed. Old Venchieredo had finally died, leaving his estate in such a mess that his wild and reckless son had no hope of sorting it out. There were rumours Raimondo might marry Alfonso Frumier's eldest daughter, but that Alfonso was reluctant to offer much of a dowry. Otherwise all was much the same: the town was indifferent; some pursued amusement, some wages; there was no trade, no life. Political events had left the great families very uneasy, but ordinary people had not been much aware; the people continued to complain about conscription, but habit tended to soften their grievances, above all because being a soldier meant eating good soup with lard in it and smoking good cigars at the expense of those who shovelled down polenta and smoked nothing but the chimney fumes.

'And in Cordovado?' I asked.

There was even less news from Cordovado than anywhere else, apart from Spaccafumo's madness[10] (he was fending off ghosts left and right). This anxiety of his led him straight into the River Lemene, where they found him drowned one fine morning. But some believed the many, many glasses of aquavit he'd swallowed were as much to blame as ghosts. So ended a man who would have been a hero if . . . Oh, I'm sorry! Follow-

I could, then, I boarded a ship out of Hydra and sailed for the Aegean's sacred waves. I felt like a sister of charity who has just nursed a dying man through his last hours and moves to another bedside where the pains are more vital but perhaps every bit as deadly. You know I'm not a fragile woman; you've seen it yourself, but I confess I wept often during that voyage. At Corfu we took on quite a few Italians who'd fled from Naples and Piedmont and who had decided to offer Greece the blood they hadn't been able to shed in their own country. I wept, I tell you, as a good Venetian; it was only when we reached the Lakonian shore that I felt the spirit of the ancient Spartan women course through my veins. Women here are men's companions, not the ministers of their pleasure. Tzavellas's wife and sister threw rocks and stones down from the Souli cliffs onto the necks of the Mohammedans, singing victory hymns. When Kostantina Zacharias raised her flag the women of Sparta came running with sticks and swords. Princess Mavrogenous of Mykonos plied the seas in her ship, roused Euboea to battle and offered to marry the man who would avenge her father's death at the hand of the Turks. Kanaris's[11] wife, to anyone who told her that her husband was brave, replied, 'And if he were not, would I have married him?' This, my dear Carlo, is how a nation is reborn.[12]

'When I had just arrived I met my son Demetrios, returning with Kanaris from the island of Tenedos, where they'd set fire to the Turkish fleet. All the Christians of Europe were against us there: the cross was allied with the Mohammedan crescent, fighting against the cross! May God sweep away the infidels, the betrayers of the faith, first. Demetrios had scorched one side of his face and breast with flaming pitch, but I am his mother and I recognized him. He had the reward of heroes in my arms, the glory of seeing his mother boast rightfully. Spiro and Theodoros were at Argos with Ypsilantis, hoping to hold back the torrent of Turks while Kolokotronis[13] and Niketas cut off their retreat, fomenting a mountain insurrection.

'Oh, Carlo, what a day it was when we four embraced on the soil of the Peloponnese, so near to being freed of our enemies. Missolonghi was being fortified; Nafplio was ours. The navy now had a port, the government a castle, and Greece towered above the barbarous tyranny of Constantinople as it did over the venal hostility of the Christian fleets. Shots will now be fired at any ship bringing arms, munitions and provisions to the Turks, and barbarism will probably obtain what glory, heroism and hardship didn't.

'All private gain here has disappeared into the common good. One possesses only what the *patria* does not need, and conserves it for tomorrow's needs. We embrace our country's victories; we suffer for her sorrows. And so I shall not speak of us in particular. I'll merely say that my health has not worsened despite our labours, and that Spiro's wounds, procured at the walls of Argos, are healing. Theodoros fought like a lion and was an example to all, but some divine aegis protected him and he had not a scratch on him. When I walk the streets of Athens where we are living in this moment of truce, my two sons browned by the sun of the fields and the fire of battle on either side of me, I feel as if the century of Leonidas, of Thermopylae, were still with us. Spiro often speaks of you, and he says to ask you to send one or both your sons to Greece if you want to make men of them. A lad of sixteen is no boy here, but an enemy of the Turks who can swim across to one of their wooden hulls and set it on fire. Oh, send us your Luciano, and your Donato too, if you will. Convince Aquilina that a soulless life is no life at all; that to die for a holy cause is an enviable fate for Christian mothers.

'Yesterday the deputies of Greece met for the second time among the cedars of Astros. Ypsilantis, Odysseus, Mavrocordato, Kolokotronis! Names of heroes who make us forget Miltiades and Aristedes, Cimon and all the other ancients whose memory lives on in the deeds of their descendants. I say it again, Carlo, and listen to your sister, who would not give you wrong advice: send us your sons. To be good Italians they must be a little bit Greek, and then we shall see results we haven't until now. If you are still in London and la Pisana is with you, send my regards to her and to Dr Lucilio Vianello, whom I admire and esteem by reputation. We have here with us an ensign with a Neapolitan ship, Arrigo Martelli, who says he has met you and that he's been in your debt from the time of the revolution. He also asks to be remembered to you and that I tell you that his brother has left for South America where there is great demand for good engineers.

'Farewell, dear Carlo! Be strong, despite your infirmity, and if they allow you to travel, you, too, must come to us! Oh what a fine dream! Come, and you will blessed by all those who love you.'

Well, this is how I am made. After Lucilio had read me the letter I had Luciano called and handed it to him, waiting for the response I knew would be written on his open, manly face. He hadn't yet finished reading when he threw himself into my arms, saying, 'Oh father, let me go to Greece!'

Aquilina had come in just at that point and sat down beside me, and I took her hand.

'What is it about?' she asked.

And so I told her about the invitations to us from Greece.

'If they feel they have the vocation, then let them go,' she said, making an effort to control herself. 'One must go where one is called; otherwise, nothing good comes of anything.'

'I thank you, dear Aquilina,' I said. 'You are the sort of woman we need to renew ourselves! The others, the ones not like you, are made to crawl in the dirt.'

Now I heard a light footstep entering the room; it was la Pisana, who had scarcely said a word for many days. I had missed hearing her voice, but by being somewhat gruff with her I hoped to repay her for her recent sourness. Lucilio asked a few questions about her health, to which she replied in monosyllables, in a feebler voice than usual. She then went out as if vexed and Aquilina followed, and Luciano, probably obeying a glance from Lucilio, went out too, and I remained alone with the doctor.

'Do tell me,' he began in a tone that announced ours would be a serious talk, 'what right you have to be so judgemental, so superior with la Pisana?'

'Oh, so you have noticed?' said I. 'Well then you will have observed how extraordinarily cold she is with me. I know I owe her a great deal and I shall never forget it; if blood could prove my gratitude I'd spend mine to the last drop. But at times I can't resist feeling somewhat scornful. Do you know that recently she has been insisting that the only reason she went to Naples was to distract herself from marital tedium, and that all the assistance she's so generously given me is owed to her feeling sorry for me and nothing else.'

'And therefore you suspect she no longer loves you as she once did?'

'I'm certain of it, as certain as I am that I exist. I may be blind, but my powers of discernment are not. I know la Pisana's nature like my own and I know she's unable to submit to certain relations and her own disquiet alone forces her to violate them. I speak to you freely because you are an expert on life and disease and you can sympathize with human frailty, especially when mixed with such great generosity. I repeat: our life together as brother and sister these two years persuades me that la Pisana has forgotten the past and I do not find it hard to believe that pity is her only motivation for such wonders of love and devotion. In any case, her temperament is too eccentric to obey some preconceived rule of fidelity.'

'Oh, Carlo, don't make such rash judgements! It is just such extraordinary temperaments that shun ordinary rules. Don't trust your discernment, I say; for bodily eyes sometimes reason better than those of the soul, and if you could see –'

'I have no need to see, Lucilio. Aren't you aware that I love her still, that I have always loved her? Did I not tell you the story of my marriage the other day? Alas, though, she has sworn to make me feel what I have lost in being excluded from her heart's intimacy, when she once let me in! Alas, she is punishing a love too docile – and yet too stubborn – with her pity. It's a terrible punishment, a very sophisticated kind of cruelty, a beneficent revenge!'

'Be silent, Carlo, every one of your words is sacrilege.'

'Every one is true, you mean to say?'

'Sacrilege, I repeat. Do you know what la Pisana was doing for you when I found her pale, exhausted, in rags, on the streets of London?'

'Well, what?'

'She had her hand out, Carlo! She was begging! Begging to save your life.'

'Heavens above! No, it can't be true. Impossible!'

'So impossible that I, too, was giving her some coin or other, when . . . Oh, but how can I tell you what I felt when I recognized her? How can I describe my distress – and hers?'

'Oh, please stop, Lucilio. I'm losing my mind. I feel faint with pain, looking back at what we've been through.'

'And you still doubt her love? Her love is boundless, unique: a love that has kept her alive and will make her die!'

'Have pity on me! Do not speak to me this way!'

'I speak as a doctor and I am telling you the truth. She loves you and is forcing herself not to reveal it to you. That effort, more than the hardships, the pain, the sleepless nights, is destroying her health. Carlo, open your eyes to her heroism and show your adoration for this woman you do not dare to trust! Adore her, I tell you: this virgin force of nature able to raise chaotic impulses to the heights of a miracle and hold that miracle suspended like an eagle floating above the clouds.'

Indeed, I was stunned to learn of her amazing goodness, more than I'd ever expected from anyone. And who would have thought la Pisana capable of such modest reserve, such humble, hidden abnegation, such saintly fiction (carried to such an extreme) in order not to disturb the harmony of a family you might say she herself had created? How wrong I'd been about her, for if she was volatile perhaps when it came to minor feelings, she was staunch and resolute in the great ones like no one else! The way she had busied herself when Aquilina's arrival was imminent; those tender impulses of hers so quickly restrained and the melancholy moods that followed; the way she'd distanced herself voluntarily from me: it all convinced me that what Lucilio had said was true. For two years I'd judged her wrongly and my error itself was proof of her fine sensibility and her tenacious heroism.

'Lucilio,' said I, so moved I could barely speak, 'I am at your command. Speak, talk to me, teach me how to save her. My life and those of my whole family are barely worth these sacrifices. The least I can offer her is what life is left to me!'

'We must think it over, Carlo. That is why I am here with you. I worry less about the health of all my illustrious patients, believe me, than about a single regret or sigh or lament from la Pisana. She deserves to live out her days in full and in happiness and to die overwhelmed by joy.'

'Don't speak of death. Please, do not speak of it!'

'And how do you know that for certain rare, excessive souls, death may not be a reward? However, let us reason as we do for the rest. The only way I can imagine saving her is to find some other circumstance demanding her patience and sacrifice. Her husband, for example: by his bedside she can regain her will to live and perhaps her native air will help to restore her health.'

'Send her back to Venice, you say? But Lucilio, why? Why must I send her away, now that I no longer need her assistance?'

'Not at all. You must go with her. Within your family she enjoys that intimate affection without which temperaments like hers cannot survive. When her wild, strong spirit finds other challenges, other sacrifices, other miracles to try, her past will cease to torment her and her impossible desires will subside into sweet, contented melancholy. You will have a friend again, a great friend!'

'Oh, God willing, Lucilio. We must leave for Venice tomorrow.'

'You forget two things. First, that I have promised to give you back your sight. Second, that you cannot return to Venice without putting yourself in danger. But while I work on getting you that permission, your cataracts will be getting ready for the surgery and I promise you you'll see the pale sun of Christmas.'

'Is there no way we can hurry things? Not for my eyes, you understand Lucilio, but for her – her alone. I think you could try to operate now, couldn't you?'

'Oh excellent, Carlo! You would like to be permanently blind so as to pay a great debt of gratitude with your eyes, perhaps? Be more humble, my friend; even two eyes are not enough. It is better to preserve them, and they will reward you many times over with what you can see. You are owed money by the Turks, but nothing will come of it if you have to rely on private petitions. Would you like me to try to sell your credit to an Englishman? England now has some claims on Ottoman goodwill, because the ships of London, Liverpool and Corfu are helping in the holy work of making a martyr of poor Greece. England is a loving mother and, above all, when it comes to getting her children paid what is due them, she's worth her weight in gold. To recover a credit of a thousand pounds, she'd have no regrets about setting the four corners of the world on fire. Leave it to me; let me untangle this question if I may.'

'You didn't need all those words to persuade me. Tomorrow I'll give you the papers; Bruto has them at the moment. There couldn't be a better man to represent me.'

'Until tomorrow then, we're agreed. I'll get busy trying to take care of the matter. In a couple of weeks I can operate, then the usual forty days of rest, and then off to Venice. I won't need very much time to get you a passport.'

'All right, but meanwhile?'

'Meanwhile, you must be humble and affectionate with la Pisana and do not praise your wife overmuch, as you were doing now. She deserves praise, but not at this time. La Pisana, I tell you, suffers bitterly to hear it.'

'Thank you, thank you, Lucilio. I have never had a better friend than you.'

'So you remember, do you? Ours is an old friendship indeed. It began when I ordered up a purgative to spare you the scolding and the slaps.'

That memory sent tears running down my face. Even the blind can be refreshed by weeping. So copious and so sweet were those tears that afterwards I didn't feel the half of my sorrows. Lucilio went out, taking my hand affectionately, and Aquilina came in soon after, telling me we had important matters to discuss. I wasn't much disposed to talking, but I wanted to do as she wished and asked her to speak, saying I was glad to listen. It was about our sons, and especially Luciano, who, after that half-conversation about going to Greece, had grown so excited it was hard to see how to calm him down. She hadn't opposed the plan in his presence, for she didn't want to disagree with me, nor openly deflate his pride and daring, but to me she confided that it seemed a reckless plan, and Luciano still too young to undertake such a venture without putting himself at risk. She thought it was better to let him mature a little and wait for a more genuine vocation.

Her observations seemed quite right to me and I agreed with her in full, and praised her for being so generous and so prudent, and said that I, too, was not comfortable with decisions made out of pure childishness, for they often lead us (and others) to lose faith in ourselves too early. And so we agreed; but meanwhile, in the other room, Luciano and Donato were talking of nothing else but Athens, Leonidas, Uncle Spiro and their cousins and how they couldn't wait to join up and go after those filthy Turks. Donato alone was somewhat sorry to have to leave his mother, while his cousins in Greece had theirs nearby to witness their great bravery.

'But our mother will be in our thoughts always, rousing us to great and noble deeds,' said Luciano. 'You know what the Spartan mothers were like? They liked to bear children so as to offer them up to their country, and they would hand them their shields, saying, "Either you come back with it or you come back on it!" Which meant: either victorious or dead; because they used to lay the bodies of the fallen on their shields.'

So the two lads stirred up their enthusiasm, one of them dreaming of Botzaris's[14] heroism, the other, Tzavellas's noble death.

The day was approaching when Lucilio would employ the finest techniques of his science to restore my sight. He no longer spoke to me of la Pisana and she avoided me no matter how much I tried to appease her with the tenderest words. Aquilina was jealous, but, knowing how much her friend had done for me, she didn't dare to complain. Lucilio's silence was not promising and I attributed the rare comforting words he did pronounce less to frankness than to a desire to keep me calm for the great day. I was overjoyed when he said, 'It will be the day after tomorrow.' And then my heart beat strong, thinking it was on the morrow; and when he said, 'It is today,' I was gripped by such impatience that I believe I'd have died if they had dragged it out another twenty-four hours. Lucilio went to work with great precision. I wasn't just an invalid, but a friend. If miracles could be expected they would certainly come from him; and his patient's trust in him never wavered. When he told me, 'It is finished,' they had already blacked the door and the windows, so that a sudden flash of light didn't bother me. Nevertheless, I thought I saw – I did see – a faint gleam through the gloom and let out such a shriek that Bruto and Aquilina, who were holding me, flinched. In reply came a weak shout from la Pisana, who must have feared some disaster had happened, but Lucilio reassured her, jesting: 'I'll bet this mountebank has already seen something! Now be sure that you don't remove this blindfold I'm putting on, and, above all, the shutters must remain closed as they are, tightly. The operation has gone very well and I can already predict that the six weeks of convalescence will be reduced to four.'

'Oh, thank you! Thank you! Thank you, my friend! Make it as short as you can,' said I, covering his hands with kisses. I thanked him not for having given me back my sight, but for the prospect that something might be done for la Pisana sooner than I'd hoped.

When everyone had followed the doctor out of the room, to thank him for such a great service and perhaps to learn how much they should believe what he'd said in my presence, la Pisana came near me and I could feel her tepid breath on my cheek.

'Pisana,' I murmured, 'your love and your compassion have been so very admirable!'

She fled, tripping over some piece of furniture, and two anxious sobs escaped from her breast. My wife, who was coming in, met her at the door.

'How's our invalid doing, do you think?' Aquilina asked.

'I hope he'll do well,' said la Pisana, making a supreme effort. But she could endure no more and ran off and closed herself in her room, before Aquilina even noticed she was upset. Once again I understood how strong and unselfish she was and I felt I could hear her sobs all the way from her room at the other end of the house, and every one of them was a cruel blow to my heart. For that entire day I never thought about my sight and those who were looking after my eyes annoyed me. This was much more important than two stupid eyes!

Lucilio often came to visit me, but we were rarely alone

together and he seemed to avoid all confidences. Nevertheless, I often asked after la Pisana's health and whether the prospect of returning to Venice had achieved the good results we'd hoped for. He would reply in vague terms without saying yes or no; and she, when she did come into my room, hardly ever opened her mouth, and I was aware of it because my sons were less noisy than usual, for her melancholy clearly imposed a certain respect. When Lucilio brought me my passport, obtained through the Austrian embassy, I asked her if our plan pleased her.

'Oh, my dear Venice!' she said. 'You ask if I would like to see Venice? After Paradise, that is my one desire.'

'Very well, then. Doctor, when will you permit me to open the windows, throw away this bandage and leave?'

'The day after tomorrow,' said Lucilio, 'but as for travelling you must wait a few more days; you mustn't go out immediately in the noonday sun.'

I endured those two days, determined not to delay my departure for a moment once my eyes were healed. But in the meantime la Pisana came less and less to my room and they told me she was almost always closed up in her own. Finally Lucilio came and took off my blindfold and the bandages over my eyes. The shutters were just slightly open and a soft, diffuse light, like that of twilight, gently touched my eyes. If the spectacle of dawn enchants us (although it happens every twenty-four hours), just think how overjoyed I was by that dawn that arrived after a night of almost two years! To rediscover those simple pleasures we pay little heed to, but appreciate so much more when they are forbidden; to revive the memory of sensations that had begun to fade, the way a tradition can fade in time and become a fairy tale; to glut oneself in contemplation of all that is beautiful, grand, sublime in this world, and translate our dear ones' love into a language obsolete to us: such pleasures can almost make a man wish to be blind in order to regain his sight. Certainly, it was one of the happiest moments of my life. But just after it came one that was very painful indeed.

La Pisana, too, had come to watch the last part of this miracle and when, after that first, sweet assault of the light on my eyes I began to distinguish the people and things around me, the first face that my gaze fell on was hers. Oh, she deserved to be the first! Neither friends nor family nor my sons nor my wife nor the doctor who had given me back my sight deserved my thanks so much. But how she had changed! Her skin was pale and transparent as alabaster; her features those of some sorrowful Virgin by Fra Angelico;[15] her back bent like someone who has shouldered a heavy weight and cannot stand upright; her eyes wondrously enlarged, shining through her eyelids like lamps behind coloured glass, the bluish tint of sorrow and the red of tears making splendid opalescent patterns in the whites. She looked unearthly; you couldn't say how old she was. You could only say she was closer to Heaven than she was to earth.

I cannot lie. I'm weak by nature and I've never hidden it from you. My breast swelled with sudden anguish and I burst into a flood of tears. Everyone thought they were tears of joy, except for Lucilio, who perhaps knew otherwise. Instead, I was weeping because my eyes had confirmed the dreadful significance of her recent silence. I saw that la Pisana no longer belonged to this world and that Venice, as she herself had said, was but her second desire, the first being Paradise. While this sad thought was shaking my breast with desolate sobs, she let go of Aquilina's shoulder, on which she'd been resting, and I watched her stumble out of the room. I now begged everyone present to leave me alone with my feelings, for the overwhelming emotion had tired me. When they had gone, a fresh fit of tears seized me even more violently and Lucilio could do nothing but wait until fatigue brought some peace. When, finally, the tears and sobs gave way to speech, how many words, prayers, promises burst forth, begging him to save a life a thousand times more precious than my own! I begged him as the devout pray to God, for I craved hope so much that I would have renounced reason and turned the world upside down to grasp at least a hint of it. Hope's pitiful wiles convinced me that the man who had brought me back the light could certainly bring back life and health to la Pisana.

'My dear Lucilio,' said I, 'you can do anything if you will it. Since I was a child I've always thought you were supernatural, close to omnipotent. Your will bends nature to incredible feats.

You must search, study, strive: for never have your genius and your science met a cause more just, an enterprise more noble. Save her, by God, save her!'

'So you have understood everything,' said Lucilio after a moment's pause. 'Her soul is no longer with us; her body lives on, but even I don't know why. Save her, you tell me, save her! And what makes you think that provident nature does not save her by pressing her to that great bosom? There is much we can do against flesh-and-blood illnesses, but the spirit, Carlo? Where are the medicines to heal the spirit, the instruments to cut out the gangrenous parts and save the healthy? What sorcery can bring the spirit back to Earth when an irresistible force is slowly drawing it into what Dante called the 'great sea of being'? Carlo, you are not a child, nor I a charlatan; you don't want to be deceived, however much your present frailty makes false and fleeting illusions seem preferable to hard reality. We come into this world certain to see our mothers and fathers die, and only someone who is afraid of his own death despairs when others die. When a friend dies, we suffer more for the company we lose than our friend suffers losing his life.

'You and I know something of life, I believe, and can weigh it at its proper value. Yes, mortality is sad, but we bear it with strength and resolution; we are not so selfish as to want to prolong another's pain and suffering merely to exorcize our own foolish fears, those of the child left alone in the dark. Darkness and solitude are the tomb; we enter the great realm of the shadows bravely; alive or dead, we are alone; when it comes to our friends, we must think only of easing the pain of parting. I'm not the sort of doctor who believes he has exhausted the secrets of nature because he's seen some nerve twitch under the dissector's knife. There is something in us that escapes the anatomist's eye and belongs to a higher reason, one that we don't comprehend with our own. We can only entrust the unknowable destiny of those we love to that supreme sense of justice that is the eternal soul of humanity. Science, virtue, life's obligations, all add up to a single word: forbearance.'

'Forbearance!' I said, more despondent than consoled by his cold but fatal reasoning. 'Forbearance is all very well for oneself, but for others? Are you so cruel, Lucilio, as to advise forbearance for ills that I myself have caused, for disasters that will torment me forever with remorse? Don't you see the boundless, hopeless grief that tears at me just to think I hastened by even one day the departure of such a noble, dear soul? Death, you say, is our fate. Well, let death come! But murder, Lucilio, the murder of that one creature who has loved you more than herself, more than life and honour: that is a crime that cannot be explained by fate or redeemed by forbearance. To redeem it, another life must be sacrificed. Death alone settles death's debt.'

'Death settles nothing, believe me. You won't have to wait forever for death's comfort, but to hasten it would be to try to escape your penance. Would you be so cowardly as that? Now, I'm not one of those cautious life-worshippers who make of their wives and children and country excuses for not risking even so much as catching a cold. But when a worthless, doubtful cause is battled by one that is sure, generous, noble; when passions leave us the time to decide: well then, Carlo, family, *patria*, humanity all command you not to desert, to fight to the very end!'

'No, this is pointless. I won't have the strength to fight! Better to clear the field of a useless encumbrance. All the rest is remorse; I am too unhappy, Lucilio! To watch her die, when I was meant to adorn her life with all my love and devotion!'

'And what about me?' said Lucilio with a roar, clutching my arm. 'Do you think I am only a little unhappy? I, who watched the very soul of my soul dry up; I, who still hot with passion, stood by at the funeral of all my hopes; I, who, have watched the suicide of love on the part of the woman I adored; I, whose thoughts have flitted desperately among my ruined beliefs, begging a flash of a smile from life in vain; I, who mustered all my intelligence, all the force of my soul, to reopen the gates of a heart that once was mine; I, who dreamed of the world upside down to extract from confusion and chaos that one thing I desired, the one that had escaped me.

'I, who have watched peerless energy and force defeated by an indifference that may well be false; I, who saw paradise so close, but could not reach it, couldn't ease my thirst with a single drop of happiness because the memory of three careless and dishonest words stood in the way; I, who thus had found the purest soul, the finest, most sensitive heart that ever lived below, and this indelible token of happiness for no reason turned into irremediably deadly poison in my hands – do you not think I had enough reasons, strength and will to kill myself? Why, tell me, would I stubbornly cling to life when the best and most perfect creature, the only one I ever thought worthy of my love, rewarded that love with betrayal and cruelty? Why wear myself out to build a *patria* for this humanity, when its loftiest specimen could lay me such a deadly trap? Why struggle, why study, why heal, why live?

'Do you want to know, Carlo, the *why*? Because I wasn't certain. Because a man furnished with reason must never stoop to any act that isn't reasonable; because I wasn't certain that my death would be just or useful to myself or others, while my life could be, in one way or another, and so I let nature pronounce a sentence I didn't feel able to. And that is why I am alive, because I pursued truth and justice eagerly, because I fought for them and for liberty and *patria*; because I forced my mind to accept that what the universal consensus believed was the good, *was* the good; and I laboured to bring peace to the troubled, hope to the hopeless, health to the infirm. Nature gives us life and then she takes it away; are you so learned as to understand and judge the laws of nature? Reform it, change it, judge it at will, then! And if you don't feel you have this authority, this power? Then obey. If you are unhappy, torture yourself; if innocent, suffer; if guilty, repent and make amends, but employ your reason and live!'

'Fair enough, Lucilio. Let the innocents live in pain, the unhappy in torment, the guilty in expiation; let all those who can't find reasonable arguments to destroy their lives, endure them. But I, Lucilio, I'm beyond your laws; and I shall die. Yes, I'll be guilty of a crime more hateful and monstrous, in my opinion, than matricide itself. But should nature order me to live, she will then rise up and show me how to take arms against her. There is but one remedy for ills that cannot be put right, and you know very well that nature does not preclude it. What is this mad hatred of the light, this fear of myself, this endless desire for sleep and oblivion that fills me? Are they not calls by which nature invites me to her great bosom of mysteries, peace, perhaps even hope?'

'*Perhaps*. That's the word that proves you wrong, Carlo. Here in life, only one thing is absolutely certain. Justice! Now reply to me honestly, for you can see that I put the question in clearer terms. Do you firmly believe you are being fair to all: to you children, your wife, your relatives, friends, country, to la Pisana herself and to your own conscience, in your desperate refusal of life? Now then, no objections, no wavering: reply!

'Oh, have mercy on me, Lucilio! I beg you, let me die. I have seen my children; I've seen all that is dearest and most precious to me in the world; I will press them to my heart and urge them to be good and true, strong and hard-working citizens; I will see them again for a last time if you permit and expire with my heart at peace. Have mercy, Lucilio. Please, allow me to die!'

'And what if your sensibility should survive you beyond the grave and show you your sons: poverty-stricken, miserable, perhaps even low and despicable, and all because of you?'

'No, no, Lucilio. They have their mother and she will help them with her counsel, which is certainly worth as much as mine.'

'And what if, after you die, your wife were to follow you? What if this were to be just the first link in a long chain of calamities that will plague your offspring down to the last generation? And if you – dead, distant, powerless but still aware – had to bear the fearful responsibility of your example? What if the shade of la Pisana were to spurn your act of reverence, marred as it must be by the blood and tears of others? What if she, strong as she was in suffering, compassion, abnegation, were to look on you with contempt; you, who had escaped life so ignobly; what if her great ambitions floating in the aery world of the spectres were to flee from yours, so miserable and vile? What if you were to be apart for all eternity, if your craven and brutal death were just the beginning of a separation that must keep on widening? What if nature – crazily considered your partner in this mad project – offers you just one means of reparation: to imitate her goodness and endurance and meld yourself with her when nature invites you into some doubtful, arcane future? Oh, Carlo. Think about it deeply. Don't insult la Pisana further by making her goodness responsible for all the ills that could derive from your madness!'

'My friend, you speak well, and I shall reflect. For the moment, I sense that cold reason can find no place in the tumult of my passions. I know myself well enough to think that time won't make me look for pretexts. A year from now will not be different from today if my spirit remains in the same condition.'

'In any event,' said Lucilio, 'I've tried to protect you as much as I can until now and I hope that if you speak with la Pisana, her manner, her words, her gaze will persuade you better than any reasoning of mine. But I don't want you to think we have already reached grave danger and utter desperation. If she could get to Venice and gain some repose by taking up her old life . . .'

'Oh, tell me the truth, Lucilio! Is there hope? You don't say this now to console me, to deceive me?'

'I'm so far from wanting to deceive you that, until now, I've allowed you to think the worst. I cannot give you much hope, apart from that which generous nature always permits, until she arrests, perhaps just as generously, life's mysterious motion. Meanwhile, I would advise you – this will seem strange – to spend as much time as you can with la Pisana. I can promise you her example will dissuade you from any desperate acts, and may what I know of her prove that I've been truthful with you.'

'Thank you,' I said, gripping his hand. 'No example from her or advice from you could be something I didn't need.'

Thus ended a memorable conversation that would pretty much decide the rest of my life to come. I was still quite troubled and dismayed, but Lucilio's strength of mind had somehow shored me up, and I decided he was right to advise I draw close to la Pisana and try to make amends for the harm I'd involuntarily done, adapting myself to her desires and thus offering the highest proof of love and devotion I could. Sadly, my first efforts at this were discouraging; poor Pisana did all she could to avoid me, perhaps because now that she was close to leaving me, she didn't want to enjoy my company and then feel anguish when the time of separation came. Perhaps it made her unhappy that I seemed to prefer her to Aquilina.

However, when I refused to be put off by her coolness, but continued in every way I could to show my gratitude (and my deep regret for not having shown it better and before), her stubborn reserve finally softened and I drew her back into our old confidence. My God, how it tormented me to watch the flame of life flare in her eyes even as her strength withered and she could barely keep her tired, weak limbs upright. What a horrid spectacle: the joy with which she welcomed my old tenderness, the sweet stoicism that made her shrug her shoulders and smile when I talked of the future. One day I spoke with Lucilio, who said that if things continued that way, we might risk travelling to Venice the following week. That evening I was all alone with la Pisana, for Lucilio had taken Aquilina, Bruto and the children to see some marvel of London. She was paler but more cheerful than usual and I continued to hope that just as her temperament was erratic, so her health might suddenly disobey the rules of the rest of us and that the festive spirits come to life in her might mean her illness wasn't fatal.

'Pisana,' I said, 'next month we could be in Venice. Doesn't the very thought of it do you good?'

She smiled and raised her eyes to the heavens, but said nothing.

'Don't you think,' I went on, 'that your native air and the peace we'll feel once we are all together will cure you of your melancholy?'

'Melancholy, Carlo? Whatever makes you think I'm melancholy? You know that I've never been happy by nature; my joy was never constant; it was fleeting, mere glimmers. I've always been a fitful creature, but most often surly and silent. Only now does serenity and calm smile on me, and I've never felt so peaceful, so content. I feel I've played my role and hope for some applause.'

'Pisana, Pisana, don't say that! You deserve much greater applause than we can give and you shall have it. We'll go back to Venice, and there –'

'Oh Carlo, don't speak to me of Venice. The *patria* I have in mind is much nearer – oh, it's far away if you will, but the voyage is quick. Above, Carlo, above! You see, poor Clara, if nothing else, has got me to believe in God's mercy. She didn't succeed in getting her theory of sin into my head, but I do believe in the rest of it and hope not to be punished too harshly for that little evil I did without meaning to. All that little good that I could do, I've done; and it seems fair that my reward should not be delayed very much. I desire that reward now and want to leave you – briefly – with a smile on my lips and, and, permit me to hope, your sympathy.'

'Don't you see, Pisana, that you're tearing me apart? How your words accuse me, remind me of how stupidly I accepted your seeming coldness these last few years? Low, ungrateful murderer that I am, I discounted your sacrifices; made myself believe you were indifferent (to pay off my debts cheaply perhaps); refused to see in your devotion that supreme delicacy that allows you to mask a great sacrifice and make it appear ordinary, everyday. Oh, curse me, Pisana! Curse the instant you first saw me, whatever led you to squander as much heroism on me as would make a saint virtuous or a martyr sublime. Curse my stupid pride, my mean suspicion, the foul egotism that let me live two years on your very flesh. Oh yes, may the punishment for this infamy fall on my head! I deserve it! I seek it! I want it! Until I have atoned with tears and blood for my crime, for all the suffering and humiliation I caused you, I'll have no peace, nor the courage to raise my head and call myself a man!'

'Are you mad, Carlo? What is this? What are you thinking? Do you no longer know your Pisana – or do you think that I'm pretending to be happy so as to avoid your pity? No, Carlo, I swear it isn't so. Whether I live or die has nothing to do with my happiness. I won't conceal from you that I believe my last hour to be very near, but am I less happy for that? Not at all, Carlo. Your tenderness and your trust were the last comfort I was expecting and you've given them back to me. Oh, bless you! One word of gratitude from you, one loving look, would repay two lives longer than mine, with three times as many sacrifices and privations! You kept your distance from me? You imposed pain and hardship on me? Never, Carlo, never. I sinned and you pardoned me. I left you and you didn't complain. When I came back you met me with open arms and sweet words! You are the noblest, most generous and trusting creature on earth. If eternity stood before me and I had to endure never-ending hardship without even the comfort of your presence, all just to spare you a single tear or sigh, I wouldn't hesitate an instant. I'd resign myself with joy, happy to think that all my days and all my toil were consecrated to you. Carlo, you alone haven't repudiated me. Your steadfast love has given me the courage to look at myself and say, "Perhaps I am not so despicable if such a heart still loves me!" Oh, Carlo, forgive me if I haven't loved you as you deserved!'

'Pisana, get up! Your words shame me. How can I ever dare to look you in the face again or ask your pardon? Oh, my God! How can I not be tormented by all those moments when a word of love from me, a meek and humble gaze, would have persuaded you I was grateful, if not repaid you? No, I holed myself up in my mean suspicions, punishing you, coldly and arrogantly, for the most noble, most costly sacrifice a woman ever made, that . . . yes, I want to say it, Pisana – that of her love. And if I thought you loved me no longer, then why did I use you like a slave, dragging you around the world tied to my tremendous destiny? Oh, Pisana! Sadly, I have been a low tyrant and a merciless executioner!'

'And I repeat: either you don't remember or after all these years you no longer know your Pisana. Don't you understand that what you call suffering, hardship and sacrifice have provided me with indescribable pleasure, a sensuous pleasure both delicious and sublime? Don't you see that my strange, erratic nature made me tire of ordinary enjoyments and search in another sphere – even at the risk of losing my way – for pleasures and happiness that went beyond those of my past life? Didn't you see that the first symptom of this, well, near-madness, was that strange, tyrannical whim of mine to marry you to Aquilina? Oh, I beg you on bended knee, Carlo! Forgive me for having loved you my way, for offering you up to that freakish, unthinkable fancy of mine, for making you but an occasion to satisfy my eccentricities! You could not understand me; you should have hated me, and instead you tolerated me. When in these last few years I found such sweetness in looking after you and in hiding my love from you, making you think only need and pity drove me, shouldn't I have known my behaviour tormented you and nullified most of the good in those few good deeds I did for you? All the same, I insisted in showing off that barbarous delicacy of mine, that virtue I was so vain about, that I'd deployed for the first time in your marriage – for I demanded my own pleasure first, whatever the cost! You see, Carlo, you see how selfish I was? Wouldn't I have done better to trust in your generosity, so much greater and better tested than mine, and say, "I've done wrong, Carlo! I've done wrong, because I was thoughtless and wild. Now, these are our duties. Let us fulfil them without hypocrisy or pride"? But I mistrusted you, Carlo. I confess it with a penitent's true humility. Your great, magnanimous love did not deserve such a mean reward, but perhaps my sincere confession will raise me a little in your eyes. You'll love me again; yes, you will always love me, and when my memory has been sanctified by death it will live forever in your sweetest, saddest thoughts.'

'Death? Don't say that word, by God, or following you will not be good enough for me – I will go first!'

'Carlo, Carlo, please don't think of leaving me in such atrocious distress. Free these last days of mine of the only fear that can trouble them. Look, learn from me! A hundred times I could have, should have, killed myself, and instead . . . instead, I die.'

'No, you will not die, Pisana. Pisana, I swear you will not die!'

'And that is true. I will not die if you live, if you honour my memory and make something of those few poor sacrifices that I made for you. If you care for Aquilina, whom I entrusted to you, if you care about the sons you've brought forth and to whom you're bonded by sacred duties, if you care about your country – my country, Carlo – for which this little heart of mine has always beaten and for which I'll continue to pray and hope wherever God's will takes me! Carlo, I urge you: live so that your life is worthy of imitation by those who come after. Then at least I can say that my dying words left noble actions behind them. I ask nothing else; I desire nothing more. All the good I could do, I have done; and so I die content and go to await you.'

'I am here, Pisana. You shall not wait a second! I am with you!'

'And if I were to tell you that these are the first cruel words I've heard from you, and that they debase me in my own eyes and destroy that tiny gratification that made me feel so blissful about departing? Carlo, if you still love me, you will not want to see me die remorseful and afraid. You know that when I want something I desire it and expect it at any cost! Very well, I desire and expect that my death, so sweet and easy for me, will not be a disaster for an entire family, nor subtract from one whole town and all humanity that good that you can and you must still achieve! Carlo, are you strong and brave? Do you believe in honesty and justice? Swear to me now that you will not be a coward, that you will not abandon your post, that happy or miserable, in company or alone, you will fight to the last for honesty and justice!'

'Oh, Pisana, how can you ask this of me? How can I believe in honesty and justice when I no longer have you at my side, when a life like yours is so miserably rewarded?'

'A life like mine is so enviable that blessed is the man who has a similar one! A life that begins in love and ends in forgiveness, peace and hope, and then soars up to join another love without end: such a life is so much more than I deserve that I thank God for this gracious gift. Just one joy is lacking, but I feel sure I'll obtain it, because it is in your power to grant it to me. Swear to me, Carlo, swear you will do what I ask. I don't believe you can deny me the only favour I ask. By all that is most sacred and dear to you, by the eternal memory of our love, I beg you.'

'Oh, Pisana, but I have never broken any oath!'

'And that is why I beg you. Don't you see? The happiness of my last moments depends on your will, on your word.'

'And so it is necessary? Your irrevocable decree?'

'Yes, Carlo, irrevocable! Just like the gift of myself that I made to you, like the oath I now repeat, that you are the noblest and most generous creature that ever wore mortal semblance.'

'Oh, but you value me more than I'm worth, and you ask me what I cannot –'

'Anything, you can do anything – if you still love me! Swear to me that you will live for the good of that family I imposed on you, for the honour of that country we both love and always shall love!'

'This is what you want, Pisana? Very well, I swear it. I swear by that wish I have to follow you, I swear by my overwhelming hope that nature soon will come and release me from my oath!'

'Thank you, thank you, Carlo! Now I am happy and once again worthy of God.'

'But there is one thing I must ask of you, too, Pisana. Do not feed so much on these gloomy thoughts. Let this new-found happiness revive your health and restore your courage; in short, conserve yourself for us, who love you dearly.'

'Oh, now you – you are asking more than I can give. Carlo, look at me! Do you see my smile of bliss? Well now, do you think that I, a poor woman, mad – drunk – with love, would be willing to leave you for ever, never see you again on earth or in Heaven, if I weren't invincibly certain that we will be united and a thousand times more happy than we've ever been, for all eternity?'

'Yes Pisana, I do believe you. Your soul shines in divine eyes. Stay with us. Oh, please stay with us!'

'And do you think that if I were to stay I would have enjoyed the pure delight of this last hour? No, Carlo, any further joy would be colourless and base. You must let me go. Admire with me God's clemency, that fires the setting sun with brilliant colours! Thank him for allowing us to taste the inexpressible pleasures of the other world in this one, for giving us this guarantee his promises are not false. Farewell, Carlo, farewell. Let us part now that our souls are strong and ready. Perhaps we will meet again many times, perhaps just one. But the last time we meet we shall never part again. I go to await you and to learn to love you as you really deserve. Farewell, farewell . . .'

Here she slipped away from my arms and I didn't have the strength to stop her, and I cried and cried as if she were really dead and that farewell her last word. My thoughts wandered far and wide, meeting nothing but darkness. Her majestic spirit was so bright that every other splendour here below appeared a mere spectre to me and every other love seemed cool and wan compared with hers. Soon Lucilio, Aquilinia and the others came in, but I could only point at the door by which she'd left and begin to weep again.

The sight of those who bound me so irremediably to life was unbearable just then. I almost hated them, and, indeed, I treated my wife and sons bestially. But when they had gone (afraid of my weeping and my cruelty) I could hear la Pisana murmuring in my ear. Her love, which you might say had fused with my soul, breathed health and vigour into me. To really love her, I thought, I must equal or at least imitate her, and sacrifice myself for them as she had done for me. Family, *patria*: they were not false words; when she spoke them they took on almost prophetic power. Be they spent in penance or in battle, our lives may at least serve others. The harder they are, the better those who take their lives to the finish. La Pisana's eyes, lit up by things mysterious and eternal, flashed before me once again and I knew that light would never dim in me, but be transformed in patient desire and joyful hope. Now I began to weep again, but my tears were no longer desperate and violent. I knew I could endure waiting for death.

After having left me alone for an hour or so, Lucilio came to tell me that la Pisana had collapsed, but then recovered somewhat after drinking a cordial and was now sleeping peacefully. He advised me not to disturb her and to let nature take its course, there being no more potent restorative. He would come in the evening to see if he could assist in any way that sleep hadn't. We then had a few days of respite, during which la Pisana's cheerful serenity never failed.

When I was able to join her and she made me swear once again I'd keep my promise, a celestial smile spread over her face. I'd never seen her so happy. And so I watched her soul of fire, forever tossed by such a proud storm of passions, little by little weaken and grow serene; I watched the purest part of her rise and glow with a limpid, sweet light; and the profane sentiments obscuring it disappear; and I saw what love alone could do, even in a nature as unruly and tormented as hers, despite a false and corrupting education. I watched all passion dim before the easy, swift flight of the spirit, and death approach: lovely, a friend, smiling, as if in response to her own smile.

Her final delirium was a deep, enchanted dream, and I, who had always thought the noble words put in the mouths of the dying were invented, decided that great souls when they arrive at the point of looking back on their lives, do really express their best sentiments in readiness for the grand voyage towards God. She mentioned Italy often, and often, squeezing my hand, murmured words of courage and faith. 'Your sons, Carlo, your sons!' she would say. 'I see them: they are happier than we are. But in this world, you see, in this world! Beyond this world we shall be as happy as they, for we have paved the way for their happiness.' Then I would hear her muttering something; I believe she was speaking of Naples and the glorious and terrible days we'd spent there twenty-four years before. After she'd indulged in those distant memories, she would fold her hands in prayer and say, pleadingly, 'Forgive me, forgive me!' Dear soul: from whom and for what did you beg forgiveness? From me, who would have given my very blood to be worthy of you? From that God who has long been watching you and could only admire the virtue and serenity attained by one of his creatures?

Oh, blessed Pisana, I hope you will revel in this last affirmation of your heroism that I (still alive after another thirty years of troubles and forbearance!) make on the verge of my own grave. Revel in this fact: if I've shown any courage in the rest of my life, if my sons have embraced any honourable causes, and if their sons ever do so, the credit belongs entirely to you. You, who begged me to remain and perpetuate your generous example in myself and others. Send down a smile on this old, fogged brain, from that high heaven where you reside, sweet soul, and show me the path by which I can join you. If in the bleak thoughts of age, bent over the tomb of my favourite son, a gleam of hope still shines, I owe it entirely to you. For you alone I had a family, a *patria*, a bold heart and an honest conscience. For you alone I keep the eternal flame of my beliefs alive and I shall add it to the eternal flame of your love, wherever that may be.

No, these are not the fancies or foolishness of a man past eighty years; I didn't endure so much grief to fall into that truly grievous state in which good and evil cannot be distinguished. There is a sphere above us, an eternal order in which the bad sinks into matter and virtues become spirit. I, who watched you shake off those fugitive, fragile remains; I, who recall you younger, happier, more beautiful than ever at the fearful moment of death; I, who love you more than I ever did, my life's companion in weakness and in error; I must, by necessity, believe humans can undergo some sublime purification, some mysterious transformation. Yes, by your grace, by your love, my sweet soul, as I put a foot in the grave, I proudly abjure that cowardly philosophy that does not believe in what cannot be seen. Why abase human reason to the senses, when it is a thousand times better to elevate it with imagination and sentiment? Thank you, Pisana, for this last comfort from the highest realms of heaven. Only you could do so much from above. I do not believe; I do not reason. But I hope.

When la Pisana came to her senses once again, Aquilina asked her if she wanted a priest.

'Oh yes,' she said with a sad smile. 'It would grieve my sister deeply to know I had died without a priest.'

'Oh, don't speak of dying,' said Aquilina. 'Religion's consolation also helps us to live by God's will.'

'Living or dying is all the same before God,' said la Pisana solemnly, and then she sent me a long glance of conviction. I turned my head to dry my eyes and saw Bruto and the two boys watching this mighty dying woman in amazement, almost envy. In that atmosphere of peace and splendour, I, too, began to think that this was but a separation of a few years; not a tragic death, merely a sad but friendly leave-taking. Lucilio came and took her pulse, and smiled at her as if to say, 'You will go soon, but in peace.' He, too, believed it. Last came the priest and she kept him there for a long time, neither cynical and contemptuous, nor ostentatiously pious. At peace with herself, she easily found herself at peace with God, too, and that first funeral rite – the one that seems so lugubrious because it is delivered at the deathbed – didn't alter her serene aspect at all.

She then began to talk to us, thanking Lucilio for his care and Aquilina and Bruto for their friendship, and blessing my children and urging them to obey and imitate their parents. She took my hand and wouldn't let me move from her bedside, not even to take some cordial from on top of the cupboard, and so it was Aquilina who brought the cup to her lips. She thanked her with a smile and then whispered in my ear, 'Love her, Carlo, love her! It was I who gave her to you.' I couldn't reply, but nodded my head, and I never forgot that promise, and Aquilina herself could attest to that, however much certain differences of opinion later caused discord between us.

La Pisana's breath grew more laboured every moment and she gripped my hand hard, smiling at each of us in turn, but when it came to me, her glance was longer and more intense. When she turned to look at Aquilina, she seemed to be asking forgiveness for those last tokens of love. From time to time she would say a word or two, but her voice was beginning to go and I felt myself going with it, but right away she would look at me to give me heart and remind me what I'd promised.

'Here I am!' she said suddenly in a stronger voice. And she tried to raise herself from the pillow, but fell back exhausted, though not dismayed, smiling at her weak effort.

'Here I am!' she murmured a second time, and then, turning to me, said, 'Remember, I await you!'

I felt a quiver through my heart: her soul departing and bidding me farewell. She was still clutching my hand, her lips smiling, her eyes still gazing, but la Pisana had already gone to her eternal prospect. If you can believe it, none of us moved; we all sat silent and immobile, contemplating how serene her death had been. Lucilio told me he, too, had wept, with something like relief, but I didn't see him, as I saw nothing that entire day. I didn't move or cry or speak until they came to take la Pisana's hand from mine and put her in her coffin. Then I myself dressed her and put her in her last bed, and when I pressed a last kiss to her lips my soul seemed to take wing with hers.

For many days I didn't know whether I was alive or dead. But it was not despair, merely life suspended, and slowly I emerged from that lethargy and regained awareness of myself and the memory of what had happened, and finally the strength I needed to obey la Pisana's last wishes. From then on I was a graver, firmer man than I had been before, and the guidance I gave my children was inspired by her noble and steadfast example. When Aquilina gently chided me, saying I was thus preparing them for a mean and dangerous future, I merely had to point to la Pisana's death and she would retract her remarks immediately. To be worthy of such a death, one must pay no heed to dangers or privations.

A few days before we left London, word came that His Excellency Navagero had gone to his just reward, leaving la Pisana his sole heir, and should she die intestate, all his assets were to go to build a hospital bearing her name. When all was said and done he was worth a pretty pair of millions, though he had lived out his last years in false penury to accumulate such a sum. It grieved me terribly to leave England, where such a large part of me was to stay behind in a country graveyard, but la Pisana had ordered me to think of my children, and so we left. Spiro and Aglaura had asked me to look after some of their business in Venice, and so I headed there, intending to settle. Bruto, after travelling to the Friuli to put his affairs in order, would join us in the city. So I sadly staked out the winter camp for my old age. Parting from Lucilio had also been painful, but when we left he'd said, 'I shall come to die among you!' and I knew he would keep his promise. We arrived in Venice on 15 September 1823. I spent the first night in those fateful rooms, where once I'd passed such carefree, happy days, sobbing and kissing two locks of hair. One I'd torn from la Pisana's pretty curls when she was a girl; the other, I'd reverently cut from her pale brow when she lay dead.

TWENTY-ONE

How I help to revive some commerce and trade in Venice, a source, if nothing else, of life, and how the elder of my two sons departs with Lord Byron for Greece.[1] *A duel at age fifty to defend the honour of the dead. A wedding trip to Nafplio and a funereal return to Ancona in March, 1831. Death claims my second son and mows down many friends and enemies, finding in cholera a potent ally. At sixty-five years, a student.*

We know the reasons why Venice fell, and those very reasons made it impossible for her to revive her material life and trade. Fate was mostly to blame, for the very apathy of the government and the enfeeblement of the people derived from the closing down of those routes along which both government and people had previously carried out their successful enterprises. Was it the fault of the Venetians if Columbus or Magellan built up new trade to the profit of new nations, or if Vasco da Gama opened new routes for goods from the East? The Venetians remained excellent and intrepid merchants, so long as they could still sell goods from far-off lands at better profits than their competitors; they maintained their warlike habits and energies, so long as their vast, bold commerce demanded vigorous protection. When the incentive of profits waned, so did the call of those ancient and glorious traditions. When expeditions to Syria and the Black Sea (where European manufactures were exchanged with the goods of Muscovy, and with those brought by caravan from India and China) became too costly and not very remunerative, the Venetians' military vocation waned with the waning trade; for them, as for the English, it was no more than a defence of their commercial activities.

So Venice lost her *raison d'être* and ceased to play a part in civilization. She went on living out of habit, *by accident*, as Doge Renier said. Nevertheless, her three centuries of slow, revered and not unhappy decadence was solemn proof of her ancient power and of the virtues instilled in her government and her people by long and glorious rule. Had the Republic of San Marco become a vigorous and permanent part of Italian life in the Middle Ages, it might have found new prosperity by enlarging its territories on the mainland. Instead, Venice was more trading partner than ruler of the mainland provinces; they weren't a true part of her, but mere colonies meant to enrich the reigning patriciate, who didn't possess land, the usual means of gaining wealth. The military men and politicians weren't interested in pushing their governing powers beyond the Po and the Mincio and paving the way for Italy; they wanted to defend their property, just as they'd defended their trading posts in Crimea and Asia Minor. Other governments, out of respect or diplomatic equilibrium or because the Venetians were prudent, allowed Venice to enjoy her mercantile possessions in peace, and, little by little, the need for armed defence declined; and, happy to cancel an item from the expenses side of the ledger, the Venetians entrusted the security of their dominion to their own acumen and others' discretion.

Perhaps, when Venice's traders were becoming landowners and her sailors moving to the mainland, had some bold faction or clever leader among the aristocracy tried to shift her course from utilitarian to political, she might have found a new path to future greatness (at some greater risk, no doubt). There might have been a fresh upsurge of national pride to compensate a traditionally weak attachment to the idea of Italy. But the opportunity or the force or the idea didn't arise. Venice, as I said before, remained a city of the Middle Ages, a modern state only in appearance. But appearances don't last forever and because she didn't want to – or couldn't – become a nation, she necessarily shrank to become a mere city. Political economy is like physiology. When a body is invaded by rotten humours it must be forced into natural parsimony, from which it can then follow an orderly path to good health.

When the first upheavals began and took away her every

foothold on the mainland and closed off the now unpractised seaways, too, Venice was, to say the least, moribund. When peace returned and the sea in front of her was free again, her forces were so frail that she could not compete with other ports grown strong during her indolence. Trieste boldly entered the fray, backed by Viennese trade and assisted by Venice's inability to rebuild the Republic. Pained and sorrowful, she closed herself within her marble docks, like a prince dethroned who would rather die of starvation than hold out a begging bowl.

She'd always prided herself on having been Europe's protector against the Turks; it was bitter medicine indeed to have to beg arms and money to send four halberdiers to Corfu to load up dried figs. There she sat, whether pondering her past or planning some future, no one knew. 'Before statistics were collected,' said some excellent writer or other, 'every country believed itself to be whatever it wanted to be.' Even in 1780 the Venetians considered themselves the natural defender against Mohammedan despotism, just because Admiral Emo took a dozen galleys and fought a few glorious battles against the Tunisians.[2] It was the only remaining excuse for Venice's existence. But then a great war brought home the dreadful statistical proof: two hundred English warships and fourteen French armies. The end of that titanic struggle revealed, if nothing else, Venice's political nullity, and the fact that Europe no longer needed any defender against the Turks, and if it ever should, the job wouldn't fall to Venice. At last she began to believe herself to be not what she wanted to be, but what she truly was. If this first examination of her conscience brought about some gloom and humiliation, that showed good civil sense and healthy shame.

At the time I returned to Venice, shame and inertia were universal. There was no trade, no landed wealth, no arts, sciences, glory or activity of any sort. The city seemed dead or as if life were suspended. As I ventured into Spiro's commercial affairs, I saw first-hand how lethargic was that very social category that had written the most splendid pages of the history of the Republic. It seemed to me vital to arouse some energy in tired commerce. Little could be done, for there was almost nothing to work with, but a good beginning is half the job. I decided that

Spiro wouldn't have opposed my plan, nor shunned risking the credit and remaining holdings of Casa Apostolus in this noble effort. The war in Greece had consumed most of his assets, but something remained, and his counterparts' trust would multiply the value of those scarce leavings. My first step would be to revive – create – the collective spirit, and here the wonderful accomplishments of the English, still fresh in my mind, spurred me on. But even giants must begin small. I quickly saw this was a dream and stepped back to avoid a disaster that would disperse the goodwill already quietly accumulating.

Our error is to measure the life of a people by the life of an individual, as I've said before. One man alone may anticipate the progress of a nation, but he cannot make the nation follow him. For his example to be useful it must be easy to imitate, and by many, and when it spreads and becomes a habit, the nation follows him by itself. The collective spirit, itself a measure of broader accord in society, must always be encouraged, like education, as a factor promoting trust and prosperity and other forms of improvement. But it can only develop by degrees: the association of a hundred is the prelude to that of a thousand; and for the hundred to be convinced, five or ten or twenty must first join together and be convinced by the eloquence of facts and numbers that the common (and individual) profit would have been less if each man had acted by himself. Once these principles had settled in my head, I made them the foundation of all my business, but without particularly suggesting that my goal was public prosperity, but rather private wealth.

A first company I set up to trade in dried fruit, oak tannin, oil and other commodities from the Levant and Greece was a great success. I had been careful not to risk too much or grow too large, so that profits were certain, however small. After this first step, we emerged from our deep somnolence. Other companies like ours were formed, and as competition expanded business, greater risks were taken in the hopes of greater gains. And, in fact, experience often rewarded the greatest risk-takers, and when the competition among us began to retard the development of single companies, several smaller businesses were fused into a few larger ones. And these competed bravely with the strongest and the oldest firms from other Mediterranean ports. Our earnings were less, and so Venice couldn't outstrip Marseilles or Genoa or Trieste, but honest profits were made and hope replaced gloom. Throw a stone and you know not where it will land; if Venice was not prosperous enough to draw foreigners and their capital, we had at least enough to get our own people moving. It wasn't much and I had hoped for more. In any event, fresh business had brought the Apostulos firm unexpected earnings and Spiro couldn't thank me enough for aiding him and Greek independence.

Local trade had resumed its natural course and, little by little, found its proper outlet in the great Po Valley. However, I don't want to take credit for these subsequent developments, like some stonemason who boasts about a beautifully designed palazzo because he laid the first stone. Enterprises grow large like children, more from the pleasure of the moment than from any direct ambition. I did, however, have an ambition, and, therefore, I am proud to have taken part in the revival, however modest, of Venetian trade. But all this magnificence took place later, and now I must double back to those first months when magnificence didn't enter my head, except as a distant, perhaps unrealizable prize.

My younger son Donato was well suited to help me in my new profession of merchant and although he was still a boy, his razor-sharp intelligence was very useful to me. He was such a wag, so energetic, that whenever my spirits clouded I had only to turn to him to cheer me up again. He was a fine companion to his mother and they often visited the house of Count Rinaldo of Fratta, where good Clara had ended up after the death of Navagero. The Count was still working in the government accounting office for a ducat a day and spent all his time in the office and the library, while his sister, who had kept up her friendships with the defrocked nuns of Santa Teresa, had a good many visitors. And, little by little, around that first nucleus other elements of society had clustered: patricians of the old or new stamp, most of them people who at heart were nostalgic about the old order of things and backed the present order only so as not to be condemned to plod through new revolutions.

Donato had carefully observed these odd types and he loved to mock them, which somewhat displeased his mother, but I was relieved, for I saw that it was only to keep her company that he agreed to sit with those old fossils almost every day, and that he didn't share their filthy opinions and miserable hypocrisy. Aquilina was keen to strengthen her ties with Clara, because, she said, who knew where my tomfoolery might lead us all? This and other such remarks usually engendered great rows, but I didn't worry overmuch, and, knowing that her intentions were good, let her do things her way. In any case our past lives justified our intimacy with the Counts of Fratta and I didn't feel I could prevent her from paying court to them when gratitude demanded the same of me. Luciano's conduct was a greater source of discord, for, unlike his energetic and more malleable younger brother, he spent his time in mischief and drinking and wouldn't listen to advice or reprimands, and when he was reprimanded, especially by his mother, for not busying himself with more useful things in life, he would reply that first, where was this life, and second, he didn't see what useful or un-useful were supposed to mean, and, whether we liked it or not, he intended to ignore all that.

'Watch out, Luciano,' I warned him. 'Watch out, for the day will come when you must look sharp – and too late you will realize you haven't become a man.'

'I'll take care of that,' he said sharply. And he didn't cease for a minute any of his rakish, intemperate pastimes and vices. Often, and rather bitterly, I had reason to mock his mother, who'd been terrorized by that juvenile bee in his bonnet when he wanted to go to Greece. If only this were Greece! Chatting with blonde Venetian ladies, another glass of Malvasia: his memory of those generous old ambitions seemed to have been expunged. Aquilina considered this my fault too; I had allowed him to be the master of his dreams, she said, and thus he no longer had any respect for his father or his friends, but took his happiness as he pleased.

'Yesterday it was Greece,' she said, 'today it's debauchery; tomorrow, God only knows! It's all because you praised him; you let him take the reins.'

'I'm sorry,' said I, 'but noble ideas cannot be snuffed out as if they were shameful. And you, too, have prepared him admirably by shaping that strong, bold temperament of his.'

'Yes, indeed, I tried to bring him up with the right beliefs, but not so that you could twist them around and permit these results.'

'Results, my dear, proceed directly from causes.'

'Above all when they are pushed in a certain direction.'

'Do you know what I think? If the results I was hoping for had come forth from your causes, I'd have clapped my hands in delight.'

'Well, that shows your hopes were faulty and that you didn't do much to assist them. You see what fine results we've arrived at! You kill yourself working at your desk; our youngest boy is there, day and night, like a martyr, too, and the eldest, instead, makes the rounds of the bawdy houses and the taverns.'

'What the Devil! Is it my fault? I, too, remember when I was a lad.'

'Well if I had spent my youth in such vice I'd be ashamed to think of it.'

'And I tell you, it's merely a passing inflammation and will correct itself.'

'And I repeat: it's an illness and it will soon be chronic if you don't do something about it.'

Thus we would quarrel, the two of us. Luciano, meanwhile, stayed out all night, and if you reprimanded him he grew even more sullen and kicked like a colt that wouldn't be tamed. In the midst of all this strife, one fine morning when I was least expecting it, he came into my room, pale and agitated, to tell me in no uncertain terms that he would be leaving for Greece the following week.

'To do what?' I said scornfully, for I no longer believed in his transitory ambitions.

'To defend Missolonghi against Mustafa Pasha!'[3]

'Ha!' I continued, equally scornfully. 'I'm pleased to see you know that a certain Mustafa Pasha is to be found in the Peloponnese.'

'I didn't know,' he replied tight-lipped, 'but Lord Byron, who also plans to leave for Greece next week, told me.'

'And where did you come across Lord Byron?'

'All you need to know is that I met him and that he deigned to speak to me and take me on as his travelling companion to Greece.'

'Is this a joke, Luciano, or are these dreams your own?'

'No, it is no joke, father; I'm very serious and the next time you write to my aunt and uncle, you must inform them of my decision.'

'Very well, if you are serious, I'll repeat what your mother said a few months ago. Have you a real vocation? You do understand that in the meantime you have given me many reasons to doubt it.'

'Father, I'm so sure this decision of mine will be confirmed by my deeds that I ask you to pardon the bad opinion I've let you form of me, and to advance me by a few months that esteem I intend to merit. I make this request both to you and to my mother.'

'We will consider it, Luciano. In the meantime you must learn to mature your ideas thoroughly and also to doubt, especially when you have many reasons.'

Here he said not a word, his demeanour making it very clear he was willing to doubt anything but the rightness of his decision. I was quite amazed, for, try as I might, one way and another, he would only reply with the following words: 'I have understood that we are duty-bound to live to the advantage of someone in this world, therefore, I pray you, allow me to live!' His mother complained loudly about his plan, for only a few months before he'd seemed quite indifferent to Greece, but she, too, obtained nothing. Luciano was immovable; he was only waiting for the call from Lord Byron to embark along with him. I knew the famous poet by name and by reputation and I had even seen him two or three times in his rare appearances in the Piazza, for he seemed to have adopted Italy as his country, and, in particular, Venice. Poets are like swallows, they like to build their nests among the ruins.

And I wasn't all that pleased that Luciano had joined forces with that supreme misanthrope. I feared he might imitate Byron's passions and, unmoved by the grandeur and nobility of the venture, he might, like the ambiguous lord, be drawn by twisted ambitions. Luciano was still quite young and easily seduced by that Mephistophelian perfection that serves only to disguise an absolute inability to make sense of life and discover its purpose. Impossible that a mere boy could truly immerse himself in that sterile philosophy of contempt, except in hopes of making himself special or of shining by another's lights. I feared then, and not wrongly, that when he was put to the test his resolve would not be one per cent as vigorous as his words. Luciano laughed at my doubts, adding that if I accused him of Romanticism, it was far better and more excusable to be a Romantic in deeds, rather than in sighs or in hairstyles.

'I won't weep over novels or wear suicide on my cheeks as if it were a fashionable cosmetic,' he said. 'Instead, I'll be the hero of some ballad, and the women of Argos and Athens will recall my name along with Rigas and Botzaris. Mine will be a Romanticism that's *useful* for something. Let me add that I am eighteen years old and you know very well that it's time for me to go. I wouldn't let myself be conscripted or buy another man to settle my debts with these unhappy times.'

What can I say? I let him go, and warmly urged Spiro, who was then at Missolonghi, to look after him, and told him what I thought about Luciano's temperament and his instability and the other things I feared. My wife neither cried nor despaired, although for three or four months she reproached me for having lost control of my sons; but, meanwhile, excellent news came to us from Greece. By common agreement they had refused to divide the country into three regions, as proposed by Tsar Alexander, and war had exploded, crueller and more ferocious than ever. The fourth Mohammedan army melted like snow under the sun on the hot soil of the Peloponnese. Luciano, along with his cousins Demetrios and Theodoris, was cited for his courage in one of the war bulletins. Spiro wrote to me in admiration and

Niceta (who also went by the name Turk-Eater) called him a hero and named him captain of his legion.

All of Europe applauded Greece's heroic victories, like the circus crowds, who, safe in their seats, applaud the gladiator who faces a lion and two tigers and comes out victorious. Few arms and few men – and even less money – went to support those superhuman efforts. The European governments glowered at one another and trembled, knowing they could never put the Turkish chains back on those Christian rebels. Meanwhile, the fighting continued and the pashas didn't seem all that devoted to Sultan Mahmud, nor did they obey his orders, while the Janissaries[4] simply refused to set foot in that land that devoured its enemies. The noblest and the best, however, backed Greece passionately. Byron gave up his fortune and raised a loan, but then he fell ill and the news of his illness was quickly followed by that of his death. Greece hastened to his funeral; all Europe wept at a death sanctified by that final year of his life; and one of the bastions of Missolonghi was named after him. Luciano wrote to me, upset and grieved that his illustrious friend and protector wouldn't be remembered as a great hero, but as a famous poet. 'Time is the enemy of greatness,' he said. But he was wrong, for Byron will never be greater for his magnificent sacrifice than when his fame has grown for a few centuries.

In Venice, meanwhile, adversity – proportionate with the location, of course – befell me, too. Raimondo Venchieredo, who had married Agostino Frumier's eldest daughter and who was enduring lean times (because money was short and his wife capricious), had taken to spreading nasty tales about la Pisana and me, and, especially, unbelievably lurid stories about la Pisana. He belonged to a circle at the Caffè Suttil, I was told, where not an evening went by that he didn't say something abominable about us, perhaps envious of my prospering business. I might have ignored the matter on my own behalf, but not when it came to la Pisana, whose memory I defended with my life. And so I, too, began to frequent that caffè. Few recognized me and I would sit all alone in a corner of the back room, seeming to read the paper, but in fact listening intently to the conversation in the front, where Raimondo was always swaggering about and boasting.

The second or third evening that I came and set my trap (the patrons and the waiters had already begun to cast me wary looks, thinking I was a spy perhaps) the caffè suddenly resounded with the clatter of sword and spurs and there was a great buzz of greetings and felicitations and a hard, guttural voice I thought I knew echoing up and down. Yes, by Jove, it must be Partistagno, and indeed I heard his name whispered by someone replying to a question, and a few minutes later Raimondo began to shout 'Long live the General!' and compliment him on his girth, and then he asked him if he'd come to tempt the reverend abbess and I had no more doubt it was him.

'Oh no, my good man, I haven't come to tempt the abbess,' said Partistagno. 'My wife has supplied me seven boys one after the other and they keep me busier than a regiment, so the nun has slipped my mind. A pity, though! I don't think she'd be so unhappy to see me, although age must certainly have played its part in making her a saint at last. And you, Raimondo, how did things go with her little sister, who didn't have the slightest vocation to become a nun, as I recall? If you remember, you were still quite besotted with her when I was last in Venice. Confound it! I believe twenty years have gone by!'

'Yes, indeed, and many things have gone by, not just years,' said Raimondo. 'I have some choice things to tell you before you are caught up. First, the end of the story: the lovely Pisana is dead.'

'Dead!' exclaimed Partistagno. 'I would never have believed it. Women don't die that easily.'

'And, in fact, la Pisana went through a good long struggle,' said Raimondo. 'Listen to this: for two years she played the servant to that lover of hers, do you remember? Carlino Altoviti.'

'Yes, yes, I remember. The one who used to turn the spit at Fratta and then became secretary of the Municipality.'

'Indeed. Well, it seems that in her own way she loved the fellow. In '99 they were together in Naples and Genoa, always with the approval of good Navagero, whom she'd married. Then, off and on, they lived together as husband and wife until, no one knows why, she stuck some country girl to her lover's loins and made him marry her. That was quite an event! Everyone had something to say about it, but we never got to the bottom of it. You, my good General, have such a rich imagination, you must resolve the problem. Let's hear: what do you say?'

'Hmm . . . one moment. Let me think. I'd wager she was tired of him and to be done with him forever she tossed him a wife!'

'Very good, General. But what would you say if I told you she then came back to Venice and devoted herself body and soul to her husband's bedsores and to mumbling paternosters and de profundises with your dear abbess?'

'What would I say? Oh, Bacchus help me! I'd say she wanted to make peace with the good Lord and that's why she got rid of the lover.'

'Excellent. You have a fertile imagination, dear General, and the brains to put it all together. The man who made you general was no fool! But what would you say if I told you that during the last revolution in Naples, our Carlino, now forty-five if he was a day, took off once again and got thrown in the dungeon, and he was losing his mind until la Pisana abandoned her husband and her kneeler to go and ask pardon for him and get his execution changed to banishment? What would you say if I told you that when he was left blind and penniless, she spent two years with him in England supporting him with the lowest sort of toil.'

'Oh, really? Mad, quite mad!' thundered Partistagno in that northern accent of his. 'Either I am mad to believe you or you are mad to tell such fairy tales.'

'It's the gospel truth,' said Raimondo hotly. 'And I'm sure you can guess in what profession la Pisana earned her wages. A Venetian maiden doesn't know many, you'll grant me. She had to make a virtue of necessity. And despite her forty years she was still so pretty, so youthful, that I swear that even many a non-Englishman might have fallen in her net. Her friend Carlino knew all about it and swallowed it happily. What do you say, some stomach, no? But, as I said, they had to make a virtue of necessity.'

Even more than Raimondo's indecent lies it was the grins and the sneers and the meanness of the whole pack listening to him that enraged me. I lost all restraint and, charging into the room where they were sitting, I leapt at Raimondo and gave him the most resounding slap in the face any slanderer ever received.

'I, too, make a virtue of necessity!' I shouted and those chicken-hearts ran about in a muddle trying to escape from the caffè or huddling in terror behind the tables and chairs. 'What you got from me was just a first instalment of justice. If you want to appeal the case, you know where I live. But slanderers are usually cowards, too.'

Raimondo was quivering and straining at the bit, but could not decide how to defend himself. A natural energy, although dispersed by many years of soft living, still heated his blood, but his voice would not obey him and he was so used to getting away with his bluster that my swift attack had shattered his composure. He was like the dog that howls and furiously chases the fleeing thief for a bit, but soon withdraws to his barn to see if that villain is brave enough to pursue him. I had already left the caffè and gone home, and for three days I heard nothing about it. On the morning of the fourth day, a certain Marcolini, who was reputed to be the best sword in all of Venice, came to inform me that Signor Raimondo of Venchieredo, considering himself deeply offended by the way I had treated him at Caffè Suttil, demanded satisfaction and granted me the choice of weapons, as was my right; and so I should make my choice and send along my seconds to set the terms of the duel. I replied that since it had been my right to challenge Signor Raimondo from the first instant I heard him denigrate a highly respectable person very dear to me (and hadn't done so only because I held particular views about duelling) I considered myself the challenger and therefore the choice of weapons was his, and I would dispatch my seconds that very day.

Marcolini thanked me for my gallantry and went off. I later learned that after I'd left the caffè, Raimondo had shouted and stormed and swore a dozen times he'd rip out my heart with his teeth, and other such things worthy of his well-known bravado, but then sleep brought milder counsel and the next day he merely repeated that he would keep all his promises and more, if he didn't have a wife and children. That last clause provoked uproarious laughter and the word soon spread all around Venice. And so Raimondo – when he took General Partistagno's arm to stroll with him around the Piazza, and the latter roughly freed himself, adding rather sarcastically that he would join him when he didn't have a wife and children – understood. He was pushed to the limit and, after thinking it over thoroughly, decided to challenge me by sending Marcolini, as you've seen. Partistagno, the other second, either wanted to avoid the trouble of coming to my house or Raimondo wanted to frighten me by sending a man famed as a great swordsman. Such things mattered to me not at all; and while I would never be as mad as to challenge anyone, I would also never refuse a duel, even one against the fiercest murderer in all of Europe.

The duel took place the following week in a garden near Mestre. I went out as if I were merely going for a stroll, my eyes clear, grip firm, not even a trace of anger against Venchieredo in my soul. I even pitied him when I saw him there, pale and trembling like a leaf. Although my attack was rather tepid, he let me push him back until his right foot rested on the brink of a ditch several arm-spans deep. I stopped, all too generously, to warn him that one more step back and he would fall and his seconds repeated the warning, but, exploiting my distraction, he lunged forward and jabbed me in the breast – and woe to me had I not taken a leap backward! He'd have run me through. In any case he pierced my breast and blood began to spurt, and that and the snarl I saw upon his face revived my fury. I went at him with two quick thrusts and, while he was stabbing left and right in terror, contemplating, I'm sure, how he might throw away his sword and flee, I sunk my blade halfway into his thigh and sent him rolling in the ditch.

If the legal code of the time punished duelling quite severely, I suffered no real consequences on account of this one. As for Raimondo, his wound healed, but he had broken his femur in falling and was to remain frightfully lame. From then on, I believe, he praised me and la Pisana as his dearest friends or else his scandal-mongering was so meek and cautious that no further unpleasant acts on my part were necessary. Aquilina learned of my foolishness and I can't tell you the scolding and lambasting I had to endure. Despite our perpetual disagreements, the birth of our third son and two years later of a daughter are fair proof that at least sometimes we got along all too well. I say too well, because after such a long moratorium I didn't at all desire a larger family, but as nature had performed something of a miracle for us, I had the good sense to be grateful. The boy we named Giulio and the girl Pisana, in memory of two dear souls who had departed before us.

By this time all of the Apostuloses' capital had been transferred to Greece, where Spiro had donated most of it to the cause of the nation, spending some to buy land near Corinth. The war of independence had now deteriorated into a diplomatic dispute. After the Turkish fleet was destroyed at Navarino, Ibrahim Pasha and his Egyptians[5] kept a weak hold on the Morea; Turkey had neither guns nor cannon to help them, and the holy war declared against the Greeks didn't frighten or disturb them much. Count Kapodistrias[6] held the country's fate in his hands and, although he was said to be a spokesman for Russian interests, necessity forced the Greeks to follow him. From Spiro's letters I could see he wasn't happy; his eldest son and my Luciano were among the Count's favourites and he didn't like it. But the young chase glory and power and we must forgive them. Theodoris was with the liberals instead, with the old insurrectionary leaders who were watched even more closely than the Turks and frowned on by the Count; but his father was very proud of him and thought his independence was truly worthy of a Greek.

Whether because of circumstances, Kapodistrias, the French or the Russians, the Morea was soon rid of its oppressors and could await with some ease the European decision about its destiny. It was the Russian army that delivered the last blow. Their victorious march across the Balkans followed by the Treaty of Adrianople[7] forced the Divan to concede Greek liberation, and Tsar Nicholas would certainly have obtained more if jealous diplomats of France and England hadn't stopped him. Spiro sent me news of these joyous events in terms that were biblical, inspired; he'd abandoned much of his antipathy for Russia and Kapodistrias, and in announcing the probable marriage of my son Luciano to a niece of the Count, he wrote, 'So your family will join a noble lineage whose name will be inscribed in the independence of modern Greece.' I then read a few lines from my son in which he asked my consent to the marriage, and finally a brief note from Aglaura in which she expressed her husband and her nephew's rather bashful desires that I be present at the wedding. 'If the spectacle of a people freed by its own heroism can embolden your affection as a father and a brother,' she wrote, 'then I urge you to come and you will see something unique in all the world; and if nothing else, it will encourage you to live and die in hope.'

My firm's trade, still tied to the business of Casa Apostulos, meant I could undertake the voyage without problems, especially since Bruto and Donato were more than capable of looking after matters in my absence. I would have liked Aquilina to come along, but the two little ones made that impossible. And so I departed alone, aboard the ship of a trading partner, at the beginning of August 1830, just as the revolution in France[8] was agitating, in one way or another, all the crowned heads of Europe. I arrived in Nafplio three weeks later and, as Aglaura had said, it was truly a very welcome spectacle: this bold, confident people who had thrown off a yoke of four centuries and had the pride of victory impressed on their brows. It's true, there was some discontent, for the government had not been kind to the old leaders of the independence war. Yes, they were hotheads, better suited to the fervour of battle than to fine legal disquisitions, but their role had been immense and it was wrong to punish them with prison and exile.

When I repeated Spiro and Theodoris's complaints about these injustices, Luciano berated me as if I were impossibly spineless. During the war, he said, the Turks had been ruthlessly slaughtered and the Phanariots with their tact and diplomacy had been ignored; now that peace and independence had been secured, every source of disquiet must be rooted out in order to guarantee the people that tranquil, orderly life that makes liberty purposeful and ensures that it will endure. Those secondary forces had played a great part in winning the war, but were badly obstructing the government's progress now and must be brought to heel. They had risked their lives on the battlefield for the welfare of their country? Well, they must be ready to lose those lives on the scaffold, unless they corrected their subversive habits. His logic was unbeatable, I couldn't deny it; but reason untempered by mercy is cruel by the standards of human logic and I listened to him in horror.

Otherwise, Luciano was so affectionate, so kind to me, that I attributed such talk on his part to a wish to be contrary. What would a young man of twenty-four want with the logic of Cromwell or Richelieu? As for the Count Kapodistrias, he seemed to me rather pleased with himself and more crafty than malevolent. I don't believe, as he insisted in his declaration, that it was only for the glory of God and the good of the Greeks that he had done violence to himself and accepted the presidency, but nor do I believe he aspired to become a tyrant like Pisistratus.[9] Perhaps he was working for Russia's interests, for Russia more than the other great powers had high ambitions for Greece, and because of the religion they shared (and the hatred) it was inclined to back the Greeks. If he prevented Leopold of Coburg,[10] England's candidate, from ascending to the throne, I see no crime of any kind. If between England and Russia he favoured Russia, there might be a hundred good reasons why, and anyway I am always inclined to distrust England and approve anyone who distrusts her, although I have nothing but good to say about the English as individuals.

My son's fiancée, who lived in quite princely splendour in the Count's house, could certainly not claim to be a great beauty. I've always had – have still, despite the sirocco of my old age – a terrible weakness for beautiful women, and at first I wasn't entirely satisfied with her. But as I studied her more, I saw goodness emanate from her calm smile. She wasn't a woman of Greece, but she would be a good wife, and so I made peace with my son for having chosen to marry the niece of a prince, or almost. It must be said, though, that Argenno was more disturbed by than proud of the opulence of her surroundings, and this seemed to promise well for her character and for Luciano's happiness.

The wedding celebrations were quite magnificent, and because Luciano was respected among the soldiers, the Count also earned some popularity. I think, in fact, he may have given Argenno in marriage with this political end in mind. But Luciano had ends of his own in mind and didn't try to determine whether his fortune was due to his own merits or to other considerations on the part of the President. I stayed for a while in Greece, admiring both the remains of ancient grandeur and the marks of recent devastation, two different kinds of monuments, both of which honour that poetic land. Luciano didn't want me to leave at all, Argenno treated me as tenderly as any daughter, the Count Kapodistrias hinted he wanted to make something important of me, the Minister of Finance, or some such. I thought of the gilded fancies of Intendente Blowhard, but I didn't take the bait and Aquilina's letters were so pressing that I was eager to return soon.

But a cruel fatality did not permit me to satisfy my wish. Aglaura's health, which even in Greece had never really been restored, took such a bad turn in just a few weeks it seemed she wouldn't survive. I alone could appreciate Spiro's desperation and her sons' grief, for in her I would lose my only sister and the sole creature who linked me to my poor mother. Treatments, medicines, prayers were of no avail. She died in my arms, while three soldiers, three heroes who had risked their lives a hundred times against Ottoman scimitars, dissolved in tears around her bed. The earth over my sister's coffin was not yet hard when another terrible blow came from Venice. Bruto wrote that Donato had suddenly disappeared without leaving any word and without any apparent motive for his departure, and they naturally feared the worst. Aquilina seemed to have gone mad with grief and my presence in Venice was badly needed. He guessed, although it made little sense, that Donato might have become involved in the revolts then shaking the Papal States, and urged me to hurry back and perhaps he might learn something before I arrived. My other children were in excellent health; they were impatient that their mamma was ill and eager to see Papa. Well, I didn't delay. I hinted vaguely to Luciano and the others that business called me urgently to Venice and that very day boarded a French steamship bound for Ancona.

It was an anguished voyage with many terrible premonitions gnawing at me, but the arrival was far worse. I reached Ancona on 27 March just as General Armandi[11] was lowering the Romagna rebels' flag, defeated but unstained, before the Austrians. With Bruto's suspicions in mind, I hastened to ask some officers if anyone knew a certain Donato Altoviti and whether he'd taken part in the uprising. Some said they didn't know him; others said they did, but no one was sure of the name. At headquarters I learned that a young Venetian called Altoviti had volunteered with the Imola Legion, fought like a lion at Rimini and been wounded there two days before. I ran to the coach stop, but all the horses had been seized by the Austrian Army, and so I left the city on foot and four miles out of town found a greengrocer with his cart and offered him all the money I had on me to get me to Rimini that same day.

We got there, me puffing and wheezing for having pulled the cart all the way, and quite fatigued. I searched the hospital, but Donato wasn't there, nor had they heard of him. You can imagine how anxious I felt going about looking for him in that ugly city, dark and deserted under war and the coming of nightfall. Asking the whereabouts of a wounded volunteer was the same as having a door closed in your face. In the end I went back to the hospital, having decided to question the doctors there, one of whom must have been called to look after him wherever he fell, unless they'd let him die like a dog. Not every doctor in Rimini worked in the hospital, of course, and the thought was distressing, but I couldn't think of anything better to do. And lucky that I went, for a young surgeon, moved by my pleas, took me quietly aside, told me to wait in the street and that in half an hour I would find what I sought.

'Oh, I beg you, how bad is it?' I exclaimed. 'I beg you, tell me the truth. Don't deceive a miserable old father!'

'Do not fear,' said he, 'the wound is deep, but I'm not convinced it won't heal. He is in good hands and could not have better care if his mother and sister were at his bedside. And he doesn't deserve less; but, meanwhile, I pray you to wait and I'll be with you in a few minutes. Above all, be cautious: these are sensitive matters and we live in difficult times.'

I didn't breathe a word, but slowly went down the stairs and when I was on the street walked up and down until the doctor emerged. He led me to a modest-looking house and, once he had spoken to my son, led me into the room where he lay. Oh, the sweetness of those first embraces! The sight of him confirmed something I've always believed: that if women hadn't been put on earth to give birth to us, God would have had to provide them to men as nurses. A young spinster, a fine seamstress barely able to scrape together a living, had found Donato on the street and had looked after him with such efficiency and sweetness the doctor was right to say that no mother or sister could have done better.

I thanked the young lady, more with tears than with words, and Donato did, too, but she merely replied she had done nothing more than Christian charity demanded, and urged my son not to torment himself, because it might worsen his condition. The doctor examined the wound and, finding that it was healing, he also urged me not to let Donato talk much, that he must rest, for his chances were good. I quickly informed Aquilina of the news and a few days later heard that she was much better now and awaited us with open arms whenever Donato was ready to travel. Meanwhile, he'd told me why he'd abruptly left for Romagna. It was because of the foul slander he'd heard in Casa Fratta in Venice against the Romagna rebels.

'All those curses and slurs turned my stomach,' he said, 'and because I didn't have the courage to refute all that ugly talk, I decided to do better and show them what I thought by my actions!'

'Oh my dear son,' I said, 'bless you.'

The man I'd once been was now completely reborn in me. A few days before, faced with my son's grave injury, I had heartily cursed all revolutions, and the only thing I regretted about my curses was that my wife would have said the same, and, as I'd often accused her of pettiness, I didn't want to convict myself too. In any case, what happened is that the sick man brought the healthy back to life. Donato's recovery took longer than the doctor had imagined and only in May were we able to travel, in short hops, towards Bologna. The good seamstress was repaid, not as much as she deserved, but as much as our resources permitted, and as there was a young man who loved her and would have married her if the two of them were not so penniless, I hoped I had helped her more than money usually does.

We stopped in Bologna for a number of days and I renewed many old friendships. Some were dead, but there were also many fathers who had been babies at the breast in my day, and pretty mothers who had once bounced on my knee. Alas, the girls I'd once courted were now unrecognizable, and for many days I couldn't look at myself in the mirror. Bologna was neither crowded nor very jolly, but I found the same goodness, the same kindness and a thousand times more unanimity and concord. The confusion and anxiety of the past were gone; all was crystal clear and only the force was lacking, but there was hope. Whether rightly or wrongly, I'm proud to have witnessed such determination.

When we arrived in Venice you can imagine Aquilina's relief and Donato's joy. But his health, which we thought would improve in his native city, soon declined. His wound began to reopen and then developed a deep fissure; one doctor said the bone was damaged, another thought a metal splinter was hidden away in some cavity. All of us were uneasy, unhappy, upset. Only the cheerful, serene invalid could console us, laughing about the joke he'd played on the faithful of Casa Fratta, and listening happily to Bruto tell how shocked they'd all been. Ormenta, recently back from Rome with many rewards and distinctions, had settled the question thus: 'like father, like son'. Personally, I thought his comment was a cause for pride, not an insult, and I had no desire to confront the old Sanfedista. Sadly, I had graver troubles. Donato's health declined steadily and, finally, in the autumn, he died. Among all the calamities of my life, this one – apart from la Pisana's death – was the most atrocious, the most miserable.

However, my grief was nothing compared to that of his mother, who treated me as if I'd been his executioner and firmly refused to forgive me for Donato's death. When, in fact, she herself had been the involuntary cause of it, by making him endure the discussions of Casa Fratta, until he finally fought back by nobly spilling his blood at Rimini! She, however, continued to frequent Casa Fratta and took along our two younger children, and, when I chided her about it, gently recalling Donato's case, she snapped at me that his wretched example would not have poisoned her life if I, with my liberal tirades, hadn't spoiled the benefits he might have gained from the Fratta salon. As you can see, because of age or friendships or maternal concern, the good woman was becoming more and more reactionary. Still, I trusted in the proverb that says blood is thicker than water and believed my children would not share that peculiar malady. Not being the sort of man to take arms against her wishes, I let her do as she wanted, merely reproaching her gently when little Pisana was caught in an outright lie or little Giulio rebelled at being corrected, and rather than admit he'd erred would let himself be pounded in a mortar. I'd ask: were falsehood, pride and obstinacy perhaps the results of her new methods of child-rearing? And she would say she'd rather have her children be proud or dishonest than murder them by her own hand, and that I should ponder the evil I'd already done and not blight her life with my reproaches. And then I'd feel bad about all she had suffered and try to be silent, much as I thought that death was better than a life disfigured by lies and swollen with presumption. And the truth was, I didn't think my children's failings were terribly grave and hoped they would disappear in time.

One day, though, I cannot remember in regard to what, she spoke of Ormenta as a shining example of a Christian man and good citizen, and I could not refrain from asking why that perfect Christian and good citizen was letting his father die, you might say, of starvation.

'That's an abominable lie!' Aquilina began to shout. 'Old Ormenta gets a rich pension from the government and he could live very well if he weren't being bled by those vices of his!'

'And if were to tell you,' said I, 'that the interest on those debts he contracted to favour his son's ambitions have eaten up most of his resources and his son knows it and hasn't made the least effort to help him?'

'Even if it were so, I wouldn't blame him!' exclaimed Aquilina. 'His father was such a scoundrel that he deserves to be punished and so do all the other vile souls like him.'

'Oh, very good!' said I. 'You're such a scrupulous Christian, but you allow men to exercise that supreme ministry of justice that God reserves for himself! And what law of charity enables sons to judge and punish the sins of their fathers, I don't know.'

'That's not what I'm saying,' Aquilina went on, 'but God can certainly permit Ormenta to turn a blind eye on his father's privations and let the old man be punished for his villainy here on earth too!'

'Fine!' I replied. 'But I certainly wouldn't want to have that blind eye on my conscience!' And in fact old Ormenta died a few days later, loathed by all. But if any feeling was more intense and more universal than that posthumous loathing, it was contempt for his son's meanness and ingratitude: he haggled over the cost of the funeral and, after the inheritance was calculated, refused to pay the doctor's bill, because the debts exceeded the assets.

The quarrels between myself and my wife on this and like matters grew more and more common, until in the end they spoiled our peace. Had la Pisana's parting words not been impressed on my mind, we might have had serious troubles indeed; but I went on being patient and probably more indulgent than my role of father demanded – for later I would repent that I'd left far too much responsibility to Aquilina, and, too late, would suffer acute remorse. Little Pisana was picking up those ultra-pious manners that make even virtue seem suspect and unpleasant. Giulio, spoiled and praised by his teachers, grew more and more conceited and so presumptuous that there was no way ever to convince him he had made a mistake. I could see very clearly where these faults were going to take him: with some flattery and adulation anyone would be able to lead him into filthy, sordid affairs and he would be convinced he was in the right.

But when it came to correcting these flaws in my children, I kept putting it off until tomorrow, and, of course, I didn't want to upset their mother and hoped that from one day to another she would open her eyes and see the truth. For example, I wasn't pleased that all their morality was based on blind obedience to authority. I'd have preferred them to think morality was dictated by conscience and the social order. I wanted God's will to be shown not just in revelation, but in the laws underlying individual conscience and public justice. As they were now, once distanced from religion, and subject as they were to its precepts only out of fear, their consciences would have no guiding light, their souls no moral courage. Aquilina didn't want to hear this. In her mind it was a sacrilege even to think that her children might distance themselves from religion; and should they be so wretched and unlucky as to fall into the abyss of non-belief, it wasn't worth trying to stop them halfway down. Once their souls were lost, she didn't care whether their actions would bring benefit or harm to society. Egoist in herself, she was an egoist in their name, too.

I thought hers was a bad system, even for believers. To begin with, nature (which shows us the mind of God) always makes us prefer the lesser evil to the greater. And then compassion obliges us to protect our fellow man's well-being against evildoers. Now, to harm others with one's actions is certainly more dangerous to society than to abide by moral law and sin only with respect to religion. Let us bring up our children so that even if they are deprived of belief, their consciences will privately obey the universal law of justice. As for whether education can change ideas, men are ever men, that is, ever mutable, and I see no sacrilege in that. You say we live in times of misbelief and tepid religious convictions? Well, then, defend society with the best remedy beyond that faith you say is lacking. I don't pretend you stop inculcating that faith and preaching it, if you must, but merely that you add a second guarantee.

As for myself, if I'd taken my every moral rule from what I learned in Doctrine, I'd be a terrible scoundrel; and if I cite myself it's neither out of pride nor shame, but to provide an example you cannot doubt. Now that you've read this life of mine, and whatever your opinions, you must admit that if the good I did was slight, I might have done far more harm. The merit for all the harm I didn't do belongs to conscience, which held me back, even when I had stopped believing in certain rules. No longer a believer, I still behaved like one, and if I was not a Christian in words I was one in deeds, every time Christian morality coincided with natural morality, which it nearly always does. If you can show me that I would have been more useful to society as a usurer, a liar, corrupt, a murderer, then you and I can only concur that it would be quite useless to think religious precepts are based on absolutes. Not to mention that with scripture one can always play the jousting match of casuistry, but when it comes to sentiments, my dear sirs, casuistry is out of the question!

I don't believe I ever had the courage to babble out such a long sermon to Aquilina (but I don't doubt I would have convinced her!) and, indeed, let me take this opportunity to say that however long-winded and sermonizing I may seem to you in this account of my life, the truth is I've always been rather stingy with words and three more listeners than usual in front of me are enough to dry up all my loquacity. However, I did raise the subject with my wife once or twice and, having lost the battle attacking on one side, came back on the other, with the same result in every case: a solemn dressing-down. And so I let her do everything her way, especially because it was a problem to decide who had more rights, father or mother. The balance began to tip in her favour with the arrival of cholera, which appeared in Italy then for the first time, bringing all the terror that accompanies rare, contagious diseases and causing the greatest alarm in Venice.

Our Giulio was struck by that terrible illness and the steely courage with which his mother looked after him gave her a second round of parental rights. I had to resign mine and it was only with little Pisana that I kept up some pretence, she being in need of a moral compass much more than her brother, and three times cleverer and more pernicious. Along with her name she seemed to have inherited something of the temperament of my Pisana, and when, just as she began to make up some farrago of lies, she would gracefully toss her head to free her brow of the thick ring of brown curls that fell on it, my mind would fly to the little sorceress of Fratta – and so I let myself be duped most charmingly. My little daughter was not as thoughtless and impertinent as her namesake, however, but knew how to calculate her own interests very well, to be docile and pious today, but confident and determined on the morrow. I watched her carefully and every day I saw that pursuit of pleasure that is a woman's fortune and her ruin growing in her.

And so I tried to direct her the right way, to make the approval of those who are good seem valuable and the admiration of the vicious seem worthless, and show her that virtue and vice cannot be recognized only by how splendid they look. However, I saw I was making little progress. They had so deeply inculcated the lesson that those who command are in the right and want nothing but the best for those who obey, that it was impossible for her to admire goodness that was poor, despised, oppressed. Merit, virtue, honours, wealth and power were all one to her and her silly head was full of fantasies and guile. She chased the light like a moth. Charming little moth, how will you fly when the candle flame has burned your wings?

This was my fear: that some terrible disenchantment would snatch all the poetry from her soul and she'd be left one of those fools who think they are bold, positive, perfect, when they are nothing but bastard human beings, fated to pollute some quantity of fresh air for a number of years and then to populate a tomb with worms. When my business permitted, I would battle furiously against that feminine nature of hers, but although I could arrest her bad instincts, I could never eliminate them, for Aquilina disagreed with me and the company my daughter kept offered quite the opposite example to what I believed.

Cholera had this advantage[12] if nothing else: it swept the world of many people who had no idea why they'd been put there. One of the first to go was Agostino Frumier, who left a great many children behind and was quite dismayed at having to go underground without the chamberlain's key he'd so long coveted. The plague also robbed his brother of the old Correggitrice, who died more of fear than real illness, I believe; and afterwards he found the world around him so new and strange, I think he marvelled he no longer had a wig on his head or saw the esteemed Doge or the Most Excellent Procuratori in their noble cloaks. In Venice they would say, 'There goes Cavaliere Alfonso Frumier, who's just come out of school.' He was about sixty-five years old and Madam Correggitrice had been past seventy when she upped and died. To match fidelity like that you'd have to go back to the dawn of the human race, when there was nothing but one man and one woman.

Doretta, too, died of that pestilence, I think; after a life of disgrace and many peregrinations she had come back to Venice to defame her old age, too. I know for certain that she died at the hospital in the summer of that year. I'd seen her many times, but pretended not to know her, for her sordid person disgusted me and it seemed a sacrilege that Leopardo's memory should be united with such a shameless creature. However, her end helped to convince me that a supreme justice rules over the things of this world, and although there are many sad exceptions, the general rule remains true: do evil and you will harvest evil. In youth, when hot and impetuous spirits have no time to consider the fullness of things but are easily attracted by details, it's possible to err. But little by little, as judgement cools and memory makes better use of its store of facts and observations, that collective reason that regulates humanity gains our trust and we can watch it ascend to higher ground. In the same way we don't see the cliff above a river from even a few feet away, but can see the whole river from up on the heights.

We had barely recovered from that fearful pestilence when one evening, in the middle of November, I believe, Dr Vianello was announced. I had always corresponded with Lucilio, but after '31, when he, too, returned to Italy but then left again soon after, our letters had become rarer. At that point I had heard nothing for a year. I found him bent, pale, the sparse hair left on his head now white; but his eyes were *his*; that incorruptible spirit still warmed his words and when he waved an arm you could see the vigour his lean, bony frame still contained.

'Didn't I tell you I would come to die among you?' he said. 'Well, I've come to keep my word. I'm seventy-two years old, but that would be nothing were it not for this bothersome chest complaint that London's climate has bequeathed me. We have to watch out, we children of the sun, the fogs destroy us.'

'I do hope you are joking,' said I, 'and that just as you cured my eyes, you'll cure your lungs.'

'No, I repeat: I've come to keep my word. We know each other well and can dispense with politesse. We know what we can expect from life and what kind of good or evil death is. If I were to pretend to act out a part that means nothing to me, you would be right to weep, but you know that I speak as I think, and if I say I shall die in peace, in peace I shall certainly die. The only real regret I have is that I won't see my own death, but that is a complaint that ten generations before me have voiced and it will do no good to moan about it. My actions and ideas, my spirit (with much study and a certain amount of effort I have trained it to love virtue, even by suppressing the passions that ruled it), all of this will serve that wondrous providence that is perfecting our moral order. Do you remember Goethe's concentric worlds? Not real, perhaps, but a powerful allegory. Our words and our sighs ripple out from us and travel far, far away, growing feeble but never entirely silent, like circles that spread out from where a stone falls in the lake. Life comes forth from contractions, death from expansion, and the universe of life contains all these movements, much the way a body contains the functioning of different organs.'

I listened to Lucilio's words quite devoutly, for there are so very few of us who can draw real comfort from the lofty speculations of philosophy, and that talent belongs to a tiny group who by nature or education or force of will have learned to put reason and sentiment in intimate accord. Although I could never fly with that eagle, I could admire his luminous flight from earth and console myself thinking that where others ascended by reason, I'd arrived by a leap of conscience.

'Lucilio,' I said, embracing him again, 'listening to you I feel reinvigorated, which means your ideas are true and salutary. And for that reason, allow me to hope you may keep us company longer than you'd have us think.'

'I promise I'll keep you good and cheerful company, no more. I could even say how long, but why risk making a fool of myself as a medical man? I'm content and that should be enough for you.'

'And do you wish to see Clara again? Or has the desire passed entirely?'

'No, no!' said Lucilio. 'I do mean to see her, so I can ponder once again the way a single passion takes two different courses in temperaments that are different and have been educated differently. To learn as much as we can: that must be the soul's highest rule. That unquenchable thirst to know that torments us right up to the last instant doesn't seem to spring from individual reason in any obvious way. But it might well derive from the demands of a vaster order that expands after death. Learn, then, let us learn! Nature seems to squander rain thoughtlessly, yet every drop, however small, however tiny, is drunk by the earth and moves along some invisible meatus to where all-powerful aridity calls it. Idleness was invented by human imbecility; nature is never idle and nothing in it is useless.'

'So, you will study Clara as the anatomist investigates a cadaver?'

'No, Carlo, but I will study her as I study myself: to be absolutely certain, despite appearances, that a single reason alone excites, moves, soothes a great and various humanity; and to demonstrate once again by my unwavering love, that love belongs to a larger existence, a freer and fuller kind of happiness than can be obtained in the human phase of our being. For if it were not so, Carlo, I would be quite mad to love someone who torments me and despises me; but deep in myself I know I'm not mad at all and that my point of view is as correct and impartial as any other man's.'

'But listen, why did you never seem either surprised or indignant about the incredible change in Clara's feelings for you? I've wanted to ask you that for a long while now, because to me it seems even more remarkable than the very constancy of your love.'

'Why was I not surprised or indignant? Clara was always prone to sublime illusions, so I could not be surprised to see her escape me that way, especially when I had other things on my mind and was feeling foolishly sure of her. Women can decamp downwards, but it's easy to get them back that way and it's the most common problem, the risk most generally feared. But woe,

woe to you, if she decamps upwards! It is pointless to pursue her, vain to beg her to return, for no pleasure is greater than the sensual pleasure of sacrifice; no reason can conquer faith; no mercy will distract her from pondering the eternal. And women, you see, are better than we are at living, well, *beyond* life. Working as a doctor convinced me that no man, however strong and tested, could match a miserable, petty little woman in her indifference to death. They seem to have a clearer premonition of future life than we do. As for not having been angry with Clara, first, anger is an emotion for schoolboys; and then I couldn't be angry, because hers was not an injustice to me but an illusion: she believed she loved me more that way and would procure me not just transient worldly pleasure, but eternal celestial happiness. In short, I was meant to be grateful to her!'

I could only admire the ease with which Lucilio made even the most fleeting and involuntary twists of his soul submit to reason. By dint of practice and resolve he governed himself like a clock, so that passions, affections, thoughts, all ran just as he planned. Still, you couldn't say his emotions were feeble; if you knew him well, you saw that only an almost superhuman force of will compressed and regulated the passions that shook him.

Lucilio and Clara saw each other almost every evening that winter, and the little circle gathered at Casa Fratta was often scandalized by the elderly doctor's violent opinions. Augusto Cisterna thought he should be forgiven because he was so old; Clara was even more indulgent, saying he had always been mad that way and that God would have his own good reasons to forgive him. She took great care never to look at Lucilio, perhaps because she'd made such a vow on leaving the convent, but otherwise her faith was so simple and her manners so ingenuous that Lucilio smiled more in admiration than in scorn.

The one who seemed most pleased to see Dr Vianello was – you would never guess – Count Rinaldo. From his daily brooding on the books in the library, something was about to be born: a colossal work on Venetian trade from Attila to Charles V, in which bold hypotheses, excellent documentation and sharp critical intelligence were masterfully combined, according to Lucilio. And the doctor proved useful to the author in examining some questions on which he knew him to be profoundly erudite, and together they corrected some points and amended others. Lucilio was quite astonished to discover such learning and such love of country in the unwashed, whining little person of Count Rinaldo, but he also guessed the reasons why.

'You see,' he said, 'how in times of error and national indolence the right and far-seeing minds, the energies that refuse to lie abed, are put to use? They waste their love and vitality bringing corpses back to life; unable to improve the society and love human beings, they dig up ancient inscriptions and broken stones and love and study them. It's the almost universal destiny of our intellectuals!'

But Lucilio exaggerated. With Alfieri, Foscolo, Manzoni, Pellico, a new family of writers was born that did honour ruins, yes, but called the living to witness and risked – or welcomed – present suffering for a better future. Leopardi, who became proud of that very reason he had cursed; Giusti,[13] who attacked his contemporaries to provoke a moral revival: they are the sons of that troubled but living family. When despairing Leopardi wrote 'Broom' and 'Brutus' he knew better than the rest that only by living a long life can a man achieve that sublime scientific gaze that takes in the whole metaphysical world.

My son Giulio might have profited greatly from Lucilio's company and conversation if the doctor had stayed with us longer. But, alas, his health began to decline at the beginning of the spring and his prediction was right, for he soon died. He died staring me proudly in the face, almost as if he forbade me to mourn him. Clara was in the other room, praying for him, and his last words were 'Thank her!' And I did thank her, for what I'm not sure. As much as she prayed, she never agreed to comfort the dying man with her presence, but I knew she made it a point to thwart her own desires and so I think I can say she wanted to. The sacrifice was offered to the greater good of his soul. I felt more contemplative than sad after we lost him, but the unabashed pleasure my wife showed at his death annoyed me fiercely. She thought Lucilio's presence in the house was endangering her children's morality and that God had answered her prayers by sending him to the last resting place he deserved.

That day I picked a furious fight with Aquilina, complete with tears and howls, but, in truth, I was too restrained, for such an injustice, when gratitude was called for, demanded a smack on the backside. I confess I never had, nor shall ever have Lucilio's serene composure. But his death, like that of la Pisana, convinced me even more that there's always something to gain by being strong and unselfish. If nothing else, you die in good spirits and that is not only a desirable outcome, but the touchstone that distinguishes an honest man from a squalid one. In life, hypocrisy interferes, but at the great moment? Believe me, my friends, you won't have time or any desire to play a part. And the inevitable punishment for a scoundrel is to die trembling.

Looking back over my life, I often think of the daisy, that humble little flower made of a golden button and white rays on which young girls foretell their loves. One by one they pluck the petals until only the last remains, and so it is with us as we go among the companions with whom we walk life's way, one falling today, another tomorrow, until we find ourselves alone and melancholy in the wilds of old age. After Lucilio, Spiro went, and when we heard the news from Luciano my sorrow redoubled. As for my son, he had decided not to leave Greece and, as I'd predicted, ambition proved stronger in him than any other sentiment. He'd been somewhat discouraged after Kapodistrias was assassinated, but when King Otto[14] took the throne he'd obtained a good post in the War Ministry and from there he aspired to higher positions, patient as a dog that puts his nose on his master's knee to get a crust of bread. Venice, Italy, us, he seemed to consider curiosities; his wife's letters were more affectionate, although I'd heard from Spiro's children that he didn't treat her very well. And, of course, my wife continued to blame me for Luciano's distance, just as for Donato's death.

However, in the two or three years that followed, misfortunes that struck her more directly made her somewhat more tolerant, and I began to feel remorse (and will always feel remorse) for the great damage caused by my own weakness and indulgence. One by one her brothers and sisters died and the only one left was Bruto, who wore his years rather lightly and only complained that destiny had settled him in Venice, where the frequent bridges were a tremendous nuisance for a man with a wooden leg. Thus we slowly declined into old age, even as the country grew youthful again, and what follows is proof that all those years were not lost, as the pessimists like to say. Nothing is born from nothing: here is an axiom that cannot be disputed.

TWENTY-TWO

In which I demonstrate, gladdening the hearts of all cultivated persons, how Count Rinaldo, writing his famous Historical Analysis of Venetian Trade, amply consoled himself for his dire poverty. The very sad direction my son Giulio's life takes and the comic temperament of my daughter Pisana. How the young of today are superior to the youth of once upon a time; and mistakes are a method for learning, so long as one knows what one wants, and wants what one should. Giulio flees; old friends visit. Celebrations, public and private mourning during the year of 1848. A return to Friuli, where, several years late, I receive news of my son's death.

Perhaps you will have noticed that among all the professions I've dedicated myself to, my own free will directed me to none of them. The will of others, the necessity of the moment, some extraordinary concordance of circumstances: all delivered the decision, signed and sealed, to my hands before I could think about it. When it came to commerce, I had only become involved as a favour to Spiro, and if I didn't quit when Casa Apostulos liquidated its assets, it was only because employing my small capital in the business allowed me to keep the family afloat. Around '40, feeling old and once again weak in the eyes, when I saw I had enough that my assets, if invested, would allow me to live, I decided to retire from trading. I'd been thinking over how to do so for some time, when the authorities in Constantinople informed me that the Ottoman government had finally recognized a part of my father's credits, and that a fair sum was due to me, if not the huge amount originally claimed.

Three or four years before, Lucilio had already advised me

that the English ambassador hadn't forgotten about the matter, that it was the Porte's miserable finances delaying payment. But I had never believed I would see the money, and so when the eighty thousand piastres arrived they seemed a great bounty, and, as for the heirs of the Grand Vizier, I left them in peace because my son Luciano, of whom I'd enquired, told me they were nasty types. Between the eighty thousand piastres and the thirty thousand ducats I had when I'd liquidated my accounts, I had a goodly sum with which I bought a nice, big farm next to Casa Provedoni in Cordovado, as well as many fields that had belonged to the Frumier estate (Domenico Fulgenzio was eager to be rid of them, for he wanted to have his own assets free to swallow those of others).

However, Giulio's education demanded that we remain in Venice and we continued to live in my father's house there, and for two months a year we rented a house on the River Brenta, where we enjoyed the fresh air and country life. Little by little I'd grown used to Venice, until I'd become the proper Venetian gentleman who couldn't go a day without seeing the bell tower of San Marco. And not just the bell tower, but the Church, the Procuratori's offices, the Palazzo Ducale: when autumn arrived and we left the country behind, I saw them all anew with pleasure and the sweetest melancholy. But Bruto with his wooden leg was far better off on dry land, and so he served quite happily as our steward, and thus spent a good part of the fine season in the Friuli, where he could also be of use to the swarm of nieces and nephews of all ages that his siblings had left behind, and whom he tried to look after as best he could. As for me, I'd taken care of all of Donato's children and those of Bradamante. The two girls had married quite well; one lived in Portogruaro, one in San Vito. One of the young men earned his living as a veterinarian; the other got enough to compensate the family misfortunes from the rent of the druggist shop and one of my plots I'd given him to look after.

The Counts of Fratta, however, were going from bad to worse. Perhaps it was foolish, but it grieved me, and still does, to see my dear Pisana's family disappear. They seemed to view their ruined fortune with the most stoical good cheer: Rinaldo buying books and neglecting his taxes, Clara with her prodigal acts of charity, both scraping the bottom of the barrel of what they owned. There were still two or three farms left, and one crumbling wing of the Castle, and two derelict towers, but the rents vanished left and right into the litigious hands of their creditors, and not a penny made it to Venice. To do some justice to the last representatives of the Counts of Fratta's illustrious descent, they were as stingy in paying out as they were careless about what came in. So Count Rinaldo and the pious Clara were reduced to one ducat a day, along with the three Venetian lire she received from the public treasury as a needy patrician. As you can see, they were no spendthrifts; the whole year was one long Lent for them.

It was a good thing that Clara, because of her seraphic ecstasies, and the Count, who was forever thinking about ideas, had no time to think about their stomachs. They grew slenderer every day, never noticing, and were getting ready to live on air like Harlequin's jackass. I do remember one day I asked the Countess Clara why she took so many coffees – wasn't she risking a paralysis? – and she told me that in Venice coffee was cheap and if she drank a lot she could get by without meat broth. Between coffee and air there is little difference in terms of nutrition, I guess. And yet, any low woman who came to their door, whimpering and paternostering, was sure to go away with a coin or a piece of bread. I feel sure that Clara, if she met her worst enemy (supposing she had one) would have shared her last coffee, and even given him all of it if he'd scowled a little.

In the meantime Count Rinaldo was searching by land and by sea for a publisher for his book, but, alas, could find none. Wealth had notably increased during those long years of peace, not as much as we might have liked, perhaps, but it increased. Civic pride and education had improved, too, although slowly, and almost in spite of circumstances; sights were still low, and public philanthropy sought present needs, wounds to heal, desires to meet – not remote glories to revive or old inheritances to claim. A Manzonian hymn to the railway then being planned to connect Milan and Venice[1] would have happily found a publisher, but a voluminous work on ancient Venetian trade did not pique the public's curiosity and didn't offer booksellers much profit. And so they all raised a hat to the Count and, having weighed his manuscript in their hands, gave it back to him without even turning the pages. His breath was wasted trying to get them to look at his work and see how extensive, how thorough, it was. They would reply that it was surely a masterpiece, but readers weren't ready for such a deep and lofty tract, and while the job of the writer was to serve his own ideas, the printer instead had to satisfy people's desires.

Count Rinaldo had the modesty that stems from real merit and the natural dignity of the man who is sincerely modest. And so he didn't – as they say on the street – stoop to lick anybody's boots, but withdrew to his study to plot noble revenge and console himself for the rejections by refining, correcting, amending, his work. Thirty years of study, research and reflection had not perhaps been sufficient: every day some passage struck his eyes demanding a broader examination to clarify his ideas or help the reader understand better the author's frame of mind. You might have thought he was deeply grateful to those publishers for having given him time to brighten up a piece of his portrait and retouch the outlines. But when he decided he had finished rewriting, and did the rounds of the booksellers' shops again with his manuscript under his cloak, he got the very same demurrals and even the odd witticism or scowl from the less polite. Advised to address himself to better-known publishers in other cities, he began a stubborn correspondence with Florence, Milan, Turin and Naples. Most did not reply; a few were courteous enough to ask him to send extracts. And there he sat, the good man, selecting, re-polishing, re-transcribing once again; but when the reply finally came it either said the style was too abstruse or the topic too distant from present interests, and he was invited to write about statistics or economics, for these paid decently, but as for monumental works of historical erudition, they just weren't right for our century.

These last plaudits, too, the poor Count put in the cupboard of deposed illusions, but he still had such a stock of good ones that quite a few years went by before he was persuaded it was absolutely impossible to find a publisher for the *Historical*

Analysis of Venetian Trade. It did occur to him that it might be quite useful to find someone well known in sciences and letters to put in a good word for him, and, as he knew no one, he consulted Cavaliere Frumier about the matter. What luck! The Cavaliere, after the death of his dear wife, had never regained his senses, and to speak to him of letters and sciences was to hear him go on about the literary history of the previous century. He came no nearer to the living than those luminaries of the Settecento Abbé Cesarotti and Count Gaspare Gozzi, and his cousin left him not much enlightened. Count Rinaldo thus decided to take matters in hand himself and began to sell whatever he had left that was saleable to begin to print something, hoping that the first sheaves that came forth would find favour with that public that could not fail to exist for a work of great historical importance ennobling their native land. From that day forward the Countess Clara drank even more coffee and even withheld the bread from her mouth to scrape together as quickly as possible those five hundred lire needed to print the first four chapters. As soon as he had them in his pocket, he went straight to the typographer and, without even trying to bargain, put the money on the counter and said triumphantly: 'Print as much as you can of my manuscript.'

'What format do you wish to order? How many copies do you want? Will you send out subscriptions or do without?' asked the printer.

All things that Rinaldo knew nothing about. But once every detail had been explained to him, they agreed that four thousand subscription orders would be sent out all over Italy with a few words of invitation summarizing the main points of the book, and that a thousand copies of the first instalment would be printed in royal octave. The Count went home, his feet not touching the paving stones, and the three weeks he spent running back and forth from house to print shop, reading proofs, correcting errors, changing a word here and there and adding a note or two were the happiest days of his life – what for an ordinary young man would be his first love. But the printer didn't much share his jubilation, for the orders weren't coming back with signatures affixed, and in Venice and other nearby cities they'd received no more than a few dozen. And these mostly came from booksellers, and they knew how grudgingly money flowed through those unreliable channels. The Count, though, certain that he would see his first instalment printed within a month, slept on a bed of roses. He did have to bicker with the censor about a phrase here, a sentence there, but they were corrections that didn't in any way detract from the importance of his work and he was quite willing to concede them.

And so finally the famous frontispiece with four succeeding chapters saw the light and Count Rinaldo had the supreme satisfaction of seeing boxes of his work in the windows of the book shops. This satisfaction was followed by another no less vital, when the book was advertised in the newspapers and mentioned with a great tolling of bells in some literary review. Milan's leading paper praised the book for its intentions and profound erudition, not to mention the great practical use it might be put to in modern trade, should circumstances ever lead the old trade routes to be revived. The review spoke of the Indies, China, the Moluccas, England, Russia, opium, pepper and rice straw, of Mehmet Ali, the Burmese Empire and plans to cut across the Isthmus of Suez, everything, in short, but Rinaldo's work on commerce and Venetian trading houses during the Middle Ages.

However, Rinaldo was content because his patriotic intent and vast, deep analysis had been named as the work's principal qualities, which was true, and the author knew it, just as he knew that the reviewer had properly read and interpreted his work. A Tuscan paper then copied the main points of the Milanese review, the writer adding something of his own, and, along with this, also acknowledging that he had barely skimmed the pages. But then a hundred reviews, a hundred opinions, one more eccentric than the other, began to turn up all over, all obsequiously copied and modified at will from those first articles. It was soon apparent that the writers knew no more of the book than the title, and perhaps hadn't even glanced at that, for a learned writer from Turin recommended the Count of Fratta's treatise as an excellent manual for traders hoping to enlarge their businesses by speculating in the modern economy.

When he read this last opinion, the poor author rubbed his eyes, thinking he hadn't seen right or that at least they weren't talking about him and his book. But then he looked again and saw that, alas, it was his.

'A pack of donkeys!' he muttered through his teeth. 'All right, don't buy it. Fine, don't read it! But not to understand even the title! To serve up a judgement pell-mell before even consulting the frontispiece! This is just too much, and I say the truth when I say I'd rather be ripped to pieces than complimented by such a mob of sour pedants.'

He had been living in the library until then, Count Rinaldo, and had no idea those were not times for *reading* books. You praised them or condemned them without reading them, because the spirit and the intent mattered more than the intellectual value or the form. You'd say to the next person, 'Read this book, I dipped into it and it looked good!' The word was passed, but the books remained in the shop. Instead, you hurried to read the latest word in some newspaper. I don't mean to say there weren't some energetic scholars who had time for both, but young people, the great consumers of new books, were too busy. To keep up with the everyday excitement, the amusements, the flirtations as well as the new passions fermenting in their young circles, you needed more than one life.

In those days Gregory XVI died and Giovanni Mastai Ferretti, Pius IX, took the papal throne.[2] Pius IX: a name that hums in the ears like a well-known melody long after you've heard it. He was a priest and a pontiff above all, but there were many who perceived him as pontiff and soldier in the style of Julius II – the way a man with some image in mind will see it in a cloud, but in vain will try to point it out to others.

The new pope didn't understand or pretended not to understand why he was being praised to the skies, and, by saying nothing, seemed ready to concede much more than he was actually willing to. Whether enthusiasm was fashionable or fashion generated enthusiasm I don't know, but there was a universal wish to stand behind a holy flag and there was no intrigue in this, merely instinct. These events, which interrupted Italy's long somnolence, didn't help Count Rinaldo in the least to resolve his typographic problems; in better times he might have sold enough from the first instalment to pay for half the second, but now he didn't earn a single *scudo*. And what was stranger, he forgot all about the book and he, too, hurried out to the piazza to shout, 'Long live Pius IX!'

His sister was among the most fanatical about the new pontiff. She considered him a great prophet and the whole Fratta salon was scandalized, for no one could believe that the old true believer, abbess emerita of Santa Theresa could approve so heartily of a pope who leaned more to the political side than to the sacerdotal (or so people thought then). But perhaps they were unaware of the reason why Clara had turned pious and a nun, and under what conditions she had taken her vows with the Almighty. I did not know for sure, but believed I could guess from a word here and there.

In the midst of all this agitation, resources grew even scarcer; finally, Count Rinaldo sent an order to his steward in Fratta requesting money at whatever cost. The poor fellow solved the problem by selling the remaining bits of the Castle and advancing the Count the money. It went to help set up a patriotic newspaper in some mainland city or other and once again slipped through his fingers, and Clara was left without coffee and there was little bread for him, but, one of them praying, the other reading and dreaming, they bravely defended themselves against hunger. From time to time I exercised my Christian charity and invited him to luncheon, but he was so vague that despite an appetite several days old, he would forget the hour and only appear as the meal was ending. However, once he got his jaws moving again they seemed to remember what fasting meant and worked at length to avoid it.

This was about as much as I could do for my cousins, la Pisana's siblings; and in any case I didn't want to be obvious about it, knowing how touchy and sensitive they could be. Whenever Aquilina sent Clara a couple of pounds of coffee, she'd send it on the sly, by the maid's hand. If I must tell the truth, in the preceding years I had found the two of them quite unappealing and had only been able to tolerate them by thinking of la Pisana, but now that the times were troubled, my antipathy waned and I saved my bile for the people in their circle. They seemed to resemble Clara and Rinaldo, but they were different: Ormenta, the Cisterna cousins and their hangers-on were thinking about their own interests and comforts behind the excuse of the glory of God; Rinaldo and Clara worked for the glory of God in everything they did and would have cheerfully sacrificed all their assets and comforts for that holy purpose. True, the glory of God meant different things to brother and sister, but in any case, they were pursuing an ideal and they clapped their hands and joined in the general enthusiasm, while Ormenta stared suspiciously out of the window and wished daggers on those cursed howlers. When necessary, though, he could shout as loud as anybody else and keep his own counsel, too.

My son, meanwhile, was getting deeply mired in bad company and for all that I tried to raise his mind from material things and keep his youthfulness of spirit alive, he paid me little heed and seemed older at twenty-two than I was at seventy. I very much wanted to instil noble sentiments in him, for I sensed the time was short and I was feeling quite doddery myself and feared I might leave him rudderless just when he needed me most. But the sickly sweetness of vice had ruined his palate and he'd been persuaded that there was nothing to be desired in this world except ease, good food and good company in bed. And he flaunted those tastes as if they were the mark of a strong spirit and independent views and despised anyone who wanted to satisfy higher desires.

This was the reaction against Romanticism, and the old foxes made use of it to draw the young to their side. When other young people of greater experience or better counsel opposed them and called it an abomination to deny all ideals in life and behave like pigs wallowing in filth, thinking of nothing but pleasure, those old masters of corruption said they were envious, said pay no attention to them, it was all hypocrisy and you must have courage and scorn those Pharisees. Giulio had a strong, decided will and never did anything by halves; for him, fighting the censure of the Puritans, as he called them, was proof of his courage, and the more the others disapproved of him, the more cynical and reckless he became. Gaming, drinking and women were his three main strengths, but he had others, too, and especially one he faulted his adversaries for: hypocrisy. As soon as he had one foot inside the door of the house, the brazenness ceased and he abandoned the usual bordello language. With his mother he seemed an angel and when I would tell her what I'd heard of his habits from the word going around, she would shout that it was all falsehoods, that you could see right through her Giulio into his heart. If he didn't lose his head chasing after the usual fancies of youth, but pursued solid affairs and established friends, we should thank Heaven! Hadn't I already had a terrible lesson in what happened to Donato? And here, the usual accusations were trotted out, and, to avoid hearing sermons all day, I could only shrug my shoulders and walk off.

However, I scolded Giulio harshly and threatened worse, when besides the usual rumours about him I heard something really quite ugly. A friend of Cavaliere Frumier warned me that he had been told about some gambling den where my son had been accused of cutting the cards all too expertly. He used his fists to reply to his accuser and few were impressed by this method of defending his honesty. When I questioned Giulio about the matter, he said quite confidently that he preferred to play cards his own way without other people telling him how, that he thought their chatter was foolish, but didn't like to be treated badly, and that anyone who didn't like his fists should get out of the way. As for the charges against him, he didn't confess or deny them, but slid over them so vaguely that I was almost convinced his accuser hadn't been wrong. However, I still clung to the illusion that his bad behaviour might derive from a distorted sense of self-esteem or an excessive taste for contradiction, and might still be repaired before petulance became habit and errors, vice.

And I was still hoping so when Pius IX conceded amnesty to all political prisoners,[3] and in the midst of the general enthusiasm Giulio was the only who dared to defy the universal jubilation and deride those who cheered and celebrated on the streets, calling them lunatics and silly females. It wasn't so much that he saw what the future would bring: he was just cynical; but in any case, even had it been his profound conviction, it was more brassy impudence than real courage that made him say so at that time, in that way. Even illusions sometimes deserve respect, and just as it isn't right to spoil a young lad's virginal hopes, it's not right to attack the noble faith of a people, for faith itself is a regenerative force. Giulio instead mocked and jibed without any respect and even those more convinced of his own convictions than he was pretended not to listen to him in public or, if drawn in, quickly tried to steal away. He would then become even more stubborn and attack both friend and foe; unmasking the hypocrisy in the one, parodying the credulity of the other, relishing being the raven of bad news, defender of the *ancien régime*.

The more others despised him, the more he prided himself on being contrary and even began to believe some of his opinions. But men too frank and absolute are often charged with all the wrongs of their side, and Giulio was universally condemned. I knew nothing of these matters (for parents are often the last to learn what their children are up to), but I sensed that Giulio was in danger and warned him. He replied that he valued life no more than it was worth and that, in any case, nothing bad could happen to him, for imaginary evils couldn't harm him.

'Be careful, Giulio!' I said, pleading, almost tearful. 'Life is not just what you think it is. Your soul may wake and want love and admiration . . .'

'Father mine,' he broke in with a sardonic smile, 'no more of this . . . poetry! It would be all very well if men were wise, just and good, but as they are, you might as well have the love and admiration of your dog. I'd gladly give it up forever!'

'Don't say forever, Giulio. You're not entitled. You're too young!' (He smiled, as young men do when their inexperience is pointed out.) 'Those you consider so wretched, so misguided, may still throw off their abjection and prove more decent and generous than you can imagine. And if they do and you have to face their contempt, believe me, it will destroy you, unless you've lost all human shame and dignity. For it won't be foul ostracism that you'll face, but a sentence of decency and generosity. You won't be able to fool yourself, to defend yourself! Against one, two, ten you may be able to struggle, but there's no defence against the opinions of an entire people. Like flames beaten down on one side they will flare up higher on the other. The only refuge Providence permits the honest man in such cases is the refuge of conscience. Giulio, can you face your conscience? What comfort will it give you? You, who have gloried in trampling everything humanly noble? You, who have declared your profound contempt for mankind and joined up with the worst of men; how can we not believe you despise yourself most of all? Come, answer me. Do you really think there is no difference between your friends and companions, Ormenta, Augusto Cisterna and his sons – and other people? If people condemn and attack them, isn't that a sign that the general conscience is superior? You should fear, Giulio, being confused with such a nest of vipers; you should fear being dragged beyond where you want to go by their contradictions, and that your desire to take centre stage will end by making you pay for all their vices and errors, even as they shrewdly fade from the scene.'

'You're very wrong about me,' said Giulio as calmly as could be and without considering my remarks for a second. 'I'm not a follower of anybody's creed. Ormenta and Augusto Cisterna are wily, shameless old fellows, no better or worse than anyone else. If I haven't renounced them it's merely out of habit and because I don't see why I should leave the frying pan for the fire, abandon vice for hypocrisy. My younger friends are those who agree most with my views; if they aren't perfect, it isn't my fault. As for being concerned about what people say, I'm not such a fool. My conscience will always tell me I'm right and that they are ignorant.'

I could see that even if I were to preach for the forty days of Lent, I would get nowhere, and so I saw him off, hoping (and fearing) that experience would accomplish what I'd attempted in vain. I'd begun to think that my neglect of his upbringing and my deference to Aquilina would be gravely punished, and that the fiercest sorrows of my old age would be caused by my children. For it wasn't only Giulio who worried me; young

Pisana, too, had begun to behave very badly and now I'd lost all paternal authority over her.

My daughter, as I said, was a very shrewd young lady, but I hoped that the example of her mother and the piousness of her upbringing would protect her from the worst. But from what I could observe, she didn't seem to be getting much benefit from her religion. She was humble and affectionate with her mother, and modest and discreet with me, and when we were present in larger company, she acted like a little saint. But with the servants she was hard and imperious; and then at times you would hear her teasing and laughing with them, as she never did when we were present. And in society, whenever her mother turned away for a moment, she would immediately start sending fiery glances left and right, and I noticed that she never erred in distinguishing the handsome young men from the plain. She would even blush and flutter around on her chair, making her sainthood all the less credible. In short, I wasn't at all at peace where she was concerned, and whenever Aquilina – for yes, she admitted that Giulio was a bit heedless – praised her good fortune and the good Lord for having compensated her a thousand times over with that fine daughter, I couldn't help but frown.

'What? What have you got to say now?' my wife would reply in that harsh, irritated voice she always used in speaking to me.

'Oh, nothing,' said I, rubbing my chin.

'Nothing, nothing! Do you think I don't see your censorious looks? All right, then, let's hear what you have to say about our Pisana! She isn't perfect and pretty enough to be an angel? She doesn't have two eyes the colour of lapis lazuli that reveal a sincere and loving nature, and hair and height that couldn't be improved upon? She isn't thoughtful, reserved and polite as a girl of marriageable age should be? She isn't as devout as a saint and as humble and obedient as a lamb? Where could you find another daughter so exemplary? I'd be happy to be a young man myself just to be able to marry her, and the one who does so will be three times happier, and I shall hesitate three times before giving her away.'

I didn't know what to say and let her go on with her panegyric, merely suggesting she lower her voice when she thought the girl might be in the next room, eavesdropping, as I had once found her.

'Well, come then!' said Aquilina. 'Don't sit there frowning like a statue! Are you her father or not? Ever since you got rid of your business and have my brother to slave away for you in the country, you've become the most feckless creature imaginable. You're good for nothing but sitting down to a coffee, reading the paper and, God forbid, nattering on with some other crazy old fellow.'

'Aquilina, if only it were possible, I swear I'd speak out more often, but –'

'And what am I doing just now? You don't think I'm telling you to speak? Haven't I been urging you for an hour to bring out your observations? Am I not standing here all too patiently listening to you?'

'Well, then, let me say that Pisana does not seem to me to behave with others as she appears before us; whenever you take your eyes off her she changes her demeanour wondrously, and I'm quite worried that all her great gifts may merely be play-acting and –'

'Do I really have to listen to this? Oh, poor me! The poor girl! And you certainly have the right to accuse her, don't you? You who look after her constantly! You, who scarcely join us in company twice a year, want to teach me, who's with her morning till night and never let her out of my thoughts or my sight!'

'Let me tell you, Aquilina, that perhaps she's always in your thoughts, but often she is not in your sight. I certainly don't join you every day, because the conversation in Casa Fratta and in Casa Cisterna isn't to my taste, but when I do come, I have no desire to engage with those people, I have all the time in the world to observe. Believe me, you think you've made a saint of her, but if things continue the way they're going, you will have made a very sophisticated coquette!'

'Sainted Mother of God! Please, go away and stop this filthy talk. My Pisana, a coquette?'

'Oh, be silent, Aquilina, so that she doesn't hear you!'

'It makes no difference at all! She wouldn't understand such wickedness in any case. I see now that you don't care for the girl at all. What you like are hard, ungrateful men like Luciano or hotheads like poor Donato, whom you yourself pushed to the brink. But discreet and affectionate young men, honest and proper young women mean nothing to you. You are perfectly right to call yourself an incorrigible Jacobin! You aren't comfortable in Casa Fratta when we are there, but when it comes to spending hour upon hour building castles in the air and inventing blasphemy and heresies with Count Rinaldo, well then, Casa Fratta suits you just fine!'

'Don't confuse one thing and another, Aquilina. Count Rinaldo has nothing to do with those old foxes that his sister's God-fearing zealotry has drawn into the house.'

'There you go again; nothing but insults and banter at the expense of all that's sacred and respectable in this world!'

'I'll repeat what I've said a thousand times: I respect and venerate the lady abbess, but I think she's somewhat easily fooled, and I wouldn't rely on her to understand men very well. And anyway, now that they are so poor, what have all their fine relatives and their passionate good friends done for them?'

'They have helped. They've helped them not much less than we have. And they would do more if the lady abbess were not so touchy.'

'Oh yes, it is her very touchiness that makes them escape like flies from the table the minute the dishes are carried away!'

'If they're keeping their distance, I'm sure they have their good reasons, and you would do well to imitate them. These are no times for chatter and conversation, especially for old men.'

'You seem to think we ought to spare the gravedigger the bother of burying us! Now that a gleam of hope has begun to shine, a flicker of life to run through our veins.'

'What marvellous prospects! What life! He who laughs last, laughs best.'

The discussion began to turn political and I left her; not, however, forgetting the main point of our dispute and promising myself I'd observe my daughter more carefully than I had done in the past. Recently, she had seemed so preoccupied, so quick to change her mind and grow confused, that I wouldn't have been surprised if, underneath, it wasn't a rat I smelled. According to my wife, those were only signs that she was passing from girlhood to youth, which tended to disturb girlish innocence. I knew something about innocence, and perhaps even more about malice, and could not accept my wife's idea, and so I spied, very cautiously, on Pisana, convinced that in the long run my old man's shrewdness would win out over the girl's cleverness. The efforts she made to seem calm and unconcerned whenever she realized she was being observed, convinced me that this was not that unconscious disturbance which her mother imagined, but the days went by and I failed to discover anything.

Finally, one evening, Aquilina went out with her brother Bruto, who had just come in from the Friuli, and I, too, was meant to be out late and had returned home for what reason I don't recall, and, entering the sitting room where the women usually worked, I didn't find Pisana. When I asked the maid, she said she was in her bedroom. Stealing up to her room very quietly, I thought I heard the squeaking of a steel pen and when I reached out suddenly to open the door I found it locked.

'Who's there?' said my daughter, sounding frightened.

'Oh, it's nothing. It is only me, come to see you.'

'Right away, Papa! I've just changed my clothes, because I perspired so much working on my embroidery tonight that I was as wet as a new-hatched chick. I'm coming to open up now.'

And she opened the door and met me with such a lovely smile that I could only kiss her – and lay aside most of my suspicions. I saw some garments tossed here and there, as if they'd just been removed, but when I approached her desk I could see her pen was still wet with ink. She must have been writing, but didn't want me to know it, and that was enough to make me quite suspicious indeed. I left her, wishing her a good night, as if I hadn't seen it. The following day when she was out attending Mass with her mother, I went to her room and carried out a diligent search of all the drawers and wardrobes. But everything was open and I found nothing to confirm any of the suspicions I'd entertained the night before. In the little chest beside her bed

I saw, among a stash of pious books, a small embroidered bag in which she kept religious medals, relics, little pictures and other things of little value. I had the impression that my fingers did not reach the very bottom of that bag and felt some papers I couldn't extract. When I turned it inside out, I found it had been sewed shut in haste with white thread. Taking apart the stitches, I found three letters that smelled so sweet they were a delight.

'Ah, I've caught you, you little scamp!' I whispered and ceased to feel remorseful about having gone through her secrets. Fathers are perhaps (or rather certainly) the only ones who have the right to do so, because a father is responsible for his children's well-being even when he must act against their will. The letters were signed by Enrico, who was Augusto Cisterna's youngest son; he wrote rather more than necessary of kisses, caresses, embraces, and I stopped wanting to know more. I put them in my pocket and waited for the ladies to come back from church. In about half an hour, Pisana came to her room to remove her hat and veil, and was quite astonished to find her father there.

'Pisana,' I began, without beating about the bush, for I was quite tired of playing the inquisitor, 'you must tell the truth now and atone with a rapid confession the sins that you've committed out of childish silliness. Tell me immediately where and how you found yourself alone with this Enrico, who writes to you so tenderly?'

Her legs began to give way and she looked so stunned that I almost felt sorry for her, but then she caught herself and stammered that she knew nothing about it, that it wasn't true, until I lost my patience and loudly ordered her to be obedient and truthful. Nevertheless, she continued to insist that she didn't have the slightest idea what I was talking about, and she did it so prettily that I was itching to slap her.

'Listen, my girl,' I said, half-fuming, half-restraining myself. 'If I were to tell you that you receive and write letters to Enrico Cisterna and converse with him at the Riva window when we are in bed, I wouldn't be an inch from the truth. But I didn't want to say it, in order to allow you the chance to be honest with me. Now that you see I know all and am still willing to treat you kindly, I hope you will show yourself to be worthy and tell me how you came to be so intimate with that young man, what it is you like so much about him, and why, if you thought your conduct was decent, did you conceal it from your parents? I know you are clever when you want to be and now you ought to see that the wisest, most honest, shrewdest course is to speak to me as to a friend, so that your cleverness and our wishes can be in accord.'

At these words my Pisana's demeanour changed: no longer was she a modest and timid young lady, but insolent and self-possessed, the way I'd often seen her with the maids or in some circle while her mother was distracted.

'Father,' she said, quite bold and sure of herself, 'I beg your pardon for a mistake I shall never cease to reproach myself for, but I was more afraid of your authority than confident of your affection. Yes, it is true: Enrico Cisterna's pleas moved me and I gave him what he asked, so as not to have him suffer.'

'And if I were to tell you that Enrico Cisterna is a dissolute fellow without any decency or integrity and that the worst punishment we could bring down on you would be to concede to him your hand?'

'Oh, don't be angry! No, please, there's no need! It's true, I pitied Enrico, but I'm not wedded to him and if he's not to your liking, anyone will do better than he!'

'And is that how you replied to his letters when you met him every night by the window?'

'Not every night, dear father. Only when Mamma put out the lights before midnight. And since she has many prayers to say over the various days of the week, the only nights we saw each other were Monday, Wednesday and Sunday.'

'That doesn't matter in the least. You mean to say you did what you did out of simple compassion?'

'I swear to it, Papa; compassion was the reason.'

'Therefore, if tomorrow some gondolier or ragged beggar comes to ask you to make love to him out of compassion, you'll say yes!'

'Certainly not, Papa. That would be a different matter.'

'Well then, you agree that you do see some particular merits in Enrico that make you feel more compassionate towards him than some other? Now, please be so good as to tell me what these merits are.'

'In truth, Papa, it's not easy for me to explain, but since you are so good to me, I shall make an effort to please you. First of all, when we went to the theatre I saw all the most beautiful ladies approving and making much of Enrico. You don't mean to say you don't think he's quite charming, at least?'

I no longer knew what world this was in which the little saint spoke like this, but I was determined to see how far she would go.

'Go on,' I said, 'and then?'

'And then he dresses so elegantly and his manner is so fine, and he's so sparkling and clever when he talks. In short, there was plenty to dazzle a girl with no experience, I would say. As for his habits, his temperament, I know nothing of that, father; to me everyone is good and I'd never be so brazen as even to ask what a dissolute fellow is!'

She was, however, careless enough to let me see that she did know. And I, in turn, replied that rather than investigating Enrico's moral qualities, she must understand that his outward appearance and charms were not sufficient to merit the affections of a well-born young lady.

'And who says he has my affections?' she replied. 'I swear to you, Papa, that I responded to him only out of pity, and now that I've seen he's not fortunate enough to please you, I shall forget him quite easily and happily accept that husband you'll be so good as to find me.'

'Oh, filthy girl!' I snapped at her. 'Who is talking about a husband? Are you in a hurry? Who taught you to bring up certain matters all by yourself?'

'No one!' she stammered. 'I only spoke that way to show you how docile I am.'

'I see,' said I, 'just how far your docility goes. But I urge you to restrain your nature and control your sentiments, for until you're ready to appreciate the merits of an honest man, the deuce

I'll let you marry! I don't want to be responsible for your ruin or that of others.'

'I promise, Papa, that from now on I shall concentrate on restraining my nature and controlling my sentiments. But will you promise me that mother, at least, shall know nothing of this?'

'And why don't you want your mother to know?'

'I would be ashamed to stand before her.'

'Well now, some shame wouldn't be bad for you; in fact, I'd like to see you suffer great shame, so you might try to avoid suffering it in the future. Meanwhile, I must warn you that I cannot allow your mother to be ignorant of something that will put your saintliness in the right proportion.'

'Oh please, Papa!'

'No, don't try to defend yourself and don't cry. Think about improving yourself instead: about telling the truth from now on, and not becoming infatuated by vanities and foolishness, and not giving out your affection so freely.'

'Oh, I swear, father!'

'Not so many oaths. At luncheon your mother will inform you what we've decided to do about you. There is no such thing as harm that cannot be redressed; you are still young and I hope you will be a good daughter once more, able to provide happiness to us as well as to the man Heaven has in mind for you, if fate wills you to marry. In the meantime, meditate well on such foolish deeds as make a daughter blush before her parents.'

I left her then, but so dismayed you cannot imagine. Those promises she would reform she had simply tossed out automatically and I had no idea where to begin to make a decent woman out of such a wanton flirt. I'll admit I always feared I might one day discover something unpleasant beneath that veneer of saintliness, but never such shocking frivolity as I'd just seen.

Aquilina nearly lost her mind when I told her at length of the muck her daughter had sunk into. At first she didn't believe me, but I had the three letters in my pocket and they convinced her, and she began to shriek and scratch her face with her nails (and would have done the same to Pisana had she been present).

I held her back, though, and succeeded after a while in calming her, so that we could think how to break off that liaison quietly and change our daughter's bad behaviour. We decided that when it came to sending Enrico away – for he was a real good-for-nothing – it was better to leave the job to Pisana, as if it were her spontaneous desire, while we knew nothing and had nothing to do with it. Then we decided to dismiss all the maids and take on new ones, for I was convinced that their company had something to do with the foolish frivolity I'd seen in her that morning. I hoped to accomplish something by encouraging her to read more and go out to the theatre and in society less; but I didn't conceal from Aquilina that the damage was far worse than I'd guessed, and that every remedy we tried might be in vain. My wife was annoyed at my pessimism and insisted that Pisana's folly had been due more to inexperience than immorality; and she was sure that she could bring her daughter around, so that I wouldn't recognize her within a month's time.

'She's so steeped in religion,' she said, 'that once her duties are recalled to her mind, she'll repent of her error and resolve never to repeat it.'

'Oh yes, trust in her religion!' said I. 'I tell you, it is all appearances; you've seen first-hand how terribly mistaken it was not to arm her conscience with something beyond the Ten Commandments.'

Now Aquilina began to fume and I began to badger her, and soon we forgot about Pisana and fought each other. Finally, I came to myself and told her to be very careful in dealing with Pisana, and I left her, hoping her maternal instinct would guide her better than her pious convictions. And that was how things seemed to work at first, for every day the girl showed improvement, and even though she still behaved somewhat frivolously, she didn't try to conceal it as before. Shame had been good for her, and I, too, tried not to encourage deceit in her, by suppressing my dismay at her natural flippancy. If not a strong and exemplary woman, at least an ordinary decent wife might come forth, I hoped. I was also convinced that she could be guided by what pleased her, and thus, if some well-brought-up young fellow should appear who was both handsome and good, I'd hand her education over to him, for I was almost sure he'd succeed in shaping a wife to his desires in a few years. What better teacher than love, who can teach even what he doesn't know?

While Giulio's wild behaviour and Pisana's questionable conversion kept me agitated, the crowds on the streets all over Italy were growing bolder and more combative. The winds of hope blew in from France,[4] which had suddenly become a republic; and revolution threatened Vienna, erupted in Milan, and in Venice took the course we all know. And in those days – old, half-blind and a father that I was – I had no time to worry about my little problems at home. I went out on the street with the others, throwing off my seventy years, and felt I was stronger, more hopeful, younger than I'd been half a century before, when I'd taken my first steps in politics as the secretary of the Municipality.

The republicans were arming our National Guard, and they wanted to make me colonel of the second legion, and I said yes with all my heart (without consulting my eyes and legs); and searched my memory for all my ancient knowledge of military tactics and put a hundred willing young men in ranks and made them march left and right, and went home with my head in the clouds. And Aquilina, seeing me got up in a uniform that made me look more like a brigand than a colonel, was almost faint with fury. Enduring her bile, I ate a hasty meal and then returned to drilling soldiers, feeling, I swear, no more than twenty years old. Only that evening, when I returned home around midnight (and after submitting to the noisiest complaints a good husband ever heard from a nagging wife) did I ask about Giulio, whom I'd been searching for, on and off, all day. No one had seen him; no one knew anything and this was another occasion for Aquilina to begin her exertions afresh. But I was too concerned about him to really pay attention to her; for I feared that his recent behaviour and his arrogant, aggressive nature had put him in serious danger. After much thought and another half hour waiting for him, I could wait no longer and went out to search for him. What a dreadful blow was awaiting me!

I called to ask about him at Casa Fratta and Casa Cisterna,

but they could tell me nothing, and then I tried Casa Partistagno, but was told the General had left two days before (cursing his seven sons, who all had decided to stay in Venice) and that they hadn't seen Signor Giulio in a week. Then it occurred to me to ask at the Guards in our own district, and there I finally forced a young student to tell me the unhappy truth. That morning Giulio had gone with them to the Arsenale, where arms were being distributed, and he had already belted on his sword when a rash fool (according to the student) began to insult him and Giulio had turned on him, but a hundred others had taken the side of the first and the shouts, insults and brawling convinced my son to flee and he'd been lucky to escape with his life. But a few decent fellows who didn't want to see fraternal blood flow had defended Giulio, sword in hand.

'I hope that once things have been clarified your son will obtain justice,' continued the student, 'and take up that post in the National Guard that belongs to him as a citizen.'

He said it in a way, however, that suggested more pity for the father than real respect for the son's side, and I understood him all too well, even what his compassion had led him to conceal. I had just enough self-possession to slip away, one shoulder to the wall, refusing the arm held out to assist me. But as soon as I was home and even before I could inform Aquilina, I was seized by violent fits. After blood was let and a cordial or two administered, I calmed down and by dawn I was able to speak. Making an effort to behave as calmly as I could, I blamed my collapse on fatigue, and I said I'd had word of Giulio and that he had just left the city on business. My wife believed me, or pretended to, but around midday a letter arrived from Padua in Giulio's hand and she opened it without telling me, read it and appeared suddenly in my room, letter in hand, shrieking like a lunatic that they had murdered another son of hers, that they were going to murder him! Our Pisana, who showed quite a bit more tenderness than I expected under the circumstances, put an arm around her mother, and when she saw she was raving, called the maid and helped her to put Aquilina to bed. For a couple of weeks, between her father's bedside and her mother's, that all too vivacious young lady was the most dedicated and loving of nurses. To say that love is the best schoolmaster was wrong, perhaps; misfortune also teaches much.

Giulio's letter went something like this:

'My dear father! You were right: one can defend oneself against ten or twenty, but not against an entire people. There are certain moments in the life of a people when their judgements are inescapable. I was arrogant, rash and contemptuous. I can no longer live in that *patria* I love so much – though I despaired of seeing her come back to life. Now that cowardly despair of mine has cost me the right to join those gathering round Venice to defend her. Father, I think you will approve of my decision, to depart and earn the esteem of my brothers with my own blood. I am going to fight, perhaps to die, certainly to atone for a mistake I confess I made. Comfort my mother; tell her that respect for your name and mine demanded that I go. I could never remain in a country where I'd publicly been called a traitor and a spy. I had to swallow the insults and flee. Oh, Father, my guilt was great, but the punishment is far worse! I thank heaven and the memory of your warning to me, which helped me accept a glorious penitence instead of fratricidal revenge. You won't hear from me often, for I want my name to remain unspoken until it can resound with honour on the lips of all. Farewell. I feel certain that you love me and pardon me, and that is my greatest consolation.'

Let me say, that letter restored me, body and soul. I'd feared much worse and was quite amazed to see someone as proud and rash as Giulio go so far as to confess his errors and seek such a worthy way to atone. It was comforting to be able to weep for my son and not curse him, and I bowed before that inscrutable justice that imposed such fierce grief on me. When I was well – although my wife's condition was anything but encouraging and at times she seemed outright mad – I returned to my post as colonel of the Guard. The news of my son's letter and his departure had spread, and so perhaps, even those very same men who had attacked him now revered my old grey head. However, I heard nothing from him until the following May, when a few lines reached us from Brescia. The location made me think he'd enrolled in the Free Corps, defending the Tyrol borders from that side, and, as we shall see, I was not far from the truth. I blessed him from the bottom of my heart and hoped that Heaven would grant his noble hopes and my prayers.

Two days later, troops arrived from Naples[5] under General Pepe's command, and two of my old friend's officers came to ask about me. One was Arrigo Martelli, a veteran of Greece who had come back in 1832, then immediately got involved in the Rossaroll plot[6] and had spent the next fifteen years in the dungeons of Castel Sant'Elmo. He introduced me to his brave friend Major Rossaroll himself, whose long years in prison had weakened his eyes but not his spirit. We were friends straight away and I told them of my old, and new, sorrows. While I was recounting the old, the name Amilcare Dossi fell from my lips. I knew he had stayed in the Kingdom of Naples, but had heard no more of him. Martelli then told me that sadly, he did know what had become of him: he had joined the war in the Abruzzi in '21, was jailed, escaped, went to Sicily and after a series of misfortunes and crimes, had ended up on the scaffold, proudly haranguing the people and cursing his executioners. This happened in 1836 and helped to fan the unrest spreading around the island, which exploded the following year in violent uprisings when cholera struck.

'Poor Amilcare!' I said.

But it was what he was destined for and I couldn't help but blame my own perverse destiny for bringing me fresh grief, even from friends long buried.

Equally dear to me, and not so sad, was the visit I received a few months later from Alessandro Giorgi, just back from South America; sunburned, old, lame, and now Field Marshal and Duke of Rio-Vedras. His huge body stuffed into a gaudy scarlet tunic encrusted with gold and ribbons, he looked like some grotesque ancestor of the Tahitian Queen Pomaré,[7] if not worse. But the heart beating under that bizarre uniform was his own: the heart of a good lad and a soldier. When I saw him, I couldn't help but compare him with Partistagno: both of them more or less of the same temperament, both pursuing the same career, but, by Jove, with what different results! On pliable natures like theirs, all advice, examples, companions and circumstances have little effect; they come out ruffians or heroes by pure chance.

'My dearest Carlino,' he said, embracing me so tightly that some of his medals got hooked in my buttonholes, 'as you can see, I left it all behind – duchy, army, America – to return to my old Venice.'

'Oh, I never doubted it.' I said. 'How many times, when I heard an unfamiliar footstep on the stair, did I think: can that be Alessandro?'

'So tell me, what has life been like in these years, Carlino?'

I briefly recounted my story and, by way of conclusion, introduced my daughter, who had just then come to the door.

'There's no denying that you have suffered great misfortunes, my friend, but you have some solid consolation here,' he said, pinching Pisana's plump cheek between his knuckles. 'With all my dukedom I haven't succeeded in doing the same, although I can assure you that all the beautiful ladies of Brazil wanted to marry me. My friend, if you have sons ready to take a wife, entrust them to me, for I can guarantee a very pretty girl and several million *reales*.'

'Many thanks, indeed, but as you can see we've got other things on our minds here than marriage.'

'Oh, you let this nonsense concern you? These things are over quickly, believe me! In America we have two revolutions a year and there's time left over to visit our country houses and cure our gout at the springs.'

Pisana stood wide-eyed, admiring that singular example of a duke and field marshal, until he took her somewhat roughly by the arm, saying it pleased him greatly to think he could still capture the attention of the young ladies of Venice.

'Oh, in our day – what, Carlino? Do you remember the Countess Migliana?'

'I certainly do, Alessandro, but the Countess is now dead ten or twelve years and all but a saint, and we ourselves are dragging our sins fairly lamely around the world.'

'Oh, as for myself, if I didn't have this nagging gout that's murdering my legs, I could dance a tarantella! . . . Bruto, my good friend! Here's another dancer! Confound it, but you've turned black! I swear, body and blood, that if it weren't for your wooden leg I wouldn't have known you.'

Bruto, who had just appeared in his civic artilleryman's outfit, was an odd figure himself, a worthy counterpart to the eccentric American duke-marshal. At the sight of his old friend, he spared no exclamations or embraces, and Pisana, watching the two whacking each other's backs and nattering on, was laughing so much she risked choking. But if they were silly inside the house, they behaved quite seriously outside, offering a nice example of military deference to all those young men who'd like to have been born admirals and generals. Alessandro, despite his dukedom and marshalhood, accepted the rank of colonel, and Bruto went back to his cannon as if he'd just left it the day before. His limping stride and cheerful humour kept up his young companions' spirits. Everyone did a stint in the Guard in those days, even Count Rinaldo, who often (I saw him!) stood guard in front of the Palazzo Ducale as seriously as one of those silent sentries who stand by the painted scenery in some stage performance. The one who didn't manage to stand guard was Cavaliere Alfonso Frumier, whose right mind had never returned after his wife died, no matter how hard he struggled. One day his manservant entered to tell him they were shouting 'Long live San Marco!' in the Piazza, and that they had a republic, and a thousand other things, one more crazy than the next. The old gentleman smacked himself hard on the forehead.

'Got it!' I'm told he exclaimed, and then, as his eyes left their orbits and his limbs began to tremble, 'Here, right away! Bring me my toga! Give me my wig! Long live San Marco! My toga, my wig, I say! Hurry! I must get there in time!'

The master seemed to have trouble getting these last words out and his legs were wobbling; his serving man reached out to hold him upright, and Frumier slumped to the floor and died of an overdose of joy. I still remember I cried to hear of that moving scene, which explained so well the decades-long lethargy of the good Cavaliere.

Meanwhile, we, too, if not happy enough to die, had our joys. The harmony among all classes of citizens; the serene endurance of Venice's fine populace in the face of every kind of disaster; a blind faith in the future; our well-drilled military preparation: everything led us to think this was the end or, as Talleyrand once said, the beginning of the end. Every sort of person was involved in public activity and this prevented indolence, greatly improved morality and not least reduced the ranks of malefactors, who, when the public spirit resurfaced so victoriously, crawled into their dens like frogs in the mud. Ormenta fled to the mainland and died, we later learned, of fear during a raid of the Free Corps. The fact that he'd worn Sant'Antonio's habit in childhood didn't help him at all; he was lucky they even gave him a Christian burial. Augusto Cisterna, now despised and forgotten by all, stayed in Venice, but even his sons were ashamed of their name, and that scapegrace Enrico regained some of my esteem when his face was slashed in the assault on Mestre.

One day when I was returning from a visit to General Pepe (he used to listen to me go on quite willingly), Pisana came to meet me, wearing a more serious expression than usual, and said she had something important to tell me. I told her to speak up and she then reminded me I'd said that she could marry a young man of good intentions, worth more for his substance than his appearance, and that she thought she had found the right fellow.

'And who might that be?' I said, rather astounded, for the clever little thing never left her mother's bedside and Aquilina was only just beginning to recover.

'Enrico Cisterna!' she said, throwing her arms round my neck.

'What? That –'

'No, my dear father, don't speak ill of him! Say: that good and generous young man; that young man who, despite a neglectful upbringing and a silly, empty life, was brave enough to have his face cut by a sword and return to his post a week later as if it were nothing! Oh, Papa, I love him more than my own self! Now I do understand what it means to care for someone. I said I loved him out of pity, when he certainly had no need of pity. And now that perhaps he deserves it, I love him out of respect and adoration.

'Well, all right, very well, but your mother . . .'

'Mamma knows everything as of this morning; she unites her prayers with mine.'

Just then the door came crashing open and Enrico himself, who had been hiding in the next room, stormed in, begging me not to send him away until I had pronounced his sentence of life or death. He was clutching onto my legs and that other little madwoman had her arms around my throat, sobbing and weeping – it was a real stage comedy.

'Marry, then, marry in the name of God!' I shouted, taking both in my arms, and never did sweeter tears of mine wet two happier beings.

And then I asked them if and how their love had carried on behind my back, and after Pisana had formally dismissed him on our orders. The young lady confessed, blushing, that she had written two letters that day instead of one, and the second was somewhat sweeter than the first.

'Oh, you little traitor!' I said. 'And so you deceived me. So that business of writing letters continued right under my nose.'

'Oh no, Father,' replied Pisana. 'There was no more need to write.'

'And why was there no need to write?'

'Because . . . we saw each other nearly every night.'

'You saw each other every night? But didn't I nail the shutters of that accursed window of yours closed?'

'Papa, please forgive me, but when Mamma fell asleep I went down very quietly to open the door for him.'

'Oh, you wicked children! You shameless girl! You took him into the house? You took your lover into the house! But what do you say if I tell you there's but one key to the door and I kept it myself, next to my bed?'

'That's right, Papa, now don't be angry; but every night I took that key away and then returned it in the morning when I came to bring Mamma her broth.'

'And I suppose you played this dirty trick on me while giving me a good night kiss and one to wake me in the morning!'

'Oh, Papa, Papa, you're so good! Forgive us.'

'What can I say? Yes, I pardon you, but on the condition

that no one ever hears a word of this. I wouldn't want to find the story had become the plot of some opera buffa.'

Enrico stood there, quite ashamed, while that brazen little thing went on confessing her treachery, half-pleading, half-teasing, until I put a fist under his chin.

'Confound you, don't play the hypocrite with me!' I said. 'Take your wife, you earned her at the Battle of Mestre.'

And, indeed, he wasn't lame about embracing her and we all went to Aquilina's room to celebrate. Three weeks later Enrico was my son-in-law, but I made him live at home with us, because I didn't want to be made a fool of and pay for it, too. All my old friends came to the wedding banquet, and once again we proved that the stomach is ever youthful when one's conscience is clear.

That was the height of our happiness, I think. After that came the bad times, the disasters in Lombardy, our own distress, long interregnums still intoxicated with hopes, but growing ever grimmer. Oh, it's not so easy to fool an old man! That winter between '48 and '49 was steeped in lugubrious reflections: I didn't believe in France any more; I didn't believe in England; and the rout of Novara[8] was less an unexpected defeat than the painful confirmation of something I'd long feared. We were fighting now more for our honour than to win, although no one said so, to keep the others' spirits up.

After the larger dismay came private grief. One day they came to tell me that Colonel Giorgi and Corporal Provedoni, wounded on the bridge, had been taken to the military hospital and couldn't be moved from there because their injuries were very grave. I hurried across the city in a terrible state and found them, lying on two pallets next to one another, talking about their childhoods, their war memories, their common hopes, two friends on the brink of sleep. They could scarcely breathe, either of them, their breasts torn by horrible wounds.

'Oh, this is strange,' whispered Alessandro. 'It's as if I were in Brazil!'

'And I'm in Cordovado on the piazza of the Virgin,' said Bruto.

They were in the grip of that delirium that comes with death, a sweet delirium that nature concedes only to an elect few to make their departure from this life easy.

'Do not fear,' I said, holding back my tears. 'You are with a friend.'

'Oh, Carlino,' murmured Alessandro. 'Farewell, Carlino. If you want me to do something for you, just say it. The Emperor of Brazil is a friend of mine.'

Bruto took my hand, for he was not as far gone as his friend, but soon he, too, began to wander, and both so revealed their good hearts and fine sentiments in their final hallucinations that I wept hot tears and grieved that I could not detain them. Each regained his senses long enough to say farewell to me, and to each other, to smile and die. When Pisana, Aquilina and Enrico came soon after, they found me on my knees between two corpses. That very day General Partistagno died on the battlefield attacking the fortress of Mestre. Only a few miles away were his many sons, but none was there to comfort him at the last.

When I'd closed the eyes of my two friends, I felt it was no sin to want to die myself, and I thought of my dear Pisana, who perhaps was watching me from the highest of heavens, and asked her if it were not time for me, too, to join her. But a voice deep inside me said no; and, in fact, there were other sad duties awaiting me. A few days later Count Rinaldo was struck with cholera, which had already begun to mow down a starving populace. The bombardments had concentrated people in those quarters furthest from the mainland, and it was a solemn spectacle, the sad patience with which they endured so many deadly scourges. The poor Count was fading fast when I arrived at his bedside; his sister, bent by the years and their privations, shone with that implacable courage that never abandons real believers.

'Carlino,' the dying man said, 'I asked for you, because in those moments when I am in my right mind, I think of my book, which risks remaining incomplete. I entrust it to you, therefore, and I want you to promise me you will have it printed in forty instalments using the same format and paper as the first.'

'I promise you,' I said, near tears again.

'Look after any corrections,' the Count went on, 'and make changes . . . if you think they are necessary . . .'

He went no further and died with his eyes fixed on me, that last gaze entrusting me with the sole fruit of his earthly existence. I made sure he had a funeral service worthy of him, and took Clara into my house, for as her paralysis worsened she could barely move around on her own. But we were only briefly content to look after her as affectionately as we could. She, too, died, in August on the day of the Assumption, thanking the Virgin for calling her on the very day of her assumption into heaven, and praising God, because that vow she had taken fifty years before on behalf of the Republic of Venice (and which had cost her so many sacrifices) had been so beautifully rewarded in the sunset of her life. I thought of Lucilio then, and perhaps she did, too, and with hope, for she had great trust in her own prayers and a thousand times more in God's clemency.

On 22 August the surrender was signed. Venice was the last to withdraw from Italy's battlefields, 'watchful as a lion when she reposes', in the words of Dante.[9] A final sorrow awaited me: Enrico Cisterna's name was on the proscription list.[10] There was my Luciano, who seemed to have forgotten us during these two years; Giulio (I'd had a letter from him from Rome in July, but the subsequent defeats had made me pessimistic about what may have become of him); now Pisana, great with child, would follow her husband into exile; and with them, aboard a ship sailing for Genoa, went Arrigo Martelli, who had buried poor Rossaroll in Venice. So many tombs, so much living grief upon them.

Aquilina and I – oppressed, dismayed and silent – were left alone, two tree trunks split by lightning in a wasteland. But life in Venice grew every day more unbearable, until by common agreement we moved to the Friuli, to the old Provedoni house in Cordovado full of so many memories. And there we lived for two years in worship of our own sorrows, until finally the poor woman, too, was visited by death in his mercy. And I was left. Left to reflect and to understand in full the dreadful meaning of that awful word: alone.

Alone? Oh no, I was not alone! I thought so for an instant,

but I quickly changed my mind and, amid my woes, I blessed that good Providence that concedes (to those who've pursued the good and avoided the bad) a restful conscience and memory's sad but sweet company.

A year after my wife died I had a long-awaited visit from Luciano and his family; he had two boys who spoke Greek better than Italian, but both they and their mother came to feel quite tenderly about me, and the moment of their departure (the sixth month after they'd come, Luciano decided, not a day longer) was quite painful for all. My son was made that way and whatever faults he had he was still my son, and I thanked him for remembering me and reflected sadly that I would never see him again. I hope he and his family will continue to prosper in their new *patria*, but when I recall those two marvellous grandsons of mine I can't help but think: why are they not Italians? Greece certainly has no need of brave, young men to love her!

After the fall of Rome's republic in 1849 Giulio sent word from the many stations of his exile: Civitavecchia, New York, Rio de Janeiro. He was now an exile roaming the world, without a home or a future, but proud to have restored his honour and to bear a glorious and worthy name. But then suddenly his letters ceased and I had only the newspapers to rely on, where I saw he'd been named as one of the directors of an Italian military colony in Argentina, outside Buenos Aires. I assumed then that the poor postal service was the reason I'd received no letters from him, and waited patiently for the heavens to restore that comfort to me. Meanwhile, I had another heartily desired comfort in those days, when Pisana and Enrico came back to Venice with a funny little infant girl named after me and said to resemble my portrait made when I was secretary of the Municipality. Finally, with my children by my side and Carolina on my lap, I felt reborn. It was like a gentle springtime for an ancient tree that's been through a long winter.

Finally, four years after returning to Cordovado, I had the courage to visit Fratta, and there, with the old Andreini's grandchildren, themselves already parents of many children, I celebrated the eighty years since I first arrived at the Castle, sent from Venice in a bread basket.

After luncheon I went out all alone to visit the spot where the famous Castle had stood. There was no trace of it; just a few ruins here and there, and a pair of goats grazing, and a girl humming to herself, who stopped her spinning to stare at me in curiosity. I could make out the shape of the courtyard and, in the middle of it, the stone under which I'd buried the Captain's dog. It may be the only monument of my memories that is still standing. But no, that's not true: everything in these beloved places recalls the sweet years of my childhood and youth. The trees, the fish pond, the meadows, the air, the heavens, all take me back to those distant days. At the corner of the moat I could still see in my imagination the tall, dark tower where so many times I'd admired Germano as he wound the clock; I could see those long corridors where Martino led me by the hand at bedtime, and his anchorite's cell where the swallows would never again make their nests. I could see, coming along the dirt road, Monsignor with his breviary under his armpit; or the great family carriage with the Count and Countess and the Clerk inside; or Marchetto's old nag that I used to ride. I could see the afternoon visitors arriving one by one: Monsignor di Sant'Andrea, Giulio Del Ponte, the Chaplain, the Rector, dashing Partistagno, Lucilio. I could hear their voices reverberating around the card tables in the dining hall, and good Clara softly repeating some stanza from Ariosto under the garden willows. And then there were noisy invitations from my childhood playmates to come out, but I did not reply, only stole away, alone, and happy to spend the day around the fish pond with la Pisana.

Oh, how devoutly, how tenderly, did I approach that memory that throbbed in all the others, making them so much sweeter and more melancholy. Oh, dear Pisana, how I wept that day and blessed you, and thanked the Lord that this octogenarian's tears are not all tears of grief. Night had already come when I left those ruins and the sparrows in the nearby poplars were twittering away before sleep, as in my childhood. They were still twittering, but how many generations must have come and gone in that little bird family? We human beings think nature is always the same, because we don't bother to observe it carefully, but everything changes along with us, and while our dark hair turns white, millions and millions of other beings have lived out their lives.

When I left that old world to rejoin the new, I sighed a bit, but the dear little hands of Carolina reconciled me. The past is sweet, but the present is better, for me and for all the rest.

The next year was a very sad one, for I learned that Giulio had died, but along with that heavy sorrow came joy: the two little children he'd left me. His wife had also died, even before I knew I had a daughter-in-law. General Urquiza,[11] entrusting to me these two orphans and all Giulio's papers, as my son had asked him to, also wrote to me to say that Colonel Altoviti's death had been a great loss for Argentina.

Pisana now became the loving mother of these two nephews of hers (whom Giulio had thoughtfully named Luciano and Donato), and so my first two sons, one far away and one dead, now came to life again in those dear creatures, while Pisana herself took on the job of resuscitating the third, giving birth to a brother for Carolina, whom she named Giulio. And I saw, then, how much delight and purpose that bloom of new life brings to old age. The pleasures of childhood as we live it are not much different from the pleasures enjoyed by those children we love and protect. The family, of all the souls in it, makes up a sort of collective soul; for what are souls if not memory, love, thoughts and hope? And when those sentiments are shared, in whole or in part, can we not truly say we live in one another?

Thus humanity perpetuates itself and becomes a single spirit in those timeless laws that make men merciful, sociable and thoughtful. My daughter had taken my one-time warning so much to heart that I could scarcely believe I'd once had that talk with her about a little stash of letters. It was nearly all to her credit, but the hard times we had seen, and her husband's strong and sensible temperament, helped too. You see, I've paid a fair tribute now to Enrico, who once struck me as a dissolute fellow, a delinquent! Better not speak ill, my friends, not even of misfortunes. According to the French, misfortunes, too, are good for something: they earn us that durable happiness that comes from strength of character.

Among Giulio's papers that arrived from the Americas there was also his journal, which serves as a kind of proof of what I say above. I wept copiously over those pages, but then, I'm his father. If they convince you to love him and rehabilitate him after all the injustice he so nobly endured, that is sufficient. I transcribe them here, without one syllable added or subtracted.

TWENTY-THREE

My son Giulio's journal: his flight from Venice in 1848 to his death in the Americas in 1855. After so many errors, so many joys, so many woes, a peaceful conscience makes my old age sweet. Here among my children and my grandchildren I bless that eternal justice that has made me a witness to and an actor in a great chapter of history, and which conducts me slowly towards that repose, that future, we call death. My spirit, feeling itself immortal, will rise from the grave to love's eternity. I close these Confessions as I began them, in the name of la Pisana, and I thank my readers here and now for their patience.

Tonale Pass,[1] June 1848

Pride was judged the worst of the deadly sins. Whoever said so knew human nature well. But there are punishments that surpass the gravity of any sin in their horror. That which I've suffered has no equal; the Sicilian tyrants couldn't have invented a crueller penance. It is true: I was proud. I despised others who were probably no less wise and no less courageous than I; I went among them with my head held high and a whip in hand, as if they were a flock of sheep; I accepted the masters' arguments because they were powerful, not because they were right; and I laughed when they were trampled on, because I thought them incapable of fighting back. Poor fool, who did his horse-trading when the horse was in the stable. The day came when the mocker was derided by the mocked and had to bow his head before the worst punishment that can befall a man: an undeserved affront that is also a just one.

It was an absurdity, yes, but it happened to me and I had to accept it. I was fortunate in this: I didn't cling to my pride, but respected the justice of that injustice done to me, preferred the hard bread of penance to the blood of my brothers. Traitor and spy! Those terrible words still ring in my ears. Oh, I wanted the gods to help me carry out Nero's infernal vow! Wanted the human race to have a single head and cut it off; wanted a silence pregnant with ruins, darkness, murder to fall on that wicked charge; wanted to be transformed into a cruel Nemesis of revenge and extermination! But the gods don't attend on the proud; the ambrosia in those eternal chalices is for heroes only; in their right hands the gods clutch thunderbolts that destroy Titans. A divine voice inside me (but certainly not in that part of me drunk with rage and pride) shook me to the core.

Yes, I was a traitor who had crushed the oppressed under my foot, murdered conviction and replaced it with scorn and contempt! A traitor who laughed at human frailty, when he should have had compassion. A cowardly spy who denounced imaginary crimes and invented depravity to ward off my shame before those I accused. Come! Cover your head with ashes, prideful one! Love those whom yesterday you insulted. Humbly accept that same vituperation they themselves suffered from you.

Thus, trembling, I spoke to myself, rage counselling me to strike, regret and humility telling me to flee. Oh, divine, unexpected humility, I bless you! How can I not have faith in humanity when we have this weapon of humility against our own passions? Bless you, sweet pain of atonement! I have no family now, no name. I am but a slave of penance and I shall only reacquire my rights as a man, a citizen and a son at the price of my life. And when my brothers see my virtue written in letters of blood, their arms will open and a thousand voices will celebrate my redemption.

Here, no one knows me. I am called Aurelio Gianni, a foundling of the human race, a warrior for justice, no more. I seek the most dangerous positions and fight the roughest skirmishes, but heaven will protect me and let me live long enough to restore my name.

Tonale Pass, July 1848

The news is grim: our army is on the run, we scouts hidden away in the mountains defend the border we've been assigned and ask no questions. Battle after battle without distinction, long hardship invisible to all, vigils that last months, interrupted by brief skirmishes and shattered sleep. This is the right apprenticeship for me. Wherever dreams of glory and danger's intense emotions compensate the risk of life, that is not the place for a man seeking pardon and penance. But atop these steep mountains that almost touch Heaven, in deep gorges and roaring torrents, sinners come to seek God in solitude and soldiers of liberty ascend to martyrdom.

When you have fought in a pitched battle on the front lines, raised a flag on the enemy's ramparts, repelled the lancers' charge, shouted victory when the cannon came to a halt, would you ever be so presumptuous as to say, 'My country owes me, give me the crown of oak leaves'?

No, your compensation lies in the renown of your deeds. Victors, thank the country that gave you a chance to show your courage and taste the joy of triumph. Don't ask for crowns: crowns are for soldiers who fight patiently, ignored, without the applause of any spectators or hopes of glory or lust for victory. When will servile posterity – which has bowed for so long before Caesar and Augustus – stand up and revere the Gauls and the Germanic Prince Arminius?[2] Courage, not fame, demands respect; the nobility, hidden in the shadow of the forest, can eclipse that which marches, triumphant and self-confident, through the streets of Rome. Once again, men are unjust, but God, lord of rewards and punishments, resides in our consciences.

Lugano, August 1848

It was true, alas. Here we are, fugitives who haven't been defeated, just as before we were victors who hadn't won a battle. It was meant to be war to the bitter end, and instead, one pace after another, across a river today, a mountain tomorrow, our captains have brought us to this Alpine retreat. We hear it said they are traitors, involuntary traitors like myself, men too proud and arrogant. But that's the usual consolation for failure, blaming your own errors on another. Meanwhile I, who was hoping for a desperate, glorious attack and a death or victory that would clear my name, here I am, once again, confined to invisible sacrifice and long waiting. What had looked like a quick victory is but endless suffering. That, too, is atonement. For sacrifice, even of life, means nothing if one hasn't shown constancy. Death alone is not redemption. Pardon must be deserved. So I go forward in the conviction that Providence will find the way for me to demonstrate my essential innocence if not my rightness. With hardship will come the strength to be silent, until one day my brothers respect me again.

Genoa, October 1848

I was impatient to fight, not because I'm young and rash, but because I didn't want to be thought lazy and idle. But here in Genoa, too, things are moving very slowly and perhaps that is not a mistake. Over-confidence can be a form of treason just as much as flight in the moment of danger. We are foolish to measure the lives of a people by that of individuals; a people must be patient because they can, having before them not twenty, thirty or fifty years but eternity. I myself was quite ready to sacrifice the fate of the nation to my frenzy to do battle. But desires must be tamed by moderation and wisdom or our ventures will never hit the mark. We must learn to wait patiently or we shall wait forever. When events permit deliberation, that is; but when the die is cast and honour is at stake, the weighing, the worries, the scruples must be abandoned. Then soldiers may – indeed must – offer themselves in sacrifice, and all belated regrets and mutual reproaches are banished. Wherever the first spark flares I shall fly with my rifle and, though I shall not hasten the battle, I shall make the danger mine.

There are some exiles here from the Venetian mainland – old school companions or fellow wastrels – who have recognized me. They were smirking among themselves, without actually confronting me, but when I saw them the next day they seemed more admiring than contemptuous. It seemed they'd understood my purposes here and respected them. I later learned that they had asked some of my fellow soldiers about me, and they told them the name I am using and testified to my bravery when fighting in the Tyrol and around Varese. It seems a dispute brewed up among them, with some insisting I was Giulio Altoviti, and some saying no; and some of the first questioned my good faith, while my companions in arms fiercely defended me, saying that whether I was Altoviti or Gianni, I was a brave soldier and an honest man.

One of those Venetians, Giuseppe Minotto, convinced his friends that if I had reacted to my state of disgrace by undertaking such a hard and noble road, that was already a fair proof I was no traitor. I thank him now – I scarcely knew him – for having raised his voice to defend me among many who only recently called themselves my friends. As a result of his words, I'm now looked upon with respect, cautious, but genuine. Grateful that Providence has supplied these consolations to help me pursue my aim courageously, I shall try to be worthy.

Two young Partistagno boys who fought valiantly when Vicenza rose up against the Austrians last April were among my heartiest detractors at first, but then I saw they seemed to be quite keen to renew our old friendship. I didn't pursue them, though. I waited. Now I hear they're leaving for Turin, where some Lombard regiments are being sent. I had an urge to go and sign up in those ranks, too, but modesty made me think I shouldn't boast of my courage, and a touch of pride, perhaps, held me back from letting my penance be observed by friends and acquaintances. I would seem to be asking forgiveness for sins I didn't commit, while instead I mean to deserve that forgiveness for my real wrongs and get redress for the ones unfairly attributed to me.

At sea, December 1848

Father, I undertook to write this journal for you and you alone. If I should die far from home, these few lines will provide a proof that I was not entirely unworthy of my name, which I shall reclaim when in my tomb or back in your arms again and blessed. Oh, in those first days of exile how I suffered to think that you cursed and damned me! Instead, when I wrote to you from Padua, you believed me and, setting aside my life of dissolution, you trusted in me, and, once you knew where to write, sent me words of praise, comfort, benediction. How many times did I kiss that sheet of paper that convinced me you loved and respected me? I thank you, Father, for having tried to redeem my honour among our fellow citizens. Your words are certainly better than my deeds, but allow me, however, to fight and win redemption by myself, so that I can truly be worthy of your tenderness. I kissed your letter over and over and thanked you deeply for your blessing, and yesterday, embarking, the tears streamed from my eyes.

'Oh, young fellow, cheer up!' said an old sailor, who gave me his arm to get up on deck. 'It will pass. Out of sight, out of mind: that's how love works!'

He thought a lover's letter made me weep like that – that there was some sad young maiden I'd left behind, waiting anxiously for me to return, perhaps even with a ring on her finger! Charmed illusions! I left nothing behind in Venice but contempt for my name and, God willing, oblivion. Only you, Father, and my mother and sister, will cherish a few decent memories of Giulio. And I vow I shall not turn your goodness to shame.

Rome, 9 February 1849.
The Roman Republic declared today.[3]

Eternal city! Immense and dreadful spectre! Glory, scourge and hope of Italy! You raise your voice and the people from the Alpine snows to the Ionian coasts listen. You are arbiter of past and future; the present is but an interval that can't be interpreted for the mass of memories and prospects. Today, this very day, the Republic of Rome was resurrected from centuries of oblivion, and unbelieving Europe won't have the courage to react with the usual sardonic smile. Whether out of respect or in fear, all will be forced to pronounce that name. But Rome's every breath demands bloody expiation. It was born of fratricide, freed by Lucrezia's blood, and Virginia butchered and the

Gracchi brothers' severed heads sullied the finest pages of Rome's history. Brutus' dagger felled a giant and opened the way to the giant's abysmal descendants.

Today, once again, a murder fuels the great endeavour.[4] May God be the judge. Conscience, too, has its inebriated moments, but they don't obscure the sanctity of moral laws. But do we reject the effect because the cause was vile? Has anyone the right to ask an entire nation to pay for the crime of one man? History is stocked with similar examples; perhaps in Providence's divine order great crimes are compensated by the greater and more general good. Even if new disgraces and ruinous falls await us, I cannot accuse an assassin's knife of destroying a people. God punishes; he does not avenge. More tears will flow for other sins and the murderer will hide his remorse in the shadows, and we will proudly show off heads covered with ashes and eyes shining with hope.

Rome, June 1849

I swore I wouldn't write a word unless it was my redemption. Here I am at last. I've taken back my name and my honour. My family and my country can be proud of me, and while I pen these lines I relish the pain of my wound and the sight of the page stained with blood.

In my legion there are some young Paduans I knew before. They didn't like me very much and I think they warned their companions against me, but I pretended to know nothing and waited until my deeds could speak for me. The time had come, however, for I feared I would lose my patience over the long run.

Ten days ago the French dug their trenches in front of Porta San Pancrazio.[5] The French forces kept growing, but yesterday evening there came a sort of truce and our side took advantage to allow the soldiers to rest. Only a small company stretched out in a chain protected the line of defence; I was keeping watch in a guard post built a few days before and already reduced to rubble by the shelling. The sky was clear and the fires of Oudinot's camp were visible in the distance. Suddenly I heard a pounding of footsteps down below; and the sentries seemed to be sleeping, for they gave no signal. 'Man your weapons!' I shouted and before a dozen legionaries could gather round me, a column of French infantrymen were up on the ramparts. With my bayonet alone I fought off the first ones; being on the heights was in my favour, and perhaps also the fact that the attackers had been ordered not to fire their guns until they were on top.

But they weren't able to hit me coming from below, and, as I backed up, I threw the first file into confusion and they, in turn, upset the second. They probably expected a heavier defence of the wall and for an instant I thought I'd fended them off all by myself. But just then the officer leading the assault, most likely impatient with their timid approach, sailed forwards and leapt on to the ramparts, shouting and urging them on with his sword unsheathed, and his men took courage and came right after him.

Now I didn't know what to do and went back to shouting 'Man your weapons! Man your weapons!' as loudly as I could; and while some of my companions began to fight back against the French column, I threw myself at the officer and, before he could use his sword, disarmed him. He had a pistol on his belt, however, and shot at me at short range, luckily blowing away nothing but one joint of my toe.

But now there was a crowd of defenders and the ramparts thundered with rifle shots, men raced to the cannon and the French soldiers (I had taken their captain prisoner) were pushed back down. At the same time there was another assault at the other end of the hill, but some of our men were able to hold them off until fresh troops arrived from the barracks. We later learned from some prisoners that a major attack had been planned for that night, but it failed when the infantry reconnaissance team was repelled.

I must hand it to my companions; they all gave me credit for that manoeuvre and called on our superiors to recognize me. The next day, when I appeared at inspection with my hand bandaged, an order was read out publicly thanking soldier Aurelio Gianni for service to his country and promoting him to standard-bearer. All turned towards me and I asked permission to speak.

'Speak,' the Captain said, for in our ranks the discipline was not as severe or obedience as mute as in other armies.

I glanced towards those young Paduans lined up not far away from me and calmly raised my voice.

'I ask to remain a simple soldier,' said I, 'with one request: to receive public recognition under my real name. I had to abandon it temporarily when forced to by one of those accusations of spying and treason that dishonour our revolutions. I hope I've now convinced my defamers of their error and I take back my name with pride. I am Giulio Altoviti of Venice!'

Applause thundered up and down the line and, if the officers hadn't forbidden it, I believe they'd have broken ranks and embraced me. Many an eye that boldly faced rifle fire was gleaming with a tear or two. When the men were brought to order again and fell silent, the Captain, after consulting with the General, spoke up to say that Italy could be proud of a native son who parried an insult so nobly, and that in reward for my fine resolve, I was to be named aide-de-camp to General Garibaldi[6] with the rank of captain.

My fellow soldiers broke out in fresh applause at this, and the review was adjourned and, marching back to the barracks, I began to blubber like a child and quite a few of those brave fellows blubbered with me. And soon I had reason to feel even more tender, when those Paduans began to protest that they hadn't known me and begged me to forgive them for their suspicions. This was the sweetest reward I had and I made this clear by embracing them one by one. That the whole legion thanked me, my companions admired me, an entire city praised me – this was proof that one can always regain esteem, and that really noble endeavours that aren't inspired by rage or pride will be recognized and rewarded without envy. Could that ever be the case if humanity were so vile and perverse as some think and as I once believed? Forced to accept humanity's esteem, I felt ashamed that I had despised it so stupidly and decided that my punishment had not been too severe for such a grave wrong.

Rome, 4 July 1849

Oh, what is the point of staying the course? Here we are, wanderers in an exile that may well be eternal. The legion has left for Romagna and Tuscany, hoping from there to arrive in Venice or Piedmont or Switzerland, but my wound, which reopened during the trials of these last few days, prevents me from walking. The General has given me letters of introduction to the Americas, so that once I've healed I can set sail across the Atlantic. Yes, across the Atlantic! Columbus went to look for a new world; I seek no more than endurance. But I sense that the honour of our nation depends on us poor fellows, flung by disaster to the four corners of the world. Action, then. Be bold! So long as virtue kindles my spirit, the spark is alive. I shall always be worthy of my name now, and of my native country. Father, whom once I hoped to see again and now fear I shall never more embrace, take this last sigh from your exiled son. From now on my love shall be without tears and sighs, like that which is eternal. I'll think of my mother and sister as two angels who one day will double heaven's bounty for me.

At sea, September 1849

Fortune supplied me a Roman family as my companions in exile: a father still young, forty years at most, who holds an important position in the provinces, Dottor Ciampoli of Spoleto. And his two children, Gemma, who is nineteen, I believe, and Fabietto, twelve or thirteen. At first sight they brought to mind an engraving I saw some years back of a peasant family clustered under an oak to pray while a great storm rages. The usual anger of political refugees is quite alien to them. They comfort each other with love and their life is that of before, minus Rome. If only I had my parents or my siblings with me! And so take most of my *patria* along. But how unjust to wish to make our dearest ones share our worst misfortunes. How would two poor, elderly souls endure such a hard, uncertain, anguished existence without any promise of repose or the tomb? Better this way, that destiny condemns me to suffer alone. In any case, distance presses us compatriots into something like family ties and I see that I already care for Dottor Ciampoli as a father and Gemma and Fabietto as siblings. This young lady is the sweetest creature I have ever known: if not very Roman, very much a woman in her grace, fragility and mercy.

Perhaps until now I've sought out only the lowest type of woman, but she seems sublime to me; I'd dream of her if I were a painter or a poet, but wouldn't have thought she existed in this world. Not a woman you fall passionately in love with (I certainly wouldn't dare to), but the sort who can guarantee a family happiness, one of those celestial beings who does everything for the others and nothing for herself. Shipboard nausea is neither pleasant to suffer nor to witness, but how sweetly she looked after Fabietto, even in the grip of the swells. When this morning she learned that a cat aboard ship had drowned, she wept.

By now we are all quite accustomed to life on the sea and to seeing nothing but ocean and sky. We talk, play games, read, and from time to time even laugh. Nature is good enough to permit us laughter, a great restorative, even when it does not pacify our spirits. When I am alone I climb up on deck and seek God in the immensity surrounding us. It makes me think of one of our popular songs that speaks of God clothed in blue: it's only now that I see how right that is. There is nothing that hints at God's hidden presence better than that blue immensity of sky and sea. I'd wager that song was composed by some Chioggia fisherman when summer's dead calm stopped his boat in the middle of the Adriatic and he could see nothing but the sea, his life, the heavens and his hopes.

I taught that song to Gemma and she sings it so beautifully with her noble Roman vowels that our tone-deaf English sailors stop their work to listen. I'd feared the voyage would be tedious, but I've begun to enjoy it. I hope I won't be less fortunate on land and that I'll find employment in New York, where Dottor Ciampoli intends to settle. They don't want for money and they won't let me go without; but I'm not made either for idleness or for the merchant's life, and all the letters of introduction I have for New York are addressed to traders. In South America it is different: Italians have begun to arrive and we are now highly valued and welcome. I'd be very happy to go there!

The very lush, virgin nature of the tropics seems inviting. In New York, instead, I expect it will be bastard Europeans, crates of sugar, bales of cotton and numbers, numbers, numbers. It seems strange indeed that someone who has sailed across the Atlantic can be reduced to totting up sums.

New York, January 1850

How I've grown tired of darting through the crowds of shopkeepers and brokers with cigars in mouth! They may be fine people but I'm hard-pressed to believe they are descendants of George Washington and Benjamin Franklin. Those great men must have died without issue, I think. I've gone on a few forays out of town, but nature is so powerful here it reminds me of a lion in a cage. They restrain it, divide it up, chop it in pieces; you must view it from quite far away and behind the almost Britannic fog that abounds here, to see America as travellers have described it. I find it hard to believe that such fog was here at the time of Columbus. Perhaps the steam engines brought it, like some mad European journalists say of the vine rot.[7] In any event, I'm happy to depart. We must go, because Engineer Claudio Martelli, who was supposed to come to New York and on whom Dottor Ciampoli depends, cannot leave Rio de Janeiro. Brazil is far away and Ciampoli has no wish to undertake another, long voyage, while I, instead, cannot wait to set sail and Gemma seems to be more of my opinion than of that of her father. As for the boy, he talks of nothing else but Brazil and is wild with happiness. My dear ones are well, my health is good, my companions love and respect me; if I could find a country where I could satisfy the craving for action that's devouring me, I would be very happy with my fate. What is life, anyway, but one long exile?

Rio de Janeiro, March 1850

Here at least we are in the Americas. You still sense Europe here and there, but it is the southern Europe of Lisbon, not the northern one of London. Engineer Claudio Martelli is a severe man, sunburned and honest and enterprising, from what I'm told.

When he heard my name he started in surprise and asked if I was related to that Carlo Altoviti who took part in the Neapolitan revolutions of '99 and '21. When he learned that I was his son, he relaxed and embraced me, and so I dared to hope that he wasn't an entirely mathematical man, for, to tell the truth, I'm as wary of mathematicians as I am of merchants. What if they put me to the terrible test of explicating the Golden Rule?

He then asked if my father had ever spoken of him and I said yes: for just then a flicker of a memory came to me of some story involving the name Martelli, but, unfortunately, I hadn't paid much attention to my father's tales and had no precise recollection. The Engineer told me that he had just received a letter from his brother – on his way to the Americas and presently living in Genoa with my sister and brother-in-law – and offered me anything I might need, saying he was greatly indebted to my father and very happy to repay him by helping his sons. I also learned from him what I already suspected: that Dottor Ciampoli, who had lost everything in the revolution, was hoping to amass a quick fortune on this side of the Atlantic and return to live on it in Genoa or Nice or some other Piedmontese city. Had I known, before I boarded ship at Civitavecchia, that Enrico had been proscribed from Venice and was living in Genoa with my sister, I would certainly have gone there instead. But now, although distant ventures tempted me, I did not wish to abandon the good Ciampoli and his little family. A young person like myself could be a great help to them and I would feel blessed if I could help him accomplish his aim. And so I remained, having decided I would share his fate.

Brazil is a new and orderly state. The Engineer was hopeful he could secure Ciampoli a lucrative position, but he needed time. And so we had to wait, but in the interval Ciampoli found a decent post in the Imperial Statistics office, while I, having demonstrated I'd held the rank of captain, was appointed a major in the border infantry. In the army I discovered another friend of my father's was remembered: Field Marshal Alessandro Giorgi, who had departed two years ago for Venice when they had word of the revolution and was said to have died of wounds there. If I can believe what I was told, he was a most extraordinary man; if not supremely clever, a man of that stubborn, sure, invincible courage that is often better than cleverness. All by himself, in a very short time and with just eight hundred regular soldiers behind him, he brought under control and imposed uniform laws and taxes on the huge central province of Mato Grosso, a territory greater than all of France. To hear of just a few of his successful endeavours in thirty years on those frontiers forgotten by civilization is to believe the Age of Wonders is still with us. If I knew anything of metrics, I would demonstrate that epic poetry is not dead, so long as heroes like him continue to provide material. The Emperor awarded him the Duchy of Rio Vedras, but he left it all behind to go to Venice. I'd like to live like that – and die like that, too. I needn't be a duke – to be remembered among the worthy is all I want.

We are now hoping that Dottor Ciampoli will be sent as Superintendent of Mines to the same province where Marshal Giorgi distinguished himself. I would follow with riflemen on foot and on horseback. But this will not take place until the autumn.

Rio Ferreires, November 1850

I no longer know why I resume this inconclusive tale of mine every five or six months. What I write here my family has already heard by letter and I'm not a man who means to have his life story printed. Nevertheless, habit insists: once I had blotted the page writing about myself, I developed a taste for it and every once in a while the fancy overtakes me. A small fancy, luckily; from the first of the year I haven't filled up two pages and God only knows when I shall take up the pen again after this. I agree, though, with my whim, that these places compel you to write about them. The written symbols of our admiration are necessary to remind us that memory does not deceive, that distance has not turned molehills into mountains or diamonds into rock. Everything here is gigantic, intact, sublime. Mountains, torrents, forests, plains, all is marked by the most recent revolution that shook creation. Nature here is as much like that in Europe as the feeble existence of an old man is like a robust and healthy youth. The mountains come in clusters and closes that draw together and lean upon one another, surrounded by deep inscrutable forests and maelstroms spouting flames upon the snow. Ancient trees, each one of which would be a wood on the hard flanks of the Apennines; valleys where the grass is taller than a person and wild bulls chase the shadow of a man; rivers that become cascades higher than the eye can measure, where the waters disperse in a mist that covers an entire valley and erects a rainbow above it; gold and silver lining the bowels of the earth; stones that reveal diamonds when split; the great river that winds, immense and tortuous as a sleeping serpent, past banks shadowed with bananas and catalpas. Lush earth, fiery sun, the heavens nearly always serene. A fresh breeze from the Andes bringing a few hours of springtime every day.

Oh, if they had the great railways of the Ohio and Mississippi valleys here! If this province were not three months by foot from Rio de Janeiro. There's no help for it: the distances make the separation keener, and, odd as it sounds, two years in Mato Grosso seem longer than ten or twenty in France or Switzerland.

We are housed like princes, but nature is mostly responsible for that. The house is built of rough stone and looks like a tent, being open on every side with balconies, porticos and entrance halls. A large garden runs down to the banks of the river; in front, a courtyard where the slaves work and horses whinny as they are driven into the stables. The city spreads out on the plain below, right up to the river banks below our garden. To the left is the barracks where I go twice a day to lead the drills and take the evening roll-call. The soldiers are quite obedient in Rio de Janeiro, but along the road their discipline falls away and they become raiders, brigands, not much different from the Indians who attack us continually.

These skirmishes are brief but bloody and dangerous. We must climb, with several days of rations on our backs, the most difficult heights, and cross tremendous precipices on trees that have been cut down on the spot and thrown across to make a bridge; pursued by enemies that hide like wild beasts in deep, dark caverns, in gloomy, swampy forests ripe with serpents and ambush. You hear something whistle by your ear, an arrow sent by an invisible hand; there are no wounded, no prisoners, for the weapon is poisoned and if it draws blood, it kills. Anyone who falls into enemy hands is slaughtered without fail and they say some connoisseurs even enjoy eating their victims. Apart from these passing entertainments, we live like wealthy country-house-dwellers on the banks of the Brenta, but with this sky and this magical nature that transforms earth into Paradise. Dottor Ciampoli, inspector of mines, goes out for two or three days prospecting; he's begun trading in diamonds from Bahia, which should bring him rich profits quickly. He usually travels with a sergeant and ten men, but sometimes I go with him. We then choose the most picturesque and poetic routes, and the last time he went out to a newly opened mine we took Gemma and Fabietto with us. I can't tell you how high-spirited that little trip was; it was like returning to those silly outings we used to take to Recoraro or Abano. When we had to cross a stream Gemma was laughing and trembling with fear, but she trusted me and put her little feet on the stepping stones, one in front of the other, so gracefully that I could have kissed her. I really couldn't love her better if she were my sister.

Often when her father is absent and I'm looking after the men – they need looking after if they are not to become the plague of the territory – we spend the nicest days together you can imagine. We read some history and I teach her what I know of Athens and Rome, and she teaches me to pick out a little tune on the harpsichord, and after just two months we already play four-handed: in Europe it would be a torture to listen to us, but here they are enchanted and her maids, two mulatto girls, never fail to dance a wild saraband to our music. These lady slaves don't fare badly at all; indeed, and if this were all the harm in slavery, one could only subscribe immediately; but I've seen the sugar plantations and I lack the courage to speak of them. Slave society, too, has its heedless, happy, hard-nosed aristocracy and these are hated by their inferiors almost as much as they hate their masters.

Gemma and I also look after Fabietto's schooling; he already speaks ungrammatical French with great audacity, and we all take Portuguese lessons from an old priest who is chaplain, bishop and effectively pope of the place. There is a bishop in the province, but it would be a miracle if once in his life he were to venture all the way out here. It is a beastly trek and our prelates would shiver even to contemplate it: no hospitable parish priests, no spacious rectories or festive processions, no bountiful tables every two miles along the way at which to dine. Ten nights of sleeping on the hard ground until you arrive at the hut, where some poor, brave missionary is risking his life to teach the natives the ABCs of civilization that constitute Christianity. Marshal Giorgi, invincible Duke of Rio Vedras, accomplished much with carbines, but I think these patient, invisible priests achieve more. Here's another case where Voltaire was mistaken. In short, if it weren't for the distances, the unreliable post and that craving for the new that grows the more new and marvellous things you see, I'd happily end my life here. But Venice? Oh, let us not think of it! Papa and Mamma, will I ever see you again? In heaven, for sure.

Rio Ferreires, June 1851

It has been many months since I added anything to these few notes, and it would probably be wiser to write one volume a month or abandon the project. Everything here is new, strange, surprising. When we return from excursions among the savage tribes, the peace and delight of the family awaits. Dottor Ciampoli is quite pleased with his business.

'One more year,' he tells me, 'and we shall see Genoa again! But why don't you join in our trade? Why don't you enrich yourself too?' he asks me.

He believes my family must be poor and would never guess why I've come to Mato Grosso, and I reply that my needs are not great, that I am young and that my sole ambition is to train myself in perilous military circumstances and return to Italy poor in money terms but rich in experience. Gemma smiles at this and Fabietto shouts that he too wants to be a soldier and command the company. The little devil is growing strong and brave; he rides beside me for half a day and when we go out hunting his aim is sharper than mine. But when it comes time to kill a bird of such beautiful plumage, sitting so confidently on its branch, watching us go by, well, mercy overwhelms me. The boy's hand doesn't tremble like mine; he is strong, fearless, almost Brazilian, and all that remains of Europe in him is the colour of his eyes and his golden brown hair. He speaks Portuguese as if he'd learned it from his nursemaid and puts us, with our limping accents, to shame.

Yesterday I had a letter from home, but Papa writes that he's sent eight or nine and this is the first I've received. I wonder what's happened to my own letters? Engineer Martelli also writes, saying his brother has arrived and they are on their way to Buenos Aires, called by the government on colonial and military business. Italians have a good reputation there; General Garibaldi was much appreciated,[8] and apparently they want him to return. If that happens before I depart, I'd like to go and see him, and also the Martelli brothers who are as dear to me as my own kin. Oh *patria*: how your bonds spread around the world! Two men born under your skies know each other in a foreign land, without even stating their names, and an irresistible force throws them into each other's arms.

Villabella, April 1852

What awful days! Two months I've been thinking about all this and I haven't been able to write a syllable. Oh, I'd have ripped out my soul with my teeth had I known last year what dreadful, grievous things would occupy this page. She is there, sleeping, and has come back to her senses. Her health improves daily; the roses have returned to her cheeks; her eyes sparkle despite the tears. How terrible to see the cold apathy, the wild delirium that overtook her. But now the storm has calmed and I can hear her breath come peacefully and evenly as a child asleep. I must write this down before the terrifying events grow confused in my mind, which still shudders with the memory.

At the beginning of August last year a certain unease began to be apparent among the Indian tribes that come down to spend the winter on the banks of the river. In fact, I had pressed the governor of Villabella to ask for reinforcements, but the distances are such that we could not hope to see assistance arrive before the following spring. I had, meanwhile, supplied our barracks with cannon, so improvising a little fort to defend the approach to our house. Until January we saw nothing more than little skirmishes, but then a more menacing revolt broke out near a mine to the west and I had to hurry off with most of the garrison to restore order. That battle kept me away far longer than I'd expected; the savages can be very clever fighters and it took three weeks to drive them beyond the river and burn their boats.

Sure now that they wouldn't trouble us for a while, we turned towards Rio Ferreires, but halfway there we met a courier who urged us to hurry because the Indians were threatening the city. Although the men were exhausted, we speeded up our pace sharply, because many had left their wives in the barracks and were quite worried. I was particularly concerned about Dottor Ciampoli, for he is such a proud fellow that he might well put himself and his family in danger. The first thing I saw when we came in sight of Rio Ferreires was the governor's office engulfed in flames. Rage doubled our strength and those last five miles were a wild race. The Indians, we would learn, had attacked the barracks, immobilized the guns and, taking the men by surprise, had slaughtered most of them and taken the women prisoners.

The few survivors had sought refuge in the residence, but now the savages were unleashing all their fury on them. They had come to kill the white-skinned chiefs who ousted them from the plain and the banks of the Great River, and their arrows and rocks were soon pounding against the walls. Ciampoli and a few soldiers mounted a courageous defence, giving time to the farmers to arm themselves and run to their aid – and perhaps we, too, might arrive in time and all would be well. But then those rabid beasts gathered great piles of cane from the nearby farms, stacked them around the governor's office and set fire to them, and, despite all efforts by those closed up inside, a great plume of fire soon enveloped the building. It was a spectacle of great courage and terrible despair: women throwing themselves into the flames, men leaping from the windows and, half-dead, pursuing the savages; slaves, both men and women, protecting their masters with their very bodies; soldiers who aimed their swords at their own hearts to avoid being roasted alive.

Dottor Ciampoli managed to get out from a side door where the fire was less intense; with him was a small escort of men loyal and ready for anything. Behind them was Fabietto, pulling Gemma by the arm, almost carrying her, a sword in one hand and a dagger in the other. They had hoped to cut through the enemy lines, but now that they had escaped the fire alive, they found an angry swarm of redskins surrounding them. The Indians looked like brawling demons in the flames of Hell: we could see their sinister outlines as we descended the mountain a mile away. Ciampoli, struck by an arrow, fell to his knees, but still had the courage to try to protect Fabietto, who held Gemma in his arms. But his wound was gushing blood and, as he fell back, the furious Indians attacked. Then Fabietto, prodigious boy, took up his father's sword and, leaving his sister (she had fainted on her father's corpse), sustained a hopeless, awful battle for a few minutes. Oh, why did that courier not find us an hour before? The lad, now struck by many arrows, collapsed and died murmuring the name of the Virgin Mary, and the savages fell on those dear bodies to carry them off as trophies. But just then the old Portuguese priest, who had learned of the massacre, came running in his surplice and stole, crucifix in hand. The sight of that unarmed man who spoke to them of peace in their native language, who faced them without fear in order to save the others, stopped the savages in their tracks for a moment. It gave us time to arrive.

What I saw, endured, practised the rest of that night God alone knows; I no longer remember. In the morning, three hundred Indian corpses lay scattered here and there on the winner's ground, but poor Ciampoli, his son and two hundred of ours – soldiers and farmers – had lost their lives. Gemma had not regained her senses, except to relapse into madness, and her delirium went on for almost two months. The ruined barracks, the scorched buildings, the Indian tribes increasing around us, while we grew fewer in numbers and in strength, convinced us to retreat to Villabella. Here it seemed likely Gemma would recover, and I promised myself that before summer I'd go to Buenos Aires, where the Martelli brothers had settled, and deliver her to safety with them and consult with them about taking her back to Europe myself. May God bless my good intentions!

Buenos Aires, October 1852

Three months of travelling, every minute of it lovely, picturesque, in places of almost unimaginable beauty. The distraction has cured Gemma and she smiles at me in thanks for all my trouble. When we arrived in Buenos Aires in the summer the Martellis had left for a city in the interior to help found a settlement there. But a captain who was great friends with the Engineer was about to sail for Marseilles and offered to deliver Gemma to her aunt in Genoa. His wife would be on board and the whole affair seemed in every way convenient. As for me, my plan was to return to Rio de Janeiro and take revenge on those accursed Indians. But when I told Gemma of my intention, she bent her head to her breast and two rivers of tears flowed from her eyes.

'What is it?' I asked. 'Does it displease you to leave the Americas?'

'Oh, yes, terribly!' she replied, sobbing and looking at me with pleading eyes.

The result was that we married four weeks later and decided to depart together for Europe. That way she didn't mind leaving the Americas, and I, in turn, gave up my thoughts of revenge on the Indians for her sake. Oh, what an adorable creature is my Gemma! May God protect me, but these two months we've been husband and wife I've thought of nothing but loving her.

We came here hoping to see the Martelli brothers and a Partistagno I've heard went with them, but as it seems they will be slow in returning, I'm thinking of making a trip to the interior myself. In the meantime I have been able to assist the government by laying out the plans for a new settlement on the coast beyond the river, to be inhabited entirely by Italians: a settlement that, because of its location, should be more suitable than the other, from which they've been waiting for the Martellis to return for a year now. But I'd like to see them before we depart to give them a report on this other site; unfortunately, the Southern provinces are in a state of insurrection and I must travel the long way around to reach them.

Saladilla, February 1855

I've been held prisoner now twenty-eight months by these insurgents, who drag me along behind them from camp to camp like a miserable slave. I have two babies, children of captivity and misfortune. Their poor mother is by my side, paying bitterly for her audacious wish to unite her destiny with mine. Alas, having left her father and her brother on the greedy soil of the Americas, she'll leave her husband, too! Fever consumes me; tomorrow, perhaps, I'll be a corpse.

Oh, Father! Oh, Mother! Oh, my sweet brothers, how happy my spirit would be to soar up to heaven by your sides. I thank the Lord that even here, at the end of the world, He has surrounded me with gentle affections. Three angels stand by my bedside and, day and night, give me hope of eternal beatitude.

Oh, Father, I feel death is approaching and that all my eternal sufferings are coming to an end. I wronged you badly and I beg you to forgive my fugitive spirit the ingratitude I showed you; to comfort me for my penance by grieving a little; to honour my memory as one who was sympathetic – if not obedient – to my country; and to take in this unlucky widow and these innocent children, whom God will guide and protect, on sea and on land, until they reach your doorstep. When they humbly knock upon your door, may your hearts tremble with feeling! May it not be necessary even to speak your names. I shall introduce you to one other, push you into one another's arms. May the thought of Giulio add only sweetness to your tears!

Thus ended the letter from my unlucky son, and he died the next day in his wife's arms. But she struggled to leave that ill-fated continent where her dearest ones were buried. First she waited at Saladilla, until the insurgents permitted her to return to Buenos Aires; she finally got back there in June, but her life force was already eroded by an incurable cancer. The Martellis wrote that she prepared for death like a martyr, every day more resigned to her fate. Her only regret was that she must abandon her children, but she was consoled to think that friends would conduct them to safety in her husband's family. The words she wrote in her own hand at the end of Giulio's journal were, and always will be, wet with tears when I read them.

'Father,' she wrote, 'I turn to you because I have no other father, nor brother, nor any relative left on this earth, only two little children who now sit on my lap and soon will frolic on my tomb. So much world separates us, Father, and yet affection, that of the dead and that of the living, joins us forever. I loved your Giulio as you loved him yourself, and now he calls me from the heights of Heaven, and it is God's will that I shall be the first to follow him. Oh, why was I not to enjoy just once the sight of your venerable face? Unknown to one another, we passed through this world, as close as a father and daughter could ever be. And this is a guarantee we shall see each other in Heaven. God cannot divide the loving from the loved forever; two spirits in the great space of the universe can find each more easily than two friends in a village. Oh, Father, be slow to join us, though: be slow for the good of our children. I know you will envy us, and the wait will be a torment, but I beg you not to leave them utterly orphaned on this earth. I am a woman: I am fragile; I pray they will learn from your example, from your words, and imitate you. Farewell, we shall meet again in Heaven!'

So that dear soul wrote to me from her death bed, laying down her pen as she laid down her mortal suffering. Oh, I dreamed on her father, I dreamed on the girl holding his hand, all eyes in the piazza on her, so angelically beautiful was she. Thus I must meet her: daughter, phantasm, grief. Thus I must lose her, even before knowing I had her; must begin to love her in order to weep upon two tombs instead of one. I could only pray to Heaven that I would soon be worthy of the love she'd brought to my son. My heart is intoxicated with purpose, my eyes are wet with tears!

I make my home now with my children and the children of my children, content to have lived and content to die. I am also pleased to be able to do some good for others. Raimondo Venchieredo, who died here in the country during the revolution, had the very decent idea of entrusting his children to me. I forgot our one-time enmity and made myself father of this other family, too; so I could benefit all men and perhaps show my goodwill. Luciano has promised me another visit this spring and the little ones will travel with their beloved uncle Theodoros, who has never married and is their delight. Demetrios, poor thing, gave body and soul to Russia, joining the Moldavian Legion as a colonel and dying on the battlefield of Oltenitza,[9] taking hopes of the Greek Empire of Byzantium with him. But ideas do not die and spirits from their secret hiding places continue to press on this unruly and bellicose world. Not long ago I took up Count Rinaldo's famous treatise again and in a month's time the second instalment will be published. The necessary payment has already been made to the printer and there won't be any delays now. I hope our native letters will benefit from it and that his analysis of Venetian trade during the Middle Ages will serve as a valuable addition to that distinguished history of Venice now being written by our Samuele Romanin.[10]

And Italy will learn of another immense, humble intelligence quietly consumed in the dust of the library and the sums in the accounts office. I, in turn, will be pleased to have carried out the last wishes of a man who merited far more than he sought to obtain.

On Sundays when I go out in the carriage with Pisana, my son-in-law and four grandchildren (getting a taste of Monsignor's sirocco, alas!) to visit the spring at Venchieredo or Fratta, a cloud of melancholy sometimes crosses my brow, but I quickly chase it away and resume my normal good cheer. Enrico is amazed to find me so serene and good-humoured after so many misfortunes and so much grief, at the not very cheerful age of eighty-three. My reply to him:

'My boy, wrongs are far more painful than any misfortunes; but those few wrongs I did I believe I've paid for, and I am not afraid. As for misfortunes, they bother us less as we near the grave, and, though I believe nothing and count on nothing, I feel sure that no worse fate nor any punishment awaits me on the other side. You only need to obtain that certainty yourself and you will die with a smile!'

Yes, die with a smile. If it's not the purpose, it's the proof that life hasn't been ill-spent – that you haven't harmed either yourself or others. Now that you have come to know me, dear readers, now that you've listened so patiently to the long confessions of Carlo Altoviti, will you now give me absolution? I hope so. Certainly, I began to write with that hope in mind and you wouldn't want to deny a bit of mercy to a poor old man after having kept him company for so long and so indulgently. Bless, if nothing else, the times I've lived through. You've seen how the young and the old were in my youth and how I leave them now. It's an entirely new world, an amalgam of new sentiments and affections boiling under the seemingly placid surface of modern society; and if the portraits and the poetry lose something, history gains. Oh, as I said once before, if we don't seek to measure the lives of nations by our own lives; if we content ourselves with reaping what good we can, like the harvester who at the end of the day rests happily on the sheaves he has cut; if we are humble enough to entrust the continuation of our work to our children and grandchildren (our own souls rejuvenated, growing stronger every day as we weaken and fade); if we are brought up to believe in our own goodness and in eternal justice, there will no longer be so many disagreements about how to live.

I'm not a theologian, nor a learned man, nor a philosopher, but I still want to have my say, like the traveller who, however ignorant he may be, has a perfect right to judge whether the country he's passed through is poor or wealthy, unpleasant or fine. I've lived eighty-three years, my young friends, and so I may say what I think.

Life is what our temperaments make it; that is to say, our natures and upbringings. Physically, necessity rules us; morally, justice does. The man who in temperament and convictions is just to himself, to others and to all humanity, will be the most decent, most useful, most noble. His life will be of service to himself and others, and he will leave a deep and honoured mark on his country's history. Such is the archetype of the true and integral man. What does it matter if everyone else is aggrieved and unhappy? The rest are the degenerates, the lost, the guilty. Let them be inspired by that exemplary man and they will find that peace that nature promises to her every particle in its right place. Happiness resides in conscience; bear that in mind. The sure test of spirituality, whatever that may be, lies in justice.

Oh, divine, eternal light, I consign my tremulous life to your never-ending rays! So the lamp seems to have expired when compared with the sun, so the firefly is lost in a mist. My soul's peace is utterly unruffled, like a sea upon which the winds have no effect; I approach death as towards a dark, arcane mystery, but without fear or threat. Oh, if this certainty of mine is mistaken, then nature likes to mock and contradict herself! I don't believe that – for in all the universe I've never found a law that both heats and cools, nor a truth that both affirms and denies.

No, I sense it within myself. I said it once with implacable faith and repeat it now with the firmest of hopes. The peace of old age is a placid gulf that opens, little by little, towards the great, infinite and infinitely peaceful ocean of eternity. I no longer see my enemies on the face of the Earth; I no longer see the friends who have abandoned me, one by one, retreating to the shadows of death. Among my children there are those who went nobly and too soon; one who has forgotten me; one who remains at my side to help me appreciate the certain benefits of this life, while I aspire to the unknown benefits of the other. In my brief days I've measured out the pace of a great people, and that universal law that brings fruit to ripen and makes the sun complete its rounds tells me that my hopes will survive and become triumph and victory. What else could I ask? Nothing, my brothers! I lay my head happily on the pillow of the tomb and watch the great, ideal horizons widen as the earthly ones of my faltering eyes fade.

Oh, brother souls in blood, faith and love, both alive and departed, my kinship with you is strong. I feel spirits fluttering, caressing, inviting me to join their airy squadron. Oh first and

Notes

ONE

1. *Castle of Fratta*: Built in the twelfth century, the historical castle of Fratta (once in Venetian territory, today in the region of Friuli) was already in ruins in Nievo's youth. Much of this portrait is based on his family holding, Colloredo di Mont'Albano, then in Venetian territory, today in the province of Udine, although there were many such ageing, extravagant, fortified manors in the former Republic of Venice.
2. *I shall die an Italian*: Carlo and his fellow Venetians would have had to wait until 1866 before their territory was taken by the Italian crown and they became Italians – an accomplishment Nievo did not live to see. The Risorgimento achieved its final victory in 1870 when Rome was captured from the papal government.
3. *Dante, Machiavelli, Filicaia, Vico*: The *Divine Comedy* by Dante Alighieri (1265–1321) was as fundamental for Nievo (and for Italian literature) as the Bible in English, and Nievo's references to Dante abound. Nievo counted the philosophers Niccolò Machiavelli (1469–1527) and Giambattista Vico (1668–1744) among those who foresaw an Italian nation. The poet Vincenzo da Filicaia (1642–1707) was prized in the nineteenth century for his patriotic sentiments.
4. *zimarra*: A cassock-like garment worn by noblemen.
5. *German wars*: The War of the Austrian Succession (1740–48) and the Seven Years War (1756–63). The Prussians under Frederick the Great (1712–86) were much admired in some parts of the Venetian Friuli bordering Austria; in others, Nievo goes on to say, the gentry favoured the Hapsburgs over Venetian rule.
6. *la corda*: The *tratto di corda* (Spanish *strappado*) was a form of torture widely practised in Europe up until the nineteenth century.
7. *libbre*: Perhaps the *libbra sottile* (literally, 'slight pound'), a measure

widely used in Italy, which was equivalent to about one-third of a kilogram.

8. *Serenissima*: Venice, the 'Most Serene Republic'.
9. *Cernide*: Militias raised by the lords to keep order in single jurisdictions.
10. *San Luigi*: Probably San Luigi Gonzaga (1568–91), who spurned a military career to become a member of the Society of Jesus.
11. *Ariosto's poem*: The great Italian romantic epic *Orlando Furioso* (1532) by Ludovico Ariosto (1474–1533).
12. *if you had also glanced at your Tasso*: The epic poem *Jerusalem Delivered* (1580–81), set during the First Crusade and written by Torquato Tasso (1544–95).
13. *Schiavoni*: These fighting men from the Venetian Republic's Dalmatian and Istrian territories were reputed to be loyal and fearless.
14. *the jurisdiction*: The *giurisdizioni* were largely autonomous fiefdoms within the Republic of Venice where sovereignty had been ceded to local lords. Land-owning aristocrats like Nievo's Count of Fratta thus had their own tiny militias and tribunals and punished offenders.
15. *laguna*: The marshy lowlands and shallow waters around the islands of Venice.
16. *as Attila had left them*: In ruins, that is. In the fifth century, the Huns attacked and laid waste to many of the Roman settlements along the coast north-east of Venice, among them Aquileia. Nievo is always alert to such symbolic reminders of the end of Roman power.
17. *I doubt that all of them understood Tuscan*: The characters in Nievo's tale would have spoken the Venetian dialect. Standard Italian, which largely derives from the Florentine dialect, would not fully come into its own until long after Italy was unified in the 1860s.
18. *His Serene Highness the Doge . . . Council of Ten*: The Doge of Venice, elected from among the patrician class, was the Republic's leader. The Council of Ten was charged with state security, espionage and policing.
19. *Signoria*: The Republic of Venice's main governing body, it included the Doge and the Minor Consiglio.
20. *Friulian statutes*: In ridiculing the laws of the past, Nievo, who studied law at the University of Padua, draws on the actual statutes here.
21. *Leeward*: Istria, territory to the leeward side of Venice.
22. *Grist Tax*: A tax imposed when grain was milled into flour – one of the most hated (and abused) forms of taxation.

23. *buli*: (Sing. *bulo*) A dialect term for bully, rowdy.
24. *four miles*: The mile referred to here is probably that measuring 1,852 metres; the English mile is 1,609 metres.
25. *San Marco*: The patron of Venice and, by extension, the Republic of Venice itself.
26. *zecchini*: Gold coins.
27. *Messer Grande*: The Venetian Chief of Police.
28. *Caporetto*: Kobarid, in today's Slovenia.
29. *Sacchetti*: Franco Sacchetti (*c.*1332–*c.*1400), a fine short-story writer in the vein of Giovanni Boccaccio (?1313–75), is best known for the *Trecentonovelle*.
30. *tresette*: A card game played with the forty-card Italian pack, traditionally popular in southern Italy and along the northern Adriatic coast.

TWO

1. *'Gentleman' of Torcello*: A patrician of modest standing, like the decayed Venetian island of Torcello.
2. *Smyrna*: Modern-day Izmir in Turkey.
3. *Cappa Nera*: The bodyguard and personal servant of a Venetian patrician.
4. *Aspasia*: The Greek statesman Pericles' companion; in Nievo's time she was reputed to have been a courtesan.
5. *'little corporal' Bonaparte*: *Le petit caporal*, as Napoleon was often called, was, in fact, commander-in-chief of the Italian campaign of 1796–7.
6. *Confiteor*: The prayer in which penitents declare '*mea culpa, mea maxima culpa*', thus an admission of guilt.
7. *Game of the Goose*: The Gioco dell'Oca, a board game in which players advanced by rolling dice, was popular throughout Europe.
8. *as I will report in due course*: A lapsus. Nievo does not, in fact, mention the matter again.
9. *If Jacob's ewes could bring forth piebald lambs*: In Genesis (30: 25–43) Jacob is promised he can keep all the young in his flock born with 'speckled and spotted' fleece and coats, so he makes the white ewes conceive dark lambs using a stratagem involving white and black reeds.
10. *Erminia . . . Angelica and Medoro . . . Brandimarte's death . . . Fiordelisa*: In Tasso's *Jerusalem Delivered* Erminia and Angelica (who loves the knight Medoro) are models of female ingenuity, escaping the knights who pursue them. In Ariosto's *Orlando*

Furioso the knight Brandimarte is slain on the island of Lampedusa, while Fiordelisa is a model of conjugal fidelity.

11. *the Great King's*: 'Louis le Grand', Louis XIV (1638–1715) of France.
12. *reforms undertaken by Joseph II*: In 1781 the Holy Roman Emperor issued the *Toleranzpatent* giving religious freedom to all Christian confessions, and, in 1782, extended that freedom to the Jews.
13. *Pantaloon*: The wealthy merchant of Venice, a figure in the *commedia dell'arte*, the popular Italian theatre in which stock characters were played by masked actors.

THREE

1. *Mutual Instruction Method*: An educational system to teach poor children, promulgated in the early nineteenth century by the Scots clergyman Andrew Bell and the English Quaker Joseph Lancaster, in which the best students were supposed to pass on to the others what the master had imparted.
2. *a cluster of hillocks, some of them crowned with bell towers*: Here, Carlo sees the so-called Bastion of Attila, where the leader of the Huns is said to have camped.
3. *Voltaire at Mount Grütli*: A mountain in Switzerland, where, at dawn one morning, the French Enlightenment writer and free-thinker Voltaire (1694–1778) was supposed to have fallen on his knees to worship God's creation.
4. *Champollion read the story of the Pharaohs at the Pyramids*: French Egyptologist Jean-François Champollion (1790–1832) first deciphered the hieroglyphs of the Rosetta Stone in 1822.
5. *Foscolo's Sepulchres*: Ugo Foscolo (1778–1827) was Italy's most important poet between the eighteenth and nineteenth centuries. Born in Venetian Greece, his life was one of exile and he died in a suburb of London. His celebrated poem *Dei sepolcri* (1807), written to contest a Napoleonic decree on burial practices, argued that the tombs of the dead are precious because they inspire the living.
6. *Mahmud*: Ottoman Sultan Mahmud II (1784–1839) ruled from 1808 to his death. In 1821 an uprising by Greek nationalists posed the first challenge to the Ottoman Empire. In 1832 the Greeks gained independence.
7. *before meeting Pope Leo*: In 452 Pope Leo I (*c.*390–461) is supposed to have met Attila (406–53), King of the Huns, on the Mincio River near Mantua and dissuaded him from attacking Rome.

8. *Candia, the Morea, Cyprus and all the Levant*: One-time Venetian possessions that had been lost to the Turks.
9. *Carletto*: A diminutive of Carlo, who is also known by another diminutive, Carlino.

FOUR

1. *the Commune*: The autonomous town governments first established in Europe in the Middle Ages and particularly widespread in northern Italy.
2. *felony*: In feudal law, betrayal of feudal vows or treason. A crime calling for the confiscation of the guilty party's land and goods.
3. *Bruto, Bradamante, Grifone, Mastino and Aquilina*: Along with 'Lion' and 'Leopard', the Provedoni children were thus 'Brute'; Bradamante (the hard-fighting female knight of Ariosto's epic poem *Orlando Furioso*); 'Gryphon'; 'Mastiff'; and 'Eagle', a girl.
4. *Aminta*: A pastoral play (1573) by Torquato Tasso.
5. *the Morea*: The Peloponnese, long contested between Venice and the Turks.
6. *Regulus*: Marcus Atilius Regulus (*c.*307–250 BC), commander of the Roman navy in the Punic wars. When captured and returned to Rome to negotiate, he patriotically urged the Senate not to compromise and, according to legend, was sent back to Carthage, torture and death.
7. *Illyria*: The far Adriatic coast opposite Venice, roughly today's Croatia.

FIVE

1. *primitive India . . . eternal metaphysics*: During the Indian Mutiny (1857–8) there was widespread interest in Europe in Indian customs and beliefs. Nievo himself even wrote a ballad inspired by the Indian rebel Nana Sahib (he also observed, however, that his poem was 'a piece of rubbish').
2. *Margherita*: A lapsus: in Chapter 3 Nievo calls the cook Orsola.
3. *planting a clean kiss on the other shore*: Unlike heroes of yore returning from long travels and bending to plant a kiss on native soil, Nievo's heroes 'kiss' the shore with their backsides.
4. *Guerrazzi*: Francesco Domenico Guerrazzi (1804–73), writer, democrat and contemporary of Nievo's, known for his fiery patriotism.
5. *valiant crusaders of Pisa*: That is, help that arrives when it is no

longer needed, like the Pisan troops of the First Crusade, who arrived in Jerusalem when the city was already secured.

6. *they vowed to press Maria Theresa to take over Venetian Friuli*: From the point of view of Venice, which controlled this territory, Venchieredo and company's request to the powerful Hapsburg ruler was treasonous.

SIX

1. *men felt themselves to be citizens*: From medieval times, *cittadino* meant a city-dweller. In the Republic of Venice a *cittadino* was a member of the middle order, below the patricians. The word took on a further meaning – citizen as a rights-bearing member of society – with the French Revolution (1789).
2. *prince from the North*: Grand-Duke Paul of Russia (1754–1801), son of Catherine the Great, visited Venice in 1782 and observed that the Republic was like a 'family'.
3. *18 February 1788*: Although the date should be 1789, the episode Nievo tells is true.
4. *Ridotto gambling hall*: The Ridotto or 'Private Room' was Venice's first casino, haunt of the nobility.
5. *Enrico Dandolo and Francesco Foscari*: Doges Dandolo (ruled 1192–1205) and Foscari (1423–1457) symbolize to Nievo the height of Venice's glory.
6. *Avogadore*: One of the three officials in the Venetian Republic who served as public prosecutors. An archaic term for *avvocato*, attorney or advocate.
7. *horned bonnet*: The Doge's distinctive peaked hat, known as the *corno ducale*.
8. *Procuratore*: The *Procuratori di San Marco* were the nine officials in Venice charged with administering the Republic's revenues.
9. *Gulf of Kotor*: In southern Dalmatia.
10. *country villa . . . So the Venetians called any house of theirs on dry land*: In his *Villeggiatura* ('Country Villa') trilogy of 1761, Venetian playwright Carlo Goldoni (1707–93) poked fun at such customs.
11. *Golkonda*: An Indian city with a flourishing diamond trade to the west; in Italian, as in English, the term also meant 'astounding wealth'.
12. *conversazione*: Nievo uses the word *conversazione* in the eighteenth-century manner to mean a salon gathering.
13. *quintiglio*: A variety of *tresette* played by five players.

14. *capot hand*: In the game of *piquet*, a hand that wins all tricks.
15. *Correggitore*: Regent. His wife is playfully called the Correggitrice.
16. *cleave unto the dust, as the psalm says*: King James Bible, Psalm 119:25.
17. *When the Society of Jesus was suppressed*: By Pope Clement XIV (1705–74) in 1773.
18. *Paolo Sarpi*: The Venetian friar Paolo Sarpi (1552–1623) upheld the sovereignty of the Republic against the claims of Rome and the Pope.

SEVEN

1. *Rocca della Chiusa*: A lapsus: in Chapter 6 Nievo calls Venchieredo's prison Rocca d'Anfo.
2. *Jesuit Bartoli*: Daniello Bartoli (1608–85) was a Jesuit poet and historian.
3. *statue of Gattamelata*: A celebrated equestrian statue in Padua by the Renaissance sculptor Donatello (*c.*1386–1466) of Erasmo da Narni, known as 'Gattamelata', the fifteenth-century captain of a hired army that defended Venice.
4. *refusing the crown as Caesar, but then accepting it as Augustus*: Saying no and yes at the same time.
5. *the rising sun as painted by Guido Reni*: a fresco, *Aurora* (1612–14), painted by Guido Reni (1575–1642) in the Palazzo Pallavicini-Rospigliosi, Rome.

EIGHT

1. *in favour of Louis*: The French king Louis XVI (1754–93) was, in fact, already dead, beheaded on 21 January 1793.
2. *fourteen centuries*: Here Nievo probably refers to the legendary founding of Venice in 421.
3. *method of Boerhaave*: The Dutch physician Hermann Boerhaave (1668–1738).
4. *in the times of Galileo . . . attended that university*: The Italian physicist and astronomer Galileo Galilei (1564–1642) taught at the University of Padua from 1592 to 1610.
5. *Congreve rocket*: A weapon designed in 1804 by the English inventor Sir William Congreve (1772–1828).
6. *Gregory VII*: The eleventh-century pope St Gregory VII (*c.*1021–85) battled with the Holy Roman Emperor over church investitures, and was also famous for repressing ecclesiastical vice.

NINE

1. *The Bruti, Cornelii and Scipioni*: Three prominent families in Ancient Rome. The Risorgimento tended to mythologize Rome's past greatness somewhat uncritically, and Nievo could count on the fact that his readers, schooled in Latin, knew that history well.
2. *cut their hair to look like Brutus*: A short hairstyle with forelocks, favoured after the French Revolution.
3. *pellagra*: A niacin-deficiency disease widespread in northern Italy and caused by a diet based largely on cornmeal polenta.
4. *Count of Provence*: The brother of Louis XVI, he had moved to Venetian territory in 1794 and enjoyed patrician status in the Venetian Republic.

TEN

1. *race to death*: From Dante's *Purgatory*, Canto XXXIII, 54.
2. *indi s'apprende . . . spesso nol raccende*: From *Purgatory*, Canto VIII, 76–8. Nievo's citation differs very slightly from the original, although the meaning is the same.
3. *canto of Francesca*: In Canto V of Dante's *Inferno* Francesca da Rimini and her brother-in-law Paolo Malatesta fall in love while reading the tale of Lancelot and Guinevere.
4. *Bassvilliana . . . Varano's Visioni*: *In morte di Ugo Bassville – La Bassvilliana* (1793) is a patriotic poem in terza rima by Vincenzo Monti (1754–1828); *Visioni sacre, e morali* (1789) is a poem by Alfonso Varano (1705–88).
5. *Liberty Trees*: Symbols of the French Revolution, borrowed from the American War of Independence (1776–83), these were trees or more often tall poles holding aloft a Phrygian cap.
6. *Had I been Pompey*: The Roman general and statesman Pompey (106–48 BC), when his assassins approached, was supposed to have covered his head with his toga and died with heroic stoicism.
7. *that fine portrait that Appiani left us*: A portrait (1803) of Napoléon Bonaparte (1769–1821) by the Italian painter Andrea Appiani (1754–1817), a gift from Bonaparte to the Vice-President of the Cisalpine Republic, Francesco Melzi. *Cisalpine*: The Cisalpine Republic, established by Bonaparte in northern Italy (Lombardy and later Emilia) in 1797, became the Italian Republic and then part of the Napoleonic Kingdom of Italy.

8. *Oh, he shaves his beard?*: Bonaparte's clean-shaven chin would have seemed remarkable during the Italian Risorgimento, when beards were a mark of patriotism.

ELEVEN

1. *Tana*: Modern-day Azov in Russia, a Venetian–Genoese trading centre near the Sea of Azov.
2. *2 April 1797*: In other words, Carlo becomes a patrician of Venice just weeks before the Venetian Republic came to an end. The Venetian populace burned the registers of the Libro d'Oro that year and the Maggior Consiglio was disbanded on 12 May.
3. *Carlino di qua . . . tutti mi volevano*: 'Carlino here, Carlino there, everyone calling me, everyone wanting me.' Nievo, a fan of the Italian composer Rossini (1792–1868), echoes the well-known 'Largo al factotum' aria from *The Barber of Seville* (1816).
4. *Cispadane Republic*: Founded in north central Italy in the last days of 1796 and absorbed into the Cisalpine Republic of northern Italy in July 1797.
5. *Veronese Easter uprising*: On Easter Monday 1797 a popular uprising drove the French troops out of Verona.
6. *The gravity and severe constraints of the present circumstances*: This phrase and the one below in italics come from the historical record.
7. *the abyss of 12 May*: On 12 May 1797 the more than 1,000-year-old Republic of Venice came to its end.
8. *Monsieur Villetard*: Edme-Joseph Villetard (1771–1826), secretary of the French Legation in Venice.
9. *Vittorio Barzoni*: (1767–1843) Author of a book on the fall of the Venetian Republic. He likened the Roman domination of Greece in the second century BC to Napoleon's Italian campaign.
10. *Battaja . . . Dandolo*: Francesco Battaja, Tommaso Zorzi, Giovanni Salimbeni, Giovanni Vidiman (or Widman) and Vincenzo Dandolo were all historical figures.
11. *Monsieur d'Entragues*: Probably Comte Emmanuel d'Antraigues (1753–1812), a French spy, diplomat and adventurer.
12. *the entire Council of Ten had appeared before Foscari*: In 1457 Doge Francesco Foscari (1373–1457) was forced to resign his office.
13. *Zante*: Today the Greek island of Zakynthos.
14. *Sulla's proscriptions*: In the first century BC Roman leader Lucius Cornelius Sulla (138–78 BC) proscribed (purged) thousands of nobles, killing and driving them from Rome.

15. *Bucintoro*: The grand barge of the doges, used in the annual ceremony in which Venice was united in marriage to the Adriatic.
16. *Romulus Augustulus*: (*c*.460–*c*.500) The last Roman emperor, defeated by the Gothic chieftain Odoacer (433–93) in 476.
17. *when Diocletian abdicated*: The Roman emperor Diocletian (245–313) abdicated in 305.
18. *abdication of Charles V*: The Holy Roman Emperor Charles V (1500–58) abdicated in 1556.
19. *Zeno and Dandolo*: Two leading patrician families in Venice's long history.
20. *Marin Faliero was beheaded*: In 1355 Doge Marino Faliero (1285–1355) was executed for conspiring against the constitution, the subject of a popular verse tragedy by Lord Byron.
21. *Suleiman and the League of Cambrai*: The Ottoman sultan Suleiman I (*c*.1494–1566), the Magnificent, although Nievo refers to him as Suleiman II. The League of Cambrai (1508) was an alliance of the papacy (Pope Julius II), the Holy Roman Empire (Maximilian I), France (Louis XII) and Spain (Ferdinand II) against Venice.

TWELVE

1. *Berthier*: Louis-Alexandre Berthier (1753–1815) was chief of staff in the Italian campaign under Napoleon, then commander of the Army of Italy.
2. *General Victor*: Claude Perrin Victor (1764–1841), the French soldier and military commander.
3. *Bernadotte*: Marshal Jean-Baptiste Bernadotte (1763–1844) became King Charles XIV of Sweden.
4. *the footsteps of Cincinnatus*: Lucius Quinctius Cincinnatus (*c*.519–438 BC) was appointed dictator in 458 at a time of crisis. After defeating the enemy, he forfeited his power and was thus regarded as a model of civic virtue.
5. *Horatio at the bridge, alone against all Tuscany*: The Roman army officer Publius Horatius Cocles' legendary defence of the Roman Republic against the Etruscans in the sixth century BC; Ariosto, in *Orlando Furioso*, writes of 'Horatio alone against all Tuscany'.
6. *hoping for a Monk*: In 1660 the Scottish general George Monck (1608–70) helped to put Charles II (1630–85) on the throne after the death of Oliver Cromwell.
7. *our Parisian Aspasia*: See Chapter Two, note 4.
8. *Mme de Beauharnais*: Before becoming Napoleon's wife and Empress of France, Joséphine (1763–1814) was married to Alex-

andre de Beauharnais, who met his death by guillotine in 1794, during the Terror. Her son Eugène Beauharnais was Napoleon's viceroy in the Kingdom of Italy.

9. *parrot-grass*: *Erba pappagallo*, as a variety of amaranth was called.
10. *the Lion's Book*: Images of the winged lion of San Marco show him holding a book in his paw, inscribed with the words *Pax tibi Marce*: 'Peace to you, O Mark.'
11. *Treaty of Campo Formio*: A treaty, signed by France and Austria on 18 October 1797, which brought an end to Napoleon's first Italian campaign.
12. *Belshazzar and his mene, mene, tekel, upharsin*: Book of Daniel, 5:25.
13. *Herostratus' immortality*: Criminal notoriety; a reference to the arsonist who burned down the Temple of Artemis at Ephesus in 356 BC to make his name famous for all time.
14. *Dalmatians of Perast*: Venice controlled Dalmatia (today Croatia and Montenegro) for hundreds of years; when Napoleon turned them over to Austria (after the Treaty of Leoben) the people of Perast, in the Bay of Kotor, burned the flag of San Marco and buried the ashes under the high altar of their cathedral.
15. *Sérurier*: General Jean-Mathieu-Philibert Sérurier (1742–1819), governor of Venice in the provisional government installed on 16 May 1797, helped to supervise the looting of Venetian galleries, churches and the arsenal ordered by Napoleon. Spelled 'Serrurier' by Nievo.
16. *the opening lines of his Last Letters of Jacopo Ortis*: 'Our native land is sacrificed, and all is lost; and life, should we be granted it, will be but tears for our insults and our infamy.' Foscolo's *Jacopo Ortis* (written 1798–1802) was an epistolary novel along the lines of Goethe's *Werther* (1774).

THIRTEEN

1. *Poe*: The American poet and short-story writer Edgar Allan Poe (1809–49).
2. *Dante's Ugolino*: In Canto XXXIII of Dante's *Inferno*, Count Ugolino della Gherardesca (1220–89) is depicted trapped in ice up to his neck in the bottom circle of Hell.
3. *Camillus . . . Sardanapalus*: The dictator Marcus Furius Camillus (c.446–365 BC) was the so-called 'second founder' of Rome. It is said that the defeated Assyrian king Sardanapalus threw himself on a pyre to die.

FOURTEEN

1. *Armida . . . Rinaldo*: Lovers in Torquato Tasso's *Jerusalem Delivered*. See Chapter One, note 12.
2. *Timoleon*: The Corinthian general sent to aid the colony of Syracuse, Timoleon led the defence of Sicily against Carthage in the fourth century BC.
3. *Coriolanus . . . Medea*: In la Pisana's mind, the Roman general Coriolanus (the subject of a Shakespeare play) and Medea, a character from Greek myth (and the subject of a play by Euripides), are stirred up together with other legends.
4. *Manlius Torquatus . . . Brutus*: The fourth-century BC consul Titus Manlius Torquatus ordered his own son executed for a breach of military discipline; Lucius Junius Brutus, one of the founders of the Roman Republic in the sixth century BC, was also supposed to have killed his sons (but not his father). The litany of names points to the way in which the Roman republic was idolized by the Risorgimento.
5. *Dalmatian maids*: Nievo refers to *morlacche* (feminine), a Balkan shepherd people.
6. *Uscocks*: Dalmatian pirates.
7. *Armida's garden*: In Tasso's poem *Jerusalem Delivered*, Saracen sorceress Armida lures Crusader Rinaldo into her enchanted garden.
8. *Raimondo's mocking, curious glances stuck in my throat*: Nievo never fears mixing a metaphor.
9. *Lepanto*: A great sea battle on 7 October 1571 in which the Holy League forces of Venice, Spain, Genoa and the papacy defeated the Ottomans, who wanted to drive the Venetians out of the eastern Mediterranean; the Venetian fleet played an important role.

FIFTEEN

1. *as dumb as Pinchbeck*: An alloy of copper and zinc that resembles gold, pinchbeck (Italian *princisbecco*) is named after its inventor, the British watchmaker Christopher Pinchbeck (1670–1732). *Rimanere di princisbecco* means to be dumbfounded.
2. *Benacus*: The name the Romans gave to Lake Garda.
3. *Virgil . . . towards the skies*: In the second part of his *Georgics* the Roman poet Virgil (70–19 BC) wrote of Lake Garda: 'Rough and tumultuous like a sea it lies / So loud the tempest roars, so high the billows rise.' (Joseph Addison's translation.)

4. *Catullus . . . wrote*: The Roman poet Catullus (*c.*84–*c.*54 BC) wrote about the town of Sirmione in his *Carmina*, 31.
5. *Bertoldo*: The shrewd peasant Bertoldo was a well-known folk character.
6. *the twenty-first of November*: Nievo collapses two historical events into one here. On 21 November 1797 the two legislative bodies of the new Cisalpine Republic (their members directly appointed by Napoleon) met for the first time. The actual inauguration had taken place on 9 July that year, when the constitution (closely modelled on the French constitution of 1795) was adopted. By 21 November Napoleon had already left Milan.
7. *Lazzaretto Green*: The Lazzaretto of Milan was a huge hospital or dying ground built between 1489 and 1509 to isolate plague victims, and a model for other such facilities elsewhere. The Lazzaretto of Milan plays an important part in the celebrated novel *The Betrothed* (1821–7) by Alessandro Manzoni (1785–1873). In 1797 the Lazzaretto grounds were renamed Federation Green and converted to lodgings for cavalry troops.
8. *Pythia*: The priestess at the Temple of Apollo who gave voice to the Oracle of Delphi.
9. *Purification . . . two pigeons to church*: As to how the nobility was to be 'purified': according to the Bible (Leviticus 12), a woman may purify herself after childbirth by making an offering of a pair of turtledoves and a pair of pigeons.
10. *Maria Theresa*: Maria Theresa (1717–80) Archduchess of Austria, the Hapsburg monarch who ruled Lombardy among her many possessions between 1740 and 1780. The *sous-chef* referred to was probably her governor; some felt that she neglected her Italian subjects.
11. *Machiavelli's great dream*: The Renaissance man of letters Niccolò Machiavelli (1469–1527) had imagined an independent Italian state.
12. *Thou alone shall rule the people . . . Any peasant, taking sides, can be a Marcellus*: Virgil's *Aeneid* (VI, 851), in Dryden's translation: 'But, Rome, 'tis thine alone, with awful sway, / to rule mankind and make the world obey.' Dante's *Purgatory* (VI, 124–6): 'For the cities of Italy are full of tyrants, and any peasant, taking sides, can be a Marcellus.' Marcus Claudius Marcellus (*c.*268–208 BC) was the Roman consul who opposed Julius Caesar's hold on his military command after the Gallic wars.
13. *Luciano Manara*: A hero of the Risorgimento who died in 1849 defending the Roman Republic.

14. *Anacreon*: The sixth-century BC Greek lyric poet's Ode V celebrated the rose and the grape.
15. *Brutus . . . Tarquinius*: According to legend, the last king of Rome Lucius Tarquinius Superbus (535–495 BC) was ousted in a rebellion led by Lucius Junius Brutus in 510 BC.
16. *Pindar's odes . . . scholiast*: The many fragmentary writings left by the Greek poet Pindar (*c.*522–443 BC) were grist to the mill of ancient commentators.
17. *Ettore Carafa*: Duke of Andria and Count of Ruvo (Kingdom of Naples), the republican Ettore Carafa (1767–99) was executed for conspiring against Bourbon rule. Nievo draws heavily on Carafa's character for this portrait, although his deeds here are mostly invented.
18. *Robert Guiscard*: (*c.*1015–85) A Norman adventurer, Duke of Apulia and Calabria.

SIXTEEN

1. *Egeria*: A minor goddess and consort to Numa Pompilius, the legendary second king of Rome.
2. *On 15 February 1798 in the Campo Vaccino five notaries drew up the act of liberty for the people of Rome*: The Roman Republic of 1798 broke the papacy's temporal power for the first time in more than a thousand years. The Campo Vaccino or 'Cow Pasture' was the Roman Forum before it was excavated, and served as a cattle market in the modern era. The British painter J. M. W. Turner (1775–1851) depicted it in an atmospheric 1839 landscape.
3. *Treaty of Tolentino*: (1797) When Pius VI (1717–99) gave up the Legations of Romagna, Ferrara and Bologna, as well as Avignon.
4. *General Duphot*: Léonard Duphot's death at the hands of papal gendarmes during a popular riot near the French Embassy in late 1797 was the pretext for the French to intervene.
5. *like Muzio Scevola*: The ancient Roman hero Gaius Mucius Scaevola, celebrated in a Handel opera (1721).
6. *Aldini, Paradisi, Rasori, Gioia, Fontana, Gianni, both Pindemonte brothers*: Celebrated early patriots and patriotic writers.
7. *May the Gonzagas rest in peace . . . Martha*: The Gonzaga family were the dukes of Mantua, the absolute rulers. In the Gospel of John, Martha, Lazarus's sister, was a loyal follower of Jesus, daily occupied in prayers and fasting.
8. *Mantegna . . . Giulio Romano . . . Tasso . . . Francesco II*: The Italian painters Andrea Mantegna (1431–1506) and Giulio

Romano (1499–1546) produced great works under the Gonzagas' patronage; the poet Torquato Tasso (1544–95) was able to leave the madhouse of Sant'Anna when invited to Mantua by Vincenzo Gonzaga (1562–1612); Francesco II Gonzaga (1466–1519) led an anti-French alliance against Charles VIII (1470–98) of France at the Battle of Fornovo (1495), after which both sides claimed victory.

9. *'Please, let us make our tabernacles here'*: Matthew 17:4.
10. *canticle to match that of Moses*: See Deuteronomy 32.
11. *third life*: The expression comes from the patriot, philosopher and radical politician Giuseppe Mazzini (1805–72), one of the key figures of the Risorgimento. After the Rome of the Caesars and the Rome of the Popes, Mazzini wrote, would come the Rome of the People.
12. *parse the erratic moral of his couplet*: the words of the song should be *somigili all'onda* ('you are like the wave') not *a Londra* ('like London').
13. *Cardinal Chiaramonti . . . homily*: In 1796 Gregorio Chiaramonti (1742–1823), later Pope Pius VII, delivered a surprising homily declaring that the gospels were not at odds with democracy.
14. *département du Tibre*: In 1809 Rome and its countryside became a First Empire *département* of France.
15. *Murat*: Napoleon's brother-in-law Joachim Murat (1767–1815), a general who fought in numerous Napoleonic campaigns and was King of Naples, was executed while leading an anti-Bourbon insurrection.
16. *King Ferdinand's*: The Bourbon king Ferdinand I of the Two Sicilies (1751–1825) ruled southern Italy for sixty-six years, during which time he was, rather confusingly, sovereign of Naples as Ferdinand IV and sovereign of Sicily as Ferdinand III, before the two kingdoms were united in 1816 and he became known as Ferdinand I. His rule in Naples was interrupted by the Parthenopean or Neapolitan Republic of 1799 and by that of Joseph Bonaparte (1806–08) and Joachim Murat (1808–15), when Ferdinand transferred his court to Palermo, where he was protected by the British. After his return to Naples, anti-Bourbon unrest forced him to briefly grant a constitution to his subjects in 1820, before abruptly declaring it void. His long survival was largely due to the protection of the British navy.
17. *Trouvé*: Claude-Joseph Trouvé, ambassador to the Cisalpine Republic from 1798, increased the powers of the Directory and reduced those of the legislature.

18. *Lahoz, Pino and Teulliet*: Leaders of the secret (and, according to some sources, apocryphal) independentist association, the Società dei Raggi.
19. *Soldiers of the Holy Faith*: The *Sanfedisti*, as the peasant soldiers recruited into the Armata della Santa Fede (Army of the Holy Faith) came to be known, were roused and organized by Cardinal Fabrizio Ruffo to fight the Republicans under the banner of Church and religion. See Chapter 17, note 3.
20. *General Championnet*: In 1798 Jean Etienne Championnet (1762–1800) was Commander of the Army of Rome.
21. *Baron Mack*: The Austrian military man Karl Mack von Leiberich (1752–1828) fought in the Napoleonic wars and was briefly commander of the Neapolitan Army under King Ferdinand. In Tolstoy's *War and Peace* (1865–9) he is remembered as 'the unhappy Mack'.
22. *Naselli . . . Roger de Damas*: The Neapolitan generals Roger de Damas (1765–1823) and Diego Naselli (1727–1809), Prince of Aragon (Puccini gave him a role in *Tosca*), failed to reach Rome during Baron Mack's 1798 assault.
23. *Rusca*: Championnet's second-in-command Francesco Domenico Rusca (1761–1814).

SEVENTEEN

1. *Acton (ruin of the kingdom)*: John Francis Acton (1736–1811) settled in Naples in 1779, becoming Secretary of the Navy, the Army, and finally Prime Minister, and, along with the British Ambassador to Naples, William Hamilton (1731–1803), exerting considerable influence on Ferdinand I.
2. *Viceroy Pignatelli . . . humiliating armistice*: Francesco Pignatelli di Strongoli (1775–1853) signed the truce with Championnet in January 1799, ceding half of the Neapolitan territory to the French.
3. *Cardinal Ruffo*: The royalist Cardinal Fabrizio Ruffo (1744–1827), scion of a titled southern family, led bands of peasants to attack and bring down the Neapolitan Republic in the name of God.
4. *Mammone, Sciarpa and Fra' Diavolo*: Brigand leaders who rode the tide of peasant revolt that was championed by Ruffo. Fra' Diavolo ('Brother Devil'), born Michele Pezza, was the subject of legend.
5. *San Gennaro the democrat*: The blood of Naples' beloved patron St Januarius was supposed to have miraculously liquefied

when Archbishop Capece Zurlo recited a *Te Deum* of thanks in the presence of General Championnet.

6. *Suvorov . . . Kray*: In 1799 the celebrated Russian general Alexander Vasilyevich Suvorov (1729–1800) and the Austro-Hungarian military man Baron Pál Kray (1735–1804) were sent to Italy to fight the French revolutionary forces.
7. *MacDonald*: French military man Jacques MacDonald (1765–1850).
8. *General Schipani*: Neapolitan Republican commander Giuseppe Schipani was taken prisoner and hanged when the Bourbons returned.
9. *Turko-Russian alliance*: The pact between these inveterate enemies which Nievo refers to was probably that of 1798, including also Austria, England and the Kingdom of Naples.
10. *Lilibeo*: An ancient city, its remains lie under Marsala in Sicily.
11. *Bayezid*: The Ottoman sultan Bayezid I (1347–1403).
12. *Chevalier Micheroux*: Antonio Micheroux (1755–1805).
13. *Judith . . . Holofernes*: The biblical Judith, who beheaded the Assyrian king Holofernes (Book of Judith 14:8).
14. *secret society*: The Società dei Raggi. See Chapter 16, note 18.
15. *massacre of the Pythagorean school*: Between the fifth and fourth century BC, the Pythagorean school at Crotone (in modern Calabria) was repressed and its members burned alive. In 1799, when Ferdinand returned to power in Naples, 99 republicans were executed and hundreds imprisoned or exiled.
16. *Mario Pagano, Vincenzo Russo, Domenico Cirillo . . . Eleonora Fonseca . . . General Francesco Federici, Admiral Francesco Caracciolo*: Among the Republicans executed were some of the most distinguished members of the Neapolitan elite. The famous words uttered on the scaffold by the Italian poet and revolutionary Eleonora de Fonseca Pimentel (1752–99) – *Some day, perhaps, remembering even this will be a pleasure* (*Forsan et haec olim meminisse iuvabit*) – were borrowed from Virgil's *Aeneid* (I. 201–2), given here in Robert Fitzgerald's translation.

EIGHTEEN

1. *Battle of Marengo*: In June 1800 the French defeated the Austrians at the village of Marengo in Piedmont.
2. *Marshal Vauban and Frederick II*: Sébastien Le Prestre de Vauban (1633–1707), the famous military engineer, and Frederick

the Great (1712–86), King of Prussia, were on the curriculum of every educated military man.

3. *Tripoli powder*: Powdered limestone, used for polishing metals and also known as rottenstone.
4. *played by Salvini*: The distinguished stage actor Tommaso Salvini (1829–1915) fought to defend the Roman Republic in 1849 and was decorated by Garibaldi.
5. *San Luigi*: Probably San Luigi Gonzaga (1568–91), referring to his vow of chastity. See also Chapter One, note 10.
6. *Ott's*: The Austrian military man Peter Karl Ott von Bátorkéz (1738–1809).
7. *The siege intensified . . . What did General Masséna want?*: Nievo reflects the views of the long-suffering Genoese, who endured two months of starvation and a plague epidemic, while General André Masséna (1758–1817) held off the Austrians and diverted their troops. Meanwhile, Napoleon crossed the Saint Bernard Pass and descended to defeat the Austrians at Marengo.
8. *Bonaparte came down . . . Melas and Suchet*: French general Louis-Gabriel Suchet (1770–1826), separated from the rest of the French forces near Genoa, was battling the Austrians, led by General Michael von Melas (1729–1806), while Napoleon was daringly crossing the Alps in May 1800 and preparing to march on Milan.
9. *tenacious hands of friends*: Rome's ally Austria held that the papal legations were hers by right of conquest.
10. *Cisalpine Republic . . . Italian Republic . . . Francesco Melzi*: The Republic was named 'Italian' and given a new constitutional order. Count Francesco Melzi d'Eril (1753–1816) served as Vice-President until 1805.
11. *Prina, an able administrator*: As in Carlo's reverie, Napoleon appointed Giuseppe Prina (1766–1814) Minister of Finance for the Italian Republic, and then for the Kingdom of Italy.
12. *Invent vermouth*: Vermouth was introduced in the late eighteenth century.
13. *Albertine Statute*: The 1848 constitution was granted by the King of Piedmont-Sardinia Charles Albert (1798–1849) and later became the constitution of the united Kingdom of Italy.
14. *Like Joseph with Potiphar's wife*: That is, he resisted temptation, as Joseph resisted being seduced by Potiphar's wife (Genesis 39).
15. *Madonna di Monte and the Montagnola and San Petronio*: Respectively, the church of Santa Maria del Monte, the public gardens, and Bologna's main church; that is, the main tourist sights.
16. *Signor Ludro!*: A Venetian huckster in the comedy *L'uomo di*

mondo (1738) by Italy's great comic playwright Carlo Goldoni (1707–93).

17. *proclamation of the French Empire*: Napoleon was crowned Emperor of the French in December 1804.
18. *Iron Crown*: The medieval Lombard Iron Crown, according to legend, incorporated a nail from the Crucifixion.

NINETEEN

1. *Napoleon left for Germany*: Where he would defeat the Russians and the Austrians at the Battle of Austerlitz (2 December 1805).
2. *Treaty of Pressburg signed on Santo Stefano*: On 26 December 1805 Austria gave up its Italian territories and Napoleon added Venice to his Kingdom of Italy.
3. *Biscottesque aristocracy*: A 'let them eat brioche' aristocracy. Nievo nods at the great Milanese dialect poet Carlo Porta's sharp lines on the *damm del bescottin*: the rich and pious ladies of Milan who distributed biscotti as charity to the poor.
4. *Cesare Balbo's and Massimo d'Azeglio's*: Piedmontese Risorgimento moderates Cesare Balbo (1789–1853) and Massimo d'Azeglio (1798–1866).
5. *Phanariots*: Greeks, many of them wealthy merchants and high Ottoman public office-holders; so named because they lived in the Phanar district of Costantinople under Ottoman rule. Spiro expresses the younger patriots' distrust of these assimilated, 'semi-Turkish' Greeks.
6. *paternity bump*: Paternal instinct. The nineteenth-century discipline of phrenology had identified a predisposition for having or loving offspring in a particular protuberance on the head, known as the philoprogenitive bump. *Avere il bernoccolo* ('having the bump' for something) came to mean an instinct, predisposition or talent.
7. *married into old dynasties*: In 1810 Napoleon, having divorced, married Marie-Louise of Austria.
8. *Rigas*: The early Greek patriot Rigas Feraios (1757–98) was arrested by the Austrians and handed over to the Turks.
9. *Ali Pasha of Tepelena*: Albanian Ottoman ruler in Ioannina (the Lion of Janina), who, when deposed, rebelled against his Ottoman superiors and spurred a Greek uprising. Byron visited his court in 1809 and wrote of his impressions in *Childe Harold's Pilgrimage*, Canto II.
10. *Leipzig*: Defeated at Leipzig in October 1813, Napoleon abdicated in April 1814.

11. *Emperor Dom Pedro*: Who, in fact, only became emperor in 1822, but had lived in Brazil from 1807 when Napoleon took Portugal.
12. *Holy Alliance*: An anti-revolutionary pact between Russia, Austria and Prussia, signed in 1815.
13. *Carbonari*: Groups of secret revolutionary societies active in Italy, especially in the south, beginning in the early nineteenth century, the Carbonari ('charcoal makers') were patriots and liberals who took their name from the ancient trade.
14. *Skyros*: Some sources suggest Nievo meant to write Chios, where revolts provoked an Ottoman massacre.
15. *Congress of the Allies in Troppau*: After Ferdinand was forced to approve a constitution, the Holy Alliance met in Troppau. Ferdinand then joined them for the Laibach Congress (1821), where the Austrians agreed to come to his aid.

TWENTY

1. *General Guglielmo Pepe's*: An officer under Napoleon and Murat, Guglielmo Pepe (1873–55) briefly became commander of the Neapolitan army in 1820, when the Carbonari uprisings he was leading forced the King to underwrite a constitution. He was subsequently forced into exile, but returned to fight for the Venetian Republic of 1848–9.
2. *Carrascosa's*: The War Minister Michele Carrascosa (1774–1853).
3. *Nugent*: Austrian Marshal Laval Graf Nugent von Westmeath (1777–1862).
4. *Florestano Pepe*: (1778–1851), brother of Guglielmo (see note 1 above).
5. *secret societies protected by governments*: In this paragraph, Nievo gives a succinct description of how the Sicilian mafia would come to flourish.
6. *Minister of Police Canosa*: Antonio Minutolo, Prince of Canosa (1763–1838), was so intransigent a reactionary that he alienated part of the conservative aristocracy in Naples and in Europe. The Austrian statesman Metternich (1773–1859) forced his resignation.
7. *Pythagorean frugality*: The sixth-century BC Greek philosopher Pythagoras and his followers had a reputation for temperance and vegetarianism.
8. *Congress of Verona*: In 1822 the European powers met to discuss anti-insurrectionary measures, particularly in Spain. The British refused to back any action against the revolts in Spanish America.

9. *Lord Byron, the poet*: Lucilio's encounter with Byron is fictional, of course, but it reveals that Nievo was well informed about the famous poet, his lame leg (probably a club foot), his writings, scandalous reputation and fiery character. See also Chapter 21, note 1.
10. *Spaccafumo's madness*: A lapsus: Nievo reports his death in Chapter 19.
11. *Tzavellas's . . . Kostantina Zacharias . . . Princess Mavrogenous of Mykonos . . . Kanaris's*: Lambros Tzavellas (1745–95) was a Greek patriot; Kostantina Zacharias was probably the daughter of the Greek patriot known as Zacharias; Manto Mavrogenous (1796–1848) was a heroine of Greek independence; Konstantinos Kanaris (1790–1877) was a patriot and sailor.
12. *This, my dear Carlo, is how a nation is reborn*: Aglaura's letter provides a rapid summary of some of the highlights and heroes of the nineteenth-century Greek independence movement against the Ottomans, for which many Italians of the Risorgimento had a lively fellow feeling. Venice, with its long-time connections to the east and its large Greek community, part of which went back to the Ottoman seizure of Constantinople, was especially sensitive. Various distinguished Italians fought and died for the Greek cause.
13. *Ypsilantis . . . Kolokotronis*: Demetrios Ypsilantis (1793–1832) was a Greek military man; Theodoros Kolokotronis (1770–1843) was a military leader and patriot.
14. *Botzaris's*: Markos Botzaris (1788–1823) was a Greek patriot.
15. *Fra Angelico*: (*c.*1400–55) Celebrated early Renaissance painter known to Italians as Beato Angelico.

TWENTY-ONE

1. *the elder of my two sons departs with Lord Byron for Greece*: Byron lived in Venice from 1816 to 1819 (a few years before the events taking place in this chapter), where he wrote the early cantos of *Don Juan*. The poet was a great philhellene and went to Greece in the cause of independence in 1823, where he died of fever at Missolonghi in 1824.
2. *Admiral Emo . . . against the Tunisians*: Between 1784 and 1792 Admiral Angelo Emo (1731–92) fought a sea war against Tunisian pirates.
3. *Mustafa Pasha*: See note 5 below.
4. *Janissaries*: The Janissary corps was the Ottoman Sultan's household guard. They were recruited as children from among the Empire's Christian subjects.

5. *Navarino, Ibrahim Pasha and his Egyptians*: At Turkey's request Ibrahim Pasha (1789–1848), son of the Pasha of Egypt, came to Greece, heading an Egyptian force to help defeat the rebels. But in 1827 a Franco-English naval unit attacked the Turko-Egyptian fleet and destroyed it. The Ottoman Porte called all Muslims to a holy war, but in vain. By 1830 Europe had recognized Greece and in 1832 the Sultan did too.
6. *Count Kapodistrias*: Ioannis Antonios Kapodistrias (1776–1831) was born in Corfu. He served as a Russian ambassador and conspired with Greek patriots. President of the National Assembly in 1827, he was accused of treason for Russian loyalties and murdered in 1831.
7. *Treaty of Adrianople*: This 1829 treaty ended the Russo-Turkish War.
8. *revolution in France*: The July Revolution (1830) that put Louis Philippe (1773–1850) on the throne.
9. *Pisistratus*: (*c.*600–*c.*527 BC) Tyrant of Athens.
10. *Leopold of Coburg*: In 1830, keen to instal a constitutional monarchy in Greece, the European powers were ready to invite Leopold of Saxe-Coburg-Gotha (1790–1865) to be king, but Count Kapodistrias is supposed to have dissuaded him. Instead he became Leopold I of Belgium in 1831.
11. *General Armandi*: Pier Damiano Armandi (1778–1855), a former Napoleonic general, led the rebel government in Bologna.
12. *Cholera had this advantage*: Recapitulates Manzoni's well-known line about the bubonic plague in *The Betrothed*: 'It was a scourge this plague, but it was also a broom.' The cholera pandemic that began in China in 1826 reached Venice in 1832. See also Chapter 15, note 7.
13. *Alfieri, Foscolo, Manzoni, Pellico . . . Leopardi . . . Giusti*: In this paragraph Nievo pays tribute to the most celebrated Italian writers of the eighteenth and nineteenth centuries: Vittorio Alfieri (1749–1803); Ugo Foscolo (1778–1827), who appears as a character in the novel; Alessandro Manzoni (1785–1873); Silvio Pellico (1789–1854); Giacomo Leopardi (1798–1837), the poet of 'La ginestra' and 'Bruto minore'; and Giuseppe Giusti (1809–50).
14. *King Otto*: In 1832 the European powers designated Otto (1815–67), royal prince of Bavaria, to be the first modern King of Greece in a constitutional monarchy.

TWENTY-TWO

1. *railway . . . Milan and Venice*: The long railway bridge crossing the laguna to Venice proper was completed in 1846.
2. *Pius IX, took the papal throne*: Liberals and reformers had great hopes of Giovanni Mastai-Ferretti (1792–1878) when he became Pius IX (1846–78), but he disappointed them gravely, especially after the revolutionary year of 1848.
3. *amnesty to all political prisoners*: By Pius IX in 1846.
4. *The winds of hope blew in from France*: In France the February Revolution (1848) gave birth to the Second Republic. The numerous uprisings of that fateful year in Germany, Poland and the Austrian Empire, including Milan and Venice, raised the hopes of Italian patriots. The revolts against Austrian control of northern Italy, initially supported by both Pius IX and Ferdinand II, were put down after those other Italian states withdrew.
5. *troops arrived from Naples*: Neapolitan troops, led by General Guglielmo Pepe (see Chapter 20, note 1), disobeyed Ferdinand II's orders and went to assist the revolutionaries in Venice.
6. *Rossaroll plot*: In 1833 Neapolitan patriot Cesare Rossaroll (1809–49) was accused of plotting to kill Ferdinand II. He died fighting in Venice.
7. *Queen Pōmaré*: Pōmare IV (1813–77) of Tahiti.
8. *rout of Novara*: In March 1849 the Austrians defeated the Piedmontese-Sardianian Army at Novara in northern Italy.
9. *'watchful as a lion when she reposes'*: In Dante's Italian: '*sguardando a guisa di leon quando si posa*', *Purgatory* (Canto VI, 66). Although the Venetian insurrection against Austrian control had failed, the Lion of San Marco remained vigilant, Nievo suggests.
10. *proscription list*: The exiled, banned from Venetian territory by the returning Austrians.
11. *General Urquiza*: The Argentine general and politician Justo José de Urquiza (1801–70).

TWENTY-THREE

1. *Tonale Pass*: A high mountain pass between Lombardy and Trentino. Giulio's journal follows the course of some of the toughest fighting between Italian patriots and Austrian troops in the revolutionary year of 1848.

2. *Prince Arminius*: The Germanic chieftain who defeated the Roman Army in the battle of the Teutoburg Forest in AD 9.
3. *The Roman Republic declared today*: The Roman Republic boasted a constitution that was quite forward-looking for its time; the Pope was granted religious authority, while the Church's temporal power was abolished and some of its property confiscated. But France, under Louis-Napoléon Bonaparte (1808–73), soon to be Napoleon III, and the influence of French Catholics, attacked Rome, defeated the Republic on 4 July and reinstated the Pope.
4. *a murder fuels the great endeavour*: Pius IX's interior minister, Pellegrino Rossi, was stabbed to death in November 1848. The Pope then abandoned Rome for Gaeta, where he remained for almost a year.
5. *the French dug their trenches in front of Porta San Pancrazio*: Louis-Napoléon sent 10,000 soldiers under General Oudinot to fight the Roman Republic: they battled on Rome's Janiculum Hill during the month of June 1849.
6. *I was to be named aide-de-camp to General Garibaldi*: A few years after Nievo wrote these lines about the fictional Carlo, he himself would join General Giuseppe Garibaldi (1807–82) on his 1860 Expedition of the Thousand to rid southern Italy of Bourbon rule.
7. *like some mad European journalists say of the vine rot*: The phylloxera aphid that all but destroyed European vineyards seems not to have been identified before 1863. However, this remark suggests that Nievo, who was alert to the current affairs of his day, knew of an unidentified vine blight (*crittogama* is his term, meaning mildew) before 1858, when he was writing the *Confessions*, as well as the 'mad' theory that it was spread by steamships. That theory effectively proved true, because the reduced sailing time allowed the aphid to survive the passage.
8. *General Garibaldi was much appreciated*: Garibaldi, the 'hero of two worlds', had left Italy after a failed insurrection in Piedmont in 1834 and went to fight for Uruguay's independence, returning to Italy in 1848. In 1849 he was forced into exile once again. After a stay in New York and several sea voyages he returned to Italy from England in 1854.
9. *battlefield of Oltenitza*: In 1853, during the Crimean War (1853–6), the Russians fought (and lost) against the Ottomans at Oltenitza near the Danube in what is modern Romania. The Tsar had hoped to bring the Orthodox Church in the Balkans under his protection.
10. *Samuele Romanin*: (1808–61) The author of a major ten-volume history of Venice.